MAY   2006

A Single Star

A Single Star

Stan Barnett

CORINTHIAN
BOOKS

Mount Pleasant, S. C.

Publishers Cataloguing-in-Publication Data
(Provided by Quality Books, Inc.)

Barnett, Stan.
   A single star : a novel/ Stan Barnett. — 1st ed.
   p. cm.
   LCCN 2002114315
   ISBN 1-929175-32-9

   1. Radioactive wastes — Transportation — Fiction.
   2. Terrorism — Fiction. 3. Radiation — Toxicology — Fiction.
   4. Politics, Practical — Fiction.   I. Title.

PS3602.A835S56 2003   813'.6
                             QBI33-811

First Edition:
   First printing, February 2003

   This book is printed on archival-quality paper that meets the guidelines for performance and durability of the Committee on Production Guidelines for Book Longevity for the Council on Library Resources.

Corinthian Books
P. O. Box 1898
Mt. Pleasant, SC 29465-1898
(843) 881-6080
http://www.corinthianbooks.com

Dedication

To my wife, Dale Cantrell Barnett, and my mother,
Elizabeth Haselden Barnett, two South Carolina
girls who have made my life rich and dear.

Acknowledgments

My deep and sincere appreciation to Doug Warner,
Louis Cantrell, Commander Mike Schumacher (U.S.N., Ret.),
Major Steven Durst (U.S.A.R.), Helen and Burrow Hill,
Robert Haines, Colonel John McNeill (U.S.A.R.),
and Truman Smith, friends without whom
this book would not have been possible.

It is a long road you have opened, for first men will disclaim their hearts and presently they will have no hearts. God help the people whose statesmen walk your road.

Thomas More to the court
Robert Bolt's *A Man for All Seasons*

Prologue

From his table, the courier stared at the window of the apartment where Khalil waited. Thickening fog infiltrated the narrow street, coating paving stones with a shiny slickness, blurring light and shadow. The blue tile that marked the building was obscured now by roiling mist that made him think of the Destroyer of Exodus, the deliverer of death to Pharaoh's city in the Jewish holy book. But no blood smeared on lintel and doorposts could protect Khalil from the plague that would soon find him. It was no divine pestilence coming through the gray mist, but men. Warning him was impossible. Khalil was a good soldier — and a man of God — but now the courier could only pray that he survived.

"You expect someone?" The waitress smiled down at him, interrupting his dark reverie.

He struggled to remember the German words. "I'm just watching the fog. It's romantic," he said, returning the young woman's smile.

Her face reddened. "More wine?"

"Please." He silently asked forgiveness for this sin. It was necessary to conceal himself among the enemy.

She hurried away with his wide-bottomed wineglass for the third time. He was drinking too much. He turned to look at the street again. The ruins of the city's castle were invisible. He hated the miserable German weather, rain and fog — he longed for the warm sun and cobalt sky of home.

The first car crept quietly onto the curb, headlights darkened. There were others behind it and more around the corner under the clock tower, all carrying German police. All came to seize Khalil. Three days before, the courier detected the surveillance of Khalil. Three well-dressed Germans alternated lingering in shops along the street, or strolling adjoining alleyways, never beyond sight of Khalil's apartment. He realized then that his mission was doomed. The Germans knew what Khalil was guarding, and they had come to take it.

In the apartment above the fog-dimmed street light, Khalil shivered and wondered if the courier would ever come. How much longer could he wait, no matter how precious the thing he guarded? He stared at the black suitcase that never left his side; when he slept, it lay tucked close under the heavy coverlet next to him, but what was inside the satchel never slept. In the night, invisible fingers reached from the black case to caress and penetrate his body.

Suddenly, nausea came again. He lunged toward the sink, tripped on the table leg and sprawled across the floor. He pulled himself up and painfully spit what was left of his stomach into the sink. For days he had grown sicker. Surely he would soon shake off the illness. He was young and strong and had never been sick for more than a few days. Pulling a towel from the counter, he fell back onto the floor wiping his mouth. He yearned for a clear head — free of the pounding pain, to feel his strength again. He laid his pistol next to the sink and stood.

Khalil dipped his face into cold water cupped in his hands, but he could not wash away the despair that overwhelmed him. The truth bore down on him — no one is coming. Khalil remembered the face of the Russian at Chelyabinsk. In the dim light of the tiny shack three kilometers beyond the fence of the giant weapons complex, Khalil saw the bitter, thin smile as the Russian took the satchel of money and, with his boot, slid the black leather suitcase across the floor.

"You needn't worry, my friend. It is well lined with lead. You may as well be carrying stones from the river," the Russian said.

Khalil picked up the suitcase. It was indeed heavy. For an instant he hesitated; he had been carefully instructed that no shielding would be needed. He pushed aside the doubt and the first flicker of fear. "There are ten kilograms?" he asked the guard.

The Russian's smile broadened and he took his hand from inside the satchel where he was fingering the American currency. "Ten kilograms of plutonium. More than enough to make a bomb for Allah." As Khalil dried his face he saw the smile on the Russian's face in the mirror next to his own weary reflection, staring at him, eyes dark and piercing. He shook his head to force the specter from his mind. Five weeks he traveled across the Russian emptiness, to Hungary, Prague, and finally back to his German apartment. Seven days he waited for the courier who would take the suitcase to Yemen. He waited and guarded the satchel.

He retrieved the pistol and fell back into the chair. His body ached. The skin of his side, his arm and his leg burned. He fought to control another surge of panic. He told himself it was only a virus. It would pass. But the fear and the doubt never left him. The fever wouldn't let him think for long. He staggered to the wall and leaned against it. Dizziness washed over him, and he feared he would collapse. He slid down the wall to the floor and pulled a blanket from the bed to cover himself and the suitcase he clutched to his chest. The pistol rested in his hand as he slipped into a fevered sleep.

The German police streamed silently into Khalil's building. The courier admired their skill. He imagined the scene behind the shutters of the second floor apartment where Khalil waited. Police lined up on either side of the locked door, finally bolting inside as the door crashed down. The courier agonized over reckless mistakes he now saw clearly — errors that condemned Khalil and denied their people a chance at salvation. Maybe his friend would only suffer a German prison. As he stared at the apartment window, flashes from the barrels of a dozen guns shattered his prayer. The ugly sound of the barrage exploded across the gray shrouded street. The waitress dropped a platter and screamed.

Soon, Khalil's white-covered body was rolled into the street. The courier raised his wineglass a final time and took a long drink, a silent toast to the young martyr who was now in Paradise. And a promise. Nothing ends here.

Chapter 1

"Objection." The word might as well have been shouted across the small courtroom. The effect was the same. Jurors jerked their heads at the defense table where the lawyer, who until now had said nothing at all, stood facing the high marble bench. Most stopped listening to the boring exchanges between the young justice department lawyer and his expert shortly after they began. Only two of the twelve could have repeated the professor's name. They got the point with the first few questions — the gray-bearded man was an expert in the soil and plants found in what the government called wetlands, "swamps, marshes, bogs and so on …" the justice department lawyer said in his opening statement.

"Doctor Swampy," the twenty-four-year-old carpenter whispered to the young nurse to his left, when he thought no one was watching.

They already knew the professor was there to confirm what the lawyer said. The defendant had grievously harmed their environment by filling up five acres of wetlands next to a ditch to expand his trailer park. That's why Dr. Swampy was there. That assumption made, they quit paying attention. Twelve separate daydreams floated about the courtroom, the young carpenter's erotically linking himself with the nurse.

But now something interesting was happening. The older lawyer had their complete attention, standing, hands folded behind his back, respectfully gazing up at the judge. Judge Richardson brushed a white strand of hair from his forehead and turned to Drew Holland, "O.K., Mr. Holland, what's your objection?"

"The government is about to introduce this report … exhibit 4." He held up a two-inch bound document. "And it is plainly objectionable."

Richardson rolled his eyes to the ceiling and smiled before responding, "Other than not being to your liking, Mr. Holland, what exactly should keep me from letting it in?" Several jurors chuckled.

The justice department lawyer, who had not moved since Holland's objection, barked, "Your Honor, the defense raised no evidentiary issues in their pre-trial brief. This is outrageous grandstanding."

Richardson ignored him and leaned forward, peering over his glasses at Holland, "Well?"

"This report is not the work of this witness, Your Honor. It contains material written by government counsel and supplied to him with instructions to include it in his report. This witness admitted it in his deposition. It's fatally flawed. It can't be admitted, Judge."

"Your Honor, it's too late for this! Your pre-trial order specifically required counsel to make objections to evidence *before* trial! They've had the report for weeks."

"The draft report, Your Honor. He gave us the final report yesterday — a week late according to your order," Holland said evenly, hands still clasped behind his back.

"Your Honor! It's the same report!"

"How was I supposed to know that?"

"All right, gentlemen," the judge said quietly. "Well, is it true?" he asked the justice department attorney.

The young man's face flushed with anger. After two forced breaths, he said, "Yes, Judge. But all of the information reflects facts confirmed by other evidence."

"It is not this man's work, Your Honor," Holland responded.

Richardson turned to the government lawyer and said gently, "I'm afraid you're going to have to just lead him through it without the report — and stick to what he knows of his own knowledge. He's been recognized as an expert. You've got pretty wide latitude. I'll sustain the objection. The report will not be admitted. Proceed."

Holland took his seat again. "Thank you, Your Honor."

No one on the jury understood. But they knew Holland had just body-slammed the government. And now they were paying attention. Now it was like a trial was supposed to be. Like TV. They tried hard to hide their smirks while the justice department lawyer, the man who a few hours before told them he would prove to them the defendant was a bad man, an enemy of the environment that sustained them all, began to question the professor again. This time, his speech was unsure, halting. They didn't have to be told his carefully prepared script had just been ripped to shreds. "7–0, Defense," the carpenter scrawled on his notepad and showed the nurse.

"Now, professor, have you been to the defendant's property?"

"Yes. On February fourth of this year I examined the site. And on the fifth, as well."

"And what did you …?"

"Objection." Holland stood, as before, facing the bench.

Two of the jurors stifled giggles. Richardson turned to Holland, smiling in spite of himself. "Yes?"

"Judge, despite three warnings from my partner here, Mr. McNeely, the government sent this witness onto my client's property without prior notice and without permission. He was trespassing. I ask the court to forbid him to testify about anything he did or saw while he was breaking the law."

"God Damn!" the carpenter whispered.

"That's a da … that's a lie," the government lawyer hissed. "We told Mr. McNeely the professor was going out there."

Richardson dismissed the jury. James McNeely rose, "May I be heard, Your Honor?"

Richardson nodded. "The assistant U.S. attorney, Mr. Emery there, told me in January they wanted to send their expert to the defendant's property. I told them … here is the letter I wrote.…" he walked to the bench and handed it to Richardson. "They had to let us know exactly when they were going to be there. This is a mobile home park. People live there."

The justice department lawyer, barely containing his fury, spat, "They've known for months about the professor's visit. They had a duty to raise this before now. This report is the key to the government's case, Your Honor."

"Then they should have been more careful," Holland answered calmly.

The justice department lawyer looked at the assistant U.S. attorney next to him, staring hard into his eyes before speaking, "Judge, Mr. McNeely was specifically told that our expert was going to the property. I wish we had put it in writing, but we just didn't. At some point you have to trust in the integrity of opposing counsel. Mr. Emery had this conversation with him exactly one week before the February fourth visit."

McNeely jumped from his chair. Steadying himself with one hand against the table, his eyes blazing dangerously at the justice department lawyer, he seethed "You're lying! You know perfectly well .…"

Holland pulled him back into his seat. "Your Honor, let's ask Mr. Emery what happened. He's the one who's supposed to have passed the message."

The judge and the three other lawyers turned to look at Emery, who was staring at his note pad. He was the only one who saw his boss, A. Bradley Sweatman, the U.S. attorney, take a seat in the back of the courtroom gallery. He glanced briefly at his colleague and said, "Mr. McNeely is correct. We did not tell him exactly when the professor was going to the property. I assumed he knew the visit was imminent."

Richardson leaned back in his chair, staring hard at the young government lawyer from Washington. "The objection is sustained. You may not ask this witness any questions about his visit to the property."

"Your Honor, we ask for a delay in the trial so that we may send our expert out to the property and then resume his testimony."

"No," Richardson said immediately. "Now, I have some questions for you. What other evidence do you have that wetlands were filled by the defendant?"

The shock of what was about to happen to his case froze the young man's face for several seconds. "None. That's all there was."

Richardson nodded, then turned to Holland. "The court grants judgment to the defendant. There is nothing to submit to the jury."

The defendant, whom the government had threatened with a $100,000 fine if it won the case, turned to embrace his wife. Tears streaming down his face, he grabbed Holland's and McNeely's hands and vigorously slapped their backs.

"Bailiff, call the jury back...."

"Your Honor, we move that our client's attorneys' fees and costs be reimbursed by the government." Richardson turned to Holland, smiling. "No."

"But, Judge, the statute ...."

"No. Don't bother me again." To the bailiff he said, "Bring them back so I can send them home."

Glad to be freed from days of laborious testimony and lawyers' antics, the jurors fled from the courtroom. Most turned to glare at the government lawyers, communicating their disgust.

"Well, Drew, Jim, congratulations." Sweatman took Holland's hand as he reached the exit. "Next time, it's our turn to win."

* * *

Richardson was still laughing when his secretary buzzed him. "Judge, the governor is on the line."

"Blackie, how are you?" He listened to the request from the son of his friend and fraternity brother. "An environmental case. Would it be in federal court? Then you'd better not tell me what it's about. It might be mine." He chuckled again. "The lawyers you want are Drew Holland and Jim McNeely. No question about it.... No, they're not with a big firm ... Holland, Rollins, Jerald and McNeely right here in Charleston....Yes, I've seen them work."

* * *

The first gulps of coffee warmed Jim McNeely as he drove along the old ferry road under a canopy of oak and sweet gum hung with Spanish moss. The sky was awakening when he reached the foot of the bridge, a bank of clouds catching the rising sun in blazing red streaks. The rivers were smooth with a morning calm. Under the first span of the Charleston Harbor bridges a huge ship quietly cut its way through the surface carrying precariously stacked rows of containers towards the port terminal. Across the harbor, the spires of Charleston's churches gleamed in the bright sun.

"Did you see the paper yet?" The booming voice in the locker room belonged to Kevin McClure, a young state prosecutor. The wetlands case won only the day before, Jim returned to his morning routine with a trip to the gym. The mark of a good lawyer, someone once told him, was to go back to work immediately after a trial. All he felt at the moment was exhaustion from days and nights of preparation. And he was still mad as hell at the lie by the justice department lawyer.

"I'm not even awake yet."

"It looks like His Excellency, the governor, is going to war over nuclear waste."

"I thought we lost that one years ago," Jim said.

"This time he says we're going to win. Seems the feds want to bring in plutonium from Russia and store it all right here. He's going to hire the best lawyers he can find and fight like hell."

"So, Kevin, is your résumé up to date?"

McClure threw his big head back and laughed. Toweling off, he turned to Jim. "This is right up your alley. Why not go for it?" The younger man's bulk dwarfed Jim's normal height and lean build.

At the sink, Jim combed his short, dark hair. He looked like a man in his thirties, instead of his real age, forty-two. "I'll tell you why. It's the feds. They care about this one. They have more money than God and twice as many lawyers. Besides, what is the governor going to do? The law is unfortunately on their side, even if God is on his." *And because they're lying bastards*, he thought.

"So? Screw the feds. Take the case. Make money and make their lives miserable. The state's taxpayers will get their money's worth." He reached over, like the athlete he would always be, and squeezed Jim's arm. "Go fight the arrogant sons of bitches."

"Damn, I forgot a tie again." Jim searched vainly in his bag. "Great, I have a hearing at 10:00."

"You know, Jim, if you're going to play with the big boys, you have to dress professionally, " Kevin said as he pulled on his pants.

"The hell with you. Get dressed and go put somebody in jail." Jim started to rush out, irritated that he would now have to drive home and then back into the city.

"Here." Jim turned just in time for the tie Kevin tossed to bounce off his chest. "Goes great with the suit." Waving, he added, "Take it, it's my extra."

"Thanks, Kevin."

*   *   *

Jim McNeely opened the office and went to the kitchen to make coffee. It would be an hour before anyone else arrived, and he used this time to skim the morning newspapers. The office of Holland, Rollins, Jerald and McNeely occupied an eighteenth-century house on one of the corners of Charleston's oldest section. Jim McNeely was invited into the firm a half dozen years before by Drew Holland, a decade older and the kind of fixture in the state's legal community he would never be. Jim's experience in environmental law came from a decade in the federal government. That's where he met Holland. In the early days of this newest branch of the law, they worked with and against each other a dozen times. When Jim told Holland he was suffocating in the bureaucracy, Holland gave him a chance to escape.

Now he was wearied by more than long hours of trial preparation. The whole business of the law — litigation, judges and lawyers — made him feel tired.

The night after their victory, he sat alone with a glass of bourbon, unable to sleep, watching lights reflected in the creek behind his house. He was glad for their client, who was a decent man, undeserving of the crude threat by the government to "crucify" him as an example. But satisfaction in the success he worked so hard to earn eluded him. Their bill would be paid — it was always those who couldn't afford it who paid. Why did he torment himself wanting more?

Maybe it was the rootlessness in him, always there, hidden just below the surface. Or, maybe just being forty. He thought sometimes of chucking it all, doing something else. But what? Then he thought of his wife and the kids, and that was that. No. There was no way out. The stream of consciousness always flowed to the same end — guilt for idle treason against his duty to those who depended on him.

Scattered around the desk were files waiting for his attention. More care taken would have prevented all of the problems concealed in the rows of folders. But care wasn't taken and attention not paid; now they were problems for him to solve.

"Thank God for the careless client," Holland said a month before, raising a beer. Jim laughed at the ancient tongue in cheek gratitude of the lawyer for the shortsightedness of those who put food on their tables.

"Wouldn't it be good to have just one case that actually mattered?" Jim asked after the laughter of his partners faded.

Holland stroked his mustache and raised his glass again. "Be careful what you wish for," he said smiling.

Jim searched the paper for the article McClure talked about. It was just as he said. Governor Haselden vowed to stop the importation of nuclear material. A spokesman for the Energy Department said there was absolutely no risk. No one, even someone standing next to the track, would be exposed to harmful radiation. And they denied there were any specific plans. The governor was not convinced. He declared, "South Carolina is not the world's trash can." *Pure politics*, thought Jim. *He knows he has no chance, but it's good press.* Jim wondered cynically if the governor was concerned that his support by the Christian Right wouldn't be enough to get him re-elected. *Maybe he's after the environmentalists.*

He answered the phone. It was Jake Rollins calling from his car.

"Have you seen the paper?"

"Why?"

"Word is the governor is coming to see Drew and wants to hire us for this nuke case. More important, Haselden will pay our usual fee." The firm's hourly rate was twice what the state paid outside counsel. "Get with Drew as soon as he comes in — is he coming in today?"

"Why are you asking me?"

Rollins laughed. "Good point. Anyway, get hold of him and tell him we need to sign up the state. This could be the biggest environmental case ever."

"Jake, the state has no chance." His mind reeled at the prospect of another, even meaner, clash with the federal establishment.

"So? They want to hire us. They're no different from any other rich, mad client determined to have their day in court. We can sure give it to them. This case will take forever and the state will pay. What could be better. Are you sure there isn't something we can do for them?"

"You mean a miracle," Jim said. "All I know is what the paper says, which isn't much. I have no idea why Haselden thinks this is any different from the last time the state tried to stop nuclear waste from coming here."

"Well, sign them up. We ought to get a lot of exposure from this. If you don't screw it up."

"Thanks for the vote of confidence."

*　*　*

The state limousine turned onto Broad Street. William Blackwell Haselden had been South Carolina's governor for a year, elected after a short career in the state's General Assembly. He was the most recent of a series of men to ride a crest of support from religious and other conservatives into the governor's mansion. Like his predecessors, he spoke often and fervently of the importance of the family and the sanctity of human life. But the issue that brought him to Drew Holland was more than a rallying cry. It was more than politics; it was personal.

He knew one of the federal government's secrets, one that only a few shared. Its plan for the plutonium was dangerous. And he knew what would happen if the government's carefully concealed fears materialized.

He was determined to keep the horror hidden in the shipments of pluto-nium from being unleashed in *his* state. That was the job he came to offer Drew Holland and Jim McNeely.

Judge Richardson warned him that the two lawyers were unortho-dox and famously unpredictable. There was as much chance, he said, of finding Holland dressed for hunting or fishing, as in the gray suit most of his profession wore like a uniform. Others told Haselden that Holland had no use for his politics and referred to him as "that sanctimonious little bastard." He couldn't have cared less. He smiled at the part about being little. At thirty-six, Haselden carried his athletic frame much as when he played college baseball. All that interested him was that these men were a team, and one that always battled to win. This was a fight he meant to win.

"Let us out on the corner, Nick, and pick us up in an hour," Haselden told the driver.

Jim walked through the park behind City Hall on his way back from the courthouse. As he passed between the iron gates and onto Broad Street, he saw two highway patrol cars leading a black Lexus slowly past his of-fice. *Oh hell*, Jim thought, *he's there now*. He jogged to the door and bolted into the foyer. A tall man in a golf shirt and windbreaker, flanked by two others in business suits, smiled broadly and extended his hand to Jim, "Bill Haselden. How you doing?"

"Governor Haselden. Welcome." Sherry, the receptionist, returned to the foyer with a tray and three cups of coffee.

Turning to the receptionist, he asked, "Is Drew here yet?"

She replied nervously, "He's on his way."

"Governor, let's go upstairs. We can spread out."

"I know we're barging in on you. I was down at Kiawah and thought I'd drop in on the way back." They climbed the stairs to the conference room.

Haselden walked around the room while his companions sat. "I love these old buildings." He ran his hand along the molding. "Do you know why I came by this morning?"

"I believe so." The two younger men seated at the table began un-loading their briefcases with stacks of black tabbed notebooks.

Jim noticed how young Haselden looked. Jim knew that he was not a lawyer, that he made a good living from a number of businesses, and described himself as a farmer. He was "Blackie" in college. Close friends and family still called him that, but politics forced him to lose the nickname. "Blackie" conjured up too many images in South Carolina.

"Governor, what brings you to our humble law office?" Drew Holland said, as he walked into the conference room carrying a cup of coffee. Jim noticed with relief that his senior partner was wearing a suit instead of blue jeans.

"I'm glad we could get together on such short notice." Haselden took Holland's hand and shook it vigorously. "You have a wonderful place here." Holland stood several inches shorter than the governor. He flashed a quick smile under a thick black mustache that showed streaks of gray and shifted as he spoke. Haselden noted Holland's well-weathered tan. The reports of his fondness for the outdoors were correct. "I want you guys to sue the federal government. I understand, you're no stranger to that sort of thing."

Holland laughed. "Bill, we love to sue the federal government." The shift to familiarity was calculated.

"You have probably read that the president plans to bring Soviet plutonium here to store at the Savannah River Plant. The government doesn't admit it, but it's true. They intend to transport it with spent nuclear fuel rods they are already bringing here from European power plants. They say there's no risk. And they're lying."

Holland looked intently at the governor. Jim knew they were thinking the same thing, that this was nothing to make a case out of. "Like I said, we love to sue the government. They make the cases take forever, and we get to bill a lot of hours." Everyone laughed except Haselden. "And we would love to represent the state. Hell, we've done it before. It's a good client." *It pays on time*, he thought.

"Drew, you don't need to give me the speech." Holland was stunned. Jim couldn't remember a new client cutting him off in the middle of his lecture about how long, costly, and potentially fruitless litigation was. He was proud of the speech. It was a well-worn means to ensure the client knew what he was getting into. Haselden smiled.

"O.K., Governor. What's going on?" Holland asked.

"The government knows there will be terrible consequences if there is an accident that breaks open the containers of fuel rods or plutonium."

"But aren't the chances of an accident very re …."

"No…They're not remote."

Holland stared at Haselden. "How do you know this? Pardon me, but the federal government keeps some secrets pretty well, and what you are saying would have to be one of the biggest."

Haselden's eyes narrowed, hinting at an anger that had been smoldering there for months. "My source has to be one of my secrets. But there is no doubt about the truth of these things." Holland nodded soberly. "An accident would be a tragedy beyond imagination."

"You say the government knows there is risk. What could cause an accident like that?" Jim asked.

"It's the plutonium. They know criminals and terrorists are planning to steal enough to make a nuclear weapon. Planning now."

"Steal it here?"

"Steal it anywhere."

"What do you want us to do? We'd love to take the state's money, but what's the goal?"

"Force them to cooperate with us. Make them stop the secrecy and work with us to eliminate any risk of a catastrophe. I want you to find an expert to explain exactly what could happen. Present it to the whole world in open court. Force them to admit the truth."

Holland studied the intensity in Haselden's face. "You already know what the consequences would be."

"It doesn't matter what I know. I want someone of unquestionable authority to get up there and lay out all the ugly details. Then there will be no way they can insist on continuing in secret. They'll have to work with us. So do you want the job?"

Holland glanced at Jim. "We don't give guarantees, Governor."

"Just do what you're good at."

*   *   *

The voices were loud. They were voices of violent men, used to quick, certain action, impatient with delay and uncertainty. The argument ricocheted around the smoky room, more rapidly as tempers grew short and faces reddened. A tall man watched from the corner as first one and then another waved his balled fist or thrust a finger angrily in the air to make his point. He had heard enough.

The tall man walked to the center of the room. The loud voices fell silent. In the years since the war against the American and Jew infidels began, they learned to respect this one among them. It was Atta, the Egyptian, who made certain they had all the pieces of the weapon that would end their struggle once and for all time. All except the plutonium. Atta let them argue, let them vent their anger at the failed mission of Khalil Dahlan. They raged against the Russians who, instead of the pure plutonium promised, gave Khalil material that was dangerously radioactive, contaminated plutonium that sickened him. It was not the rich, uncorrupted fuel they needed and had paid for.

Atta folded his arms and calmly stared at his fellow soldiers, the leaders of their holy jihad. "By the New Year we will have the weapon." He searched their faces. "We have learned from our failure. This time we will use others to get the fuel. I have already made the deal with the men who will take it for us. By November, we will have twenty kilograms, more than enough to make the weapon."

They were silent, but he understood that they wanted to know who.

"Russians. Who better?"

How would they control these men? The question came from more than one of the angry men.

"Like criminals. For money, they will agree to do anything. When we have the plutonium we'll deal with them like the criminals they are. And, God willing, we will give Islam its greatest gift."

Chapter 2

A late spring snow was falling in heavy, wet flakes as Mikail Plekanov drove alone, winding through the low hills around Lake Onega. He came here often with his father and mother as a child. The city where they lived then, and where he did still, was Petrozavodsk, only a few kilometers behind him at the base of the hills. In that long-lost time, the forests of birch and fir around the wide lake were their refuge from the confinement of the industrial city two hundred miles north of Leningrad. How much it looked the same. *But only the lake and the trees are unchanged*, he thought.

The Russia of his youth was as extinct as the empire of the czars. Then, Mikail and his family lived crowded into a flat at the heart of a beehive complex of apartments — no bigger than one room in the house he built the previous year. The city's factories were only a shadow of the great engines of the communist era. Most of the families he knew as a child now lived close to starvation. He employed as many of the friends from his youth as he could trust. At least that had not changed.

As a boy, Mikail longed to be a great soldier. It was easy enough to get into the army. He flourished in the academy for officers. In his first posting to the East, he saw his men machine-gunned in clashes with the Chinese. In Afghanistan he found what the barbaric enemy left of his men, wishing they had died from bullets. On the night he watched, angry and disbelieving, as the Berlin Wall was smashed into rubble — under orders to do no more — he joined the army he still served. The army of Mikail Plekanov.

It was a profitable enlistment. He was rich at thirty-nine, even by the standards of Russia's new American masters. In the New Russia, he was like a Czarist prince. The drugs his army sold in St. Petersburg and the hundreds of little cities and villages of the north paid very well. So did the guns. He did not soil his hands with prostitution, leaving that for the petty thugs and the AIDS-ridden women they abused into servitude. Lately, he had discovered the miracle of money handling, the quintessential capitalist venture. Four banks were now his, including one of the largest in St.

Petersburg, and many others did his bidding. Their legal business alone was remarkable and would support him in luxury. But the real value of the banks was their ability to launder illegal profits — his as well as many others', even to hide the bribes to government officials so necessary to the success of the army of Plekanov.

The meeting he called for this night was to initiate a new venture, one which would bring huge profits and achieve a goal almost as dear to him. It would strike a savage blow against the Americans and their sycophantic allies.

He stopped the Mercedes outside the gate of the dacha and waited for the security signal, then drove down the lane, now completely white with snow, past two men with machine pistols slung over their shoulders. Inside the old log house, a fire blazed and his men waited. Mikail stamped the American western boots he favored to shake off the snow and brushed flakes from his jeans. Tossing his leather jacket onto a bench, he strode across the room. They rose to greet him, and he searched each face for the appropriate look of deference and loyalty he demanded from his soldiers. In the face of one he saw fear.

"Misha, you look well," he embraced the first, an ox of a man, a cold and ruthless killer recruited from the army. "And you are prospering I see," he said to the second, chief of his drug operations, slapping his belly, "Your customers are still hungry for your products, eh?" The man nodded, clearly pleased with himself. Mikail led them to a table. "Now, my friends, we have a new opportunity to make great profit."

As he spread out a map, Alexis, a thin bespectacled man in a suit, the image of a prosperous businessman, handed each a diagram of what looked like a military compound. "I have received word that our Arab friends in Yemen wish to purchase a sufficient amount of plutonium to make a nuclear weapon. Not that we are concerned, but I think we know why they want it." The men laughed heartily. "We are going to get this material for them. As you know, our country and our former Soviet brothers no longer feel the need to keep so much of it. There are plans to give it to the Americans. I propose to take some of it off their hands. The Arabs will pay us in gold — twenty million American dollars worth for our trouble." Mikail let them absorb the figure.

"This will require that we take the material from Kazakhstan. Alexis will explain the plan; then we will discuss it."

The men pored over the plan until late into the night. When they were done, Mikail handed each a vodka, and they toasted their success. "My friends, we will do this thing, make money and hurt the Americans in the process." Alexis gathered up the maps and diagrams from the table.

Mikail stood and walked behind Misha. He placed his hands on the powerful shoulders. "Misha, you and I have served together a long time." The big head nodded, smiling in agreement. "It pains me to know that you have stolen from me." As he said this he held out his hand to Alexis who placed a .38 pistol there. Terror flashed across Misha's face as the barrel came to rest against his temple.

"No! No! Mikail Nicholaevitch, this is a lie, never—"

The blast flung the great head to the side and much of its right half was sprayed across the room. Misha's hulking body slumped over the chair and pulled it to the floor, the crash echoing through the dacha. "Yes, Misha. It is true, but will never be true again," Mikail said to the body. He wiped his hands on a damp towel Alexis traded him for the pistol. "Good night," he said, "We will meet again soon." With that Mikail retrieved his jacket and left his shocked associates in the room. One of the guards had started his car for him and it was already warm.

He drove back to the lake road and towards Petrozavodsk. Of course, it wasn't true. Misha had never stolen from him. He was loyal as a dog and too stupid to steal. As long as he could have enough money to keep him in liquor, food and women — particularly women he could brutalize — he was happy. But he could not be trusted with such a perilous secret. It was necessary that they have complete secrecy, and now Mikail was certain they would.

*　*　*

Despite the cold, sweat poured from Alexis as he drove over the snow-covered streets to his apartment. Mikail told him before the meeting what he planned to do and the reason. Knowing was one thing; seeing the brutal death was quite another. Alexis had no experience with war or violent death. He had much experience with Mikail Plekanov, however. Mikail was his brother, older by eight years.

Alexis was terrified. Not only by what he had just seen but also by what he knew his brother was capable of. Alexis knew his brother trusted him completely. The idea of family was inviolate to Mikail — betrayal by his brother would never occur to him. Mikail made him a part of his enterprises from the start, placed him in charge of the money — laundering it, hiding it, and determining which ventures were most profitable. Now Alexis ran their banks and all the new businesses. Only rarely did he have to confront the true nature of Mikail's activities.

What worried Alexis now was the same thing that had robbed him of sleep for a month. He knew the man would contact him again. He knew he could not hide and could not run away. The hour was late and his wife and son were long since asleep. Alexis shed his overcoat, coat and tie and poured himself a long cognac. He softly stepped down the hall and peeked into his son's room. The six-year-old was curled around the giant stuffed bear he called Niki. Alexis gently slipped the covers over his son.

Next door his wife slept the sweet sleep of the innocent, the unknowing. *If she knew, if only she knew half of the truth*, he thought. The sharp, stabbing pain in his stomach came again. Alexis knew the man would call again.

Mikail has his wife, too, Alexis tried to reason. And daughters — delightful, lovely girls. They protected their families so well from the harshness they knew as children. *Why can't we let go of the horror now; why can't we be content with what the banks and the stores can make for us? They will keep us rich.* An overwhelming sadness came over him as he remembered. Mikail wanted more, needed more. Sadness gave way to panic when he remembered the call that would surely come, the message to pick up some obscure public telephone in the city. And then the man would tell him all over again the impossible thing he must do.

*   *   *

"What does the FBI in Moscow report?" The voice belonged to the national security advisor — the "NSA." Gathered around him was the team assigned by the president to ensure — the president's word — that none of the Russian mobs stole any of the plutonium already being collected across the former Soviet Union for shipment to the U.S.

"Our representatives have been working hand in hand with Russian State Security. They assure us that each of the groups capable of mounting a raid has been penetrated, and that if there are plans for a raid, we will have warning." Leo Scardato was deputy director of the FBI. He spoke with the cool confidence of a seasoned veteran of Washington.

"Exactly how have we been assured?" C. A. Moore was special assistant to the president for policy and security. He functioned without a formal duty description. In fact, he was the president's "fix-it" man. His facility for solving problems made him indispensable when Roger Seekings successfully sought the nomination for president. Seekings confided to more than one close friend that in the brutal world of high-level politics in America, you could not succeed without a C. A. Moore. In the first two years of Seekings' administration, Moore became known as a man who spoke directly for the president. No one asked him questions any longer when he made a request. The few who inquired too closely in the beginning were no longer around. The rest got the point.

"The Russians have isolated what they believe to be the weakest link in each of these organizations and sent them all the same message," Scardato answered.

"Which is what? Or do we know?" Moore said sharply.

Scardato paused. *God how he hated this piss-ant.* "They have told each that if there is a raid by that person's organization on plutonium without the government receiving warning, the individual will be killed, as well as each member of his immediate family. No questions. No ifs, ands or butskies."

"My God," the NSA sighed, rubbing his forehead.

"Do they believe this will work?" Moore asked.

"They do. So do we."

"Are there any indications of a plan by one of these groups?" Moore's stare bored in on Scardato. Scardato knew that Moore had already asked the Defense Intelligence Agency the same thing.

"No. But we believe, as do the Russians and the Defense Intelligence Agency, that if there is an operation, the warning will come anonymously. Unless they catch one of the bastards, or come up with a body they can ID, they'll never know which group it was." Scardato returned Moore's stare.

"What is the likelihood that one of these groups will try to take the plutonium in the U.S.?" Moore asked the group at large.

Scardato answered, "Zero."

"Zero." Moore cocked his head slightly. "Does this mean there are no precautions being taken against it? We've given up the idea of flying the stuff, right? So, we have to move it by truck — also an idea we've rejected — or by train across hundreds of miles of open territory. Are we going to let the South Carolina Highway Patrol protect it?" he laughed.

"It'll never be far from the coast. A helicopter out to a ship — poof, it disappears. Hell, I think I could come up with a plan to pull it off."

"Well, C. A., thank heavens you're on our side," the NSA said smiling. "All right, let's stay on top of this with the Russians. C. A., why don't you and I get with the energy people and take a look at tightening up security in the Carolinas? I see in each of your reports that you agree this is still a very low grade threat." Each man nodded soberly. Except Moore.

As they all stood, Moore spoke to the men around the table, the scowl gone now as he vigorously shook the hand of each. Scardato fumed silently. *The most offensive thing about the son of a bitch*, he thought, *is the way he smears on the honey just after playing the bastard.* It occurred to him that Moore was actually assuming the role of the president, powerful enough to look you in the eye and say, "If I want, I can spit in your face one minute and expect you to kiss my ass the next — and thank me for the privilege." Scardato smiled broadly as he took Moore's hand.

"I'll brief the president this afternoon and let you know his feelings on how to proceed," Moore said pleasantly to the NSA.

*   *   *

"Good afternoon, Mr. Moore, the president is running just a little behind." The voice belonged to the president's long-time secretary, the woman who kept him out of more embarrassments than he liked to think about. Roger Seekings' natural tendency was to ignore the clock. It was one of the reasons he gladly abandoned a senior position — in one of the Midwest's largest banks — to run for congress. Politics did not run on the clock, and the more important you were, the less it mattered. He loved the freedom from slavery to the schedules of others that public service gave him.

After three years he was still exhilarated by the enormous power of this greatest of positions. Historians and biographers loved to speak of the terrible burden of the presidency. He felt no burden. He loved it all.

When he called, people answered. When he spoke, people listened. His every public pronouncement was analyzed and evaluated by pundits and editorialists. Crowds greeted him wherever he went. This was an addiction more powerful than any drug. It made him understand what drove men through the ages to make such power permanent.

As the door to the Oval Office opened, Moore saw Seekings standing by the large polished desk fronting the presidential seal woven into the carpet. Tall and perfectly proportioned for a man of any age, with exactly the right amount of graying at the temples, Seekings was the image of an American president. The image was no accident but the product of relentless attention. He waved Moore into the office and motioned him to a chair. "Where are we with this plutonium thing, C. A.? Anything to worry about?"

"There has been a tremendous effort by the FBI in Russia, Mr. President. There is good reason to be optimistic, but I'm concerned that this may be a bigger problem than we have acknowledged."

"Why?" Seekings asked. Seekings had long ago learned to respect the instincts of this peculiar man. He was quiet. Flawlessly efficient. Intensely, perhaps morbidly, serious concerning the missions Seekings gave him. His private life, if he had one, was a mystery. He knew Moore lived more than an hour out of town in a farmhouse on several acres of land. He had children, teenagers, Seekings believed. But the president long ago stopped asking about them. The questions only elicited uncomfortable and incomplete answers.

About one thing there was no doubt. C. A. Moore was the best political operative he had ever known. More important, unlike so many of the slick campaign organizers and position architects who came to Washington, Moore knew how to function in the government. He knew exactly what power was, and he had no inhibitions in its use. Give him an order, and it got done. It was as simple as that. And he lacked the flaw that brought down so many in this city; he had no desire to be in the limelight. In fact, he shunned it. Seekings was well aware of Moore's reputation as someone to fear and it pleased him very much. The president needed someone like him to cut through the questions and nettlesome, time-consuming coordination that Washington would demand, if you let it. Moore didn't let anything delay or deter him — and that was exactly what Roger Seekings wanted.

Seekings idly wondered how long he would remain in office if the details of all of Moore's projects were discovered. Not long, he was certain.

"Mr. President, we have known for some time that there are many governments in the world that would like to acquire enough plutonium to fabricate a nuclear device. All of the Western powers have expended considerable effort to stop them. As you are aware, we have been bringing nuclear fuel rods from Europe back to the U.S. to avoid having them stolen by terrorists. Now, we are seeing the accumulation of large amounts of weapons-grade plutonium in the republics of the old Soviet Union. Quantities of stolen plutonium have been seized in Germany, Italy and Russia. This winter the Germans found enough in one suitcase to fabricate a bomb."

"O.K., so far this is information I can glean from *Newsweek*," the president interjected.

"Sir, I believe there is great risk. The money to be made from plutonium is quite large. But there's more here that should worry us than the money. Many organized crime groups in Russia are built around a core of former military men. I've read and reread the profiles on these men. They have a particularly dark and vicious hatred for us. Maybe it's bitterness over having been beaten and humiliated. My fear is that some of these men would like to see plutonium enter the market of terrorists, not for profit, but for the sake of harming us."

"Is there any evidence these groups plan to take the stuff?"

"Nothing solid."

"But you feel something is going on?"

"Yes, Mr. President. I believe it. So do the Russians. Their security agency has selected the weakest members of each criminal organization and bluntly threatened them. The FBI is confident this will prevent a raid."

"Are you?"

"No. We should never underestimate such groups. They will try like hell to get their hands on it. Perhaps even once it gets here."

"Come on. Here! How in blazes would they get it out of the country?"

"Mr. President, this country has failed for three decades to stop the importation of illegal drugs. Our society does not permit the measures that would be necessary. The same is true here. With solid planning and enough money, one of these groups could take anything out of the U.S. they wanted. The goal should be to absolutely stop them from taking the material in the first place."

"All right. I'm not convinced, but God knows the risk of being wrong on this one is too great to take chances. I want you to stay on top of the FBI and the others and keep me personally briefed on what happens. As far as domestic security, do whatever it takes to stop the theft of this damn stuff. You get with the FBI and the lawyers in Justice. Get with whoever does railroad security and so on. Do this with my direct orders. Get me whatever authorization you think you need, and I'll sign it."

"Mr. President, on a related note, the governor of South Carolina, ah... Governor...." Moore searched his notes.

"Governor William Haselden. One year into his term. Farmer. Baseball player at Clemson. Darling of the Religious Right," the president added.

"Yes, sir." Moore looked up and continued, "He wants to meet with you to discuss the shipments of plutonium we plan to send to the Savannah River Site in Aiken. Of course, he's right. We have been planning for some time to send the material there for permanent storage. But we aren't sure how he knows this. We haven't finished structuring the legal requirements, and there has been no public release of information."

"C. A., come on, someone up here told him." Seekings chuckled. "Find out who it is and tell me immediately."

Moore saw the tightening of muscles in Seekings' face signaling that he was angry. "Now when does the governor want to come, and what does he want to do... exactly?"

"He's been making a lot of public noise about these shipments of plutonium. And he's hired a private law firm to represent them — maybe to sue us."

The president laughed.

"Several years ago, South Carolina sued to stop the shipment of spent fuel rods from Europe. They lost, of course," Moore continued.

"A redneck governor wants to make a little political hay by fighting with us. Big damn deal. Is there anything new here?" Seekings was amused by Moore's concern over such a transparent bit of political grandstanding.

"We can't afford any delay, Mr. President. And we can't afford to be made to discuss the details of our security plans with state and local politicians."

"You have my support. Get with Justice and make sure they understand the White House wants any legal challenge killed as soon as possible."

Seekings walked over to the large desk that faced the presidential seal woven into the carpet. Picking up a football he kept on the desk — it was an effort to evoke the image of JFK — he walked to the window and tossed the ball lightly from hand to hand. "And tell my secretary to schedule the meeting with Governor Haselden for a date I won't be in town. Have the vice president attend instead." Smiling, he added, "Don't tell Haselden. It'll be a little lesson in where he fits into the big picture."

"Yes, sir."

*   *   *

It was nearly nine o'clock at night when C. A. Moore headed home. He passed the illuminated Washington Monument and stopped for a light. The imposing centers of American government were lined up on both sides of the broad avenues bordering the Mall, anchored by the Capitol at one end and the Lincoln Memorial at the other. It never failed to thrill him. It was the center of the world.

A satisfied weariness filled him. His entire day had been consumed with study and analysis, meetings, and more study of the problem posed by the plutonium being collected in Russia. There was no doubt this would become a major project — and that he would have a free hand to solve the problem. *Focus. That was what gave life meaning.* As he crossed the Potomac into Virginia, he exulted in the knowledge that he was one of the few men lucky enough not only to be free to concentrate himself totally on a problem but also to possess the power — albeit power as an extension of Roger Seekings — to do what was necessary to solve it.

Now, he was anxious to get to the farm. It was only a farmhouse, really. He had neither the time nor the desire to plant anything or care for animals. He liked the image, however, the idea that he was leaving Washington behind. Going to the farm. In truth, he never left Washington. His mind never retreated from a mission once it was undertaken, no matter where he was. And there was an endless succession of missions. Nor was he ever separated from contact. The computer, fax, and secure phone ensured continual control.

The drive was too long, but he knew that only out here could he ensure the solitude he needed as badly as the frenetic and important work he did. Tonight, he was especially anticipating seeing his current housemate.

He would have thought it odd to say "lover." He needed to unwind, to feel the warmth of another human being. The letting go would wash over him, carry and lift him along, leaving behind for the briefest of moments all thought and concentration. And he would feel refreshed again.

C. A. Moore was forty-seven and retained the dark good looks that had always enabled him to attract a companion for a night, or longer, as he chose. Those same looks and the intensity he brought to romance, as to everything else, swept the young graduate student who became his wife, completely off her feet. They stayed together for ten tempestuous years, through most of his career in the navy, and long enough to have two children, now grown. Moore's intensity was capricious, however, and the focus he brought to bear on the problems of people, he did not apply to individuals, even to the woman whose love for him languished for the lack of it.

Their divorce was a sad admission of failure for her, a relief for him. His sons had never really known him and did not object to his leaving. It had been three years since he had spoken to her. The pictures of their children in his office were older.

He liked the navy at first, but grew weary of the numbing routine. The demands of leadership required an interest in people he lacked. Constant compensation for this deficit left him exhausted. He liked the sea, and the absence from home gave him breaks from the demands of his family that were, as it turned out, necessary for him to stay married.

When he met Roger Seekings during a detail to the navy's Office of Legislative Affairs, Moore was immediately impressed with the congressman's drive and with all the machinations of Washington. At the time, Seekings was an important member of the House Committee on National Security. Seekings saw Moore was looking for a way out of the service, and he was in need of a man with his qualities. Moore jumped at the opportunity to join Seekings' staff.

Moore's marriage lasted only eighteen months longer. From that time, Moore had been free to pursue whatever mission he was given. It did not concern him that the missions were generally decided upon by someone else. They were important, and they were his challenges.

The farmhouse gate appeared in his headlights. He flicked the security wand and the gates slowly opened. He stopped in the yard and noticed that the house was nearly dark, but he saw that Terry's little Honda was parked in the back. Terry, an army sergeant, was the third in a series of young soldiers he had lived with. How easy they were to find and to win over with the promise of the great power he could bring to bear to advance their careers. It was so clean and neat.

He climbed the steps to the bedroom. Quietly, he slipped out of his clothes and into the bed. Terry murmured, but didn't wake. Moore slipped his arm around the firm, warm body. That was O.K. Morning was soon enough.

In the front yard of the old farmhouse a lone figure returned the camera to his coat pocket. The man could return and install his equipment later. His colleagues were already tracing the tag number of the Honda. The man walked down the lane to his own car parked a hundred yards beyond the gate.

Chapter 3

Laughter and screams from children floated up from the yard. A ten-year-old boy chased another between the folding tables set up earlier in the morning on the expanse of grass behind the farmhouse. In fact, children seemed to be running everywhere. Women were in constant movement, carrying pots and dishes of food from cars and vans into the kitchen and platters loosely covered with cellophane out to the tables in the yard. Groups of men idled here and there, some enjoying a last cigarette or cigar before they were ordered to sit down to the reunion dinner.

The Haselden farm was old. The land had been theirs since the Revolution; the house dated from three decades before the Civil War. It was two stories with a porch across the first floor on the front. In the rear, shed rooms were built out from the original two stories. Through the years, more rooms had been added to the rear so that now it rambled haphazardly. From the foot of the back porch, a yard spread out for an acre to a stand of pecan trees. Along the right side stood a row of cypress outbuildings of unknown age. Their origins rarely mentioned anymore, they were actually single-room slave cabins, more recently used to store seed and tools. Beyond the pecan grove stood the vegetable garden and beyond that fields, spreading across hundreds of acres of black, sandy soil.

For as long as anyone could remember, the Haseldens hosted the reunion at their farm. It wasn't so much a family reunion. Many families participated, all rooted in this section of Florence County.

"Blackie, they're going to be calling us up to eat soon." Watson Harris — "Bud" to friends and family — sat on the edge of the dock, his feet dangling toward the black waters of Welch's Creek. The creek was wide enough to make a fine place to swim. He and Blackie grew up swimming in this creek and fishing in the Great Pee Dee River, five winding miles downstream. Watson looked forward to the dinner he knew included all the things he loved but which were now deemed unhealthy and, therefore, permitted only on special occasions. Nobody wanted to put pork in the butter beans anymore, or even wanted to cook the damned things.

Watson could almost taste the well-cooked gray beans, spooned over rice with diced hot pepper.

The governor stretched out across the bench on the dock, eyes closed, enjoying the feel of complete freedom. No calls. No meetings. Nobody wanted anything from him, not today. "I've got the cellular. June will call when they want us." As Haselden spoke, he opened his eyes and watched the gray moss gently swaying among the cypress and tupelo gums in the swamp across the creek. The sun was warm and the sky clear. A perfect day. "Bud, we'd like Billy to come up and stay with us for a week when school's out, if he'd like."

"Sure. Just don't spoil him too much. Last time he came back he thought Dottie and I were supposed to tend to him like those fellows you have there in the mansion. You know, 'Mr. Harris, what will you be having for lunch, sir? Will you be having dessert now or would you like it brought to you by the pool?' We didn't mind waiting on him, but we just wouldn't wear those little outfits."

"Why don't you just get...?" The cellular phone on the dock interrupted him. Blackie lazily answered. "The feast is ready, boy, let's go." The two men pulled themselves up and walked towards the truck. "Do you think Billy will want to come?"

"Are you kidding? What could be more fun for a thirteen-year-old than hanging out in the damned governor's mansion?"

William Blackwell Harris was Watson's son and Blackie Haselden's godson. Blackie and his wife, June, had a son at the same time that Billy was born. After a year of terrible sickness, the infant died. They learned soon after that there would be no more children. Their marriage nearly died with the tortured infant. As Watson Harris was like a brother to Blackie, Billy was like a son.

Blackie and Watson had known each other since before they could remember. The woods, fields, and swamps were theirs to explore. Blackie's father called in favors from the local school board and arranged for Blackie to attend the city schools in Florence with Watson. They learned about mathematics, girls, and liquor together. Their only real fight came when they left high school. Blackie was going to Clemson to play baseball. Watson could have gone, too. If Blackie was a good baseball player, Watson was extraordinary — his powerful arms could send a ball farther, and his legs carried him around the bases faster, than anyone Florence had ever seen. Clemson begged him to take a full scholarship. Blackie was furious when his friend refused to join him. But Watson was struck with an attack of wild independence that summer. He joined the army. All he would say was that he had had enough of classrooms and books.

Watson spent five years in the army and came home to Florence. One year and two jobs later, he joined the city fire department. A year later, he married Dottie. With her salary as a teacher, they did fine. Life had been good to him. When Blackie told him privately — returning from fishing to the dock on Welch's Creek — that he intended to run for the state senate, Watson told him he was out of his mind — that all politicians were criminals, or worse. Why would anyone with so much to enjoy in his life waste so much of it by associating with such scum? He said exactly the same thing a few years later when Blackie confided to him, while they gathered peanuts to boil, that he was going to run for governor.

But Watson was immensely proud of his friend. After June and Blackie lost their son, he was also relieved that Blackie was able to focus on politics. Those were days when he worried Blackie might not make it. The night his son's weak heart finally failed, Watson held Blackie while he sobbed great, heaving cries of pain. He feared the man's heart would fail, like the baby's. Two months later, June left. Through long nights of too much bourbon, he sat in the old farm house kitchen, listening to Blackie. One morning, he found Blackie asleep in a chair on the back porch, reeking from the liquor. Watson kicked the chair over. He grabbed his groaning friend by the shoulders and dropped him heavily onto a bench. "When are you going to get tired of being pitied, you son of a bitch!" The blistering speech didn't stop. His wife was his responsibility. She hurt even worse and it was his job — his job, he yelled   to go get her and put their lives back together.

Later, Blackie tried to thank Watson for what he had done, but Watson stopped him. "Some things don't need to be said." That's where they left it.

"Bud, how many people are coming this year?" Blackie asked as the truck followed the sandy road through the woods and along a newly plowed field.

"Well, you know, since you got yourself elected governor, we keep discovering more people with connections out here in Welch's Creek. This year, Dottie tells me they got back nearly three hundred confirmations."

"We ought to do more to help set this up. It's a lot on you and Dottie," Blackie said.

"Bullshit. Don't you have enough to keep you busy in Columbia?" Wild dogwoods filled the pine and oak stands with clouds of white. The hardwoods were sprouting light green blossoms. As they pulled up next to the old smokehouse, they could see the crowd lined up before the tables, loading their plates. "Man, I hope they leave a little for us." They stepped down from the cab and approached the end of the line. "In a miraculous transformation, ordinary guy Blackie Haselden becomes — in the twinkling of an eye — Brother Bill, Man of the People." Blackie turned his head and mouthed an obscenity, before offering his hand and a greeting to an elderly woman he did not recognize.

The tables held a tremendous feast. Casseroles and salads of every description lined one table. Bowls of rice awaited marriage to gray butter beans, black-eyed peas or steamed tomatoes. Smaller bowls of diced green peppers sat next to these. Corn on the cob, fried chicken, ham, and the centerpiece of any celebration in this part of South Carolina — pit-cooked pork barbecue — weighted down two entire tables. A dozen women hovered back and forth from the house to the tables, exhorting each one approaching the food to take plenty and declaring, "Save room for dessert!"

The governor located his wife and the seat she had reserved for him. "Lean over here a second," she whispered. "You're going to be asked to speak after dinner. So don't be surprised. And think of something to say."

"Oh my God," he groaned, not losing his smile. "Speak about what?"

"Governor stuff." She kissed his cheek. "I'm sure you can handle it. Don't blame me. The minister at Welch's Creek thought it would be a great chance for everyone to catch up — you know, on the issues of the day." Her husband groaned again. "The best part is that he will invite folks to ask you questions."

"Hey, just like a campaign," he whispered back.

"Who's ready for dessert?" Blackie's aunt called out from the porch. A chorus of children yelled back.

Blackie picked out a piece of pecan pie and returned to the table, but he was lost in thought about what in hell he was going to say. He wondered if any press had slipped in. So much for relaxation.

The reverend walked to the porch. From the top step, he called out for everyone to give him their attention. Wiping his mouth with a napkin, he continued, "As you know, we all owe a great thanks to Governor Haselden for hosting this wonderful community gathering again this year. We really ought to give June and Bill a big thank you." With that the well-fed crowd applauded warmly. "And let's don't forget all the cooks for this marvelous food we have been blessed with today." The crowd offered more, even heartier applause. "We really shouldn't let this opportunity go by without asking Bill to say a few words."

Haselden pushed back from the table and joined the minister.

"Give your attention to the governor, please." The crowd, fearing a speech, welcomed the governor with less enthusiastic applause.

After shaking the minister's hand and slapping him on the back, Haselden waved to the assembled family and neighbors. "Isn't this a terrific day? You just don't find food like this anywhere else but here in Welch's Creek."

The crowd couldn't disagree with this and clapped loudly.

"Reverend, thanks for giving me the opportunity to say a few words — a few, I promise. The election's not for three years."

This brought relieved laughter.

Now what to tell them about. How about the budget negotiations in the General Assembly? That would be deadly, he thought.

"The biggest challenge we have to face is getting our schools back on track." He summarized his education plan in three sentences from his stock speech. More loud applause.

The little crowd loved this stuff. Maybe this wasn't such a bad idea. He decided to stop while he was ahead.

"Now, that's enough from me. What's on your mind?" *Maybe just getting a nap,* he hoped.

No such luck. "Bill, is anyone going to propose legislation to protect the unborn in South Carolina?" The question came from a pretty young woman he didn't recognize.

Oh hell, he thought. Watson was leaning against the truck behind the tables barely able to control his laughter. At least someone was enjoying this.

"That's hard to say. As you know, we have to keep in mind that the federal courts will strike down any law they believe is unconstitutional. But I have always been pro-life and I will continue to fight any effort to make the bad situation we have now even worse." *Why did people make you do things like this? Did anyone really want to make girls get abortions illegally again?*

Another speaker stood, a tall, elegantly dressed elderly woman he recognized as his mother's cousin from Kentucky. "Blackie — when did you decide to be called Bill, by the way — why should the state get into the business of making it harder for a young family to avoid a problem pregnancy? Would you actually make it illegal again if you could?" Now he remembered her, in the vanguard of progress. Never married. Outspoken.

"How are you? It's been a long time. It's so good to see you. My campaign advisors thought 'Blackie' sounded too much like a Labrador retriever." The crowd howled. They knew the truth. "All I'm saying is that all of us in public office need to look out for the family as much as we can. The courts have told us what the law is, and we're going to obey the law in South Carolina."

Was this almost over? He spied Billy's hand held up. "Yes, Billy."

"I saw in the paper that the government was going to send a lot of nuclear stuff from bombs in Russia all the way to South Carolina, and we'd have to keep it here. Does it have to come here?"

This was a pitch he could hit out of the park. He could kiss his godson. "No, Billy. It does not have to come here. And if I'm any judge, it won't, at least not until we have done everything we can to prevent it. And one thing I can promise you — none will come here unless we are absolutely certain that our citizens are safe. The time has long passed when this state will sit idly by and take any waste that New York City or Washington or Kentucky" — *take that, Cousin!* — "wants to send us because they don't want to take care of it themselves. We are not the nation's dumping ground, and I will not let us be used as the world's." The crowd erupted into applause. "The president has agreed to meet with me. I'm sure we can reach an understanding. Our sister states that were supposed to take over the job of storing this lethal nuclear material are dragging their feet. It's so easy to avoid the problem — just send it to poor old South Carolina. Who cares what happens down there?" Loud and raucous applause erupted.

"I tell you now that we are of one mind in this state." He was in the groove now. "We have pulled this plow long enough. There must be an end, and I promise you there will be. No resource will be spared to take our case to the president, to the courts and to the nation. Enough is enough." They were on their feet, applauding vigorously now.

This issue would definitely play. Besides, he knew he was right.

* * *

They put the last glasses in the cupboard. June Haselden pulled down five mugs, poured four with the coffee that was just now ready, and mixed hot chocolate in the fifth. "Billy, here's your hot chocolate." He bounded into the kitchen from the den and grabbed the mug. June noted how his shoulders were broadening and his arms becoming stronger. He was growing up to be the same powerful man his father was. She never failed to be grateful for his presence. It didn't hurt so much anymore to remember that her own son would be turning into a man just about now.

"Thanks, Aunt June." He kissed her cheek and dashed back into the den.

She joined the others at the table. "We always gather in the kitchen."

"There's no TV in here," Watson observed. "I talked to Billy. He'd love to come up any time you all are ready to have him."

"It'll be great," said June. "You guys can take a breather for a while."

Dottie spoke up. "Blackie, what is all that about more nuclear waste? I thought it had been coming in for several years now."

He nodded. "That's true." He paused to think. It was still awkward for him to guard what he knew was sensitive without offending those close to him. "Remember that first train of nuclear rods? Remember how they ran the train right through downtown Florence without telling anybody they were going to do it? It shook us all up knowing they didn't need to tell us what was going on and didn't give a damn what we thought.

"The plutonium is worse. This is what every terrorist in the world wants to get his hands on. The only way I know to make sure they are careful enough is to force them to come out in the open."

"When are we going to go fishing again?" Watson interjected. He knew there was more to the story, and he knew why Blackie had to keep it to himself. "Let's all go down to the lake and put the boat in."

June added, "Let's do it. We need to get out of Columbia."

Blackie brought the coffeepot to the table and added some to each of the mugs. "When you bring Billy up, why don't you and Dottie stay?"

"That's a great idea. Will you come?" June added.

Blackie Haselden was never short of people to talk to. Yet only with these people was he at ease, confident. He supposed it was a weakness, but he had long accepted in himself the need for someone he trusted absolutely. It balanced his judgment, gave him perspective. He was convinced he could deal with the impersonal life he led only because deep inside himself he could hold onto these people he loved so completely.

"It's a deal. This time, we'll do it. Hell, you might not be reelected and then we would've blown our big chance to schmooze in the mansion," Watson said, gathering his mug and Dottie's and placing them in the sink. "We better go. Some of us have to work."

"What happened? Aren't you still a fireman?" Dottie burst into laughter.

"Very funny, Your Excellency." Stepping behind him, Watson slipped his large forearm around Blackie's neck. "Just remember I could always whip your ass."

"Yeah, but now trigger happy state troopers will track you down like a dog."

"Dad, I think it's a felony to choke the governor." Billy laid his mug on the table. "I guess this means we have to go, huh?"

Watson released Blackie's neck. "Yeah. Let's saddle up," he said. He bent to kiss June. "You're still too good for him, honey." He tousled Blackie's hair, as he had since they were six. "Stay out of trouble. No bribes and stuff like that, O.K.?"

*   *   *

The navy blue mini-van stopped at the security gate. "Henrico Heating and Air — Fairfax County's HVAC Professionals," it said in fancy white letters on the sides. The driver climbed out and stepped to the gate lock. Reaching into his overalls, he retrieved what looked like a remote control wand. He passed the wand over the electronic lock once, and it clicked open. He pushed the gate open, drove the van through the gate, and closed it again.

At the little farmhouse, he casually ascended the steps to the front porch and within five seconds had opened the door. He was professional.

Wasting no time, he found the large bedroom on the second floor. Carefully opening the toolbox on the bed, he laid out the instruments he came to install. With even greater care, and with surprising speed, he completed the installation, closed his toolbox, and left as he had come.

On the main highway, the van turned to the northeast, toward Washington. It was certainly nothing unusual this time of year. It would soon be hot in northern Virginia, and it was prudent to get the air conditioning system inspected. At the first stoplight, he peeled the invisible plastic gloves from his hands. They were tight and uncomfortable, but they would ensure that no fingerprints were left anywhere in C. A. Moore's farmhouse.

* * *

It was already 6:00. The streets outside his window were mostly quiet now. A pair of birds chattered in the tree next to the curb. Jim McNeely was the last one in the office again. For a week he had been wading through documents from the state's first futile effort to stop shipments of European nuclear material to the Savannah River Site. Then, it was the rods used to fuel nuclear reactors in power plants; depleted to the point they could no longer power the reactor, they still contained deadly radioactivity. The state complained the government was hiding the real risk hidden inside the rods and that it was violating one of the oldest environmental statutes. The requirement to disclose the dangers of a project was intended to end the secrecy blamed for so much environmental degradation in the past. The law gave voice to the idealism of an entire era, something that seemed increasingly remote to him.

A carriage pulled to a stop next to his window, and the driver pointed to the steeple of St. Philips. The two songbirds flew away.

What he found in the stacks of reports and statistics and affidavits was simple, and inescapable. The government argued there was no danger from the spent fuel rods. They claimed the rods had to be removed from Europe to prevent theft by terrorists. The material in the rods could be used like plutonium itself to fabricate a weapon. It was an emergency! The government won the case when the court found there was no proof that bringing the fuel rods to South Carolina was dangerous. Jim remembered that the first train carrying the fuel rods rolled through the middle of Florence, a city of thirty thousand people. The message from a triumphant federal government was clear.

Jim read the affidavits of the government experts. He knew they would hear these arguments again. There was no *significant* chance, they said, that an accident would occur that would release dangerous radioactivity.

But what was the danger hidden in the casks of fuel rods? What if there were an accident that shattered the heavy casks? Would deadly radiation escape? And how dangerous would it be? The questions were like the wail of a siren, but there was no answer. "Don't worry," the government said, "It won't happen. Trust us." *It's dangerous. It's safe. It's an emergency.* His head pounded.

He thought angrily of the governor. The man claimed he *knew* what the danger was. And they were supposed to find an expert to testify about what *Haselden* already knew. Testimony to confirm the illusions of a politician. He wondered bitterly where that expert had been in the first case? They were wasting their time.

The phone rang, a merciful interruption.

"So, when are we coming home tonight?" It was his wife, Alicia.

"I'm done. I thought I'd go by the hospital and see Rex on the way home."

"Tell him I'm bringing the children by tomorrow."

He gathered his coat and flipped off the light. He glanced at the affidavits on his desk. His battles with the government were always the worst. Their lawyers wielded an arsenal of weapons to delay or derail any challenge, to drive the costs of opposition beyond endurance. And sometimes, they took up more menacing tools. He remembered the effortless lie the justice department lawyer told Judge Richardson. He looked at the stacks of documents around him, and he knew the government was lying when it said there was no danger from the spent fuel rods. No, there was no doubt that the government would lie this time, too. And much more.

How much more, he could not imagine.

Chapter 4

Rex insisted on going to the naval hospital. Many friends pleaded with him to go somewhere else when the cancer first appeared. The army was his career for twenty-five years, and military doctors would go on taking care of him. He was unmovable. Now, it looked as though this was the place he was going to die. Jim paused for a minute in his car, gazing up at the illuminated windows. He hated coming to such a dismal, doom-ridden place to see a person so filled with life.

He walked out of the elevator into the seventh floor lobby.

"Colonel Skanchy's room," he said. He didn't need to be told visitation was permitted. It was always allowed when the end was near.

"He's just finished eating." The nurse led the way the few feet to the room. "Colonel. Here's some company. How was that dinner? Pretty good, eh?"

"You must be talking about the guy down the hall. That's where you send the chateaubriand and your fine wine. What you gave me was gruel." He began to cough badly. Jim's gut tightened.

She ignored the coughing and laughed. "Don't believe him. He's in the lap of luxury here. He just likes the attention." She slid out the door, pulling it gently closed.

Rex flashed him a smile, full and wide as ever. Only the face that framed it showed the ravages of the victorious disease. His eyes were bright. A careful look revealed that they were also tired. "Hey, Jim, it's good to see you."

"Are they taking good care of you?"

"I couldn't be better off. How are the children? Ready to get out of school?"

"They were ready in September. Alicia's coming by tomorrow with the kids. They miss you."

"Are you sure they want to see me like this?" He held up his arm bearing the intravenous needle.

"They love you. It's important to them."

Rex nodded.

"Rex, have you thought anymore about contacting the army?" For many months Rex's friends had encouraged him to file a claim as a victim of Agent Orange. He refused, but admitted that the cancer overtaking him was hatched in the clusters of dioxin molecules that invaded his body when he was exposed to the herbicide during the Vietnam War.

Though it knew of the effect on humans, for years the government stubbornly denied any connection between the poison and the illnesses of veterans. It acknowledged the truth only after public outcry. Still, Rex would not add his name to the list of victims. He was a soldier. If the cancer was a wound from that long ago war, he was happy to have lived so full a life. He would not turn on the government he served for so long.

"How's that case for the state coming?" Rex asked, ignoring the question.

Jim was glad to have someone to listen to his frustration, and he explained what he found in the boxes of documents from the earlier case. "I know they weren't telling the truth. And they still won." He shook his head. "I'm dreading this. I'm supposed to go find an expert to …. Hell, I don't know what he's supposed to say. It's a waste of time."

"Lately, every time you get into it with the government you sound like you're shopping around for a militia group to join." Rex's laugh was cut short by more coughing.

Jim smiled thinly. "The crazies. Anyone who wonders if the government is a bully or a liar gets to keep company with every lunatic tortured by nightmares of black helicopters … or little microchips secretly implanted in the brains of God-fearin' Americans. Jesus!" Rex was laughing again. "The trouble is I'm right about what they'll do. And I hate it. I really hate it." They sat in silence a moment.

"I heard from Matt." Rex said, referring to Matt Reicher, Jim's oldest and closest friend.

"Isn't he leaving New Mexico this month to go somewhere?"

Rex smiled, "He's coming here to be the executive officer of the weapons station. Can you believe it?"

"You're kidding."

"No, he's got his orders. It'll be great to have him back. But I guess we won't be going sailing." There was the first sign of sadness in his eyes.

The image of Rex and Kitty, his wife, with he and Matt on Rex's boat would always be fresh in Jim's mind. They filled a summer navigating the harbor on the *MISS KITTY*. The navy left Matt to cool his heels in Charleston the summer after college. Rex adopted the two young men. "The Skanchy Boys," Matt called them. There was special truth in the title for Jim.

Rex filled much of the void left by Jim's father, a distant and lonely man who could never give enough of himself. That and a childhood spent following his father from one assignment in the air force to the next, left him with a fundamental sense of detachment. Rex's fast-approaching death would be more than the end of a friendship.

"This is a real gift, Jim. Time is always in short supply. And this time is important. Use it." There was strong conviction in his voice.

"I know, Rex. We always find out there's never enough for what matters." Jim stared into the fatigued eyes.

"After Matt gets here, talk to him about this plutonium case. He's been at a lab where they study radiation hazards. He can help."

"You know Rex, he sort of works for the other team. This is going to be ugly."

"The government has a lot of secrets. Some aren't too pretty." Jim said, wondering if Rex was thinking of himself. "Talk to Matt."

"Thanks." He took the hand lying on the flawlessly white hospital sheet. It looked so much older and thinner than it had just a year ago. Much too old for a man of only sixty-seven, too old for a man with so much life. "Get some rest. I'll see you again soon."

*   *   *

"How was Rex?" Alicia asked him from across their den. Jim was always sullen after a visit to the hospital.

"He's about the same." He ran a hand over his forehead and closed his eyes. "The doctors don't give him much longer."

She crossed the room and slid her arms around him from the back. "There's nothing we can do. We have to be glad he was such a wonderful part of our lives." Holding his hands and looking into his eyes, she said, "I know what he means to you."

"He was so excited that Matt's coming back." He turned to her. "Do you know that even now he's trying to help me. With this nuclear case." Jim shook his head. "He wants to convince Matt to help me find an expert."

He was beginning to feel useless. Everyone around him was trying to take care of him. He was always reluctant to accept help, and the realization brought its own pressure. But he was tired. He took her in his arms. "I love you."

They had been married for twelve years. When their oldest started school, Alicia left her job as a professor of nursing at the medical university. She was pretty as well as smart. He had no doubt that he was a lucky man.

They went up the stairs and looked into the children's bedrooms. Both were asleep. John, eleven, was sprawled across his bed. Jim stepped through the collection of Lego ships and forts to the bed and covered his son. Eight-year-old Katherine was carefully curled in her comforter surrounded by a menagerie of stuffed animals. He bent and kissed her forehead. "Goodnight, Daddy," she murmured.

*   *   *

C. A. Moore pulled into the yard of his farmhouse.

He was exhausted and stressed. The dinner he shared with Sergeant Terry Wilkins that night began to relax him. The bottle of wine with dinner and vodka tonics afterwards left him calmed and ready for bed, but not for sleep.

The sensors installed in the master bedroom detected Moore and Wilkins as they walked in. Responding to the signal transmitted instantly, and silently, from the sensors, the cameras turned themselves on and saw Moore begin to strip off Terry's clothes, then kiss and caress the body underneath.

The eyes of the cameras watched dispassionately as the two naked bodies grasped and tangled themselves on the bed below. The microphones in the cameras captured and transmitted the sounds of voices excited, more breathless and strained as they neared the apex of their passion. Finally, the camera caught Moore roll away and drift off to sleep. One hour after the sensors told the cameras to activate themselves, they, too, went to sleep, as they were programmed to do, to wake again the next time the sensors detected anyone weighing 150 pounds or more walk across the old wooden floor.

In a trailer park five miles down the main road towards Washington, the man who had installed the sensors and cameras also slept. Tomorrow, he would find the transmission from his cameras carefully recorded on the receiver in the next room. Part of what made his job so rewarding, besides the excellent money it brought, was the opportunity to watch the kind of tape he would find.

* * *

Jim summarized what he found in the boxes of documents while he drove Bob Geddings to Columbia. He and Drew Holland were scheduled to meet with the lawyer who led the state's team in the first case. He was a man they had both known for years, a member of the small, tightly knit family of lawyers who specialized in environmental litigation. Geddings had a quick wit and razor sharp legal mind. They respected him, and they liked him.

"Do you have any ideas on where we can get an expert?" Geddings asked Jim. "We didn't have any success doing that before. Most of them outside the government have no credentials — or no credibility. The government has guys who've spent their whole working lives studying what happens with nuclear materials in all kinds of conditions."

"I've got one lead," Jim said as he pulled a sheet of notes out of his file. "A lot of the environmental contamination problems in the old Soviet Union are from accidents with radioactive waste. Teams of professors from the U.S. are over there studying it. Hell, maybe we could get hooked up with some of those guys."

Holland nodded. "Can we get the funds to pay for this kind of help?"

"As long as it's not exorbitant, that won't be a problem. The governor has rallied all the support we need. Which is another thing we didn't have going for us before."

Holland put his hand on Geddings' shoulder, "Look, Bob, you did everything you could last time. We can't make chicken salad if all our clients give us is chicken shit. This time, let's go out and get a nice, fat Rhode Island Red."

* * *

They turned the corner and passed the state capitol building. The soldier on top of the confederate monument stared defiantly north along Main Street, a street lined with gleaming office towers.

The governor's office set up the meeting at the mansion, where he was preparing for his trip to Washington. They were ushered upstairs to the den, a room in the front of the house, flanked by windows overlooking the landscaped grounds. Haselden was going over a notebook with his press secretary and his secretary of commerce.

"Come on in fellas. Do you all know each other?" Everyone shook hands and the lawyers picked seats among the well-stuffed chairs. "Get us some more tea, would you, please," Haselden addressed a man standing in the door.

"Tell me what you've got. Any leads on finding an expert?"

Geddings answered, "That's liable to be tough, Governor. We didn't have any success in the first case."

"You didn't have the support I'm going to give you this time, Bob. Do whatever it takes." He looked at the three lawyers. "Is there any other argument we can make other than their failure to reveal the real dangers of their plan?"

"Governor, I think we might be able to claim that the fuel rods and the plutonium itself are hazardous waste." Jim explained the scheme he and Holland mapped out on the drive to the capital. It was nothing more than a complex diversion. A "rabbit" they would release to lead many of the government's legion of lawyers on a pointless chase. He didn't tell Haselden that part.

"There is a catch. If the government really digs in its heels, it can have the president declare this stuff exempt from our regulation. And the General Assembly will have to pass regulations," Jim continued.

Haselden thought for a minute. "What do you think they'll do over there in the General Assembly? Will they go for this?" he asked his press secretary.

"Absolutely. You will have to send them the regulations, and lead them by the hand," she replied.

"Draft them right away, Jim. I want to get them over to the capitol in three weeks." He stood and walked to the corner of the room. "I'm meeting with the president tomorrow. So far, my primary goal is simply to get him to admit that the administration is planning to bring the plutonium here. Beyond that, it would be nice if he told me how they plan to do it." Picking up a baseball bat from a table under the window, he began stretching, pushing the bat over his head. "But Roger Seekings is a notorious, insufferable asshole. I don't think he's going to tell me a damn thing. In that case, I'll tell him we're not going to roll over. Any thoughts …?"

The press secretary started to speak. "Governor, I think we need to be careful. We have …."

Drew Holland interrupted, "Bill, are you in for the long haul?"

Haselden stopped, holding the bat hard in his right fist. "Yes."

"Then you tell that arrogant son of a bitch that you are the man elected by the people of one of the states of this republic to be their governor and that you are *not* going to give up until you have answers to your questions."

There was complete silence in the little room. Jim stared at Holland in surprise.

"O.K., Lawyer. That's just what I'll say." He patted Jim's shoulder. "Let me have those regulations. Make them tough."

* * *

C. A. Moore cracked open his eyes. The sun was just over the horizon and the bedroom was faintly visible. There was no rush to get up. His first appointment in DC was not until one. Still, the tension of the day before began to dig into him again, as the memories flooded back. It always did. It was the price he gladly paid.

Moore long ago accepted the truth about himself. He no longer wondered about the sense or normality of his drive to accomplish the tasks set for him by Seekings. It was simply how he was. What life held for him after Seekings left the White House seldom occupied his thoughts. That was a diversion, a distraction. He had low regard for those he saw all around him who constantly plotted their next career move. He knew it was impossible for such people to focus on getting something done.

The sooner he got the program in place to bring the plutonium out of eastern Europe, the sooner he would register this task a success, like all those before it. The night before, he had lost himself in sex again. It was only a temporary escape, a momentary haven. He recalled the sex and savored the still-fresh images. Some of the tension began to recede. *Give yourself a morning*, he told himself. *Relax.*

Sergeant Terry Wilkins' back was turned to him, rising and falling with the rhythm of sleep. The covers had been tossed off during the night and were gathered at the foot of the bed. Moore watched his young friend sleep, admiring. There was nothing out of shape about the young soldier. Wilkins was devoted to exercise and faithful to a daily regimen that preserved a trim and attractive body.

Moore pulled himself over and slid his arm around to stroke Wilkins' chest. Wilkins rolled over, looking up at him. Moore slid his hand up and ran it over Wilkins' cheek and jaw, feeling the day's growth of stubble. He stretched, raising his thick, strong arms over his head, flexing while Moore watched. "Like that, huh?" Wilkins said sleepily.

Moore caressed the young man's biceps and broad shoulders. "Yeah. And I know what you like."

*   *   *

"C. A., come in, come in. How are you?" Vice President Michael O'Connelly ushered Moore into his office. "I see from the president's memo that he wants me to meet with the governor of South Carolina. I understand you can brief me on what this is all about." He leaned back on the couch while Moore took a seat.

Mike O'Connelly had been around Washington a long time. But he had never seen anything quite like C. A. Moore. Sometimes he thought it was his age that made each wave of young functionaries who came to the capital seem less human than the one before. But the coldness and strange intensity of the man opening his briefing book on the table between them was real enough.

O'Connelly came to Washington as one of the young liberals of the 1960s. After several terms in the House, he won election to the Senate. He became an expert on welfare and had long been respected for his mastery of foreign affairs. His wry wit and ebullient personality made him sought after as a guest on television's political forums. O'Connelly was in his fifth term and sixty-eight years old when Seekings asked him to be his running mate. Seekings wanted a "real liberal" to get the disaffected left wing of the party out to vote; besides, O'Connelly scored very high in the focus groups and pre-campaign polls. Roger Seekings was a creature of public opinion. More than any of his predecessors, he lived by the polls.

O'Connelly hated presidential campaign politics. But he was ready to retire, and, as he joked with his many friends, what better way to retire than to be vice president? There was another reason he accepted the offer from Seekings, whom he barely knew. After four decades in Washington, Mike O'Connelly still believed. He was as crafty as any when it came to political horse-trading. And he was not naive. But the core of the ideals he brought with him to congress was still solidly in place. He didn't like what government had become. It was important for him to try to fix as much as he could. And if Roger Seekings wanted to give him a chance to do that, he would take it.

Mostly, his experience as vice president had been disappointing. Seekings had no apparent use for him except for the odd job here and there, none of which amounted to very much. This had always been the lot of his predecessors, and he accepted that fact. After all, he had been serious about retiring. But something else was starting to bother him. A foreboding was beginning to infect him about the administration he was a part of. The more he watched Seekings, the less substance he saw. With Roger Seekings, the public image was no more than a carefully painted screen. Behind that screen, O'Connelly was coming to believe, was only a man determined to keep power and enjoy the privileges that came with power. He was unsure what the president believed, if anything at all.

The gutter tactics of the campaign that had surprised and distressed him he now knew were fully approved by Seekings. Although O'Connelly was isolated from significant decisions, he was still well connected in the capital. He knew the same tactics were often a part of the administration's way of getting what it wanted.

And then there was C. A. Moore. O'Connelly knew Moore had been responsible for the resignation of officials who angered the administration. The president never got involved. O'Connelly believed Moore bullied them out, using information collected from government files — FBI, Secret Service, IRS, Military Intelligence — all files to which he had unlimited access. As he was during the campaign, Moore was Seekings' point man when he decided to fight dirty.

"Mr. Vice President, the administration is currently engaged in very delicate planning with European governments. Our goal is to bring plutonium from dismantled nuclear weapons in the former Soviet Republics to the U.S. for safekeeping. We believe there is grave risk that criminal organizations will steal this material and sell it to terrorists."

"What does this have to do with Governor Haselden?"

Moore paused as if pondering what information he should share. "Sir, the governor believes that we are planning to send the plutonium to South Carolina."

"And are we?"

"There aren't many places we can satisfactorily store it."

"Well, are we planning to send it to his state?"

"At this time, security concerns require that we not make public the details of our planning." He paused again. "The president wanted me to relate to you that he feels you should be fully briefed on this matter. South Carolina is the site that has been chosen. The president does not feel that it is in the national interest to share this information with the governor."

O'Connelly placed the palms of his hands on his knees and leaned back on the couch. "So, am I expected to lie to the governor?"

Moore retrieved a single page from his notebook. "The president feels that this summary will provide Governor Haselden with the information that is appropriate."

O'Connelly read the sheet. "This doesn't answer the question at all."

"We do not believe we can afford to include locals in the planning process. For security reasons. There's too much at stake."

"The state and local people may know more about things affecting safety than we do," O'Connelly replied.

"The president feels we need to keep this federal. And that we should not reveal our plans until they are complete."

"What does the president intend to tell Governor Haselden regarding the selection of his state as the site for the plutonium?"

"Nothing. We need to tell him we are still studying the matter. Shipment of this material must be done according to a schedule and along routes that we, and we alone, select. The details must be kept secret," Moore replied.

"The president's memo says nothing about that type of ... statement," O'Connelly said smiling. "I can't believe that Roger intends for me to deceive the governor." He laughed good-naturedly. "I can't imagine he would be dishonest with the governor himself, if he were here. Do you, C. A.?" O'Connelly knew exactly what Seekings intended.

Moore glared at the vice president, and then started to speak, but was interrupted by O'Connelly, "Look, what I take this to mean is that I need to be discreet with Governor Haselden and emphasize that this will be a ... top secret — do we still use that term? — operation of utmost importance to national security. I think what Roger wants is to convince him we will do everything possible to ensure safety." O'Connelly rose. "Now, won't they be here in about thirty minutes?" Looking down at the pages in his hand, he answered himself, "Yes, that's what the memo says. Why don't you come back then and we'll meet with them together."

After Moore left the room, O'Connelly sat down on the couch again and laid his head back on the comfortable cushioned back. *How did things get to be like this?* he wondered. *Did he really want to disregard what the president clearly planned for him to do? Could he? Could he look a governor straight in the eye and lie?* For a fleeting moment he thought perhaps Moore was right, that national security dictated complete secrecy, even from the chief executive of the state where they were planning to send this awful relic of the Cold War.

He reached toward the end table and picked up the framed picture from the top. *I wish you were here*, he said to himself. The woman who smiled up at him from the silver frame had not only been his wife and lover all those years, she had been his most trusted friend. How he longed for her counsel now. Well, there was really no doubt what she would have told him. He replaced the picture carefully on the table.

*   *   *

"Governor Haselden from South Carolina," the driver of the car said to the guard at the White House gate, "Here for a meeting with the president."

The guard looked perplexed as he studied the appointment list on his clipboard.

"Yes, sir. I see it right here. Welcome to Washington."

The governor and his party stepped onto the covered walk. The uniformed aide at the entrance didn't show his surprise, nor did he say that the president had left for a long-planned speaking engagement in Chicago that morning. After glancing at his own appointment list, he smiled at the governor, "Come right this way, Governor Haselden."

They followed him down a hall and into an office. The secretary rose and greeted them. "Come in and make yourself comfortable, Governor." She opened the door and let them into the Oval Office. As she had been instructed to do, she said no more. Mike O'Connelly greeted them.

"Bill, welcome to Washington." He motioned for all three to sit down. "How was your trip?"

Haselden was visibly confused. He was reluctant to ask where Seekings was. He didn't have to.

O'Connelly said, "I'm sure you would have preferred to meet with the president. As you know, Roger had to go to Chicago."

Haselden smiled, concealing the anger, which had now replaced his confusion. "I'm always glad to see you, Mr. Vice President. But to tell you the truth, I didn't know we'd be seeing you until just now."

It was O'Connelly's turn to be surprised. As he returned the governor's smile, he saw what had been done. Seekings set Haselden up to humble him. And, of course, he was the tool being used.

"I thought you knew," he said quietly. "Well, I hope we can make your trip worthwhile." Whatever lingering doubts he had about what he should do were swept away by the disgust he felt.

"This gentleman who has joined us is C. A. Moore, the president's special assistant for policy and security." Without waiting for Moore to exchange greetings, O'Connelly turned to Haselden. "I understand that you are concerned that South Carolina is to be the site for storage of more nuclear material, specifically plutonium from the former Soviet Republics."

"Yes. I've heard rumors for some time, but my inquiries haven't been answered. I really think it is appropriate that, as governor, I be informed of these plans."

"I agree with you." Glancing briefly at Moore, he continued. "What you have heard is correct. South Carolina has been chosen as the storage site for a large quantity of plutonium that will soon be brought from Russia."

O'Connelly noticed that Haselden was stunned at his frankness.

"There are serious security concerns with this plutonium. It is being sought by terrorists who will do almost anything to get their hands on it," O'Connelly continued. Haselden was nodding, but he was trying hard to figure out what was going on. O'Connelly decided he might as well enjoy this.

Motioning to Moore, O'Connelly went on, "Now, C. A. here is the most knowledgeable about the details of our plan. I'll let him summarize what he can without breaching security."

O'Connelly let his guests absorb this information before going on.

"C. A., explain — to the extent you can — our concerns." He gazed calmly at Moore.

Moore said nothing for a full minute. He was marshaling every ounce of his self-control to keep from lashing out at this old fool. Gathering his composure, he smiled at O'Connelly and said quietly, "Beyond what you have said, Mr. Vice President, I really shouldn't elaborate at this time. There are many things we don't know."

"O.K. Thanks, C. A." O'Connelly laughed, "I guess you did a better job of briefing me than I gave you credit for." His stare bored into Moore. Turning back to Haselden, he said, "There are clearly a number of security concerns that we need to work out with your law enforcement agencies. You know your state better than any of our people."

Still confused, but pleased by the unexpected openness, Haselden responded, "I appreciate that. If this is something that must be done, we can offer a lot of help in making it safe. No one has more of an interest in doing that than us."

"Precisely." O'Connelly motioned to Moore again. "Now, you should stay in direct touch with C. A. As this develops, as the environmental documentation is prepared, and as final details are crafted, we need to work very closely with the state. If there are any problems along the way, feel free to contact me."

"Thank you."

"All right, are you clear on that, C. A.?" Moore stared at the vice president.

"Good. Is there anything else we can do for you, Governor, while you're in Washington?"

Haselden and his party thanked the vice president and left the Oval Office. When the door was closed, O'Connelly turned on Moore, "Get out."

* * *

A few miles down the highway from C. A. Moore's farmhouse, as evening fell, the man returned to the trailer that was temporarily his home. He poured a cup of the coffee that had just finished perking. After a few sips of the strong dark blend he favored, he positioned himself in front of the television and inserted the tape transmitted by his cameras from the farmhouse.

He was shocked. His clients' contact said nothing of who the presidential aide's live-in was, only that it was a soldier. They certainly didn't tell him it was a man. He watched dumbfounded as Moore took off the man's clothes, revealing a large, well-muscled body. The young man was clearly enjoying Moore's attention but was not reciprocating. It was one-sided lovemaking, to be sure. The presidential aide was enthusiastic. The man chuckled out loud to himself as he watched Moore work on the soldier's body. He laughed as he rewound and watched the tape a half dozen times more.

He didn't know who this guy was, but it didn't take a genius to figure out what was going on. He had seen most of the base, even ugly, things that could be found in people's lives. His work brought him close to the truths hidden behind the most carefully cultivated facades. He recognized the essence of the relationship between Moore and the soldier. Moore was a powerful presidential aide. It wasn't necessary to know his position. The soldier was young and ambitious, and knew Moore could write whatever ticket he wanted to punch. All he had to do was let Moore have some fun. It was probably nothing the soldier hadn't done before anyway, when he was lonely and without a woman. Hell, maybe he likes it. With this arrangement, the soldier scored a huge career advancement, at no cost — at least at no cost he was unwilling to pay.

And the aide. There he was on the film, so secure in his house, enjoying his secret pleasure. And boy was he enjoying it. The reality was that this guy was toast, unless he did whatever the men who would soon have the tape demanded. I'll bet it won't be cheap. His professionalism told him never to wonder such thoughts, but he couldn't help speculating on who this guy was and what his clients wanted from him. As the tape flickered again, and the soldier's head slowly moved from side to side, his eyes closed, the man wondered about him as well. *This'll finish him for sure*, he concluded. It was too bad.

He rewound the tape and packaged the small cartridge as he had been instructed in the envelope that his contact provided. The tape would be in Richmond by Tuesday. Beyond that, he didn't know where, or to whom, it went. He would keep the backup tape just in case, and for his own collection. You never knew when something like this would come in handy.

On Tuesday, after the tape arrived in the tenth floor offices of Tidewater Investors Centre, it would be delivered to an international courier. By Thursday morning, the tape would be in Petrozavodsk.

Chapter 5

"Alexis?" There was no mistaking the voice. "Alexis? I know you can hear me, my friend. Aren't you glad to hear from me again?"

Alexis Plekanov was fully awake now. His heart pounded, and the pain shot through his stomach.

"Alexis Nikolaevitch..." the voice sang, "talk to me."

"What do you want?" Alexis said with more strength than he felt.

"Go to the Republic Park. The phone by the gate will ring in twenty minutes. I know you will be more comfortable speaking with me outside of your flat." The receiver buzzed as the voice hung up. Alexis glanced at his watch.

Twenty minutes later Alexis sat in his car next to the stadium gate watching the public phone. Two minutes later it rang.

"Very good, Alexis. I was certain you would want to speak with me. How is your little son?"

"He is well."

"So, Alexis, let us come straight to the point. I am sure you wish to return to your family." The voice mocked him. Hatred welled up inside Alexis, mixing with the fear. "We must know if you and your brother are planning a raid on the state's supply of nuclear material. You recall our arrangement — our partnership?"

"I recall." The skin on the back of Alexis' neck crawled when he remembered the first call from the voice. They would kill his son and his wife if Mikail tried to take plutonium in any of the old republics, unless he warned them first.

"Is there such a plan, Alexis?"

Alexis was silent.

"When and where, Alexis?"

"There is no plan. I told you before."

"Ah, but if one is hatched, you will tell me, won't you?" The voice laughed. Alexis thought of Misha's head exploding and wanted to do the same thing to this animal. "We will talk again soon, my friend. Go home and take care of your family." The phone buzzed.

Alexis turned to walk to his car. The streets were silent. He was cold, but not from the evening chill. It was the inescapable decision he must make that made him shiver. I will take care of my family, he told himself.

* * *

The fist slammed down on the desk again, the thud loud enough to send an echo even in the thickly carpeted office. It was not the first time Roger Seekings brought his balled fist down onto the desk since this tirade began; with each blow the men in the Oval Office cringed.

"I want someone — anyone — to explain to me why that dried up old son of a bitch thought he was in a position to screw with me," the president seethed at the small group assembled on the other side of the great desk. "C. A., did you not make it perfectly clear to O'Connelly that I did not want our decision revealed to that meddling redneck governor?"

There was no answer from Moore. None was necessary.

"But he still screwed it up." Seekings rose and marched to the mantle across the room. "Now... I... will... have... to... deal... with... that... puffed-up... little... bastard... for months! Instead of making it plain that he was out of his league, our benighted *vice* president invites him to take part in the process." Seizing a small model of a shrimp boat, a gift from the Boy Scouts of Texas, he hurled it across the room where it crashed into a portrait of Harry Truman, shattering and tearing the canvas below Truman's jaw.

Dropping into a chair, he snarled at the men in front of him, "Sit down and get this straight." They all sat. "I will not tolerate anyone from South Carolina participating in *any* way in this business. To hell with them!"

The oath hung in the air for a moment while the president caught his breath.

"All calls from those crackers will be forwarded to C. A." Turning to Moore, he continued, "And you will tell them that NO decision has been made as to a storage site for the nuclear material. Tell them that no decision is imminent. When they remind you of what that dumb ass O'Connelly told Haselden, tell them they must have misunderstood. Tell them it is impossible for the vice president to have said anything like that." He glared at Moore. His meaning was clear. *It should have been impossible, if you hadn't blown it.*

"I want O'Connelly completely isolated from any information regarding this matter." Pacing back to his desk, he turned on the youngest of the three cowering staff, "I want solid recommendations for a new running mate. That old fool is finished as far as I'm concerned." Waving his hand, he dismissed the two men with Moore.

When the door had closed, Moore thought Seekings' anger would subside. "Judas Priest, who does he think he is!" Beyond any concern with the effects of what Mike O'Connelly had told the governor, Seekings was outraged that his wishes had been disregarded, his decision subverted.

"C. A., I want him isolated completely."

"Yes, sir. The vice president will not have access to any information on our plans for the shipment of the plutonium."

Slamming his fist again on the polished wood top of the desk, Seekings yelled, "No! God damn it, I mean thoroughly cut off — ostracized — turned into a highly paid orphan. A frigging vagrant. I want it made as plain as it can be made to the media that he's lost it — he's senile. Gone. I want people to believe it. This is what you know how to do better than anyone in this town, C. A., and it's what I want done. I want him to be the very embodiment of uselessness. Do you understand me?" Moore saw the malice in the president's eyes. He had known Roger Seekings long enough to know that this was not a fit of anger that would pass. His boss and patron meant what he said — he intended for Mike O'Connelly to be destroyed as a figure in American politics.

"Yes, sir."

"Then do it."

* * *

The Hotel Byelorusse occupied a modest building a dozen blocks from the Kremlin on Gorki Street. Mikail nursed his second cup of coffee and a cigarette in the bar while he waited for the Arab. There were many finer hotels in Moscow these days, but none more discreet. He watched a couple at a corner table as they started on a new bottle of wine. He idly guessed them to be lovers, not husband and wife, as their rings would suggest. *In Moscow for a tryst, away from Ivanovo or some damn place*, he thought.

Marwan Atta stood a moment, searching him out, his tall, broad form blocking the bar entrance, then he strode to Mikail's table. The old-style suit fit the man poorly. Mikail thought he looked like one of the old socialist leaders. Poor clothes for a servant of the people.

"Plekanov, good to see you," Atta said, stretching out his long arm.

"Sit down, have some coffee before we talk business. So, Marwan, how are things in Yemen?" Mikail motioned to the bartender for a cup for his guest.

"The same. We're neither one thing nor the other. Everyone is master of our fate except us."

Atta sipped his coffee, glancing casually around the room. He was clearly a man accustomed to caution. He needn't bother, Mikail thought. Every entrance to the hotel, indeed every street leading to the hotel was under surveillance by his soldiers.

"Nothing will change until we can demand the respect of the West. It has always been so for us. Only power can solve our problems," Atta said coldly.

Mikail nodded. "That's what we will give you, Marwan. Let's go and discuss the details." He led the Arab to the elevator and then to a third-floor room.

"It isn't important for you to know how I will get the material," Mikail said, responding to the Arab's repeated demand that he divulge the exact plans for stealing the plutonium. "What does it matter to you? As long as I give you what you need, that is all that matters. Telling you can only lead to more complications."

"Then when? I must know by what date we can expect delivery."

"Your needs will be met. You say you must have it in Yemen by November 15, and you shall." Mikail looked at the other man taking a long draw on his cigarette. "Tell me, Marwan, do you have the other pieces you need to make this toy of yours — the trigger mechanism, the shell, and so on? They are very complicated, are they not?"

"We have it all. All but the plutonium." He had carefully overseen the collection of the many requirements himself. Most had come from Russian military organizations, anxious for money. Some, the basic parts, their own engineers and technicians had fabricated. They were not such complicated devices after all. It was the rare fissionable material that was so difficult to come by, and this Russian thug would take care of that for them. Again for money. All awaited the plutonium, secreted in caves, guarded by men who had no idea what the crates hidden there contained. In fact, no one in the world suspected that the Arab holy warriors would soon possess a nuclear weapon. It was what the infidels feared the most, and soon they would know more than their fears.

They should suspect, Atta thought. *What else should people be expected to do when they had been treated as the Arabs had been?* They had been hounded by the unholy Americans and Jews for fighting a war of self-defense. He was called a murderer for doing what soldiers are supposed to do. He remembered the thousands of the enemy killed in New York and Washington. And he had killed many enemies of Islam himself. In Kashmir. In Afghanistan against the American devils and their allies. In Palestine against the hated Jews. They would have killed him, if things had been different, and would do it now if he were found. But that was in the hands of Allah. *The rest of the world will never see the truth of it, though, and they will never let us have decent lives. Lives that we deserve.* Muslims would have to take their honor and respectability in the only way such a weak people can. Hadn't their history been one of constant struggle against those who would enslave them, or worse?

"Very well, Marwan. It will be delivered to you by November 15. And the gold?"

"Yes. The gold will be delivered to your bank in St. Petersburg the same day. Twenty million U.S. dollars."

Mikail produced two crystal glasses and filled them with mineral water, in deference to his partner. "A toast to a good venture for us both."

* * *

When the Arab left, Mikail stood by the window watching Gorki Street below. The sidewalks were crowded with people hurrying along in the warm May sunshine. Moscow spread out before him, the ornate spires of Stalin's skyscrapers rising on the horizon. For an instant the idea of providing men like Atta with a nuclear weapon unsettled him. *But this is the world the Americans have created*, he reminded himself. *Boundless chaos they have the power, but not the courage, to control.* More Marwan Attas would acquire more nuclear material from others like him. No one could prevent it. Ancient enemies from the Baltic to the Indus would seek out their own ultimate weapon, most in the name of God, all in the name of protecting themselves from those they insisted would murder them.

Ultimately, Mikail didn't care what Marwan Atta and the other madmen in Yemen did with their weapon, so long as they paid him the twenty million dollars. And ultimately, no matter what the Arabs did with the device they would surely build, the Americans would suffer, and that made Mikail very glad. The same Americans who had driven his country to disintegration.

Still, it was an awesome thing he was about to do. One should reflect on it, and savor the thrill. Mikail poured himself a vodka and stretched out on the bed. He glanced at his watch. The woman he had arranged for would arrive in another fifteen minutes. The excitement of the deal with the Arabs made his desire all the more ardent.

* * *

The loud crack of the bat making solid contact startled the small crowd of parents gathered on the aluminum bleachers. A good hit in a baseball game always electrifies the crowd. But in an eleven- to twelve-year-old Little League game, a good solid hit is so rare, that when one comes, it's a shock. The ball arched slowly toward right field then, reaching its apogee, began to drop quickly toward John McNeely, scrambling to place himself in the right spot. The only thing more rare than a good solid hit at this level of Little League was a successful catch of a good solid hit.

"Oh God," James McNeely whispered to himself.

"Come on, John. You got it!" his coach yelled.

Realizing too late that he was a step-and-a-half too far to the left, the boy hurled himself where he thought the path of the ball would take it. For a second, his body seemed to hover horizontally, the glove thrust as far as he could reach. Giving way to gravity, he fell hard on the grass and rolled over once before leaping to his feet — holding the ball.

The bleachers across the diamond groaned. Jim and his fellow parents jumped to their feet roaring their praise for his son's magnificent — and surprising — catch.

It was John's turn to be retired from the game and let another player finish in his place. He ran from the dugout to the concession stand.

"When are you leaving?" Jim asked Alicia, who was seated next to him. She and the kids were going to be spending the upcoming weekend with her parents while Jim did his monthly duty with the army reserves.

"About noon. There's no need to rush. Do you want to meet us for lunch on the way out of town?" There was another crack, this one landing next to the left field fence. The parents around them rose as one and cheered madly. Now the score was tied. Parents in both stands silently worried that the game might go into extra innings.

"Yeah. I wish you and the kids could help me welcome Matt."

"Tell Matt we'll have him over for dinner soon. You two need to catch up. And you need a break from this radiation case, don't you?" She slipped her hand into his and smiled slightly.

He studied her face and saw she was serious. He leaned over and kissed her.

"Have I gotten too wrapped up in it. I'm sorry."

She touched his chin lightly and smiled broadly. "Maybe just a little. Try not to lose it."

* * *

"I know this may be a silly question, but is there any way to get in touch with Drew today?" It was Geddings from the attorney general's office.

Jim smiled as he answered, "It's a Friday. It's May. The weather's perfect. Where would you look for Drew?"

Geddings laughed, "O.K. I tried. You're my witness."

"What the hell is going on anyway?" Jim asked.

"The governor called me about fifteen minutes ago and insisted I talk to you and Drew at once. You all know about his trip to D.C., right?"

"It went great. And we may have nothing left to do."

"Not so fast. A couple of days ago Haselden tells his staff to contact this C. A. Moore guy to start coordinating with him. They call Moore's office and leave messages. None are returned. Ten messages in two days. Yesterday afternoon, Haselden calls the vice president. O'Connelly tells him that he won't be playing a role in this issue any longer. He's polite and all that, but was clear that any contacts would have to be with Moore directly. You with me so far?"

"Yes," Jim replied.

"O.K., so Haselden calls the president. No calls are returned all yesterday. Finally, last night Haselden calls and says it's an emergency. Seekings comes on the line. He tells Haselden that he is very sorry. There is no plan to ship plutonium to South Carolina or anywhere else. He appreciates the governor's interest in national security. When Haselden pressed him on what O'Connelly said, Seekings apologized for any misunderstanding. Said he was sure that as a chief executive, he knew he could appreciate that things like this happened. That it was sad. *Sad*. Then he asked him if South Carolina was expecting a good soybean crop this year. *Soybeans!*"

"Jesus."

"Haselden went ballistic. He called me at home last night at 11:30 after he had calmed down enough to make only marginally unrealistic demands. One of them was to tell me he wanted us to get ready to 'go to war,' I believe were his words."

"Well ...."

"No, wait, there's more. Seen this morning's paper yet?"

"No."

Geddings continued, "An article ran in yesterday's *Washington Post* about the vice president. It claims that 'sources' report that O'Connelly is no longer actively participating in the administration — that he might even be senile, Alzheimer's or something. It says, 'The White House issued a statement today categorically denying that the vice president's health was anything but perfect, for a man of his age. An administration spokesman said it was important to refute rumors, which he said were currently making the rounds in Washington, that Mike O'Connelly is no longer included in major decisions or briefed on important issues. The vice president continues to be a vigorous and vital part of the administration.' The article goes on to note that, prior to the announcement, no one seems to have heard the rumors. Odd, don't you think?"

"I guess it doesn't matter at this point if we can figure out Washington."

"What can I tell Brother Bill?" Geddings asked.

"Tell him we need to go to the next phase. The regulations we sent him need to be circulated in the General Assembly and enacted as soon as possible. Then we need to get ready. There's a lot of work to do." Jim saw his daughter Katherine stick her head around the corner and wave at him. "Oh, and tell him that Drew took a rare Friday afternoon off to go fishing and is not reachable."

Katherine slipped into his office and gave him a hug, handing him a note she had written, "DADDY WE HAVE TO GO TO LUNCH NOW. I LOVE YOU."

"I'm being kidnapped by my family, Bob. I'll be back this afternoon if you need me on this. Bye."

"You forgot us." Katherine affected an exaggerated pout.

Pulling her onto his lap, he hugged her. "I could never forget you. You're my favorite and sweetest daughter."

"I'm your only daughter."

"Smart, too."

After lunch, Alicia loaded the children into the car for the long drive to her parents. She kissed Jim through the window of the van. "Have fun tonight. Mature, sensible fun." She laughed.

"Don't worry. I'm a big boy."

* * *

Jim lay on his back on the floating dock trying to convince his head to stop spinning. The stars overhead seemed to be swaying back and forth. The warm night air floated over his bare chest and legs, drying the droplets of water that remained from his swim in the river.

"Hey, get back in here, you wimp! Let's swim to the other side."

Jim lifted his head up enough to see over the edge of the dock. Matt Reicher was treading water a few feet away. Light from the pole at the end of the dock illuminated a small circle in the otherwise inky blackness of the Cooper River. Beyond Matt lights from one of the station piers danced on the river's surface. He glanced at the Jim Beam bottle sitting on the bench. There wasn't much left.

"You're nuts."

"Come on, Wimp."

"All navy divers are nuts."

"It isn't far. We can make it."

"It is far. But that's not the reason I got out. There's a much, much better reason I got out."

"Yeah. Like what, cause you're a wimp?"

"Nope. The alligator."

"You're lying," Matt said, but his voice didn't sound sure, and he was turning his head from side to side, scanning the dark waters. "What gator?"

Without turning his head to look, Jim pointed to the left. "That gator. The one with bright red eyes over there."

Matt followed the pointing finger. There they were. Two red dots glowing in the reflection from the dock light. As if propelled, his body launched itself to the steps of the dock and he scrambled over the side, his naked body falling heavily on the wooden planks. He lay on his stomach for a few seconds breathing heavily.

"Jesus, why didn't you tell me sooner?"

"What are you, a wimp? No gator is a match for a deep-sea diving, explosive disposal stud like you. I was afraid you might go over and hurt him. Or her. Whatever. They're an endangered species, you know. Those of us in the environmental community are very protective of ...."

"You are drunk."

"It wasn't me talking about swimming across the Cooper River at 1:00 a.m. with no clothes on."

Matt got up and stepped into his shorts. "Boy, we did a job on this bottle. Here finish it," he said handing it to Jim.

Jim lifted himself on one elbow and took the bottle. After a swallow, he handed it back. "How about some coffee. I'm afraid my head is going to spin right off my shoulders."

Matt tilted the bottle back and gulped the last of the brown liquor. Wiping his mouth on his arm he looked down at Jim, "Wimp. Wimp. Wimp."

* * *

It had indeed been a long night, just as Matt Reicher promised when Jim met him at the Weapons Station that afternoon. Matt hailed him from his jeep outside the gate. He shook Jim's hand and pulled him into a crushing bear hug. "You look great."

"So do you. Still keeping in shape, I see," Jim said.

Matt was still one of the strongest men Jim had ever known. His legs and the arms that hung from his broad shoulders were extremely powerful. He looked much the same at thirty-seven as he had at twenty-two.

As they made their way into the officers' club dining room, Jim patted the short thatch of hair on Matt's head. "Letting your hair grow out, there, Matt?"

"Hey, quit that. I'm the XO. It's part of the image."

They were practically alone in the dining room. "So how's the practice?" Matt asked.

When Jim didn't answer, he stopped eating and peered at him. Is something bothering you? Talk to me."

Jim spoke slowly, "I've been at this for twenty years now. I just don't feel like I'm going anywhere ...This sounds like bullshit. You don't want to listen to this."

"Have you ever turned a deaf ear to me?" Matt stared hard at him. "Remember me? I was there when you started this lawyer thing. So, now you don't feel like you're going to set the world on fire, is that it?"

"I don't even have a match."

"You're right. This is bullshit."

"Even when I win, it's a failure for both sides. Only we win."

"No one's going to give you a medal. Do you do a good job for the people who hire you? Then that's enough. At least that's all there is. If you want recognition, run for office." Jim started to laugh. "At least nobody's trying to toss you out into the street."

"What do you mean by that?" Jim asked.

"I'll tell you later. Now, what's this case that Rex was telling me about?"

"You mean the plutonium case. We're taking on the federal government, your employer. Are you sure you ought to be talking to me about this?"

"I'm no lawyer. Don't confuse me. I know you need to find an expert on what could happen with those spent fuel rods and plutonium. Right? I got to know a few out in the desert. Now, tell me the problem."

Jim looked at Matt for a moment, wondering how he ever came to have a friend like this. Then he explained the case. "They lied in the first case when they said there was no danger. And they'll lie again this time."

"Fire. Or an explosion. Or both."

"What?"

"Fire. That's the thing to worry about. Fire is what will cause a release of radioactive particles. Do you understand the different types of radiation?"

"Not really," Jim replied.

"Well, that's the first step. You need to get educated. Then you need someone who really understands this crap to lay it all out for you. Anthony DeSilva."

"Who?"

"Tony DeSilva. He's the guy you want to talk to. He left Energy last year. He lives in a little place called Cloudcroft in southern New Mexico. That's where he's from. He spent fifteen years studying what you want to know. Want me to call him? He and I were pretty tight."

"How did you get 'tight' with a nuclear physicist?"

"Titty bars in El Paso. He got real sick right after I got there. I don't know why, but he started telling me how he just hadn't gotten crazy in a long time. So, I took him to the strip bars in El Paso. He was a wild man. It's a good thing I didn't take him to Juarez, or we'd both have ended up in a Mexican jail. After that, he and I were pals. He's just living there in the mountains. If I ask him to, he'll talk to you. Is that what you want?" Jim didn't answer. "Do you want to know the answer or don't you?"

"Will he help us? This is a fight."

"You won't have any trouble convincing him to help you fight the government. O.K., it's settled. I'll call Tony." Leaving the club, they got into Matt's jeep. Passing through the security gate, he pointed to a small, long white building on his right, "That's the office." They turned onto a short road leading to three houses, two of nearly identical ranch-style design from 1950s.

"This is home," Matt said as he pulled into the carport of the first house. "Wait 'til you see this view."

He led Jim past the small kitchen and breakfast nook into a glass-walled den. Behind the house, the yard spread down gently to a bank that dropped off to the river. The wide river was bright blue in the late afternoon sun. Marsh formed the opposite bank, spartina grass stretching for miles into the distance. On the horizon the marsh met a pale line of trees.

"This really is fantastic."

While Jim studied the scene, Matt returned with two glasses. They clinked them together, "To friendship," Jim said. The bourbon and water warmed his throat.

"What the hell is in all these boxes?" Stacked around Jim were dozens of cardboard boxes that left only a small open area in the large den.

"Books. I don't know when I'm ever going to get them put up."

Picking up two of the heavy boxes, Jim answered, "Let's do it now. Where are the shelves?" An hour and several glasses of bourbon later, they slid the last handfuls onto the shelves.

"Now let's get much less serious," Matt said. "We're going for a swim."

"It's midnight. And we're drunk."

"Come on." Matt's eyes were lit with boyish excitement.

"Have you got some trunks I can wear?"

"You're not going to wear any."

"Oh, man, we can't do that. What about these other houses?"

"The captain is gone for the week and the other house is empty. No problem."

He was already out the door and jogging to the dock. "Bring the bottle," he called over his shoulder. Jim followed, laughing. Why not?

At the dock, Matt was already shucking his shorts. "I wonder if this place is ready for me to be the XO." With that he dove into the dark river.

"Not a chance," Jim hollered and joined him, the cool waters of the Cooper River flowing swiftly around his naked body. Maybe you don't have to quit having fun when you turn forty, even if you are a lawyer. They swam and made trips to the dock to take a swallow from the bottle. Finally, the bourbon began to overwhelm Jim and he climbed out of the river, his head spinning wildly.

Now, Matt stood over him. "Let's go, Wimp. Get your shorts on."

Over coffee, Jim's head finally began to clear. Matt pulled ham out of the refrigerator and made sandwiches. Jim remembered how Matt loved to fix people food. He was grateful and devoured the sandwich. Slowly, he began to feel normal again.

"What's the story with you and the navy?"

Matt cracked a hesitant smile. "They've pretty much decided they're through with me."

"You just made full commander. How can that be?"

"I got passed over by the command board. One of the members told me, all things being equal, I didn't go to the Persian Gulf for Desert Storm, so I didn't make the cut. There aren't as many slots as there were. After three years here, another tour will be the end. I'll get my twenty and then get invited out."

Jim was incredulous. "The Persian Gulf! What kind of bullshit is that? You were in the Persian Gulf. Have those bastards forgotten about the missile in that oil tanker you disarmed?"

Matt laughed. "That was before it was cool to be in the Persian Gulf. You, Mr. Reservist, are the one who got to go to the gulf when it was cool." He put his hand on Jim's shoulder. "Look, it ain't fair. But what can I do? I thought I punched all the tickets. The navy just doesn't need as many guys like me anymore." He didn't sound convincing.

"At least this will be a good tour."

"I'm not so sure." Jim looked confused. "When I reported on board yesterday, the captain said, 'Reicher, you're not my pick. The Ordnance Command gave me no choice. If you screw up I'll be your worst enemy.' Then he told me how he ruined some guy's career who pissed him off. This is not going to be easy."

"What an asshole."

"Doesn't matter. He's the boss."

Jim's anger was rising again. "When is Linda going to join you?"

Matt didn't turn to face him. Looking out the window toward the river, he answered softly, "She's not."

Jim stared at his friend's back and watched his head sink slightly.

Matt turned around. "She told me she was through with the navy, and when I was, too, to call her."

Jim started to speak, but Matt waved his hands. "It's complicated. We kept arguing over things. I guess she was convinced it was the navy. Long hours. Trips out of town. Entertaining people she couldn't stand. After a while, we couldn't even talk."

He approached the table and finally sat in front of Jim, who was watching him intently.

"Maybe it was just me. I'm a pretty weird guy."

"I think you're the most normal person in the world."

"How did I end up here? We haven't spoken in two months. I talk to my girls."

"Is there anything I can do, Tiger?"

Matt looked at him a long while, expressionless. "Just don't stop being my friend."

Chapter 6

Few things were more painful to C. A. Moore than being castigated by Roger Seekings. Try as he might to put it out of his mind, he knew that the nagging sense of failure would not leave him until he had solved this new problem. For a week, a stream of revelations, all personally crafted by Moore, found their way through his usual sources to the media. All were reported verbatim; all cited sources close to the White House. In another week, he would complete the first phase of isolation of the vice president. Every center of power in the government would understand that Michael O'Connelly had crossed the line into the realm of sad, pitiable incompetence. When Moore was finished, the old man would be regarded as more of a curiosity than a political force. What was more, the bastard would know why.

It was O'Connelly, after all, who was responsible for Seekings' anger. And that was unforgivable. Again, Moore felt the stabbing reminder of the harsh words, the sarcasm, the fury and frustration. He marshaled the painful memories as motivation to complete the task that would teach O'Connelly one final lesson in the politics of power. Reclining behind his desk, he swallowed one of the little red pills he knew would help control the pressure. He smiled as he reminded himself how most people lacked the strength to use the powerful medication without sliding into addiction. *It's all about control,* he thought.

*   *   *

Alexis' breakfast of sausage and rolls churned in his stomach. The steaming cup of tea he sipped as he stood by the window did nothing to relieve the burning. Today was one he had feared. But it would not be the last. This morning, he and Mikail would meet with the men who were planning the project — it sounded so civilized — *project* — to steal the nuclear material from Kazakhstan. They were coming to explain to his brother exactly how they would take the plutonium. The project would be laid out in great detail for his brother's approval and Mikail would again be the soldier, assessing strengths and weaknesses of the enemy, the best strategy. The men would tell him and Alexis how many rubles they must have.

He knew the schedule. He knew when the fate of his family would be sealed by this mad thing they would set in motion. The project would condemn his young son and his trusting wife to death. Russians know in their soul that government is capable of any savagery necessary to achieve its ends. It had always been so, and Alexis had every reason to trust that the anonymous voice of his government meant to murder his family exactly as it threatened.

His rational mind screamed for an end to his nightmare. There was no choice except to force Mikail to give up the plan. Mikail would never doom his own flesh and blood to certain murder. Alexis despised himself for failing to tell Mikail about the calls.

Outside the window, traffic on Nevski Prospekt flowed six floors below him. He was in St. Petersburg, in the headquarters of his growing chain of banks. The building dated to the end of the last century, zenith of Imperial Russia. Its revived grandeur appealed to the spirit of modern Russia exactly because of its origins in that distant, mythical past. It appealed to Alexis because it seemed real and solid. The old building's architects had known how to inspire confidence with their orderly arrangement of stone and precise balancing of embellishments. Here in the heart of the old city, he felt most at ease with the world. He loved the canals and cathedrals, and the ornate city palaces of the long-dead nobility. Confidence, celebration of beauty and power resonated from the city that proclaimed with every dome, cupola and gilded statue that it was the capital of empire. Never had pride in Soviet power — even at its peak — inspired anything approaching confidence.

Alexis reveled in the power of the money he commanded. The ways of marshaling its power came easy to him. How amazed he was when the money, which he thought would merely be stored in his banks to hide it from the government, began to take on a life of its own. Men paid a premium to borrow his money. Alexis no longer needed the money from the criminal enterprises Mikail ran. He longed to leave that part of their lives behind and guide this remarkable economic engine as far as it would take them.

The intercom on his phone buzzed. "Mr. Plekanov, Mr. Werner has called to say he will meet you in fifteen minutes." It was the message from Mikail. He would be waiting with the men in the basement.

When the elevator reached the bottom of its run, he exited into the small room that only he and Mikail could access. This was a room normally used only by he and Mikail for discussions of the finances of their businesses. It was austere, accommodating only a cheap table and chairs. When Alexis entered the room, Mikail was standing with two other men, one older than Mikail, and one younger. The older man Alexis recognized as Yigor Matveev, formerly an officer and, in Afghanistan, Mikail's commander.

Matveev pulled from his attaché case a military style map. His associate helped him spread the map out onto the table and he began to detail his plan. It was not one dependent on force. Rather, Matveev had conceived a rapid and stealthy swoop into the facility to simply pick up the plutonium. He and his men would not have to fight for it because of a generous and calculated pattern of bribes.

"Who will you be bribing?" Alexis asked.

"The assistant director and the chief of security, as well as the guards themselves, for good measure." Matveev's roughly weathered face betrayed no feeling. He spoke with detached professionalism, but he was clearly pleased with his plan and the painless theft of nuclear material it promised. "We do not expect any trouble at the facility. These men are like so many today. They are paid little, when they are paid at all. The guards are never paid and often given only cabbage to eat. Our money will keep them comfortable for years. They will have enough to deflect any inquiries from their superiors with bribes of their own. It is the trip to Syria that concerns us."

Matveev took some sheets of paper from the young man and continued. "The records of how much plutonium is kept at Zarmayevka have never been accurate. Even in the old days, the ministry officials often were required to re-audit the accounts of uranium 238 or plutonium. I am assured that the amount we require is so small that it will be a simple matter to jiggle the numbers a little, and no one, even if they are not being bribed, will ever be able to tell that anything is missing. Much of the nuclear material removed from our weapons has been sent to Zarmayevka, so their records are even more confused than before. The entire store of uranium 238 and plutonium is scheduled to be removed from this place by autumn, and the facility will be closed. The staff has no prospects for employment after they are cashiered, and this has made it even easier to recruit their assistance."

"We will encase the plutonium balls — slightly larger than soccer balls — in boxes lined with lead. The boxes will be put onto the helicopter, and we will fly to Semipalatinsk. A small cargo plane will take us to a small field in eastern Syria from there. The Syrian customs officials will be easy to settle with. If they knew what we are bringing, they probably wouldn't even ask for a bribe." The colonel laughed heartily at his own joke. "In Syria, our Arab friends will meet us and lead us to their God-forsaken little camp on the coast. From there, they will take their cargo by sea to Yemen. And our work will be done. Bad weather or mechanical problems with the plane could cause us serious trouble. We will have to rely on the Arabs to provide us security.

"For the trip to Zarmayevka and to Yemen, I will take only ten men, including Sasha here. This will require just under one million dollars. That's a small part of the twenty million we will be paid. A good profit. Most of the money will be for bribes, of course."

There was silence as Mikail stared at the map and Alexis at the sheet of figures Matveev handed him. "How have the officials at Zarmayevka been contacted? Do they know it is you they are dealing with?" Mikail jerked his head up to look at Alexis. Never had his young brother spoken of the details of an operation.

Matveev smiled at Mikail, then turned to Alexis. "Alexis Nikolaevitch, I have not dealt with these men myself. They have been approached by an intermediary who has been a trusted associate of mine for many years. And a good soldier of the Spetznaz. I can assure you no one we will pay — or see — will ever know who I am, or the identity of any of my soldiers." He chuckled slightly as he turned back to Mikail. His eyes told Mikail what he was thinking. *The damn banker wants to play in the game with us.*

"This plan will work, Colonel," Mikail said. "When can you do it?"

"After we have the money, we can move very quickly. The plutonium will be in Yemen by July 15, if all goes well." Matveev never made predictions without this caveat. How many plans had he seen come to disaster because of the unknown — the fatal surprise?

"Very good. Alexis will have the money ready for you in any currency you require."

"Alexis, I need $300,000 in American dollars, $200,000 in rubles, and $500,000 in Saudi ryals." Alexis made notes in a small notebook he took from his vest pocket.

"Two days and it will be ready for you in the usual way." Alexis returned the notebook to his pocket.

As Matveev and the other man made their way out of the room, Mikail signaled Alexis he wanted to remain and talk alone with him. With the door closed, Mikail motioned Alexis to take his seat again and Mikail sat next to him.

"What worries you, Alexis?"

Alexis looked at his older brother. The dark eyes that inspired fear in so many others were the same eyes that had looked after him from the time he took his first step. Mikail, older, larger and tougher, protected Alexis and taught him to make his way in the world. Now Alexis would ask him for protection again.

"We cannot do this thing, Mikail."

The dark eyes stared silently, the hard face rigid.

"If we take the plutonium, my family, all of us, will die."

"You are talking nonsense, Alexis"

"Two months ago I received the first telephone call, and I have received three since. They are always the same. A man calls me and tells me to go to a pay phone in Petrozavodsk. Then he calls. He says the government knows someone is planning to steal some of the state's plutonium or uranium 238. He says if our organization tries to take it, and the government has not been warned, our wives, our children, all of us will be killed. I believe him."

The dark eyes blazed. Anger swelled inside Mikail. "Bastards!" he railed. "Who are they?" he yelled at Alexis.

"I don't know. It's just a voice."

Mikail paced about the little room, finally tossing one of the chairs against the wall with a vicious sweep of one arm. "Why did they call you? They cannot know anything!" He was irrational, shouting.

"That's the point, isn't it? They don't know — so they are threatening me so that I will be their alarm bell."

"But why you? Why us?"

"Suppose they have also threatened each organization they suspect could plan a raid." Alexis had spent many sleepless nights analyzing the calls — at last reaching this conclusion. "In this way the government inoculates itself against surprise. Who would risk their families as well as their own life when the threat is so clear and certain?"

Mikail leaned against the wall, head tilted back and eyes closed. "How will they know it was our organization that makes a raid? If there is no fighting, but we simply take what the facility gives us, they could never know we had done anything at all."

"I don't know, Mikail. They may never know. If I were gambling in the casino, it would be a good bet. But it's my family we gamble in this game."

"Alexis, there has always been risk in our business. We can't run from every apparatchik in state security. We just have to be clever and careful."

Alexis stared deep into his brother's eyes. Why couldn't he see?

"Little brother, let me think about this. I'm sure we ...."

"No!" Alexis exploded across the table. "No! I don't want you to think about it! I don't want my son's life to be one of your risks! Not for plutonium and not for $20 million!" Alexis stared at his hand and realized he had been striking the table. He gripped the edges of the table and he closed his eyes. "No, Mikail."

There was no sound for several minutes, save for the labored breathing of Alexis. "You are right, Alexis." Mikail sighed.

Alexis felt tears of relief suddenly well up inside him.

"But this is complicated. These Arabs won't like being disappointed." He saw that his brother did not understand. "Alexis, these are men who murdered thousands because they were of a different faith. They slaughtered them with airplane missiles and suicide bombs. Not for power, or money or even for political advantage. But just because they hated the way they worship God. They're crazy, Alexis. They're insane killers. You have to understand how vindictive they will be if we fail them."

He read the question in Alexis' face.

"We have to get it for them, Alexis, or they will kill us."

"It just isn't possible. It was never possible. The Arabs must find another way."

Mikail laughed bitterly. "What a businessman you have become, Alexis. This is not a question of balance sheets. It's blood and survival —

and a fanatic's image of God. Do you think men who believe they are the instruments of God and history will give a damn about risk? Do you think men with so much blood on their hands will pause a second before murdering all of us?" *I have protected him too much*, Mikail thought. "Alexis, our world isn't one of order," he said quietly. "It's chaos. Typhoons and blizzards and earthquakes. Others may strive for 'order,' but not us. Can you imagine how many deaths, how many guns, how many ruined lives sent you the money in this bank? I can't give you what you want. All we can do is survive, and to do that we have to be cleverer and stronger than the wolves. Do you understand?"

"Yes," Alexis lied.

Mikail patted his cheek. As Alexis watched his brother leave, helplessness washed over him. Their lives were wholly dependent on how well Mikail could shield them from the madness swirling around them.

* * *

Vice President Mike O'Connelly walked along the narrow path of the garden behind his official residence. It was a pretty place, and never more so than now in early summer. "Fanciest Retirement Home in Maryland" he called it when he first moved in. It was a grand house, really, and often filled with the friends and colleagues from his decades in Washington. How his wife would have loved living here. No one could throw a Washington party like her, and this would be a perfect backdrop for her finest. He cherished the many people who came to see him and enjoyed their laughter at his bad jokes. But nothing seemed to fill the void left by Helen's death five years ago.

In the last few weeks, his "job" had become more aimless than ever. It was no mystery to him what was going on. Several times a week, ever since the meeting with the governor of South Carolina, a story appeared in *The Washington Post* containing denials from the administration that he was becoming incompetent. This was Roger Seekings' retribution against him for not lying to Governor Haselden. If it all weren't so transparent, he might be more concerned. There were certainly a lot fewer meaningless little assignments doled out to him by the president's chief of staff. He confided to friends that he had mixed feelings about it. He seemed finally to have found that retirement he was looking forward to.

Nothing deterred the people who still flocked to visit him. Many senators' wives were still anxious to be his hostess for one of his frequent informal parties. The advent of the bizarre stories in the Post had so far only served to provide him with raw material for jokes. Tonight, he was expecting two of his oldest friends, Washington journalists. He felt lucky at the end of his political life to be surrounded by such illuminating and loyal companions. With unconcealed pride, he championed his daughter's new career in the raucous world of politics he had inhabited for so long. Next year, she would stand for election to his old seat in congress. His son, recently promoted to major in the air force, still gave him nervous moments flying the fastest fighters in the skies.

"Mike, you make being vice president seem almost something worth doing," Brent Manzi teased as they carried the dinner dishes into the kitchen. Manzi had been the White House correspondent for the largest wire service in the country for most of two decades, and his short, plump form was often featured at presidential news conferences, rising to press the hard questions that made him famous. There was a staff at the official residence, but one of Mike O'Connelly's idiosyncrasies required that at these informal gatherings everything be kept as near to what he considered normal as possible. The bemused staff waited in the kitchen and accepted the dishes and glasses for washing from the vice president and his famous guest.

"Good. Why don't you try it after Roger fires me? Brent, you'd be great at it. You possess exactly the right combination of vacuousness and fecklessness."

"That must be your problem at the moment, Michael. You're neither vacuous nor feckless."

"It's lousy what the White House is trying to do to you, Mike," Howard Casselman said when Manzi and O'Connelly returned to the den. His deep, stentorian voice and square jaw were recognizable to every American over the age of ten after two decades as anchor of one of the network's nightly news shows. "I don't know what you did, Old Boy, but somebody on Pennsylvania Avenue is clearly pissed off."

"My God, Howard, somebody in that house is always pissed off. It's the nature of the place." O'Connelly did not want to get into this. He was, after all, still a part of the administration. Disloyalty was respected by no one and despised by everyone. He didn't want that to be his epitaph.

"He's right, Mike," Manzi offered. "We get these releases unbidden and a few make it into the paper, buried, but there nonetheless. It stinks."

"Look, Mike, you have so many friends in this town. You shouldn't have to take this sort of crap. Why don't you go public and talk about it? Give us your medical records, or authorize your doctors to give interviews," Casselman suggested.

"Is the news so slow these days, Howard, that you need this puny little consommé of a story to fill up the nightly news? Not enough red meat out there?" In truth, O'Connelly had been thinking about doing exactly what Casselman proposed.

"You should think about it, Mike," Manzi said.

"And what good would it do, boys?" He filled their glasses with more brandy.

"It might save your daughter's chances for congress." Manzi's statement hit O'Connelly like a knee in his stomach.

"What the hell do you mean? My daughter has nothing to do with this!"

"You ran with Roger Seekings. You've served with him for a couple of years now, Mike. Do you mean to say that you don't know what he and his crowd are capable of? Especially that hit man of his, Moore."

"What is going on with Marilyn? Do you fellas know something or not?"

"Mike, we just hear things. It's our job to be snoops, you know. These nonsensical leaks about your slipping into an early state of drool and snooze isn't all Roger has in mind. We hear the White House intends to bury you completely, and that includes a smear that'll stick on your daughter. He's a mean bugger, your running mate. Whatever you did to cross him must have been a gold-plated pain in his presidential ass." Manzi got up as he finished speaking and refilled his own glass, offering more to Casselman and his host. "You always have the best damn brandy, Michael."

"What do they plan to do to Marilyn?" He was no longer the glib vice-president-in-exile. Now, he was the worried father.

"No one has heard any specifics. It's just rumblings now. But if I had to guess, I expect they will just make you out to be such an embarrassment, that she catches enough fallout to be ruined in the primary," Manzi replied.

"What about you, Howard?"

"We hear exactly the same. The man to watch is that reptile Moore."

O'Connelly was silent. He drained the last of his brandy. What a fool he was to think this smear by the president wouldn't affect anyone but himself. How callous he was to treat it all as a joke. "Boys, I'll be holding a press conference in two days. I'd love to give you two the scoop, but I'd like the broadest coverage possible. My physician will be there, and you fellas can all have copies of my medical records." He walked to the mantle. "What the hell was I thinking of?"

Brent Manzi and Howard Casselman nodded to one another, proud their old friend was deciding to fight back.

In the kitchen, the two cooks and the maid listened through the door to every word and were delighted. The cooks raised their hands in a loud high-five.

* * *

Moore watched the computer screen flash from page to page, as he scanned one of the files he had just retrieved from the FBI data bank. Marilyn O'Connelly looked almost pure. Almost. The thing that made the FBI's files so valuable was their infatuation with allegations of any sort of financial, political, or moral impropriety. The allegations weren't often proven, or provable, but they were always detailed. Sources and leads were carefully catalogued, providing a clear trail to anyone willing to search a little further.

Marilyn O'Connelly. Wife of a lawyer in an Albany firm, still using her famous father's name. Mother of two boys. And soon to be candidate for their party's nomination for her father's old seat in congress. It was a story made for the Sunday Supplement. You could always count on the FBI, though. If it were there, if it were alleged, whispered about, and if there was anything at all to it, the dirt would be right here in the Bureau's files. Here was the scar on Marilyn's reputation, in a memo one-and-a-half decades old, written when her father was being touted as a possible candidate for president. In college, she joined a radical feminist organization. The memo explained that she and one of the group's leaders moved into an apartment together. The roommate, the agent went on to report, was well known as a lesbian. After three months, Marilyn moved out. In an off campus bar, shortly after, she was confronted by the roommate, who was reported to be a little drunk, demanding that Marilyn return several hundred dollars the angry woman accused her of stealing. The few witnesses to the ugly scene recalled that the woman's bitter accusations left no doubt that the two had been lovers. The story never made it into the press. Only three people were present other than Marilyn and the shouting ex-roommate, and they were friends of both, anxious to have the whole thing go away. Here were their names, and the name of the bitter roommate.

He clicked twice and the FBI file gave way to the personnel records of the air force. In less than a minute, he was staring at the last promotion picture of Major Michael O'Connelly, Jr., USAF, a fighter pilot. He stood erect and sober, decorations colorfully adorning one half of the breast of the blue uniform jacket. He hadn't bothered to ask for the FBI file on Mickey O'Connelly, as he had always been known. It was not necessary to have any dirt on an officer in the military to ruin a career. It only required that the officer displease someone in power. The reason mattered not one whit. The officer's choice of a wife was sufficient. Or the officer's hometown. Or looks. It didn't matter. This would be no trouble at all. Moore was accomplished at undermining a military career.

While he was in the data base neighborhood, he decided to check on an old acquaintance. Three clicks and the navy personnel records system logo rolled itself down the screen. He entered the name, even the social security number, which he had committed to memory, and clicked "search." In seconds, the file presented itself, again with the most recent photograph — the first thing to appear — this one of a stocky, dark-haired navy commander. The man looked remarkably unchanged despite more than ten years having passed since Moore had laid eyes on him. His shoulders were still square, his face as pugnacious as he remembered. He flicked through the biographical details to the awards. Navy Marine Corps Medal, two awards. *It would have been three, if it hadn't been for me*, Moore thought. He moved to the assignments list. He paused here, remembering, still able to feel the sting of humiliation. He scrolled down to the "current" block. Naval Weapons Station, Charleston — Executive Officer. "Hmmm," he said. Although he knew what was there, he clicked to the career progression section of the file. Command Selection Board — convened the previous fall. "Non-selected for command." Moore laughed out loud.

Indeed, he thought to himself, there was no better example than Commander John Matthew Reicher of a military career sabotaged by someone in an important position.

* * *

"I'm telling you, this is going to be a problem." The deep bass voice on the phone spoke in a rapid, street-wise Brooklyn style. "I've known you a long time, so I'm trusting you not to quote me, honey, but this guy just ain't got all the bolts screwed down tight. Know what I mean?"

She never said "ain't." In fact, the accent she grew up speaking was long ago jettisoned as baggage that would impede her career. "I know what you mean. And where do you get off calling me 'honey,' Leo? I ought to turn your oversexed Italian ass in for sexual harassment. What a headline — FBI Deputy Director the Subject of Serious Sexual Allegations. Tomorrow's Post. What do you think?"

"You can kiss my Italian ass, honey. Look, Julieanne, we need to talk about C. A. Moore. My people are telling me some pretty wild things about this guy. He's running the show, and he's gonna cause a problem, I'm telling you."

Julieanne wondered why Leo spoke so freely about his contempt for Moore on the phone. Perhaps it was deliberate. Maybe Leo had something on Moore and was hoping he got wind of it.

"And now Moore is out to find out whether some guy is leaking information to the governor of South Carolina. Seekings is on his ass to find out, and if it's true, to get the guy. Moore is going to use that putz over there — what's his name — Felix — you know, the army intel guy."

"Felix Hubbard."

"Yeah, yeah. Anyway, that'll be another zoo. This is nuts. We can't keep this a BIG SECRET. Why try?"

"Leo, run for president. When you win, we'll do what you think makes sense."

"O.K., O.K. Very funny, Julie. Very sweet. Now, when are we going to meet."

"How about Friday, lunch?"

"It's a date — no. I didn't mean that. A proposition. A rendezvous. My God, no, not one of those. It's a … deal. Friday for lunch. Your place or mine?"

"Goodbye, Leo."

Julieanne Harris wasn't surprised that the president and his security thug, Moore, had decided to try and find the leak. Moore was bound to figure out sooner or later that someone was talking. Still, the knowledge gave her a sharp chill. Now the risk of discovery was real. She wondered if her anger and her resolve to follow her conscience would seem foolish now. No matter. It was done, and she was no less convinced she had been right.

She loved Washington. She had shed so much of her original self to succeed here. The young southern girl from Florence who won a scholarship to Georgetown University would not have made it. When she discovered the allure that the world of intelligence held for her, Julieanne made a deliberate decision to change because only in this city was it possible to live in that world. Her shy charm, the reflexive grace and manners absorbed from her mother, like the gentle, easy Carolina accent, she had peeled off and replaced with a new skin, harder, but more practical for her chosen life. Julieanne was greeted by the same attitudes as many women who entered a mostly male profession. She didn't shrink from the tough language and rougher attitudes. She thrived. Without pretending to be a man, she found her place in the culture of men. In fact, she had never lost her striking good looks and was as attractive at forty-one as she had been at twenty-one.

Now, there were fifteen men who answered to her, as well as eight women. She knew that many women suffered in their jobs from the type of masculine pressure they weren't equipped to deflect. And she knew, from personal experience, that some men would manipulate the work relationship to dominate a woman for sexual reasons. But those problems had seldom been very important to her, and never deterrents. By the sheer will to stay and succeed, Julieanne simply marched through it all.

Leo Scardato, like many of Washington's intelligence virtuosos, was a friend and confidant. Years before, he became much more for a while, before she discarded the notion of romance all together. It was one more sacrifice to her chosen life. Now her hard-won membership in the fraternity was threatened.

She recalled the day in a conference room in the Bolling Air Force Base headquarters of the Defense Intelligence Agency that her anger boiled over. After months of analyzing the situation in the former Soviet republics, most of the team she assembled was convinced that a major theft of nuclear bomb material was imminent. The president's man told them they had to devise a blueprint for bringing the material to the U.S. The first step was to decide where it should be stored. Her staff recommended a site selection study — taking into account security as well as environmental safety. C. A. Moore had a very different idea. Julieanne remembered clearly how Moore coolly introduced the question of the proper site. Then, without pausing or asking for their ideas, he informed her team that the administration had made the decision.

"This is an entirely political question," he had said. "This stuff can be stored anywhere, Energy tells me. We just have to have the right containers. And security. The risks have been studied to death, and there aren't any." Julieanne had turned to catch the perplexed looks on the faces of her engineers. Only a few days before, they had explained how dangerous the balls of plutonium or spent fuel rods could be. Moore continued, "But the public thinks there are. And that's what matters. Perception may not always be reality, but it sure is what determines elections. We have looked at the same options Energy considered when they brought the fuel rods in from Europe for the first time. It seems to us the same decision as the one made back then makes sense now. South Carolina's got three million people and eight electoral votes. When it comes to national politics, they don't count. They didn't vote for us and wouldn't no matter what we did. Besides that, what happens there just doesn't matter to the rest of the country. It's already a dump for all kinds of waste from all over the U.S. As a state, South Carolina is marginally important. It just doesn't matter. That's where we are going to put it. All of it." Then he stood up from the table and left.

She was shocked at Moore's crudeness. But more than surprise stirred in her. Something basic deep inside her rebelled against the ugliness of what Moore said. South Carolina was not a place she thought about a great deal. She loved her brother, and her nephew, Billy, was one of the joys of her life. Yet the state that gave her birth seemed largely an abstraction. Until she listened to C. A. Moore.

Shock turned to outrage as the inescapable import of his words sunk in. Moore's pronouncement could only be dealt with in two ways, she finally concluded. Either she accepted it — ignoring it was only a weak synonym for accepting — or she rejected it. To accept Moore's premise was to brand a part of herself as "marginally important" — inferior. She had never allowed anyone or anything to cause her to do that — and wouldn't now.

In the weeks that followed, as Moore decreed total secrecy about their plans, she made her decision, and the newborn rebel in her began to form a strategy. It was the secrecy that most offended her. Not only was her home unimportant to this bastard from the White House, the people who lived there were to be denied even the knowledge of the danger their government had decided to inflict on them.

No one knew better than she the vast intelligence apparatus that was being mobilized to find her. No longer could she speak to her brother freely on the telephone. She began to consider options that were secure from the meticulous scrutiny she now knew surrounded her. She was certain she could avoid detection. This was her world, after all.

She considered, as she had when she decided on her rebellious course, that she might have to leave her career. What had been only a theoretical possibility before was now made very real by Scardato's call. And the reality frightened her as nothing had for many years. Leo was trying to warn her. How transparent was her little sabotage, she wondered. Only three more years until she was eligible for retirement. No matter how exotic the world of intelligence, when it came to money and retirement, she was still a federal bureaucrat, depending on a pension. She would be careful, but she would go on getting word to Blackie Haselden. She was determined, but she was also frightened as she gazed from her window across the Anacostia River at the Capitol dome.

* * *

The tape reached the end of the three erotic scenes recorded on the hidden camera in C. A. Moore's farmhouse. Yigor Matveev pulled another cigarette from the pack in his vest pocket and lit it from the lighter on the table in front of the couch where he and Mikail Plekanov had watched the tape.

"So, Mikail, how can we best make use of this dirty little show?"

"Information, Colonel."

"Obviously, but exactly what do you have in mind? Will you try to blackmail the White House apparatchik?"

"No. He is too strong willed. His obsession is pathological. Not him. The soldier. We will squeeze the soldier. He is the type who will be terrified of being labeled a homosexual. In his eyes it would be the end of being a man. If we approach him correctly, he will tell us anything to avoid being found out," Mikail explained.

"All we want to know is when the Americans intend to remove the plutonium from Zarmeyevka. Surely, that is something we could find out easily."

"Yigor, we must know more. We must know exactly how and where they plan to take it in America. We must know the schedule."

Matveev stared for a long time at his old colleague. "What have you not told me?"

"Our job is going to be much harder than we thought. The plutonium must be taken from outside the motherland." Mikail explained to Matveev the threat by the government to kill anyone involved in a theft, to murder their families. "So, Colonel. You see, we are caught between our government who will kill us if we steal the material and the Arabs who will kill us if we do not." He leaned back on the couch. "We must devise a plan to take it from the Americans — in America."

"It's mad, you know that, Mikail," Matveev said, smiling. After a long draw on his cigarette, he added. "Now we can put to work all those theories we had about how easy it would be to raid the American homeland. When will we have the information?"

"Our friends in America say they believe they can prime the young soldier to be ready to tell them all the details as soon as his powerful friend has them."

"We will cancel our raid on Zarmeyevka, then."

"No."

The colonel's face betrayed his confusion. Then it darkened. He began to see.

"There must be a raid, but it must fail. And it must not be tied to us in any way," Mikail said.

* * *

"Hi, Daddy!" the soft little voice called out to him from the telephone receiver. "Daddy, I wish I could crawl through the phone and give you a big hug. I miss you."

Matt Reicher's heart swelled and tears flowed freely down his cheeks, though his voice betrayed no hint of it. "I miss you, too. How's your sister? Are you taking care of her for Mommy?"

"No!" the four-year-old protested. "She takes my toys and breaks them."

"That's how little sisters are, baby. In a few years you two will be best playmates."

"Well, maybe." She was unconvinced. "When are you coming to see us?"

His stomach felt as though it had been sharply kicked. "I don't know, Annie. Mommy and I will have to talk about that." This was so hard.

The girl's voice became more distant as she talked to someone else in the room. "Daddy, Mommy had to go. You talk to her soon, O.K., so we can see you." Matt knew what had happened. Linda had left the room to avoid speaking with him.

"O.K. You better get some sleep now. I love you. Give your mom a big kiss for me, all right?"

"Night, Daddy." The phone buzzed as the connection was lost. He held the receiver in his hand for a full minute before returning it to the cradle. He lay back on the carpeted floor and gazed at the framed photo on the bookshelf above him. It was a happy family that smiled back at him … the past that mocked him.

The pain he felt turned to anger. The tears stopped. He climbed up from the floor and retrieved his wallet and keys from the desk. *I don't want to be alone tonight*, he thought bitterly.

Chapter 7

The air was free of clouds and the ground hundreds of feet below him was clearly visible. Brown and empty. Nothing was below but tan soil spotted with green dots — tumbleweed, he remembered. In summer it was green, the long strands, prickly, but soft. As summer ended, it dried, the root weakened and the bush broke from its anchor, rolling across the desert with the wind. A ridge of pale blue jutted up and came into focus as a range of mountains. As the jet passed over the mountains, already well into its descent, El Paso appeared, blocks filled with the green of trees, alien and alive only because they could share the city's water.

Walking from the air-conditioned terminal to find his rented car, the hot air enveloped him, incredibly dry. It pulled the moisture from his skin.

Three decades had wrought no change in the landscape that had been Jim McNeely's home for five years. This had been only one stop as the son of an air force sergeant, but it was the place where his life began in earnest. As he drove into the New Mexico desert, a line of treeless mountains rose on his left, shadowing him. *Traveling back in time*, he thought whimsically. Even the silhouette of the mountains in this long abandoned place was familiar to him; a sense of belonging washed over him.

He came to the gate at Holloman Air Force Base. He was enjoying this. The appointment with Anthony DeSilva wasn't until the next morning, and he was tired of traveling.

He found the officers' club and took his time having lunch. In the early 1960s the base was the scene of testing and research for America's space program. Before the Mercury capsules carried men into orbit, the monkeys that preceded them came here for training. A rocket chair, called a sled, was built in the desert to carry the astronauts along a stretch of railroad track at supersonic speeds to test their resistance to the grueling gravitational force they would experience during blast off. On Armed Forces Day weekends the sled was fired up for the crowd, streaking across the desert, its passenger emerging to the cheers of spectators.

Once he had taken that remarkable time for granted. During the "space race" of the '50s and '60s, this was home to scores of scientists and technicians laboring to bring America the future of space flight. Sixty miles to the north, at the edge of the Tularosa Basin, near a massive prehistoric lava bed called the Valley of Fires, lay Trinity Site. On July 16, 1945, the first atomic device was detonated there. It was no exaggeration to say that the dawns of both the nuclear and rocket eras had broken here. The pioneers of man's most advanced and potentially destructive technologies came to this place to make the vast, empty landscape their laboratory, and to push the limits of flight and power further than mankind's most fanciful dreams — or most horrific nightmares.

North of Alamogordo, he drove into the Sacramento Mountains. The road snaked back and forth as it carried him rapidly higher through hills covered with sagebrush and cactus. Then a few scrawny trees appeared amongst the desert growth. Suddenly, around a sharp curve he saw the mountains rise high behind a tunnel, deep green, covered in a thick forest of evergreen and aspen. In his rear view mirror he still saw the brown, desiccated desert. On the other side of the tunnel, he emerged into a different, lush world of mountain meadows and orchards of apple and cherry trees. A stream spilled over boulders and cascaded in shallow falls at the bottom of a beautiful valley that bordered the road on his right.

He fought off the urge to spend the afternoon exploring. Two thousand miles was a long way to come, and he wasn't ready to do the job he had come for.

Matt Reicher had given him an entire file of information to study. With folders of photocopied material laid out on the bed of his hotel room, Jim tried to absorb the basics of ionizing radiation. He once heard a friend of his from law school say that being a lawyer was the business of learning other people's jobs. It wasn't true, of course. They never really learned another's skill, but the perception lawyers projected that they *thought* they had done so was one of the reasons they were routinely despised. More than one engineer has fantasized during a deposition about impaling the lawyer on the pencil he was using to point at details on a set of plans, details the lawyer tried to make the engineer believe he understood better than the man who produced them.

With only a break for dinner, Jim continued to study the articles — neat, academic descriptions of how neutrons and protons and other subatomic particles flew away from atoms, smashing into other atoms, knocking more particles from their orbits. As the particles flew wildly about in ever-greater numbers, the phenomenon called radiation was created. It seemed remote from the films of the dark, billowing mushroom clouds of nuclear blasts. It sounded no more harmful — and no more unnatural — than photosynthesis. It was a sterile presentation. What he came so far to find was a witness who knew not only the mechanics of what happened when atoms disintegrated, but the consequences. The long day began to overwhelm him. He opened the window, still amazed at the coolness of the air of the mountains, and quickly slid into a deep sleep.

Not long after midnight, Jim woke to distant howling. A coyote. Out of the window he saw the silver crescent shining through the trees, and he wondered if the animal was singing to the moon. Without an answer to his question, the exotic sound still drifting through the window, he fell back to sleep.

*   *   *

Jim sipped his coffee slowly, as the waitress cleared away the dishes from a magnificent breakfast. Below the Lodge restaurant, towering fir trees spilled down a steep slope. Beyond the basin on the horizon, the San Andres Mountains rose, a faint, jagged buffer between the desert and a brilliant morning sky. A thin, luminescent white line shone under the mountains, gypsum dunes known as White Sands, that ran the length of the basin.

"Jim?" Standing next to his table was a man dressed in denim jeans and shirt. He was shorter than average with grayish white hair pulled into a ponytail. His tanned face was spare. Jim noticed that the man was thin, and not in a healthy way. The face and the accent were Hispanic.

"Yes. Dr. DeSilva?"

"Call me Tony. Man, I'm having a hard enough time getting used to this witness thing. Let's be informal, O.K." *I've got a retired hippie*, Jim thought. *Great.*

Jim laughed, but didn't feel relaxed. The difficulty of the job he came to do was suddenly tangible. DeSilva took a seat at the table and the waitress brought him a saucer and cup of coffee. Next to the saucer she laid a shot glass filled with an amber liquid.

"Thanks, Maria. You are all aglow this morning. Chuck must be back from deployment." The young woman laughed and her face blushed brightly. "Thought so."

As Maria retreated to the kitchen, DeSilva explained, "Her husband's a technician with a fighter squadron down at the base."

He picked up the shot glass, dumped the contents in the coffee and winked. "Don't worry. I don't drink it for the buzz; I just like the flavor."

Jim smiled, but images of his expert witness passed out the night before trial raced through his mind. "So, Jim do you like New Mexico?"

"I lived here for five years when I was a kid. My dad was stationed at Hollomon."

"Damn. This must be really cool for you. Coming home, like."

"Yeah. A lot of memories."

"We'll take you around and get you reacquainted with the old neighborhood. Matt didn't tell me. And you haven't been back since? Cool." He coughed, his thin shoulders shaking. Jim noticed for the first time a weakness in his eyes that seemed familiar, but for a reason he couldn't grasp. "Sorry, I've got this thing I'm trying to get over. Please excuse me."

Jim nodded, wondering how he was going to tell his witness not to say "cool" during his testimony without hurting his feelings. "Tony, I know I've explained this before, but we're looking for an explanation of what the effects on the environment would be from an accident with plutonium."

"Tell you what, let's start from the beginning. Have you read up on ionizing radiation?" DeSilva waved to Maria. Maria filled his cup and laid another shot glass next to the saucer.

"Yes," Jim quickly added, "but I won't say I understand it."

In between coughs, DeSilva laughed. "Neither do 99 percent of the people walking around out there." He waved at the basin below and poured the second shot glass into his refilled coffee cup.

DeSilva began to speak, his voice suddenly authoritative, "The radiation we need to be concerned about is the type that produces ion pairs by knocking electrons out of their orbits in atoms." Jim began to take notes as his companion began a private lecture. "Particulate ionizing radiation consists of portions of atoms — subatomic particles — which are traveling at very high speed. They could be the nuclei of a small atom —

you know, a proton, an electron, or some other particles." He paused, gazing at Jim scribbling rapidly across his legal pad. "So you were ten when you left Alamogordo?" Jim nodded, surprised at the diversion. "Did you want to leave?"

"No ... I really hated leaving."

"O.K.... Now, some elements have very unstable nuclei, and their atoms can be induced to break up artificially by the introduction of particle accelerators. These unstable elements emit a high-speed particle and/or a gamma ray. Of course, even stable elements can be made unstable when bombarded by too many radiation particles. The loose particles intrude into the stable atoms and knock the orbiting particles out of sync until some fly off into space. Then the stable element becomes radioactive, too. Each radioactive element will remain unstable — or radioactive — for different periods depending on the circumstances. Remember Three Mile Island?"

"Yeah."

"The radioactive waste from that accident will be dangerously radio-active for ten thousand years. It's being stored in Idaho. Imagine watching over something for ten millennia? Just producing some form of record to describe what it is and why it's so dangerous would be a challenge. What do you do?" DeSilva paused again. When Jim looked up he said, "Where'd you go when you left here?"

"Baltimore. Everything was different." Jim laughed. "You know here I wore jeans and cowboy boots to school. Couldn't do that there. That was the last time I ever wore a pair of cowboy boots. Even when everybody was wearing them, I didn't. I never forgot showing up in that school, being told I couldn't look like myself anymore." The sound of his own words surprised him.

"Let's go." DeSilva rose from the table. "Shit, man. It's been long enough. There's this great store down the mountain called Boot Town."

"Tony, maybe we'd better make some more progress here first."

DeSilva was already laying a ten dollar bill on the table. "Let's go. You really ought to put on some jeans. That suit will look really weird with the shit-kickers we're gonna fix you up with."

*   *   *

"Man, you'll knock 'em out back in.... Where are you from?"

"Charleston...."

"Yeah man. Those look cool."

Jim held up the new boot on his left foot and inspected it. He pictured his return to Broad Street wearing these black, hand-tooled specials from Boot Town. "Tony, maybe the boots. But I'm not sure I can walk down Broad Street in this hat." He placed the cream-colored Stetson on his head using the store window as a mirror. "O.K., Dr. DeSilva, we need to get back to work."

"There's plenty of time. It's not every day a cowboy comes home. Let's go see the old neighborhood. What was the address?"

"You really don't have to do this."

"Man, this is a kick. Hop in the truck."

A half dozen blocks further, they stopped in front of a small stucco house. "My mother planted that tree," Jim said, pointing to a tall elm at the corner of the front yard, by far the largest tree in sight. "She was a South Carolina girl who couldn't stand it that there were no trees. As soon as the rocks were dug up from the yard, she planted that tree and nursed it like a baby for five years."

"She did a good job."

"I'm boring you."

"This place meant a lot to you." DeSilva looked at him, his eyes seeming to know more than he could.

Jim gazed at the front door. "It was a great place to be a little boy." He turned to DeSilva, "I had forgotten ... so much." He looked at the window of what had been his room and remembered the day he came home after the movers emptied the house. Suddenly, leaving was very real. He stood by the window of the empty room and cried. He could see that boy, his heart breaking behind the stucco walls. He knew the boy had reason to cry. Here he had been a boy in a natural wonderland with no doubt of his place in the world. "Before I left, my friends and I hiked up to the mountains," he pointed to the foothills across the desert that faced the house, "We went up farther than we ever had. I looked down at the town, and I told them I'd come back and climb to the top of the canyon. Big promise."

"Well, you're here now, aren't you? Let's go get a little bite to eat and then we'll keep your promise."

* * *

"Tony, do you feel up to this? You look a little under the weather."

"Man, I live here, remember? This is just an afternoon's exercise for me. We'll do a little more work on the way up the canyon."

They left the truck where the road ended in a rocky hill. DeSilva retrieved a shotgun from the box behind the cab of the pickup. "Planning on doing a little hunting?" Jim asked.

"No. I just don't want anything to hunt us. Since you left, my eastern friend, the law has protected the mountain lions and the bears that live here. There are a lot more of them than there used to be." Noticing Jim's surprise, he patted his shoulder. "Don't worry. They don't like to come out in the heat of a day like this. Only humans are crazy enough for that."

They followed an arroyo, a dry streambed filled with rocks of all sizes, carried into the depression by water rushing down from the hills after a heavy rain.

"Plutonium is often considered one of the most poisonous substances known to man," DeSilva said. "It certainly makes one hell of a powerful bomb. But if you just sat it on the street, there would be little harm to anyone. So long as they didn't handle it, or worst of all, ingest some. Then it would be fatal. That's what makes it so different from the spent fuel rods that are being transported to your state now. Those rods contain actual fission material."

"Do you mean that there is an actual risk from the spent rods?"

"Absolutely."

Jim tried to follow DeSilva, but the landscape around him was too fascinating. At the head of the canyon, he saw the remains of a quarry and a thin stream of water falling a hundred feet from a crease in the adjoining hill to a pool. On top of the foothills, the scattering of fir trees thickened into the edge of the mountain forest.

"They did experiments burning plutonium at Sandia while I was there. Nothing dramatic happens. Just don't breathe any of the smoke," DeSilva continued.

"So, there's no danger unless there's a fire."

"I'm not sure I'd say that. But a fire is certainly going to be a problem with any radioactive material. You have to remember that any normal, stable matter is going to become radioactive itself if it is exposed to too much bombardment from radiation. Smoke is no different. It's just particles of ash and dirt that get carried up with the hot air from a fire. If that fire is burning highly radioactive material, the smoke is going to become irradiated. Are you following me?"

"Yes," Jim said, staring at the horizon behind them.

"Beautiful, isn't it?"

Jim looked down the canyon. "It's much greener than I remember."

"People like your Mom have been watering trees for thirty years."

They sat under a ledge near the pool at the head of the canyon. The waterfall splashed against the rocks and ran quickly into the pool. DeSilva began to talk about himself. Jim felt clumsy for not asking him sooner. The mountains and desert of southern New Mexico were his home. The government gave him a scholarship to pursue a doctorate at Stanford in return for his promise to return to work at Sandia Laboratory, part of the huge complex of nuclear research facilities that stretched across New Mexico from Los Alamos to Las Cruces. It was a promise he was glad to keep. For twenty-two years, he worked in the thin, rarefied atmosphere of cutting-edge research. Then, three years ago, he became sick and retired to Cloudcroft. Jim was afraid he saw what the illness was and hoped he was wrong. The lines in DeSilva's face seemed to have deepened, and his shoulders sagged more than before. Jim was concerned.

He needn't have worried. DeSilva strode through the rock-strewn ground with little apparent effort. At the edge of the desert, he carefully unloaded the shotgun and placed it back into the truck. "Man, I could go for a cold one. What do you say?"

"You nuclear scientists really know how to live."

DeSilva burst into laughter, seizing on an irony that Jim didn't intend. They headed into the heart of Alamogordo to what DeSilva assured him was the "coolest" bar in that part of New Mexico.

* * *

At the drive of the Lodge, DeSilva stopped the truck. "Look, man, I'd like to have dinner with you, but I'm a little worn down." Reaching behind the seat, he pulled out a small satchel. "These are some things I grabbed from my little collection that you need to look at. There's some reading and a videotape. They should have a VCR set up in your room by now. We'll talk about them tomorrow, and before we're through we'll put them in context for you, O.K., man?"

"O.K., Doc. Thanks for the tour."

"Don't mention it. Hey ... cool boots."

Jim waved as he watched the dusty pickup truck head down the drive and disappear in the trees. He poked around in the satchel as he made his way up the stairs to his room. The doctor had given him quite a load of homework. He stretched out on his bed and picked up the folder with "#1" penned on the cover. It was a long excerpt from a medical text on the effects of radiation on human tissue. "Acute effects are those which appear within a short time after radiation exposure," it began. "Most notable among these are redness of the skin, a prompt fall in the number of white blood cells in the blood, which may be followed by anemia, sterility, chromosome aberrations, organ atrophy, and radiation sickness. These early effects are manifested only after a dosage of several hundred rads and may appear within a few days after exposure. They are a prelude to other effects that will appear later."

The article was written in the bloodless language of medical literature, clouding the true horror. But even to the unschooled, it was not difficult to imagine the savagery of the scourge ignited in the human body by the assault of the pieces of dying atoms. Soft tissue was simply cooked by the particles that raced into it. Too many of them, and it burned beyond recovery. Doses of 600 to 3,000 rads would severely damage the salivary glands, skin, the lining of the blood vessels, growing bone, the lining of the gastrointestinal tract, and most connective and elastic tissue. The list read like a biology primer. All of the body's systems were subject to destruction. The kidney, liver, endocrine glands, mature bone, cartilage, muscle, brain, and nerves succumbed to 3,000 rads or more. But these were only the direct effects of *acute* radiation exposure.

Later, if the subject survived, the mutating effects and long-term damage from the rampaging particles would manifest themselves. Cataracts might develop, or atrophic skin begin to break down — to rot. The very DNA of cells was violated by the attack of protons, neutrons, mesons, and gamma rays. Mutated cells often bred genetic "aberrations" and cancer. The text reviewed in painful detail the ghastly variety of mutations that might be spawned. Increased tendency to cancer or other diseases, biochemical abnormalities, or any of a range of macabre physical deformities. Prenatal children were especially fragile. The experience of Japanese children in Hiroshima and Nagasaki was catalogued and analyzed. Mutations from a single exposure could be manifested two or three generations into the future.

Most significant, the authors suggested, was the growth of malignant disease — cancer. The incidence of peculiar cancers in certain groups of people was, in fact, how the world had come to discover radioactivity. Silver miners in Europe were known for centuries to suffer and to die in large numbers, as high as 50 percent, from "mountain sickness." It wasn't until 1879 that the sickness was recognized as lung cancer caused by radiation from the rock lining the mineshafts.

Workers in the industry that produced luminescent paint for application to watches and other instruments were other early examples. Phosphorus was irradiated with Radium 224 to make it glow and then applied by hand. Many workers ingested small amounts of the harmless-looking paint with violent results. The most seriously afflicted were stricken with anemia, widespread hemorrhaging, and destruction of their jawbones, with the jaw ultimately becoming horribly infected. All of these people died within a few years of beginning their work.

The nuclear age itself provided many other examples of the long-term effects of radiation doses below the *acute* level. Radiologists, atom bomb survivors, uranium miners, and patients overexposed to x-rays shared the same array of malignant tumors and other cancerous illnesses. Two of the study groups coolly analyzed in the text were particularly shocking to Jim. Children in the State of Utah exposed to fallout from nuclear tests in Nevada had been found to share higher rates of leukemia with soldiers deliberately placed in the zone of worst fallout from test blasts. These groups experienced doses of only 3 to 20 rads and still manifested a great increase in the disease. He wondered how it could ever have been possible for the government to *intentionally* expose people to something so horrible. He thought about the children in Utah, people who would be his age, if they had lived.

There were many kinds of cancers the authors linked to long-term effects of excess radiation. Skin, breast, lung, thyroid — particularly likely to afflict young children — and leukemia. One of the groups found to have unusually high rates of the form of leukemia induced by radiation

— the most deadly type, which affected the bone marrow, called myelo-cytic — were workers in the nation's nuclear laboratories. This disease attacked the body's ability to produce red blood cells. As with so many radiation-induced afflictions, the immune system was diminished and often completely destroyed. The treatments themselves were cruel, making the patients sick — sometimes violently — and debilitated. Those suffering from the disease became markedly thin and drawn. They were frequently sick with a variety of infections and viruses. They were weak. They were like Anthony DeSilva. He closed his eyes. "My God," he whispered.

*   *   *

"Mr. Moore, come on in." Felix Hubbard closed the door behind his important visitor and offered him a chair. Hubbard was more than a little self-conscious this morning. His office in the Defense Intelligence Agency was a small, windowless square. He was acutely aware that C. A. Moore was accustomed to the spacious, well-appointed offices of Washington's power elite. Hubbard had long ago lost any fascination for any part of Washington. After nearly three decades in various compartments of the nation's intelligence bureaucracy, the sole focus of his working life was preserving the comfortable retirement he longed for.

"Felix, I don't have much time. Tell me about the leak. Are we close to finding it?" Hubbard noted Moore called the leak "it." It was a person they were looking for, of course, a person Felix Hubbard could almost pity once they found him.

"None of the wire taps have turned up anything. But remember, we haven't been at it too long." Moore's eyes bored into him. "This person is leaking information for a reason. Maybe he has ties to some anti-nuclear or environmental movement, or he has it in for the president or the government generally. Maybe he's from South Carolina. I've cross-referenced lists of everyone who had access to the information that we know has gone out — everyone from secretaries and maintenance workers and up. Now, I'm checking each of these to see if there are any matches with possible motives. I'm betting the matches will include the snitch."

"How long, Felix?"

Moore was pressuring him. "In two to three weeks."

"One week. No more."

Felix swallowed hard. "Yes, sir."

"Now, what about these lawyers who've been hired by this son of a bitch Haselden?"

"It's common practice down there for the state to hire outside counsel to handle important litigation."

"I don't give a damn, Felix! What are they up to?"

"Well, I can only surmise that the governor intends for them to sue us."

Moore stood up and, leaning over Hubbard, gently patted his pale, fleshy cheek. "Felix, I can read the papers. I don't need you to tell me what they say. Your only reason for being, Felix, is intelligence. That's what I want from you. I want to know exactly what they're doing. Exactly. Do you understand me, Felix? Do I have to diagram it for you?"

"No, sir. I'll take care of it. Mr. Moore, is this likely to be a long-term operation?"

"As long as it takes. I don't want these crackers to interfere. I want no surprises. None. Get two more men to work with you. Make sure they're military officers. And make sure they are reliable."

"I can tell you that one of the lawyers has gone to New Mexico to interview a retired nuclear physicist, a guy named Anthony DeSilva. I assume he is supposed to be some kind of expert witness for the state."

"When did you learn this?"

"This morning. I have this contact at ...."

"Don't tell me about your contacts, God damn it!"

"O.K. Of course ... ah ... I have gotten a file on DeSilva. He worked at the nuclear labs at Los Alamos and Sandia until a few years ago when he developed leukemia and retired. Energy has always denied any connection between his disease and their labs, although it was the type associated with radiation exposure. But he was clearly angry, and he believes the radiation in the lab made him sick. About ten years ago there was an accident. Incompatible chemicals were mixed and exploded. DeSilva was the only one of four men who weren't knocked unconscious. A container of nuclear fuel was broken open by the blast. DeSilva dragged the open container out of the chamber and into a sealed safe. Then he dragged the men out of the chamber to an uncontaminated room. He believes the cancer was caused by the radiation he absorbed that day. He believes it, but has never filed a claim, not even a letter bitching to the DOE brass."

"I want to know everything about him. Everything. Understand?"

"Yes, sir."

"Felix, the *USS DEYO* will be making a prolonged visit to Charleston to conduct a surveillance exercise. The ship will monitor telephone calls and faxes from the governor's office, the governor's mansion, and offices of the lawyers involved with the case. All of this information will come to you. You will provide me with a daily summary of all the information we collect. Are you clear?"

"Yes, sir."

"Good. Find the leak, Felix."

*   *   *

The view down the mountain was just as breathtaking as the morning before, but Jim took no notice. He was thinking about DeSilva. All the signs seemed to point to leukemia. Jim hoped against the evidence that there was another, more benign explanation for his illness. Surely this quirky, delightful man wasn't doomed to that terrible fate. Maria interrupted his somber thoughts with a pot of fresh coffee and a plate of rolls.

As she laid the platter holding the coffee on the table, Jim noticed a full shot glass next to the pot. "Maria, Tony isn't coming over for breakfast this morning."

"Yes, I know. He called this morning and told me to put this on the table for you. He said you'd need it." Her face betrayed her confusion at the message. "And ... oh," she reached into her pocket for a note, "he said to be sure and watch the video before he comes to pick you up at 11:00."

Jim laughed and poured the bourbon into the coffee. "O.K. You run a tight ship."

When he returned to his room, he picked up the tan envelope holding the videocassette. "USSR Trip: Mar 88" was scrawled on the side. He opened the window to the cool morning air. The only sounds were from birds and tires on the gravel drive.

The tape had been made with a camcorder. The voice narrating it was DeSilva's explaining that it was made during a visit to the Ukraine to view the effects of radiation released by the 1986 accident at the nuclear reactor in Chernobyl. "Precipitated by a massive failure of the reactor's safeguard systems, the reactor exploded, launching parts of the building as well as a fifty-ton chunk of the reactor's core into the sky. The fifty tons of fuel evaporated and became the plume of radioactive particles that spread across Russia and Northern Europe.

"The radioactivity of the ejected fuel was in the range of 15,000 to 20,000 roentgens per hour. A field of radioactivity with the same intensity was formed around the reactor, fed by the open reactor core, where fifty more tons of fuel was at the center of a ferocious fire. It was this intense radiation that killed the firemen and reactor workers who rushed to the scene. Fourteen of these men were dead within three weeks. Ultimately, over thirty persons died within a few months from acute radiation exposure at the site of the accident.

"These are photographs of three of the firemen, Dima, Nikolai, and Vladimir." The pictures were of three husky young men in their 20s. Their faces were Slavic, the smiles reserved and typically Russian. "Dima was bathed by the radiation beam for only 3 minutes and is estimated to have received 400 rads. The radiation came at him from below, damaging most severely the soles of his feet, shins, perineum and buttocks. He was admitted one hour after the exposure, already with a fever of 102 degrees, nauseated, chilled and glassy eyed." The next picture showed Dima's skin, a dark, ugly brown — the nuclear tan. "Four days after the accident, terrible pain began due to the severe injuries to the mucous membranes of the mouth, esophagus, and stomach. Sores also appeared on his tongue and cheeks. The mucous membranes began to fall off in layers. Dima didn't eat for a week." Pictures of the disintegration of the young man's mouth filled the screen. Jim felt the urge to look away. "His shin began to swell and the pain became unbearable, feeling, the man said, like his leg would explode. Blisters appeared on his buttocks, back and perineum. His hair fell out after two weeks. But on the fortieth day he began to improve and lived, suffering only a limp. His long-term prognosis is not known."

"Nikolai was exposed longer and received some 10,000 rads. He lost consciousness and was taken to the hospital. His temperature was 104 when he was admitted." The picture showed the same brown skin as before. "He vomited continually and immediately began to show swelling of his neck, face and arms. His arms swelled so much so that the normal cuff could not be used to take his blood pressure." A photograph on the screen showed the fireman's horribly deformed and bloated body. "Four weeks after the accident his blood pressure suddenly dropped to zero and he died. This picture was taken of the heart tissue under a microscope.

Note that the tissue is unrecognizable, a mass of torn fibers. Nikolai's heart was utterly destroyed — as if it had been microwaved.

"Vladimir's pain was the worst of the three. His entire body was seared by the radiation. He was wracked with debilitating high fever. His body was swollen everywhere because all of it had been intensely irradiated. The physicians noted that he might have survived, had it not been for the underlying death of his skin — and the pain. Nuclear pain is especially merciless and unbearable." The pictures sickeningly catalogued the man's deterioration. "As he approached death, all of his skin was gone. All of it." The narration was less detached now, his voice betraying his compassion for these men. Jim turned away; the image was too horrible. "His salivary glands were also destroyed, leaving him unable to speak and with a continual, unquenchable thirst. His nuclear tan darkened, until his body, withered and dried up, was entirely black. This last picture of Vladimir illustrates how the body tissues and skin of radiation victims actually becomes mummified. When he died he weighed no more than a small child." Jim stared transfixed and horrified at the image on the screen, lashless and sightless eyes staring from the blackened, shriveled face.

"The Russians discovered soon after the first deaths that the bodies of the dead were radioactive, so much so that there was fear that the decaying corpses would carry the contamination into the groundwater. Thereafter, the most radioactive bodies were sealed in lead coffins." Jim turned the tape off, unable to watch anymore.

*   *   *

It was almost noon and they had been driving for an hour. They chatted about everything except radiation. DeSilva was interested in Matt Reicher, aware that his wife, Linda, refused to accompany him to his new assignment.

Jim studied the horizon while they spoke. "Are those volcanoes?" He was pointing to a series of conical mountains in the distance.

"Extinct. This is the Valley of Fires, and all that rock out there is lava. The desert was covered in the ancient black flows, beautiful and eerie."

DeSilva turned onto a single-lane road marked as a gate to the White Sands Missile Test Range, "Authorized Personnel Only," a large sign said. A short distance beyond, they came to a gate manned by a single airman.

DeSilva produced a piece of paper; the airman made a call from his phone in the guard shack and waved them through.

Fifteen minutes later, DeSilva stopped the truck at a small obelisk monument. "What is this?" Jim asked.

"This is where it all began," he answered. "This is Trinity Site." DeSilva got out of the truck. "This place is normally open to the public just two days a year, the first Mondays of April and October. But I still have a few connections. Did you do your homework?" He grinned.

"I didn't finish the tape. The last picture of Vladimir was it for me. You have a real knack for the cinema arts, Doctor."

"You should have finished it. But I suppose you see the point."

"It's horrible."

"It's more. An earthquake is horrible."

"I don't get it."

DeSilva tossed him a box-like device. "Turn it on."

Jim flipped a switch to on and it began to emit rapid static. He shot DeSilva a startled look.

"This place is still radioactive."

"Then why the hell are we here?" Jim yelled.

"It isn't so much as to hurt you. If we don't stay too long. But even after fifty years it's still hot."

"You have a point. What is it?"

"You say you want to know what's dangerous about nuclear fuel rods or plutonium. You have to understand. Radiation isn't just any force of nature. It *is* nature. It's the energy from existence itself. When we split the atom, we unleashed the energy that holds atoms together. Think about that. The energy that binds infinitesimal, hurtling particles together to make all matter. The problem is that once we set that energy free, we can't control it. The particles smash into other atoms and knock more particles loose. And it goes on and on. It's chaos to us because we weren't prepared to handle it. Maybe only God is prepared to control the primal force. But we were driven to try to make this force our own. We pried open the fingers of God. And what came out of His hand is a fury that disintegrates everything it touches, mutates life, and changes the very nature of energy and matter."

DeSilva was speaking rapidly, his eyes wild, pleading with Jim to grasp what he was saying. "You know about hurricanes. Have you been in one?"

"Yes."

"What was it like?"

Jim didn't have to think. The memory of huddling filled with terror with his small children and Alicia in a motel room was one that would never fade. "It's howling, mindless destruction. You just hope you live through it."

"That's what radiation is. It has no mind or reason, just terrible force. But it doesn't howl. And it doesn't stop. The violence of all those loose neutrons and protons continues for hundreds or thousands of years, passed from one mutated piece of matter to another. That's why it's more than a tragedy. It's profound." His eyes blazed. "The soil and the food chain will be dangerously radioactive around Chernobyl for over a hundred years. Seventeen million acres of land are contaminated with cesium 137. When the radioactive cloud from Chernobyl was formed, the Soviet government ordered it to be secretly seeded so that the rain would wash the radionuclides out before it reached Moscow. They succeeded. But when the radiation was washed out with the rain, it fell into the drinking water of Kiev, a city of two-and-a-half million people. Since the accident, there have been over 375 cases of infantile thyroid cancer in the Ukraine and Belorussia, almost four-hundred times the number that should have occurred naturally. Probably something like fifty thousand people will eventually die early deaths, most from cancer, as the result of this *one* accident in *one* power plant. What could possibly be worth the risk that only one mistake could cause such profound devastation?"

Jim saw suddenly that DeSilva was condemning not just the folly of man, but his entire life's work. "I understand Tony. Can anything like this happen from shipments of plutonium and spent fuel rods?"

He jerked his head to look at Jim. "Yes ... take a last look at this holy place so we can get out of here."

*   *   *

DeSilva talked as he drove, again the teacher. "Remember the picture of Vladimir. That is the worst case you asked for. The only question is how many Vladimirs or Dimas any accident will cause."

"But really, what is the chance of something happening? Why did the government make such a strong argument in the earlier case that there was no chance of a serious accident?"

"You come pretty naive for a lawyer. Do you read the papers at all? Do you honestly believe the government would tell you if there was a serious risk if it didn't have to?"

Jim was silent, stung by DeSilva's harshness.

"Let's talk about government. First, the old Soviet one. After Chernobyl the Soviet government didn't tell people to take iodine tablets. The tablets would have prevented the thyroid cancer."

"Nuclear fuel is the same. Ours is no different than the Russians'. If it is released, it will kill and contaminate, like any fission material. My favorite anecdote from American handling of spent fuel is about the driver of a truck hauling spent fuel rods from California to Idaho for storage. He stopped off in LasVegas at a casino and left the truck in the parking lot overnight. But what do you expect when we keep saying that there is no danger from spent fuel?

"Remember the thousands of soldiers ordered to stand close to blasts *just to see what would happen to them.* The thousands of children in Nevada, Colorado, and," he glanced at Jim, " New Mexico who were exposed to dangerous fallout were just unintended, what is the military term — collateral damage." A chill crept along Jim's spine. "Do you think our government, our scientists, generals, and leaders didn't know the risks they were inflicting on our own people?" He spat out the answer. "Of course, they knew. They knew the danger ... and like the Russians they never told anyone ... never even told them to take iodine tablets, even though they knew the radiation clouds carried dangerous levels far from the test sites. We'll never know how many cancer deaths could have been prevented if they had just told people that one simple thing."

They rode in silence for a while. Jim watched the lava beds of the Valley of Fires spreading out to the horizon, the strange triangles of the ancient volcanoes, pale shapes in the distance. His mind was reeling. DeSilva spoke again, "Even if we lay aside the occasional perfidy of all governments, there is risk from simple human error, from ignorance, mistake or sloth. The facility in South Carolina where this stuff is going illustrates this well enough. The tanks the DOE intends to use for storage have long been known to be leaky. And there are risks of explosions. A senate commit-tee heard testimony a few years ago that the tanks are 'the most current threat to the public.' Plutonium and highly enriched uranium have often been found to be escaping, even into the local municipal water supply."

"Do you have an opinion as to what the worst case of an accident involving shipping fuel rods and plutonium across South Carolina would be?" It was the ultimate question he had come so far to ask. Now, he found he was frightened of the answer.

"If the train crashes and there is an explosion or an intense fire, fission material will be released, as well as alpha particles and gamma radiation in fallout from the fire. In the immediate vicinity of the fire, all persons will be irradiated with doses likely to be fatal in weeks or months. These would be persons who happened to be present at the site, or firemen ... like Vladimir ... who arrive to fight the fire. Worse, a plume of highly radioactive smoke would rise from the fire and spread contamination so severe that within one mile of the site, persons remaining for a year would die. The area contaminated badly enough to require evacuation and decontamination could exceed 750 square miles."

"My God." Jim slowly shook his head. "Are these your conclusions, or are you relying on work done by others?" He asked the lawyer's question.

"Both. Look, let's take a break. I have a final package for you. After dinner, I'll explain where these conclusions came from. I'm a little tired right now."

"Sure, sure. I'm sorry to be so pushy. This is ... just so much to take in."

"Do you shoot?"

"Shoot?"

"Guns, man. Do you hunt?"

"Some. Not much."

"Let's go blast some clay. You'll get a kick out of this place. We can have dinner there later after some therapeutic shooting. Then we'll finish up. And, hey, you'll know all that I know."

They were back in the mountains again, leaving behind the desert and shimmering heat. DeSilva turned off the highway at a sign for The Inn of the Mountain Gods resort.

"This is an Apache facility. It's become quite the chic place. Gambling, skiing in winter, swimming, great food, and skeet. It's got it all." They parked at the range and armed themselves. DeSilva was well known here, too. For an hour and a half they shot countless rounds at the clay disks that were hurled in front of them. Jim's shoulder throbbed long before they finally quit, but the pain was a small price to pay for the release of tension it brought.

"Let's go eat, man. I'm starved. These treatments I'm taking don't leave me many windows of opportunity," DeSilva said. They still had not spoken of DeSilva's illness. Jim knew he must ask before he left, and he dreaded confronting what he felt certain was the truth.

Inside the lodge, they were ushered to a spacious dining hall, with high glass walls on one side offering a view of a beautiful lake and a high mountain rising above its reflection in the blue water. The setting sun illuminated the side of the mountain in a reddish glow. "Sierra Blanca," DeSilva said.

"Old Baldy," Jim replied.

"You have a good memory."

"We used to ride up here and see if the snow had melted from the top. There was nothing here then."

"You mean nothing but poor Apaches. My cousins, man. I'm one-fourth Apache. They aren't poor anymore. The Mescalero have figured out how to make money from the White Man." The food was spicy south-western and delicious. When they were done, DeSilva said, "I need to drag you to one more place. Tonight the Mescalero Apaches begin a festival to celebrate the coming of age of girls into womanhood. It's right up the road."

*   *   *

They took seats in stands that lined one side of an arena the size of a football field. On the facing side small trees and branches had been formed into a wall of greenery. A fire blazed in the center of the field. Hundreds of people sat in the stands or roamed about the area, lining up at concession stands, or just visiting. Jim noted that they were the only non-Indians he could see. "People come from all over the country to this. It's like a huge family reunion." In the arena, a group of girls, dressed mostly in white, escorted by older women in shawls shuffled in a dance together around the fire. Drums beat out a rhythm. From behind the barrier of greenery, a lone dancer rushed onto the field. His body was painted black and he wore a headdress of tall, thin wooden slats in a perpendicular pattern. His face and headdress presented a fearful appearance in the reflection from the flames.

"You asked where my conclusions came from. In the box I'll give you tonight, you'll find a package of three thousand pages that was submitted to DOE in 1991 by Greenpeace. Greenpeace argued that the spent fuel rods were too dangerous to be transported the way the government proposed to do it, and ought to be left where they were. In that package is a report by an expert in radiation who calculated the likely contamination from a fire aboard a ship carrying the casks of fuel rods. My figures come from his report, and from my own work.

"The DOE environmental assessment that concluded there was no risk in bringing the rods to South Carolina was done in 1991 and their policy was published in 1993. So they knew about these conclusions."

"They knew," DeSilva said smiling.

"Why didn't Greenpeace help the state in the first lawsuit if they were so concerned?" Jim was thinking out loud, not really expecting DeSilva to know the answer.

DeSilva continued, smiling at Jim's surprise, "Other environmental groups supported the government. Perhaps Greenpeace was worried it might be labeled a fringe group. No group like Greenpeace can survive with that stigma, and they backed down." Jim's face could not hide the fury he felt. "South Carolina was simply regarded as expendable, the risks from an accident there worth taking for the greater good."

The dancers moved around and around the fire, their white dresses illuminated by its orange-red glow, sparks drifting into the night sky above them with the smoke. The black dancer raced, leaping and gesturing imaginary threats in time to the incessant drums.

* * *

At the lodge Jim was restless. Sleep would not come. He dressed and walked down the steps to the bar. He took a table near the bar and ordered a bourbon and soda. The crowd thinned as he finished a second. The whiskey began to take hold and the fearful images of the day started to recede. Before heading back to his room, he studied the old stuffed bear in the corner. It was raised on its hind legs, front paws held fiercely, as if ready to strike.

He lay back on the bed, feeling the whiskey soothe and pull him into sleep. *The wind roared, shaking the door of the little motel room. Things banged against the door and the large plate glass window. Sticks, pine cones, God only knew what all was hurled by the furious wind from the monster hurricane. An oak tree fell on top of the building next door, crashing loudly. The ground shook under his feet and under the bed where his two small children lay in the corner away from the window. He thought they had traveled far enough away from the coast to be safe from the hurricane — and now it had followed them, its fury unabated. The metal tower on the roof of the motel fell into the parking lot. Suddenly, the wind subsided. He wondered if it were the eye of the storm. There was a sharp knock on the door. Jim looked at his wife huddled in the corner with him. The knock came again. He rose and unlocked the door. Slowly, he pulled the door open, fearful the wind would start again. Outside, immediately in front of him was the ghastly image of the Apache dancer, his face painted in an evil mask. Jim drew back in horror, his heart racing. Drums beat in the distance and the dancer swayed and waved his sticks threateningly at Jim. Alicia screamed, and Jim slammed the door shut, rushing to fasten the latches. The sound of the drums grew louder. He turned to see his ashen-faced wife bent over their children. They had lost all their hair, and their faces were burned the dark and ugly brown that he knew to be the nuclear tan. Their eyes were sunken in their faces, the lashes gone. Their lips were swollen, blistered, and they raised their burned arms for comfort, unable to cry for the pain in their throats. The scream began to rise in his chest when the wind came again, rocking the window and shaking the door. Over the wind, he heard a coyote howling loudly, as if the animal were just below him. He wondered how the coyote could be outside in the terrible wind, his mind fumbling frantically for an answer, when his eyes opened and he saw the open window of his room.*

The coyote was below him singing to the moon shining clearly overhead through the tall fir trees. Slowly, his heart calmed, his breath came more easily, the terror subsided, and the frightful images now were only a dream.

* * *

He drank his coffee, again gazing down into the basin from the lodge dining room. His mind struggled to overcome a night with so little sleep. And so much terror. He found the answer he came for, one of unimagined fears. Over another breakfast of coffee and rolls, DeSilva told him about his leukemia, myelocytic and probably caused by radiation.

"You can help us win this case, Tony," Jim said.

DeSilva's eyes betrayed his doubt, but more than that they were filled with a profound and unsettling sadness.

"I'm sorry, Tony."

"So am I. But I knew the score. I'm not like those kids in the Ukraine — or Colorado. Now, I just want to tell the truth."

Chapter 8

"Officerrrrrs!" The major's booming bass voice called out while he raised one hand in the air. The many groups of camouflage-uniformed men and women broke from the little groups engaged in small talk and filed into formation, as the 1189th U.S. Army Transportation Terminal Brigade assembled for its monthly drill weekend. Sleepier than most, and tired from the trip to New Mexico, Major James McNeely claimed a place in the first rank of officers.

As the morning wore on, Jim lounged with several of the unit's officers in a corner office. Captain Nathan Engle flung open the door, sauntered into the room, and took a seat on one of the desks.

"I miss Billy the Kid," he sang, pausing to spit into a coffee cup.

"Nat, you're the only Jew I know who chews tobacco and sings country music. I thought you people were supposed to be so damn smart." Captain Mark Killian, the only unit officer bigger than Nat Engle, was jabbing his finger at the tobacco-filled coffee cup. "Man, that's disgusting. Look, it's dribbling out of the edge of your mouth. Yuk!" Mark exclaimed.

Nat daintily brushed the brown drop of juice from the edge of his lip. "I truly beg your pardon, Mark," he responded in his heavy drawl, "I wouldn't for the world offend your fine Irish-Catholic-Charleston-Jock sensibilities." The rest of the room erupted into laughter, joined, despite his best efforts, by Mark Killian. "Shit, boy, I'm probably the only Jew you know. You should just be glad you got to know a real down home country Jew." Nat punctuated this statement with a long jet of tobacco juice into the cup. And then joined his friends, breaking up into a hearty laugh.

"I got something to tell you boys," Nat said swinging his long legs back and forth. "This is my last drill with the old 1189th."

The room suddenly went quiet. Nat had been with the unit for over five years. Announcements like these in the close knit group had the same effect as news that a family member was moving to the Indian subcontinent.

"What's going on?" Mark asked.

"I think it's time to go back to the infantry, fellas."

The other officers looked stunned.

"The National Guard?" Jim was incredulous.

"Bubba, you know that they sleep in tents ... in the woods. And eat those things. What are they called? MREs! They eat that stuff." Mark stood in front of him and grabbed Nat's broad shoulders. "Don't do it, man. I take back everything I ever said about Vince Gill and Garth Brooks."

"I appreciate that, big boy; but ... I have a chance to join a Bradley unit right there in Kingstree." He was referring to the Bradley fighting vehicle, a fast armored vehicle made famous in the Gulf War for successfully killing Iraqi tanks. "In fact, I'll be the commander. I couldn't turn it down. The Bradley was my baby back in the real army."

"Commander? How in the world did you swing that? You haven't, as they say, paid your dues in Guard politics."

"Connections."

"O.K., Nat. Listen to me, now." Jim McNeely had taken Mark's place in front of the young captain. With palms pressed together, he waved his arms to his left, "Over here we have the National Guard staying in the field — you remember, the woods, ticks, and slit trenches? Stay with me, now." He switched his arms to the right. "Over here, we have the 1189th, staying in hotels in nice coastal cities where we can load our nice clean ships. You can see lots of Bradleys then. Abrams tanks, too. Over here we have the guard eating really bad-tasting, cold MREs. Over here we have the 1189th eating in the hotel restaurant. You're smart, Nat. You've got an MBA from NC State. You and your dad run the largest independent bank left in the state. 1189th — Guard. What's to choose?"

"Bradleys." Nat spat again. He smiled at Jim's show of frustration and disbelief. "Tell you what, though. It's tough to leave you all. Nobody can load a ship like the 1189th." This was the unit mantra. They could load a huge ship with hundreds of military vehicles and send it thousands of miles across the sea. Out of chaos, they brought order. They always made it work. When one of them moved on, particularly one like Nat Engle — who was so good at their rare, part-time trade — it was like losing a family member.

"Well, I know you'll do great, Nat. And when you get this foolishness out of your system, you can always come home," Jim slapped his shoulder.

"Well, I think you're gonna suck," Mark offered. "You'll come crawling back. Are you sure you're Jewish? Maybe you're adopted."

"The sound you hear the next time you're in the confession booth, choir boy, will be my Bradley coming up the steps of the cathedral."

The door swung open again, this time hesitantly. A sergeant stuck her head through the opening, "Major McNeely, the colonel is ready for his meeting now, sir." Jim and everyone in the room but Mark and Nat grabbed a notepad and filed out into the drill hall.

"Damn, Nat, it won't be the same around here. And it sure won't be the same at AT," Mark said. AT was short for Annual Training, the two weeks when the unit went on duty for training, usually to load a ship. "Remember Beaumont two years ago? Man, we really tore it up down there. 'Specially you. That was some woman you hooked up with."

"Yes... she... was," he agreed, nodding and smiling broadly. "And as I recall, you nearly forgot you were married. That CPA was hot to cozy up and do more than the two step with you. What was it she said, 'I just luvvvvv football players!' They do love their football in Texas."

"Hey, now, we don't talk about that, remember?"

"It's too bad. Beth should be real proud. If you didn't stray out of the pasture that time, she's got nothing to worry about."

"Why don't you come eat dinner with us tonight, unless you have other plans not fit for polite company?"

"That would be nice, thanks. Do you mind if I bring a friend? I'm kind of staying in town with a girl I've been dating."

Mark laughed. "Sure. Who's this one?"

"Her name's Susan Ryan. She's a nurse in Florence. A nice Catholic girl, you'll be glad to know."

Nat continued to stare at Mark, who noted the uncharacteristic embarrassment in his friend's face. He tilted his head to one side finally and exclaimed, "Oh, no, don't tell me!" Nat was silent. Mark closed his eyes and threw his head back, "I'm right, aren't I?... Aren't I?"

"O.K., O.K., you're right. Be quiet. I've got a reputation around here."

"Not for much longer, Stud. My God, Lion Loins is gonna settle down! Come on, let me hear you say it.... Come on."

"All right, I'm engaged. There. Feel better, asshole?"

"This is great! This must be some woman to cool your jets."

"Hey, now I want to let the news out in my own time, O.K." Spitting into his cup again he said, "Can you imagine the hell I'd catch if all these bastards around here knew?"

"Yes, I can."

"Well?"

"O.K., I promise I won't tell them."

"There's one more thing."

"Yeah. Man, you're full of news today."

Nat paused for a moment. "How 'bout be my best man?"

"Sure. It's an honor." Mark's smile widened and finally exploded into a loud, deep laugh. Grabbing Nat's neck in his large arm, he rubbed the closely cropped head, "There's just one thing. Do we get to jump on that glass and dance in a circle?"

"Screw you, Mark."

"Officerrrrrrs!" the major yelled from his spot at the corner of the officers' formation. This was the signal for the end of the drill day. The weekend was half over.

The morning's arrangement was repeated, more hurriedly this time. Nat Engle sang as he worked his way into the second rank.

The adjutant read a list of reminders. Then he pulled out the note Captain Killian had handed him just before formation. Smiles crept across the faces of the commander and his deputy standing behind the adjutant.

"Listen up to this last announcement. All members of the 1189th will please congratulate Captain Nat Engle on his recent engagement to Miss Susan Ryan of Florence, South Carolina." Hoots rose from officer and enlisted formations alike.

"Lion Loins bites the dust!" a voice called out.

Nat closed his eyes and dropped his head, as hands began to slap his back.

* * *

In the communications room of the USS *Deyo*, the technician noted that the indicator light on his panel was lit. Another fax was being intercepted from Test Location Number 1. He pulled the first page off the printer, a header sheet from the same law firm as a number of the other faxes from the morning. These people really burned up some paper. This one was something called a "complaint" with "D-R-A-F-T" written at the top of the first page. It was being sent to two other guys, both in Columbia, according to the header. The petty officer second class read the first three pages. It was all legal-sounding mumbo jumbo to him. This was really a peculiar exercise. He began to feed the pages into the secure fax machine for transmission to Exercise Control at the Defense Intelligence Agency, as he had the other dozen faxes from the law firm, and a half dozen others from Test Location Number 3. He wondered what sort of game this was. For the last week they had been intercepting faxes and telephone calls from several designated locations, all recorded and sent on to Exercise Control. The test locations included what were supposed to be the offices of the governor of South Carolina and a law professor.

Well, he thought, *it's no weirder than a lot of other oddball things the navy thinks up to keep us busy.* He glanced at his watch. Three more damn hours in the windowless little room and he'd be relieved, in more ways than one he hoped. Two nights before, he had met a real beauty at a place called Vickery's. Tonight she was picking him up for dinner at her place. Blond hair, bright blue eyes, real class. And legs that went on forever. Weird or not, he hoped this exercise kept him in Charleston for a long time.

*   *   *

Music blared from speakers in the Killians' den. The two men performed a passable two step across the carpet and sang along with the tape, "Jose Cuervo was a friend of mine ...."

"I'll bet they'd be great in a karaoke bar," Beth Killian mused to Susan Ryan while she filled her glass with more white zinfandel. Beth was a little concerned that the noise might disturb some of the neighbors, but not enough to do anything to dampen Mark and Nat's celebration. The house was in a good subdivision, and it cost more than many people thought a couple in their late twenties could afford. But Mark did well in the stevedore company. With her teacher's salary and his reserve pay, they made a better-than-comfortable living. Most of their neighbors were older. They got along with them all. Mark regularly played coach in the games of soccer and football that sprang up among the gangs of neighborhood children that seemed to gravitate to their house.

"This will definitely have to be it for tonight," Susan said. "As you can see, I've got to drive us back downtown." Beth looked around the corner into the den again where her husband and Nat, arms draped around each other's shoulders, belted out the final lines to country and western's anthem of tequila oblivion. She would never know that it was also the ballad of Mark Killian's and Nat Engle's wild and, so far as Beth was concerned, secret time in Beaumont, Texas.

"I see what you mean. They sure are having a good time," Beth said.

"Nat's going to miss Mark a lot. He's told me so much about the both of you. If he didn't want this command in the guard so badly, he'd never leave the 1189th," Susan said.

"Mark feels the same way. When he got home this afternoon, he went on and on about what a mistake it was for Nat to leave the unit. God, THE UNIT. You'd think it was a religious cult or something. What's really going on, though, is he can't stand to see Nat go. He's really going to miss him." Beth sipped on her wine. "It's funny, isn't it? They can do anything. They can build things, fix things, work outrageous hours, and of course, as they remind us repeatedly, they can *load a ship*. But they can't say they care about one another. When Mark told me Nat wanted him to be best man, he just beamed, like a little boy who won the prize at the fair."

Susan laughed. "It's true. But you know, I don't really want them to hug each other and talk about each other's feelings. Is that too backward?"

"Yes." Beth turned to look at her husband and his best friend again. "We'd love that, but face it — it's not in them. They'd make lousy imitations of us." The two women burst into laughter. Mark unsteadily poured two more shots of tequila and handed one to Nat. The little glasses swept up as the two men tilted their heads back and threw the liquor into waiting mouths. Beth grimaced, turned back to Susan, and said, "Tell me about the big wedding. Is it going to be a religious ceremony, civil, or what? I thought we had in-law problems."

"Religious. Doubly religious. We're having it at my parents' church, St. Nicholas' in Florence. The priest will do part of the service and Nat's family rabbi from Kingstree will do the rest. The wedding will be no problem; it'll be fun. The problem is everybody wants to know how we're going to bring up the kids. Nat just says, 'As Americans. We're going to raise them to be Americans,' and thinks that's enough." Beth laughed. "It isn't, of course. We can put this off for a while, but sooner or later I'll be pregnant, and then we'll have to figure something out."

"That is a tough one."

"He's like a big kid sometimes, and it makes me wonder if he's just putting off a problem that'll blow up in our faces; but then I talk to him, and he tells me that all we have to do is love our children, and they'll love God the way they believe is best. That's when I know everything will be O.K." She smiled at Beth. "I've got it bad, don't I?"

"Real bad, honey."

* * *

Susan navigated the pickup truck into the parking garage next to the hotel. Nat was sound asleep in the passenger seat, as he had been since they left the Killians' drive. Not too gently, she shook his head from side to side. "Wake up soldier boy. We're home, and I'm not carrying you to the room."

"That was quick," he said yawning.

"I guess so, since you slept the whole way. Can you walk?"

Reaching for her across the cab, he leered at her and slurred, "Baby, I can do more than walk."

She slapped his hands away. "Walk first, run later."

Stumbling and unsteady, Nat made his way on Susan's arm across the foyer of the grand old hotel. He leaned his head against the wall as they waited for the elevator. "Don't worry, Nat, I'm not embarrassed. If anyone comes by, I'll just pretend you're a drunk street person trying to assault me."

"Yeah," he giggled.

As the lock of the room clicked open, Nat nearly fell into the room, tripped over the combat boots he had left there that afternoon, and tumbled into the king-size bed. "Ain't this romantic?" he laughed.

She didn't respond, but walked to the bed and peered down at him, his eyes closed, smiling stupidly. "Are you all right?" Without responding, he pulled her down and across him, rolling quickly so that he hovered over her, his outstretched arms on either side of her shoulders.

"There's nobody more romantic than this cowboy," he said thickly, lowering his mouth to hers. She took his tongue as he ran it between her lips and rolled it around her mouth. Sliding her arms free, she cradled his stubbly face in her hands and returned his kiss. "I love you, cowboy."

They embraced and kissed more passionately, now pulling clothes free from one another. Out of their clothes completely, they poured themselves onto one another. "You're sure you're not going to be sick?" she whispered.

He paused long enough to answer, "Baby, I'll never be too drunk or too sick to love you." Again, he took her into his arms, wondering at the small, gentle creature that had captured him so completely. She rose to him, taking his powerful body to her, her arms tight around his thick neck.

"Come here, Lion Loins."

He paused above her, "Where'd you hear that?"

"On NBC."

Later that night, Nat woke, Susan curled and small in the comparative massiveness of his arms. He watched her sleep in the light from the street below that leaked through the drapes. *I have the best woman any man ever had*, he thought. *And the best friend.* He laid his head back and slipped again into a sleep of contented confidence.

* * *

Morning broke in Columbia to a perfect day. The brutal heat and humidity of summer were weeks away. This final Sunday in May was destined to be ideal for a boat trip to Lake Murray. On the first floor of the governor's mansion, Billy Harris led his friend, Hal, on a tour.

"Come in here." In the next room was a huge portrait of Francis Marion and below it, in a glass case, a broad-bladed cutlass.

"Wow. Was that his? Really his?"

"Nobody knows. But I'll bet it's from the Revolution." On the wall behind them was a print of the Battle of Cowpens. "See. These guys are carrying some just like it."

"One whack from one of those and you'd be deader than shit," Hal exclaimed.

"Man, watch the cussing!" he hissed under his breath. "You'll get us busted."

From the top of the steps Dottie Harris called, "Billy, where are you? You and Hal need to be ready. Your dad's going to want to leave. Answer me."

"Down here, Mom. We're ready!"

From the back of the house, Watson Harris came into the foyer and called up the steps. "O.K., let's get this show on the road ... Dottie ... Anybody home up there?... Hey, First Lady.... Anybody?" He was joined by Blackie Haselden. "I think they've left us. Probably ran off with some of the trustees."

"No. I think they had their eyes on a couple of highway patrolmen," Blackie said. Spotting Billy around the corner, he waved to his godson. "Billy, is everybody about ready?"

"O.K. boys, let's go," June Haselden said, hurrying down the stairs, followed by Dottie. Both were dressed in shorts and polo shirts.

"A couple of visions aren't they?" Watson offered.

"Dazzling. Let's go."

An hour later than planned, the four adults and two children loaded the suburban, and Watson slowly navigated out of the back gate and onto the street, taking care for the boat and trailer they were towing. This was the second day of a long weekend he and Dottie would spend with their friends in the mansion. It was only the second time since Blackie's election that they had accepted an invitation. At first the idea of staying there intimidated them both. In retrospect, they agreed it was silly. These were special times, and it would be foolish to let the trappings of the governor's office keep them away.

The long suburban and the boat headed north to Lake Murray. Watson was concerned about Blackie. Though he was starting to unwind, he was still tense about the trip to Washington. Watson knew he had been humiliated.

Politics was a world that Watson knew little about, and, except insofar as it concerned his friend who had gotten himself elected governor, he didn't much care about it. He knew enough, however, to understand that no one succeeded in that world without two things: a tremendous ego and a ferocious will to win. Blackie had both, although it seemed odd to say so. There had been other times when he watched his friend start talking about some fight he was in — they were always fights, never just issues — when his eyes burned with the fire of the confrontation. *God help anyone*, Watson thought, *who takes him on.*

But Blackie's fixation on the matter of the nuclear material worried Watson. The night before, he and Blackie stayed in the upstairs den, and Blackie told him of the trip to Washington and the offensive telephone conversation with the president. He saw that his friend was far beyond angry. He was bitterly determined to beat these people. The reasons he gave were all about what was good for the state — public safety, and all that. Watson often teased him that his reasons had as much to do with "the fight" — with winning. Watson was worried that this time it was also about winning, and this time his friend could not possibly win. It galled him to hear of the president's insulting treatment of Blackie as if he were some hick. Watson had listened attentively to everything his friend said, and when he was finished, Blackie asked his opinion, as he always did.

"You can't beat them."

Blackie's eyes flashed, for an instant showing real anger.

"You can't. Whatever else you can do — and I'm sure that's a lot — they'll win. Don't fool yourself."

"It isn't right to treat us like this."

Watson thought, but cared too much for their friendship to say, that what Blackie meant was that *he* didn't like being treated this way.

"I know it ain't right. But face it, it's their bat, their ball, and their field. They make the rules."

"They're not following the rules." Blackie was standing now, facing the window. Columbia's skyline illuminated the dark above the wall beyond the grounds.

Watson took another swallow. "You're hopeless. Fight them 'til your heart's content, Ace. I'm just a goddamned fireman from Florence." Blackie turned around smiling, and Watson added, "Just don't get ulcers over it.... Life's too short."

The wind rushed past them as the boat cut through the lake water. Watson was adept at steering the boat, and in deference to Blackie's "august office" as he called it, did so without his usual ration of beer. Hal was making a good show on the skis, crossing the wake back and forth with ease. Billy had already had one turn, but was anxious for a second so he could try to outdo his friend's performance. Hal signaled he was ready for a rest and let the rope free, sinking slowly in the boat's wake. Watson maneuvered the craft to retrieve Hal, and Billy jumped in to take his place. "O.K., no showing off," Watson called back to his son.

The boat slowly increased speed, pulling Billy to his feet. He wasted no time trying to outdo Hal. As he crossed the wake, he leapt over the little waves. "He's good, Bud," Blackie said to Watson. The governor watched his godson sailing over the little waves, crouched to absorb the bounce. He was growing so fast now, and full of a boundless love for life. What a rare and precious part of his life this boy was.

"Bud, I think he's getting a little carried away." Dottie said to Watson. "Maybe we should slow down."

Watson turned around to look. Floating at the surface and unseen by Billy was a submerged timber. Watson spied the shape too late to pull the boy out of its way. Billy's left ski struck the timber. His leg splayed out behind the rest of him. The effect was to destroy any control Billy had over his body, as it hurled along behind the boat. In an instant he bounced crazily off the surface of the water, and, finally letting go of the tow rope, he flipped once and landed hard upside down, his head plunging deep into the water of the wake.

"No!" Blackie yelled. Dottie and June screamed. Watson immediately pulled the boat around and inched his way to a spot near his son. Blackie was in the water before the boat stopped and quickly swam to the motionless boy. When he reached him, it was clear that a large amount of water had been forced down his throat from the force of the fall. He lifted the boy's head out of the water and held it there until the boat came alongside them. Positioning himself under the boy's back, he pushed his arms up so that Watson could grab them and pull Billy onto the deck. By the time Blackie hauled himself back into the boat, Billy was coughing and gagging, finally hanging over the side to vomit.

"You gave us a terrible scare, Boy," Watson said, his arm around his son.

His face was white, Blackie saw, but he looked like he was otherwise unharmed.

"I'm sorry, Dad ... Mom. Sorry, Uncle Blackie."

Suddenly, the image of Billy's body tumbling out of control into the water seized Blackie. The cold realization of near loss crept along his neck and spine, and he felt himself shiver. "Billy, don't worry about it. Do you feel all right?"

"Yeah. I might pass on the skis for the rest of the day, though."

Blackie laughed with the rest. But the feeling wouldn't go away. Loss was always so close. It couldn't happen again. *Please God.*

Watson pulled the boat onto a small point with a wide beach, and they piled out to have the lunch they had packed that morning. Slowly Blackie began to shake the terrible fear that seized him after the accident.

The sun was warm. He forced himself to see that everything was fine.

While the boys followed the wood line along the water's edge, the adults finished lunch and reclined on the warm beige sand. "Will I have to wait for you to get a real job before we can drink beer on the boat again?" Watson mused.

"Bud, I think you've got a problem," Blackie answered.

"I think we've all got a problem." It was June who spoke, standing now and staring at the sky around the point. The rest pulled themselves up and saw the blue-black cloud that covered the horizon. There was no wind yet, but the cloud was moving resolutely in their direction. A brilliant streak of lightning shot out of the cloud to earth. Dottie shivered and urged Watson to get them back to the marina quickly. She guarded the secret closely, but lightning filled her with a nearly debilitating fear. As the rest gathered the scattered clutter from lunch, Blackie ran along the lake to find the boys. As he ran, he saw that the cloud was particularly large; its blackness projected menace. He could feel the wind beginning to rise.

The cloud caught up with them halfway back to the marina. Lightning seemed to explode on each side of them at once. The wind swept up behind the boat and stirred the lake into a dark, churning sea of waves that threw the bow into the air as the boat fought towards shore. A flash of electric light and a deafening, ripping crack of thunder immediately in front of the little boat pushed Dottie to the edge of panic, and she grabbed her son's arm. Surprised by his mother's fear, Billy took her hand and shouted to her that everything would be all right. The rain began to fall immediately in sheets, stinging their faces as the boat rushed along. The density of the cloud now filled the sky and blotted out the sun of midday so that it seemed dusk.

More orange streaks of lightning shot in front of them as they entered the breakwater of the marina. Highway patrolmen waited in the driving downpour on the dock to take the bowline from Blackie and pulled the boat alongside. Dottie scrambled onto the dock and, fighting the nearly overpowering impulse to run to the suburban, waited while bags were handed to her by the boys. The governor left the boat to be tended by the patrolmen, and he and his companions made their way into the small restaurant. He watched Watson comfort his wife, fully aware of her fear of the storm. Billy approached his mother and offered gently, "Mom, it's just nature. It's O.K."

Chapter 9

He liked to run in the morning, especially in the summer, before the heat and humidity set in. Two or three miles of pushing himself, and he felt alive again. He refused to be one of the people who stumbled into the Pentagon in the early morning half awake, struggled to Starbucks in the mall, and slowly awoke to the day. Not even the bitterest winter mornings kept him from the tracks and roads around the Pentagon. When the herds of glassy-eyed commuters were streaming into the black-tiled corridors, Staff Sergeant Terry Wilkins was already sorting the morning's message traffic for his boss.

This morning a drizzle of cool rain kept most other joggers away. He nearly had the track to himself. On the highways around him, a slow-moving river of headlights flowed toward the bridges across the Potomac. The dark pavement passed quickly under his long, even strides. He was two miles into his run when he noticed another runner cutting across the grass between the track and the parking lot towards him. The runner was another young man like himself with the close-cropped haircut of a soldier. Wilkins noticed that the man was taller and very strong. He had the solid, steady gait of a football player. The man fell into a pace behind him and ran for a tenth of a mile before speaking. "Terry Wilkins, right?"

Wilkins shot a glance at the man, who had moved up next to his shoulder. "Yeah. What can I do for you?"

"Nothin'. Just wanted to meet you. We have a little something in common and I thought we might talk."

"You in the army?"

"Marines."

"Not trying to recruit me are you?"

The other man started to laugh. "No, I don't want to recruit you. But I thought I might have a little advice to pass on to you."

Wilkins stopped running. Irritation at the interruption of his morning ritual showed on his face as he stood breathing hard and glaring at the marine now walking back to join him. "What's up?"

"You've been living at the farm for how long now ... four months? How is C. A.?"

He stared at the tall marine, shaken. *How could he know?* He was suddenly very afraid.

"I know, Terry, O.K. I know all about the farm. You can't imagine how anybody knows about you and Mr. Moore." Wilkins stood motion-less in the light rain while the marine spoke to him. "I know because I was you. I was a farm hand, just like you, Terry," he said jabbing his finger into the young soldier's tee shirt. "Until a year ago. He's nuts, Terry. C. A. is crazy as a loon. And it ain't just the pills." The young man looked out at the traffic inching along the highway. "You can get hurt. I just wanted to warn you."

"I don't know what you're talking about."

"Yes, you do. I'm talking about letting C. A. have his fun with you so you can take the fast track to a hot career. Don't bullshit me. I've been there. How do you think I got assigned to the Chief of Naval Operations?"

Wilkins was unable to speak. His mind raced. *Was this a shakedown? Was he in the middle of some Washington power game?*

"Why did you leave the farm?" The pretense was gone from his voice.

"He just started to scare me, you know? I wanted to get the brass ring, but I just had to get away."

"What scared you?"

"He ruins peoples' lives. He's a predator. If his boss says take some-body down, he just goes out and does it. Nothing's past him. I didn't want to be close to that anymore. So I asked him to help get me the assignment quick, and told him I needed to move on. I didn't sleep for three months after I left."

He stared at the marine, and then sputtered, "Look, I'm not gay, all right?"

"I figured you're not. It doesn't matter to me. I am." He saw the shock in the rain-streaked face. "Look, I don't want to throw my career out the window any more than you do. Just watch out for yourself. Take my advice." The marine started to jog back towards the Pentagon, but stopped and turned, "Name's Paul Gregg, Platoon Sergeant. I'm in N41 in the CNO's Office. If you want to talk, call me. It gets pretty lonely being the only farm hand. I know." Wilkins watched him jog away as the rain began to fall hard and steady. He knew there was only one thing that mattered now. He had to get away from the farm.

*   *   *

C. A. Moore walked up the front steps of the clubhouse. The gray stone Tudor-style building looked more like a mansion than a golf club. Ornate oriental rugs covered most of the polished pine floors that led from the foyer to the cluster of meeting rooms in the wing opposite from the bar. The conspicuous secret service agents flanking the door marked the room where he was supposed to meet with Roger Seekings. The president asked for an update on Moore's plans for the Russian plutonium. But Moore knew what he wanted was the name of the leak.

Moore held up his White House pass. In the room, a table had been laden with a variety of juices and coffee. He waited patiently next to the table. As the campaign season neared, Seekings spent more and more time playing golf and hosting morning coffees with wealthy visitors. The games and meetings were nothing more than repayment to wealthy contributors to the party, or to his own reelection fund. The right amount of money purchased access to the great man, and access meant the chance to lobby him.

An agent entered the room and held the door for Seekings, who hurried towards a chair at the corner of the table. An aide fussed over a cup and saucer, preparing the president's coffee, while a second handed the president his golf shoes and a pair of clean socks. Seekings ignored Moore while he removed his loafers and the black dress socks he wore. "Wait outside, gentlemen," he said. When the door was closed, he looked up. "So what have you got? I need to get out there. A million-dollar donor is anxious to whine to me about the serious problems he is having with imported sugar products. I don't want to disappoint him."

"Mr. President, we will have an assessment within the week of South Carolina's plans to file suit. They plan to sue. I've arranged with Justice for Fred Muldoon to handle our side of the case. He's the most experienced lawyer over there. Seven years ago he won a case against the same lawyers the state plans to use."

Seekings walked to a mirror next to the door and brushed his hair. "C. A. that's exactly what I expect from you. Good job." Turning to face him, he added, "Now that is the last I want to hear from you about this. Just handle it. You know what to do."

"Yes, sir," Moore replied. Seekings continued to stare at him signaling he wanted to hear about Moore's more delicate project. "I have received some information concerning the vice president that may be of interest to you, sir."

"Yes?"

"Mr. O'Connelly's daughter is about to announce her candidacy for her father's old seat in congress. But there may be a problem. My sources tell me that an old college roommate of hers once claimed that they were lovers. This story may hit the papers soon. Of course, this will put her campaign in grave jeopardy. It also seems that the vice president's son has been the subject of an internal air force investigation into allegations of inappropriate behavior. You know, too much to drink, wild women, and so on. These are real problems for an officer who has been in the top of his peer group and expects to be promoted. I know you are concerned about the vice president."

Seekings smiled. "C. A., I want you to go and speak to Mike. Tell him I am deeply concerned about these things and that I stand ready to help. Tell him I want us to be committed players on the *same team* from here on out. That it's important to us both. Do you understand?" His face hardened, the smile retreating. "I saw his press conference a few weeks ago. His insistence that his health is strong was impressive. And, of course, his medical records confirm he's in fine form. Tell Mike that we stand behind him a hundred percent to fight any suggestions that he is anything less than ... competent. Make sure he understands exactly what I intend to do. Understand?"

"Yes, Mr. President." He paused a moment, "I believe we will soon know the identity of the person who has been communicating with Governor Haselden concerning the plans for importing the plutonium ... within the month."

Seekings took a final sip of coffee from the china cup. "I expect you to take care of these things."

* * *

Sasha Dunitsev did not understand at all. The words were clear enough. Colonel Matveev had explained precisely what was expected of him. The colonel had always been direct, never ambiguous. Dunitsev had been his aide in the old army. He could not understand why the simple plan had to be abandoned. The bribes had been arranged; some were already paid. All that remained was to pick up the containers of plutonium and pay the rest of the bribes. Now, the colonel expected him to launch an assault on Zarmayevka — an assault that would fail, and from which none of the men would return. But Matveev had so far failed to tell him the reason for such madness.

"Colonel, you know I have never questioned your orders."

"Then do not do so now," Matveev sighed. He anticipated the young man would have to be told. *It was never like this in the old army*, he thought, tiredly.

"Is this a feint?" Dunitsev's face was firm.

"The government must believe that this was a serious raid. And they must not know it was us. That's why we are going to recruit the Chechen scum. No one will associate them with us, and they won't be missed." Matveev lit another cigarette. "You want to know why this is necessary? It is because the government is in league with the Americans to prevent any of the nuclear material being put to — productive uses. The government will round us up and kill us if they suspect we have taken any of the plutonium." He stared into the young man's eyes, searching for his reaction. "So, we will let them think the Chechens have made a clumsy attempt. And then we will take it in America."

Dunitsev was shocked, but Matveev saw in his eyes the spark of excitement. "I see," he said nodding slowly. "Who will lead the real raid?"

"I will, with Mikail. And you, Sasha. That is why you must return from Kazakhstan." He slapped the young man's back. "When I have sketched out the plan, you and I will go over it and fill in the details. It will be a challenge, but it can be done."

"It's like the game from our exercises."

"Yes, Sasha, like the game."

When Dunitsev left, Colonel Matveev returned to the maps spread out on the table. They were map sheets of the area from Sunny Point, North Carolina, just south of Wilmington, to the Savannah River Site, all the way across South Carolina. The most likely railroad routes had been highlighted. There weren't many choices. But he had to know the exact route. And he had to know the schedule.

Already, their American contacts were speaking with the most likely group to work with them. There were so many anti-government groups in America, and they were so easy to find. It amazed him that such a large country could be ruled when its government tolerated such enemies among its own people. The prospect of possessing bomb-grade material would be irresistible to many of the so-called "militia groups." Matveev smiled and shook his head. The challenge would not be finding the help they needed within America. He studied the maps more closely. No, the challenge would be the escape. If security for the train was as poor as that for most shipments of fuel rods in America, taking the plutonium would not be too difficult. Americans still believed the oceans protected them from the chaos of the world. The trick was to find a means to get to the sea. He traced his finger along the railroad from Sunny Point across South Carolina. The farther along the line, the greater the distance it was to the ocean. The key was to make the raid early in the journey. He spread the map sheet out, scanning the terrain between the small city called Florence and the Atlantic. Stretching along the coast under his fingers was a densely built-up strip labeled with pleasant-sounding names, like Myrtle Beach.

It was the only practical choice they had. They could not hide in America. The escape must be clean and swift. And they had to get to sea as soon as possible. A helicopter would take them from the train to some remote place where they would take a small boat to a ship offshore.

It was time to squeeze the young soldier in the videotape. Matveev flipped on the terminal of his computer. In his electronic mail file he composed a short message to the e-mail address of Tidewater Investors' Centre in Richmond. "Regarding the investment we discussed on Thursday, make the inquiry and let me know the response." The man at Tidewater would know what to do.

*　*　*

Erick walked to the rear of the building and unlocked the door that faced the driveway. He carried a bag and a bucket of cleaning supplies inside with him. He locked the door behind him. It was still daylight, and would be for another hour. Plenty of time for him to do his work without turning on any lights. Tim was across the street setting up a camera, apparently trying to adjust the angle and light meter to catch the perfect shot of the steeple of St. Michael's church against a picturesque sunset. From his vantage point, Tim could see all the approaches to the offices of Holland, Rollins, Jerald and McNeely, and if anyone began to enter the building, he would warn Erick by whispering into the speaker in his camera. Erick was a professional who went about his work quickly and calmly.

He was amazed at the computer system these people had. It was archaic. He shook his head. *How could lawyers function like this?* It would be impossible to tap into their computers directly. "Shit," he said aloud.

Plan "B," he thought. Finding McNeely's office, he placed his folding stepladder under one of the recessed lights. Fitting the tiny camera took less than five minutes. The camera would send an image of the screen on the lawyer's computer to a receiver in the office that he and Tim had rented across the street, and from there to Washington. This would have to do. Holland's office didn't even have a terminal. *What a bunch of rubes.*

In each office he placed listening devices so that the entire building was covered. In the room containing the copier, he spotted a list of files and account numbers. He made himself a copy, as well as one of the names, addresses and phone numbers of all the attorneys and support staff in the office. In the closet-like shelves outside the kitchen he found the files arranged in neat numerical order. Running his finger along the labels, he came to the file entitled, "South Carolina v. United States Department of Energy." It wasn't too thick. He had time. Carefully he copied the contents, coming to a typed set of notes with the heading "Interview with Anthony DeSilva — Proposed Testimony Outline."

His microphone was keyed. "Erick, two men standing next to front entrance," Tim whispered into his camera. Erick's heart skipped. He stopped copying the file and turned off the machine. He retrieved his can of furniture polish and began to clean the desk used by the firm's runner. "All clear," Tim whispered again. Quickly, Erick finished copying the file and tucked the copies into his bag.

The job done, Erick let himself out the back door and locked it carefully. *You never know who might be in the neighborhood,* he laughed to himself. He threw the bucket loudly into the back of the truck, got in the cab and drove back to the hotel. After changing clothes, he joined Tim in the bar downstairs.

"What the hell were you doing in there, redoing your will?" Tim — Captain Timothy Giordono, U.S. Army Intelligence — was still agitated from the delay. He had worked with Erick — Lieutenant Erick Gilbert — several times before, but would never get used to his penchant for freelancing, particularly when it led to delay.

"There was no rush. The last thing on these people's mind is being broken into. Do you know they don't even have locks on their file compartments. These guys can't be heavy hitters. You should see the place. They have the same computers they had when Reagan was president! Can you believe it? I don't know what everybody's so concerned about. These guys are losers. I copied their whole file. Felix'll be a happy man."

"Fine."

"Tomorrow, we'll test the system," Eric said, draining his drink. He was having fun.

* * *

The dive boat slowly moved to a position away from the main shipping channel, but where the river was still deep enough. Captain Wallace Kratz and Matt Reicher were already in their gear for the dives, which they were to make in sequence. The exercise, called "Dive Qualifications," was required once a year to maintain their status and pay as navy divers. Kratz elected to go first.

The atmosphere on the boat eased at once with the disappearance of the captain into the silty waters of the Cooper River. Tension surrounded all commanders of a military installation whenever they were around subordinates. But in the case of Captain Kratz, there was justifiable unease.

The day was bright, and not yet hot. Matt studied the gentle swells that rolled the dive boat. He welcomed the quiet. The dive crew stirred as Captain Kratz began to make his ascent to the boat. Matt readied himself for his own dive. The crew pulled the captain on board. Kratz stood on the deck, freeing himself from the heavy tanks, water spilling around him. "How was it, Captain?" Matt asked.

"Dark," he snapped.

Matt rolled backwards into the river, sinking slowly below the surface. The light above grew more opaque as he sank deeper. Below him was a void of blackness that seemed to swallow him as the weight of his gear drew him down. As his flippered feet touched the soft bottom, he looked above where only a dim light marked the surface of the river. The boat was a long silhouette rippling far away. The water was cold at the bottom. He stood still, looking in vain around him. There was only an inky invisibility. He hated not being able to see. How different it was from his dives in the Pacific, where he could see rays, sharks, and even whales at great distances. Here, anything could be inches away and he would not know it. As the emptiness closed in on him, his mind recounted the teaming dangers lurking in the dark waters: snakes, sharks… and alligators. Inside his mask he smiled at that one. He glanced around at his feet. Maybe the big son of a bitch was right here. The current was swift, and he found it difficult to maintain his footing. Something scraped his leg. He jerked, panic flickering in his stomach. He stood motionless, every sense alert for another alien and unseen contact. His watch alerted him that his time was up, and he slowly rose to the surface, resisting the urge to rush away from the eerie darkness below.

Matt climbed into the boat with studied casualness. He fooled no one. Every member of the crew had also stood in the inky depths, and all had felt the surge of relief when they escaped back to the surface. "Who brought the beer?" he yelled to the crew gathered in the bow, sparking restrained laughter. Kratz looked at him silently, unsmiling. Matt removed his gear quietly as the boat headed back towards the dock.

"Take us up river. I want to look at the new piers," Kratz called to the helm.

"Aye, sir." The seaman brought the boat about and headed up the river. On the shore off the port side, the mouth of Goose Creek passed. Ahead lay the Weapons Station piers where the USS *Deyo* was moored. She had completed ammunition loading days ago but remained to conduct some sort of exercise, Matt recalled from the Monday security briefing. As the boat approached Storm Point, the captain motioned for him to sit with him in the rear of the boat.

"Matt. I want to talk to you."

"Yes, sir." *Crap*, he thought.

"Is your wife having some trouble arranging to move out here, Matt?"

"No, sir. But that's a fair question." *It's nosy and none of your damned business*, he fumed to himself. "It's a personal thing, sir. We'll work it out. We're just readjusting to some things."

"O.K. Matt, this is a little base, you know." Kratz spoke in low, measured tones. "There aren't really any secrets here. When the XO is living alone, he gets a lot of attention. I think you know what I mean. People watch. You're not a young kid anymore. Besides, things are different these days." He paused, studying Matt to see if he was following him. Matt was struggling to force the anger he felt building to a safe place, deep inside himself. "There's a new morality out there. Look, this makes me uncomfortable just like I'm sure it does you. Do you know what I'm talking about?"

"I think so, Captain."

"You need to stop the running around. If I notice, so does the base. The XO can't do that shit. Period."

"Yes, sir."

Kratz wondered whether to ask him about the things he was hearing "off line" from Washington. In a way, he wished things could be different for his new XO. You couldn't help but like the guy. He worked tirelessly. There was a physical toughness and mental confidence in him that won the respect and loyalty of sailors and civilians alike. Kratz knew he could easily come to value him as an officer ... and as a friend.

But none of that mattered. Kratz's superiors had already selected an early replacement. In a month or so, he'd tell Matt to expect a transfer by the spring. He carried some heavy baggage, and the navy was through with Matt Reicher because of it. There were people in Washington who didn't want him around any longer than necessary. And that was all Wallace Kratz needed to know.

* * *

Mike O'Connelly dreaded the telephone call to his daughter, but after the visit from Moore, he knew he had no choice. What Moore told him — and, more frightening, how he said it — made O'Connelly fear for his daughter. The certainty that his own conflict with the president had spawned the threat to her made his anxiety worse.

Moore came to see him, bringing neither briefcase nor notebook. O'Connelly thought he looked like an amputee without them. He immediately came to his purpose. "Mr. O'Connelly, the president has asked me to discuss a couple of things with you. He is very distressed over the irresponsible reports that keep cropping up in the press suggesting that you are not ... well."

"You mean the ones that say I might be drooling all over the table at cabinet meetings? Are those the stories you mean?"

"Yes, sir. I'm glad you can keep your sense of humor about this. It must be terrible."

"That's one word for it, C. A." The man's disingenuousness was deliberately obvious. There was no smirk on his face and no sneer in his voice, but they were there all the same.

"The president wants you to know that he has full faith in your ability to fulfill the office of vice president. These scurrilous stories are no more than sensation-seeking by the press."

"'Scurrilous'? C. A., you've been reading too many Victorian romances."

Moore ignored the joke. "Mr. O'Connelly, the president has also learned that some news organizations may be working on a story about your daughter that would be very harmful to her campaign for congress, and, he is certain, quite painful to her and her family." O'Connelly's heart began to race. A threat to the daughter he loved more than life.

"What is this about?" O'Connelly detested needing anything from this man, but he had to know how to protect Marilyn. "I want to know everything you have learned."

"Someone at one of the wire services picked up on an old story about your daughter and a public confrontation she had with her roommate in college. They are working hard right now to confirm the details, but what they have been told is that your daughter's roommate was quite an active lesbian. This woman became angry with your daughter and accused her in a very public argument of being an unfaithful — I'm sorry, Mr. Vice President — lover. Clearly, this is trash journalism, but it's dangerous. We wanted you to know."

"That's bullshit," O'Connelly said, seething. What his instincts told him was too outrageous to believe, even for C. A. Moore.

"We know. We know, Mr. O'Connelly. But it is a real threat to Marilyn. We will do everything we can to monitor the situation and, of course, will keep you informed. And I'm afraid there is more. Your son, Mickey, I believe he's called, is also the subject of some intense press attention. Unfortunately, there is an Air Force investigation, just internal and very close hold for the moment, of some allegations — I'm certain unsubstantiated — that Mickey sexually harassed several enlisted women. We are concerned that interest in your daughter's campaign, and, of course, in your own situation might lead the press, particularly the tabloid shows, to highlight this nonsense. You know how the military can be. This could ruin his career."

O'Connelly was silent, overcome by rage and fear.

"Mr. O'Connelly, President Seekings is determined to stand by you in this." Moore paused to be certain that O'Connelly was following him as he prepared to deliver the real message he brought from Roger Seekings. "The president feels that it is vital that you and he present a united front. As you may know, the State of South Carolina is preparing to file suit against us over the shipments of plutonium. President Seekings understands that you have strong, legitimate views that are different from those of the administration. He feels that if we are to prevent these smear stories about your children from going public, you and he must be seen to agree on all-important public issues, like the matter of the plutonium. As you know, we have considerable influence with the media, but we need to set the right tone to be effective."

For hours after Moore left him alone, O'Connelly was lost in the grief of a father who knows he has placed his children in danger. Seekings intended to threaten him with harm to his son and daughter, that much was clear. He struggled to restrain the fury he felt. He had to find what needed to be done to protect his children. The first step was the call to his daughter.

* * *

"Now, aren't you glad you came?" Jim McNeely asked. Matt Reicher took the two drinks from the uniformed bartender and handed one to Jim.

"Yeah, boy, this is a regular bash. Do you lawyers always have so much fun, or is this your annual orgy?" Jim listened while he sipped from his glass and surveyed the ballroom of Hibernian Hall, which was crowded with many of Charleston's lawyers. The band on stage began to play a set of Motown hits.

"No need to be sarcastic. We'll go get dinner soon. If you're going to be stationed here in the Holy City, you need to be exposed to a little society."

"Well, that's exactly what this is. Very little society."

Alicia approached them from the hall and, taking Jim's hand, said, "All right, I've danced with Matt. What about you?" They walked to the small group of couples in the center of the floor and soon disappeared among the dancers. Matt looked around the hall, a babbling sea of strangers.

"My God, I don't believe it's you. Matt Reicher?" Matt turned to see the pretty aquiline features of a face he had not seen in fifteen years. "Do you recognize me?"

"How could I forget the fairest belle in Charleston?"

She laughed a little too loud, he thought. He wondered how many glasses of champagne she'd drunk before the one she was holding. "You haven't changed a bit. I haven't seen you since you left The Citadel," she said.

"The navy's kept me moving. I just reported as the XO of the Weapons Station." She nodded, not seeming to hear what he said. "But more importantly, what have you been doing all these years?" he asked.

She swayed her head to one side as she answered, "Married, of course. To *the* Belton of Hollis, Mayers, Belton, and Rush. A *very* nice firm here in town."

"That's wonderful."

"Wonderful," she repeated taking another drink from the long champagne glass and smiling thinly at Matt. "That is my husband right over there," she said, pointing to a balding man in a blue suit that did nothing to hide a body too accustomed to expensive lunches. "He's trying to iron out the details of a deal with one of his *colleagues*." She reached for his hand. "Tell me, Matt, why didn't you and I ever get together?" Her eyes searched his, looking for an answer to their invitation.

Matt laughed softly and, delicately withdrawing his hand from hers, replied, "It could be that you were dating my best friend."

She smiled and sipped more champagne. "Jim," she said, glancing at Jim and Alicia sliding across the floor. "He always was a nice guy," she said wistfully to Matt, "but it just didn't work." Matt could see now that she was drunk. "He was solid. There was never any doubt about that. But he was *so intense*. You know, I just didn't need anybody then to be devoted to me."

"He was crazy about you," Matt replied.

"I was still looking for what *I* wanted."

Matt, downing the last of his bourbon, said, "I know. You were looking for Mr. Belton."

"Don't be mad at me, Matt. Not after all these years. Jim didn't need someone like me. He was looking for someone to return the same kind of devotion he's always needed to give. I think he needs to do that to keep his balance or something."

Matt looked at her. She was as beautiful as when she had been a student at the College of Charleston. He told Jim then not to waste his energy on this one and thought that Jim's enraged response was the end of their friendship. Jim was so focused on her that he wouldn't, or couldn't, see things in any other light. Matt could still hear Jim's angry words when she finally ended the relationship, a tirade of anger, but one turned on himself... for not being enough of whatever it was he thought he needed to be.

"You're still so loyal, Matt. I never understood how you two could be such friends; you're so different. Where he's so focused and trying so hard, you seem to have enough power to just glide. You know, when I used to look at you, Matt, which was often, it seemed to me there was enough energy inside you for several men. Maybe, that's why there always seemed to be more than just one Matt. One of you might be quoting Rudyard Kipling, while another one was beating some guy up with a lacrosse stick." She looked at him wistfully again and said, "You always looked good in those shorts, too."

Suddenly, the fine columns and chandeliers of the old hall seemed to be closing in on him. He spotted Jim and Alicia walking from the floor. "I have to go, and... thanks for the compliment."

*   *   *

Sergeant Wilkins was right on time. *This guy is really an eager beaver,* the man watching him from the parked car thought. Wilkins never left before the crowd had cleared most of the Pentagon parking lot. It was the perfect place to make contact. The man watching him was parked five rows away from Wilkins' Honda. Wilkins walked briskly across the lot, anxious to leave. The man got out of his car and began to walk slowly toward the sergeant's car. He looked no different from the thousands of other bureaucrats that emptied out of the giant tan office building every afternoon. Wilkins' first thought was the man needed a jump for a dead battery.

"Sergeant Wilkins," the man called out to him. Wilkins wondered if he should know the guy's name.

"Yeah."

"Name's Carl, Terry. I'd like to talk to you about a little investment opportunity."

Wilkins glared at the man, who was now standing directly between him and the Honda, and did not take the hand offered to him.

"It's important to us both that we talk."

"I don't want to invest. And I don't want to talk. Now, excuse me." Wilkins' instinct was to shove the creep out of his way, but there was no way to tell who he might be. A lot of important people in the Pentagon acted pretty strange.

The man stood squarely in front of the car door. "Look, Mac, I'm going home. Get out of my way," Wilkins declared.

The man smiled and stepped aside and waited while Wilkins opened the door.

"Sergeant, I won't take any more of your time, now." Lifting a brown manila envelope, he tossed it into the open door. "Look this over, and I think you'll change your mind." Wilkins jerked his head from looking at the folder to watch the man striding back towards his car. The man turned and, calling over his shoulder, said, "I'll call you, Terry."

In the car, Wilkins watched the other car drive out of the lot and toward one of the entrance ramps. Then he opened the envelope, just as the man had known he would. Inside was a single 8½-by-11-inch color photograph. His hands went numb as he saw the remarkably clear image of the bedroom at the farm and of himself and C. A. Moore.

Chapter 10

Walking through mostly empty halls, Matt Reicher found the elevator. On the seventh floor of the hospital, he approached the nurse's station.

The pretty young navy nurse was on duty again. He motioned for her to listen as he asked very quietly, "How is he?"

"Oh, today's a good day. Come on."

She led Matt into the room where Rex Skanchy's last fight was drawing inexorably to a conclusion. "Hey, Colonel, the navy's here."

The thin face turned from the window and the bright blue eyes widened. Rex, beaming a smile, said, "Matthew, it's good to see you. Sit down." His laughter was broken by ragged coughs.

"I've got my eye on a nice twenty-four footer, Rex. You need to come give her a try with me. We'll take a sail up to Beresford Creek."

"Lieutenant, get your psych department down here. Commander Reicher is having a bad hallucination." The nurse chuckled as she backed out of the room, managing to catch Matt's eye before the door closed. He returned her wink with a smile.

When the door pulled closed, Rex rolled his eyes back and shook his head, "I saw that, you dog. You haven't changed."

"That's right, Rex. I'm still just the clown they want to entertain them."

"So, how are things at the Weapons Station?"

Matt held his hand out and rotated it back and forth.

Rex studied him in silence for a moment. "What's wrong?"

He hadn't come here to confide the turmoil his life had become, but he felt drawn to the safe haven of Rex's genuine concern. Still, he was reluctant. "Matt, I don't have much time, you know," Rex said, his labored laughter filling the sad little room.

"O.K., Colonel." Matt recounted his wife's refusal to join him. He wanted to describe the pain of separation from his daughters. He was tempted to explain the desolation of a failing marriage. But he allowed himself to speak only the facts.

"Give her a chance; she'll come around," Rex advised Matt, who was now staring through the window. "Give yourself a chance. Now, what about the job?"

Matt shook his head. "It would be great if I did *anything* right."

"You didn't come here to hand me that crap, did you? You know I could be watching *Jeopardy*. Hell, what's wrong with you?" The voice was suddenly strong.

"I don't know, Rex. I work my ass off. I'm there early and stay late. It's never enough." He didn't say what he really felt — a dark conviction that his career would quickly be over.

"You're beating yourself up for nothing. You just have to keep plugging away. There have been guys like this captain before, and will be again." Rex began to cough. Finally regaining his voice, he added, "You're lucky, you know. You don't have to face any of this alone. Jim would do anything for you."

"I know. With you and Jim I can kick anybody's ass." He wished it were true, but the conviction in his voice was false.

"And Jim needs you."

"He's a big shot lawyer, Rex. He doesn't need anybody," Matt laughed.

"You know better. He doesn't see what you see. I've gotten philosophical lately. It must be because I'm dying." Matt winced. "There are two things I know. No one is whole — we all have missing pieces. And there's no guarantee of a replacement part. Friendship is a priceless gift that, if you're lucky, makes up for some of those missing pieces. But it can end in a moment — and you don't even see it coming."

Matt smiled thinly and thought he understood — that death could steal the lives men cherished most. He didn't yet understand that death was only one of the enemies of men's hearts.

*   *   *

"Terry, it's for you," the receptionist called out across the room.

"Hello, Terry. Carl here. I wonder if you've had time to think over my suggestion by now."

"Yeah."

"I know it's hard to talk during the work day, so much going on." The voice was cool, businesslike. "Why don't we link up someplace on your way home. Do you know the Fox and Hounds Inn, on the Pike?"

"Yeah, I know it."

"How about 5:30 this afternoon? I'll be in the bar."

Terry was silent for a moment. The voice seemed remote, almost an echo, far away from the real world.

"Terry? Terry? You there?"

"O.K., 5:30's fine. I'll be there."

The few dim lights in the bar of the Fox and Hounds did little to brighten the dark paneled walls. There were only two other patrons, men seated at the bar and looking like they were intent on serious drinking. He guessed them to be truck drivers. The inn's customers were usually interested only in using their rooms, and more often than not, for less than a full night's stay. The man he met two days before in the parking lot waved to him from a booth in the far corner.

"Sergeant, I'm glad you accepted my offer," Carl said. Wilkins took a seat across the table.

"What do you want?"

"We don't want to talk here." Looking around the deserted room, he added, "It looks empty, but we want to be sure we can have a free and open discussion. I've gotten a room. Number 205. That'll be more private."

"Damn you. I don't know what kind of guy you think I am, but I —"

"Terry, I know what kind of guy you are. Remember? Don't worry. I only want to discuss a business arrangement with you. It's in your best interest to believe me." Carl walked to the bar and handed the waiter a ten dollar bill. Glancing back at Terry, he headed out the door and walked across the paved lot to the two-story row of motel rooms. As he expected, the soldier followed a short distance behind.

Inside the sparsely furnished room, Carl motioned to the chair by the window and seated himself on the dresser in front of the bed. "Terry, you know that your friend, C. A. Moore, is a very powerful man. He works at the highest levels of the administration. I'm sure this is no surprise to you."

"What do you want from me? I'm just a staff sergeant."

"And hope to be much more, don't you, Terry? Isn't that why you took Mr. Moore up on his offer?" Wilkins glared at him, his fists clenched, tight with the desire to use his strong hands to break Carl's neck. "Well, that's not my business, is it? I hope you get exactly what you want. I expect you've earned it."

Wilkins wasn't sure how much more of this he would be able to endure. Forcing down the fury that threatened to overwhelm him, he said, "You want something. What the hell is it?"

"Your friend is the man in charge of our government's plan to bring a very large amount of plutonium from the old Soviet Republics back here to keep it out of the wrong hands. I represent a group of very wealthy people who want to know exactly when the plutonium is to be shipped and the route it will take. Has Mr. Moore discussed this with you by chance?"

"Why do you want to know this? And no, C. A. doesn't tell me national security secrets."

"My clients are committed environmentalists. Not enviro-terrorists, or anything like that. But they are very devoted to the anti-nuclear movement ... and, like I said, very rich. They want to know where they can tell their favorite environmental group — The Blue Ocean Fund headquartered in Richmond — to stage a big demonstration. These folks want to make a big point that all nuclear stuff is deadly. You know the drill — signs, line the track, sing folk songs, all that bullshit," Carl said, laughing derisively. He'd seen it all before, his manner said, and had no use for such foolishness, except to take their money. "They'll make it worth your while to the tune of $50,000."

"C. A.'s no fool. What if I think it's just too damned risky?"

"Then these folks will insist that I send a copy of the video tape — the one the picture I gave you came from — to the army ... and to your wife." He paused to let the threat sink in. Carl knew, of course, that Wilkins' wife and son were staying with her parents in Iowa. The cost of living anywhere near the capital was too much for a staff sergeant. "These tree huggers can be pretty mean. You know, the end justifies the dirty-low-down means, and all that stuff."

"I don't know if I can get this kind of information. C. A. doesn't have me around to talk about shit like that. I'm there just for ...," he said, his throat having gone dry, "for his idea of fun."

Carl's face softened. He understood, his expression said. He nodded slowly, then said, "I'm sure you can do it. Moore is a mean son of a bitch. But he's kind of pathetic, isn't he? Lonely, I mean. I'm sure that's why he wants you around. Talk to him. He'll tell you, and he'll be grateful you wanted to know what great things he does for the nation," Carl said, smiling. "I'm sure you'll do it."

Walking to his car, Wilkins began to shake with the fear he had kept at bay in the motel room. He wiped away the sweat that was pouring from his forehead.

* * *

"Leo, I appreciate you coming over. We should both be out playing golf." The vice president had telephoned Leo Scardato from his plane and asked him to meet at his residence. Scardato had been perplexed by the request, but he was always happy to oblige Michael O'Connelly. It had been O'Connelly who paved a clear path so many years ago for him to advance from the FBI's New York City office to the Bureau's Washington headquarters. And besides, Leo Scardato liked the good-humored Irishman as much as he did any man in Washington.

"My pleasure, Mr. Vice President. You look well. This job agrees with you."

"Leo, there's no liar like a Brooklyn liar. I need some help."

"New Yorker to New Yorker, Mr. O'Connelly?"

"As a father, Leo. I need help because I'm worried about my children. It's a little delicate, Leo, but I have to ask. I hope you'll understand." Leo always understood about family.

"Whatever I can do, I will; you know that," Scardato said, sitting patiently and watching O'Connelly.

O'Connelly suddenly found it hard to ask for help from his old friend. It wasn't that he doubted that the stocky, gray-haired FBI veteran could do what he was about to ask. It was the threat that made his help necessary that was so painful. O'Connelly related the details of his conversations with Moore and with his daughter. Marilyn had assured him that after the terrible scene between her and her roommate in the bar, they had reconciled and parted as friends. "The type of thing that Moore says is being reported would ruin her chances to be elected to congress. I need help finding this woman. If Marilyn can find her and talk to her, I think we can kill this story. What do you think, Leo?"

"You mentioned your son?"

Again, O'Connelly set forth what Moore had reported. "I don't know what to do about that. If I intervene, word will get out, and he'll be finished in the military. There will be no doubt that he's guilty of everything they say about him." He looked away from his guest. "It hurts, Leo, but I feel powerless to help Mickey."

Leo Scardato knew that his old patron was not telling him what he really thought, although the concern for his children was real enough. "Mr. Vice President, have you considered that there may be another explanation for what C. A. Moore told you is happening?"

"I've considered the possibility. I was hoping you could help me find out what is really happening. I know that's asking a lot."

Scardato thought he already knew. He wondered if O'Connelly did, too, and guessed that he probably did. How was he supposed to go about telling the vice president that the president of the United States was trying to destroy the reputations and careers of his children? Scardato was certain O'Connelly already knew that Roger Seekings was capable of exactly that and worse. It was another matter, he well knew, for a father to accept that his children were in such serious and unreasoning danger. "Yes, I can help. And we can find your daughter's college roommate. That will be simple enough. I should have that information to you in a few days."

"Leo, I would like you to keep this as discreet as you can. Do you understand?"

"Yes, sir. I understand." He understood not only that he was being asked to protect Marilyn O'Connelly from an embarrassing lie but also that he was being asked to check up on one of the projects of the president's hatchet man. It was vital that he keep as low a profile as possible to protect himself. O'Connelly needn't have worried.

As they exchanged goodbyes in the large foyer, Scardato remembered the stories in the national media, absurd reports that O'Connelly was losing his grip, maybe even slipping into early senility. You didn't have to be an FBI agent to figure out that the president was gunning for O'Connelly. Leo Scardato survived and prospered in Washington by learning to recognize these things and by striving assiduously to stay clear of such clashes and the shrapnel that invariably tore into anyone too close to the eruption. Walking down the path from the porch, he already knew he would take these risks to help Mike O'Connelly.

* * *

Jim drove unhurriedly up Highway 17. The twin rivers of the Santee delta passed slowly beneath the car. Past the entrances to rice plantations, long ago reduced to hunting playgrounds, he drove on towards Georgetown. Thirty miles farther lay the tourist sprawl of Myrtle Beach bulging with its summer crowds. But here at the southern end of the long curve of beach called the Grand Strand, the barrier island communities were much as they had been when he was a child, and none was more unchanged than Pawleys Island.

Clustered on an unreasonably thin strip of high ground, an eclectic collection of houses either faced the blue Atlantic or backed onto the rich green marsh of the creek that wound behind the island. Some were older than the republic, and some were quite grand. Others were new and merely cottages. "Arrogantly Shabby," the bumper stickers said. A dozen generations of childhood memories had been born here, so rich they matured into lifelong devotion that brought the faithful back year after year.

Near the center of the island the Pelican Inn stood next to the road facing the marsh. The old building had served as an inn of one sort or another since the 1840s, the only condescension to modernity being the addition of electricity and a single phone in the lobby. The lack of air-conditioning did nothing to deter its patrons, who returned, anxious for the peculiar serenity of the place. The sun was sliding below the pines across the marsh as Jim grabbed their bags and called out through the screen door leading from the wide porch to the sitting room. "Anybody home?"

"Sure, as long as you're not selling anything or running for office."

"Neither. I'm Jim McNeeley. We have reservations for tonight and tomorrow night." The woman holding the margarita glass retreated to a desk in the far corner of the room darkened by the setting of the sun.

"Here you are," she called from the desk. "You're down for breakfast and dinner, is that right?"

"The works."

"Terrific. Here's your key. There's ice downstairs and a fridge you can use. Breakfast's at eight."

"Do you think Matt's O.K. with the children?" he asked Alicia.

Turning around, he saw that his wife was swinging slowly in the hammock at the far end of the porch. He walked towards her, his footsteps on the old floorboards the only sound. "Sure. Sure. You deserve a break. Want to go down to the water before it gets dark?" she replied.

They walked down the boardwalk that led from the porch, a hundred yards under a canopy of oak branches and moss to the barrier dunes. At the top of the highest dune, the walkway widened to a deck flanked on the left by a gazebo where another hammock was slung. The retreating sun still barely illuminated the waves, and a breeze blew across the dune. Jim sprawled in the hammock, "Come over here a minute."

"Why?" she asked, tucking herself into the hammock without waiting for an answer. They arranged themselves comfortably in the rope web. Jim watched her face in the fading light as she gazed at the waves breaking on the beach below. It seemed odd to study such a familiar thing as Alicia's face. The fading light lent a special softness to the gentle lines. He reached a hand to trace the shape of her cheek. She looked at him, briefly surprised. Alicia slid her arm around his waist and snuggled her body next to his. Jim took her chin in his hand and kissed her. The dozens of files and deadlines that usually filled his thoughts faded far enough away to be forgotten. He even forgot for a while the images of the firemen of Chernobyl.

*   *   *

It was not a big story for any of the reporters who gathered at the Capitol. Most carried Styrofoam cups of coffee and either scanned the morning paper or chatted with other reporters. The cameramen tuned and focused their equipment. Many of the seats were empty. The word had certainly gone out in time. It was old news. We've "been here, done this" some of the reporters joked.

Without being noticed by most of the reporters, Governor Haselden walked to the podium adorned with the state seal.

"Ladies and gentlemen, thank you for coming." He waited for the little crowd to take their seats. "As you know I wanted to speak to you this morning about an important step we have taken as a state to protect the health and safety of our citizens."

Young pages on either side of the rows of seats began to pass out photocopied documents to the reporters. "On Friday, South Carolina filed a lawsuit in United States District Court in Florence against the federal government. It is always a sign of failure when our state must engage in litigation. In this case, I do not believe the failure is ours.

"Months ago I sought to discuss with the Seekings Administration its plans to ship large amounts of Soviet plutonium to this country, land it in North Carolina, and transport it by rail to the Savannah River Site in South Carolina for semi-permanent storage. I was first told this was the plan of the administration. Only a few days later I was told that there were no such plans. Recently, I have learned that these plans are very real and, most disturbing to us, that the federal government does not intend to inform us or to consult with us in any way regarding these shipments. This means that a train laden with highly radioactive weapons-grade fuel will simply appear in our state with no prior warning and, I fear, without proper safety and security measures in place. I believe this course of action poses grave risks.

"This state sued the federal government in 1994 challenging the shipments of spent nuclear fuel rods across our state. In that suit the government claimed there was absolutely no risk. We now believe that the government knew in 1994, and many years earlier, that there was a grave risk of terrible catastrophe. We are demanding that the federal agencies involved in this plan fully comply with both the National Environmental Policy Act and the recently enacted South Carolina Nuclear Materials Transportation and Disposal Regulations.

"This is not an academic exercise, my friends, but a vital effort to prevent a horrible tragedy. It is too easy to forget the dangers of highly radioactive materials. These most hazardous of all substances are like nothing else known to man." Behind him a screen was suddenly filled with the image of Vladimir, the Chernobyl fireman. His blackened, shriveled face stared out at the stunned reporters and cameramen. "This is what lies hidden in the casks of nuclear material the government intends to haul across our state. We will pursue all means available to ensure that this horror does not escape.

"Thank you ladies and gentlemen."

As Haselden walked away, hands shot up from the little audience. Loud voices called out to him, but he was already gone. "Jesus Christ," someone said.

*   *   *

The camera that Giordono pointed at the governor transmitted the scene to Felix Hubbard in his office at Bolling Air Force Base. *What a performance*, Hubbard thought, *he's a natural*. He picked up his phone and called the point of contact he had been given at the Justice Department by Moore. By this afternoon, Fred Muldoon would be on his way to Charleston to meet with Bradley Sweatman, the U.S. attorney for South Carolina. Sweatman had been every bit as helpful as Moore said he would be. Typically ambitious, Sweatman possessed, for reasons Hubbard didn't know or care about, the extra incentive of a personal animosity against Drew Holland. And Sweatman had no scruples about using whatever means were available. Muldoon would find a very complete file on the case when he got to South Carolina and an answer already prepared, as if Sweatman had known for weeks what the state's complaint would say. He laughed out loud.

* * *

Fred Muldoon had been with the Justice Department for all but four of his years as a lawyer, and most of that in the section that litigated environmental cases. He was the first of his family, black farmers from Kentucky's tobacco country, to make it through college, let alone law school. In the department's environmental defense section, Muldoon made his name as a premier litigator for the United States.

This was his fourth case in South Carolina. The last had been against Drew Holland in a suit on behalf of the state challenging the environmental impact statement (EIS) for a turbine in one of the Savannah River dams. The case received widespread publicity due to wholesale destruction of fish when the unit was tested. The complex of pumps simply sucked in thousands of fish and ground them to shreds. He smiled when he remembered a cartoon Holland sent him during the case. The turbine unit was depicted as a huge blender. "The Bass-A-Matic," the caption read. It was a pleasure to litigate against some lawyers. Drew Holland was one of those.

As the cab took him into Charleston and towards the federal courthouse, Muldoon read over the state's complaint. They alleged a simple violation of the National Environmental Policy Act (NEPA) because the government had failed to prepare an EIS, choosing instead to analyze the risks in a summary fashion.

This kind of argument was familiar terrain to Muldoon. He knew the state had an uphill battle, unless it could show the government completely disregarded information. The complaint asked the court to enjoin the government from bringing the plutonium into South Carolina until a full-fledged EIS was done. It also claimed that the state's Nuclear Materials Transportation and Disposal Regulations required the government to keep the state fully informed of its plans, coordinate with state law enforcement, and even manifest the material. He knew the courts would never tolerate the "federal sovereign" being subjected to this type of regulation by the states. Handling nuclear materials had always been entrusted to the sole discretion of the federal government.

At the courthouse, Muldoon found Sweatman's office.

"Brad, are you planning to participate directly in the case?"

"Yes, I am."

"Great, that will be a tremendous help," Muldoon replied, doubting that Sweatman would actually do anything or that he would be any help if he did. "I think we have a very strong position here."

"My goal is to bury these guys. They have to know they can't hamstring the United States government with this sort of absurd litigation."

"Yeah," Muldoon said, looking carefully at Sweatman to see if he was serious.

"Holland has ginned this case up to grab some headlines for the governor, and that's all this is about. It's about time he had his tail kicked." Sweatman was pacing in front of his desk, hands sweeping through the air while he spoke.

"I see."

"Here is an answer that was drafted by our office with help from Washington."

Muldoon looked at it as if it were a first draft of *Blackstone's Commentaries*. In fact, he assumed it had to be practically worthless, drafted only two days after the case was filed, probably by a staffer with no experience. As he glanced at the text, however, he saw that the draft contained all the defenses that he had outlined in his notes on the plane and a few he had not thought of but which he saw had merit. His thoughts about this extraordinary sequence of events were interrupted by the entry of two young men. "Fred, these are two investigators with our office. I have found them to be very helpful in all of our big cases."

Muldoon, not sure how to respond, said, "Brad, you know in a case like this, most of what we will deal with will be documents. We don't have a lot of investigating to do."

"Well, we've got them if we need them. Look, Fred, I'm giving a press conference tomorrow on this case. Here's my statement. I don't think we can let the governor monopolize the press on this."

"Thanks," Fred said, taking the sheet from Sweatman, who rose and moved behind his desk. Muldoon took this to be a sign he was being dismissed. Over the years he had seen many U.S. attorneys, and one of the least endearing qualities most of them possessed was a highly inflated sense of their importance. He found it nearly impossible to engage them in conversation. As he liked to say to friends, one did not so much converse with a U.S. attorney as one started listening when he spoke to you and got up and left when he quit. There were many things he knew he should discuss with Sweatman, not the least of which was the reason the U.S. attorney felt he might need investigators, but that could wait until tomorrow morning. Judge Richardson was holding a status conference in two days, and the federal team was assembling to plan its strategy. That would be the time to straighten out Brother Sweatman.

Muldoon retrieved his briefcase and left. Holland's office was only a block away. He decided to walk down and greet his old adversary. As the receptionist announced him, he heard Holland's voice booming from the rear of the building, "My God, lock the safe and hide the files, the feds are here! Tell that black Irishman to come on back!"

Sherry's embarrassment was obvious. "Mr. Muldoon, you can—"

"I heard," he said, laughing.

"Damn, Fred, they drafted you to come down and beat up on poor old us again."

"Drew, I still have bruises from our last fight."

"Yeah, but yours don't show."

"Holland, you're still an asshole."

"And proud of it. Why do you think people drag bags of money in here to hire us? To be nice? How the hell have you been?"

"Can't complain. Still doing God's work. If it wasn't for the consistent righteousness of my client, I'd retire."

"Fred ... Fred, come on now, boy. If you believe that, it's time for you to retire."

"Drew, you're not supposed to call my people 'boy.' Don't you read the papers?"

"Bullshit. How was Russia?"

"Interesting. And very depressing. I wonder if there is any part of that huge country that isn't contaminated, and all of it caused by their own government. We'll be long dead before they recover."

Wagging his finger playfully, Holland teased, "There's a lesson for us all. So, are you on the case?"

"When the department saw it was you on the other side, they knew only I could put up with your incredible crap. So, here I am. Tell me, the governor's horror show aside, what does your client really want?"

Holland smiled. He was going to enjoy battling with Muldoon again. "Fred, we just want the government to abide by the law. It's really simple."

"Drew ... suppose I just give you my word, how's that?"

Holland whooped.

* * *

Hubbard dialed the number to C. A. Moore's direct line. He was very disturbed by what he heard from the microphones in Holland, Rollins, Jerald and McNeely. Muldoon and Holland acted as though they were long-lost cousins. This was not good at all. How could this important detail have been missed?

Chapter 11

Alexis eased the door to his office closed. He unlocked the special compartment under the middle drawer of his desk and retrieved a small memo book. Flipping through the pages, he came to the number he needed. This was the number that the voice of the government man had given him, the "insurance policy for his family" the man had said. Alexis' hands trembled as he laid the memo book on the desk and began to dial.

The line rang many times, so many Alexis was tempted to hang up; then he heard a series of clicking noises, and a new ringing began. "Hello. Who is calling, please?" The voice was not the one that had terrorized him so often.

"Alexis Plekanov."

There was a pause. "Yes, Alexis, one moment." There was the sound of footsteps on a tile floor.

"Good afternoon, Alexis, my friend. And how are you?" The low, mocking voice was the same.

"Not in a mood for pleasantries."

"So sour, Alexis. You wound me. Why, then have you called State Security, if not to pass the time of day? To report the writing of a bad check, perhaps?"

State Security, Alexis thought, *so that is who these bastards are.* "There is a plan to seize plutonium. Are you still interested in such information. Or are you too carried away with your own wit?"

Suddenly, all business, the voice said, "The details, Alexis. Tell me what you know."

"At Zarmayevka there will be a raid on the store of plutonium, or perhaps uranium 238. I am not certain which. It is my understanding that both substances are kept there."

"When?"

"Within the next ten days."

"This is your brother's raid?"

"No. We have nothing to do with this, as I told you. Such folly is for fools and madmen."

"Who then?"

"Even State Security will be able to solve that mystery when you capture these idiots. In any event, the time and place is all I know. I will not share such dangerous speculation with you."

"Fair enough."

"I want no more calls from you. I have done as you asked."

"And the Motherland is grateful, Alexis Nikolaevitch. And I am grateful. Perhaps, I shall move my modest savings to your bank. Is there a prize for opening a new account?"

Alexis slammed the receiver down, his hand shaking. From the cabinet on the wall by the window overlooking Nevski Prospekt, he lifted a glass and a bottle of vodka. He quickly downed the first glass, the liquor searing his stomach. The second, he took more slowly, in three smaller swallows. His hand stopped shaking enough for him to call Mikail.

* * *

Moore spent most of the afternoon laboring over a backlog of work he hated, administrative minutiae. His habit was to accumulate it, bring it to the farm and do it there, where he could finish without interruption. The sound of the front door opening echoed below him. He glanced at his watch. It was only 4:00, early for Terry to be home. Stepping out of the small converted office, he leaned over the rail and called down. "You're home early. Want to help?"

Moore was joking, but Wilkins walked up the steps, pulled off his shirt and stood behind him. "What is all this?" Terry asked.

Moore looked at him skeptically, and then explained, "These are personnel evaluations. The president's chief of staff requires that I prepare these once a month for everyone who works in the White House itself. Here," he said, selecting a file from the menu, "this is a lieutenant's. He's easy; all the security information on him is pretty much static. And he's army. The only thing I'd be looking for with him is trouble with his marriage, or signs he was getting into debt. None of them change much. It's mind-numbingly boring." He looked up at Wilkins, who sipped his beer, looking genuinely interested.

"Is that what all these are?"

"No. These over here are worse. These are fund reports for my part of the budget. I'd rather lie down on an anthill. My part of the budget is classified. So I have to reconcile the figures personally."

"That stinks," Wilkins replied, picking up a form with a number of tally sheets attached to it. "This is the same form we use. I reconcile our office budget. Want me to do this one?"

Moore looked at the stack of ledger sheets, and back at Wilkins who was already leafing through them, sorting by date. "Knock yourself out." He watched as Wilkins took a seat and leaned his broad back over the desk, lining up the stacks of forms in perfect order.

Wilkins, pointing at the calculator on the edge of the desk where Moore was working, asked, "Are you using that?"

Moore finished a memo and glanced at Wilkins jamming the calculator keys with his thick finger. "Ready for another beer?"

"Yeah. Thanks."

When he returned with the beers, Wilkins was entering the final sheet's tally onto the form for reconciliation. He handed the soldier one of the bottles. "I really appreciate your help."

Wilkins put the calculator down and smiled at Moore. Squeezing Moore's shoulder gently, he said, "I'm glad to do it. Hey, it makes me feel like I'm working in the White House."

Moore's pager began to beep insistently. He picked up the secure phone, dialing Felix Hubbard's number.

"Mr. Moore, are you on a secure line?"

"Yes, Felix. What's up?"

"I've just monitored a conversation that gives me a lot of concern. Muldoon, the hotshot lawyer we've got on the case, visited Holland about an hour ago. They were very chummy, too friendly. It sounds like they go back a long way."

"Felix, you know lawyers. They all think they're in some kind of fraternal society or something. Are you sure they weren't just being polite?"

"No. They were real pals. Now maybe Muldoon can still go in there and try to cut his ass, but my gut tells me these guys are soulmates, and that ain't good. I got a bad feeling about this guy. Do we need him? Can't we get along with that Sweatman fellow? He's a team player."

"They say every cop starts to think he can be a lawyer. Is that what you're thinking, Felix?"

Hubbard was silent.

"It's a problem, that's all. We got a lot going on in this operation. I get the feeling that Muldoon won't play by our rules; know what I mean?"

"All right. I'll go down to Charleston and sit in on the lawyers' meeting tomorrow. Maybe the hearing. If things aren't right, we can still make changes."

He hung up and immediately made reservations for the evening flight to Charleston.

"What's going on?" Wilkins asked him. "It sounds like a big deal."

"It is a big deal," Moore answered. "It's a lawsuit the State of South Carolina has filed to try and dictate how we bring the Soviet's nuclear weapons material into the country. It's a bullshit suit, but we can't take it lightly. There's a lot riding on this program." He began to gather his files together. "I've got to hurry."

"Don't worry. You get ready to travel. I'll put all this stuff back in order and back in these little folders here, and they'll be right here when you get back."

Moore looked at him gratefully for a moment, and then hurried to his room to pack.

Wilkins walked with him onto the porch. As Moore drove down the lane to the highway, Wilkins sat on the top step. The evening breeze blew cool across the bare skin of his chest and arms. He marveled at how readily Moore had shared the details of his work. With no more effort than the interest he feigned in Moore's administrative drudgery and the little help he volunteered, he had insinuated himself into the details of Moore's responsibilities. Maybe Carl was right. This might not be too hard after all, and then he could get out of this nightmare for good, with his career intact.

* * *

Malcolm Richardson was old school. He revered the office he held. The United States and its laws were not abstractions to him. No one who spent time in his court failed to understand that Judge Richardson strove to make the nation's court a haven of equity and civility. A raised voice was as rare in his court as good-natured banter was common. And it was a mistake.

Richardson leafed through the handful of papers in the case of *South Carolina* v. *United States*. He asked one of his law clerks, "Did you notice when the government filed its answer?"

"Yes, Judge. The next day. Pretty odd isn't it?"

"Yeah. Odd." He stood and pulled the black robe from its hanger. "Well, let's go see what these people have to say." He pulled on the robe as he led the way into the narrow corridor from his office to the courtroom.

"All rise," the bailiff announced well before he was in the chamber. Both sides were gathered in force, he noted with a smile. It was bound to be interesting having Holland and Muldoon fighting it out in front of him again.

"Mr. Muldoon, welcome back to Charleston. It's always a pleasure to see you," Richardson said in a gentle, honey-smooth voice.

"It's good to be back in Charleston."

"I've been following the progress of that power plant over on the Savannah River. It sounds like it still has an unfortunate tendency to grind up fish," the judge said smiling. Most of the lawyers in the room burst into laughter. Bradley Sweatman did not. "Mr. Holland, it's good to see you as well." Holland stood and nodded to the judge. "Now, you know I like to have these conferences early on to get a feeling for where we're headed in a case, particularly one with as much interest as this one. The issues in the pleadings are pretty well laid out, so I don't think we need to dwell on what they are...."

"Your Honor, if I may address the court." Sweatman was on his feet, his right hand raised limply in the air.

"Certainly, Mr. U.S. Attorney. I don't want to presuppose anything. Go ahead."

"Thank you, Your Honor. The state has alleged that the United States plans to bring a large quantity of highly radioactive materials into this state. Setting aside for a moment the matter of whether there is any basis whatsoever on which the state could properly challenge such a plan, there is this important fact that we must bring to the court's attention. There are no such plans at the present time, none whatsoever. That is a seminal issue in the case that must be addressed."

"I saw your press conference last night on television, Mr. Sweatman. It was very impressive. Do I take it that the government says that the project of which the state complains doesn't exist?"

"That's correct, Your Honor. There is no such plan."

Muldoon slowly rose from his seat and, waving his long arm slightly, said, "Your Honor, we want to be completely frank with the court." Sweatman shot him a piercing look. "There are no specific plans *at this time*. But we don't want to mislead the court. The government intends eventually to bring a substantial amount of plutonium and other nuclear material to the Savannah River Site here in South Carolina. What Mr. Sweatman and I would like to emphasize is that, all things being equal, the state's case is premature. It's just too early to be having this argument at all."

"All right, gentlemen."

Holland rose. "Judge, we are prepared to prove, if we have to, that they have a plan, a very specific plan. We will be putting up the governor of this state who will testify that the vice president of the United States told him exactly that."

Richardson nodded and turned to look at the federal table. No one moved to respond.

"We need to talk about what sort of evidence the court will hear. Mr. Holland, what do you anticipate you will need to put forth?"

Holland stood and came around in front of the table. "Judge, we have received proof that the government has not considered a very large quantity of evidence revealing the serious dangers posed by the materials that we believe they are at this very moment planning to ship, in an unsafe manner, across this state. We intend to present documents that were provided to the government years ago and live testimony from a witness who will testify that the government knowingly disregarded this evidence in its decision-making process. In addition, we will present an expert in the hazards of transporting hazardous materials. As Your Honor knows, this evidence may be received in the court's discretion. We will show that the government has long been aware of exactly the dangers we seek to guard against, but has cavalierly refused to address any of them in planning this project. The state's goal in this case is to force the United States government to *ensure* that the transportation of such dangerous material is made as safe as is humanly possible."

Before Holland was seated again, Sweatman was responding, "Your Honor, none of this evidence can properly be brought before the court. I really must caution the court about departing from the well-established rules governing review of federal administrative processes."

"Mr. Sweatman, I appreciate your efforts to keep me on the straight and narrow. But you know I've heard one or two environmental cases in the last twenty years. I've found that sometimes, Mr. Sweatman, the government — like Mr. Holland says happened in this case — doesn't look at everything it ought to. That's sort of what I'm for, I believe, to see to it that in important matters, they do look at those things. It's also my practice, as Mr. Muldoon knows, to let things into the record liberally, and then see what relevance they have to the question."

Sweatman was not to be deterred. "Judge Richardson, the government is very concerned about giving the state a free hand to explore areas of national security without setting narrow boundaries on what can be exposed in open court."

Holland offered good-naturedly, "Your Honor, I can tell you all the documents we plan to offer out of the government's files are public information already. There's no security problem with those."

Sweatman, still standing, responded immediately. "Judge, it isn't just the documents. It's the witnesses they plan to bring in. For instance, Judge, Dr. Anthony DeSilva is a former Department of Energy employee. We are concerned that he will be asked to testify in violation of clear law and policy governing former federal employees and their divulgence of information gained in federal service." Holland and the entire state team stared in shock at Sweatman. How did he know about DeSilva? No one had mentioned his name. "Judge Richardson, the United States has an important interest in exactly this type of situation with a former employee." Richardson looked down and over his glasses at the two tables of lawyers. Everyone on both sides was staring at Sweatman. As Sweatman took his seat, the courtroom became strangely silent. Richardson looked from one side to the other, not certain what had caused the surprise that was obvious on both sets of faces.

"All right, ladies and gentlemen. This is what I'm going to do. All the issues in the pleadings are going to be aired completely. I'm not going to bar any evidence at this stage. Mr. Holland, you are free to pursue your theories with whatever evidence you think is appropriate. Mr. Sweatman, if you and Mr. Muldoon think any of that evidence is improper, or needs to be heard in chambers, you are free to state your position. The state has a motion for a preliminary injunction pending. I want you both to be ready to present your cases on this motion in two weeks. O.K. I think that about takes care of things."

As Richardson rose, everyone stood with him. "Your Honor," Sweatman called out to him.

"Mr. Sweatman, I have to go have lunch with my wife. Excuse me, but I'm loath to be late for that appointment." Bowing slightly to the two crowds of lawyers, all of whom except Sweatman were chuckling, Richardson disappeared behind the bench.

In the first row of pews behind the federal team's table, C. A. Moore remained seated as the judge left the courtroom. His impudence was noted by the bailiff, who decided not to make an issue of it. The man was clearly with the U.S. attorney, and there was no reason to go looking for trouble. Moore was stunned by the failure of the federal team to achieve even one of their goals with Judge Richardson. Moore had directed that Sweatman do the talking for the government. He saw clearly, as had Felix Hubbard, that the U.S. attorney was the tougher fighter. But none of Sweatman's demands or legal research had impressed this judge. Once again, the people who were supposed to help him accomplish his mission were failing. Hubbard was right. He would have to take charge of the situation himself.

*   *   *

"We have a free hand!" Geddings said, tossing his briefcase onto the conference table. "This time, we've got a fighting chance."

The rest of the state team filed into the conference room. They were all excited by their success. All, except Drew Holland. "Who was that guy sitting behind the federal lawyers?"

Jim answered, "His name's C. A. Moore. He's the administration's man in charge of the whole plutonium project. Special Assistant for Policy and Security."

"Security," Holland said softly.

"Two weeks isn't much time," Jim said to the group, "I guess, we need to decide who's going to do what."

"How did Sweatman know?" Holland asked, staring out the window at St. Philips' steeple. The room became silent. "How did he know?"

Before anyone could answer, the door opened. Jake Rollins stepped just inside, smiling broadly. "Well, boys," Jake said, "I hear you kicked Uncle's ass all the way up Broad Street."

"News travels fast," Jim laughed. "We got everything we went for. Now, the hard part begins."

Holland finally grinned. "We're not finished kicking yet."

*   *   *

Muldoon stayed in Sweatman's office after the other members of their team left. "How did you know the man's name, Brad? DeSilva, wasn't it?"

Sweatman shot Muldoon an angry and nervous look. "We did our homework."

Muldoon smiled and looked at the carpet. "How'd you know, Brad?"

"What difference does it make? I've got a squad of investigators in here. They dug it up somewhere. Why do you need to know details like that?"

"Because I'm a lawyer on this team. And because I'm not going to jail for anybody. Not for you, Brad. Not even for Roger Seekings."

*   *   *

Moore closed the door to the office he had borrowed, unpacked the secure telephone from its case, and dialed.

"Yes, sir." The voice belonged to one of the president's secret service agents.

"I need to speak to the president. This is Moore. Priority Alpha."

"Wait one."

Seekings' came on the line, "What is it C. A.?"

"I'm in Charleston, Mr. President. The federal judge has ruled for an open hearing. The goddamned governor is going to testify about his visit with O'Connelly. He's going to be a real problem. I need your approval to get Richardson off the case."

"Do it. Get the U.S. attorney down there to figure out a way. Is that all?"

"Yes, sir." The line went dead.

Moore packed the phone into its container and walked down the hall to Sweatman's office.

* * *

Sasha Dunitsev squatted low, bending over a map spread out over the rocky ground. On his right, Gregori Donskoi held a flashlight filtered with a red lens to minimize detection in the Kazakh night. Donskoi was eight years his senior, but still deferred to Dunitsev, who had been his lieutenant in the last terrible months in Afghanistan. Donskoi thought uncomfortably that the terrain reminded him of that cursed place, never mind that this land was only a short time ago part of the Motherland.

Arrayed in front of Dunitsev were the leaders of the four teams of Chechens who would enter the compound of Zarmayevka a few thousand meters away in the valley below them. Dunitsev explained again the plan they had drilled over and over and were now prepared to set in motion. Each of the teams would report only to Dunitsev. The team leaders wore small headsets. All of the men were dressed entirely in black, their faces and hands smeared with camouflage, making them all but invisible to the naked eye in the moonless night. Positioned at vantage points that gave them clear shots at the nine surveillance towers, nine lone Chechens waited with RPG-22 rockets, ready upon receipt of Dunitsev's signal to blow the towers and the guards inside them to oblivion.

"In the confusion caused by the destruction of the towers, your teams will blast their way into the rear of the compound and secure this building here," Dunitsev said, pointing with a stick to a black rectangle on the map, "and seize the plutonium casks. You will move them by hand outside the compound to a point... here. The helicopter will pick you up there." Dunitsev looked at the faces dimly lit by the red light's reflection. There were no questions. They knew exactly what to do. "Take your positions."

The Chechens each slid away into the dark to join their five-man teams and move to their positions a few hundred meters from the rear of the compound fence. When they had been gone for ten minutes, Dunitsev pulled his night scope from his pack and scanned the hillside sloping down to the valley floor. He spotted the first team in seconds, stealthily moving through the trees and brush. In only seconds more, he detected the other three teams as well. He wondered if the State Security forces that were certainly in the compound were also watching the teams with similar devices. "Goodbye, little lambs," he said taking a final look at the four columns of men.

"Let's go, Gregori," Dunitsev slapped Donskoi on the shoulder. They rose and moved along the path chosen weeks earlier that led them higher up the hill to a spot where they could observe the compound. Donskoi removed the brush and rocks that covered the place where he and Dunitsev had buried two backpacks. He pulled them out of the shallow pit and brushed off the loose dirt. Inside the packs were two sets of clothes, which he removed and carefully stacked on rocks nearby. Quickly, Donskoi and Dunitsev removed the black clothing they wore and donned the clothes from the pack, typical clothing for two hikers on an adventure tour. Donskoi placed the black military-style clothes into the pit and buried it, replacing the rocks and brush over the hole. Dunitsev continued to monitor the progress of the Chechens, although he now had to use magnification. It would soon be time.

In the compound, the leader of the state security force sipped a cup of hot tea. With his headset, he was in communication with each of the pairs of men who, from the nine surveillance towers, scanned with night vision devices the valley around the fence. He hoped all of the night vision devices worked. It was getting more difficult all the time to keep any sort of sophisticated equipment working. This was the night his superiors had been told there would be a raid on the compound. He chuckled to himself as he wondered if it wasn't all a big joke or, more seriously, a diversion. In addition to the eighteen men in the towers, he had thirty-five others, more than enough to stop any raid. His headset began to crackle.

"Major, Tower Number Four, two small groups of men are approaching the rear of the compound ... correction, there are four altogether ... they have stopped ... about four hundred meters from the fence."

"What do the other towers report?" Each reported in turn seeing no additional men outside the perimeter.

Before the major could speak, an explosion rocked the compound, shaking the pictures from the walls of the office where he sat. The first rocket found its mark in the northwest surveillance tower. The blast illuminated the night with a scene of fire and concrete block tumbling to the ground, carrying the men who had been standing in the tower to their deaths. Just as suddenly there were two more explosions, as the northern and southeastern towers were blasted to rubble. Six more explosions followed in succession, throwing orange-red flames and broken pieces of the tower walls into the sky and signaling the destruction of the remaining towers and their occupants. The compound broiled with confusion in the wake of the fiery eruptions. The major's security soldiers ran in every direction. Gazing on the scene of chaos, he realized he must communicate to the leaders of his remaining soldiers where the intruders had been spotted. "All teams, all teams," he shouted into his microphone, "intruders are in position beyond the rear of the fence. Take defensive positions now!"

Now the soldiers ran with purpose to their positions, designated in advance for this contingency. Seconds later more explosions rocked the night air, this time from the perimeter fence at the rear of the compound. Through gaping holes left in the fence from the detonations, the Chechens raced toward their target building. As the lead team reached the door and blasted it open with a grenade, the first of the security force arrived and began laying down fire at the intruders. The second and third teams of Chechens formed on the flanks of the first and covered the security force with withering fire. Six of the security force, which had not taken adequate cover, fell at once; the remainder returned fire as best it could.

Inside the building the Chechens recognized the casks they had come for and dragged two of them to the door. Placing them on roller devices fabricated for this purpose, they prepared to tow them back the way they had come. The Chechens on either side of the door frantically motioned for them to get out fast. More security forces were joining the fight. They rushed from the door, pulling the casks on their rollers. The greatly increased fire of the security forces struck the Chechen pulling the second cask. The bullet ripped his left shoulder and knocked him to the ground. The man regained his footing and continued to run, pulling the cask toward the hole in the fence. Chechens not already felled by fire from the government men retreated, maintaining a deadly covering fire.

At the spot where they had been told to meet the helicopter, the Chechens who fired the rockets into the towers established a semicircle and prepared to cover their comrades with automatic weapons and rocket-propelled grenades. On the ledge overlooking the valley, Dunitsev's headset sizzled with the cries of the team leaders. "Bring the helicopter now!" one screamed. "We have the casks!" Dunitsev and Donskoi watched the fight, the orange flashes of gunfire marking the path of the battle. Dunitsev was amazed that the Chechens had retrieved the casks at all, much less that they were able to actually get them to the pickup zone.

The two Chechens towing the casks reached the defensive arc at the pick-up point and dropped into firing positions. Quickly, the remaining Chechens retreating from the compound joined them. Seven lay dead or dying inside or on the grassy ground outside the fence. With all their comrades inside the arc, the Chechens loosed a volley of rocket grenades that landed among the security forces with devastating effect. The surviving team leaders pleaded for the copter, but Dunitsev could no longer hear them. He had removed his headset.

For nearly half an hour, firing raged across the ground outside the perimeter fence. With less cover, and with their supply of rocket grenades gone, the Chechens were finally overwhelmed. The last three Chechens alive were mortally wounded when the security forces managed to land a grenade in their midst. They died cursing the Russian bastards who had abandoned them.

As the last orange flashes flickered in the valley outside the compound, Dunitsev and Donskoi slung the backpacks on their shoulders and made their way along a predetermined path away from the valley and the Zarmayevka compound. Approximately one kilometer ahead a cave was stocked with sufficient provisions for them to lay in wait for ten days. By then, two hikers would not be noticed in the woods and mountains of the Irtysh Valley.

Chapter 12

The major walked from the rubble of the corner surveillance tower to the hole in the perimeter fence. The bodies of his state security soldiers lay in neat rows covered by tarps of various colors that flapped in the strong morning breeze. Twenty-one of his men were dead from the night's fury, and twelve were being treated by a doctor from Semipalitinsk. At the spot beyond the fence where the Chechens gathered, their twenty-nine bodies lay in the sun. *Why had they stopped there? They must have expected to be picked up. By a helicopter, no doubt. It was impossible. There was never a chance to get away after such a spectacular attack. An aircraft would have been reported immediately.* He looked from the bodies of the raiders, scattered chaotically across the brush, to the smoldering towers of the compound. It didn't make sense, and his agile mind, so long devoted to solving the riddles posed by criminals, labored to find the meaning that he knew was there.

His report was already in Moscow. They seemed less interested in his unanswered questions or in the corpses under the brightly colored tarps than in the successful interception of the raiders. They were anxious to report triumph to the Americans. He wondered idly if the FBI would claim credit with their government bosses in Washington. The major rubbed his unshaven chin and puffed deeply on the bitter-tasting cigarette he carried. No matter. His report would be complete. *Perhaps the Americans, with their genius for success in all things, would solve the riddle of the mad Chechens.* He laughed at his private joke.

* * *

The second morning after the raid at Zarmayevka, the Russians were prepared to report to their colleagues in the American FBI. The FBI agent in charge of the operation in Moscow read through the report and called Leo Scardato immediately. He paid little attention to the questions raised by the Russian major.

157

Though it was nearly eight o'clock in the evening, Leo Scardato wasted no time contacting the other members of the task force to report the success of the FBI's operation. The call to Moore would be the sweetest of all.

"C. A., Leo here. We have good news from the Russians," he said, speaking even more rapidly than normal, unable to conceal his pride in the success.

"Do the Russians have any idea how the Chechens thought they were going to get away?" Moore asked.

"No. A copy of the report is on its way to you by fax now. It makes sense that it was the Chechens. They've been bragging for years that they could get their hands on nuke stuff."

Terry Wilkins leaned on the bar that separated the kitchen from the den and listened. "Big news?" he asked, when Moore hung up the telephone.

"You're a soldier. Does it make sense to launch a raid on a highly secure installation — shoot rockets, blow up the fence, generally put on a big show — and not have a quick way out?"

"Not unless, you're in Hollywood. Or you just want to create a diversion."

Moore looked at him. "That's right. A diversion. Pretty basic, isn't it?"

"What the hell is going on? Or should I wait for CNN?"

"A bunch of Chechens tried to steal enough plutonium two nights ago in Kazakhstan to build several nuclear weapons. They never had a chance to get away. They just waited outside the fence and got blown to pieces."

"It sounds like they got left high and dry by somebody. They must have expected a pick-up that never came."

"Sure sounds that way, doesn't it?"

"So, what happens now? Are we still going to bring the plutonium out?"

"Absolutely." Moore walked to the bar and leaned across the surface, gesturing excitedly as he spoke. "Something's not right."

Wilkins listened carefully as Moore earnestly explained his dark suspicions about plans to steal the plutonium while it was in transit to a permanent storage facility in America. Stabbing the air with his right hand, Moore insisted, "Nobody's going to get any of this stuff. I'm going to make damn sure of it."

*   *   *

From habit he woke early. Through the opening in the curtains, he could see the sun easing above the horizon. He felt her next to him before he could see her in the dim light of dawn, still sleeping soundly, her long auburn hair framing the face that had so captured his attention the night before. What luck had brought him here, he wondered. She was probably the most beautiful woman he had ever been with, certainly the classiest. She was a paralegal with some big law firm, and from the looks of her little condominium, he figured she must do all right. He looked around the bedroom in the spreading light, studying each picture on the walls and each piece of furniture. He would have been happy just to sleep anywhere else than his cramped bunk on the *USS DEYO*, but this was like paradise for the young sailor. The digits of the clock flipped, taking him closer to the time she would leave for work. She moved, gently stretching her soft leg against him. He turned to her, circling her with his arm, pulling her back close to his chest.

She purred as his hand stroked her. Her hand reached behind her to caress his thigh. She turned and pulled him down to her, taking his stubbly face in her hands, kissing him softly. He lowered himself to her, and she wrapped herself around him. They moved together, the lazy, easy rhythm giving way to a passion nearly as frenzied as the night before.

He lay back on the pillows when they were finished, and she rested her head on his chest. "Do you know all the lawyers in Charleston?" he asked her.

"Most of them. Are you looking for an attorney?" she asked, stroking his arm.

"No. What about a group of them with a name ... it's something like 'Holland, Rollins ...' I can't remember all the names. There's four of them."

Her interest now piqued, she said, "Holland, Rollins, Jerald and McNeely." She knew them well.

"That's it."

"They're not after you, are they?" she asked, her bright, green eyes teasing him playfully. "They don't take any prisoners. Those guys are some of the best hired guns around."

"So, they're a real outfit. I just wondered."

"How did you hear about Holland, Rollins?"

He looked at her pretty blue eyes and wondered if he ought to keep his mouth shut. *It's just an exercise, but the navy takes this shit seriously sometimes.* He felt her hands again. He wanted only to stay there and feel her hand stroking his leg. "We're doing this exercise where we're practicing intercepting faxes and telephone calls. They gave us three fax numbers and we get whatever is faxed to or from those numbers. These guys are one of the numbers."

"You can do that, Dave?" she asked, genuinely amazed.

"Sure," he answered, proud to explain his skill. "There are two numbers in Columbia and the one here. We've been at it ever since we got here. I'll tell you what, these lawyers keep their faxes busy as hell, at least for this exercise. One of the numbers in Columbia is where they send things addressed to the governor. The stuff doesn't make any sense to me. I figure they're just running a test of different systems to see if we can pick it up. You know, so we can tell what works."

Her mind was spinning. *Why would the navy be intercepting faxes from Holland, Rollins?* The young man seemed to think it was all arranged, just something set up to test his ship — and his skills. She watched him as he explained the details of his surveillance technique. *So strong, so handsome,* she thought. But so unaware of how strange and incredible a story he was telling. "Dave," she said, "could you give me one of the sheets you get from that law firm's fax? One with some of the legal mumbo jumbo on it. Their paralegal is a real good friend of mine. I'd like to show her I know that you guys were able to pick up their stuff. That would be really cool."

"Oh, man, I don't know. I don't want to get myself in a crack." Her hand felt so good. He looked at her eyes again. "O.K., sure. Can I bring it tonight? That ought to earn me a little reward, hey?"

"Absolutely," she said, lowering her mouth to his.

* * *

"Hello. Samantha, this is Carol. Are you all doing any work with the state right now?"

"Carol, don't you read the papers? We're representing the state in the case against the government over bringing plutonium from Russia to store at the Savannah River Site. It's a big deal for us. I'm hurt you haven't noticed," she laughed.

"I've been kind of busy."

Samantha had known Carol a long time, and lived through the roller coaster of her romantic episodes. She could tell from the sound in her old friend's voice that Carol was on another ride. "Yeah, who is he?"

"I've met this guy in the navy. He's pretty nice."

"Carol, another sailor?" Samantha cooed.

"So what's your point?"

"Carol, I thought you swore off sailors after they closed the base."

"Dave's pretty nice."

"You said that."

"Yeah, well. Look, Samantha, let's get together tomorrow for lunch, O.K. It's important."

"All right. Is anything wrong?"

"No. There might be something I need to tell you."

*   *   *

"Do you hear anything in the community about a replacement coming down here to relieve me early?" Matt Reicher asked, holding the receiver, afraid of what the answer might be from his old friend at the Pentagon. But he needed to know if there was more to Captain Kratz's attitude towards him than bad temper.

"Matt, this really stinks. You shouldn't hear this from me. Kratz should have told you. What the hell is he waiting on? The asshole."

"So it's true."

"I understand from the detailer that they've tabbed someone to come down there in March to relieve you. He's supposed to be a real star. They should have already talked to you about where you'll go next. Wait 'til I get my hands on that little shit in personnel!"

Matt was quiet — the hurt sinking, leaden and hard, in his stomach.

"Matt, you still there, bud? Those bastards. I can't believe this."

"Hey, take it easy. Some admiral might hear you raising your voice. That makes those guys nervous these days."

"I wish there was something I could say, Matt. Nobody is a better officer than you."

"Yeah."

"Listen, Matt, let me ask you something. I don't know what this has to do with anything, but have you ever had a run-in with a guy named

C. A. Moore? He's a heavy hitter around here. He hiccups and all these people jump. Anyway, he dropped in on the admiral about a month ago. His admin officer is a friend of mine. She told me Moore came over to talk about working with the German intelligence folks, but then he mentioned you. And it wasn't real nice. What did you ever do to this guy, man?"

Matt froze. He hadn't thought about C. A. Moore in a very long time. *Jesus Christ*, he thought.

"Matt ... Matt ... you there? What's wrong, man?"

"Yeah, I know him."

* * *

Matt picked up the phone and dialed the familiar number. "Hello," the voice that answered seemed more distant than the seven hundred miles to Harrisburg. "Hello," his wife said again.

"Linda, it's Matt. How are the kids?"

There was a tense pause before she spoke, "They're fine. But they're not here. Mom took them to the pool."

"That's fine. We need to talk anyway, Linda."

"About what?"

"About us."

"There is no 'us' right now, Matt."

"What are you trying to say?"

"We need to leave things the way they are for a while."

"The way they are sucks."

"You need to adjust. I'm sure the job takes most of your time."

"I need you and the kids to be here," he blurted out. "I'm dying."

"You don't mean that literally?" There was a hint of concern.

"No. Don't get out the life insurance policy. I just need you to be here with me. The house is really great; you'll like...."

"No, Matt. I've been there and done that. I told you I didn't want to do it again. Let me guess. The C.O. is a real asshole. There's more work than you can do, right? The station is mostly civilians ... so the people who work for you are lazy and shiftless and you have to do most things yourself, or they get all screwed up. Am I close?" Her voice was strained and she spat out the words rapidly.

"Linda...."

"Matt, I want the same thing you do ... but I'm being realistic. If I come down there, we'll be at each others' throats in no time." She was crying now. "I can't take that again. Besides, it wouldn't be good for the children."

"Linda, don't do this—"

"Goodbye, Matt." The receiver buzzed in his ear.

*   *   *

Jim McNeely was alone at the conference room table. His notes on Anthony DeSilva's testimony were spread to his right. Across half the remainder of the large table were articles, memos from other members of the state's team, the pleadings, and photographs, most of which Tony had recently mailed to him. Jim had called home and told Alicia he would be working until nearly midnight. Drew Holland wanted all the questions for direct testimony completed by the next morning, complete with exhibits. It was a tedious project.

He was creating the equivalent of a script that he would memorize and practice with DeSilva several times before the hearing, now only seven days away. As he wrote the questions, he annotated the script to show the time when each exhibit would be introduced.

He leaned back in his chair and rubbed his eyes. He needed a moment to stop thinking about radiation, fatal dosage, and cancer. It was already half past eight, and he would be at it at least three more hours.

*   *   *

As Matt pulled on a pair of blue jeans, Ann — he couldn't be sure of her last name without looking at the card in his wallet — slept soundly. Her naked legs were curled up in a fetal position among the tangled sheets. *At least she got what she wanted tonight,* he thought bitterly. Why wasn't it enough for him? Certainly, it was all he was going to get, so he might as well be satisfied. He wanted to shower, but the sound would wake her, and he didn't want that. Folding up his uniform, he quietly stole into the kitchen. The bottle of Jim Beam he brought with him the last time he visited was still in the cabinet. With the bottle and a glass he took a seat on the couch and poured his first drink — at least the first drink of bourbon, he remembered.

God damn Linda. And God damn himself for letting this happen. Why didn't the bourbon stem this tide of black thoughts? He was alone to face what he knew was coming. All he ever wanted to be was the best damn officer in the navy. Now they were going to fire him, run him out of his job in humiliation. But why? Was it that crazy bastard Moore after so many years? The third glass of bourbon disappeared in one long swallow. He ached with the pain of indefinite separation from his children — and his wife — and now with guilt, too. *I'm drunk*, he realized. *Well, that's progress.* He gathered his khaki uniform and shoes and, with the Jim Beam dangling from his fingers, slipped out of the apartment. Maybe he would send Ann a card tomorrow.

Piling his clothes into the jeep, he knew that he couldn't drive. He walked unsteadily to the corner of East Bay Street, still carrying the bottle of bourbon.

*   *   *

Jim was nearly finished. "God," he groaned, "it's 11:30." He should give it one more read, he knew, while it was still fresh in his mind, but his brain was too weary. He could do it early in the morning. As he arranged the notes, articles and other papers scattered across the table, the phone rang. A flash of panic came over him as he feared that something had happened to one of the kids.

"I'm Officer Russell with the Charleston Police Department. Your wife said you were at your office. Do you know a man named Matt Reicher?"

"Yes, I do. Has he been in an accident?" Jim asked, worried.

Russell laughed. "No. But he's drunk as a skunk and sitting on the gatepost of the Custom House. Singing. I saw him when I was making my route." Russell began to chuckle again. "He's a real Buffett fan, but he sure can't sing worth a damn."

"I know."

"Normally I'd call for a patrol car and they'd take him to the drunk tank, but when he said he knew you, I wanted to call first."

"I appreciate that."

"Listen, I just have my motorcycle. Would you be able to come and get him? Oh shit, there he goes...." As Russell put the mike down on the seat of the cycle, Jim heard him in the distance, "That's enough Matt.... Hey, man cut it out. Help's on the way."

As Jim grabbed his keys and started to hang up, he heard Matt bellow over Russell's pleading, "Why don't we get drunk and...?" He cursed under his breath and sprinted for the door.

*　*　*

Five o'clock. Jim winced at the sound of the alarm. Less than five hours sleep wasn't enough. But he had to get Matt up, make him presentable and get him on his way to the Weapons Station. It wouldn't do for the XO to be late because he was plastered. He couldn't remember seeing Matt Reicher so drunk and wondered if he'd be able to move. Jim asked himself what had driven his friend to such excess. He didn't — couldn't — say much the night before, except to mumble something about the navy firing him. What the hell did that mean? Even more bizarre, he said that C. A. Moore was out to get him. Jim wondered if it could possibly be the same man who was an advisor to the president.

Matt was just stepping out of the shower when Jim stuck his head in the playroom door. Grinning, Jim said, "Well, Tiger, I wasn't even sure I'd be able to wake you up. I underestimated you."

"We're not all wimps like you," Matt answered toweling off. "Just don't make any loud noises."

"So, you're at least part human after all, Superman. Here's a razor and toothbrush." After I get dressed, I'll take you out for a little breakfast and a lot of coffee. Maybe a champagne breakfast ... or some Bloody Marys...." Matt's hand shot out from the bathroom, the middle finger extended. "Hey, this is a family household."

On the short drive to Alex's Restaurant, Jim said, "Last night, you mentioned a guy named C. A. Moore. You said he was out to get you. What the hell was that all about?"

"This guy I knew in the navy — who's now some big shot in the White House — has been trashing me to the brass in the Pentagon. Look's like the bastard's part of the reason I'm getting canned. He and I had a bad run-in a long time ago. I guess he never forgot."

* * *

Persian Gulf — 1988

A decade of brutal war filled the gulf between Iraq and Iran with death. Driven by the madness that passed for logic on both sides, jets from the two countries attacked the tankers that came for the crude oil pumped from the deserts. In the early hours of a moonless and steamy July night, one of those jets spotted a Greek-flagged tanker two hours out of Ad Dammam on the Saudi Arabian coast. Locking the fire control mechanism onto the tanker, the pilot unleashed an Exocet anti-ship missile at the unarmed vessel. Seconds later the crew of the tanker felt the impact as the missile's tip bored its way through the inches of steel of the ship's hull. With the hull peeled open, the missile's warhead passed into the ship and fell into one of the holds. The frightened men waited a full minute of terror for the explosion they were certain would follow. It didn't come. In a matter of hours, news of the attack had been relayed to owners of the tanker in New York, and to the Navy Department.

On the USNS *Kilahuea*, an ammunition ship hundreds of miles away, Lieutenant J.G. Matthew Reicher was just beginning to shower after a morning workout in the ship's exercise room. He and his Explosive Ordinance Disposal (EOD) Team were on a six-month deployment, so far remarkable only for a complete lack of excitement. "Lieutenant, Lieutenant!" called the excited voice of one of the bridge crew who had clearly rushed to find him. "You've got a call you need to take right now. It's CINCPAC. Come on. Captain says come *right* now!"

"Like this?" Matt spread his arms to illustrate his nakedness.

"Right now, sir."

Matt pulled a towel around his waist and followed the third class up the ladder to the telephone. Under the bemused stares of a half dozen officers and crew, Matt took the phone with one hand and held up his towel with the other. He listened a moment before yelling into the receiver, "And I'm Ronald Reagan. Gotta go catch Air Force One." Slamming the phone down, Matt looked at the stunned faces on the bridge. "Some wise guy."

He was only a few yards down the passageway when a voice called him back to the bridge. "Lieutenant, it's the admiral ... really." Matt walked quickly back to the phone. Taking the phone, he listened, sheepishly this time.

The message was as sobering as the realization that the commander in chief of American forces in the Pacific had called him to deliver the orders personally. Matt and his team would be picked up and taken to a cruiser near the tanker where they would disarm the Exocet missile in its hold. The Exocet was a new French anti-ship missile, and the French had taken pains to protect their secret. His mind and his gut churned as he contemplated approaching the dangerous warhead of the missile without diagrams or a clear understanding of what they would find inside.

The aqua blue waters of the Persian Gulf slid beneath the chopper as it made its approach to the USS *Billings*. In the distance Matt spotted the tanker at anchor. Once aboard the cruiser, Matt and his team were presented a briefing on all that was known to the Pentagon about the Exocet. It wasn't much. The briefer explained that the French had been asked for the diagrams of the missile, but had so far not produced a set. He did not explain why the U.S. Navy had decided to risk four lives to save the Greek tanker. At the conclusion of the briefing, the captain of the *Billings* introduced Matt to his executive officer, Lieutenant Commander C. A. Moore. "Commander Moore will accompany you to the tanker and coordinate any assistance you require from us. There are hostile aircraft in the area. We'll do what we can to keep them away."

The cruiser's launch carried the men to the tanker, riding easily in the calm waters of the gulf. "Take us around the ship," Moore ordered the crewman operating the launch. He pointed to the jagged hole in the tanker's hull and said to Matt, "There is where it hit. Most of the missile was destroyed on impact. Only the warhead passed through the hull and survived intact." Matt noticed with some irritation that Moore was trying to appear to be more knowledgeable about what had happened than he was. As the launch passed around the stern of the big ship, Matt glanced at the white lettering below the blue-and-white Greek flag. *Helena* was her name, out of Piraeus. The rusted black hull loomed over them as the launch eased next to the ship's ladder. *I hope you're worth it*, he thought as he started the climb to the tanker's deck. A handful of the tanker's crew and one of the ship's officers greeted the Americans and helped carry their tools. Only the Greek officer spoke a little English. He indicated he would take them to a cabin where they could work.

Moore said, interrupting him, "I think Lieutenant Reicher and the team should see the warhead right away. Every minute counts." The Greek smiled pleasantly and gestured for the Americans to follow him in a new direction. It was becoming clear to Matt that Moore intended to make sure there was no question that he was in charge. *As long as he stays out of our way, I can put up with it,* he told himself. The Greek led them through a series of passages and into a stairwell. They descended the stairs and exited through a door that led to the main deck of the tanker. He directed them to a hatch that stood open.

The smell of the oil struck him at once, sharp and fetid. The darkness made the hold seem cavernous. In the pencil-thin beam from the flashlight, he could see the sides of the hold coated with the black goo of crude oil. At the bottom, lying in a thick deposit of the same residue lay the warhead of the Exocet, the shiny metal surfaces reflecting brightly. Matt descended slowly on the oil-slicked ladder toward the bottom of the hold, his three team members following closely behind. The atmosphere in the bottom of the hold was suffocating. The acrid petroleum fumes mixed with the stifling, humid air made the men feel as if they were being choked. Matt felt drops falling on his neck and arms. He wiped his forehead with the back of his hand, and realized the drops were not water but oil dripping from the top of the hold.

Looking at the side of the hull, Matt saw the gaping hole left by the missile as it tore its way into the tanker. He bathed the warhead slowly in the beam from the flashlight, studying it, struggling to see it only as a technical problem to be solved, not as a machine that could be the instrument of his own death. When he had seen what he thought he needed to begin making plans, he turned to his team, "How 'bout it guys? Seen enough?"

"Aye, aye, sir. Can we go back to Hawaii now?"

"Very funny. Maybe, we'll let you do it solo. Give you a nice medal."

"No thanks, Lieutenant."

"Sir, what gives with the asshole — excuse me — the exec from the cruiser?" another of the team asked in a low voice. "Aren't you in charge?"

"We're all in this together. Let's just do the job."

On the deck, Moore waited for Matt to climb out of the hold. "Lieutenant, you and I need to confer on exactly how to proceed with the mission."

"I need to confer with my team."

Moore fixed him with a cool stare. "Very well. Report to me this evening by 2200 hours."

In the cabin offered by the Greek officer, Matt and his men began to exchange their ideas on what they would do. It was clear from their visit to the hold that they would have to work in short shifts. The fumes were too foul. The consensus was that they would begin working toward the firing mechanism from the rear of the warhead, not the tip. It was 2245. Matt made his way to Moore's cabin.

"You're late," Moore said without looking up from a stack of papers he was leafing through.

"I'm sorry. It took this long to hash out what we might find."

"It's important to keep appointments. Especially when they're made by a superior." Matt noted he didn't say "superior *officer.*"

"Commander, it's important that we don't get blown up. This is going to take time."

"As long as time's not being wasted shooting the bull. So what's your recommendation?"

Matt explained what he intended for the morning.

"Why not start tonight?"

"We've had a long day. And I want us all to have time to think about what we might find inside that thing. We're going to have to base each step on what we find along the way. There's no road map here, Commander."

"I want you to keep me informed of every one of those steps, Lieutenant." Moore looked at Matt, watching his face for a reaction. "That's all," he said, picking up the stack of papers again. Matt swallowed hard and left the small cabin.

On the first day of work, the team fell into a pattern. They found they could work in the hot, oil-contaminated air for only thirty minutes before being relieved. With light sets in place, they studied the exterior of the missile and made sketches of the details. In their first caucus, they decided to begin removing the outer shell at the rear of the warhead. By the end of the day the rear plate and cylinder were removed. The team assembled to discuss the next step. Moore entered the cabin. "Lieutenant, I'd like to talk to you, please."

"Commander, we're at an important point right now."

"It will just take a minute."

Moore led Matt to a point where he felt the other team members would not be able to hear, and turned to confront him. "Lieutenant, I told you to report to me at *each step* of the process. From here on out you will follow orders. Is that clear?"

"Commander, I don't think you understand—"

"No. You don't understand. I'm in charge here."

"This is a very delicate business. We don't know what's inside—"

"Just follow orders, Lieutenant. Report to me when you get ready to take the next step." Moore walked down the passageway and out onto the deck. Matt wiped the oil and sweat from his face with the front of his shirt as he watched Moore leave.

On the afternoon of the second day, they removed three smaller plates and brackets to reveal a pair of wire coils and a rectangular sliding mechanism. It was the detonator. Matt found Moore.

"Lieutenant, when will you know what to do?"

"That isn't clear, Commander. We still don't know how the detonator is activated."

"You guys went to EOD School, didn't you? How many ways can there be for one of those things to function? I think you EOD jocks make more of this stuff than it deserves."

Matt felt his control slipping away. Too much tension — maybe too much of the petroleum fumes — and too little sleep were taking their toll on him. "In the morning we will make a decision." He turned and walked away from Moore.

Matt assembled the team in the ship's dining room. One of the men called out from the refrigerator, "There's no more Coke. I'm dying of thirst." The Greek officer, who was finishing his dinner, laughed and opened a cabinet. "No problem," he chuckled. He pulled a case of Heineken beer from the shelf and placed it on the table in front of Matt. "Enjoy," he said flourishing his hands at the case.

Matt pulled open the box and handed out the bright green cans to his team, and their discussions continued. As Matt was handing out second cans to each of the men, Moore entered the dining room. "Commander Moore, join us for a beer?"

"No thanks. I'll save it for when we're back in port," he answered tersely and left.

"What a prick," the sailor next to Matt whispered.

"Knock it off. Let's get back to work," Matt said. "Then we can get off this tub and away from that prick."

In the morning each of the team members described again what he thought was the best plan. Moore joined them and listened intently. The team members disagreed as to whether they should remove more of the casing from around the detonator before trying to disarm it, or whether to immediately begin to detach the detonator from the 345 kilograms of explosives in the warhead. Matt favored exposing more of the mechanism before trying to disarm it. "Lieutenant, I'd like to see you outside for a minute, please," Moore said.

Matt followed him onto a small deck outside. "I will make the final decision as to how to proceed, Lieutenant. I've listened to all the proposals, including yours. I'll let you know in two hours what to do."

"Commander, you have no training in this field, and—"

"Lieutenant, I haven't exactly been impressed with your expertise. I've told you what we're going to do and that's how it's going to be. That's how we do things in the real navy. I'm turning in a report on you for drinking on duty last night. If I were you, I wouldn't make me add insubordination to it."

Matt took two steps away and stopped. He turned and quickly lunged at Moore. Grasping the shoulders of the smaller man, he lifted him off the deck and slammed his head and back against the bulkhead of the ship. The coffee mug Moore had been holding crashed loudly to the deck and shattered. With his face a half inch from Moore's, Matt hissed at him, "You're going to get the hell out of my way and let me finish this job without anybody getting killed, or I'm going to kick your ass out of my way." He let go of Moore's shoulders, letting him slide down the bulkhead until his feet met the deck. Matt stood in front of Moore, his chest and arms flared out, as if ready to toss him over the side of the ship. Moore stared at him, shaken and frightened. Matt stabbed his index finger in front of Moore's face once and walked slowly back to the door to the dining room. "O.K. guys. This is what we're going to do. We're going to go down and start taking off more shit from around the detonator."

In the hold again, Matt felt the drops of oil raining on his hands as he knelt in the oily sludge next to the warhead. One of the sailors knelt across from him. Matt had instructed the Greek officer and his few crewmen to prepare to abandon the ship. He alerted the *Billings* to prepare the launch to pick them up just in case. Matt wasn't sure where Moore was, and didn't care. He forced himself to stop wondering if the missile would blow him to pieces. At least he would never feel it. They worked even more carefully than before, never taking their eyes from the sliding rectangular arm of the detonator. Matt removed two small screws from a section of thin sheet metal while the sailor held it in place. Like a doctor and nurse, they traded tools and gently operated to remove pieces of the deadly device. Trading roles, Matt held the next piece to be removed while the other man slowly unscrewed one of the screws holding it in place. Suddenly the quiet of the hold was pierced by a sharp whine from inside the warhead. The rectangular sliding arm of the detonator flew forward toward the point where it would detonate the warhead. After sliding only a quarter of an inch, the arm stopped, jammed in place by a bend in the slide, apparently the result of the missile's violent impact with the ship.

* * *

"After we got over the shock, we removed the rest of the detonation device. The missile was safe with that done."

"What about Moore?"

"He put me on report for the Heineken, and for insubordination. He didn't mention striking a superior officer. I guess he was embarrassed about that part. They probably would have screwed me good. But the CNO sent a message out congratulating the team. After that, everybody backed off."

"You know Moore is the man in charge of the plan to bring plutonium back from Russia. He was in court here a few weeks ago."

"I should have thrown the crazy bastard overboard when I had the chance."

Chapter 13

"Tell the president, I'll be along in five minutes," Mike O'Connelly said to the secretary. He didn't wait for her to respond. He already knew the president was in his office between appointments. There was no doubt that Seekings did not want to see him. O'Connelly replaced his phone and gathered his coat from the couch next to the desk.

Leo Scardato had found the address for his daughter's college roommate. Marilyn's report on her long discussion with the woman had removed any lingering doubt that O'Connelly held concerning what Moore had told him. No reporter had been digging into the history of his daughter and her college roommate. After his daughter's call, O'Connelly had visited Leo Scardato at the FBI headquarters to discuss his son. There was no sexual harassment charge against Mickey, and never had been. An investigation had been commenced by the Air Force, but it had been prompted not by any charges of misconduct. It was begun after an inquiry from the White House.

Scardato had said, "Mr. O'Connelly, our records show that the computerized files on your children, and many other people over the last three years, have been accessed by the White House. Our system is designed to record the source terminal of each inquiry. It was Moore who reviewed the files on your children."

The vice president had rested his hand on Scardato's shoulder. "It's enormous power, isn't it Leo?" O'Connelly had said gazing from Scardato's window at the complex of government buildings that bordered the FBI Headquarters.

"What's that?"

"The White House. A question from there, planted in the right place, is all it takes to ruin a career or a reputation. In that world, truth is relative — or, maybe a complete abstraction." He turned to look at his old protégé. "Thank you, Leo."

Scardato had seen the anger in O'Connelly's eyes. But it was anger mixed with resignation. "Mr. O'Connelly, I wish it were you in the Oval

173

Office," Scardato had said, surprised at his own words. O'Connelly had smiled and shook his head slowly.

As O'Connelly walked the short distance to the Oval Office, he remembered angrily the visit from Moore at the beginning of the week. "Mr. Vice President," he had said, "our case in South Carolina has taken a very unusual turn. The judge will be permitting testimony from the governor in which he will claim that you told him the administration has plans to bring the plutonium to South Carolina." Moore had paused and watched for his reaction before continuing, "It's important that you testify that the governor misunderstood what you said. That there are no specific plans to bring plutonium from Russia to South Carolina." The unscrupulous bastard wanted him to lie under oath in a federal court. O'Connelly had told Moore that he understood and to tell the lawyers to call him.

O'Connelly sported his best Washington smile as he casually walked into Seekings' secretary's office. "Is the president still in, or have you ushered him off to some other important function?" He brushed his unruly white hair to one side and walked to the door leading into the Oval Office without waiting for a reply.

"Mike, come on in. I just have a few minutes. We're going to Camp David for a couple of days. The prime minister of New Zealand is joining me there tonight."

O'Connelly's stare was steady and cold, though his smile remained bright.

"Mike, what can I do for you?"

"Tell that pet cobra of yours to get out of my children's lives."

"Mike ... this is...."

"Look, Roger, you and I both know what he's been doing. He's manufacturing scandal concerning my kids. He's doing it to keep me in line. And he's doing it with your knowledge — everything he does is with your blessing, isn't it Roger?"

"Who do you think you're talking to?"

"The poorest excuse of a man to sit in this office in my political career. The thought that I helped put you here is a burden I will carry all my life."

"I—"

"You and that crazy son of a bitch have threatened my children to get at me. It's going to stop, right now, or Roger — and you must know I mean this — I will bring your administration down. You know I can do it. I know this city better than you ever will. I was in congress when you were learning to fill out loan applications in Minnesota. Now listen to me. Here's how it's going to be. I will not lie for you in your lawsuit in South Carolina, or anywhere else. But neither will I tell the world what's going on in the sick little world you've created in this house. In return for my deference, you will leave my children alone. Or so help me God, Roger I'll end your political career."

"You have no idea what you're saying, Mike."

"Yes, I do. What are you going to do? You can't fire me, can you? Only the congress can do that. And an impeachment trial would not be healthy for you." His eyes burned into Seekings. "Believe me, *Mr. President*, I mean what I say."

Seekings seethed, silently gripping the arms of his chair.

* * *

"O.K., Carol, what's the big mystery? Did you go and get engaged to this sailor?"

Samantha tossed her purse into one of the empty chairs as she joined Carol at the table. "No. But thanks for the thought. I ordered for you already."

"So, come on. I've been on pins and needles. What's going on?"

Carol picked up a manila envelope and opened the flap. "This is going to be hard to believe, Sam. I've put my friend in a bad situation by asking him to bring me this. But it's important...and I couldn't just do nothing...."

"Carol, what in blazes are you talking about?"

Carol laid her hand on Samantha's and said softly, "You need to promise me that you'll do everything you can to keep David from getting into trouble. He doesn't understand what's going on."

"I don't know what I'm promising, but if it's that important to you, you've got my word."

Carol pulled the fax sheet from the envelope and handed it to Samantha. It was the first page of Jim McNeely's proposed direct examination of Anthony DeSilva. Samantha had faxed it to the attorney general's office and the governor only about twenty-six hours earlier. "Where did you get this, Carol? This is part of our preparation for the hearing next Wednesday. I faxed this out myself yesterday morning."

"Dave gave it to me." She saw the shock on her friend's face. "He's a communications technician on the USS *Deyo*. It's a navy warship that's been docked at the Weapons Station for weeks. They've been intercepting all of your faxes and calls, as well as the governor's and the attorney general's. He thinks it's a game — he calls it an 'exercise' — just something to test their skills. Whatever he gets, he sends to someplace he calls 'Exercise Control' in the Defense Intelligence Agency in Washington." Samantha sat frozen, speechless. "The government is spying on you, Sam."

"My God."

"Sam—"

"Jesus, I've got to tell Drew and Jim. This is unbelievable." It had not yet occurred to her to be frightened.

"Sam, you have to protect David." She saw that Samantha wasn't listening and grabbed her arm gently. "It's important to me. He doesn't deserve to get hurt.... I like him a lot."

Samantha saw the look of fear in her eyes ... and something else. "Carol, you've fallen for this sailor haven't you? Don't worry, honey," she said picking up the folder and sliding the faxed sheet back inside.

*   *   *

Drew Holland leaned back in his chair, feet propped on top of his desk. It was two hours after lunch on a Friday afternoon. He watched the tourists idly strolling past his window. *Why are so few of these tourists pretty women?* he asked himself. There was more he could do to prepare for the hearing on Wednesday. He could read his notes again for his examination of the governor, and thought probably he should. When would he have the job of presenting a governor's testimony again after all? But the perfect summer afternoon called to him, an irresistible siren song he rarely failed to answer. He gathered his notes, slid them into the file folder and tossed it onto the table that occupied the opposite end of his office. The back door to the building was only a few feet from his office door, and his jeep waited immediately outside. His back porch facing the beach at Sullivan's Island would be a great place to pass the rest of the afternoon.

Holland was in his jeep, sliding on the dark sunglasses he kept in the visor, when his secretary dashed from the rear door and waved him to stop. "What is it?" he called from the open window of the jeep.

"It's Samantha. She says she has to see you now."

"Did you tell her I was gone?" he asked irritably.

"She says it's an emergency." Holland couldn't imagine what their paralegal wanted on a Friday afternoon. "She's on the way and should be here in five minutes."

Holland slammed the jeep back into park and stalked back into his office. *What the hell,* he told himself, *maybe she's got a new client.*

Samantha hurried into the foyer of Holland, Rollins, Jerald, and McNeely, the heavy door slamming behind her. "Is Drew still here?" she asked the receptionist excitedly.

"Yes."

Samantha glanced at the manila envelope she had carried back from her lunch with Carol, and rushed back to Holland's office. She opened the envelope and slid out the faxed copy of Jim McNeely's outline for Anthony DeSilva's testimony.

"Drew, look at this." Then she told Holland where it came from.

* * *

Bradley Sweatman was not accustomed to being questioned as he was now by C. A. Moore. He was angry at this glorified gofer making him explain his judgment. But he wanted nothing so much as to be a federal judge, and he knew the secret to achieving that goal was to make the White House grateful — even if that meant mollifying the president's lackey. "C. A., I really think we'll be fine in this case. We have to be patient, and keep our eye on the final goal."

"What about Muldoon? Didn't you say he insisted you tell him how you knew about Anthony DeSilva?"

"I can handle him. In the final analysis, he's nothing but a bureaucrat. His biggest concern is keeping his nice, fat, secure federal job and retiring on his pension. If he wants to know, I'll tell him. What's he going to do? He can't ethically tell Holland. He'll toe the line."

"All right. You'll be ready by next week then. O'Connelly will not testify."

"We'll be O.K."

*   *   *

Fred Muldoon finished his breakfast leisurely. His room was more than the government per diem, but it was a luxury he allowed himself. He sipped coffee and reviewed his notes. This was a case that should be won, but he was fearful that Sweatman and the White House would screw it up. Soon, he would walk down Meeting Street and meet with the U.S. attorney, and he didn't relish the prospect.

Muldoon pulled on his coat. It was the lightest suit he owned, but Charleston's mid-summer, sultry atmosphere made it feel like heavy wool. He could feel the sweat forming. The bells in St. Michael's tall colonial steeple chimed nine o'clock. Already, tourists were being towed through the historic district in carriages. Even with the humidity, it was such a beautiful day. Why couldn't he shake this feeling of foreboding?

In the courthouse he emptied his pockets and sent his briefcase through the x-ray machine. He remembered — had it been just a few years, or was it longer? — when there were no such machines at any of the courthouses he visited. Now, they were everywhere. Passing through the ugly electronic frame never failed to make him feel old.

As he handed his cell phone to the Marshal, it rang. "Damn," he laughed and took the phone back.

"Fred," — it was Drew Holland — "I'm going to tell you to do something I have never told another lawyer." Muldoon was stunned by the tone of barely contained fury in his old friend's voice. "Make Sweatman tell you how he knew about DeSilva."

"Drew ... I—"

"Just do it, Fred!" Holland breathed hard and added, "I'm sorry, just make him tell you. Then come to Bob Konigsburg's office." The line went dead and Muldoon numbly handed the phone back to the Marshal.

*   *   *

"I think we need to hit DeSilva hard, Fred," Sweatman launched into his strategy of the case. Spread across the table were summaries of anticipated cross-examination of DeSilva and Governor Haselden. "The governor is predictable. We know what to expect from him. We just have to live with that, since the vice president isn't going to testify."

"Now, if we have to live with the fact that plutonium is being brought into South Carolina, what do we say?" Muldoon asked.

"We show there's no danger."

"How do we do that?"

"We attack the assumptions in their testimony."

"And how do we know what those assumptions are, Brad?'

"From what they've said publicly."

"Oh. And what's that?"

"Why are you fighting me, Fred?"

Muldoon's voice was soft, but his eyes burned into Sweatman. "I'm not fighting you. Holland is a good lawyer. If we give him any room, he'll clobber us — again. Now, tell me what you think our position is, Brad."

"DeSilva is dying of cancer. All of his testimony is suspect because he hates the government. And aside from that, it's an implausible doomsday scenario."

"Just tell me, Brad. How do you know what DeSilva is going to say?"

Sweatman looked at Muldoon for a moment, then he turned to look out the window at St. Michael's. He turned and leaned on his desk and faced Fred Muldoon. "Fred, you need to understand that this is an important case for the administration. A lot of things have been done to ensure that everything goes right."

"What things?"

"It isn't important that you know what those are."

"How'd you know?"

"The government believes this is an issue that is vital to national security, and that's all that's important?"

"How, Brad?"

"All right, God damn it! Army Intelligence is working for Moore on this. They bugged the offices of Holland, Rollins, Jerald, & McNeely. We've had access to their communications for the last five weeks. We've listened to every conversation in every office. Read every fax they sent out. Watched everything McNeely's done on his computer. The USS *Deyo* intercepted all the faxes and phone calls between the offices of the state team, including the governor." Sweatman leaned back in his chair, as though he was exhausted. "So now you know. Does it make you feel better?"

Muldoon's face betrayed no hint of surprise — or fear. Or the ache he felt deep in the pit of his stomach. "I see, Brad."

Sweatman regained his composure and returned to the table where Muldoon sat. "We've got work to do. Let's get on with it." He presented the outline of the government's case while Muldoon listened silently. At noon Muldoon told Sweatman he needed to have a conference call with his office and a judge at the court of federal claims. It was a lie. Muldoon walked back to his hotel, certain of only one thing — he was not returning to the U.S. attorney's office, and he was no longer representing the United States, at least, not in the case of *South Carolina v. U.S. Department of Energy*. He threw his briefcase on the stuffed chair next to the bed and turned the thermostat down. His body was drenched in sweat. He felt sick.

Stretching out on the bed, he loosened his tie and let the cool air dry the sweat that was still beading on his forehead. The sounds of the street below filtered up through the walls of the old house. Of all the cities he visited, Charleston inspired the most vivid conflicting emotions in Fred Muldoon. He often wondered how many of his ancestors first looked on these streets as they were pulled from the stinking hold of a slave ship on their way to the auction block. *The gracious houses, inns, and restaurants would have been closed to me only forty years ago*, he often remembered. They were like reminders throughout America; only here, where the past was so meticulously preserved, they were alive on every corner. Among the sweet-scented gardens and ancient live oaks, it was as though there were whispers he could hear, just barely, saying, "Such a short time ago you would have been nothing but a *nigger*." His whole professional life, he had fought to escape the burden of *proving* something. It was just too much work trying to *overcome*. He had simply wanted to be a lawyer, not a black lawyer — just a lawyer. In the world of environmental law, he found an oasis free of racial overtones where he could make a name for his work alone.

And now, all that was in jeopardy. He knew what they — what Moore, Sweatman, and Seekings — expected from him. It galled him, as it would any man, but it galled him more. Because he knew, as only a black American could know, that what they wanted him to be was a *Good Nigger*. They assumed he would do as he was told, when he was told. *How high you want me to jump, Massa?*

Through clenched teeth, he said aloud, "Fuck you. I ain't jumping for nobody." Muldoon reached for the telephone next to the bed. He grabbed the telephone book and turned to the address for the office of Robert L. Konigsburg, Esquire.

* * *

In Konigsburg's office Holland sat in a chair facing Muldoon.

"Did Sweatman tell you?" Holland asked.

"I want you to believe I didn't know anything about this until two hours ago. And I want you to know that I am withdrawing from this case."

Holland nodded.

"The administration installed listening devices and at least one camera in your office over a month ago. They have overheard everything said in your office and monitored Jim McNeely's word processor." Muldoon paused, as if struggling for breath. "In addition, a navy destroyer berthed at the Weapons Station has intercepted all your faxes and calls, and those of your associate counsel in the attorney general's office and the governor." Muldoon leaned back into the soft back of the couch when he had finished. The bare facts seemed all he had the energy to speak.

Holland had not moved since Muldoon began to talk. "Who?" He asked angrily.

"C. A. Moore. He grabbed a few men from Army Intelligence. They bugged your office. Navy just did what they were told. He is a very powerful man in Washington."

"Washington!" Holland snarled. "The sons of bitches." Muldoon stared blankly at the window. "Fred, what are you going to do?"

"I don't know. I'm qualified to retire. It looks like a pretty good option right now."

"It took guts to do what you just did—"

"No! It didn't take guts, Drew ... I just won't be anybody's nigger, that's all."

The ugly word hung in the air between them. "I don't want to get you in any trouble, Fred."

"Screw it. Just do what you think best with what you know. If I had real guts, I'd go to the judge."

Holland put his hand on Muldoon's shoulder. "That wouldn't change anything. You know that. You're one of the good ones, Fred Muldoon."

*   *   *

Around the antique table, Drew Holland and Jim McNeely huddled over a speakerphone. Jake Rollins was at his farm. "Jake, we're going to have the whole place checked out. Find whatever these bastards put in our office and yank the damn things out."

"Are you sure that's a good idea just yet, Drew?"

"I don't follow. What the hell are you getting at, Jake?"

"Well, look at it this way. Sweatman and the other feds don't know we know, right?"

*   *   *

It was already four o'clock. Kevin McClure had assured Jim he would wait at his office, but Jim couldn't keep the sense of urgency from making him race along the road to the courthouse. As he drove, his mind was alive with Holland's startling news. Holland would even now, he realized, be contacting the governor. Before he left the office, they had decided how to get the governor to a phone they could be sure was safe. If there was such a thing.

At the entrance to the solicitor's office, Jim was buzzed in to see McClure.

"Jesus Christ!" McClure exclaimed when Jim finished recounting what Muldoon had said about the bugging of the firm's offices. "And they have the navy intercepting your faxes? Christ! I know they can do that. I was on a ship like the *Deyo*. But to use it to spy on American civilians. Damn!" he said shaking his head.

"Can you help us, Kevin? We need to locate all their little spy toys. I remember you telling me about a guy with SLED who helped you out." He was referring to the State Law Enforcement Division.

"Sure..." McClure flipped open his Rolodex. "Here. Tommy Littlejohn." McClure reached for the phone and began to dial. "You want to get him right away don't you?" Jim nodded.

"Tommy? Yeah, too busy like always. You know how it is....Yeah, me too. Look, Tommy, I need your help with something. It's an emergency.... Yeah, this afternoon.... Probably a while ... high profile ... the governor.... O.K. See you in a bit." Hanging up the receiver, McClure shoved his chair away from his desk. "Let's go. He loves to get involved with the big shots."

An hour later, Kevin and Jim sat in Jim's office discussing an opening at Holland, Rollins, Jerald & McNeely for an associate. Shortly after they began their conversation, the man who said he was from the pest control company entered through the front door carrying an aluminum spray tank and a black box. Jim excused himself and walked through the foyer to the front door and locked both doors. Now all doors to the building were secured. He watched Tommy Littlejohn set the spray tank aside and open the black box, removing a device unlike any he had seen before and several screw drivers. The ladder, used by the firm's runner to replace light bulbs, was waiting in the foyer next to Sherry's desk. The three men were the only ones in the building. As Jim returned to his discussion with Kevin McClure, Littlejohn began a thorough scan of the foyer. McClure motioned to Jim to look around the corner when he saw Littlejohn removing the canister of one of the ceiling light fixtures. Littlejohn pointed to a spot on the outside of the canister. Carefully, he replaced the fixture in its original position and moved on to the next office. While the two lawyers talked on about the details of working at Holland, Rollins, Littlejohn methodically made his way through every office of the firm, identifying a listening device in each. Finally, he pulled the ladder into Jim's office.

Jim greeted Littlejohn, "Henry, thanks for coming over." Littlejohn had removed the work shirt with the pesticide company logo stenciled on the front, and wore only a tee shirt. The tiny camera hidden in the corner light fixture showed only a blurred figure, focused as it was on the screen of his computer monitor. In minutes Littlejohn had identified both the camera and the microphone hidden in the same light fixture. "Thanks, Henry."

Littlejohn noisily dragged the ladder out into the foyer. In his best Gullah accent, he responded to Jim, "Don't mention it, Mr. McNeely. Be seein' you, now."

It was an hour after the three men left the firm's offices. They sat on a bench in a corner of Washington Park, their backs to the high brick wall that surrounded the park behind City Hall. "So what do you make of those things, Tommy?" McClure asked Littlejohn.

"They're common enough. It's impossible to say who did it. Whoever put them there didn't try to hide them too much. Either they didn't care whether you found them, or they assumed you'd never look."

*   *   *

"Every office! Every single one!" Jim seethed across the table on Drew Holland's porch. "And a goddamned camera in mine — pointed at my computer!" The drive to Sullivan's Island had done nothing to calm his fury. If anything, it had grown more fierce.

"And they're all still in place?" Holland asked, sipping his beer and staring at the surf crashing onto the beach below the house.

"Yeah. They're still there. And still working."

"I guess we have a case that really means something now," he said, turning to meet Jim's angry glare.

Jim stared at him, his teeth clenched tight.

*   *   *

Blackie Haselden stepped onto the front porch, letting the screen door slam. June wouldn't be back to the farm for an hour. He struggled to remember the charitable group sponsoring the function she was attending. He tried to focus on the name, but it wouldn't come to him. Rocking slowly in the old chair, Haselden labored to force the shock from his mind. What was the name of the society? It had something to do with early childhood development. His wife was interested in anything to do with young children. The rockers made the old boards of the porch floor creak. It was the only sound, save the crickets in the grass at the edge of the lane in front of the farmhouse or the distant whoosh of a car on the highway. Blackness filled the scene in front of him. There was no moon to silhouette the trees. The bowl of boiled peanuts lay untouched on the table next to him.

Inexorably, the shock of Drew Holland's telephone call intruded into and commanded his consciousness. How could the government of the United States be capable of such perfidy? He rolled the question over and over in his mind. *Am I so naive*, he thought. As he began to accept the truth, shock gave way to anger. *They broke into my lawyers' offices. They eavesdropped on them. On me. They pilfered confidential messages from my office. The bastards spied on me like a common criminal.*

Suddenly, Haselden wondered what else these people were capable of. A hint of fear flickered somewhere on the edge of his consciousness. He worried about Julieanne Harris.

Chapter 14

The rod flipped forward expertly, the weighted hook and bait arcing high over the water, the reel whirring as the line spilt into the air. Finding its mark, the bait splashed into the shallows at the edge of the tidal creek. A snowy egret wading among the spartina grass nearby jerked its long neck upward and floated over the marsh to a lonelier spot. A second hook took flight, less expertly, and landed yards short of the first.

Mark Killian turned to look at Nat Engle. "I think you've had enough beer, if that's the best you can do." Nat handed him one of the two cans he had retrieved from the cooler and fitted inside coozies. Mark pulled the tab back and took a long drink of the cool beer. It was mid-morning, and the July sun was burning hot. He and Nat had been on the creek in a half dozen spots since just after dawn, with little success.

"O.K., choir boy, let's see who gets a bite first," Nat said. The tide pulled on the boat and it swayed gently against the anchor. The gossamer lines from the two rod and reels cut narrow ripples through the smooth surface as the water ran toward the creek mouth and on to the Atlantic beyond the ridge of Dewees Island. The two men sat in silence, enjoying the quiet of the marsh, the sun beating down on their bare backs. No fish rose to the bait on either line. Three more casts failed to entice the shy sea bass and flounder.

Mark began reeling in his line as he spoke. "Let's give it up; it's too hot for the fish. If we want to get any shrimp, we'd better try now."

"You're the captain." Both men laid the fishing rods in the bottom of Mark's Whaler, removed their baseball caps, and pulled a large net from a side compartment.

Mark directed Nat in arranging the net in preparation for taking it over the side of the boat. The net was about four feet wide and some twenty feet long, each end attached to a wooden pole. The two men jumped into the creek and each took one of the poles. Mark took a position on the bank at the edge of a smaller tributary where it joined the larger creek. "Take your pole and straighten it across the mouth of the creek as far as it'll go," Mark said. Nat began sliding through the soft pluff mud. In the middle of the creek, the water became too deep for him to stand and he swam, carrying the pole to the opposite bank.

Nat looked nervously around the chest-deep water flowing around him. "Are there sharks out here?"

"Sure.... Now take the pole and pull it up the mouth of the creek and across to this bank. Then pull it back to me."

"Why am I doing all the work?"

"You're the crew." Mark steadied himself on the bank of soft mud, making footholds as secure as the squishy black sediment would allow. As his hip sank into the mud, it seeped into his shorts and he felt the cool, gritty texture of the mud and tiny shell fragments against his skin. "That's good. Now pull the net across the creek," he called out in encouragement to Nat, who was struggling to navigate his large frame through the unstable creek bed. Nat positioned himself to back across the creek, the muscles of his arms flexing as he strained to pull the net after him.

"It feels like it's getting heavier," he said searching for a foothold on the opposite bank.

"That's because it's filling up with stuff."

"What kind of stuff?— Shit! There's things crawling all over me! Damn, what's going on?" He yelled, breaking into laughter.

"It's the shrimp and crabs and fish that're trying to escape the net, dumb ass!" Mark chuckled. "And the little sharks... and stingrays... and killer barracuda! Keep pulling before they all get away." The laughter of the two men echoed across the empty marsh. Nat backed across the mud bank towards Mark, dragging the ever-heavier net to close the circle. His broad back and neck were smeared black, indistinguishable from the muck he was sliding across. They tugged the net up onto the creek bank and pulled the cooler between them. With short-handled nets, they scooped the trapped shrimp and blue crabs into the cooler until it was full. Mark eased the cooler to the boat. The tide was so low now he could stand next to the hull and lift the cooler up onto the side. They gathered the net in open water and washed off the mud before loading it back into the Whaler.

Mark slipped off his shorts and washed the mud and shell from the inside, then tossed the shorts into the boat. Nat followed his example, glad for the chance to clean away the gritty, slimy material from his own swimsuit. Both men washed the mud from their bodies and hair in the water of the creek, which was now running fast with the retreating tide. They climbed over the side and into the boat. Standing in the bright midday sun, their nakedness shone white and untanned next to the brown of their legs and bellies. As Nat picked up his swimsuit and began to slip it back on, he smiled at Mark, "We ought to just ride back to the landing like this."

"The sun's cooking what little bit of brains you've got, country boy."

Mark dropped into the seat behind the wheel and replaced his Stingrays ball cap. He started the engine and slowly took the Whaler toward the landing at Gold Bug Island. "So, are you about ready to come back to the 1189th, or what?"

"Afraid not. You know, I'm taking my company to the NTC next week." He was referring to the National Training Center in the California Desert, where army units underwent intensive training in combat maneuvers. "We'll get back just in time for the wedding. I'm looking forward to this." Mark saw the excitement in his friend's face as Nat explained the challenge Mark had so long coveted. "This is a great outfit. It really is. My first sergeant keeps everything humming. All I have to — Man, you don't want to hear all this crap. I sound like I'm full of myself, don't I?"

Mark laughed. "No, you're just full of *it*." He extended one large hand and patted Nat's chest twice with the back, "Go out there and knock 'em dead, cowboy."

As they drove along the causeway, Nat said, "I need to ask you something."

"Shoot."

Nat paused, searching for the right words. "Being married. Has it been what you wanted?"

"What do you mean?"

"Have there been times when ... you wished you weren't?"

"Oh. I see. Gettin' cold feet, Lion Loins? You can't do that. I've already gotten my dress blues dry-cleaned. And I read the script for that weird ecumenical service you and Susan cooked up." He looked at his friend's face, the hard lines locked in seriousness. "Come on, tell me what's wrong?"

"I'm afraid ... I'm afraid I won't be able to be like you." He shot an embarrassed glance at Mark. "I know myself well enough to know I'm going to wish sometimes there were no obligations, no promises...."

"No ties?"

"Yeah. I've thought about all those times I was with some girl when you could have been doing the same thing. Only, you weren't. If it'd been me, I just don't know if I could have done that. I don't want to hurt Susan. She deserves better."

Mark Killian wasn't a man easily moved, but just then the back of his throat tightened. "You're afraid of not being perfect. Nobody can live up to that standard. I haven't." He saw that Nat was looking at him in surprise. "Trust yourself to be a good enough man to make it work. That's all any of us can do." They drove in silence for a few moments. "There's one more thing you need to know, Nat. No woman could deserve a better man than you. There aren't any."

*　*　*

"It's beautiful!" Beth Killian exclaimed, waving her hand at Susan Ryan, who had laid out her wedding dress across the bed of the Killians' guest bedroom. "It's perfect for you."

Susan spread out the fabric, feeling the cool softness of it against her fingers. "It is, isn't it? Mom helped me pick it out." She rolled her eyes and added, "Dad paid a bundle."

"So, is everything all set for the wedding of the century?" Susan folded the dress back into its box while Beth sipped her coffee.

"Now it is. This was the last thing I needed to do. I had to get this let out a little. Now, it'll be fine." Beth wondered at this comment. "Just three more weeks. I can't believe it's time. I keep waiting to feel nervous, but I haven't been anything but happy." She closed the lid on the dress box and laid it next to her suitcase on the floor.

They returned to the kitchen and sat by the window overlooking the backyard. Susan picked up a stuffed toy giraffe from the chair and held it. She declined when Beth offered her coffee, and Beth recalled that Susan had accepted neither coffee nor wine since she and Nat arrived the day before.

"Beth, I want to tell you something."

"Sure. What is it?" Handing her a glass of orange juice, Beth suddenly saw a peculiar look in the other woman's eyes. Where had she seen that look before?

"I need your advice about how I can tell Nat something."

Beth looked at Susan's eyes more closely and realized what the news was. *Oh my God*, she thought.

"I think I'm pregnant, Beth. I'm not sure, but pretty sure."

"That's terrific! I'm so happy for you." She reached across the table and took Susan's hands in hers, masking her surprise.

"Great. So, now, how do I tell Nat?"

This was not an answer to rush into, Beth thought. "Well, just tell him.... But don't tell him you told anybody else first! I speak from experience. Talk about male ego." She laughed. "Look, Susan, I've never seen a man as head over heels as Nat is for you. He'll be ... unmanageably, hysterically proud and happy. Trust me."

"I want this to be true so badly. I'll know for sure Wednesday."

"Call me, right after you tell Nat and peel him off the ceiling. The biggest problem you'll have is keeping *his* mouth shut, that is if you want him to keep it shut."

"Yes! I don't want to have to get into this with my dad!" They both burst into laughter.

"Susan, this is wonderful. No two people are more ready to be parents than you and Nat." The two women embraced. Mark came through the garage door carrying the cooler, followed by Nat.

"Whoa. Did we interrupt something?"

Beth and Susan turned to look at the two sun-browned men in sunglasses and ball caps, one carrying a cooler, the other dangling a six pack of beer from one finger — and burst into even more raucous laughter. It was just too funny.

*   *   *

On Monday morning, promptly at 9:00, a runner walked up to the counter of the federal district court clerk's office and presented the motion on behalf of Trident Intermodal Carriers, Ltd. seeking to intervene in the case of *South Carolina v. U.S. Department of Energy*. Trident was asking Judge Malcolm Richardson for permission to help the United States defend its decision to import Soviet plutonium and uranium 238 stocks into South Carolina. The company held the exclusive contract with the United States government to ship all nuclear materials from Europe. Counsel for the United States, it explained, did not object to the intervention. After leaving the federal courthouse, the runner walked down Broad Street and dropped a copy of the motion at Holland, Rollins, Jerald, & McNeely.

Jim read through the request and carried the motion to Drew Holland's office. Holland printed a message on the legal pad in front of him and held it up for Jim to read, "SO WHAT? EVEN IF WE OPPOSE IT, THE JUDGE WILL HAVE TO LET THEM IN. ASK SAMANTHA TO FIND OUT WHO TRIDENT IS." Jim nodded and walked back to his office. At his desk once more, Jim glanced at his watch. It was nearly ten o'clock. As he waited for the call that had been scheduled for ten o'clock, he pretended to read a xeroxed copy of a case, randomly highlighting sentences in yellow. He resisted the temptation to stare at the light fixture where he knew the tiny camera watched him. He began to imagine that he could actually feel the lens resting on the side of his head. Where else was the government watching him? His mind raced with dark possibilities. Were there microphones in his home?

The phone rang. Ten sharp. He knew before he heard Sherry announcing the call that it was Geddings.

"O.K., Bob. Are we ready to go to war?" Holland's voice was animated, even jovial, but his eyes were narrow and dark.

"There's a problem."

"What is it?" Jim asked.

"Dr. DeSilva called me last night. He said at first he was sick from his treatments. But I didn't buy it. Finally, he told me he was just plain scared. He started to come apart."

Holland interrupted him, "Is there any way we can calm him down?"

"Well, that's the other half of the problem." There was a pause, as if Bob were reluctant to tell them the rest of his news. "He says he can't say a lot of those things because they just aren't true. He understands the Greenpeace report, but says he hasn't done any independent research to verify what would happen in an accident. It's pretty ugly. The bottom line is he just won't testify. DeSilva's out."

"God damn it!" Holland yelled at the speaker. "The simpering little coward! What the hell are we going to talk about on Wednesday, the goddamned weather?"

For fifteen minutes, Holland, Geddings, and Jim talked about how to salvage the case. Geddings suggested, and Holland agreed, that their only hope was to force the issue of the state's new regulations on the shipment of all nuclear materials. There simply wasn't any evidence to argue that the government hadn't honestly considered the real risks of its plan. DeSilva had been the key, and now he was gone.

"Drew, I was just thinking about your question. I'm afraid you're right. Without Dr. DeSilva there is no NEPA case ... Yes." He cleared his throat. Holland looked at Jim and rolled his eyes.

"All right, Bob. We will see you here tomorrow. I imagine we will see the governor on Wednesday morning."

"Right."

"See you, Drew."

Holland replaced the phone. He and Jim stared at each other in silence. Holland cocked his head toward the ceiling and thrust his middle finger into the air towards the light fixture over his desk.

* * *

Late that afternoon, the runner for Holland, Rollins, Jerald, & McNeely followed the signs in the Columbia Airport to the gate where Delta Flight 1145 from Dallas was expected. When the passengers began exiting the plane, he held up a cardboard sheet with a single name printed in black magic marker, "Dr. DeSilva."

As they began the two-hour drive to Charleston, Tony DeSilva turned to the young man, "Do you happen to know why Mr. McNeely made my reservations to Columbia instead of Charleston?"

"No, sir." It was entirely true. He hadn't the slightest idea. And he knew enough not to ask.

* * *

"Drew, we have a real problem here! Our case is gone! The whole thing is just a farce." Jim dropped onto the couch in Holland's office. For good measure, he tossed a volume of the Southeastern Digest onto the conference table. The heavy book landed with a loud crack.

"It's no farce. We're going to bill the state for a huge amount of time... and at our normal rate. What's wrong with that? It isn't our fault there's no real case to be made. Brother Bill will get his day in court. And a lot of press. Isn't that what we're being paid for? We're about to give it to him." Holland laughed loudly, and added cynically, "Tomorrow, we all get what we want. We make a lot of money. Bill Haselden makes big points with the voters. And Brad Sweatman gets to pay us back for making a fool of him."

"It still sucks."

"Making money never sucks."

"Do you want to look at the exhibits we've got ... the ones we can still use without DeSilva?"

"Why not? It's more billable time, right?" Holland walked around to the edge of his desk, picked up one of the chairs next to the conference table and tossed it into the corner of the room. As the chair smashed loudly against the wall, he stamped his foot on the floor and dropped to the carpet. He clutched his neck and began to gasp. His secretary rushed into the office to find Holland still holding his neck, choking, trying to draw a breath, and holding the other hand over his heart. He rolled his head violently from side to side. Jim was already on the phone, yelling directions to the EMS operator.

"That's right ... Hurry, for God's sake. Yes, that's the right address. HURRY!" he yelled frantically. Slamming the phone down, he knelt on the floor next to Holland. He quickly loosened his partner's tie and reached for his wrist to take his pulse. In less than a minute, two paramedics appeared in the office door. Jim retreated to a corner. The secretary covered her mouth with her hand, fighting to stay calm. The EMS paramedics carefully placed Holland on a stretcher, placed an oxygen mask over his mouth and nose, swiftly moving him to the ambulance.

Jim faced the three secretaries gathered in the foyer of the annex, outside Holland's office. "I'll follow the ambulance to the hospital. When I know something, I'll call you. It shouldn't be long."

The ambulance slowed as it passed the medical university. The paramedic who was driving turned off the lights and siren and drove up the ramp to the bridge and away from the hospital. As they crossed the river, Holland pulled off the oxygen mask and swung his legs over the edge of the stretcher. "How'd I do, guys?"

In minutes, the ambulance entered the gates of the state park. At the drive marked "Private" it left the main road and slowly made the way to a large antebellum house. Holland slid out of the rear of the ambulance. He thanked the driver, an old client, for the help, and promised to pay him back. On the porch, he was greeted by Geddings. Inside the door, Governor Haselden waited for him. "O.K., Governor, let's get to work," Holland said.

* * *

Rex Skanchy was awake when the nurse eased the door open. He was gazing at the window, the lights of the Cooper River Bridge twinkling in the distance. At the sound of the door, his head turned toward Jim. As broad a smile as he could still muster spread across his ever thinner and whiter face. Jim suppressed a flinch at the sight of the opaque plastic tubes extending from his nostrils. Rex lifted his arm and held his hand out to Jim.

"I'm glad to see you, Jim. How are you?" Jim took the hand, so small it seemed. He thought of the fine carvings of birds Rex loved to make. Wrens. Gulls. Mallards. And the unfinished herons that sat next to the fireplace in the house Rex would never see again.

"Great, Rex, but a little tired tonight. I just left Matt's place. Our witness is staying with him, so I went out there to prep him for the hearing tomorrow. We wouldn't have him as a witness without you."

Jim McNeely saw more than the frailty of Rex Skanchy in the metal-rimmed hospital bed. Before him, slipping away from him, was a man who embodied a soldier's strength of simple decency. In the pain-wracked face, Jim imagined he saw the last of Rex's kind of dignity, of his natural honesty. They were withering and inexorably disappearing from the same government this exceptional man had served so well. *Where were the new soldiers?* he thought bitterly.

"Give 'em hell tomorrow."

Jim looked into the tired eyes, still so bright. He nodded and took Rex's hand again, holding tight to the man who was so quickly fading.

* * *

Agent Tommy Littlejohn opened the rear door of Holland, Rollins, Jerald, & McNeely. It was almost midnight. Methodically, he carried the firm's ladder from office to office. In each room, he opened the light fixture, which he already knew contained the microphone and removed the foreign device. When he had completed his work, the cardboard box he carried contained eleven small, very sophisticated microphones and one tiny camera. He sealed the box, replaced the ladder in the closet, and let himself out the back door.

Chapter 15

Brad Sweatman walked from his office in the older part of the federal courthouse to the new wing. No one was in courtroom one. He liked being the first person in the courtroom. Behind him were the three assistant United States attorneys who would assist him at the hearing. C. A. Moore would arrive in a few minutes, along with the witnesses: Dr. Werner Herring from the Energy Department and Dr. Sylvia Phillippi, a leading researcher and frequent witness for the Natural Resources Defense Council. Sweatman could smell a quick and sweet victory. Since Monday, he had known that Holland no longer had an expert witness. The only argument left for the state was the bullshit about state regulations aimed at controlling nuclear materials. It was a loser, on its face, doomed by overwhelming precedents from the federal courts. The notebook he opened in front of him was filled with those cases, tabbed and highlighted for easy reference.

Most pleasing to Sweatman, was the report that Drew Holland was in the hospital. The opponent worth taking seriously was off the battlefield before the fight even started. This was almost too easy. For hours, he had worked to achieve the right appearance of sincerity. He would not seem too confident, only conscientious in his presentation of the honest cause of the government. He would be the bringer of truth. His tone would be instructive, but deferential, and he would be patient and polite to Holland's colleagues, acknowledging that they were burdened with an impossible case — and, he, a brother lawyer, understood how difficult it was for them. In the final prepping sessions with his witnesses, he carefully instructed each to strive for that quiet serenity identified with one who is clearly in the right.

At the corner of his table, he placed a copy of the *Federal Rules of Civil Procedure and Evidence*. C. A. Moore entered the rear of the courtroom and joined Sweatman on the other side of the gate. The two witnesses took a bench several rows back and began to chat. Sweatman glanced at his watch. It was already 9:55. The hearing was scheduled for 10:00. He wondered where the court reporter was. And the bailiff. At 10:10, Judge Richardson's clerk entered the courtroom and called to Sweatman, "Mr. Sweatman. We're in the main courtroom. Didn't you get the word? Judge Richardson is waiting on you."

Sweatman's stomach went cold. *The wrong goddamned courtroom!* Calmly, he replied, "No. Who was the message from?" He began to pick up the stacks of papers and exhibits. His assistants did the same, with the result that they were now completely out of order, scattered confusingly between the folders of all four men.

"We gave the message to Mr. Holland and he agreed to pass it on."

The son of a bitch, Sweatman thought.

As she led the federal team down the hall, she continued, "Mr. Holland called on Monday to say that the governor's press secretary predicted that a large number of reporters would be here. Judge Richardson has agreed to allow a camera pool set up, and they really needed the bigger courtroom. Besides," she added, cheerily, "it looks so much better."

When Sweatman entered the main courtroom, he saw that the benches were nearly full. A camera was set up in the corner of the jury box. Sweatman didn't have a chance to relish the prospect of so much public exposure before Judge Malcolm Richardson called out to him from the bench, "Nice of you to join us, Mr. United States Attorney." The crowd of reporters in the rear of the courtroom chuckled. Sweatman forced himself to join in the laughter, hiding the fury he felt.

"I didn't get Mr. Holland's message, Your Honor. Like we used to say in the army, there's always that one percent who don't get the word." More laughter rippled behind Sweatman. "We certainly are sorry to keep the court waiting."

"Your Honor, I left the message with Fred Muldoon. I thought he was the government's lead attorney." Holland turned smiling to face Sweatman.

Sweatman was stunned. *What the hell was Holland doing here?* Sweatman stared at him as though he were a phantom. Holland faced Malcolm Richardson again, "I'm sorry, Your Honor, we really should have sent word to Mr. Sweatman also."

"Mr. Sweatman, where is Mr. Muldoon?"

The question from Judge Richardson shook Sweatman out of his stupor. "Your Honor, Mr. Muldoon was taken suddenly ill," he lied. Holland stared at him furiously.

Judge Richardson continued, "All right, gentlemen, let's get started. First, I have the motion by Trident Intermodal Carriers, Ltd. to intervene in the case. The government does not oppose the motion. Mr. Holland, what is the state's position?"

"No objection, Your Honor."

"O.K. Trident will be allowed to intervene. Are we ready, then, to proceed with the state's motion for a preliminary injunction?"

Holland and Sweatman, still on their feet, assured Richardson they were ready.

"Let's hear who you have with you on both sides, gentlemen. Some of these faces are familiar to me."

As Holland turned to motion for the state's team to stand, he looked Sweatman straight in the eye and smiled again. "Your Honor, you know Bob Geddings from the AG's office and my partner, Jim McNeely. And you know, I believe Governor William Haselden. Governor Haselden will be testifying for the state this morning."

Richardson nodded, "Welcome to Charleston, Governor."

"Thank you, Your Honor."

"And we also have Mr. Fuller from the Department of Transportation. Finally, Judge, this is Dr. Anthony DeSilva from Cloudcroft, New Mexico, who will also testify for the state." With that, Holland and the entire state team sat down.

Sweatman was still staring at DeSilva in shock when Richardson cleared his throat and said gently, "Mr. Sweatman, could you introduce the folks you've brought with you."

Sweatman stood, "Yes, Your Honor." He turned to look at the two witnesses seated behind him. In panic, he realized he could not remember either of their names. He peered blankly at their faces; he could feel the silence in the high-ceilinged courtroom surrounding and choking him. Dr. Phillippi saw the paralysis in his eyes and quickly stood.

"Dr. Sylvia Phillippi, Your Honor. I'm with the Natural Resources Defense Council." As she resumed her seat, her colleague, Dr. Herring, stood and introduced himself, followed by C. A. Moore.

"Mr. Holland, it's your motion."

"Your Honor has our brief. If it please the court, we'll get right to the evidence in support of the state's request for a preliminary injunction."

"Proceed."

"Our first witness will be Governor Haselden." Haselden walked through the short gate that separated the gallery from the front of the courtroom and took his place in the witness chair. The cameraman focused and adjusted the camera. The reporters readied their pens and leaned forward slightly in their seats.

Quickly, Holland moved to the time when Haselden learned about the importation of large amounts of plutonium into South Carolina from Russia. For weeks they had labored over how to address the question of exactly how he had come to know that such plans existed without endangering Julieanne Harris. After the discovery of the government's spying, the answer came easier.

"Mr. Holland, I received a very unusual letter in the mail in February, anonymously. It was a memorandum that appeared to be from the Department of Energy in Washington outlining such a plan." The lie seemed small compared to what the government had done. Only Bob Geddings at the state's table shifted in his chair.

"Did this cause you concern?"

Haselden was more comfortable now. His answer was the truth, "Not at first. I began to worry when I couldn't get anyone in the administration to answer my questions as to whether these things were true. The federal government is very large." He turned towards Judge Richardson, "It occurred to me that it was possible plans were being put in place without the president being made aware. What worried me the most was the chance that the government would not take adequate safety precautions."

The governor recounted his efforts to get the attention of the president. "President Seekings agreed to discuss the matter in Washington, and I went there expecting to learn the truth."

"And did you?"

The governor smiled at Holland. "What I had been told about the government's intentions were confirmed, but not by the president. Vice President O'Connelly and a member of the White House staff — Mr. Moore, seated there behind the U.S. attorney — met with myself and our party."

"What did the vice president tell you?"

"He told me that the federal government was indeed planning to bring the Soviet stockpiles of plutonium and uranium 238 to the United States — and store it in this state at the Savannah River Site. I believed he was being honest with—"

"Objection. The witness is speculating on the mental state of the vice president." Sweatman held his right hand up toward the judge.

"Mr. Sweatman, everybody appreciates the risk inherent in speculating on the mental state of any politician — no offense, Governor—" The gallery exploded with laughter. "I understand what he means. Go on please, Governor."

"Mr. O'Connelly promised me the closest possible coordination with the federal authorities. And he offered Mr. Moore there," he pointed to C. A. Moore, "as our point of contact."

"Well now, that sounds like a pretty reasonable arrangement. Was there a problem, Governor?" Holland asked.

Haselden continued to stare at Moore. "Only that Mr. Moore ignored our efforts to coordinate with him about the government's plans. Finally, I called President Seekings directly."

A long pause had been programmed into his testimony for the benefit of the reporters. Every pair of eyes in the large courtroom was on him when Haselden continued. "The president denied that the government had any plans to import nuclear material from Russia. He told me I misunderstood the vice president."

"Did he tell you anything else?"

Anger flashed across Haselden's face. "He thanked me for my interest in national security ... and he asked me if I thought South Carolina would have a good soybean crop this year."

Holland returned to his seat.

Sweatman was handed a thin notebook containing his carefully prepared questions for the cross-examination of the governor. The interlude of Holland's direct examination had given him the opportunity to calm himself. He had not listened to the testimony. There was no need, after all, since he had known for days the exact questions Holland would ask, and the answers Haselden would give. He opened the notebook and appeared to study it intently before walking slowly to the podium in front of the bench. He buttoned his suit jacket. "Good morning, Governor," he said pleasantly.

"Morning, Mr. Sweatman," Haselden responded.

"With all due respect, Governor, you don't know whether the federal government is planning to bring nuclear material to South Carolina or not, do you?"

"You mean other than the tons of spent nuclear fuel rods you are currently importing from Europe?"

Sweatman appeared stung by the response. "I mean plutonium and uranium 238."

"I only know what the vice president of the United States told me."

"An assertion you admit was denied by the president, isn't that correct?"

"Mr. Sweatman, if the United States will stipulate right now that it will not now or ever import Russian nuclear weapons material into South Carolina, we can all go home."

"So, the answer to my question is a 'no,' isn't that right?"

"There can be no definitive answer until the federal government stops playing games and answers the question honestly. Until then, neither I, nor anyone else in South Carolina, know what the government intends to do."

"At last, an answer. Thank you, Governor." Sweatman flipped the page of his notebook. "Now then, sir, didn't you just testify that your press secretary was with you when you met with the vice president, and if so wouldn't she be able to substantiate your testimony?" Sweatman knew that the woman was not in the courtroom.

"No, I didn't mention who was with me, Mr. Sweatman. But you are correct; she was there. If you would like to ask her what the vice president said to us that day, I can ask her to come over." Haselden retrieved a tiny cellular telephone from his coat pocket and began to open it. As he pulled the antenna up, he added, "She is down the street at Mr. Holland's office."

Sweatman's anger was obvious as he continued. "Governor, this case is based on your speculation, isn't that right?"

"No, Mr. Sweatman." Haselden folded the telephone closed and slipped it into his pocket.

"This case is based on your suspicions and assumptions, isn't it?"

"No."

"Governor, didn't you just testify that your goal in bringing this case was to force the United States government to employ state and local police in the plans which *you* believe it has to transport nuclear weapons material across South Carolina, and *force* the United States to provide funds to those agencies to offset their costs?"

"I wasn't asked about my goal in bringing this case," Haselden responded politely. Sweatman's face reddened. His experience told him to stop, but he had seen the outline of Haselden's testimony. He *knew* what Holland had planned to ask the governor and exactly what the answer would be. Holland's outline of the testimony showed that there were actual estimates of the amount of money the state hoped to force the government to pay county sheriff's departments along the route of the shipments. All he had to do was get the governor to admit this single fact, and he would be able to convince the court their case was nothing but a tawdry effort to bilk the government of millions of dollars.

"Governor, I remind you, sir, you are under oath." Sweatman closed his notebook and laid it aside, as he fixed the governor with a cold stare. "Isn't it true, sir, that your office has prepared estimates — estimates that exist right now in your files — of the amount of money you plan to demand from the United States government in return for what you intend to claim are the costs to local sheriff's offices in South Carolina for providing security for plutonium shipments? And that your intent in this suit is to force the government to pay millions of dollars to state and local police agencies?"

"None of that is true. And I resent the implication. If you have proof of such estimates, you need to produce it, or apologize to the people of this state, Mr. Sweatman."

Sweatman was seething now. The man was lying to him, and making a fool out of him. Turning on Haselden, he shouted angrily, "Then what are your intentions, Governor? To earn publicity for your reelection campaign?"

Haselden was silent for a moment. Judge Richardson peered over his spectacles at Holland, expecting an objection. Holland's eyes grew dark and angry as he sat quietly behind the state's table watching Sweatman. The governor glanced at the judge and began the speech that had been so carefully prepared. "Mr. Sweatman, my goal in this case is quite simple." As the camera rolled and the reporters' tape recorders were clicked on, he continued. "In a little while, you are going to see pictures of men horribly burned by radiation from a nuclear accident. And you are going to see charts of how large an area can be contaminated — for thousands of years — by nuclear radiation from an accident. You will hear exactly how such an accident can occur — how accidents have actually occurred in the

Soviet Union. Mr. Sweatman, as the governor of this state, I simply want to do all in my power to prevent these things from happening here."

It had not yet occurred to Sweatman that he had been set up. But Moore saw exactly what had happened. *They know,* he thought. *They know.* He smiled, as he watched Sweatman's debacle continue to unfold.

In response to Sweatman's silence, Holland stood. "Your Honor, the state has no further questions for the governor, if Mr. Sweatman is finished."

"No more questions, Your Honor."

For the next twenty minutes, Geddings questioned Fuller about the safety of railroads in South Carolina. The charts he presented showed the many unsafe bridges and crossings with histories of failed warning devices. Fuller ran a pointer along one of the black lines on the map, "When the government made the first shipment of spent nuclear fuel rods, they ran the train right along this line, right through the middle of Florence."

"And was that necessary, in your opinion?" Geddings asked.

"No, sir, it was not. There were a number of other alternatives they could have used to avoid heavily populated areas."

"Mr. Fuller, have you formed an opinion as to how a rail shipment of dangerous nuclear material could be made safe."

"Objection, Your Honor. There's been no foundation for this," Sweatman said as he stood.

"I think there is. Go ahead, Mr. Fuller," Richardson replied.

"Well," Fuller peered across the room at Sweatman. He had not testified before, other than at his sister's divorce trial, and the U.S. attorney's objection unnerved him. "I believe all of the significant dangers could be removed by taking several precautions. The least populated route should be used. All intersections with the rail line should be closed for the transit of the train. All flammable containers and vehicles should be kept a safe distance away. This, as well as general security, could be carried out by local police agencies along the path. The downside is that you give up secrecy with respect to the route, but the increase in safety, I believe, is worth it."

"Thank you Mr. Fuller."

"Mr. Sweatman?" Judge Richardson asked.

"No questions for this witness, Your Honor."

Jim McNeely felt the nerves in his stomach suddenly tighten into a knot. He hated this part of trial work, the inevitable fear prior to a performance. He rose, "The state calls Doctor Anthony DeSilva." DeSilva stepped into the aisle and strode toward the bench. Jim noticed that Matt Reicher had been sitting with DeSilva. DeSilva's black, sharp-pointed boots made loud clunks as he made his way to the witness chair. *Boot Town*, Jim remembered with a smile. *If I had any guts at all, I'd have worn mine.*

DeSilva explained his degrees and his work with the Atomic Energy Commission, and later with the Department of Energy. He described his study of the hazards posed by nuclear materials, particularly plutonium and other weapons fuels. Sweatman pulled his copy of the outline of DeSilva's testimony, sent to him by Felix Hubbard, and followed it as Jim examined DeSilva. It had been retyped, and didn't resemble the original intercepted fax. But it was the same, nonetheless. As Holland had paid him to do, the TV cameraman panned the lawyers' tables, pausing to focus on Sweatman and the outline he kept to the right of his legal pad.

"Your Honor, the state offers Dr. DeSilva as an expert in the field of the study of the hazards of nuclear fuels and their byproducts." Jim waited for a response from Sweatman.

"I object to the qualification of this witness, Your Honor."

"Now, Mr. Sweatman, Dr. DeSilva seems to be very well qualified to me. Explain your concerns."

"All of his experience was gained as an employee of the federal government. Now he comes into this courtroom as a witness against that same federal government in a case involving the very agency for which he worked. For him to testify would be a violation of the standards of conduct that he agreed to honor as a condition of his long employment by the people of the United States."

Without responding to Sweatman, Richardson turned to DeSilva, "Doctor, did you ever work on the government's plan to bring plutonium back from the former Soviet republics?"

"No."

"O.K., Mr. Sweatman, the only lifetime ban I know of is the one that prevents former employees from testifying about something they worked on. We don't have that problem here. I'm going to let him testify."

"Your Honor—"

"I've made my ruling," Richardson snapped uncharacteristically. "Dr. DeSilva's qualifications as an expert witness are accepted by this court."

Jim discreetly began his questions again. "Doctor, are you familiar with the energy department files concerning the studies of the safety of shipping spent nuclear fuel rods."

"Objection, Your Honor. We're not here to retry a case the state has already lost."

"There's no jury here. If we're wasting time on extraneous matters, I'll say something about it. Go ahead."

"Yes," DeSilva replied.

"Were there reports in the department's possession that explained the effects of a release of nuclear materials from the fuel rods?"

"Yes. Several. In addition to the 1991 report by Dr. Resnikoff, the department had its own reports. Of course, the disastrous effects of such a release have been known for some time. They are neither a mystery nor a secret."

"What sort of an accident is addressed in these reports?"

"An accident that causes the containers of nuclear materials to be broken open. Breaking open a cask would cause a release of fission material."

"Describe the casks, Doctor."

"They are very impressive. The exterior cask is seven feet tall and made of stainless steel some ten inches thick. The rods are further encased in aluminum baskets that sit inside the casks. The whole thing weighs about 45 thousand pounds, and it's quite sturdy. The DOE has tested them under extreme stress. They've been dropped from great heights, even crashed on a freight train. Always without cracking the casks."

"If the casks have tested so well, what sort of accidents do these reports you mentioned talk about?"

"Any sort of explosion, or high temperature fire, that would cause the casks to crack open."

"What would happen, Doctor?"

"Anyone who came close to the ship and the open casks would be exposed to fatal doses of radiation. Death would come in one to thirty days for most of these people. Sadly, those most likely to fall into this category would be the crew on a ship, or firemen and police if the casks were breached on shore. But far worse, the fire and its smoke would carry highly radioactive particles far from the scene. A fire like that studied by

Dr. Resnikoff would contaminate an area of 10.96 square kilometers —
an area one mile around the site — with such a high dose of radiation that
anyone residing in that area for a year would die. An area of 750 square
miles around the ship would require decontamination, or simply have to
be abandoned altogether to human habitation."

DeSilva's words hung in the great courtroom. There was no sound save
the creaking from his seat as he turned from side to side, in each direction
finding all eyes fixed on him. Jim allowed the silence to continue a moment longer before asking, "And the energy department's own studies?"

"We found the same thing as Dr. Resnikoff."

"What was done by the DOE with these reports?"

"Nothing. The department simply told everyone that an accident
couldn't happen. They avoided the subject of what an accident would
mean *if* it happened."

"And what would such an accident mean in human terms?"

"The release of fission material is a horrible thing. We don't have to
speculate on the human health impacts. All we need to do is look to
Chernobyl." DeSilva proceeded to describe the events leading up to the
explosion of the reactor in the Ukraine, and the release of fission material
to the immediate area, as well as the transport of radioactive contamination in the large clouds of smoke from the fire. Jim asked him about his
personal observation and study of the results of the disaster. And then Jim
introduced the tape of the firemen in the hospital in Kiev. With courtroom lights slightly dimmed, the four television monitors flickered with
DeSilva's videotape. The first pictures brought gasps from some of the
reporters in the rear of the courtroom. Some began to turn away, as the
images became more grisly. "Oh, my God!" someone groaned, as the tape
showed Vladimir's mouth — a bleeding, blistered mass. Richardson
watched it all calmly, although his clerk was clearly becoming sickened.
Finally, mercifully, the tape wound to its conclusion. Vladimir's shriveled,
blackened body — which had been the picture of strength and health
before the accident — lay curled in a skeletal, fetal crouch, no bigger than
a child. His eyes, bereft of lashes and life, stared out from the television at
the horrified courtroom.

As the lights came on, Jim walked closer to DeSilva, "Doctor, can
you compare these pictures we just saw to what could be expected from
an accident like the one described by Dr. Resnikoff?"

"The same thing is entirely possible. It is all the more likely if nuclear materials are transported in secrecy, so that fire and police agencies don't know that radioactive fuels are present. The firemen who fight such a fire will surely die — like Vladimir."

"Doctor DeSilva, what, in your opinion, should be done to make shipments of nuclear fuel safe?"

"Sanity dictates that every conceivable accident involving an explosion or fire should be anticipated and the chances reduced as close to zero as possible." DeSilva paused for a moment, watching the attentive, ignorant faces surrounding him. The plea he made was not in the rehearsed testimony; it came from his heart. His eyes blazed as he spoke. "You have to understand that radiation isn't like anything else. It isn't nitroglycerin. It isn't liquid nitrogen. It is energy itself. It's the primal force that Man in his madness has stolen from its place in the natural world. We have no real control over it. Once it's released, it is servant to no one. It tears apart the very fiber of matter, whether rocks and dust, or living tissue, and it goes on destroying for an eternity." DeSilva held up his hand to the courtroom. "When we say an area is 'contaminated,' we mean that the very atoms of the land and all that lives on it are altered. Altered and mutated so severely that they fling out their own nuclear particles. The bombardment is so dangerous we can't survive it.

"You ask me what should be done? Nothing is enough. Nothing that removes even one chance of such a hideous thing from happening is too much to ask."

"Your witness," Jim said softly.

Sweatman rose confidently. "Doctor DeSilva, all of your testimony has concerned casks of nuclear fuel rods. This case, I think, is about plutonium and uranium taken from weapons stockpiles. Nothing you have said has any relevance to the issues in this case, does it?"

"Is that a question?"

"Yes, sir. Please answer it."

"You *want* me to answer that question?"

"Yes. That's why I asked it," Sweatman sputtered.

"Plutonium is recognized by many, if not most, scientists as the most poisonous substance known to man. Do you know why?"

"I'm asking the questions, Doctor."

"Because it's very radioactive. Can you imagine what would happen in a fire? Or an explosion that scattered the particles of plutonium over a wide area?"

"Doctor, please...."

"A catastrophe. Aren't those pictures enough for you, Mr. Sweatman?"

"Those pictures are from the Soviet Union. What relevance do they have for a program of the United States government? Are you asking this court to judge the government of this country by the standards of the Soviet dictatorship?"

"American radiation is the same as Soviet radiation. I suppose your point is that our government wouldn't take terrible risks with the lives of its people like the Soviet government."

"Yes. I would hope that every American would join me in rejecting the suggestion that this government — one of their own making and a government that is their servant, not their master — is capable of such callous acts as those that led to the tragedy at Chernobyl." Sweatman postured for the camera as he delivered his speech to DeSilva.

"I wish it were so simple, Mr. Sweatman. But the truth is so much more complicated. Our government once ordered its own soldiers and sailors to place themselves near a nuclear blast, just to test the effects they experienced. What a horrible price to pay for an experiment! Did you know that one of the leading studies on the effects of radiation deals with the great increase in cancer rates for *children* who lived in parts of the West nearest the nuclear test sites? No one knows how many of those children died of thyroid cancer because of the radiation or how many would have been saved if the government had told them what it knew — that they had been exposed and needed to take iodine tablets. The issue you raise about the relative integrity of governments isn't a simple one, Mr. Sweatman. But what is clear to me is that the more secrecy shrouds the handling of nuclear material, the more chance there is of our own accidents like that at Chelyabinsk in 1957. Several thousand people were killed there when nuclear fuel rods spontaneously released fission material. Eleven thousand were evacuated and four hundred square miles were contaminated." The words came faster and louder as he struggled to explain the desperate truth that was so clear to him.

"Doctor DeSilva, don't you...?"

"Radiation tears more than atoms apart, don't you see?" DeSilva ignored Sweatman. "It rips apart lives … communities … nations."

"Nations, Doctor?" Sweatman smirked.

DeSilva paused and continued calmly. "Nations. For a thousand years the Ukraine was part of the Russian nation. It was the birthplace of Russian religion and culture. But it is no longer a part of Russia. The outrage over Chernobyl, I cannot help but believe, drove them to sever themselves from Russia."

"And now you are offering opinions on international politics. Well, tell me, Dr. DeSilva, isn't it true that you suffer from cancer, which has been diagnosed as terminal?" Sweatman had intended for this question to be solicitous of DeSilva's condition. Instead, it sounded caustic and demeaning.

"That is true."

"And isn't it true that you blame your illness on the radiation you were exposed to at the labs in Los Alamos and Sandia?"

"My leukemia is consistent with overexposure to radiation. But I place no blame on anyone."

"Come now," Sweatman bullied, "you blame the Department of Energy for the fact that you're dying, don't you? And you're only here to testify to get even, isn't that right?" The lawyer swaggered in front of DeSilva. He did not notice the flush spreading across Judge Richardson's face.

"No."

"Doctor DeSilva," Sweatman continued in the same aggressive vein, "you haven't been honest with this court, have you?"

Judge Richardson held up his hand. "You don't need to answer that question, Doctor. Mr. Sweatman, do you have any more relevant questions for this witness?"

Sweatman was stunned by the force of the judge's rebuke. "No, Your Honor."

Holland rose and shook DeSilva's hand as he stepped through the gate and back into the gallery. Facing the bench, he said, "Judge Richardson that concludes the state's evidence."

*   *   *

At the end of the brief lunch recess, the lawyers, witnesses and reporters began trickling back into the courtroom. Matt and DeSilva approached the entrance to the courtroom just as Moore and Sweatman rounded the corner from the hall that led to the U.S. attorney's office. "Matt, I thought that was you. My God, it has been a long time," Moore called out as Sweatman opened the door and entered the courtroom. "I hear you're at the Weapons Station. Good assignment."

Matt stared impassively at Moore.

"Hope you enjoy it," Moore added, patting Matt's shoulder.

Judge Richardson was already behind the bench. "Are we ready?"

Sweatman first called Doctor Herring from the Department of Energy. Herring was nervous. The central theme of Herring's testimony was that even if large amounts of plutonium were shipped across South Carolina, there was no chance of a serious accident involving the release of radiation.

When Sweatman had completed his direct examination, Holland approached the witness chair, stopping directly in front of Herring. "Doctor Herring, do you disagree with anything that Dr. DeSilva said in his testimony? Anything at all?"

Herring looked trapped, and he searched frantically for a signal from Sweatman. Sweatman did not look up from the notes he was studying. Finally, Herring turned to Holland. "No. I could not take issue with anything that Tony DeSilva said."

"Thank you, Doctor."

Judge Richardson leaned over the bench towards the witness chair. "Doctor Herring, do you know anything about any plans by the government to bring Soviet plutonium stockpiles to South Carolina for storage?"

Herring fidgeted nervously with a button on the front of his shirt. "No, Your Honor, I don't know of any specifics," he lied.

As Herring left the witness chair, Doctor Phillippi made her way across the middle of the courtroom. She was an elegant and attractive woman, obviously comfortable in a courtroom. She joined Dr. Herring in rejecting the possibility of any serious accident. But she went further, and emphasized the importance of removing stockpiles of nuclear weapons fuel from the old Soviet Republics.

"It is impossible to overstate the seriousness of the risk of these stockpiles falling into the hands of terrorists. The Soviet government maintained upwards of forty thousand nuclear warheads and stockpiles of fuel. Now these fuels are simply being warehoused in poorly secured facilities that are open invitations to theft by any number of criminal organizations. It only takes some three pounds of plutonium to make a bomb to destroy a city — and the old Soviet stockpiles contain *one thousand tons*. It has been estimated by Harvard University that since the fall of the Berlin Wall, more nuclear material has been stolen from the old Soviet Union than was produced by the United States in the first three years of the Manhattan Project. It is a terrifying prospect, to say the least, to imagine these pilfered materials even now being implanted in bombs capable of annihilating New York or Washington, D.C.

"The NRDC has consistently maintained that the interests of the world's environment can only be served by collecting these horribly dangerous materials and storing them in a safer place. The United States offers the only locations with sufficient security." Dr. Phillippi went on to support Dr. Herring's conclusion that the mere transport of nuclear materials by rail posed no threat to the environment.

Holland walked straight to the witness box. "I have just one question, Doctor. Is there anything that Doctor DeSilva said that you disagree with?"

Phillippi leaned back in the chair and regarded Holland thoughtfully. She had anticipated the question. "I'm not sure I understand what you mean, Mr. Holland."

"Then let me be clear, Doctor. If casks of spent nuclear fuel rods are broken open, would there be a release of fission material with lethal consequences?"

She searched in vain for guidance from Sweatman. "Yes."

"And, if there were to be a fire that consumed the broken casks, highly radioactive particles would be carried by the smoke with devastating consequences for hundreds of square miles, would they not?"

"Yes."

"And if containers of plutonium were subject to a similar accident, the consequences would be similarly terrible, wouldn't they?"

"They would."

"So, the wisest course in your opinion would be to eliminate all possible chances for such an accident?"

"Yes."

"Thank you, Doctor." Holland returned to his seat.

Sweatman faced the bench. "That is all the evidence the government wishes to present to the court, Your Honor."

"Very well. As I said, gentlemen, the court will now call Mr. C. A. Moore as our witness. Mr. Moore, please come to the stand." Richardson motioned to the witness chair as he spoke. Moore was shocked, not warned that he would be called to testify, much less by the court. He walked slowly to the witness box.

"Now, Mr. Moore," Richardson began, "there has been testimony that you were present when the vice president met with the governor. Is that correct? Were you there?"

"Yes."

"Describe the substance of the statements made to Governor Haselden by the vice president."

"They were as described by the governor."

"And were the remarks of the vice president correct?"

"No," he lied.

"Explain."

"There are presently no plans to bring any nuclear materials out of Russia to South Carolina. The vice president misspoke."

"As of now, there are no plans to ship it here to South Carolina?" Richardson asked.

Moore looked at Richardson directly. "No. There are no plans at present."

"Therefore, Mr. Moore, if this court issues a preliminary injunction, the government will not be affected in any way, as there are no plans in existence, isn't that right?"

Moore paused watching Sweatman's eyes. "That is correct, as of today."

"Very well. Do you gentlemen have any questions for Mr. Moore?" Sweatman declined.

"I have a few, Judge," Holland answered. Jim handed him a printed document. "Mr. Moore, at the first hearing in this case, how did Mr. Sweatman know the name of the state's expert witness, Anthony DeSilva?"

Moore looked confused. "I don't know what you mean."

Holland opened the bound document to a tabbed page and read, "'It's the witnesses they plan to bring in. For instance, Judge, Dr. Anthony

DeSilva is a former Department of Energy employee.' Do you recall Mr. Sweatman saying that at the hearing we had last month?"

"No."

"And Mr. Moore, do you know how Mr. Sweatman got the copy of Mr. McNeely's outline for Anthony DeSilva's testimony that he was reading during Dr. DeSilva's testimony this morning?"

"I don't have any idea what you're talking about."

"Oh?" Holland lifted a tape from the state's table. "Let's look at this." He slid the tape cassette into the VCR and pushed the power button. The image that appeared on the screen was clearly made from the camera in the jury box. Holland waved the remote control wand and the film stopped, frozen in place. "Now, Mr. Moore, take a look at this picture. See Mr. Sweatman's hand there," he said, pointing to the screen. "And look here. It's hard to read upside down, but if you take your time, isn't that actually a copy of the questions that Jim McNeely asked Dr. DeSilva only a few hours ago?" Holland's eyes flashed, his voice sharp and loud.

Moore was silent, his stare boring into Holland. "And, I'll bet if we were to look through Mr. Sweatman's papers here, we'd find that very paper, wouldn't we?" Holland continued.

Sweatman was on his feet, but before he could speak, Richardson waved him down. "Now, Mr. Moore, you are in the security business. Tell me how Mr. Sweatman came to have the name — and even the outline of testimony — for one of our witnesses." Holland stood before the witness box, his arms folded across his chest.

"I don't know what you are talking about." The reporters in the rear of the gallery were transfixed, a dozen tape recorders recording the drama in the front of the courtroom.

Holland walked back to the gate behind the state's table where Tommy Littlejohn then handed him a cardboard box. He walked back to the witness box. Reaching into the box he picked up a tiny metal button with a wire attached to it. "Let me help you out. Do you know what this is?"

Moore was silent. Holland continued, "There are eleven more just like it in here. What are they?"

Moore stated at Holland, immobile. "How about this?" Holland asked, picking up a slightly larger object, a long tube of metal with a small box and wire attached. "What's this?"

Moore glanced at the object, but said nothing. "This is Tommy Littlejohn, an agent with the South Carolina State Law Enforcement Division." Littlejohn stood and nodded to the judge. "He removed these devices from each of the rooms in my law firm's offices. This is a camera that was pointed at Jim McNeely's computer, and these are little microphones capable of broadcasting to a receiver located nearby. Now how do you suppose these things got into my building, Mr. Moore?"

"I have no idea, Mr. Holland."

"Just an amazing coincidence, eh, Mr. Moore?"

"Amazing."

"I'll tell you how they got there. You had them put there, didn't you? You've been spying on us for weeks while we prepared this case, isn't that right?"

Sweatman was on his feet yelling at the bench, "I protest, Your Honor! This is outrageous!"

Holland faced Judge Richardson. "Judge, my office has been bugged. It looks to me," he said, his voice rising into a shout that echoed across the courtroom, "like the government of the United States of America is responsible. The State of South Carolina respectfully asks this court to investigate. If Your Honor concludes that I am correct, we believe sanctions should be imposed."

Richardson glared at the box Holland held in his hand and said, "These devices and the tape Mr. Holland presented will be turned over to the marshals. In addition, Mr. Sweatman, I want you to take your file with the marshal and let him make a copy of all of it, is that clear? I will decide what further action to take. As to the state's motion, I am granting the state a preliminary injunction. As the government maintains it has no plans to bring any plutonium into the state at this time, it will suffer no harm from an injunction at this time. My order will be issued within the week."

Richardson remained seated for a moment after he spoke. As he rose he turned angrily to Sweatman. He appeared about to speak to the U.S. attorney. Instead, as though he suddenly could not think what to say, he turned wearily and left the courtroom.

When he had disappeared, the reporters charged for the exits.

Chapter 16

Mike O'Connelly sipped a little more cognac and admired his garden. The French doors across the den were open allowing him an unfettered view of the roses and tulips. It was unseasonably cool, and he took the opportunity to trade the air-conditioning, which he hated, for fresh air. The phone on the desk interrupted his reverie. "Mr. O'Connelly," his secretary announced, "Brent Manzi is on the line for you." O'Connelly picked up the receiver.

"Mike, are you watching the news?"

"Do I have to?"

"Turn on CNN. Then call me back." The phone buzzed as Manzi hung up.

O'Connelly picked up the remote control. A story was in progress on CNN. He recognized South Carolina's governor speaking to a gathering of reporters. His face was determined and angry.

"The people of South Carolina have a right to know that their safety will not be sacrificed for any purpose. Today, the federal court has taken the first step toward ensuring that goal. We will continue our efforts in any forum available to us to ensure that the terrible scenes of victims of a nuclear accident you just saw in that courtroom are never repeated here. I am confident of our ultimate success." Haselden paused, surveying the group of reporters crowded around him, some of whom were thrusting microphones close to him. "And I want to assure the people of this state that I will not rest until there is a complete explanation for the shocking discovery that the offices of our attorneys as well as my own have been spied upon. As you just saw, the evidence suggests that the United States attorney and the White House arranged to have the offices of our attorneys broken into and planted with secret cameras and microphones. The people of this state — of any state — have the absolute right to be free from such outrageous abuse of power by the federal government," he declared, jabbing the air with his finger, his eyes flashing as he spoke directly into the camera. "We will never accept it. Never!"

The film of Haselden on the courthouse steps was replaced with a picture of the CNN reporter speaking live next to a fountain. "We have been unable to speak with the U.S. attorney since the hearing concluded. I tried to get a statement from the White House press office a few moments ago, and they are saying they will not comment at this time. This is really an extraordinary turn of events here. This case wasn't expected to go anywhere. Clearly, the revelations we just saw in court make this a very different ballgame. I was in there, and I can tell you, the fear from the federal lawyers was palpable." The reporter reached for the microphone fixed to his ear, "... I understand we have a result on the comparison of the videotape of the U.S. attorney."

The screen switched to two women, one holding a blowup of a frame from the video taken of Brad Sweatman. The second woman pointed to a hastily prepared transcript page, also blown up. "There is no doubt that Mr. Sweatman was reading a copy of Dr. DeSilva's testimony prepared *BEFORE* it was given.

"That is certainly consistent with the state's claims that the microphones and cameras they found in Drew Holland's office were put there by the federal government.

"We haven't seen anything like this since Watergate. This story is a long way from being over." O'Connelly picked up the phone and called Brent Manzi.

"What the hell is going on, Mike?"

"You're asking the wrong guy."

There was silence on the other line for a moment. "What the shit do you mean the wrong guy? You are the vice president of the United States."

"Accent on the word 'vice,' Brent."

"Do you know what this means?"

"Of course."

As he hung up, the phone buzzed. It was his secretary again, "It's Howard Casselman, Mr. O'Connelly."

Damn, he cursed to himself.

* * *

"You fool," Moore laughed bitterly. He leaned over Sweatman, slumped forward in one of the wingback chairs in his office, his head held in his hands. "It was obvious from the start that they knew."

"How?" Sweatman moaned.

"Muldoon told them. He told his pal Holland. Do I have to draw you a picture?"

"That's unethical."

"Yes, it is. But on balance not as unethical as using the power of the federal sovereign to spy on lawyers opposing you in important litigation, not to mention the governor." Moore chuckled as he spoke to Sweatman, but his disgust was plain. "Denying a charge by Muldoon, in the unlikely event he had ever made one, would be one thing. Refuting documentary proof is another. One day, Brad, you really must tell me why you took McNeely's draft of DeSilva's testimony into the courtroom."

"What are we going to do?" Sweatman had managed to raise his head.

"Well, Brad, I'm going to clean up this mess. As for you ... the final word will have to come from the president. But I think it's a safe bet that you'll be resigning in the very near future."

Sweatman jumped from the chair and said, "Wait a goddamned minute, if you think, I'm going to—"

"Take the fall. That's right. All the way to the bottom of the gorge." Moore collected his briefcase and made for the door. Without looking back, he walked out of Sweatman's office. "Bon voyage."

* * *

"My God, Jim. When did you all realize they were spying on you?" Alicia McNeely asked her husband.

"Friday."

"It's scary. I watched the CNN broadcast right after the hearing."

"They didn't know we had found the mikes and the camera. So we set them up. We got the cameraman to shoot Sweatman while we examined our witnesses, just on the chance he would be looking at our outline of the testimony. Who would have thought he would be stupid enough to actually bring those things with him to court?"

"It's frightening," she said quietly. "Do you think they were spying on you anywhere else? I mean ... like here?"

"No. No reason to." Jim hadn't thought about fear. For so many weeks now, his focus had been the hearing. Microphones and a camera in his office had been just one more factor to consider. He considered what

Alicia said for a moment. Maybe when the adrenaline wore off, he would be intimidated by what the government had done. But not tonight.

"Let's don't talk about all that right now. I need to take a break for a while. Tomorrow will be a circus."

"Is all this stuff as dangerous as the governor says it is?"

"If you listen to our expert, it is. You should have seen him. He was really worked up ... talking about radiation ripping apart nations ... nations, for God's sake. It was eerie. This whole thing feels like it could get out of control."

* * *

"*FEDS CAUGHT SPYING ON GOVERNOR, LAWYERS,*" the headline on the front page of the Charleston paper blared. The headline from Greenville said pretty much the same thing. Another demanded to know, "*WHAT KIND OF A GOVERNMENT SPIES ON ITS OWN PEOPLE?*" Without exception, newspapers across the state cried out in editorial outrage.

"There must be an investigation that shies away from no question, and fears no answer," an editorial said. A second lamented, "... the next descent by the federal government from that plane of respect and integrity, which a national government must occupy to remain effective — even stable. Even the most sanguine observer must fear for the future in such a climate where abuse of power by the federal sovereign has become unexceptional."

The Florence paper asked simply, "Does anyone remember how to secede?"

C. A. Moore paid no attention as he walked past the row of newspapers displayed outside the hotel gift shop on his way to meet Frank Kennerly at Trident Intermodal Carriers.

Trident Intermodal Carriers, Ltd. was a new company. The driving force behind its expansion was Frank Kennerly, founder of Romain Shipping. The success of Kennerly's company attracted the attention of a European consortium based in London, and the merger proposed by its board gave birth to Trident. Kennerly ran the American side of Trident.

Moore spotted the three-story brick building and the Trident logo over the door. Inside the entrance were heart-pine floors, partially covered with three oriental rugs. Moore's footsteps across the wide foyer echoed in the high-ceilinged old building. He studied the ornately framed oil canvases that occupied the center of each wall — each one of a great sailing ship. Every painting depicted a graceful, sleek vessel on a violent sea of dark aquamarine waves capped in white foam, masts and sails straining against a storm-filled charcoal sky.

"Mr. Moore? I'm Frank Kennerly. Good morning." The refined and Southern-accented voice belonged to a slim, tall man. The rough hand he held toward Moore would have been at home tending nets on a trawler.

In Kennerly's office, Moore thanked him for his time and quickly came to the purpose of his visit. "Frank, the Soviet plutonium project is a very high priority of the administration."

"And for us. This contract is a major account for us." In fact, the contract to ship the plutonium, as well as spent fuel rods, was Kennerly's richest deal ever, ensuring Trident's profitability for years. So much of the company's assets were devoted to it that the contract was vital to Trident's survival.

"Frank, didn't you know Judge Richardson pretty well?"

"I knew him when he was plain old Malcolm. Don't ever play poker with him, unless you plan to lose. Malcolm was my lawyer when we started Romain Shipping. He got us through some terrible times. He kept me clean and out of trouble right up until we merged. That was when he became a judge."

"Judge Richardson is the judge in the lawsuit the state has brought to try and stop us from bringing the plutonium out of Russia."

"I wasn't aware."

"Trident has just been allowed to intervene in the suit."

"No one has briefed me about that."

"Your London office arranged to ask the court for permission to become a party." Moore saw that Kennerly was confused by the news. "As of yesterday Trident is in the case on our side, defending the government's position."

"Well, I'm certain this will all blow over. It's just early election politics by the governor."

"Unfortunately, the judge is not inclined to let it blow over. He enjoined the government from proceeding with the project yesterday." Moore paused to allow Kennerly to absorb the surprising news. "If we can't get this turned around, we'll have to curtail the whole project, including your contract."

Kennerly watched Moore in silence, beginning to understand why Moore was in his office.

"It seems to me that if Judge Richardson was your lawyer, and not very long ago, he might not want to keep this case. It might not look right ... ethically."

"I bet he doesn't even recognize the name 'Trident.' He was on the bench before we launched the new company. He probably doesn't realize he owns stock in Trident. He agreed to accept stock as final payment of the fees we owed him when he left his firm to go on the bench. By the time it was issued, it was Trident Intermodal stock, not Romain. Malcolm is no money manager. He probably never even saw the stock."

"Frank, it isn't good for Judge Richardson to stay with this case."

"Why are you telling me this? I'm not involved."

"But you are." Moore leaned forward. "You were Richardson's client. And now you're a principal in Trident, a party to this case. It's important that you prepare an affidavit with your lawyers to present to the judge explaining that he has a conflict of interest in the case. Like you say, he probably has forgotten about your connection to Trident and even the stock he owns. He just needs to be reminded. He'll reach the right conclusion after that. He'll withdraw."

"My lawyer can just explain the whole thing. If Malcolm thinks there's a conflict, he'll step aside. If not, you can be certain he'll be fair."

Moore shook his head. *I wish it were all that simple, Frank.* "I'm not good at beating around the bush. We need you to do the affidavit. If you aren't willing to do that, we will have to assume the injunction will stand, in which case the government won't need Trident Intermodal Carriers, Ltd. as a shipper. We'll invoke our cancellation rights in the contract." He held up his hands in a helpless gesture.

When Moore left Kennerly's office, he walked alone to the foyer, leaving Kennerly behind the long antique table he favored as a desk. A cold cloud enveloped Frank Kennerly. He knew he had no choice, but his powerlessness made him feel no cleaner.

* * *

This meeting was inevitable. That certainty did not make Mikail Plekanov any less uneasy about seeing Marwan Atta again. News of the bloody raid at Zarmayevka brought an immediate demand from the Arabs for an explanation. Mikail had no choice but to agree to see Atta. The warehouse where Mikail paced waiting for the Arab was owned by one of the companies Alexis set up to handle the blend of lawful and criminal commerce that made up their business. It was largely empty at the moment, and its nearness to the St. Petersburg airport made it a good place to take care of this disagreeable and necessary chore. He glanced towards the opened warehouse door. One of his soldiers kept watch on the road at the edge of the trees. "Mikail!" he heard the Arab's deep voice echo in the warehouse behind him.

Atta was standing alone under the roll-up door, smiling broadly. Mikail walked toward his visitor, "Marwan, how was the trip?"

"Long, but worth it to meet with you again, Mikail."

Mikail reached the door and extended his hand toward the Arab. Suddenly, two men on either side of the door lunged at him, both holding machine pistols aimed at his chest. Mikail raised his hands slowly. A third man searched him, retrieving the pistol he carried under his coat. It was then that he saw his man sprawled in the dirt at the edge of the road. A red pool was spreading next to his shoulder from the deep gash that had severed his neck from ear to ear.

"You're making a mistake—" Mikail didn't finish speaking. The back of Atta's hand caught his head and sent him to the concrete floor of the warehouse. One of the men dragged him back to his feet.

"You don't understand, Mikail. You haven't understood from the beginning. I'm not one of the thugs you sell guns to. I'm a leader of the army of God. Unlike you, Russian, we still know how to fight. I don't have the time or patience to play games with you."

Mikail wiped blood from his mouth, the taste salty and bitter on his tongue. "What do you want?"

"Tell me how you will get the plutonium. And tell me why I should trust you when you failed in Kazahkstan."

"I didn't fail. I told you in Moscow it was not wise to tell you the details of our plans. It is even less wise to tell you now with so many other ears to hear."

Atta grabbed one of the machine pistols from the man on his right and thrust the barrel into Mikail's face. "You will tell me, you Russian bastard!" He pushed Mikail away.

Mikail regained his balance and faced Atta. "The raid was a diversion. It wasn't supposed to succeed. Eventually, someone will figure that out, but by then it will be too late. We will take it while it is en route to the Americans," he lied. "It will be delivered as we agreed, Marwan. Your concern is unnecessary."

The big Egyptian regarded him contemptuously. "Understand me, Russian. I have killed far too many men to give a shit about killing a few Russian thugs. If you fail us, you will die, Mikail. I promise. You and your banker brother and your families.... Don't fail." Atta walked out of the warehouse. One of the others kicked Mikail to the floor of the warehouse and pushed his face to the cool concrete with his boot.

"Lie still, Russian. If you move too soon, I will kill you now. Don't move until your guards come." He rubbed the muzzle of the machine pistol against Mikail's face. "They will see how weak you are." He laughed as he backed out of the building. Mikail lay on the floor, motionless. *After these animals pay me for the plutonium*, he thought, *I will kill Atta myself.*

* * *

Alexis Plekanov walked briskly along Nevski Prospekt, making his way back to the bank after lunch at the Astoria Hotel. Investors from Italy wanted a secure bank to finance a venture in shoe manufacturing. Alexis thought the deal would surely come to him. This was the kind of business Alexis wanted more than any other. It was solid. The clients paid in hard currencies. And it was exciting. This was the future of Russia.

In the lobby of his headquarters, he was intercepted by one of his chief assistants, who talked to him as they walked to Alexis' office. He was soliciting Alexis' approval for an expansion into Vladivostok, Russia's Pacific port. Alexis waved his secretary away as she tried to speak with him.

Still intent on the expansion plan, Alexis suddenly saw that there was a man seated at his desk, his back to them. It was Mikail. "Let's finish this later," he said to his surprised assistant.

When the door closed behind them, he spoke to Mikail, still facing the window overlooking the busy street below. "What brings you here, Mikail? Is there a problem?"

The high-backed chair swung around, and Alexis saw his brother's face, marked with the cut and bruise from Atta's hand. His brother had been in many fights, but Alexis had never known a hand to leave a mark on his face. "What ... happened?"

"The Arabs came to see me. They thought we failed at Zarmayevka, and they wanted to know how I planned to get their plutonium." Rubbing the spot on his mouth where the blood had dried, he added, "Atta wanted to impress me with his seriousness. He succeeded."

"Mikail...."

"They killed two of my men. Slit their throats like cattle, although they've had more experience with Jews and Hindus, I imagine."

Alexis was silent. He knew Mikail had something to tell him, or he would not have come.

"We must be even more determined to get their damned plutonium, Alexis. There mustn't be any delay in the funds we will need. These men aren't like the criminals we deal with, or the police. They are soldiers at war, the most dangerous of all animals." He turned to stare from the window again. "There is another thing, Alexis." Mikail paused. "You are right. It has to end. After we rid ourselves of the Arabs, I will end all of it. The drugs. The guns. All of it. There's plenty of money already. I don't want to die on a cold concrete floor with my throat slit." The two brothers looked at each other in silence. Alexis nodded.

* * *

"Mike, what the hell's going on? Has everyone down there gone mad?" Howard Casselman regarded Mike O'Connelly across the patio table. "Microphones and cameras spying on lawyers hired by a governor. Christ!"

Brent Manzi didn't wait for O'Connelly to answer. "This must be hell for you, Mike."

"What is this all about?" Casselman pressed.

O'Connelly needed his friends nearby. The humor that sustained him had vanished. The stench of scandal was all around him. He understood, even without knowing the details. A president out of control and obsessed with his own power had abused that power, and not for the first time, he was sure. He knew, in fact, or should have known, that this — or something like it — would happen. There was something about this business with the Russian plutonium that was driving Roger Seekings to extremes. Or perhaps all of this was the work of his protégé, Moore. If that were true, a greater scandal could be avoided. If this were all Moore's doing, Moore would pay the price alone. A generation of scandal emanating from the White House was as much as the institution could withstand, Mike O'Connelly believed. Public opinion polls routinely recounted that America's voters didn't believe that "character" was an important issue in presidential elections. O'Connelly knew it wasn't because they believed this to be true. They had simply given up. The silence of the electorate in the face of corruption and abuse of power by national leaders frightened him much more than the corruption itself. *How long*, he often asked himself, *could the institutions of American government, so delicately balanced, survive the disdain of the people?*

"It's about abuse of power. Isn't that clear enough?" O'Connelly's response was sharp and angry. "Or is it? Maybe Americans expect their leaders to spy on one another, like courtiers of a Roman emperor."

"You don't know, do you, Mike? You really don't know. And it's killing you," Manzi said, studying the strain in his friend's face. "It's bad, though. It reeks. And it's explosive as hell."

"Mike," Casselman added, "have you thought about resigning?"

The words struck O'Connelly — hard — because they said what he had felt for some time. Why should he stand in the path of this flood, after all? The forces eroding the foundations of the government he loved were like a swollen river. They rushed around him, powerful, carrying all in their path away to whatever destination gravity pulled them. Still, the thought of resignation saddened, and angered, him.

"No, Howard."

"What are you going to do?" Manzi asked.

O'Connelly refilled their glasses with cognac. "I need you guys to listen to what I have to tell you. I need you to be my friends tonight, not reporters." They nodded.

"I made a deal with Seekings. I agreed not to make trouble for him, if he agreed to what I wanted."

"What in God's name was that?" Casselman exclaimed.

"I told him to leave my children alone." O'Connelly saw the shock on their faces. "When I didn't play along with Seekings' deception over this plutonium project, Moore spread stories about my kids. You fellas warned me months ago. I asked some friends to look into it." Manzi and Casselman knew O'Connelly could only be talking about Leo Scardato. "What I learned was that Moore was crafting stories and innuendo that would ruin my daughter's campaign and my son's career in the air force. The son of a bitch let me know in pretty clear terms that the point was to make me play ball with the administration. They wanted me to lie in court."

"I refused. I told Seekings I wouldn't lie for him. And I told him to leave my kids alone or I'd bring the administration down. If he backed off, I told him I'd be silent; otherwise I'd expose every rotten, corrupt thing going on in the White House. So, you see, I've made my deal."

Later, in Manzi's car, Casselman remarked, "You know Brent, we're sitting on one of the biggest stories in the last quarter century."

"Yeah. Unfortunately, we gave our word to one of the finest men to come to this godforsaken town in our lifetimes."

*   *   *

The dinner Carol served was one of her best. The shrimp in the Creole was fresh, and the peppers were hot. It was her mother's recipe revved up to satisfy her taste for hot, spicy dishes. It was a taste she shared with Dave Walensa, and she was delighted when he raved over her food. This was the first time she had seen the sailor from the USS *Deyo* since the press coverage of the government's spying on the state's lawyers. That morning she called him, anxious to keep their relationship alive, but very much afraid it might be over. When he wanted to see her, she began to hope.

She picked him up at the Weapons Station gate, and they stopped for a happy hour margarita at the hotel near her condominium. He didn't mention the news over their drinks at the hotel or during dinner at her place. She knew from past experience that sailors lived in a world of their own. It was possible that he hadn't even heard about the explosive story. As they cleared the dishes from the table and carried them to the small kitchen, he asked her, "How come you didn't call me this week?"

She looked into his eyes, thought again how incredibly blue they were, and struggled to lie. "I wasn't sure you wanted me to hound you. I thought you might want a breather." She felt his arms slip around her from behind and pull her to him. His lips kissed her neck and his hand found her breast. As she felt his tongue licking underneath her ear, she let the dish she was drying slide into the sink.

"You should know what I want by now." He turned her around and crushed her to him, his mouth covering hers, his tongue sliding between her lips. She returned his passion, relieved that he wasn't going to slip away, at least not yet. Her hands caressed his back and the strong arms that were holding her so firmly. She pulled the shirt free from his pants and over his head. Freeing her lips from his, she kissed his neck and chest, finding his nipples with her lips and gently with her teeth. He moaned, deep and barely audible. As she licked and kissed his chest, he removed her shirt, taking her breasts into his hands and rubbing the nipples, the way he knew excited her.

Their hands loosened belts and zippers. He lifted her onto the counter next to the sink, shoving the dishwashing liquid across the narrow surface with one broad forearm. With her shoes kicked free, he yanked her jeans down and off her legs. She shoved his own pants below his hips, and pushed them down his legs with her feet. He kissed her again, lost in a fierce desire to make love to this wonderful woman who had fallen into his wandering life. Her fingers slid between them and folded around his hardness, moving along its length, and lower, between his legs, exciting him more than he thought he could bear.

He pulled away from her, looking down between them, smiling at her, and then letting her guide him into her. She took him deep inside, and wrapped her legs tightly around his waist, her arms locked behind his neck. He moved quickly. There would be time enough later in the night for more leisurely lovemaking. She gasped as he increased his rhythm. The force of their frenzied movements rocked the cabinets behind her. Glasses slid and fell inside the cabinet doors. She cried out her excitement, throwing her head back and rapidly bringing it back to lock him in a tight kiss again. "I love you," she breathed.

"I love you," he said, sweat pouring from his forehead and down his chest. He grabbed her, suddenly more rigid and took her mouth, holding her, pulling her to him, a part of him. As the wave of passion crashed over them and subsided, he pulled his face back enough to say again, "You're terrific."

A shower and a bottle-and-a-half of wine later, they lay naked together on the couch in her den. "I can't believe you did that to me on the kitchen counter," she said.

"Believe it." He drank from his glass. His head was already swimming from the wine. "Maybe next, the utility room."

"The crawl space under the stairs."

"The roof."

"Hold on big boy, not without a rope."

"Ropes. I like it."

"You're drunk."

"Not too drunk." He smiled thickly at her. "Carol, all that shit this week about the government putting microphones and cameras in that law office. That was the same group we were listening too, wasn't it?" Without waiting for an answer, he continued, "We were part of the same surveillance. It wasn't an exercise at all."

"Right."

"But they didn't mention us. We talked about it on the ship. The rest of the guys figured they just didn't know about us." He leaned over her, his big jaw brushing her cheek. "But they did know, didn't they?"

"Yes." This was what she had feared for a week. Now he would be gone for good. She betrayed him, and he would desert her after a good—

"And you protected me. You did ... didn't you?"

Relief spread across her face. She gazed at his face, full of life and alive with fascination for ... her. "Yes," she said and the tears began to come. "Yes."

He laughed softly, the deep, strong sound sweet to her ears. "By all rights they should have been talking about us on the news. Boy, the shit would have really hit the fan then. What a stupid fucking thing to do, spy on a bunch of lawyers."

She took his head in her hands, stroking the short black hair and pulling his mouth to hers. "I love you Petty Officer Walensa."

* * *

"A perfect morning, Tiger," Jim said.

"Pour yourself some coffee," Matt responded.

His first sip of Matt's coffee confirmed that, as usual, it was one-fifth bourbon.

"Whoa. Nice blend, there, Matt."

"Thought you'd be in the mood to celebrate after the way you and Tony kicked ass last week."

"Yeah, we did a pretty fair job."

"Bullshit. What a bunch of false modesty. You guys were awesome."

They loaded their bags into the back of Matt's jeep. They had the golf course to themselves. As they approached the middle of the course, Jim noticed a change in Matt. It was as though the air was slowly escaping from him. He grew quieter and, finally, sullen. The sun was well into the sky, fueling another steamy August day. Jim pointed to a dark line on the horizon across the river. "Looks like trouble."

Matt's swing caught the ground in front of the ball knocking his ball into a short hop to the left. "A mulligan," Jim said.

Matt set up a second ball. This time his swing carried the ball on a high curving path to the right, into the hundreds of balls scattering the adjacent driving range. "Should have taken the first one," he said flatly.

At the next hole, after Jim had teed off, Matt climbed back into the driver's seat of the cart, "Come on. I'm going to skip this hole."

Jim was silent, studying Matt's face. Matt was in pain. That was clear. Jim played the hole alone. When the cart stopped next to the next tee, Jim tossed him the plastic container of spiked coffee, "Take a swig of this juice, and come over here and sit down a minute." He dropped down on the wooden bench next to the tee, this one shaded by an old live oak. Matt joined him on the bench and took the plastic bottle. "What's wrong?" Jim asked.

"Two nights ago I stayed in the club until one o'clock. I don't know how much I drank. I woke up at three in the mud next to the ditch. I've lost my family and it looks like my career is over. I don't want to end up a disgrace."

A black cloud filled the horizon behind them, billowing rapidly toward them. Orange pencils of lightning shot from the cloud to the tree line across the river. Thunder rolled over the marsh. A gust of cool air swirled up from the river, pushed ahead of the storm, announcing that it would be on them very soon. "Better go, Tiger."

They drove the cart along the road between the edge of the course and the narrow woods by the river. In Matt's quarters, Jim made them coffee without bourbon and carried it to the den. In silence, they watched the spreading black storm blot out the morning sun, chasing the last yellowish rays before the enveloping darkness. Streaks of lightning arced erratically along the front of the cloud. Thunder boomed in time to the orange flashes, violently shaking the walls. Sheets of rain flew against the glass.

Jim watched helplessly as his friend stared at the torrent moving up the river.

Chapter 17

"'The greatest evil,' C. S. Lewis once wrote, 'is not done now in those sordid 'dens of crime' that Dickens loved to paint. It is not even done in concentration and labor camps. In those we see its final result. But it is conceived and ordered (moved, seconded, carried and minuted) in clean, carpeted, warmed, and well-lighted offices, by quiet men with white collars and cut fingernails and smooth-shaven cheeks who do not need to raise their voice.'"

Judge Richardson began reading his order for the final time before he signed it. It was a short and forceful document. And it was meant to convey a clear message:

> This Court is to some degree tempted to resolve this dispute in the simplest fashion. The government has maintained vigorously that there is currently no definite plan to remove stockpiles of Soviet nuclear weapons material to the State of South Carolina. Therefore, they have argued, there is no need for it to prepare any evaluation of the risks, and the alternatives available to ameliorate those risks, as required by the National Environmental Policy Act. This is not such a simple matter, however.
>
> Congress intended the Act to prevent the perpetration of 'evils' such as those described by C. S. Lewis, by quiet men, in secret, out of the sight and scrutiny of the public, lest the public demand answers to troubling questions, or even challenge the decisions themselves. It is clear from the record that the government intended to make its plans to import Soviet nuclear material in secret. For that reason, this Court directs that no plan be implemented until a full environmental impact statement is prepared in compliance with the Act. This Court further orders that, after the government has prepared its EIS,

that the EIS and the record compiled in its preparation be submitted to the court and to counsel for the state for review.

There can be no question, but that the shipment of the
materials, clearly contemplated by the government, poses a risk
of significant impact on the human environment — in fact, it
is a risk of profound horror. The government exhorts this Court
— and by extension, the people of South Carolina — to trust
them to take such precautions as will render the risk of catastrophe minute. There is nothing in the record, nothing in the
demeanor of its representatives, and nothing in the history of
its handling of nuclear materials from which this Court can
take comfort that these assurances can be trusted. Certainly,
this Court will not rest its judgment, or risk the safety of the
land and people of South Carolina, on the assurances by this
government.

In one short paragraph, the judge declared the state's regulation of
nuclear material to be in conflict with the Atomic Energy Act and, therefore, void. Finally, the order turned to the matter of the strong evidence
that the government had spied on the state and its lawyers.

This Court will conduct its own investigation. The evidence already revealed raises a strong inference of the most
serious criminal behavior on the part of the government's representatives. While that possibility pains this Court deeply, the
Court will not flinch from the truth. If there have been crimes
committed in the course of litigation before this Court, there
will be sure and swift accountability for those crimes.

Malcolm Richardson lifted the old-fashioned pen he routinely used
to sign orders and swirled the loops and jagged lines that had for so long
been his official signature. He was resolute in his decision, but he had no
sense of satisfaction. The truth of what had been done by Sweatman and
the administration was ugly, depressing and frightening.

"Judge, this just came in. You might want to look at it before we
send out your order. It's an affidavit from Frank Kennerly, one of the
principals of Trident Intermodal Carriers. He thinks you have a conflict

of interest in this case and ought to recuse yourself. There's a motion asking you to recuse yourself," Richardson's clerk said.

Richardson was bewildered. He scanned the affidavit and motion. *Stock?* Now, he remembered. Kennerly paid him the balance of his fees in Romain Shipping stock when Richardson took his place on the bench. If he ever had known it had been converted to Trident stock, he had long since forgotten. He read the papers over again. The conflict of interest was clear and could not be remedied. He would have to step aside.

The case would go to his newest colleague, Steve Green, the only other judge who heard cases filed in Florence. "Set up a conference call with Drew Holland and Brad Sweatman," Richardson said.

"Judge, you haven't heard? Brad Sweatman has resigned," the clerk explained.

Richardson nodded, his eyes dark and sober. "Then with whoever is left."

* * *

Captain Nat Engle waited in the small conference room with his executive officer, Lieutenant Cooper, and his first sergeant, Henry Staggers. They were waiting for the colonel, who was the senior evaluator and who would give them the results of his evaluation of their performance during the two-week exercise. Staggers was tense; the occasional looks he shot Nat were icy. Cooper was just nervous.

"Sir, I know you want to make a big impression," Staggers told Nat before the exercise began, "but this don't make no sense. We've never done nothing like this before." Staggers glared at Nat, his black face glistening in the sweat from the desert heat. They had been at Fort Irwin for two days. This remote location in the California desert was the army's National Training Center — called "NTC" for short. Here units were rotated for intense training in tactics and maneuvers. National Guard units were notorious for their failure to measure up during the grueling two-week exercises at the NTC. Nat was determined that this trip would be different.

For weeks, Nat searched for exactly what the evaluators would be looking for. He telephoned the active duty command — called his "War Trace" — to which his unit would be attached if it were mobilized. His phone calls, a dozen when he stopped counting, were not returned. The last thing the active army was interested in doing was spending time assisting National Guard units. Frantic to find the key that would allow Charlie Company to beat the odds, and beat the NTC, he began searching the Internet. What did he have to lose?

To his amazement, he stumbled on an entire web site devoted to lessons learned at the NTC. Past failings of Bradley units like his were explained in meticulous detail. It was like finding the answers to the exam slipped under his door.

His excitement was *not* shared by his first sergeant. Staggers scoffed at the notion that anything pulled from "that bullshit machine" was of any use to them. "Captain, we just got to do what we always do. We just go to do it better." His frustration with the young captain, an unknown foisted on him by some political figure, and from the *reserves*, for God's sake, was obvious. His language was respectful in word, but the tone left no doubt he was furious with this transportation interloper playing at being a "War Fighter." For a week before the exercise, he railed about the outrage he was forced to endure, always careful to bend the ears only of guardsmen outside of his chain of command. Staggers was proud, but he was a professional. He would suffer a lot more ignominy than this before he would be responsible for undercutting the authority of any commanding officer, even a fool. "Captain, you got to understand. These active duty types are never gonna say we do anything the right way. That's just how it is."

But Nat insisted he had broken their code. He took each of the recommendations for training in the Internet article and drilled the company over and over. The article decried the poor training, in all respects, of Bradley units in coordination of the armored vehicles with dismounted soldiers. If the army wanted to see dismounted soldiers — those moving on foot outside of the Bradleys — coordinating with the Bradleys, then he'd show them a veritable ballet of coordination. He knew that Staggers thought he was crazy.

The final week of the exercise culminated in mock combat with the active army components acting out the role of the OPFOR, or opposition force. Armed with Soviet-block equipment and the most modern surveillance and detection equipment, they stalked the guardsmen across the desert. Nat's goal was to trap and "destroy" them before they did the same to him. All of his movements were monitored by the evaluators, watching and annotating their notebooks in preparation for the evaluation that would mark his efforts a success or failure. And determine his future in the guard.

Carefully following the lessons he pulled from the Internet article, his scouts, equipped with the observation post bags that Nat ordered prepared, sought out positions to give them maximum concealment. Not one was found by the "enemy." Instead, on the second day of the final phase, they used their anti-tank weapons to destroy two of the OPFOR tanks.

On the final night of the exercise, his scouts reported to Nat that the OPFOR were positioned to flank and overrun Charlie Company, the normal fate of guard units at the NTC. Staggers, Cooper, and Nat hovered over the map of the "battlefield." Over Staggers' virulent protests, Nat ordered a full one-third of his men to maneuver dismounted and assume positions on either side of a deep creek bed. Third Platoon, he ordered to take up reserve positions in the rear.

As his scouts alerted him to the approach of the OPFOR tanks and armored personnel carriers, Nat dispatched First Platoon to engage the right flank of the enemy. On his orders, the Bradleys of First Platoon noisily fired star clusters that lit up the desert around them. As the OPFOR tanks lunged forward to engage them, the Bradleys retreated toward the creek bed and took up prominent defensive positions on the opposite end.

Sensing another triumph, the tanks and armored personnel carriers of the OPFOR rushed up the creek bed. Elated — and shocked — the South Carolina guardsmen rose from their positions on either bank of the creek bed and bathed the creek in volleys of simulated anti-tank fire. The evaluators declared three-fourths of the OPFOR armor destroyed. The remainder established covering fire and began to withdraw across the plain at the end of the creek bed. Suddenly, the night turned to day as Third Platoon fired star clusters. Arrayed in the path of the surviving OPFOR vehicles, they fired in unison on the column. The rest of Charlie Company's Bradleys closed in on the confused OPFOR tanks from the rear, trapping them. In minutes, the evaluators declared the last OPFOR vehicle destroyed by the withering fire of the guardsmen.

From behind Third Platoon's noisy celebration a Humvee roared up to the evaluators and braked to a sudden stop, throwing up a thick cloud of the fine dust that covered the desert floor. It was the OPFOR commander, a full colonel. Even in the dim lights of the armored vehicles, it was clear his face was flushed a deep red. Hurling rich oaths at the evaluators, he yelled his complaints about the unorthodox tactics of the guardsmen. The exercise was intended to test tactics "*of the Bradleys*" he said. It wasn't supposed to be a game of cowboys and indians for a bunch of goddamned hick National Guardsmen.

The South Carolinians fell silent before the tirade of the furious colonel. The OPFOR soldiers smirked and shook their heads at the dense reservists who thought they would beat the NTC. The evaluators, all junior to the outraged colonel, dutifully noted his complaints and said they'd take it up with the evaluator. In the command tent of Charlie Company, Staggers read Nat the riot act. "I told you, man. I told you," he said and left Nat alone in the tent.

The door to the conference room opened and the colonel walked in, followed by the two majors who had supervised the evaluation of Nat's exercise. Nat called the room to attention.

When they were seated he handed Nat a folder. "Captain, here's your evaluation for this exercise. You can read as well as I can read it to you. Have a look and then tell me if you have any questions." The first sheet was a series of blocks next to a list of standards. The first one was labeled "Command and Control." The block on the far left was checked indicating "Exceeded Standards." It was the highest mark he could have received. He saw, incredibly, that all the blocks were marked the same way. The second page was a narrative extolling Charlie Company's flawless employment of dismounted soldiers, both in fire and maneuver, and in observation posts. The last sheet was a letter of commendation addressed to Nat's battalion commander, with a copy, he noted ironically, to his War Trace commander at Fort Stewart.

"Well, Captain," the colonel asked unsmiling, "do you have any questions?"

"No, sir. No questions."

"Good. Have a good trip home." The colonel stood, prompting the others to stand as well. As Nat reached for the door, the colonel called to him, "And, Captain, guess you see that in the active army, we have a ways to go in making the One Army Concept work." Nat saw that both majors were smiling broadly.

"Not for me to say, sir." He realized it was the closest any reservist would ever get to an apology from the active army.

Already, his Bradleys were lined up at the railyard waiting to be loaded onto railcars for shipment home to Kingstree. He ordered Staggers to drive them to the railyard. Staggers was confused, but today Henry Staggers wasn't about to question anything *this* commander did. At the railyard, Nat walked to the Bradleys, staged in neat rows next to the tracks. One by one, he walked to the vehicles and examined the three-by-five-inch white label glued to each one. It contained the data that would ensure his Bradleys returned to Kingstree. Without the label intact, he knew from his years with the 1189th that his Bradleys might be scanned out of the system and end up in a depot. Five of the labels were damaged, the bar code torn through by a deep scratch. Nat turned to Cooper, "Get the installation transportation officer to print new labels for these vehicles." He pointed to the one-story building next to the tracks, "In there. Go in there and find him. Tell him you want them to print new labels for these Bradleys RIGHT NOW. If they give you any shit, tell them if they're not ready to put them on in five minutes, I'll have somebody's ass! I'm not going to wait six months for the army to find five of my Bradleys that get lost because some asshole is too lazy to print a new label. Tell them I'm not leaving the railhead until it's done."

Staggers watched his commander, a bemused smile creeping across his face. Nat returned the smile, "Look, I didn't spend those years in a transportation unit for nothing." Staggers threw his head back and laughed loudly.

At the recreation area, before the hamburgers and hot dogs began frying on the grills, and before the cans of beer were passed around, Nat climbed onto one of the picnic tables and read all three pages of the evaluation. When he was done, Nat thanked his troops for a great job. The sound of the cheer that roared from the hundred guardsmen would never leave him. It was the sound of men who would do anything for him.

* * *

It was hot in Charleston, but it has to be hotter here, Samantha thought. She was in Florence to research land records in the county courthouse for one of Drew Holland's cases. In addition, she carried a box of records to file with the federal court, including some for the new judge, Stephen Green. The federal courthouse was her first stop. As she exited onto the walk, she thought the figure approaching was familiar. The man was well dressed and handsome. But it was his carriage that struck her as familiar. He walked with utter confidence. Or was it simple arrogance. She pretended to search her purse for something, while he came closer. When he was nearly to the door, she recognized him as the man who sat behind Brad Sweatman at the hearing. The White House staff member in charge of the whole plutonium project. C. A. Moore. What the hell was he doing in Florence?

After Moore entered the building, she paused outside the door, continuing to stare into her purse. She saw him finish signing in with the guard and enter the elevator. Samantha walked up to the guard, "I left something upstairs. This heat is just too much for me." The guard chuckled and waved her on.

Samantha took the elevator back to the floor where Judge Green's office was located. Nervously, she paused outside the judge's office door. What would she say to explain why she was back so soon? What if Moore recognized her?

"Hi. Did I leave my glasses case in here? I just can't keep up with the thing," Samantha prattled to the receptionist. At the corner of the bookshelves that divided the reception room she saw Moore entering the judge's office. One of the new judge's law clerks was closing the door behind Moore.

"Samantha? Are you all right? Samantha?" It was the judge's receptionist leaning forward, looking at her quizzically.

"Oh, yes. I'm fine. I guess I didn't leave my glasses in here after all," she said and turned quickly and left.

She found the nearest telephone and called the firm. Holland was at a deposition, but Jim McNeely was in his office. "I have to talk to him *right now*," Samantha demanded.

"I'll tell him you're on hold."

In a moment, Jim came on the line. "Jim, that guy Moore — yeah from the plutonium case — he's here in Florence. I saw him at the federal courthouse. He was going in to meet with Judge Green."

"Did you see them together?"

"Yes ... I saw Moore go into Green's office not thirty minutes ago."

Jim was silent, trying to fathom how this could be true.

"Jim, there's a sign-in sheet in the lobby. A guard at a little table has a clipboard and everyone has to sign in and out. If they save those sheets, there's a record he was here. I followed him to the judge's office. I saw him go in to see the judge."

"Samantha, before you leave Florence, go back by the courthouse and ask them what they do with the sign-in sheets." As he hung up, Jim felt the same icy hand on his spine, the same chill he felt the afternoon he learned his office had been bugged.

*   *   *

"Judge Green, I appreciate your seeing me on such short notice." Moore smiled at Stephen Green across the large antique desk, which had only recently been moved from Withers, Green, & Sellers five blocks away. The pill he took on the drive to Florence was working, and, in spite of the extraordinary thing he was about to do, he knew it would keep him completely calm.

"It's my pleasure. The work is starting to come in finally, with all the new cases the other judges don't want to handle. It's hell being the new guy," Green laughed good-naturedly. "But to tell you the truth, I haven't had much to do around here for the first week. What can I do for your this morning?" Green had never met Moore, at least he didn't think he had. His contact with the White House staff had been perfunctory. His appointment was shepherded by an old friend from his work for the party.

"First, President Seekings wanted me to congratulate you on your confirmation."

"That's good of him. I'll try to live up to his faith in me."

Moore glanced around the office. Pictures of Green's wife and children were displayed prominently. The boys were in their high school years. Leaning against the wall on the floor were a number of diplomas and certificates. At fifty-two, Green was leaving private practice at the peak of his success. But Moore knew that something other than money drove the man. It was the reputation and respect Green earned through the law. He cherished his status as a powerful member of the state's legal community, and relished the chance to mold the law from his seat on the federal bench.

"I have also been asked to go over some business with you. It won't take long."

Green looked puzzled. The lines around his eyes deepened. He could not imagine what business he had with this White House aide. He ran his hand over the thinning gray hair on his forehead, a nervous habit he had failed to break.

"It's the state's case against the Department of Energy. I believe it's just been reassigned to you."

The judge stared in silence at him for a moment. "I don't think it's a good idea for us to talk about any of the cases on my docket."

Moore pursed his lips and nodded slowly. "I know it makes you uncomfortable. Believe me, we understand. In a year, President Seekings expects to make another appointment to the Fourth Circuit. As of now, if you're interested, you are that choice, Judge." He smiled pleasantly at Green.

The judge stared at him, his expression clouded and sober. "I'm flattered to be considered."

"Now, this case about the nuclear material. It's very important—"

"Mr. Moore! We can't discuss anything about a case that's before me." He softened his expression and his tone. "Look, maybe you should speak to the U.S. attorney's office. They can go over why it's such a serious problem for us to have a conversation about ongoing litigation, O.K.? My secretary can find the name of the lawyer handling the case for the government and set up the call." He reached for the phone on the corner of his credenza.

"I already know who he is, Judge. And I am well aware of how unethical this conversation is." Moore was still smiling.

"Then you understand why we can't talk."

"Now, Judge, as I was saying," he continued, ignoring Green, "this project is one of the most important things on the president's agenda. It—"

"Look, Mr. Moore. This has gone far enough. If you speak to me again about this case, I will hold you in contempt. Do you understand?" Green's face was red and twisted into a snarl. He didn't care who the man was; he wouldn't tolerate such a brazen challenge to his office.

"Did you threaten me, Judge?"

"Yes," Green seethed.

"Have you ever heard of an organization called Pee Dee Health Systems?"

Green froze.

"Sound familiar? Didn't you represent them when they were trying to get a license for their hospital — over on the west side of town, isn't it? Didn't they have a lot of trouble with that state agency?" he asked, studying the ceiling as though searching. "Didn't they have a really hard time getting their certificate of need?"

The judge stared ahead in silence.

"I can see that you do remember, Judge. And you got them their certificate, didn't you? It was an amazing accomplishment for someone who didn't do that kind of work. After you got them the certificate and they built their new hospital, the owners of Pee Dee Health Systems — an insurance consortium, I believe — were very grateful, and gave your law firm all of its defense work. I understand their work accounts for almost $2 million annually to the firm's gross revenues. It was a singularly profitable piece of work for you."

Green's stare drifted to the edge of his desk as he listened and waited for what he feared.

"Just how did you pull it off? The state bureaucrats recommended against the certificate. There was no public support for a new hospital. Remember?" Moore stood and leaned on the desk with his outstretched arms. "Don't be modest, Judge. I'll tell you how you did it. Pee Dee's owners offered a very generous donation to several state senators with a lot of influence. And you figured out how to transfer the money to them — should we say launder it — so that no one got caught. As I understand it, you actually took care of that part of it personally — the bag man. And except for the money trail — all those normally confidential bank records — it would be as if nothing ever happened. Just the state board doing the right thing."

Green, raised his head, "How ...?"

"How'd I know?" Moore rolled his eyes. "Come on, Steve, you can't be that naïve. We're the White House, remember? We knew about all this when we appointed you. None of it turned up in your FBI file. But the Secret Service can be much more ... thorough, let's say. They spend a lot of time with money, banks, and all that. This was right up their alley. The president felt this didn't affect your ability to be a fine judge." He laughed.

"I've already been confirmed."

"Well, exactly. We don't want you to step down."

"What do you want?"

Moore pointed his finger directly at Green's face. "You will dismiss the state's case. Completely. Do it so that they can't bring any more like it. And do it fast." He was no longer smiling. "If you don't have the stomach for it, think about this, Judge. All of the files about your petty bribery will be released. First, to the Senate; second, to the Justice Department for appropriate action; and last, but not least, to the press." He laughed again. "The press. You can't live with 'em. You can't live without l'em."

"I can't...."

"Sure you can. You have no choice." Moore walked around to the bookshelf behind the judge's chair and picked up the picture of his family. He dropped the picture onto the desk in front of the judge. "Think about them."

Green lifted the picture, his wife and two sons smiling up at him through the shattered glass.

* * *

Sailing is what he wanted to do. The thought of it made him feel alive, exhilarated. He walked down the narrow wooden pier carrying the cooler. It was a warm day, and they would need the cold drinks. Kitty followed behind him. It would be a perfect day.

"Rex!" Matt called to him from the boat. They must have cleaned her up. The *Miss Kitty* hadn't looked this good in a long time. The woodwork gleamed. He made a note to spend more time working on her himself.

Jim was forward, lifting the jib through the hatch and rigging it so it could be raised. "Hi, Rex. She's ready to get underway."

He took the tiller and started the motor. They glided along the creek on a rising tide toward the river. With the boat riding the gentle waves in the river, Rex cut the motor and secured it. Matt raised the mainsail and Jim did the same with the jib. The wind filled the bright white sails, pulling the boat fast over the swells. How long had it been since he'd felt the wind blowing through his hair like this? Kitty handed out drinks, beers for him and the guys. He heard their laughter mixed with the sound of the bow slicing through the river, the flapping of the canvas, and the metal lines clanking against the mast.

The river spread before him, wide and blue in the reflection of the clear summer sky. "Oh look!" Kitty said. "Dolphins."

A pair of dolphins surfaced off their bow, their curved, black bodies sliding beneath the water.

"This is as far as we can go, Rex," Matt pointed to a dock at the end of a long walkway across the marsh. They lowered the sails and the hull slid gently along the edge of the floating dock. Matt and Jim stepped off the boat. They both shook his hand. He raised the sails and the hull again rode swiftly through the waves. He turned to look at the dock as he took the tiller. The two young men watched them sail away. He traded salutes with them.

His arms felt so much stronger. How much this seemed like those other times, so long ago on the Chesapeake, just he and his family. The *Miss Kitty* passed under the soaring twin spans of the Cooper River bridges. Off the starboard bow was the low skyline of Charleston, marked by the spires of her churches. He loved this warm place, this adopted home of rivers to sail, and so many friends.

Kitty's hand was on his arm. "Rex, we need to stop there at the park." She gestured to the pier of the park at the end of Vendue Range. The one with the fountains, he remembered. Kitty embraced him, oblivious to the people strolling or lounging on the swings and benches of the park. "I'll always love you," she said, and kissed him again, long and sweetly. He held the boat steady as she gingerly crossed onto the pier. He stood and pulled the sails back up the mast. On the dock his wife waved and blew him a kiss.

He turned the bow to the mouth of the harbor. The wind strengthened, and the little boat cut even more quickly through the water, rougher as he approached the ocean. He tacked past Castle Pinckney and sailed through the narrows between Sumter and Moultrie, leaving the harbor behind. The Atlantic beckoned beyond the jetties. The lighthouse on Sullivan's Island blinked at him. He couldn't remember when he felt so strong. The years fell away like petals in a summer wind. It was as though he were a young man again.

On the horizon, the ocean's surface was suddenly calm and smooth. The sun reflected there, he supposed that was it, and lit the sky in a bright, golden light. He steered the boat out to the great sea, salty wind rushing over his face.

In the hospital room, miles behind him, the monitor at the nurses' station sounded the alarm indicating that Rex Skanchy was gone.

Chapter 18

They pulled the casket from the rear of the hearse along the rollers until he could grab the metal handle. An American flag was carefully laid over the surface. On the other side, Matt Reicher took the handle. In turn, each pallbearer lifted part of the weight of Rex Skanchy, and they carried him into St. Mary's Church. Jim McNeely noticed it was full. Many uniforms were scattered among the mourners. Matt was in his dress whites. At the last minute, Jim pulled his dress blues out of the plastic wrap. They seemed like the only appropriate thing for him to wear to honor a casualty of America's wars.

It was the first time that his children had lost someone they loved to the mystery of death. He had known this day was near for so long, but he was unprepared to explain to them that Rex was gone. His own grief was, at once, magnified, and pre-empted by the anguish of his children. He and Alicia gathered them together and told them that Rex had finally lost his fight with the cancer. Katherine burst into a desperate, wailing cry and would not be consoled. Alicia took her from John's room and held her in her lap, as she had when Katherine was a baby.

John sat in silence for a while, trying to absorb the unthinkable. The delightful man who had always been part of his life, who had loved him like a third grandfather, the man who carved wonderful birds from blocks of wood, and who could answer any question about the things that grew and lived around them... had now left him forever. The boy lifted his head to look at his father, "I don't want Rex to be gone." He began to sob. "He'll never hug me anymore."

The Skanchy's house was crowded after the funeral. The Catholic priest spoke warmly of the man who would be missed by so many. In the backyard, Matt and Jim walked along the path around the formal garden Rex had designed. "What did Rex say about those bastards spying on you?" Matt asked.

"I didn't tell him. I couldn't. He called me after the hearing and congratulated me. If he saw the news, I guess he knew about the rest. He loved this country so much."

"I love this country, too, and I hate what the bastards do to it. Give Rex credit. He knew there has never been any shortage of bastards." They walked in silence to the edge of the garden. "What the hell is this?" They stood at the end of a long rectangle of shorter, softer grass."

"It's for Bocci Ball."

Matt smiled. "Only Rex."

"I don't know why I've waited so long to say this, Matt, but you need to go to her."

Matt shot him an angry look. "What?"

"Linda. Your wife. Quit being stupid. Go to Harrisburg and tell her you're dying here without her. It's true, so you might as well tell her." He saw Matt was only glaring at him. "Rex can't tell you anymore not to be a fool. But he would, if he were here. So, I'm telling you. Go."

Matt shook his head and walked stiffly from the yard.

* * *

Jim drove alone to Florence. Holland and Geddings would meet him at the courthouse for the hearing before Judge Green. The purpose was to hear the government's motion to vacate Judge Richardson's order issued only the previous week. Green had granted the government's request for an expedited hearing, causing Jim to spend three long days and nights preparing the state's brief. What the government was seeking was extraordinary. Instances of a federal judge granting a request to revise an order already issued were rarer than a solar eclipse. Jim felt confident that a new judge like Green would never vacate the decision of the second most senior district judge.

The highway wove through broad fields of cotton and soybeans and a series of small farm towns to the outskirts of Florence. He found the courtroom and entered to wait on his colleagues. Already seated at one of the tables were Art Emery, from the U.S. attorney's office, and a man he did not recognize.

"Hi, Art," Jim said.

Emery introduced him to the other lawyer, the chief of environmental defense at the Justice Department.

Jim shook his hand, "Welcome to Florence."

"Thanks." The justice lawyer smiled. "It looks like a cute little town. I don't get to come to many quaint places like this."

"Quaint. That's Florence to a tee." Jim glanced at Emery, who looked away in embarrassment.

"Is Drew Holland joining us?"

"He is."

"You know," Emery continued, "in studying the transcript from the last hearing, I have to say that Drew is fortunate to have been before such a sympathetic judge. In most parts of the nation, our federal judges would not have tolerated such theatrics. I can think of one in California who would have slapped him with contempt for some of the things he did."

Our federal judges, Jim thought. *The arrogant prick.*

"I find that in many backwater locations lawyers regard the rules of procedure in federal court as only advisory," he laughed, "not what they are intended to be. The structure that preserves the ... the real majesty of the courtroom. You know, without that, we can't have a real functioning—"

Jim, having reached his limit, said, "Tell me, what would *your* federal judges in most of the nation think of breaking and entering the offices of opposing counsel, and other *cute, quaint* little acts of low life spying? Pardon me, but I'm just not in the mood for a sermon from a sanctimonious federal lawyer this morning. Maybe some other time."

The justice department lawyer stopped smiling. He lifted his chin and peered down his narrow face at Jim, who fixed him with a vicious stare.

"Jim," called Geddings to him from the door to the courtroom, "Drew wants to chat a minute outside."

In the hall, Holland addressed them. "Who is that guy?"

"That pompous ass is chief of environmental defense at main justice. He's Muldoon's boss." Geddings chuckled.

"It didn't look like he was an old college pal," Holland said, smiling.

"Where do they find these guys? Jesus, if one more starts preaching to me, I swear I'm going to tear his head off."

"O.K. Feel better? Let's go to work." Holland led them into the courtroom just as the bailiff walked to the bench.

"Oyez. Oyez. This court will come to order. The United States District Court for the District of South Carolina is now in session, the Honorable Stephen Lamar Green presiding. God bless the United States and this Honorable Court." The bailiff walked to the front of the bench and took a seat, as did the court reporter and the deputy clerk. Green strode quickly to the high-backed chair behind the bench.

He picked up a folder and leafed through to a tabbed page. "All right gentlemen, please tell me who is here for each side." After the lawyers introduced themselves, he continued, "This morning I want to address the motion to vacate by the government in the case of *South Carolina* v. *The Department of Energy.* The order under consideration is the recent order by my colleague Judge Malcolm Richardson granting a preliminary injunction and forbidding the government to proceed with plans to transport nuclear weapons material from Russia to this state without first preparing an environmental impact statement. Gentlemen, I have read both parties' briefs and the entire record. Have there been any changes in the facts since the first proceeding?"

Holland and the justice department attorney assured him there had not.

"Very, well, gentlemen, I see no need to belabor this issue with oral argument. I'm ready to rule." He lifted a page from the front of the folder. "Having reviewed the arguments of both parties, the motion by the United States will be granted. The order by Judge Richardson will be vacated."

Holland rocked back in his chair, stunned.

Judge Green continued. "The testimony of Dr. Anthony DeSilva will be stricken as a violation of applicable regulations and statutes governing post-employment activities of former federal employees. This is necessary to protect the integrity of the multitude of federal agencies.

"Without this testimony, the state's argument concerning a worst-case scenario fails for lack of proof. There is, therefore, no showing of an existing or likely future NEPA violation by the United States. Judge Richardson was correct in his analysis that the state's regulations governing importation of nuclear material are inapplicable to the United States. As neither basis for its suit survives, the preliminary injunction granted in favor of the state will be dissolved.

"Further, as this is the third time in less than ten years in which the state has filed nearly identical challenges to the same federal policy, this court will enjoin all future suits as an unwarranted burden on the resources of this court and of the United States government. The court is mindful of the strong emotions that can be sparked by the subject of nuclear materials, but we are a country founded on the proposition that we should be governed by law, and not emotion. And the law clearly marks the path that we must follow in this case.

"Not mentioned in the government's motion is the latter portion of the order in which Judge Richardson ordered an investigation by the U.S. Marshals Service into the evidence indicating improper activities by the United States. This court has reviewed the results of that investigation to date and concluded the interests of justice and judicial economy will be best served by terminating the inquiry. The resignation statement by the former United States attorney, A. Bradley Sweatman, shows that he was the sole person responsible for these outrages against the state and her attorneys. The investigation is hereby ended and sanctions imposed on the United States, to wit: The United States will pay all costs and attorneys' fees incurred up to this date, with applicable interest. The state will provide a complete accounting of such costs to the U.S. attorney's office within fifteen days, and they will be paid by check from the United States not later than fifteen days after receipt of the accounting."

"Your Honor," the justice department lawyer said, rising from his chair, "the government would like to note its objection—"

"Sit down. Be glad I'm not ordering someone to go to jail.... Does anyone have any questions about my order?" he said, laying the paper down.

"Yes, Your Honor." Holland stood glaring at Green.

"Yes, Mr. Holland?"

"Your Honor, did a man named C. A. Moore from the White House visit you last week?" Holland's eyes flashed.

"You are in contempt of court, Mr. Holland," Green said evenly. "You will make payment of one thousand dollars to the clerk of court by Monday at 5:00 p.m. or you will be arrested and confined until payment is made. Are there any other questions?"

Holland was silent.

"No, Your Honor," the justice department lawyer said quietly.

Holland responded tersely, "The state notes its objection, for the record, to the revision of Judge Richardson's order, Your Honor."

"Fine." Green slapped the gavel loudly. "This matter is ended." He stood and walked rapidly to the exit behind him.

The justice department lawyer picked up his briefcase. As he walked toward the aisle, he paused in front of the table where Holland, Geddings, and Jim collected their things in shocked silence. He watched them and smiled when Jim looked up. He shook his head and walked to the exit behind the gallery.

* * *

Stephen Green walked calmly back to his office, forcing down the urge to run. His hands didn't start to shake until he closed his door. How did Holland know about Moore coming to see him? The nervous twitching in his hands spread along his arms. His whole body began to convulse in waves of tremors. Just in time, he clutched the trash can beside his desk and vomited. Wiping his mouth on a handkerchief, he covered his face with his hands and laid it on the top of the fine, antique desk. "Oh, my God," he moaned.

* * *

In the solicitor's office at the county courthouse, Holland called the governor. Blackie listened intently. When Holland finished, he asked if Green's decision could be appealed. He assured him that it could. Blackie directed them to prepare the appeal.

"You all did everything the state could have expected. I need to make a public statement, but I want to coordinate it with you guys. The press will have already reported Green's decision."

That's not all they're going to report, Holland thought.

After Bob Geddings and Jim McNeely left, Holland found a phone where he could have privacy. He had made a decision that would haunt him all his life.

For many years, one of Drew Holland's most frequent fishing partners had been a regional reporter for one the wire services. Holland closed the door of the tiny office he'd borrowed and dialed the number. "I've got something that might be a story for you."

"Drew, you're not going to reveal to the public the location of the best fishing spot behind Dewees Island, I hope?" The reporter was intrigued. Not once in their friendship had Holland given him so much as a lead.

"What I have is a story that needs to be told. It's important that you never tag me as a source. It's vital. Can you agree on that?"

"Sure. But I need to be able to verify what you tell me." He noted the anger in Holland's voice. "Is this something you're involved in as a lawyer, Drew?"

"Yeah. Don't worry about verification. I can give you that. Remember Judge Richardson's order enjoining the feds from bringing any plutonium into the state without doing an EIS?"

"Yes. That was a big win. He was going to look into who spied on you guys, too."

"The case was transferred to Judge Green in Florence. Today Green vacated Richardson's order. He threw out the injunction and forbade the state to ever bring another challenge to the importation of nuclear material. He also terminated the investigation into the feds' spying. He claimed that Sweatman's resignation ends the matter."

"Damn, Drew. That's a tough one to swallow."

"Listen to me. Here's the real story. Last week the White House aide in charge of the whole plutonium project visited Green in his office in Florence. *Last week!* This morning, after he screwed us with his ruling, I asked him if this C. A. Moore guy had visited him. He fined me a thousand dollars for contempt."

"Jesus Christ.... How do you know this?"

"My paralegal saw the son of a bitch go into Green's office, saw them shake hands and go behind closed doors. But you want to be able to verify? They make you sign in with the guard in the lobby of the federal courthouse up here. The sheets are on file in the U.S. Marshals' office. All you do is ask for them under the Freedom of Information Act."

"Shit. You know what this looks like?"

"It's a goddamned set up, that's what it is! It doesn't just look like one. It smells like one."

When he hung up, Drew Holland leaned back in the chair. His head hurt. *The bastards*, he thought. *The no good bastards!*

* * *

The reporter immediately called the U.S. Marshals' office. No, they didn't have the sheets from Florence yet. They wouldn't come in until the end of the month. If he would like to ask for them, he could write to the Florence clerk's office. They gave him the name, address, and phone number.

He called the clerk's office in Florence. They would be glad to send him the sheets for the previous week, if he would ask in writing. Yes, they could fax them out right away if he would fax his request. There wouldn't be many sheets.

In one hour, his fax machine began to beep as it received a call, and the digital data streamed across the phone line. Twenty sheets slid from the tray of the machine. He scanned them as they appeared. On the eighth sheet, he saw the firm name of Holland, Rollins, Jerald, & McNeely next to that of their paralegal. Five lines down were the printed name of C. A. Moore and a scrawled signature. "White House" was printed plainly in the last column.

"Jesus H. Christ!" he said aloud. He reached for the phone and started gathering phone numbers — for Stephen L. Green and for C. A. Moore's extension at the White House.

* * *

Matt Reicher had almost forgotten how green it was in summer. He looked for the exit while navigating through the busy traffic on Interstate 83. Almost too late, he spotted the sign for Camp Hill and turned onto the exit ramp. The two wrapped presents slid across the seat and dropped to the floor of the car.

The road wound through the base of the mountains south of Harrisburg. He drove through wooded hills and down a steep slope. An old metal bridge crossed a creek at the bottom of a little gorge, the water cascading over scattered boulders.

Linda's parents' home was suddenly on his right. Matt pulled the rental car to the curb. The doubts about his coming to Pennsylvania came rushing back, now that he was actually there.

After his anger receded, he saw that Jim was right — that he had no choice but to go to Linda and ask her to come back. Now, standing at the door, he wasn't sure. As he stood frozen, unable to reach for the knocker, the door suddenly flew open.

Linda started to hurry through onto the porch, when she saw him and screamed in surprise. She stumbled and began to fall backward into the hall. Matt grabbed her by the waist.

"My God, what are you doing here? You scared me half to death! Is something wrong?"

This wasn't how he planned things at all. Still holding her halfway from the hall floor, Matt blurted out the truth, "Everything is wrong without you. I need you to come back." She pulled herself free and stood facing him, smoothing her dress. "Please—"

"Matt, this isn't—"

"Don't say it. Don't say anything except you hate my guts and can't stand my ass anymore. Say that and I'm gone for good. But if you can't say it, don't give me any other reason not to put our family back together. I can't stand it any longer."

"Matt, what's this about?"

"I can't live like this. I love you. You and the girls are my life."

"The navy, Matt."

"It's trying to throw me out, but I'm not going without a fight. It's part of me ... and I need you to share all of my life, including the navy."

"Who told you to come up here and do this?"

Matt stared at her in silence, but she saw the answer just the same.

"Jim told you to come, didn't he? You are a lucky man to have a friend like him." She grabbed a napkin from the counter and dried her eyes.

"I almost forgot the presents I brought." He ran to the car and returned with the wrapped presents and a plastic container. "This one is for you from Jim. Just a little taste of South Carolina. See what you're missing."

"Boiled peanuts. You did come up here to seduce me."

*   *   *

In the dim light he saw a dozen men sprawled in various positions, all watching the large television at the end of the room. All of them were drunk, except Morey. Nat promised his aunt that his cousin from New York would not get drunk, and he sincerely agreed with her that nineteen was much too young. He didn't say anything about the movies.

"Ooooh. Yeah!" The men shouted in unison as another sex act was culminated on the screen. Nat was at the bar. He fixed himself another drink and scanned the crowd. He wasn't drunk, exactly. The last thing he needed on his wedding day was a hangover. It would have surprised most to learn that this large, powerful man suffered a particularly virulent reaction to alcohol. Nat leaned on the bar and watched the revelers. There were men from his National Guard company, including Henry Staggers. Next to Morey was another cousin from Boston. Mark Killian and six other officers from the 1189th had been trying to organize a trip to a topless nightspot, but were now content with the x-rated videos. "All right!" they cheered as another couple — or maybe it was three, he couldn't tell — got down to business.

"Nat, this is great, man!" Morey dropped into one of the bar chairs next to Nat.

Nat leaned closer to his cousin. "Morey, you've been drinking, pal. I promised your mama."

"I won't tell," he confided in a heavy, and slurred, Brooklyn accent and rejoined the others on the floor in front of the television.

"Yeah, but we've got to show these gentiles how to dance tomorrow." He looked into the crowd of gawking men. "Shit," Nat said to himself. He patted Mark Killian on the shoulder, "Can you give me a hand? Dad's passed out over here." He and Mark made their way to Nat's father and lifted him over the heads of the men, laying him down on the couch in the adjoining living room. "Boy is he gone."

"Your mom is gonna cut your ass."

"Not if you're the one who shows up with him at the hotel. Here's the cab fare. Thanks, I knew you were perfect for Best Man."

Mark looked at the bills Nat shoved in his hand and frowned.

*   *   *

The little Catholic church was packed. With the exception of his cousin, all of the groomsmen arrayed next to Nat wore army dress blues. A dozen more guests wore the uniform as well, including Jim McNeely. At the altar were the priest from the small Florence parish and the rabbi from the even smaller temple in Kingstree. They were clearly enjoying themselves. In the racks in front of each pew were programs explaining the unique service. Nat and Susan, neither deeply religious, had labored to blend elements together from both the Jewish and Catholic ceremonies.

After the final exchange of vows, Nat accepted a crystal goblet from Mark and wrapped it in a large cloth. He laid it down on the step next to the altar rail. With one quick movement, he smashed the glass. Susan Ryan's family looked at one another but thoroughly enjoyed the show.

They left the church under six arched swords, including one held by Henry Staggers, who could not remember when he had as much fun at a wedding. The reception was a short drive away. Food was spread on two groups of tables. A band greeted the guests with music that spanned the spectrum, but it was heavily weighted in favor of country and western.

At a table surrounded by Nat's appreciative family and many curious guests, the couple signed the Jewish wedding contract, an intricately decorated document provided by Nat's Uncle Aaron. After the food tables were taken away, the dancing began and lasted for another two hours. Every effort had been made to make these disparate groups feel at ease, and it showed.

The band finished a Garth Brooks song, and the large crowd on the dance floor applauded loudly. After a brief pause, they began a piece that was very familiar to half the guests, and exotic to the other. Nat walked over to Mark Killian, "It's time to dance, big boy." Nat arranged the men in a circle. After an awkward start that brought raucous laughter from the observers, Nat and his cousins managed to whip the dancers into shape. Royal blue uniform trousers and dress pants alike moved rhythmically in a circle, dipping and swaying in the ancient dance of the children of Israel. The crowd began to clap in time to the lilting melody.

Susan slid up beside Nat after the dance as he toweled the sweat from his forehead. She took him in her arms and said quietly into his ear, "I don't want this to end."

He kissed her, every part of him alive with happiness he had never imagined. "It won't. I promise."

*　*　*

The shouts from the crowd — it seemed that no one had left — as the couple ran to the car under a shower of rice were still fresh as Nat drove along the dark highway. Susan — now Susan Engle, he reminded himself — rested her head against his shoulder. In Charlotte they would stay the night in the honeymoon suite of the best hotel in the city. The next day they would fly to Quebec.

He had never felt as alive as he did that night. He felt he truly understood what all of the endlessly repeated descriptions of marriage meant. He recalled the scenes from the day. Images of the faces of his friends and the men he loved and respected came back to him ... and there was the woman whose head rested on his shoulder as he drove, the woman he loved more than life itself and who would be with him forever. All of life seemed spread out before him, exciting, warm, and happy.

In the hotel suite, he and his new wife made love with a tenderness he had not known before. He felt he could go on forever.

She rested her head on his chest, running her hand through the hair that ran to his stomach. "Nat, I'm going to have a baby."

"I know. We'll have a bunch."

"No. I mean I'm going to have one. I'm sure of it."

"What ... what are you saying?"

"I'm pregnant, Nat."

He jerked himself to a sitting position. "Really! You're sure?"

"Sure. By March we'll be Mom and Dad."

He circled her in his arms. She saw there were tears streaming down his cheeks. "I love you so much," he said, and he pressed his mouth to hers.

* * *

It was almost seven o'clock when Jim pulled into the drive behind Matt Reicher's jeep. He wondered why Matt wasn't waiting outside, as he normally was, studying the morning paper and nursing a cup of coffee. He rang the bell next to the kitchen door. The second ring also went unanswered.

As Jim turned to walk back to his car, the kitchen door latch clicked and the door opened. Matt was there, dressed only in a pair of shorts, and obviously right out of bed. He waved Jim into the kitchen without speaking. Perplexed, Jim stepped up into the laundry corner and followed Matt to the kitchen, where he was pouring a large mug of coffee. He handed the mug to Jim. "What's wrong with you this morning?" Jim asked him as Matt splashed several handfuls of water onto his face. He grabbed a dishtowel and dried himself. Over his shoulder, Jim could see at the end of the hall a figure was walking toward them in the darkened passageway. "Oh, shit, Matt," he whispered. "Why didn't you say something?"

He smiled and waved his hand dismissively. As the decidedly female figure moved slowly toward them, Jim said, "O.K. I'll take a rain check. While I'm up here I think I'll go and try to beat the crowd." He put the mug down and turned for the door.

"Hold it," Matt laughed, grabbing his shoulder and pulling him back.

"Hi, Jim." He turned around to see Linda Reicher, also just out of bed, and wearing one of Matt's uniform shirts.

Jim stared in surprise for a moment. Then they all began to laugh. "You came down here just to ruin my golf game?" Jim teased.

"Sorry."

"Are the girls still asleep?"

"They're not here. Mom's keeping them while I... check out the terrain." She gazed at the den. "I've got to do something with this furniture." She was beside Matt, and slipped her arm around his waist, nuzzling close to his bare chest. They smiled at each other, and then at Jim.

"O.K. Think I'll hit the course. Call me when you come up for air."

Matt followed him from the house. At the car, Matt squeezed the back of Jim's neck, "Boiled peanuts... I never would have thought of that. And thanks."

Chapter 19

There were no signs among the crowd. But the number of people had grown since the night before. No planning brought the thirty angry persons to the parking lot, but there was purpose. They faced the door where they knew U.S. District Judge Stephen L. Green would exit, and they were determined that he would hear what they had to say.

The story by Holland's friend was featured on the front pages of the morning papers the day before. It described in detail a meeting between Judge Green and a member of President Seekings' staff, a man named C. A. Moore, and said that Mr. Moore was in charge of the plan to bring Russian plutonium to the U.S., probably to South Carolina. The meeting occurred only one week before Judge Green reversed the order by Judge Richardson halting those plans until the government complied with environmental laws. The story implied manipulation of the judge by the president. But the governor's spokesperson did more than imply wrongdoing; she read a statement explicitly accusing the administration of a pattern of wrongdoing, including spying and shameless interference with the federal courts. The governor promised an appeal and a full investigation. Judge Green refused to speak to the reporter.

The television news led with the story. Local stations reported little else. Press offices of both United States senators from South Carolina announced that a meeting of the full congressional delegation from the state would be held soon and a full accounting would be demanded. The congressman from the Sixth District called for a special prosecutor. That night a crowd had formed at the parking lot, but had merely stood and watched Stephen Green walk to his car. But the larger crowd that was assembled the second night was anything but quiet. At the first sight of Green, a trio of young construction workers nearest the building began whistling at the nervous judge. Others moved up to surround Green as he walked towards his car. "What kind of a judge are you!" a voice shouted. Others mocked him.

"What did the White House promise you, Judge?"

"Are you corrupt or just stupid?"

Finally, his path was blocked completely. Frantic, he looked around to find he was encircled by the angry group of young men. "Let me pass!" he yelled, his voice cracking.

The crowd was unmoved. "Tell us what you did, you asshole!" A burly mechanic demanded.

"I won't be bullied. Get out of my way! Do you want to go to jail!" Green noticed at the rear of the crowd a television cameraman holding his camera on his shoulder, filming the specter of the federal judge trapped in the parking lot. The sight of the camera shored up Green's courage. "I won't warn you again. Let me pass, or I promise you will each be charged with threatening a federal official." Many of those surrounding Green saw the camera, too, and began to move away from the judge. A narrow path opened from Green to his car. Safely in the car, Green jerked the shift into reverse, and lurched out of his parking space and away from the mob and their catcalls. He sped onto the street from the lot.

Green's wife was not at the house when he arrived. He rushed to his bedroom and started the shower. The spray of water massaging his neck did nothing to relieve the terrible sense of dread. He had already resolved to request protection from the U.S. Marshals until this hysteria passed. His wife had been alarmed by the images on the television news of the ugly scene behind the courthouse.

"It's just a bunch of thugs blowing off steam. I'll bet half of those rednecks were drunk," Green said bitterly.

That night, Green tossed fitfully, denied sleep by fear. "Two thirty," he moaned to himself. He turned over and then heard the terrible sound of shattering glass, followed by a loud thud. The crash of the brick through the living room window caused his wife to awaken screaming. Green leapt from the bed to look at the street below. Under the street light was a non-descript pickup truck. He couldn't even make out the color as the truck noisily disappeared into the darkness. In the living room, he gingerly stepped around the shards of glass from the shattered picture window strewn across the floor. The brick was wrapped in a piece of notebook paper. He pulled the paper from the brick, his hands trembling. A single word was printed on the paper in black magic marker: "*JUDAS.*"

* * *

Terry Wilkins stopped at the intersection and checked his directions. The motel shouldn't be far. This was only the second time that the man who called himself Carl had asked to meet him. On three occasions Carl left messages at his office in the Pentagon to call various repair shops: one an auto mechanic, one a stereo shop, and one a tire store. All were signals Carl wanted to speak to him. Each time he stopped at a pay phone on the way back to the farm and made the call. And each time he reported what C. A. Moore had revealed about his plans for bringing the plutonium out of Russia.

He was surprised at his success. After only a couple of drinks to smooth the way, Moore responded to his casual questions about the project with enthusiasm. As he sat up nights listening to Moore describe the surveillance of the governor and his lawyers, he recalled what the marine at the Pentagon said about Moore's capacity to destroy anyone who stood in the way of his mission. When Moore talked about the intricate scheme to remove one judge and the blackmail of the second judge, the young soldier had to hide his fear.

Carl had been right. It was all too easy to become the confidant of this strange, intense — and frightening — man. He wondered how he would ever cut these new ties forged so effortlessly. Before, it had all been neat and uncomplicated. But things were very different now. He shivered with a chill that ran down his spine as he thought of Moore's hands on his body, grasping him with a new, more intense need, one that outlived his sexual release — a need that scared Terry Wilkins to death.

He turned into the parking lot that surrounded the motel pool. It was an old-style roadside motel, with a row of one-story units that formed a semicircle around the parking lot and pool. A small restaurant adjoined the office. He slowly drove around the lot until he spotted room number 105.

"Come in. Come in, Sergeant Wilkins," Carl greeted him at the door. "Sit down." He retreated to a table next to the sink and returned with two glasses, one of which he handed to Terry. "Have a little Scotch."

Wilkins accepted the drink in silence. "So, you have some important news for me, Terry."

He drained the glass and put it on the table. "I think so. C. A. says most of the details have been decided."

"Excellent. Tell me ... Wait, let me turn this on." He retrieved a small tape recorder from his briefcase and sat it between them. "Go ahead."

Terry looked at the recorder for a moment, then shrugged. "The route is fixed now. The trains will run from Sunny Point in North Carolina to Florence by way of Mullins and Marion. From there, they go to Sumter, Orangeburg, Barnwell, and finally end up at the Savannah River Site near Aiken. The first ship will arrive in the middle of September; the second, in the first week of October. After that they'll run every two weeks until the end of the year. They won't resume until the middle of next year. Each ship will leave from the army's port at Rotterdam and take about six days to reach Sunny Point."

Carl listened patiently as the young soldier spoke. "There is no way to know exactly when the train will leave until the ship is unloaded. That's when the CSX dispatcher will assign the train a number and a schedule."

"Won't that be kept secret?"

"Not the train number or its schedule. C. A. has decided that the trains should be unmarked and treated as though they were empty cars leaving Sunny Point. They will not be marked in any way. It'll look just like a freight train anywhere. No hazardous cargo placards or anything." Wilkins walked to the bottle and ice bucket and filled his glass again.

"What about security?"

"None that's visible. The whole idea is to make the train inconspicuous. Now that they don't have to do any of that environmental bullshit they've been fighting about, they don't have to tell anybody. The railroad will think the cars are empty. They won't ask any questions. The rate will be three times what they normally get, and it won't even be their cars or engines. What do they care?"

"Isn't there a requirement that they keep a nuclear response team alerted to the location of material like this?"

"Look, Carl, or whatever your name is, I'm an E6 operations sergeant. How the shit would I know about regulations like that? What I told you is what I know. No security. No monitoring by anybody except C. A. and some guy named Felix Hubbard at Bolling Air Force Base. Got it!"

"O.K. O.K. Calm down. It just seems a little odd."

"Is there anything about this that isn't odd? "

Carl studied him for a moment. "It sounds like that's the most you could tell us, doesn't it Terry?"

"That's right."

Carl turned off the recorder. "No need to waste the tape. What are you planning to do?"

"I'm getting off the farm," he blurted out. He turned away, embarrassed, and stared at the door.

"I see." Carl picked up the recorder and packed it into his briefcase. "I have spoken to my clients with the Blue Ocean Fund. They're very grateful for your help."

"What goddamned choice did I have?"

"I understand. In any event, they think you may need some more cash." He pulled a manila envelope from the briefcase. "In there you'll find what you need to access a bank account we've opened in your name at Commonwealth Bank and Trust. You'll find it has $100,000 in it, courtesy of my clients. There are also papers to prove you inherited the money from a man in the Bahamas. His will explains that he was indebted to your grandfather. Did you know that your grandfather once spent some time in Nassau? Those should help you explain the money to the IRS or anyone else who gets curious."

Wilkins pulled the ATM card from the envelope and stared at it.

Carl continued, "I imagine it's occurred to you, too, by now that getting away from your friend poses its own challenges."

"Yeah, I've thought about it." *Every time I see him, every night when I can't sleep, when I look at him and wonder what he might do.* When he slept, he lived through a dozen different versions of Moore's revenge, waking feverish and sweating from a nightmare tragedy inflicted on his wife and son. He castigated himself. *How could I have let this happen?*

"Terry, you need to stay on until the first train leaves. I'll talk to you then. After that, you'll never hear from us again."

"Fine." Wilkins picked up the envelope and left the room. In his car on the road back to Route 66, he glanced at the manila envelope next to him. *Money. Now, I'm the complete whore.*

*   *   *

He picked up the glass next to the laptop computer. The Scotch was good. It slid easily down his throat, and he poured another. Carl read the text of the message he was preparing to send to the e-mail address his clients gave him. Soon, the information young Sergeant Wilkins gave him would be transferred instantly to Petrozavodsk. Liquor and business never mixed well. He knew that. As he stared at the screen, he knew he shouldn't think. He needed only to click on the icon, and his job would be nearly done. The money he would earn would be more than he had cleared in his best two years.

But still he sat and stared at the glowing screen. Ready to be encoded and transmitted to his clients was the information they sought. All of it from an unimpeachable source. Why was this so difficult? A hundred other times, Carl had pried information from unwilling mouths. His tools were always the sordid secrets people left lying around, so easy for him to pick up, sharpen, and use for his purpose. The soldier had been gone now for an hour. And Carl was drunk. The Scotch was nearly gone.

The extra money had been his idea. His clients accepted his explanation that their source would be more willing to cooperate if he knew he had strong financial insurance against a possible ugly and dangerous separation from his powerful friend. The soldier, he knew, would have never asked for it. Carl knew soldiers. He didn't like what he had done to Staff Sergeant Terry Wilkins. He knew Wilkins would be lucky to survive.

And there was a smell about the business with the plutonium he didn't like. None of it added up, despite a lifetime spent analyzing people and their schemes. He smelled danger, subtle and furtive, but real enough, he was certain. After the job was over in October, he would take a long vacation. Somewhere he could drink good Scotch and watch the news to see what happened to Moore's goddamned trains. He clicked the mouse, and his report on the information from Terry Wilkins went instantly to Colonel Yigor Matveev.

* * *

"We will need to watch them closely, Yigor. When they load the trains, we must see exactly what they put inside the cars. Our American soldier tells us there will be no security, but that is very hard to believe. We'll watch the bastards from start to finish when they run their first train. And then we'll know exactly what they do and don't do." Mikail Plekanov leaned over the seat to speak to Matveev, who was in the back of the car. Sasha Dunitsev was driving the three men south along U.S. 17 through the fields and crossroads of the southeastern corner of

North Carolina. They spent the day touring the small riverside town of Sunny Point and the area around the army's Military Ocean Terminal to the west of town, where the army operated its only major ordnance terminal on the east coast. They were headed back to their hotel in Myrtle Beach.

"It shouldn't be difficult to get inside and watch the place where they will load the train," Matveev said, studying the aerial photographs provided by the state library in Raleigh. Blown up, they illustrated in perfect detail the location of all of the rail lines on the terminal. Dunitsev would stay behind with Donskoi, and together they would prepare the points of entry through the slender security fences around the terminal for use in September when the first train was scheduled.

As they crossed into South Carolina, the highway broadened to four lanes and the sprawl of Myrtle Beach replaced tobacco and soybean fields. The Russians were silent, fascinated again by the chaotic profusion of restaurants, tee shirt shops, bars, water parks, and golf courses, particularly the miniature ones, which seemed to be everywhere.

Dunitsev stopped for a red light at an intersection across from an artificial "mountain" laced with multicolored waterfalls and adorned with huge, garishly tinted dinosaurs. Winding across the surface of the mountain, swim-suited tourists carefully bent over putters clutched in their hands, and knocked golf balls across wildly twisting Astroturf courses. Under the claws and menacing plaster mouth of a purple Tyrannosaurus, a heavyset middle-aged man in pink swim trunks coaxed his ball toward the hole. As the ball sank into the PVC cup, the man suddenly dropped his club and leapt into the air, letting out a loud yell. Dunitsev smiled at the peculiar scene.

"How did we lose?" he said.

"What did you say, Sasha?" Mikail asked.

Motioning to the dinosaur mountain, Dunitsev repeated, "How did these people beat us?"

"I don't know. What do you think Yigor? Perhaps we should have built water parks and golf mountains with orange waterfalls, instead of so many tanks." Mikail slapped the young man on the shoulder and laughed. Dunitsev was already laughing.

Yigor Matveev didn't laugh. "The two peoples in the world most often underrated are the British and the Americans. The British have not lost a war in two hundred years. And the Americans now rule the world. In Vietnam, I watched our Vietnamese comrades torture American prisoners beyond tolerance, only to be 'rewarded' with propaganda photographs of the same men signaling with their middle fingers 'Fuck you!' I imagine those men once chased little white balls across these same silly mountains, under purple dinosaurs. Drive us to the hotel, Sasha. Never take these people for granted." He returned to the study of the photographs and maps spread across his lap.

At the hotel Gregori Donskoi waited in the room for their return. Earlier in the afternoon Donskoi met with the Americans who would help them take the plutonium from the train. The Americans were members of what they called a militia group. Donskoi was confused. In Russia, the militia was the police. But these men clearly hated the American government, although he could not understand the reason. They belonged to the Northwest Territorial Militia, and they came from places called Indiana and Illinois. They were peasants. He could tell their background from their hands and their backs. Farmers, they called themselves. They enjoyed talking to him about growing wheat and barley, what he had done as a boy in the Ukraine before the army.

The Americans regarded him as a curiosity and asked him many questions, but they were not interested in discussing anything of substance with him once they realized he was not in charge. Donskoi was not offended. He was content to wait for Mikail and the others to return. The hotel room was pleasant, and the staff quickly brought whatever he ordered from room service. It amused him that they so readily accepted his accent as French. He remembered Mikail telling them they would get a car with Quebec license plates. "The Americans will think we are French Canadians. They will never know the difference in our accents. All foreigners sound French to them." He was amazed that it was true.

He sat by the bed and propped his feet on the table by the window. The ocean spread before him, seven floors below, blue and extending forever across the horizon. This was a strange place. All around him were gaudy and vulgar buildings and businesses catering to throngs of American and Canadian tourists. Yet here was the Atlantic bounding it all, unmoved, majestic, as mighty as time itself. *No wonder so many people came here*, he thought.

"I'm Thaddeus," a tall blond man said, extending his hand to Mikail. There were three of them. The same three who met with Gregori earlier. "This is Thomas, and this is Alvin," he said, introducing his companions.

The Russians shook hands. "So, Thaddeus, you want to do business with us?" Mikail said.

"We want to be partners. There's a lot we can do to help you out." Thaddeus was forthright and earnest. His two friends eyed Mikail intensely.

"And what payment do you want for your help?"

Without hesitation, the young man answered, "None. We want part of the plutonium. No more ... and no less."

Mikail smiled and nodded his head slowly. He glanced at Matveev who stood in the corner of the room. The Americans' demand was not a surprise. "Done. There will be plenty for us both. Now, let us talk about the details of the job."

For hours the five men poured over Matveev's maps. "The train will slow as it passes through these towns, no?" Mikail's finger traced a path along the map. "That is where it will be the most vulnerable. If we are prepared, it can be taken in minutes."

The train would be stopped in one of the towns along its route. The keys would be control and time. Thaddeus argued that they should create a justification for stopping the train. But they would have to control the local police for the short time required to make the plan work. The Americans had enough men to provide phony police in the vicinity of the train. Thaddeus assured Mikail they would have no trouble duplicating the uniforms of the police of whatever town was selected.

"We must each provide for our own escape, Thaddeus," Mikail cautioned.

"That won't be a problem."

Mikail wondered at the confidence of the young man. The Americans would scour every corner of the country to find stolen plutonium. No matter. The question was academic. "Then we are agreed. My friends and I will do some more investigation here, and I will select the place. We will communicate this to you, and we will complete our planning in the next weeks. Are you certain you can keep up with us, Thaddeus?" The insult was intentional. Mikail wanted to see if his would-be ally was too hotheaded.

The young man regarded Mikail calmly. "Completely. You have no need to worry."

"Good. This will be a profitable venture for us both."

Thaddeus shot back, "Profit isn't what we're about."

Mikail was silent for a moment and then said, "Tell me. What are your goals, my friend?"

"Liberty. The end of an oppressive government will give us back our freedom."

Mikail gently patted Thaddeus on the shoulder and led the Americans to the door. When it was closed behind them, Mikail leaned his back against it and closed his eyes, smiling.

"Bolsheviks," Yigor Matveev said.

"Lunatics," Mikail answered, shaking his head.

"So, Mikail Nikolaevitch, are you going to share the plutonium with our militia friends?" Matveev asked.

"Yigor, I don't think it would be safe."

The Russians laughed heartily at their joke.

* * *

"Felix, you promised me a name a month ago. I still don't have it. What am I supposed to tell the president?"

Felix Hubbard narrowed his eyes as he faced C. A. Moore's angry glare. "I can give you a name. And I can tell you there is no longer any doubt who leaked the information to Governor Haselden. What I can't give you — yet — is proof anybody could take into court."

"Who asked you to be a goddamned lawyer? I don't give a damn about court! Who is it?"

"Julieanne Harris. Can't be anybody else."

Moore tilted his head to one side. A smile cracked the scowl that darkened his face. "Julieanne. That mousy bitch."

"She's from South Carolina, some little backwater called Florence."

"Well, Felix, is that all? That's a pretty slender reason to suspect someone of violating national security."

"Her brother is the governor's best friend. They're like brothers. Her nephew is the governor's godson, named after him. He spent a week in the mansion with Haselden just... two months ago," Felix added, consulting his notes. "Julieanne has been in D.C. so long, no one thinks of her as being *from* anywhere. She worked hard to lose her accent, and whatever else might hold her back. There's nothing left of any southern belle in her."

"Damn, Felix." Moore beamed.

"She must have gotten pissed off. That's all I can figure. She has absolutely no reason to care about this project. It isn't politics. The governor is her brother's friend, not Julieanne's. My theory is that she got mad enough to feed what she knew to Haselden figuring he would bring down some kind of heat. So she told her brother — a fireman — and he passed it on to his pal, the governor."

"*My, my, my,*" Moore drawled. "What a bunch of hicks! A fireman! That's great."

"I can't prove any of this. She's too smart, and she's been around the intelligence game too long to get caught, at least up until now."

"Do you think she's still passing information to the son of a bitch?"

"I don't know. It would make sense that she would, if there were anything to tell him."

"Well, let's give her something to tell him. Set the bitch up, Felix. Fabricate something really outrageous. Otherwise, she's out of the loop on anything to do with the Russian nuclear material. Is that clear?" Felix nodded. "When she gets fed the bogus information, and she runs and tells the governor, we'll catch her. *Mah goodness, Felix, Ah believe it's agin the law to leak national security secrets.* Seekings will cook her redneck ass crispier than southern fried chicken." The pills he was taking now were stronger; they brought composure so complete that he was detached from the turmoil surrounding him. With calm, he could control it all.

Hubbard wondered what he would be able to make up that was more outrageous than the truth of what they had actually been doing for the past three months.

"Now, Felix, I have another mission for you. The plutonium and uranium 238 will be arriving in the middle of September. The president wants to ensure that the shipments are entirely secure from theft by terrorists. And we want you to handle the job."

"I thought there wasn't going to be any security with the train."

"Exactly. The train is to look like any other. In fact, I want each train to be as large as a normal freight, even if that means pulling a bunch of empty cars. Put in some tanker cars. Whatever. But no guards. No notice to police or anyone else. Once the train is on the track, it's just another train in the system. Got it?"

"Yes, sir. But I don't exactly understand what you can do to ensure there can be no theft, if there aren't any guards, and no contingency for security forces to be called in. Disguise and camouflage can only take you so far."

"That's right. Now think a minute. If you wanted to be *absolutely* sure no one could ever get their hands on what's in those railcars, what would you do?" Moore stared at Hubbard, his eyes bright and intense and eerie, the incredible message beginning to penetrate Hubbard's consciousness.

Hubbard blinked nervously. "Do you mean to ... you want to rig the cars with explosives?"

Moore winked at him and jabbed his index finger in his direction. "Now, you've got it. I want the cars rigged so that if anybody tries to get in without the right combination, they'll blow sky high, at least so badly that the plutonium is no good to the bastards."

"There are a lot of scenarios to consider here—"

"No, Felix, there's only one to consider. And that's the one where you do what I tell you."

Hubbard knew he should ask about the many unexpected things that could cause a petty thief, or a stowaway, or even an official of some kind to try and pry open the rail cars. What if the cars were derailed in an accident? But he could see in the violent expression on Moore's face that the prudent course was to keep his mouth shut, and do as he was told.

"Let me know when you've got it all arranged. O.K., Felix? Use army railcars. You'll find plenty down at Fort Eustis." He handed Felix a manila envelope. "Here are the contacts you'll need to provide the right supplies."

"Yes, sir."

"There's one more thing I need you to do for me. I want to know all the big clients of Holland, Rollins, Jerald, & McNeely. Just the big ones. The ones they can't live without. And I want to know what kinds of ... *things* ... these clients need from the federal government."

"Things?"

"Yeah. Cooperation. Favors. Permits. Licenses. Access. *Things*. Understand, Felix?"

"Yes, sir."

"Excellent. Get me the list of those clients tomorrow. Keep in touch."

* * *

Moore drove through the main gate, leaving Bolling Air Force Base. He turned onto the ramp of I-295 and headed back for the bridge across the Anacostia River and Pennsylvania Avenue. He was confident Hubbard would carry out his orders. And it was more important to him than ever that he do so. He especially wanted to hand Roger Seekings the head of the "bitch" who went behind all their backs to try and sabotage their plans. That would make up for some of the humiliation her little game had caused him. He remembered the meeting with the president after his return from South Carolina.

"What ... you were drunk? Is that it, C. A.? You signed in to the lobby of the federal courthouse and created a record that you were there *and that you work in the White House.* Amazing." Seekings had waved the front page of *The Washington Post* in his face while he yelled and paced in front of his desk. The administration's press secretary had stood silently in the rear of the president's office, trying hard to blend into the wall. "First, those idiots got caught *spying* on the opposition like a bunch of common thugs. And now I get to read how one of my staffers — *my security advisor, no less* — gets caught talking to the judge *one week* before he rules in our favor in the same case. Shall I read it to you, C. A.? 'Calls for a special prosecutor became more numerous this week with renewed allegations by South Carolina's governor. Conventional wisdom in the Capitol is that Roger Seekings cannot avoid the embarrassment of a special prosecutor if there are any more revelations about administration misconduct in this case....' Now, do I need to tell you what your future will be if that happens, C.A.?" Seekings had stopped in front of Moore, his face flushed, eyes blazing. He had turned away, then swung back quickly, slapping Moore's chest with the newspaper, letting it fall at his feet.

"Mark my words, C. A. Nothing you may have done in the past will matter one whit if there is one more story about this bullshit. One. Am I clear, C. A.? You will be gone from here. I need people I can count on."

"Yes, Mr. President."

"Get this over with! Do you realize that because of these crap stories in the press, I am now being asked by the Europeans when we will have all that shit out of Russia. I have a NATO meeting in two months, C. A. I want this all over by then. All of it, God damn it!"

The memory burned. He could hear the president's shouts as clearly as that morning a few days before. A bitter taste filled his mouth, as the searing pain of humiliation returned. But coupled to his degradation was a furious determination to get even with those responsible — Julieanne Harris and Drew Holland.

* * *

"It is even hotter here. It feels like Iraq," Dunitsev complained, returning from paying for a full tank of gas.

"Like Vietnam," Matveev corrected him. "The humidity reminds me of that cursed place."

"Sasha, we have one more police station to see ... and a highway patrol headquarters. Then I want to see all of the rail crossings. Gregori, I want plenty of pictures of those. Don't worry about being discreet." Mikail sat in the back with Matveev. As they glided slowly past the satellite station of the Florence police, Donskoi snapped a single photograph from his window.

"Mikail," Matveev spoke to him while still looking at a map of South Carolina, marked in yellow with the route they knew the train would take. "This is the place. The last thing on the minds of these people is an attack on a train in the middle of their city, much less a professional military assault. Have you ever seen a more placid place anywhere? And it is a hundred miles from the nearest military base capable of posing any threat to us. Look here, here and here. This air force base," he said pointing to Shaw in Sumter, "is close, but not equipped to respond to what we have in mind. The diversions our friends have planned will plunge the entire city into chaos. They will barely notice us."

Dunitsev reached the first rail crossing. He parked the car in the lot of a hardware store. Mikail went inside to ask the clerk if they could park the car for a short time. The tracks ran behind what appeared to be the main business and shopping district of the small city. At the point immediately in front of the city's police headquarters and its city government building, they began running. Down the tracks from the police headquarters was an overpass. An empty field lay behind the row of little businesses that included the hardware store. Matveev glanced at the city map, sent to him by the Chamber of Commerce, as he walked with Mikail along the track. Behind them, Donskoi was taking another picture.

A police cruiser slowed and parked next to the city government building. The uniformed policeman exited the car and walked slowly toward the side entrance. He hailed the two Russians, "Hey fellas. You all with the railroad?"

Mikail answered, smiling, and walking toward the policeman, "No, officer. We are Canadians. From Quebec. We are with the Ministry of Transportation. Your city has been written about in trade journals as a model for rail/highway interface in medium-sized cities. We came to see for ourselves, eh?"

"You picked a hot one for it," he said, pulling his cap from his head and wiping the sweat from his face with the sleeve of his shirt. "Well, welcome to Florence. You fellas ought to go over to Myrtle Beach while you're here. It ain't far."

"Officer, I'm afraid you have found us out. We are staying there. It seemed like a good idea to kill two birds with one stone." Mikail appraised him conspiratorially.

The young policeman laughed loudly. "Oh, I get it. Good idea." Reaching for Mikail's shoulder, he said, "Say, you boys need to go to the Crazy Horse while you're there. They've got some babes in there. Here," he pulled out his wallet and began searching, "take this. It's a free pass. It'll get you and one of your buddies in with no cover." Handing the card to Mikail, he strode to the door, smiling broadly, "Y'all have a good time."

Returning to the car, Mikail stuck his head into the hardware store as the others climbed into the car. "Merci!" he called to the clerk.

Dunitsev turned to follow the map to the next crossing. He looked worriedly at Mikail's reflection in the rear view mirror and asked, "What did the policeman say to you, Mikail?"

Mikail was studying the card, grinning. "He gave me a free pass to a striptease bar."

Chapter 20

Felix Hubbard walked across the long expanse of concrete that lay between the fence and the warehouse. The chalk-colored surface shimmered in the fierce midday sun, a final blast of heat from a summer he would be glad to see end. He mopped the sweat from his face with a handkerchief. At the warehouse door he saw Erick Giordono and Timothy Gilbert, the two army officers assigned to his team, and two civilian men he did not recognize, but whom he knew to be their contacts for the placement of the explosives.

Inside was a single boxcar. Giordono began to explain how the cars would be loaded. "Each train will carry casks of spent nuclear fuel rods. These casks are large — about seven feet tall — and they weigh 45,000 pounds. The casks carrying the plutonium are smaller. We've pulled an off-the-shelf detection system — laser triggers at the doors of each of the cars carrying plutonium. Cars without fuel rod casks or plutonium won't have any detection installed. About half the cars in every train will be empty and will travel with their doors open. Four tanker cars will be incorporated in every train."

"Tankers empty?" Hubbard asked.

"I guess so. It wouldn't make any sense to haul anything in them."

"O.K. What else?"

"The detection system will activate the detonation of the explosives wrapped around the casks."

Hubbard continued, "All right, I think you guys have the idea. Just be sure these things aren't too sensitive. I don't want them blowing up because there's a rough place in the tracks." The army officers watched the older man sweat. It was plain to them he was suffering from much more than heat. "Look, don't ask for empty tanker cars. Get cars filled with fuel. Deisel, or gasoline, I don't care. If you ask for empty cars to go to Sunny Point, someone's going to start asking questions."

Giordono wrote down the change in a small notebook he pulled from his pocket.

"O.K. Is that all?" Hubbard asked. *This is all just bullshit*, Hubbard thought. *If it ever gets out what we're doing, there'll be hell to pay. But that's what they pay me for, isn't it? To do the things that must never be known.*

"Don't worry about the explosive rigging, Felix. It won't be easy to trip the laser triggers. These are 'Special Cargo Railcars' designed to carry special weapons," he said, referring to nuclear weapons, "and the doors will not be breached by a normal collision or a derailment. Crowbars won't pry the doors open. And if the train is stopped unexpectedly, metal spikes will deploy from the rear of the car, locking it into place right where it sits on the track. No one's gonna tow one of the these babies anywhere," Giordono explained.

"How many of the cars on each train will carry nuclear material?"

"Four."

"Let me know when you've got it done, but don't go into detail in your message. Just say 'package wrapped,'" Hubbard said. He then walked nervously from the warehouse back to his car. *God damn, how'd I get involved in this?* he asked himself.

When he had gone, the two civilians turned to Giordono, and one of them asked, "Tony, so we're wrapping the fuel rod casks in explosives, too, or just the plutonium?"

"The fuel rods are weapons-grade material, just like the plutonium. Felix said to rig the casks of nuclear material for destruction. That's what we're going to do. He didn't say just the plutonium."

"It just doesn't seem likely that anyone would be able to steal a forty-five-thousand-pound cask."

"It doesn't seem likely that anyone would be foolish enough to try to steal any of this stuff in the middle of North or South Carolina. But we don't give the orders; we just carry them out. And, I'll tell you this, I'm not asking Hubbard for any more clarification. He just wants it done, understand? He doesn't want to be any closer to this than necessary. I'm not going to piss him off. Do you think I want my career ruined because some piss-ant bureaucrat thought I asked too many questions?" The two civilians snickered. "Besides the fuel casks have *nothing in them but spent fuel ... spent.* It ain't dangerous. Load the motherfuckers up so that all the casks will be fractured, then none of this shit will be any good to anybody who tries to take it."

"We should put one of the tankers next to each of those cars. It'll look more like a real train that way, and it'll space the rigged cars. That way, if one goes up, they won't all go up," Gilbert added.

"Will do," one of the civilians replied.

"You guys make sure the cars come with the explosives already inside. After they're loaded with the fuel rod casks and the plutonium, the train will be assembled in the railyard at Sunny Point. Erick and I will connect the detonators and the laser triggers there. We'll be covered as DOE inspectors. At the end of the line two men will unlock the doors, thereby deactivating the laser triggers and the attached detonators. It's foolproof," Gilbert added.

"Who'll ride with the train?" the civilian asked.

"Just the engineer, the conductor and the trainman" Gilbert replied.

"They are not to be made aware of the special security precautions installed in the railcars," Giordono added.

"Right."

"What happens if there is a derailment, or some other accident?" the other civilian asked.

"If the train goes off schedule for any reason, a response team from Andrews Air Force Base will be automatically alerted. OPER NAVY BLUE is its code name. There are also assets at Fort Bragg. They will get the word simultaneously," Gilbert said.

"Remember, under no circumstances are the state or local authorities to be alerted for any reason. Is that clear?" Giordono asked.

"Roger."

"All right. Good job. The first train rolls in two weeks," Gilbert said.

Giordono and Gilbert left the two civilians in the warehouse with the boxcar. They sat in the open door and began to calculate the amount of explosives to wrap around the casks. "That seems like an awful lot," the younger man said.

"You heard those guys. They want these things to go up ... they're going to go up. Besides, how the hell are we going to find out the specs on these casks without making a whole lot of people suspicious? Screw that." He held up the sketch he had drawn on his notepad. "This'll blow them up, no matter how tough they are."

* * *

"Hell yes. We'll keep appealing until we run out of places to go," Blackie Haselden said in response to Watson Harris' question. Watson was slowly navigating the small creek boat around a fallen tree. The black waters of Welch's Creek were flowing swiftly, fed by a month of regular rainfall. The limbs of the tree swayed is if with the wind, pulled by the current that made ripples in the surface of the water. In the center of the boat, Billy sipped a soda and listened as his father and the governor talked about his frustration over the failure of the state's case concerning the plutonium the federal government was bringing into South Carolina. "Isn't it clear that Judge Green simply did what the president told him? We're supposed to have an independent judiciary in this country, God damn it!"

"Blackie, how are you going to prove Green did anything wrong?"

The boat nosed past a bank of tall reeds and grass that disappeared under moss-laden oak and tupelo branches. "I don't know if we can. But I'll be damned if I'm going to just roll over and play dead. Seekings and that asshole ... Sorry, Billy...."

"I've heard that word before, Uncle Blackie."

He continued, chuckling, "O.K., no more soapboxing. Let's just say I'm going to make them explain at every step why all the evidence proves they've subverted the justice system. I've told our lawyers to have at it, to pull out all the stops they can think of."

Watson didn't say what he thought. All this was futile, and worse. It was needlessly depressing for Blackie, and it probably distracted him from other matters where he could actually accomplish something, although Watson could not name a single such issue. Such was his lack of interest in politics. But he knew his friend was driving himself crazy in his battle with the federal government. Blackie couldn't fathom the depth of its willingness to wield every power at its disposal, legal or illegal, to achieve its goals. For Blackie Haselden, the public arena had always been a world of tough combat, but combat governed by rules understood and obeyed by all. The brutality and amorality of naked power, stripped of constraint and constitution, was foreign to him. Watson just smiled at Blackie. *At least it will all be over soon*, he told himself. "Go get 'em, Brother Bill."

Billy snickered into the back of his hand.

Blackie turned a mock scowl on his godson, "You know, I've been considering a proposal to eliminate summer vacation in public schools.

We need to compete with the damned Japanese. What do you think, Billy?"

"Bad idea, Uncle Blackie. Real bad idea."

The boat slid alongside the dock. Blackie jumped from the bow and pulled the boat to a stop, tying the bow and stern lines to cleats to secure the boat. Billy noisily landed on the dock and dragged the fish cooler from the boat. Watson lifted the drink cooler with one hand and laid it next to Blackie. "There's two beers left. Here, Guv. Take one."

Blackie took the can, ice cold and smooth in his hand. He opened the tab and took a long swallow. From the corner of his eye, he saw Watson, head tilted back draining his own beer. In the fading afternoon sun, his large frame was silhouetted against the orange-and-blue-streaked sky. For an instant, Blackie Haselden was struck with the uniqueness of the moment, the rarity of his friendship with the man he knew before he could spell his own name, with love for this brother ... and the son he shared. Watson grasped the empty can in one large hand and crushed it. In that act, he was the same boy who shared first stolen tastes of beer in those long ago, but not lost, days of their youth. "To the last beer," Watson said.

"To the last beer, Bud," Blackie replied, and crushed his own can.

They began cutting and scraping the scales from the fish they caught in the Pee Dee River. "Uncle Blackie, can I ask you a favor?" Blackie could tell the question was a prelude to one long and carefully considered request by the boy.

"Sure. Anything."

"My Boy Scout Troop is having a campout the first weekend in October. I was kind of hoping you would come by and talk to us.... It's not out in the woods, or anything. It's right here in Florence. We're going to set up camp behind the hardware store next to the railroad tracks. On Saturday morning, we're going to go down Evans and Irby and clean up the streets, you know, litter and bottles and stuff. It's our public service project this year. Can you come?" His eyes were full of hope and doubt, and he would never be denied by Blackie Haselden.

"You bet. The first Saturday in October?" Billy nodded. "O.K. You got it. I'll be there."

Billy's face beamed as he returned to the fish he was cleaning.

* * *

"Damn it! Those assholes at the EPA told me all I needed to do was get the state's approval. I got it and now they say they can't approve my permit because it's not 'water dependant.' What the hell does that mean?" The voice on the telephone belonged to a long-time client of Jim McNeely's. He had been trying to get a permit to construct a marina store on his property near Hilton Head Island for eighteen months. "I thought I had the best environmental lawyers in the state," he yelled. "But if you can't deliver anything better than this, maybe I'm with the wrong team."

Jim shook his head as he left his office and walked up the stairs to the conference room. This was the third time in three weeks he had received a call like this one. He wondered what the reason was for the rare firm meeting called by Jake Rollins.

Jake took a long draw on his cigarette. "Drew ... I don't know," he laughed, "maybe we can just do wreck cases." Drew Holland wasn't laughing.

Jim asked, "What's going on?"

Jake flashed him a bitter smile, "We're wondering what we're going to be doing in two years."

"Jake, we can't walk away from this," Holland answered.

"Drew ... they're strangling us. How long did we work to get the insurance company business we have now? Three big companies. Two of them have pulled the business and given it to those clowns at Olde and Waters. We have to face up to it. The White House hates our fucking guts. They're out to get us."

"I've had three clients screwed by three different federal agencies in as many weeks," Jim said, looking at Holland.

"The state wants to appeal," Holland said.

"There are still lawyers at the attorney general's office, aren't there?" Rollins asked, puffing nervously.

"It was our case," Holland said.

Rollins crushed the cigarette in the ashtray and closed his eyes.

"If we run now, what are we?" Holland asked.

"We still get to be successful lawyers making good livings," Rollins laughed.

"Who's to say the bastards will leave us alone even if we get out?" Holland asked.

"They might not give a damn one way or the other."

"They do," Rollins said, looking out the window. The general counsel for Granite Mutual called me yesterday. He told me the White House wants us out of the case. As long as we're in, our clients like Granite won't be able to get a tour of the White House, much less the access they've enjoyed for so long. As long as we're in the case, our name is a curse to anyone who wants anything from the United States government."

"So, we just bag it and run?"

"Who'd blame us, Drew? We have to survive. This is a business."

Holland walked to the window and stood next to Rollins. "Jake, we're good lawyers. We'll make it."

Rollins pulled another cigarette from the pack and lit it with his lighter. From the first puff, he exhaled a blue cloud of smoke. For over fifteen years Rollins and Holland had practiced their brand of law together — rougher and sometimes wild by Charleston standards. They were more than partners. "Drew, you're crazy.... O.K., we go on and make the best of it. Just make sure your friend Brother Bill knows we need all the help we can get down here."

*   *   *

"Have you got your military identification with you?" Matt Reicher turned to ask Jim McNeely as Matt drove the jeep down the road through the center of the sprawling Weapons Station.

"Sure. What the hell for?"

"I'm going to show you something you've never seen before, and will never see again." Matt turned the jeep onto a road with a brick guardhouse and tall fence topped with barbed wire. Two marines emerged from the guardhouse as the jeep approached. Each carried machine guns across their chests. "Let me have your ID."

The first marine snapped to attention and cracked his arm in a sharp salute. The second marine stood to the rear and watched in silence, clutching the machine gun in front of him. They young man carefully examined the cards, going through a mental checklist, Jim thought had probably been drilled into him. "Commander," he said, "What is your destination, this afternoon, sir?"

"Area Delta. Container Three, Corporal."

"Very good, sir." The marine returned the IDs and saluted again.

Matt slowly drove away from the guardhouse down a road that was entirely empty. They might have been on a country road, miles from nowhere. "These guys will all be gone in a year."

"Why?"

"The reason they're here will be gone." Matt smiled. "The special weapons are the only reason we have marines."

"What are 'special weapons?'"

"Nukes, my friend. Nukes."

The road passed through woods that crowded both sides. Four more marines waited along the road, next to an armored personnel carrier. Matt stopped at the signal from one of the marines, two men and two women, and all carrying the same machine guns slung over their shoulders. Again he produced their ID cards for inspection and told the marine where they were headed. A short distance later, they arrived at a large, squat structure with sloping sides. In the front was a square metal doorframe under a short overhang from the roof. Two more armed marines stood guard in front of the door. "Let's go take a peek," Matt said softly.

At the door, Matt presented their IDs. This time the marines demanded, in a firm but respectful tone, an explanation of exactly why the commander was inspecting Container Three, Area Delta. Matt said he was there to check the temperature control and the transponder. It was a spot check, he said, dictated by headquarters. Satisfied with the explanation, the marine opened the heavy metal door and flicked on an overhead light switch. The dark came suddenly alive with an array of racks, each one occupied by a shiny, cylindrical object, unmistakably a bomb. "There they are," Matt whispered, "the terror of the world."

Jim was speechless as he gazed at the weapons.

Matt walked to one of the racks at the rear of the bunker and placed his hand on a small disk affixed to the side of the bomb. "This is a transponder. If this little baby ever gets lost, this would let us find her location in less than six hours. It's amazing technology. A satellite network continually monitors the location, so long as the transponder is functioning. Even trucking companies use these now — although not as fancy as this one — to protect their equipment. Of course, these are a whole lot more sophisticated than those on the commercial market." He ran his hand along the smooth side of the weapon. Unconsciously, Jim reached out and did the same. The steel skin of the nose was cold, and he drew back his hand. Matt laughed. "It won't bite."

"They're just spooky, that's all."

"They're bad news. The worst news on the planet," Matt added.

"How many of these things are out here?" Jim asked as they drove away.

"Now, that's a secret ... but there are twenty-five bunkers. They're all in this area, and, hell, you can see 'em from an aerial photograph. Some bigger than this one. There are all types out here. Tactical nukes. Strategic nukes, too, for the subs. They are all here." He waved at the empty pine groves. "We have a reinforced company of marines here just to guard them. When the 'specials' leave, so will the marines. It'll be a big headache my successor won't have, that's for sure."

"The nukes?"

"No. The damned marines!"

Jim looked behind them as they exited the gate. He shivered from the chill that settled along his spine.

*　*　*

"You look lovely this afternoon," Leo Scardato said, greeting Julieanne Harris. He rose and held her chair as she took her seat at the elegantly set table. "In an otherwise drab Washington world, you bring such class to any occasion."

"Leo, you are so full of shit."

Scardato snickered. "Julie, Julie, Julie."

"Your Cary Grant imitation is no better, Leo."

"I've taken the liberty of ordering your favorite, my dear ... and just the right wine from their reserved cellar."

The waiter brought their iced teas and a basket of bread.

"Leo, in Brooklyn, is it necessary for every boy to grow up with such a monumental talent for the absurd? I mean, do you get beaten up or something if you can't shoot a line of incredible crap."

"Every region has its own unique cultural rites of passage. In South Carolina, for young women I suppose it was being able to name every known piece of silverware, and the top twenty styles of china."

She blinked in surprise. In all the years she had known Leo Scardato, he had never so much as mentioned South Carolina. Julieanne didn't know if Leo was even aware that was where she was from.

"Why certainly, doesn't every well-brought-up girl know those things?"

They made small talk through their lunch of soft-shell crab sandwiches. As the waiter removed her plate, Julieanne looked Leo in the eye and asked, "So, Leo, what did you want to see me about? No jokes."

"Moore knows it's you, Julieanne."

She felt as though Leo had slammed his large fist into her stomach. "That weasel Hubbard has been snooping around everybody over at Defense Intelligence Agency for months. He doesn't have any solid proof. But he knows it was you."

She was staring at the wine list. "Julieanne? Are you O.K.?"

"I'm fine. How do you know?"

"Trade secrets, Dear."

"Come on, no jokes."

"I can't tell you that. Really. There's been a lot going on around here lately. We've just been trying to keep current, you know."

"I know."

They sat in silence for a moment. Leo had apparently said all he had to say to her.

"So, Leo, are you just going to drop this little bombshell on me, or what?"

"There's more, Julie. Moore wants to set you up. Hubbard will be feeding you some incredible bullshit, and if you pass it on to the governor, they'll arrest you. No joke."

"I see."

"Julie, these are really bad people, O.K.? Don't mess with them. Nothing you hear is reliable. You are out of the loop. The only people working that project now are Moore and Hubbard and some army goons with Hubbard. That's it."

"Leo, why are you telling me this?"

He smiled at her. "Come on, Julie. Do you have to ask?" Why didn't she see what he felt?

"Thanks, Leo."

"Be careful, sweetheart." He wished he could make himself say so much more.

*   *   *

Carol Hicks leaned against the stone wall of the embankment at Fort Moultrie. A light rain fell from the gray sky. She watched the narrow stretch of water between Moultrie and Sumter, the main shipping channel. She glanced at her watch. Soon, Dave told her, the *DEYO* would pass through the stretch of harbor in front of her, and out to sea.

Dave called her one week before with the news that the ship was leaving Charleston. How had she let herself forget this was inevitable? The news tore into her with unexpected force. She pictured a return to her world as it was before the young sailor came over to her in Vickery's Restaurant, brash and clumsy ... and charming. The thought of her life before seemed bleak and colorless. The bow of the great ship appeared from around the row of houses that lined the beach, cutting through the slate-colored water. Her heart jumped as she watched it move, so graceful, and so hated by her for taking him away.

Every night since Dave brought her the news, he stayed with her. They fixed wonderful meals and drank delicate wines, and made love, every time with new intensity. But each night brought the day he would leave closer, and forced her to confront the feelings that were spinning wildly inside her, completely out of her control... forced her to ask the question she dreaded more than any other. Were her feelings reciprocated by the handsome, sensitive man who had wandered into her life, and brought her such a lust for life? She could not bring herself to ask and was resigned to his departure as a final goodbye. But on the last night, the answer to the question she feared came to her, unbidden.

With her head resting under his chin, he said softly, "I love you, Carol."

The words were so lightly spoken that they merged with the couple's breathing. But she was certain she heard them. Before she could answer, he said more loudly, "I love you. Now what are we going to do about it?"

Her eyes filled with tears and she lifted her face to kiss him. Their kiss became renewed passion, and the question hung unanswered as their hands and mouths covered each other one more time.

In the morning, as they waited for the sun to rise on the day that she cursed, Carol answered him, "I want to be with you. Whatever that means, I'll do it."

"Marry me, Carol. Do you want that? I've never been as sure of anything in my life. We'll work out the details."

"Yes. Yes." She kissed him, his face, his chest, and his stomach. "Yes."

As she watched the warship disappear into the vastness of the Atlantic, all Carol Hicks knew for certain was that the next time she would be truly happy was when she watched the USS *Deyo* enter Norfolk harbor in six weeks. Then they would decide how they would arrange their lives. "Our lives," she said aloud as the rain rolled down her face.

* * *

Sasha Dunitsev, clothed in black-green from head to foot, his face made invisible with camouflage paint, lay unseen in the brush a hundred yards from the railcars, watching as six of the cars were loaded with the casks he recognized as the fuel rod containers. Three casks were placed in each of the six cars. Along with those, four of the smaller containers of plutonium were loaded. When the six cars had been loaded, all the laborers were driven away. Two men remained wearing jackets labeled on the back in large white letters "DOE" for Department of Energy. The men entered each car and remained for twenty minutes. His night scope, aimed through the narrow opening left in the railcar, couldn't detect their movements. He assumed they were making a final safety check.

When the two men left the train, they closed the doors and secured each car. The engine arrived a half hour after the men finished locking the cars and the train was ready. Dunitsev silently made his way back the way he had come to the passageway through the security fence. He joined Donskoi minutes later. Donskoi drove them through the moonless night to the first spot where they would watch the train pass through Florence. On the way, Dunitsev used the soap and water in the back seat to clean his face and hands of the paint, and he changed clothes.

In Florence, they watched the train approach the overpass near the city/county government building and noted the travel time from Sunny Point. The train moved very slowly as it neared the overpass. Dunitsev noted that it would not be difficult at all for a man to drop from the overpass onto the roof of the engine as it passed underneath. The train continued to slow as it came near the intersection at the center of the business district of the small city. *No more than ten kilometers per hour,* he noted. No police were evident anywhere near the train, except for the ones coming and going from the station next to the tracks. There was no one in the cab of the engine except the engineer. He noticed that the engineer traveled with the window of the cab open, and he smiled.

No vehicles other than theirs had followed the train. No one paid it any notice as it slowly crossed the highway and left the city. The same was true in each of the towns where they watched the train pass with its deadly, precious cargo, unnoticed, and unknown to anyone but themselves.

Chapter 21

This was his favorite season of the year. The searing swelter of summer in Washington was over, and the nights were chilly with the first hints of the coming winter. But Leo Scardato didn't notice the coolness of the morning air or the color appearing in the trees. He was headed for a meeting with the vice president to do the most difficult job of his life.

He drove along the entrance to the vice president's house. The rambling Victorian mansion was a place he had been to visit only a few times before. It was a poor second to the White House, not as grand or imposing — or frightening.

Mike O'Connelly waited for him in the library. Scardato found the vice president lounging on a couch, flipping through the latest edition of a newsmagazine. O'Connelly greeted him, "Come in. Sit down."

As he took Mike O'Connelly's hand, he remembered it was October, and he ought to be concerned about who might be going to the Super Bowl, or at least about the World Series. When they were seated in front of the tall stacks of books, O'Connelly said, "Leo, what is it you want to talk about? I know this isn't a social call."

"Something very serious, I'm afraid, Mr. O'Connelly."

"What is it?"

"Some of this, you already know. Some of it will surprise you. But it is all, beyond question, the truth. You should know that this room and, in fact, every room of this house is entirely secure. We can speak without fear of being overheard. We've made sure of that."

O'Connelly smiled, but he was genuinely shocked. "You've debugged the official residence of the vice president?"

Scardato ignored the question. "And you needn't worry about your secret service detail. They would resign before they spied on you."

O'Connelly sat quietly, disbelieving.

"You must understand, Mr. O'Connelly, I have taken the steps to determine these things for good reason. I hope you will understand why, when I have finished my briefing." O'Connelly nodded. "The administration is engaging in acts that are dangerous and illegal. I have placed myself and a number of my agents in positions of extreme risk in order to learn the truth."

"Leo, you understand, I am still a member of this administration."

"In name only. I know you are aware that some things have been done that are a disgrace."

"Go on."

"Everything reported in the press concerning the surveillance conducted on the governor of South Carolina and his lawyers was true. It was not done by the U.S. attorney, although he has taken the fall. And not by Moore alone. It was all done with the full approval of the president."

Leo took a deep breath. "After the first judge ordered the government to coordinate its plans for importing the plutonium with the state, Moore contrived to have him conflicted out of the case. The judge they knew would inherit the case is someone Moore knew he could control."

"Control?"

"Blackmail. They knew this guy once helped bribe state officials. He obviously caved in, and gave them what they wanted. You've seen the press reports, I'm sure. Moore was there a week before the second judge reversed the earlier order."

"Leo, I know it's bad. But it's over. They got what they wanted. Things will just simmer down after this."

"No, sir. It isn't over. Moore has been authorized by the president to have total discretion over how the plutonium is transported. The steps he is ordering are extremely reckless."

"What do you mean?"

"The train is booby-trapped with powerful explosives. The purpose is to destroy the plutonium so no one can steal it. Mr. Vice President, rigging nuclear fuel rods and plutonium with high explosives is madness." He pulled an envelope from the pocket of his coat. "This is an abstract of the testimony of a former energy department researcher who testified for the state. It explains in detail what detonation of those railcars would mean."

O'Connelly walked to the garden window, his hands thrust in his coat pockets. Looking at the plants he had nursed so carefully, now slipping into their autumn sleep, he asked, "Why are you telling me this?"

"Mr. O'Connelly, I have been in the business of national security and law enforcement all my adult life. I know that what I see is a grave danger to the country. You are the second ranking official in the government. The first ranking official is the person creating this danger. Who else would I tell?"

"What do you really expect me to do?"

"I wasn't elected to your office, Mr. O'Connelly."

"Damn you, Leo!" O'Connelly turned on Scardato, exploding. "It's so easy for you to report your dirty little secrets! But now what? You have the gall to tell me I'm *supposed to just know* what to do! The hell with you!"

Scardato accepted the blast from the vice president in silence. "Mr. O'Connelly...."

"Leo, how do you know for sure these things are true?" O'Connelly asked angrily.

Without hesitation, Scardato replied, "We have conducted close surveillance on Moore and his operatives since this began. There is no question about their activities."

"Leo, I've made a deal with the president. Or did you already know that?" Without waiting for an answer from Scardato, he continued, "I agreed to leave him alone, if he left my children alone. Nothing is more important to me than my children."

"What about the country?"

"How dare you!"

"Well, what's the answer?" Scardato shouted back. "Do you really think that Marilyn would tell you to turn your back on the nation to protect her race for congress? Is that how your children think?"

Mike O'Connelly stared at the gray sky.

"I think you know they're better than that," he went on. "Maybe nothing will happen. All I know is, this country needs you to be ready. There isn't anyone else."

* * *

Moore was looking forward to getting home. The air was cool, but not yet cold. The thought of grilling steaks outside appealed to him. He'd like to sit on the deck behind the kitchen with a drink. He found the thought of spending time with Terry appealed to him, as well. Lately, the time he spent with the young soldier seemed more important to him. It was the stress, he supposed, of all that had gone wrong.

Things wouldn't be going wrong anymore, at least with the goddamned plutonium. The first train went without a hitch. Now it was a system. The second train should be leaving — he looked at his watch — in about eighteen hours. And soon he'd be able to pay back the "bitch" who had caused him so much trouble in the first place. That made him smile.

Terry wasn't home yet. In the back of the house, Moore turned on the gas grill. He fixed himself a Scotch and soda and carried it with him upstairs to the shower. The warm jets of water felt like fingers massaging the tension from his muscles. He stepped from the shower and grabbed a towel from the rack. As he dried himself off, he watched his reflection in the mirror behind the door. *Still in good shape*, he told himself. Pulling on jeans and a heavy sweatshirt, he felt whole again.

In the kitchen, he made himself a second drink and transferred the steaks to the grill. "Hey, what's cooking?" Terry Wilkins asked, standing in the open kitchen door, still in uniform.

"Steaks. Get a drink and join me. It feels great out here."

Wilkins returned to the deck with a glass. The Scotch was straight. He needed all the help he could get for what he had to do. He emptied the glass quickly.

"I've got news."

Moore looked at him expectantly. "O.K."

"My wife called me, C. A. She and my son are coming to live with me."

Moore seemed unfazed. "It's expensive," he replied. "How are you going to make it on a staff sergeant's salary?"

Wilkins struggled to maintain his composure. A hundred times he had rehearsed what to say about the money. He could feel the muscles of his face twitch. "We inherited some money." It sounded better than saying he was the heir. "She thinks I need to be with them all the time. A week here and there isn't much. My tour in D.C. will only last two more years. We can hack it that long."

Moore nodded, but the lines around his eyes deepened. "Let me fix us two more drinks," Wilkins said, taking Moore's glass and disappearing into the kitchen. He came back with refills for them both. He had intended to be very drunk tonight, and to take Moore as close as he could get him to the same oblivion.

"I'll miss you around here. When will you leave?"

"In a week or ten days."

Moore was quiet as he tended the steaks. "C. A., I want you to get drunk with me." He walked over and took the glass from Moore's hand, tossing the mixed contents into the yard. "Here," he handed him his own glass of straight Scotch. Moore took a drink and handed it back.

"O.K."

The fear began to subside, anesthetized by the liquor. His plan was going well, so far. He would memorialize the end of his "special" relationship with Moore in characteristic male fashion — with a fraternal drink. It ought to work. Soon he would extricate himself from the nightmare once and for all. It had to work. The toughest part of the plan would be later — at night. But it would be one of the last.

*   *   *

"Mikail, the second ship is on the berth. That means the train will be ready to leave in eighteen hours."

Mikail Plekanov listened to Sasha Dunitsev over the secure phone. "Well, Colonel," he said to Matveev, "it won't be long now."

Dunitsev would watch the train being loaded, and report to Mikail exactly which railcars contained the plutonium casks. When the engine arrived at the railyard, Dunitsev and Donskoi would leave for Florence to join Mikail and the others at the farmhouse outside of the city. It would require several hours of hard driving, but they would make the trip well in advance of the train. Mikail and Matveev and two dozen other members of Mikail's army waited in the rented farmhouse — Canadian tourists on a hunting trip, a short detour from their golf vacation in Myrtle Beach, Mikail had told the realtor.

Miles away, Thaddeus and the Northwest Territorial Militia also waited for the signal to begin final preparations for the raid on the train. Thirty members of the militia nervously anticipated the call to change into their police uniforms and begin staging themselves to take over the four police stations scattered around Florence. The explosives that would provide the diversion were already in place, carefully located the night before, and awaiting only the signal from the remote control device to begin the chaos. The final alert would come from one of Thaddeus' men, stationed thirteen miles north of the city along the railroad tracks. That signal would set it all in motion.

At the rented farmhouse, Mikail watched the pilot fuss over the engine of the helicopter. He laughed to himself. It was just like the army. *He has no reason to check the engine. But the tension drives him to do something. It will all begin soon enough,* he thought. *Then they will have plenty to attend to.*

* * *

"Mom, where are my extra Scout shirts?" Billy called from his room. Dottie looked at Watson across their kitchen table.

"Right where they should be."

"No, they're not! No, wait. Here they are."

She smiled, and Watson shook his head, chuckling, "You'd think they were going to Indonesia instead of downtown."

Dottie walked to the steps in the hall and leaned over the newel post, "You need to be ready in an hour, Billy. Is everything together?"

"Not yet. I'm close," he answered. "Where are my socks, Mom?"

"In the drawer," she yelled up the stairs. "Hurry up. They'll be here to pick you up soon."

She walked back to the kitchen, where Watson was finishing his dinner. He hurried the last bites of pork roast into his mouth. She watched him from the hall, gulping iced tea, his muscular neck pulsing as he swallowed. He wore only a tee shirt, and she admired him, as solid as when they married. Watson put the glass down on the table and grabbed his uniform shirt from the back of the chair.

"Will you be able to make it for Blackie's visit to the troop?" Dottie asked him.

"Unless there's an earthquake, I guess I will. Hell, Dottie, this is Florence; when was the last time anything happened on a weekend?" Watson said, then leaned up the stairwell and called out, "Goodbye, Billy. I'll see you tomorrow, O.K.?"

"O.K., Dad. Mom, where's my sleeping bag?"

Dottie rolled her eyes as Watson took her into his arms. His powerful arms pulled her to him and he kissed her. Like we were kids, she always reminded herself. "See you at Brother Bill's speech," he joked, and pushed the screen door open with his foot.

The sun was sliding below the horizon by the time the Scouts completed their camp in the lot behind Ferris' Hardware. They had a bathroom that opened to the rear of the store, and Ferris agreed to leave it unlocked for the boys during their campout. The line of tents began a hundred yards from the railroad tracks. Mr. West, the Scoutmaster, hammered poles into the ground and attached a rope to form a safety cordon separating the tents and the tracks, in case any of the boys walked toward the tracks during the night. As night fell in earnest, seven of the Scouts set up the Coleman stove and began preparing supper.

It was nearly half past nine by the time they finished cleaning up from the meal. "All right, boys, let's call it a night by ten o'clock. We've got a lot of work to do in the morning," West said loudly as he walked among the eighteen Scouts. He watched as the flashlights were turned off, one by one. Only then did he climb into his own tent and fade into an exhausted sleep.

* * *

"I want to get a picture. Everybody get over by the mantle," Linda Reicher called out to the noisy crowd in the Reichers' den. Nearly all of the men and two of the women wore military dress uniforms. Most were navy mess dress. A few were air force, and one — worn by Jim McNeely — was army. They were gathered at the Reichers' for a pre-party in advance of the navy ball, the annual celebration of the service's "birthday." Against his better judgment, Jim agreed to wear the uniform to what Matt assured him would be "one helluva party." The breasts of all the uniform jackets were hung with ribbons and medals.

"O.K., now move closer. Everybody needs to get in."

"I'll take the picture, Aunt Linda," John McNeely offered. She handed him the camera and joined Matt in the front row. One flash illuminated the tightly packed group. Then John took another picture, just in case. The McNeelys would sleep over to avoid what promised to be a late drive home.

Most of the junior officers on the Weapons Station were at the Reichers' house, though Captain Kratz was hosting his own smaller gathering. "Commander, where's the kilt?" a lieutenant yelled from the kitchen.

"Taken care of, shipmate!"

Jim leaned close to Matt and asked quietly, "Kilt?"

"It's an old navy custom. You wouldn't understand."

"There is no kilt. You don't have the ... well ... you won't do it. I've got ten bucks that says you won't," the lieutenant said.

Jim watched Matt's face for a few moments. Turning to the young officer, he said, "Kiss your money goodbye, Lieutenant."

*   *   *

For hours, Dunitsev watched as the same black longshoremen he remembered from his first visit loaded the railcars with the same mix of huge casks containing nuclear fuel rods and smaller casks of plutonium. Just as before, when the loading was complete, the railyard was abandoned by all but the team of men wearing the DOE jackets. Once again, they climbed into each of the cars carrying the nuclear casks and emerged about fifteen minutes later, carefully locking the doors behind them. This time Dunitsev noticed a pattern he hadn't seen before. Next to each of the cars loaded with nuclear material was a tanker car so that there were two tanker cars between each of the "target" cars. For a moment he wondered what, if anything, that revealed about the Americans' intentions. Nothing, he concluded.

Dunitsev noticed that the sun was sinking to the tree line. The night air was turning chilly. When the last car was locked by the DOE inspectors, he silently backed away from his vantage point overlooking the railyard. As before, he crawled through the dense woods and swamps, again hoping to avoid the snakes that infested this soggy place. At the edge of the trees, past the fence under which he had crawled, was Donskoi. This time he smoked a cigarette, the tip glowing brightly in the dark. Standing and walking from the trees to the Land Rover, where Donskoi leaned casually against the hood, Dunitsev pulled the watch cap from his head. "Gregori, have you lost all your soldier skills? Smoking on watch?" Dunitsev slapped Donskoi's shoulder with the watch cap. "Do you want to be arrested and rot in an American jail?" Dunitsev was smiling.

"A man has to relax, Lieutenant."

"Something which has never been a problem for you, Sergeant." Dunitsev, standing next to the vehicle, removed his dark clothes and replaced them with the dark shoes and blue pants of the police uniform they would all wear later. He pulled a sweatshirt over his head. Printed on the front was the seal of the 22nd Canadian Regiment and the motto of Quebec.

Donskoi parked the Land Rover in the concealed spot selected by Dunitsev and him days before, and they waited. He glanced at his watch. It was 7:30. When the train passed them, they would alert Mikail and drive quickly to the farm outside Florence, arriving an hour ahead of the train's approach to the overpass.

* * *

"Your house is wonderful," Beth Killian said, following Susan Engle to the table, carrying a tray of iced tea and glasses.

"It's a good thing you have taste," Mark called to her from the den of the Engle's new home, "Because this clown you married sure as hell has none." Looking out of the front window, he said to Nat, "Damn, it's dark out there. Are you sure you two want to live this deep in the woods?"

"Don't worry, Mark. We won't let the boogey man get you," Nat said.

Walking to the dining room, Mark picked up a newspaper from the couch. He pointed to the headline across the top: *"First Nuclear Shipments Could Come Soon."* "Y'all know that Jim McNeely was one of the lawyers in the case about this nuclear stuff."

"Sounds like they got screwed," Nat said. "Jim's a good guy. I hate it for him."

"Well, I hate it for us, if something goes wrong." Mark said. "You can't help but wonder what would really happen if there's an accident."

"When are you due?" Beth asked Susan.

"March," she answered, touching her rounding belly.

"Are you going to work much longer?"

"Not long...." Nat started to say, but was interrupted by his wife's hand gently squeezing his own.

"I'm starting to feel it, but I want to keep working at the hospital as long as I can," Susan said. "In fact, I'll be on duty all day tomorrow."

"Well, I don't blame you," Mark said. "Anything beats sitting out here staring at trees all day."

* * *

The waitresses began clearing away the dishes in the club dining room. It was time for the ceremony of the navy's birthday. "Do we have to leave the room?" Jim said quietly to Matt.

"Go get us some more champagne, Grunt."

"We'll all need it to endure what I am certain is about to be a torrent of bullshit." Jim headed for the bar, and returned minutes later with four bottles of champagne. *Thank God, I don't have to drive tonight*, he thought. Alicia shot him a bemused glance as he returned. He leaned over to her ear, "I'm O.K."

"Enjoy it." She kissed his cheek.

Captain Kratz gave a short speech, praising the staff of the Weapons Station for a successful year, and singling out Matt Reicher for special compliments. *The disingenuous bastard*, Jim fumed silently.

On cue, the band, which had assembled quietly on stage during the toasts, began to play. Matt walked quickly to the table, and took Linda's hand. Taking her in his arms, he whirled her across the floor to the strains of a waltz. Couples flooded onto the dance floor. Bemedaled uniforms and gowns of all colors swirled around the floor. "It almost makes the idea of war seem like fun," Alicia said to Jim as they danced.

"Yeah, bring on those Yankees, Scarlett!" Pointing to Matt, he added, "There goes one now!"

After the first obligatory waltz, the band quickly took up more contemporary music. The band struck up a Springstein hit. Laughter rippled across the room as people saw that the base's XO had, in fact, donned the kilt he had been promising for a week. He and Linda kept the floor to themselves as the crowd began to clap in time to the music.

* * *

Donskoi snored in the driver's seat of the Land Rover. It was two o'clock in the morning. Dunitsev saw the headlight of the train moving slowly toward them along the track that led from the Sunny Point terminal toward the switch connecting the spur with the main rail line. He knocked Donskoi's shoulder. "Here she is, Gregori." Donskoi rubbed his eyes while Dunitsev watched the train's light brighten as it closed the distance between them. Still moving slowly, the train passed them, the ground trembling under its weight. When it had passed, Donskoi headed down the narrow access road to the paved road outside the army property fence. There he activated the vehicle's lights and accelerated to the legal speed limit, heading for the main road that would carry them to Interstate 95 and then to Florence.

"Mikail. This is Sasha." They had elected to dispense with code names and used the cellular phones openly. Time was more important, Mikail had said, than needlessly worrying about American surveillance, which they could assume was nonexistent. "The delivery is on its way. See you soon." When Mikail acknowledged the news, Dunitsev pressed the button to end the call.

"It won't be long now, Gregori," he said.

* * *

Mikail looked at his watch — 6:00 — it was time to dispatch his militia friends. He picked up the phone from the table next to the couch in the little farmhouse. "Thaddeus, it's time, my friend. Are you ready?"

"Ready."

"Let's go."

Thaddeus hung up the phone and signaled to the men surrounding him in the house several miles away. All were dressed in exact replicas of the uniforms worn by the Florence police. An unusual light flashed in his eyes this morning, the same strange light that was reflected in each of the men that surrounded him. They removed their pistols and loaded them with the clips. Several opened large bags that sat at their feet and extracted machine pistols. Affixing the drums of bullets, they checked the weapons, loud clicks resounding in the old house. The men filed out the back door and walked to the car shed at the rear of the yard. Throwing open the doors in the pre-dawn dark, Thaddeus turned a flashlight on the first white van parked in the shed. The light illuminated an exact copy of the seal of the Florence Police Department. Thaddeus glanced at his watch. The train would be at the crossing in ninety minutes. The vans began to roll slowly out of the shed toward the highway leading to the city one hour away.

* * *

"Time to get up, guys," West called out as he walked along the line of tents. "Let's get a move on. Up, up, up! We've got work to do before breakfast." Slowly, the Scouts crawled out of the tents. Other tents were illuminated by flashlights, the figures inside making strange shadows against the fabric as the Scouts struggled to pull on their uniforms. When most of the Scouts were outside brushing their teeth, he reminded the four boys selected for the breakfast detail to begin their preparations.

"All right, boys. We'll walk over to Irby Street and make a sweep up one side before we come back here and eat. We've got a lot to do before the governor gets here this afternoon. So let's get moving." He checked the time. It was 6:45 and the sun was easing over the horizon. He noticed clouds gathering in bright red and orange streaks and hoped it wouldn't rain before time for them to pack up. "We'll be back at 7:45 to eat. You guys be ready for us."

"Yes, sir," the boys called back to West, as he led the rest of the troop across the railroad tracks toward the government center and the street of shops on the other side. Billy Harris finished tying the laces of his sneaker, jumped up from the ground in front of his tent, and sprinted after West and the other Scouts.

* * *

Just before 7:15 the white vans of Thaddeus' militia arrived at their target locations. One van pulled to the curb next to each of the three satellite police stations, and one stopped next to the state highway patrol headquarters. The van with Thaddeus slowly drove up Highway 52 to the railroad tracks and to the front of the city police headquarters. A second van followed the first and parked along the street. As they crossed the tracks, the van driver saw to his left the headlight of the train. His pulse quickened. "What's that?" He pointed to the row of tents behind the hardware store on the other side of the tracks.

Thaddeus studied the scene for a moment. He saw the four boys cooking at the table with the Coleman stoves. "Boy Scouts," he answered.

"Shit," the driver said. "Where are the rest?"

"I don't know. It's time. Forget about the Scouts." The headlight of the train was just beyond the overpass. Thaddeus calmly opened the door to the van and placed the police cap on his head. The other militiamen climbed out of both vans until only the drivers were left. As they walked towards the police headquarters, the drivers reached under their seats and retrieved machine pistols, checking to make sure the weapons were ready to fire. The driver of the lead van picked up the portable radio. "All units, make ready. Cargo delivery imminent."

Mikail listened to the transmission. "Toy soldiers," he said to Matveev. They sat in a car parked along the highway next to a vacant lot. The colonel chuckled. On the overpass, the Range Rover pulled to a stop, the morning sun reflecting from the window. Sasha Dunitsev casually stepped from the passenger door and walked to the concrete guardrail. He could feel the train shake the earth as the nose of the cab approached. Quickly, Dunitsev jumped onto the guardrail and lowered himself over the side. The nose of the engine passed under him and he dropped from the overpass. His boots struck the top of the engine hard, and he fell onto his hands and knees.

In the cab of the engine, the engineer heard the heavy thump. Thirty seconds later a concussion grenade landed in the cab and detonated, exploding his eardrums and knocking him unconscious. Dunitsev swung himself through the open window of the cab from a rope he had tied to the roof of the engine. Unfastening the rope, he rushed to apply the brakes of the engine, finding the lever exactly where he had learned it would be from the diagrams he had studied. Pulling his pistol from its holster, he shot the engineer once in the temple, scattering blood and brain tissue across the floor of the locomotive.

The driver of the lead militia van saw Dunitsev drop himself into the engine and picked up his radio. "Go! Go!" he shouted. At each of the satellite police stations and the highway patrol headquarters, the vans emptied, and the militiamen, in police uniforms, walked into the stations. Inside, before the desk officers recognized they were strangers, the militiamen pulled their machine pistols from the bags they carried and sprayed the office with bullets. As officers rushed to the sound, they were cut down. After securing each of the stations, the militiamen made rapid searches of the buildings to ensure that no officers were left. In each building, one militiaman opened the satchel he carried and set the timer of the explosive device for five minutes. The white vans sped away from the stations, followed by the roar of an explosion that collapsed each police station into a smoking jumble of timbers and bricks.

The engine of the train slowed to a stop just beyond the city/county government building, blocking Highway 52 completely. Thaddeus walked into the police headquarters followed by six of his men. When they were all inside the outer office, they pulled their machine pistols from the bags and trained them on the officers behind the desk. "On the floor," Thaddeus said calmly. The shocked policemen dropped to the floor, and one of the militiamen retrieved their pistols. The rest of the militiamen fanned out in the building, rounding up remaining officers and herding them at gun point to the front foyer. In five minutes, sixteen policemen were gathered in the front of the headquarters building. "All you guys, on the floor with the rest!" Thaddeus shouted. Without hesitation, he leveled his machine pistol at the blue uniformed officers laying face down on the floor and opened fire. In seconds, his bullets were all discharged into the bodies of the policemen. As the clatter of the gunfire stopped, the muffled moans of the dying men filled the room.

Across the city, fire engine sirens screamed as they raced to the scenes of the explosions. Dunitsev jumped from the cab of the engine. Donskoi had driven the Range Rover to the tracks and joined him alongside the train. From the car, Mikail and Matveev walked calmly to the front of the engine, and watched their men approach the first "target" railcar in which they knew the plutonium waited. By then, seven other members of Mikail's team were present. Three men fixed a small shape charge to the doors on the first car. Three more men did the same to a second. Thaddeus' militia took up positions on either side of the highway and at the entrance to the city/county government building to intercept any curious onlookers. They were to play the role of the police, keeping the public at a safe distance from a train mishap.

West and the Scouts heard the subdued rattle of gunfire from the police headquarters. They walked to the corner of the government center and were stopped by a policeman. "Better go back, kids. We need to let the railroad get this cleaned up."

"I've got four boys over there in that lot, Officer," West said.

The policeman seemed confused and looked nervously across the tracks between the engine and the first railcar. "I can't let you—" He didn't finish his sentence. The twin blasts of the shape charges made him jump. The Scouts and the policemen turned to look at the train.

Exactly five seconds after the shape charges forced the doors into the paths of the laser triggers in each of the two cars, the air was torn by deafening blasts as the explosives wrapped around the plutonium and nuclear fuel rod casks detonated. The two railcars disintegrated in balls of flame and flying, shredded metal. The twelve casks containing the fuel rods were shattered, pieces of the casks and the nuclear fuel hurled in every direction by the blast. The plutonium casks were blown apart, the plutonium scattered into the air. Pieces of the boxcars, heated by the explosion, were blown into the tanker cars, and a second later, the tanker cars exploded, billowing balls of flame following the ignited gasoline and diesel fuel as it cascaded from the air onto the wreckage and bodies that littered the surrounding ground. The six Russians who had placed the shape charges were killed instantly, ripped apart by the explosion of the railcars. Gregori Donskoi, who had been watching from the edge of the road next to the police headquarters, was decapitated by part of the door of the first car. Sasha Dunitsev, knocked to the ground and screaming in agony from the metal shard that had impaled his stomach, was covered with burning gasoline that rained down from the tanker car explosion. His screams stopped as the burning mass melted his face.

Mikail and Matveev instinctively felt the massive explosions begin, and took cover behind a concrete wall at the edge of the highway. When the explosions stopped they leapt over the wall and surveyed the scene. Shells of six of the huge casks that contained the nuclear fuel rods were scattered on the ground. Mikail could see no sign of the smaller plutonium casks. The entire scene before him was on fire, the gasoline and diesel mixture creating an inferno, sending thick, inky clouds of smoke skyward. He ran to the edge of the police building. He noticed that all the windows in all the buildings that lined the tracks were blown out. Matveev ran after him. They looked for Dunitsev and Donskoi in the wreckage as the flames seared their faces and hands. They did not see or feel the gamma particles from the fuel rods bathing them, racing through their skin, tearing at the organs of their bodies. "Mikail, we have to go!" Matveev shouted. "They are lost!"

Mikail and Matveev ran from the fires and the dense, choking smoke. The sound of a helicopter overhead made Mikail raise his head from the ground, where he had fallen, unable to breathe. The helicopter. It was their escape. "Yigor!" he called to Matveev. Several other Russians saw the copter as well, and ran to the designated landing zone. When Mikail and the others were on board, the pilot lifted the aircraft from the field, and flew rapidly to the east through the spreading black smoke, along the prearranged route.

The Scouts and the policeman who had stopped them fell to the concrete, knocked over by the force of the explosion. Pieces of hot metal struck several of the Scouts, Billy saw when he raised his head after the explosions. West was still lying on the concrete, face down. Billy shook him violently. "Mr. West, we have to get out of here! John and Frank are hurt bad! Mr. West!" Suddenly, he saw the red pool flowing around the head of the Scoutmaster. His face had been crushed by a chunk of one of the nuclear fuel rod casks. Billy recoiled in horror from the dead man. He saw that the policeman was pulling himself up from the pavement. "Officer! We need to get my friends to the hospital! Can you call someone?"

The man shoved Billy away, and he fell to the ground again. "Help yourself!" His eyes were wild with terror. The policeman began running from the scene. The van was in flames where the militia had parked it, the gas tank exploded by the flames licking the vehicle, the driver's body burning into the seat. Billy ran to the other side of the tracks to find the four Scouts hiding behind the hardware store. The ground where their tents had been was now in flames, huge pieces of metal lying under the burning gasoline. "Come on with me! We need to get help. There are people hurt all over the place."

The rest of the Scouts stood watching the burning rubble from the corner of the government center. They watched, frightened and confused, as policemen ran from the police headquarters, away from the burning train. Once again, the angry roar of an explosion filled the air. The two tanker cars on the other side of the next railcar in line had been bombarded with burning gasoline and diesel fuel and had exploded. The force of the blast had crushed the railcars next to them, tripping the laser triggers, activating the explosives in both cars. Twelve more fuel rod casks rained down alongside the remains of the train, and ten more casks of plutonium were shredded, throwing their plutonium into the air. "Let's go to the police station!" Billy yelled to the Scouts shivering around him. The boys ran to the station, staying as close to the side of the buildings

· along the tracks and as far away from the tracks as they could. The fire was hot on their skin, and they were covered in a black film from the oily smoke. They didn't feel the other fire that burned around them, through their clothes, their skin ... their futures.

They sprinted past the fleet of police cars, many of which had been crushed by falling wreckage, and up the steps to the entrance of the central police station. The glass of the doors and windows lay across the entrance. The Scouts stopped at the door, frozen by the sight of the blue-uniformed bodies piled on the tile floor. Blood was everywhere — on the floor around the dead and dying policemen and on the walls with the torn plaster left by the bullets. Some of the Scouts began to cry. One of the policemen reached toward the Scouts, his arm stretched out from under the lifeless body of another. His face was red with blood, and when he tried to speak, more blood spilled from his lips. Billy could see he was motioning for them to call for help. He ran for the phone at the desk, stepping over the clutter of shattered bodies, slipping on the red slick floor. Grabbing the phone, he dialed 911. There was no answer. He dialed the number for his father's fire station. A harried voice answered, "Billy?"

"Yes, sir. We're at the main police station. All the police have been shot! There's blood everywhere. A bunch of police ran away, Mr. Waters. Someone needs to come here now. Everything is on fire!"

"Stay away from the fire, Billy, and wait there for help. A lot of units are on the way now. Watch for the fire engines, O.K.?"

Billy told the others help was coming. They took turns walking outside to the front of the station to scan the street for the firemen. Five minutes after Billy's call, they heard the wail of sirens. Three large units of the city fire department lurched to a stop at the edge of the wreckage. Firemen in full gear leapt from the trucks and began to attach hoses to the water hydrants. In only a few minutes three wide streams of water were pouring onto the fires. The heavy smoke spread like a dark blanket over the area so that no one could see that it was raining, a steady soaking downpour. As they raced toward the fire, Watson Harris learned that Billy and the other Scouts had taken refuge in the police station. He jumped from the truck before it stopped and sprinted through the blazing debris to the station. His relief at finding his son was quickly replaced by horror when he saw the extent of the carnage.

"Dad, some of these men are alive."

He grabbed one of the boys, "Go to the truck at the corner. Tell them I said we need paramedics, and right now. Hurry, son!" He checked the pulse of each of the bodies. Five of the sixteen policemen were still breathing. A couple moaned when they saw Watson peering down at them. "Billy, help me here. You guys lend a hand." Billy joined him, as did two other boys, and they lifted dead bodies that lay on the living. Watson judged that the men had been shot together, some falling on others and shielding them from the bullets that would have been fatal. Six paramedics rushed in and began treating the policemen. "What happened to Mr. West?" Watson asked Billy.

"He's dead, Dad."

"My God!" Watson looked at the tracks, where the other firemen battled to subdue the stubborn gasoline and diesel fires. "Billy, I have to go and help out there. Are you all right, son?"

"Yeah. I'm O.K." Watson hugged his son and turned to run to the place where his unit was slowly progressing toward the train, the heavy cascade of water suffocating the flames. As he ran, he saw that eight railcars had been blown to pieces, four of them tanker cars. It had been forty minutes since the railcars and their cargo of nuclear fuel exploded. Billy and the other Scouts felt their skin burn, they thought from the savage flames that had been too close. They began to feel nauseous, and believed it was from the smelly, greasy fumes from the fire they had breathed for too long.

They could not know the unseen and far more pernicious evil that had invaded them. For nearly thirty minutes, the Scouts had been exposed to the full fury of the radiation released when the casks were destroyed in the explosions. They had each absorbed 8,000 rads throughout their bodies. Outside the station the firemen were being bombarded by the same raging particles, gamma and alpha radiation that penetrated freely the heavy gear they wore. They walked over and through the fission material spilled from the casks, as they fought the flames. After nearly an hour, the site of the ruined train smoldered, but no longer burned. Like the Scouts, the firemen began to feel heat on their skin, even skin that had been shielded from the flames, and an uneasiness in their stomachs. By the time the ambulances began to carry the policemen to McLeod Hospital, the firemen had absorbed 10,000 rads.

Chapter 22

The helicopter flew to the Southeast. Below them, the wide swamps of the Pee Dee River flanked the brown water of the great winding channel. Mikail Plekanov lay against the padded seat. Sweat covered his body. His temperature was already 101 degrees and climbing. He struggled for control against the sickness, but finally succumbed — at first, merely leaning forward to rest his head in his hands. The skin of his forehead felt hot, the burning intensifying. His legs and feet felt as though they were on fire. He was seized with the urge to rip off his shoes and socks, even his pants — anything that touched his suddenly unbearably sensitive skin. He glanced at his comrades. He could see that Yigor Matveev and the others were suffering the same as he was. *God help us*, he thought, as he saw the color of their skin, a dark tan. Jerking his hands in front of his face, he saw the same color on his hands and arms.

Now, the burning on his skin had meaning. In a burst of realization, he knew what had happened to them. The turbulence that had been swirling in his stomach quickly convulsed him. He snatched the bag on the seat in front just in time to avoid spewing his vomit over his legs and feet. Mikail no longer was aware of his comrades seated around him and was oblivious as they began to vomit as well. The pain throughout his body began in earnest. And the vomiting continued — he no longer knew or cared where it went — each time causing the terrible pounding in his head to flare in agony. But for the seat belt, Mikail would have thrown himself to the floor of the helicopter.

The pilot was a professional, but he was unnerved by the sickness of his passengers. He steered the helicopter to the alternate landing zone — a local airport surrounded by a pine forest — the Georgetown County Airport, his chart said. His comrades had not been able to secure the cargo they came for, so there was no reason to rendezvous with the boat, which would have taken them to a waiting freighter. The alternate plan called for him to deposit the men at the airport where they would board a charter jet for Bermuda and from there a flight home to St. Petersburg.

He wondered why they were so sick. All of them. And in exactly the same way. It was eerie. His job would be completed once he returned the helicopter to the rental agency in Myrtle Beach, but he worried nonetheless. His future was tied to Mikail Plekanov, after all.

Mikail was unaware that the helicopter had landed at all, until he felt arms lifting him from his seat. Pain shot through him with each touch of the hands that helped him to stand and exit the helicopter. The skin, and worse, the tissue itself under the skin, screamed in agony. He was dimly aware of voices moaning, begging for relief. One of the voices was his own.

The ground crew and an assortment of a half dozen people milling around the sleepy airport watched curiously as the five crying men were helped aboard the jet. Mikail and Yigor Matveev each had received a total of 700 rads in the short time they walked across the wreckage from the exploded train, and highly radioactive mud coated the pants and boots they wore, even now irradiating the skin, muscle and bone of their feet and legs. The other three Russians had been exposed more directly and had absorbed nearly 900 rads.

*   *   *

The rain that had been falling lightly since dawn was now pouring from the dark clouds that stretched from the Pee Dee over Florence. Watson Harris watched as the rainwater flowed from the puddles that formed near the railroad tracks, through the smoldering wreckage. Muddy with the loose dirt around the tracks and the lot behind Ferris' Hardware, the water ran to the nearby storm drain, filling it and rushing to merge with the rest of the storm water on its way to Jefferies Creek and the Pee Dee. Invisible, but raging among the water and suspended sediment was the radioactivity released from the train's shattered cargo.

Overhead, Watson noticed that the dense black smoke from the fire was nearly gone. Only slender threads of smoke drifted up from what had been the raging fire around the train. The heavy rain dissipated the smoke quickly, carrying the particles of ash, cinders, and dust to the ground, only a short distance from the scene of the conflagration. Like the water rushing to the river from the wreckage of nuclear fuel and plutonium, the smoke was highly radioactive. As the rain washed the air clean of the irradiated particles that composed the smoke, they fell onto the streets, trees, lawns, and roofs of Florence's center city. The angry particles, freed from the confines of the rods and the giant casks, roared and smashed into the healthy atoms of the matter that made up the city. Violated and mutated by the stray neutrons and other parts of decaying atoms, everything the smoke particles fell on became radioactive also.

Watson surveyed the scene of the ruined train through the drenching downpour. He noted the four sets of wheels where the freight cars had been, and the four adjoining sets from the tanker cars. What had happened here? The explosions had come from inside the railcars; that was evident from the pieces of the railcars scattered around the area. What confused him were the ragged fragments of what had been huge, thick metal containers. And why were all the police shot, the other stations bombed? The answer — the horrifying truth — came to him with the question itself. His mind rebelled, not wanting to accept the facts now so plain. He bent to the ground where a puddle of water an inch deep had gathered and washed the black film from his hands. His hands were dark brown. Some things you never forgot from army training, like the symptoms of radiation exposure. The burning that he now realized was getting worse, the nausea he felt stirring in his stomach. *God in heaven,* he thought.

Watson ran to the truck where the other firemen were packing the last of their gear. Frantically, he snatched the radiophone from its cradle and dialed the number for the police. A still shaken young voice answered. Watson shouted, "This train had radioactive fuel on it! The whole area needs to be cordoned off right now! Yes, I'm sure, damn it! Call the hospital and tell them to get ready to evaluate people for acute radiation exposure ... all the firemen ...," then the worst fear of all struck him, "and the Scouts! They were here too long!" He immediately called home.

Dottie answered, her voice strained and fearful. "Bud, this is awful. Are you all right? What happened?"

"Dottie, you've got to get Billy to McLeod right away. Has he been sick at all?"

There was a pause, as she tried to absorb what this meant. "Yes ... he's been throwing up since he got home, from all the stress and the heat, I guess."

"His skin. What's his skin look like?"

She paused again, fear flooding around her, pulling the ground from under her. "It's brown — like a sun tan. And he's feverish. I didn't take his temperature — I thought it was the fire."

"Dottie, take him to McLeod right now. I'll meet you there. I'll explain. It's important. Hurry!" Watson replaced the radiophone and saw the shocked looks of the other members of his team. "That train was carrying nuclear fuel rods! We've all been irradiated! Look!" He held up his hands for them to see. "Let's go; I'll call the others and tell them to get there as soon as they can." As the engine raced along the wet streets towards McLeod Hospital, Watson called the other units. Already, two firemen in the other teams were incapacitated with nausea.

At the hospital the fire engines lined up on the curb. The emergency room was chaotic. The staff had not recovered from the delivery only an hour before of nearly one fifth of the entire city police force, all with serious machine gun wounds, most dead and the rest in critical condition. The firemen gathered calmly in the waiting area, although several were repeatedly vomiting. Now the parents of a dozen Scouts were arriving with their sons, all of them beset with violent nausea and raging fever. And all the white boys had a peculiar dark tan. The young emergency room doctor examined the first boy to arrive, removed his shirt, and found the brown discoloration covered his chest and back. Perplexed, he opened the child's pants and fearfully noted that it covered his entire body. The child's fever was 104 degrees. What the hell was this?

As the room became crowded with men and boys, all apparently suffering the same bizarre symptoms, the doctor ordered the chief nurse at the desk to call for help. Watson Harris approached the harried doctor, "It's radiation, Doctor. These Scouts were all at the rail crossing at Highway 52. A bunch of railcars exploded and scattered nuclear fuel and probably plutonium all over the place. Check your books, Doctor. These are the symptoms."

From behind him, Watson heard his wife's anguished cry, "Bud, he's so sick." She was helping his son, Billy, to walk toward them.

"Dad...." His son's voice was weak. He took the boy in his arms and held him. The fever raged in his body; Watson could feel the heat radiating from him.

"Come on, Son. Let's get you some help. I'm real proud of you. You were a real hero today." Billy collapsed at the edge of the desk, and Watson caught him. He looked at the doctor, begging for help with his eyes. Watson laid Billy on the examining table and watched as his clothes were removed, revealing the ugly dark brown covering him. His temperature had climbed to 105, and he hovered on the edge of consciousness. Horrified, Watson saw that his son's hands and feet were showing signs of swelling.

The doctor ordered an IV and medication to reduce the fever. Dottie walked alongside as the nurse wheeled his son down the hall. The firemen waited for the Scouts to be examined and admitted, trying to maintain their composure. Finally, their strength was not enough to restrain the demon that had invaded them. One by one, they collapsed in the chairs, in the bathroom, and on the floor. Watson helped the nurses get them onto gurneys until he, too, was overcome by the fever, the nausea, and the growing pain that permeated his whole body. Too late, he reached for the edge of the counter as the sight left his eyes and fell heavily onto the tile floor.

One of the nurses that had come to the emergency room to help deal with the flood of men and boys saw Watson fall and grabbed his head in time to keep it from smashing into the hard tile. Susan Engle had been about to leave for home after an already extra long night shift when the madness began. She knew she needed to think about the baby she carried. She was approaching exhaustion and was straining herself in ways she knew she shouldn't. Never could she have imagined the most serious threat now poised to strike at her child. Unseen and unfelt were the radioactive particles viciously racing into her and her baby, flying from the muddy clothes and boots, and from the very body of the big fireman she helped to roll onto the gurney.

* * *

When the explosions ripped the casks of plutonium and flung their pieces into the air, the transponder signals emanating from each cask stopped. At OPER NAVY BLUE on Andrews Air Force Base outside of Washington, D.C., the screen monitoring the casks flashed the alarm. The officer on duty, called the response team at Fort Bragg. In minutes, he had also notified the designated contact with the Defense Intelligence Agency, Felix Hubbard.

At Fort Bragg, the response team commander alerted four helicopters to make ready to take off. The last known location of the casks was in the center of Florence, some one hundred miles away. Andrews had also told them that all of the casks in two of the railcars were still transmitting their signals.

His orders were explicit. He was to secure the area where the casks were last known to be present and determine if the other casks, the ones still transmitting signals, were still intact. If so, he was to protect them until they could be transported to whatever location and by whatever means his superiors determined. While he never questioned his orders, he thought the final part of his orders was odd. He was absolutely forbidden to coordinate in any fashion with state or local authorities. Well, it wasn't his job to figure out *why* he was ordered to do something, was it? Not on a captain's pay.

The Black Hawk helicopter gracefully lifted itself from the tarmac. Inside, the twelve soldiers clutched their rifles between their legs. None of them thought this would be much of a job. Alongside the Black Hawk, three Apache attack helicopters flew in escort. The troops joked at the overkill. *What the fuck do they think is in Florence, anyway?*

*   *   *

The call came to the governor's mobile phone from the headquarters of the state law enforcement division in Columbia at 9:30. Blackie's car was still thirty minutes from Florence. The information was for the governor himself, the officer said. "... Explosions scattered material that the hospital staff says must have been radioactive. They have over a dozen Boy Scouts, and as many firemen, admitted now with symptoms of acute radiation sickness. They were all at the scene for an extended period of time."

"Oh my God," Blackie moaned.

"Governor, I'm afraid there's more, sir. Just before the explosions, there were attacks on all the police stations, including the main one in Florence, and the highway patrol headquarters. All the officers present at that time were shot. Most, fatally. A handful are also in the hospital in critical condition. The immediate area of the explosion has been cordoned off from the public."

"Do we have anything that can measure radiation?" His mind reeled in shock. He prayed Watson and Billy were all right.

"We're looking. We asked the Savannah River Site, but they haven't answered us yet. Clemson and USC are possibilities."

"Keep looking. Has anyone called the White House?"

"No, sir."

"Call them and call me back as soon as you talk to them, no matter what they say."

He called the number for Watson and Dottie Harris. No answer. He called information for Charleston and got the numbers for Drew Holland and Jim McNeely. He wanted them to get in touch with Anthony DeSilva. God knows they needed his help now — if he would come. There was no answer at Holland's, so he tried McNeely's number. The ring clicked slightly as the call was forwarded from McNeely's home to Matt Reicher's, rang again, and a strange, sleepy voice answered. "This is William Haselden. Is Jim McNeely there? It's an emergency."

"I'll wake him. Just a minute."

Matt slipped on a pair of shorts and knocked softly on the guest room door. "Jim? ... You have a call ... a guy who says he's William Haselden."

Jim clawed his way to consciousness and looked at his watch. 9:35. Jesus. What did Haselden want? He slipped into the hall and followed Matt to the phone in the kitchen.

He picked up the phone. Matt poured two cups of cold leftover coffee as he watched and listened.

"Yes, Governor. I have Dr. DeSilva's number." Blackie's voice was taught with stress... and fear.

Jim's eyes widened and he gulped the coffee as Blackie explained about the train. "It's the plutonium train! I can feel it. The bastards ran it right through town and didn't tell a soul. Damn them to hell!" He listened to the governor's rage. "Doesn't your friend have experience with nuclear materials?"

"Yes," Jim said, looking at Matt.

"Let me ask him a few questions."

Jim put the phone down and repeated what Haselden had just told him. Then he handed the phone to Matt.

"Yes, Governor," he said taking the phone.

"Commander, I'm in bad need of help right now. I know you guys have never admitted you keep nukes at the station, but I've got a serious problem. I need some kind of device to measure radiation. It looks like a whole lot of people have already been exposed to high doses. But nobody knows how much is out there. Does the Weapons Station have something we can use?"

Matt thought only for a second before answering. "Yes, sir. I'll bring them myself."

There was a pause on the other line. "O.K., Commander. I'll have a National Guard helicopter pick you up."

"Yes, sir. Let me ask you something? Do you have reason to believe that nuclear fuel was released."

"Yes."

"Governor, I suggest you keep everyone at least one-half mile from the scene. Everyone."

Blackie's blood ran cold. "All right."

Matt drove to the headquarters building and dashed inside while Jim waited in the jeep. Thirty minutes after Haselden's call, they boarded a helicopter at one of the station's baseball diamonds.

*   *   *

Blackie's calls to Watson's home number still went unanswered. Still, he hoped.

As the car exited the ramp from I-20 for downtown Florence, he called the National Guard commander, his fifth call to General Harrison Demers in an hour. The general confirmed that a cordon was being set up one-half mile from all parts of the train. He said the press was starting to ask questions.

"The last thing on my mind right now is answering reporters' questions."

"Governor, I know how you feel. But soon we may need to use the press to communicate to the people of the area."

Blackie was chastened by the remark. Fear was overwhelming his ability to reason. "You're right, General. We'll talk to them soon. Please tell them that."

Blackie wanted to tell the driver to go straight to McLeod Hospital. But he knew the priority was to see the train. The limousine approached the roadblock of National Guardsmen on the highway. In the distance he could see the engine sitting across the road. He got out and walked to the rope. The soldiers, all from Florence, ordered to report to duty only hours before, saluted sharply. Blackie did not even see them. He stared at the city beyond the train. Anger turned to rage as he watched the still smoldering ruins of the railcars in the morning stillness. The soldiers standing next to him looked up at the sound of helicopters making a low pass over the train. Blackie followed their gaze.

"Are those guard air craft?" he asked.

"No, sir. Those are active army."

The governor watched the helicopters circle overhead and finally approach the large parking lot a hundred yards behind them. When all the helicopters were on the ground, soldiers spilled from the Black Hawk in full battle dress. "Is your gun loaded?" Blackie asked the stunned guardsman.

"Yes, sir."

The soldier leading the group from the helicopters approached the roadblock. It was the captain in command of the response team, who ignored Blackie and walked up to the National Guard staff sergeant. The sergeant saluted him and the captain waved a response. "I'll take over from here, Sergeant."

The guardsman looked at the governor, utterly confused. Blackie walked up to the captain, struggling to suppress the fury that was coursing through every fiber of his body, trying to see the young officer as just another man sent to carry out his orders. And not the enemy. "I'm Governor William Haselden. What are you doing here, Captain?"

The captain was surprised, but answered quickly. "I am ordered to secure the site of this train and to hold it until federal authorities arrive to retrieve the undamaged cargo." He glanced over the governor's shoulder at the site of the damaged train he had already seen from the air. *No wonder the transponders stopped working*, he thought. "I'll take over from your National Guard now, sir."

Blackie shook his head slowly. "I don't think so, Captain."

The captain's eyes blinked, and then the lines tightened around them. His stare narrowed. "Sir, I have my orders."

"This is my state, Captain. Besides, that area is contaminated with radioactivity. You don't really want to go over there. Stay in the parking lot." He turned away from the captain and spoke to the frightened staff sergeant. "Sergeant, call your commander. Tell him these men are not to be allowed to leave the parking lot. If they stay for a while, see they are fed. Have a Port-o-let delivered." Blackie saluted and walked back to his car. The furious captain strode back to the Black Hawk to call Fort Bragg.

Blackie called General Demers. "General, a group of active army soldiers has arrived and attempted to take charge of the site of the train. They are not to be allowed to do so. Is that clear? They are to be kept in the parking lot where they landed."

Demers smiled. It was the first time on this godforsaken day he had seen any reason. "Yes, sir."

"And have the railroad tracks blocked on both sides of the site. Use armor."

"Yes, sir."

Blackie climbed back into the car. "Take me to the hospital."

The emergency room was empty by the time Blackie got there, but the air of chaos had not yet dissipated. The faces of everyone in the building carried the mark of fear. The emergency room doctor and the chief physician at McLeod, who had been summoned by the anxious young doctor an hour before, greeted the governor. In a small sitting room, they told him what they knew. "Governor, we have about a dozen firemen and a bunch of Boy Scouts admitted, all with the same symptoms. They have very high fevers, terrible nausea — which doesn't respond to any of the usual treatments. Worse, they are beginning to show signs of swelling. I have no way of knowing how far these symptoms will progress. Without a way to measure the radiation field they were exposed to, we can't know how many rads they've absorbed, but there is no doubt in my mind that this is the source of their sickness. The instruments we do have on hand all confirm they are emitting radiation. We've removed their clothes, all of which are radioactive." The doctor stopped. It was such a horrible thing to describe. Could language alone convey what had happened? "Their bodies are actually radioactive, Governor." He described the treatments being administered — IVs for dehydration and nourishment, medication for the fever and for the pain that each of the patients was beginning to suffer, terrible pain from the assault on all the tissue of their bodies. Some blisters had started to form on some of the boys. The governor understood. He remembered the firemen from Chernobyl.

"Do you have a list of the patients?"

The doctor handed Blackie a list. His finger followed the list of hand-written names until he found them. Watson and Billy were both there. He felt the floor turn to vapor under his feet. He was falling, spinning through air into the abyss. He looked at the faces of the two doctors and his own staff. They watched him, wanting him to give them direction. He grasped for something deep inside to steady himself. In his mind he summoned a picture of Bud, his powerful arms cocked, the bat ready to punish the little white ball the pitcher would try to slide past him. Then he saw Billy, the imprint of his father, in the same stance. He heard the words of his friend again, all those years ago on the porch of his house, demanding that he put his life back together, yelling at him to be a man. "O.K., Doctor. May I visit the patients?"

* * *

The National Guard Humvee raced from the landing zone set up south of the site. Matt Reicher and Jim McNeely sat silently. They saw that the one-half mile cordon recommended by Matt was in place as they approached the roadblock. The driver explained to the soldiers who his passengers were. Matt unpacked the radiation detector and climbed from the Humvee. Standing at the rope, he switched on the device. The reading came at once, 10 roentgens per hour. Nervously, he climbed over the rope and started to walk along the road toward the train. When he was a thousand yards from the engine, the dose reading suddenly shot off the scale. He turned around and ran back to the rope.

Four more times he repeated the sampling of radiation emissions from the wreckage. To the north, the circle of heavy radiation extended much further from the train. All of central downtown was contaminated. "Where's the governor?" he asked the driver when he had returned to the Humvee for the last time. The driver checked with his commander while Matt removed his shoes and socks and replaced them with fresh ones he carried in the bag he carried. He tossed the ones he had worn, now contaminated, over the rope.

"He's at the hospital, sir. I can take you."

"Thanks. Lieutenant, I don't have any authority, but you need to move this cordon back another half mile. On the north side, another full mile. It isn't safe for your soldiers to be here for long."

The young officer stared at him for a moment, then picked up his radio and called his colonel. The colonel told him to take no chances, and move the cordon back.

*   *   *

Blackie was led by the floor nurse into the room. Watson Harris shared a room with another fireman. Both men were attached to IV bottles. The doctor explained that the bottles also administered medication for the pain, which would otherwise be unbearable. Watson turned his face to Blackie as he approached the bed. Blackie noticed that his eyes sparkled with an unusual brilliance — from the fever and the drugs, he realized. Blackie was shaken by his appearance. Already, the nuclear tan was darkening as his skin continued to break down. "Bud, are they taking good care of you?"

When Watson spoke, Blackie saw that his tongue was swelling. Still, his words were clear, though Blackie wondered for how much longer. "Guv, you made it. I wish someone had let us in on what was on that frigging train. I'd have let the son of a bitch burn, myself." He coughed, the pain clear on his face.

"Me, too, Bud. Me, too."

"You tried, Blackie. You did all that could be done. The assholes are just too damned powerful. Didn't I tell you?"

"Yes, you did."

"How many rads did we soak up, Blackie? Do they know yet?"

"They don't know, but we're working on it."

"Have you seen Billy? He was pretty sick. I hope he didn't get the worst of it."

"He's next on my list." Watson turned his head to one side, unable to hide the pain tearing through his disintegrating body. "Bud, I'll be back later. You rest now."

Watson nodded, but did not speak for fear the scream crawling up his throat would escape.

Blackie was pale and shaking as he left Watson's room. But he was terrified of what awaited him next. On the floor below, the nurse led him to Billy Harris. The room was much larger than the other, and really more of a ward. There were six of the Scouts here, separated from each other by cloth partitions. His stomach turned when he saw his godson. The boy's skin was darker than his father's, but more frightening to Blackie, Billy's lips and face were blistering. His hands were swollen, already grotesquely misshapen. Like his father's, the boy's eyes twinkled with an unnatural light. Billy turned when he heard Blackie walk to the foot of his bed. Incredibly, he smiled when he saw Blackie.

"Uncle Blackie," he said, the words slurred by his badly swollen tongue. Blackie saw that he winced, each word he spoke inciting more pain in his blistering lips and throat.

"Billy, I'm proud of what you did today. There are five policemen who owe you their lives, Son."

"Thanks. How's my dad?"

Blackie summoned all the courage he could find and lied, "He's going to be all right, Billy. You just worry about getting yourself better, O.K.?"

"O.K."

"I'll be back to see you later, Son. I need to go talk to your mom."

"Uncle Blackie, I need to tell you what happened." He whimpered at the pain. Blackie turned back to the bed, fighting the tears.

"Billy, you need to rest now."

"No, please listen. We're the only ones who saw it. Mr. West is dead, and the firemen didn't get there 'til it was over." He was fighting terrible pain, Blackie saw, and was desperate to tell what he had seen.

"All right, Billy. Tell me."

"We were with Mr. West when we heard a funny noise from the police station. We came to the corner and this policeman wouldn't let us cross the street. The train was sitting on the highway. While we stood there, these men walked up to the train and put something on the doors of the cars. Then they ran away and there were little explosions. The doors of the railcars fell inside. And right after that, there were gigantic explosions, but this time from inside the train. Two of my friends were hurt by stuff flying in the air ... and Mr. West was killed by some. The policeman pushed me to the ground and ran off. After the railcars blew up, the tanker cars exploded and it started to burn everywhere. I got the troop together and we went to the police station, only all the officers had been shot. Most of them were dead. I called the fire station and they said my dad was on the way."

"Thanks, Billy.... You rest now, and get better."

"It was the nuclear stuff on the train wasn't it?"

Blackie stared at the boy, his heart pounding. "Yes, Billy. It was."

"So we're all sick from radiation?"

"Yes."

Billy started to cry. "This is awful painful, Uncle Blackie. This shouldn't happen to people."

"I know."

"You tried to stop them. You were right. They just wouldn't listen."

"No, they wouldn't listen."

Blackie walked from the room to the hall in a daze. At the end of the corridor, he saw the door of a small chapel and walked in. His staff waited outside. In the cool dark room, he let the fear and grief finally wash over him. His hands gripped the fine-grained wood of the pew in front of him. Slowly, he lowered his head between his hands, resting it on the edge, and began to sob. When their son died so long ago, how wrong he had been to think he would never again feel such pain.

*   *   *

Matt Reicher and Jim McNeely ran up the steps to the hospital. The National Guard driver told them the governor was waiting for them in a conference room on the second floor. "Before we go see him, let's do one thing," Matt said walking to the front desk. To the nurse he explained, "We're here with the governor. I have a radiac to measure the levels of radiation. Can we take a reading from some of the patients?"

The woman regarded them with surprise, but led them to two rooms, one with firemen and one with Boy Scouts. In each Matt held the radiac next to the patients and took readings. "Shit!" he exclaimed when they were once again in the hall. "Ma'am, these people are very radioactive. You need to limit the time any person spends with them. No pregnant women should be allowed in the room with them."

The woman's eyes widened with fear. One more horror to confront before this terrible day was through. "Yes."

"Get them out of here. Right now!" She ran to the hospital director's office and relayed the message. In ten minutes, another nurse found Susan Engle in the ward with the Boy Scouts and told her. Her face went pale, and she rushed from·the building.

*   *   *

Hours of chaos in the hospital finally ended. The young emergency room physician who treated the wounded police — and fifty minutes later the largest number of cases of acute radiation sickness in American history — sat in front of his computer. His search on the Internet located several articles on the experience of doctors in the Ukraine after the Chernobyl accident. There was no question that what he saw was reliable. The firemen and the young Scouts were doomed. All he and his colleagues could do was ease the pain of their dying. But there was something that could be done for the living. Iodine. Cases of thyroid cancer in the Ukraine and Bellorus increased 8,000 percent after Chernobyl. Use of iodine tablets by all those exposed within twelve hours after exposure would have prevented most of the cancers. Iodine tablets.

The doctor grabbed the articles from the small printer and ran down the hall and up the two flights of stairs to the office of the chief of surgery, the ranking doctor in the hospital. He flung them down on the desk of his superior and explained what had to be done. "We don't have much time. Everyone with any exposure must be given the tablets... right away."

The chief surgeon picked up the phone and called his contact with the governor's staff. Next, he called the pharmacy and directed that all the police and the patients from the train explosion be administered the tablets. He saw the peculiar look on the younger man's face. "You never know," he said.

"We have to assume that exposure will spread beyond the site of the train. The family members of the victims will receive exposure just visiting the patients. And until the area is cleaned up, contamination will migrate to other areas. The least we can do is make sure as many children as possible who might become exposed get the tablets," the young doctor said tiredly.

"You're right. I'll ask the pharmacy to get us an emergency supply and we'll get them out through the Department of Health and the schools."

The young doctor turned to leave. "Did you ever think you'd be treating victims of a nuclear disaster?"

"Have you seen those boys? They don't teach us how to deal with that. And it's only started." He looked the chief surgeon in the eyes and held up his hands. They were dark brown. For hours he had treated the men and boys who came from the train, and his hands had absorbed enough radiation from their radioactive bodies to acquire the nuclear tan.

*   *   *

It was noon when Moore's beeper went off. The number on the screen was the secure line for Felix Hubbard. Terry Wilkins leaned on the counter and watched him pick up the secure phone line.

"What is it, Felix?"

Hubbard ran through the information he had just received from OPER NAVY BLUE at Andrews: "... And the response team from Bragg has been on the ground for an hour. The state is preventing them from approaching the train. They have been told the area is highly contaminated and that a number of firemen and Boy Scouts have been hospitalized for radiation exposure. And that it may be fatal."

"Who kept them from going to the train?"

"The governor."

"Son of a bitch!" Moore shouted. "Boy Scouts! What the fuck were Boy Scouts doing there?"

Hubbard ignored the question for which there was no answer. "Two of the railcars with plutonium are still on the ground surrounded by National Guard troops."

"Are they still rigged?"

"Yes."

"How badly is the area contaminated?"

"We don't know. The response team leader says some guy showed up with a radiac device and made measurements of the site. The guard soldiers told him it was a navy commander from Charleston named—"

"Reicher!"

"... That's right."

"He's the XO of the Weapons Station. Call the bastard and find out what the readings were. Then call me back. He can't refuse to talk to you."

"Yes, sir."

"Is it true about the people in the hospital? Are we sure they have radiation sickness?"

"Yes. I called the hospital myself. There are about a dozen firemen who put out the fire from the tanker cars. And about fifteen Boy Scouts who were camped out near the railroad tracks."

"Did they find any of the men who attacked the train?"

"No one has been back in the cordon since the explosions."

"Felix, tell no one about the special security precautions that were taken. No one. So far as we know this was just a terrorist attack."

"Yes, sir." The last thing that Hubbard intended to do was to let it be known he had been involved in sending booby-trapped nuclear fuel into an American city.

Moore sank into a chair at the corner of the den. He had to think — had to calm himself and reclaim his ability to reason this out.

"What's wrong?" Wilkins asked.

"Wrong? Wrong?" he screamed. Wilkins recoiled from the violence of the outburst. "Some assholes have blown up a train full of nuclear fuel rods and plutonium in the middle of a city in South Carolina!" He grabbed a porcelain figure of a dolphin and threw it against the wall of the den. The dolphin shattered loudly, scattering shards of the figurine across the room. "How did they know?" he shouted. "How?" He turned glaring at Terry Wilkins.

Wilkins saw the violence in the eyes fixed on him and fought to suppress the panic that was building inside him.

"I've got to go to D.C. right away," Moore said calmly and headed up the steps to change clothes. At the top step, he leaned over the rail. "Terry, I'm sorry." He disappeared into his bedroom.

The young soldier laid his head in his hands and rested it on the counter, searing pain arcing through his stomach. "*My God, what have I done?*" he whispered softly.

*   *   *

Mike O'Connelly looked across the table. Both of his children were there. How long had it been since he saw them like this? Just them. It was a priceless moment. If only Helen could be in her seat, there on the left. He glanced at the empty chair, an involuntary gesture that didn't escape the eyes of his daughter. The staff brought their lunch from the kitchen and fussed over every detail. They knew how pleased the boss they loved was to have his children home.

"Mr. O'Connelly, I know you didn't request a wine with lunch," the cook said as he laid the chilled bottles of Pinot Noir on the table, "but I thought these might go just right with lunch today."

O'Connelly shot a glance at the cook leaning over the table. "You're fired."

"Thank you, sir."

"Wine, Marilyn? Mickey?"

"You're a hard man, Dad," Mickey said.

O'Connelly turned and yelled over his shoulder, "Good help is impossible to find these days."

As they finished their ice cream, Marilyn rested her chin in her hands and asked her father, "Dad, you said you had some family business to discuss?" O'Connelly picked up his dishes and began walking to the kitchen. The cooks took the stacks of dishes from the vice president and his children at the door.

"Sit down. This isn't a long story, but it's a hard one for me to tell, kids."

Mickey smiled. *Kids.* They would always be his kids.

O'Connelly began to relate the development of his reservations about the administration, and how it grew into suspicion of outright wrongdoing. He told them of his conflict with Moore and the president over the matter of the plutonium. Looking at Marilyn, he explained Moore's efforts to smear them both to get at him. Their faces were grim. *Am I doing the right thing*, he wondered.

"I made a deal with the president," he said. "I told him I would be a loyal and quiet member of the administration, so long as he left you alone." He watched the shock spread across their faces. "Now, I'm not so sure I did the right thing." He paused studying the children he loved more than life itself. "I thought it was just mean-spirited politics and spying and so on. But it's more than that. There has been manipulation of the federal courts. Blackmail of a judge. Misuse of the military to spy on American citizens. And I believe the administration is taking grave risks in the way it's shipping nuclear materials."

"Dad ... Dad, are you going to ask us if we want you to protect us?" Mickey asked.

Mickey looked up, over his father's shoulder. O'Connelly turned to see one of his secret service detail standing behind him. The agent handed him a message. It was from Leo Scardato, asking that he call the number at once. "Excuse me. I need to make a call."

In the adjoining office, he called Scardato, who answered immediately. O'Connelly listened in appalled silence to the news from South

Carolina. There was no mistake, Leo assured him. It was all true. All confirmed. O'Connelly thanked him and hung up the phone. He sat still for several minutes before he could move his legs at all. Finally, he returned to the room where his son and daughter waited. They were startled at the change in his appearance. His jaw was set in an angry lock. But his eyes were filled with a sadness they had not seen since the day their mother died.

"I've received some terrible news."

* * *

"Jim, are you all right?" Alicia sat next to him. She was unnerved by the look in his eyes, one of bitter detachment she had never seen. "It must have been awful."

"It was just like he said it would be."

"Who?"

"DeSilva. At the hearing. He told them exactly what would happen." He buried his face in his hands. "Those men and the kids. You never think you'll ever have to see…. It's horrible."

"Will they live?"

"I don't know. I'm not sure the doctors there know. Who ever thinks about this? They're learning like the rest of us. The boys are John's age. What if he was there… like that? I don't know what I'd do."

She shivered from the unthinkable image, shaken, knowing that there were parents even then facing a nightmare become real.

"Nat Engle's wife was in the hospital. She was there for an hour or more with the firemen and the Scouts and all the radioactivity."

"My God. She's pregnant, isn't she?"

* * *

On Saturday evening, Governor Haselden walked to a podium in the Florence County Emergency Operations Center. A handful of cameras were there.

"Many of you have already heard of the tragic events in Florence today. Early this morning a train loaded with nuclear fuel rods as well as plutonium bound for the Savannah River Site near Aiken was attacked.

During the attack four of the cars carrying the nuclear materials exploded and their contents were scattered over the ground. Also, four tanker cars carrying gasoline and diesel fuel exploded and caused a fire to burn among the wreckage, including the radioactive materials. The result has been to contaminate the entire center city of Florence. In addition, firemen battled the fire, not knowing it was radioactive," he said, his eyes flashing furiously, "and they, along with a group of Boy Scouts who were performing a public service project, were exposed to high doses of radiation. They are currently in McLeod Hospital. Help is being sent now from the Medical College Hospital at the University of South Carolina and the Medical University in Charleston. An area roughly one mile around the site is absolutely quarantined. No one may enter for any reason. The area may be expanded when we know more about the degree of contamination. All persons who have been exposed — who have been in this area, or who have visited loved ones who were exposed — are advised to take iodine tablets as soon as possible to avoid the possibility of developing thyroid cancer. You may get these tablets from your pharmacy or the hospital. Do not delay in taking this important precaution for yourself and your family.

"To the families of the police and highway patrolmen who were murdered today, and to the victims of the radiation, I promise you I will not rest until I have exhausted every effort to find and punish those who caused this outrage." He paused, his eyes boring into the camera. "To Roger Seekings, let me make it clear that I hold you personally responsible. To the people of South Carolina, I give you my solemn promise that there will be no more trains of nuclear poison." He walked away from the cameras.

* * *

When Blackie opened the door to the house at his farm, June fell into his arms, crying bitterly. She clung to him, desperate for strength and security in a world suddenly become mad. As he held her, he felt a bulge in the vest pocket of his suit coat. It was the outline of the speech he was supposed to give to the Scouts. A speech for another world, now remote and forever lost. Slowly, he began to cry. For the moment, his was grief apart from anger. The hatred he felt for those who robbed him of half of his life waited, resting on the far border of his cognizance. Now, his tears were for the friend of a lifetime and the boy he loved as fully as any father ever loved his son.

Chapter 23

It was a story the world's media knew how to cover. A fear spoken about for decades had become reality. And it was in America, where they could observe the tragedy in all its morbid detail. The elements to capture an audience — and keep them for days or weeks — were all here. A small American city, the terrorist murder of so many policemen, the grisly sickness from radiation that the experts solemnly said was killing the firemen and the Boy Scouts. One ambitious reporter for a syndicated TV program interviewed the grieving parents of the dying Scouts, before they understood that the agony of their sons was being hawked as spectacle — before they learned to hate all reporters. The young man learned from one of the fathers, as he wept into the microphone, that one of the boys, Billy Harris, was the godson of Governor Haselden, the son of his lifelong friend, who, incredibly, was one of the firemen dying from the same radiation. Father and son became symbols of the story. A picture appeared of Haselden with Watson and Billy at the landing on Welch's Creek, Billy proudly holding up a string of redbreast.

In Europe, the story was more parochial, especially where the Soviet plutonium was collected and shipped to America. Unlike Americans, Europeans knew that terrorism was an ever-present threat, all the more so because of the immeasurable value of the plutonium to such people. The prime minister of the Netherlands called Roger Seekings immediately after confirming the story with his security advisor. The prime minister diplomatically emphasized that his country could not afford to risk the continued transportation of such materials across its territory and the use of the port at Rotterdam to load it onto ships. As soon as the ship then being loaded sailed, there could be no more, he had said. Minutes later came the call from the chancellor of Germany. He understood that the Dutch were closing their port to further shipments and politely asked for the Americans' intentions. Did they intend to use Bremerhaven? The prime minister firmly insisted that the stockpiles of plutonium the Americans had collected at Bad Kreuznach must be moved as quickly as possible. As soon as it convened, the Bundestag would demand no less, he predicted.

In the days that followed the explosion, South Carolina learned about radiation. Anthony DeSilva arrived and encouraged reporters for the local press to print fully and accurately the precautions he told them people must take. He handed them articles that explained what had happened when the casks of fuel rods and plutonium were scattered, making them promise to report the details. He let them follow him as he surveyed the wreckage and measured the level of contamination. He made them wait at the ropes as he donned a protective suit and walked to the ruined railcars, and in ever-widening circles as he measured the radiation around the cars, in the empty lots, in the abandoned police station and the city/county government building, and in the deserted streets lined with empty shops. Once the governor approved his recommendation to remove the contaminated wreckage and soil at the site, he explained it all to the reporters, telling them it was important that they get the word out to their citizens. The only thing he would not talk to them about was the sickness of the firemen and the children. That was for the doctors, he said, though he knew full well the extent of the horror unfolding in McLeod Hospital. DeSilva also did not let them see the bitter tears he could not hold back after his visit to the dying men and boys.

As soon as the story appeared in the papers of Kiev and Minsk, half a world away, the governor's office began to receive a flood of offers of help from doctors, engineers, and technicians, all with experience from the disaster at Chernobyl. Blackie asked Jim McNeely and DeSilva to serve on a team to organize the cleanup. Jim's job, Blackie said, was to manage how to make use of the Ukrainian and Byelorussian volunteers — and to make sure DeSilva was able to get what he needed. Other members of the team included leaders of the legislature. They watched closely but stayed out of the way, ensuring that all efforts to deal with the tragedy remained united behind the governor's leadership.

On the afternoon following the explosion, after dozens of calls from his staff went unanswered by the administration, Blackie Haselden suppressed the terrible rage boiling inside him and called the White House himself. The president's chief of staff explained how concerned the president was and offered to personally coordinate any assistance the state needed, once the two remaining cars containing the plutonium were recovered from the site. "Any further tragedy must be avoided," he said solemnly.

"I'm going to find out how this happened, and the cars stay here until I know. Tell that to your boss," Blackie said and slammed the phone into the receiver. Fighting back anger that threatened to overwhelm him, he dialed the number for the vice president's residence. Shortly, the voice he recognized as O'Connelly came on the line.

"Governor, I can't tell you how sorry I am."

"Thank you," Blackie said tersely. "I have been unable to get Seekings to speak to me directly, Mike. So, I'm calling you."

O'Connelly was silent for a moment. "What can I do to help?" he said evenly.

"My godson is dying from radiation. His body is so burned that every word he speaks causes him terrible pain. But he still told me what he saw yesterday. He saw those railcars blow up from *the inside!* Now, terrorists don't blow things up from the inside, do they? Know what I think, Mr. Vice President? I think they were rigged to blow up. What do you think?"

"Bill—"

"Tell that bastard in the White House I'm going to find out what happened. We'll take care of ourselves. *Fuck him and his assistance!*" The line buzzed as Blackie crashed the phone down again. O'Connelly closed his eyes. He called his secretary and told her to find out where Seekings was. Then he called for his car.

* * *

O'Connelly arrived at the White House unannounced. Taking salutes from the marines at the entrance, he walked straight to the president's informal office that adjoined the Oval Office. He walked in to find Roger Seekings alone in front of a television. CNN was broadcasting a live feed from South Carolina. Seekings glanced briefly as O'Connelly walked toward his chair. "Sit down, Mike." After the reporter stopped speaking, he turned to O'Connelly, "It's awful."

"Yes, Roger. It's very serious. We should see what can be done." He studied the president's face carefully. Seekings did not look him straight in the eye, but continued to avert his gaze to the television picture across the room. When Seekings did not respond, O'Connelly said quietly, "Roger, we should talk. Maybe there is something I could do."

Seekings jerked his head toward O'Connelly, finally looking straight at the vice president. "Yes, Mike ... I'll collect reports from the staff.... We'll find out what happened ... I'll need your help...." Mike O'Connelly had seen many things about Roger Seekings since his inauguration that concerned, and even disgusted, him but nothing before had alarmed him like what he saw now in the president's eyes. It was panic.

* * *

Julieanne Harris was a news addict, like most senior government people in Washington. But long ago, she adopted a policy of ignoring the news on the weekends. It provided a respite from the intensity of a week's worth of analysis of news from every troubled place on earth. She finished a leisurely run along the streets of old Alexandria. The air was cool and fresh. The trees that bordered the close, centuries-old houses were bright with autumn reds and golds. When she entered the front door of her townhouse three blocks off of King Street, the phone was ringing. Before she could reach it, the answering machine delivered her invitation to leave a message ... then it was her sister-in-law, "Julieanne ... Julieanne ...," she was crying now, "...call me quick. It's Bud ... and Billy, too—"

"Dottie," Julieanne picked up the phone, "what's wrong?"

"Come home, Julieanne. It's terrible! What's happened is terrible!"

An iciness formed in the pit of her stomach. "Dottie, what's happened? Please tell me." The ice turned to fire as she heard the terrible details spill from the phone.

"Was Bud hurt in the fire?"

"No! Julieanne ... the train was radioactive. All of them are so sick. The radiation is making them all so sick. Julie, I'm afraid they're going to die!"

The intensity of the pain inside her now was from more than the monstrous fear of loss. It was fueled by rage. She already knew what had happened in Florence, even before she called Leo.

* * *

Felix Hubbard was at his desk as usual at 7:30. In front of him lay extracts from all the major news organizations. They all read the same. All asked the same question — why had the train exploded from the inside? This was going to be a bad week, and it was going to start in a few hours when he met with Moore.

He looked up from the articles when a knock sounded at his door. "Come in," he called, resentful that his morning quiet was now disturbed.

Julieanne Harris peeked through. "Felix, have you got a minute?" she asked.

Now this was a weird surprise. "Sure. Come in." He smiled as she slid into one of the chairs in front of his desk. In her hands were two of the largest Styrofoam cups that Starbucks offered.

"Felix, I brought you some coffee. I hope you like the flavor I picked. And a little cream. Here's some sugar in case you like that, too." She was smiling at him, and it made him nervous.

"That was nice. Thanks, Julieanne." She carefully removed the lid from the second cup and sat in front of Hubbard holding both large cups uncovered. The steam swirled from the hot muddy liquid. The aroma was nice, he thought.

"Felix, I'm leaving the DIA and I wanted to say goodbye. We never got to work together, but I feel as though I really came to know you very well." Felix noted that behind the smile her eyes were suddenly hard, sharp points boring into him. "There are two things that I wanted you to know before I go." She stood and reached her right hand forward, as though to offer him the coffee. "First, I was born and raised in that little town where your train blew up on Saturday." As she said it, she flung the scalding coffee into his face, covering his head and shoulders in liquid fire. Hubbard howled — a high, piercing wail that carried throughout the nearby offices. He fell from his chair slapping the burning coffee from his face. Julieanne walked to the edge of the desk, leaned over him, and said, "The second thing is ... my only brother and his son were exposed to the radiation. I wanted you to feel just a small part of what they're feeling now." Quickly, she poured the second large cup onto his writhing body, causing him to scream again. She dropped the empty cups on the floor next to Hubbard and walked from the office, past the small crowd in the hall.

She drove to National Airport, dropped her car in long-term parking and one hour later boarded a plane for Columbia, South Carolina. As the jet rose from the runway, sailing up and over the Potomac, it turned and glided over the great city. Sweeping past her window, passing behind her, were the giant obelisk of the Washington Monument, white and gleaming in the morning sun, and the Capitol. She didn't bother to look.

* * *

The admiral and his two aides waited impassively in the anteroom of Governor Haselden's office at one end of the Capitol. If he was nervous or impatient, there was nothing on his angular features to show it. He was a veteran of scores of combat missions — most in unknown, secret places. His career had been spent in the netherworld of national defense. This mission was certainly not the most dangerous of his career, but it was the oddest. His goal was no less than to convince the governor to release the two railcars and their cargo of spent fuel rods and plutonium. He reminded himself that there had never been anything in any of the sharp young staffers' briefing books about a situation like the one he now faced. He silently cursed whatever moron had created such a remarkable screw up.

The secretary in front of the window looked pleasantly at the admiral and asked him if he was sure he would not care for a little coffee. The accent reminded him of a girl with whom he had enjoyed a brief, but memorable affair in Pensacola. He smiled back at her, and declined. He glanced at his watch. *Thirty minutes late.* In Washington, he was accustomed to being kept waiting by self-important people, but he still hated it. The tall polished door across the room opened and a man in a blue suit walked toward him. "Admiral," he said holding out his hand. "Come in, please."

The three officers filed into the governor's office and took seats around a small table. Already seated at the table was a man who did not great them, but only watched. The admiral guessed him to be Hispanic, surprised at that fact and by his appearance. The man had a graying ponytail and wore jeans, hand-tooled boots, and a string tie. *Everybody has a spiritual counselor these days,* he thought.

"Governor Haselden, I want to thank you—"

The man in the suit held up his hand and the admiral stopped speaking. "I am James McNeely, a lawyer and a member of the governor's disaster team. This is Dr. Anthony DeSilva, a retired nuclear researcher from the

Sandia Laboratory, and a consultant for the state. Governor Haselden has asked us to meet with you."

"It was my understanding we were to meet directly with the governor."

"I know that. Admiral, our governor tried very hard to contact the president after the tragedy in Florence. President Seekings has so far not seen fit to respond. Why should he take time away from his busy schedule to meet with you?" Jim fixed the admiral with a firm stare. Under the studied composure of the veteran warrior, he saw the flash of anger.

"I see."

"I understand," Jim continued, "that you have come to ask that we return the rest of the train that has made the center of one of our cities unlivable."

The admiral sat quietly for a moment. *A goddamned lawyer.* "Yes."

"Very well, we will be glad to give it back to you." Jim reached into a leather folder on the table and extracted several copies of a document. "On these conditions. First, we must be allowed to examine the interior of the railcars and confirm what is there. We require your people to open the cars, as there may be ... some risk due to the manner in which they were apparently ... sealed, shall we say. Second, we must be provided with the exact quantities of plutonium and the degree of radioactivity in the fuel rods that were on the two cars that exploded. Third, we must have the president's assurance, made publicly, that he will turn over the names of all persons known to have been responsible for the explosions."

The admiral smiled broadly, his best Capitol face. "Jim, I'm sure we can work something out. It's probably best the governor couldn't make it this morning. The worker bees, like you and I, are always better at getting to the practicalities of a problem."

"The conditions are not negotiable, Admiral."

DeSilva broke the silence that followed, "Do you remember me? You were just a commander in Spain when we lost those two specials in the ocean. I was on the team. You know, just in case." He remembered now. The thermonuclear devices had fallen into the sea, lying on a narrow shelf. There had been real concern over the release of the nuclear fuel into the sea. DeSilva had been there for that reason. "You know what has happened here — you, better than most. These people need our help, not political bullshit. I need to know what we're dealing with so I can help them get it cleaned up. The longer that fuel sits out there, the worse it is."

"I don't have that authority," the admiral replied. Turning to Jim, he added, "Mr. McNeely, the president insists that we must have the cars back unconditionally. They are federal property of the most sensitive type."

"We've seen how sensitive they are."

"They must be released immediately."

"Or what?"

Jim's eyes flashed bitterness he could no longer hide. "We are a nation of law, Mr. McNeely, as you know. We will seek an order from the appropriate court. I am sure you understand there is no question but that we will be granted custody of the cars."

"Admiral, we have nothing else to say—"

"For God's sake," DeSilva interrupted, "you can't hide what happened here."

The admiral jerked his head to look at DeSilva. To Jim, he said simply, "I'll take your message back to the president." Rising from the table, he turned, again facing Jim, the lines of the officer's face no longer hard. "Be careful, guys. Be careful."

* * *

Exhaust spewed from the bulldozers as they lifted the wreckage around the train with one scoop of the blade. The machines moved backward and then lurched toward the container. The blades hovered over the opening for a second and then tilted, spilling the metal and dirt inside. When the container, to which lead plates had been quickly welded, was full, the truck on which it rested pulled it to a mobile crane beyond the safety cordon. There the crane lowered a lead top, matching the plate that covered the bottom of the container. As quickly as they could, the welders sealed the top onto the container.

All the workers wore protective suits. Their time near the radioactive material was limited by DeSilva. With him were Ukrainian and Byelorussian technicians, all veterans of Chernobyl and all sent by their governments to assist.

As soon as the container sitting on one truck was sealed, the truck left for Charleston, escorted by a highway patrol car, for the trip to the marine terminal. At the pier three hours later, a long, low ship waited to receive the containers. Pier-side cranes would lift the containers from the trucks onto the ship's deck. At the rear of the ship stood a crane capable of lifting the containers. When the containers were loaded onto the ship, a dozen per trip, the ship would make her way toward the open sea. The captain of the ship had identified the spot on his chart one hundred miles off the coast, where the continental shelf drops into the deeper sea to a depth of five hundred feet. There the containers would be lifted by the ship's crane, swung over the side, and dropped into the gray waves. It took a full day to get the first load of containers filled and loaded onto the little ship. One of the Ukrainians continually took readings of radiation from the containers. The lead would work well enough for this limited purpose, but he knew that in the ocean, the radiation burning in the wrecked metal and soil would eventually free itself and escape.

In the darkness of the second container, among the scattered twisted sheets of metal, was the blackened body of Sasha Dunitsev, his chest still skewered with the spear thrown by the exploding railcar. The container was barely slowed in its descent as it splashed into the ocean, sinking into the utter blackness, and finally landing heavily, digging a trench into the sandy bottom.

* * *

Reports of the state's ocean disposal of the radioactive debris quickly reached the Atlanta offices of Region IV of the U.S. Environmental Protection Agency. A hastily assembled panel of section chiefs of the offices concerned with hazardous waste met with a little-known section responsible for threats from radiation. They were unanimous in their concern. The state had not received, not even sought, the required approval from their agency for such measures. There were treaty obligations to consider. And the United States was at the forefront of a campaign to ban all ocean-disposal of radioactive materials. What was happening off the coast of South Carolina had to stop.

The senior member of the panel dictated a one-page memo to EPA headquarters in Washington recommending immediate legal action. Within two hours, the memo was on the desk that used to belong to Fred Muldoon. Since Muldoon's surprise retirement several months before, the office had belonged to a rising star in the environmental enforcement section of the Justice Department. The young man studied the memo.

The state's actions were illegal and taking place in federally protected waters. It would be simple to craft a motion for a temporary restraining order, a rarely granted form of relief, but one that, in this case, was certainly called for. In a few hours he polished off a memorandum that ought to convince even the dullest federal judge to grant an order requiring the state to cease the ocean disposal until a full hearing on the merits of the case could be held.

* * *

They all stood as President Seekings entered the Cabinet Room. Only a select group of advisors surrounded the highly polished table. Secretaries of state, defense, and energy as well as the national security advisor, the administrator of the EPA, the chairman of the joint chiefs of staff, the attorney general, and C. A. Moore took their seats after the president. Seekings considered asking Mike O'Connelly to attend, but thought better of the idea. He didn't have the time, he told himself, to cater to the old man's sensibilities.

"I want options to resolve this problem." The president's eyes scanned the table.

The attorney general spoke first. "We are filing motions in the district court asking the court to order the state to release the railcars and halt ocean disposal of the radioactive waste."

"That's very interesting. What happens if the state simply ignores us?"

The attorney general smiled. "That would mean they would be in a state of rebellion."

Seekings glared at him. "And what do we do then?"

No one around the table responded. "I want options. Now, what do we do if they 'rebel' as the attorney general puts it?"

Still, there were no answers. "Let me tell you something. Plutonium is stacking up in Germany. We have been forbidden to use Rotterdam by the Dutch. Am I starting to make my point? We have to get this wrapped up, folks."

General Norman Cramer, chairman of the joint chiefs, said calmly, "Mr. President, it is a simple matter to plan an assault to seize the remainder of the train. More than adequate forces are available at Fort Bragg."

"Yes, General."

Cramer looked at the president for a moment before adding, "Before I prepare our forces to take such action, I believe we must know that we are prepared to use deadly military force against the government of one of the states. Have we reached that point, Mr. President?" Cramer fixed Seekings with a steady, cold stare, waiting for his response.

There was no sound in the room. The president and General Cramer stared at one another. "Prepare the plans, General. All I want from you right now is a viable option. Understood? I'll take care of the political considerations."

"Yes ... Mr. President."

"I want to give the courts a chance to act. When we get the orders the attorney general says we are sure to get, then we'll move to compel compliance, using the best means at our disposal. I want to be kept fully informed."

Seekings rose and left the Cabinet Room. The men and women around the table began to file out. The secretary of energy looked down at the notes she carried with her, thinking the president would discuss the best measures to clean up the area contaminated with radiation. But he hadn't mentioned it at all. She knew that the radiation at the site of the wrecked train was very bad and needed to be addressed very quickly. She knew it was wrong to dump the radioactive waste into the ocean, but she understood the state's desire to get it moved quickly. She noted the absence of the vice president and wondered what, if anything, it meant. No matter. When she returned to the department, she decided, she would call Mike O'Connelly and ask for his advice on getting federal help for the cleanup. It never occurred to her that the president was simply indifferent.

* * *

Nothing Mike O'Connelly saw in the face of the willful, egotistical man that stood before him reflected concern for the risks people would go on facing until the radiation was cleaned up. "We have to do something. Only the federal government can get the job done. The longer that nuclear fuel and plutonium are exposed, the more contamination will spread."

"Mike, I have a governor down there who is closer to open rebellion than we've seen in this country since the early 1960s. The integrity of the federal government is at stake. I'm not going to be remembered as the president who let us slide back to where states believe they can nullify decisions of the federal government!"

"These people aren't arguing with you about tariffs. Their city has been poisoned by radioactive waste and weapons fuel that *we* brought to *them*. It's the survival of their city and their children they care about now, not political philosophy. We have no choice but to do both things — preserve federal prerogative *and* clean up the contamination of American soil."

Seekings looked out of the window for a moment. Leaves were drifting to the ground, the light wind stripping the bright color from the trees that bordered the lawn. He turned to O'Connelly. "I'll think it over." O'Connelly nodded and walked to his own office. It disgusted him that he had to beg the president of the United States to help clean up the deadly disaster, a mess that he knew was caused by Seekings himself. He picked up the picture of his wife on the table next to the couch in his office and looked into the frozen image of her eyes.

*   *   *

Dottie Harris sat exhausted at the glass-topped table in one of the hospital snack bars. Only yards away, her husband lay, separated from excruciating pain by ever-increasing infusions of powerful medication, the cells of his body continuing to die. And a floor below was her son. She was so tired. Yet she couldn't think of anything else. Hours and days merged, and still she was trapped in a nightmare too horrible for even the strongest woman. How would she bear her life when this nightmare ended the way she knew it would, for she clung to no mad hope of a miracle that would give her back her husband and her son — her life? She hadn't been back to their house since she brought Billy to the hospital. She was terrified to go there, afraid of the empty rooms frozen in a world that was gone forever.

"Dottie ..." Julieanne Harris walked through the door and across the tile to Dottie. She extended her arms, reaching for Julieanne. The swollen red eyes filled with tears yet again, her sobbing substituting for words that would have been inadequate. Julieanne took her sister-in-law's hands and held her as her body shook with the grief she could now release in all its terror and grotesqueness.

Dottie at last found her voice and, choking back tears, said "Julie, it's really bad...."

"I know, Dear. I've already spoken to the doctor downstairs." She patted Dottie's shoulder. "Why don't you wait here while I go in and see Bud." As Julieanne Harris walked to the door of her brother's room, Dottie covered her face with her hands.

Julieanne knew she was not prepared for what she would see in the little room, that it was impossible to be ready. The man under the thin white sheet couldn't be her brother, her eyes told her. Already his hair was falling out, and was nearly gone in many spots. The back of his neck, she saw, was dark brown. He turned his head towards the sound of the door closing behind her. His eyelashes were gone. His face was so darkened she could not see his eyebrows. His lips were a mass of reddened blisters that seemed to be spreading across his face. When he spoke, it was less a voice she heard than pained gasping. "Julie ... thanks ...." He held up a blackening hand. She took it gently. The swelling shocked her.

"Bud, I'm so sorry." Finally, it was too much for her. She jerked a hand to her mouth and whispered, "Look what they've done to you."

He closed his eyes — straining against the pain, she knew. "Dottie ... take care...."

"Yes, Bud. I will."

He rocked his head back and forth, "Both of us ... too much ...," he said, his voice overtaken by an anguished cry.

Julieanne steeled herself with what courage she could muster and found Billy's room. Standing at the door were three policemen, two with arms in slings. She followed them into the room. The tallest one, a blond man who looked no more than twenty-five years old, spoke to the boy in the bed. "Billy, we wanted to come and thank you personally. They're letting us out today. If it weren't for you we'd have bled to death back at the station." His voice began to falter as his eyes took in the horror of the radiation's assault on the young boy. "There's two more guys upstairs who wouldn't have made it without you either. You're a real live hero."

The policemen stood a moment. Billy nodded his head, before he forced a single painful word from his dry and burning throat. "Thanks."

The young policemen realized the boy could not speak to them. Each leaned down to touch his shoulder gently and turned to leave the room. In the hall they walked to the elevator before each man began to cry. The image of Billy's bright-blue, lashless eyes staring at them from his radiation-burned face was permanently seared into their memory.

Julieanne made herself smile at the boy as she studied the frightful mask his face was becoming. His skin was dark, his lips and mouth blistered. As she spoke to him, his eyes shone at her. When he smiled at her, her heart broke. In the morning she would go and see Blackie and tell him what Leo had told her.

* * *

On the third day after the explosion of the train, the unnatural calm that had seized Florence vanished. The city began to slide toward panic. Rumors multiplied. The water supply was contaminated. Radioactive particles had been blown over all the city's residential areas. The government was planning to capitalize on the disaster and turn the entire county into a repository for radioactive waste. Managers of the large industrial plants that ringed the city sought guidance from their corporate headquarters. "Wait and see" was the position universally taken. The investments were too huge to abandon so quickly. It was all that saved the city from utter hysteria. The local media reported the removal of the contaminated wreckage and debris at the site of the explosion in meticulous detail. It became the symbol of the cleansing of the terrible poison. It's progress was the measure of their return to normalcy.

When the EPA announced that the ocean dumping of the radioactive wreckage would be halted, shock soon turned to anger. How could they consider halting the process that would ease this horror? Descriptions of the horrible deterioration of the victims of the radiation spread across the city. How, the angry city asked, could these bureaucrats think about letting such danger stay in the middle of their city even one second longer than necessary? News of the lawsuit filed by the United States in federal court to halt the cleanup was followed by a report that a second suit demanded return of the remaining cars of the train. But their anger turned to cold fury when the lawsuits were assigned to Steven L. Green, the same judge who had cleared the way for the train to come to their city. Appeals for calm from the mayor, speaking from the emergency operations center, did little to stem the tide of bitterness. The police denied requests from the U.S. Marshals office for protection of the judge's house.

They were short of personnel, they said. Quickly, the Marshals Service called in reinforcements from their offices in Fayetteville, Columbia, and Charleston. The show of force seemed to work. No crowds gathered and no bricks were thrown, but hatred was in the air nonetheless, and Green began to examine options to relocate his family.

* * *

Jim McNeely lost count of the laps as he jogged around the track of the wellness center. This morning he wanted to run as long as he could; he wanted exhaustion to excise the terrible images he carried from Florence. He wanted to run away. On the level below him, familiar figures completed their morning rituals on bicycles and weight machines. It was a scene that was normal and reliable, part of a solid and predictable world. It was a lie. After twenty-five minutes, the exhaustion he sought overcame him but brought no relief from the mental pictures of the stricken city and dying men and boys.

He stood under the cool jet of water from the shower, hands braced against the wall, letting the water fall on the back of his neck. From behind him, a voice called across the shower room, "You look like hell, man."

"I've been in Florence."

Kevin McClure's face darkened. "I see." The young state prosecutor looked outside the shower room to see if anyone was near enough to hear. "Jim, we need to talk, this morning if you have time."

At the end of the entrance to the gym was the door to a small cafeteria. Jim bought them two cups of coffee and they took a table in the far corner.

"Jim, you know we never stopped our investigation of the break-in at your office. Last month we found out the bank on the opposite corner has a surveillance camera, and the way it's positioned, it photographs the intersection across from your building. Tommy Littlejohn looked at the tapes going back to the spring. About the time Muldoon says the feds started spying on you, these two guys show up on the tape. One guy sets up a camera on the sidewalk, like he's taking pictures of St. Michael's or something. The other guy drives up to your building in a pickup truck, parks, goes into the building from the back door, and leaves about forty minutes later. The truck had South Carolina plates and a sign on the door for Aaron's Commercial Cleaning. There is no such business. As soon as the guy in the truck left, the guy with the camera packed up and left, too. I think it's our spies."

"That's impressive, but we already know they're feds. The government isn't going to help us ID them."

"That's the really strange part. About three weeks ago, Tommy started getting calls from somebody at the FBI. This guy tells him they're anxious to help out in the investigation, but it has to be very discreet. A matter of serious national security, he said. So, Tommy tells them about the pictures from the bank camera. He figured what the hell. There was nothing to lose. The guy at the FBI asks him if we have any prints and says they can run a match. Now here's the most bizarre part. He says maybe they can match up the prints to some file photos."

Jim watched McClure. He had clearly been thinking about this for some time. "But we don't have any prints."

McClure nodded his big head quickly. "O.K. So call this a hunch, but I think we might. I read about those railcars in Florence. They blew up from inside, right?" Jim nodded, not at all sure what Kevin was getting at. "So, let's get prints from the doors of the two cars the feds want back so bad. Let's see if the FBI can tell us who owns the last fingers that were on those doors." Jim stared at him blankly. "What if it's the two guys in the video?"

It was incredible. But in his strange new world, a world where a train blew up and flung nuclear terror into the middle of a city, it might make sense. "O.K. Is there someone who can collect the prints? He'll have to wear a lead suit to do it."

"We'll get them today," McClure said.

* * *

When Jim finally reached the governor, he told him about McClure's hunch. Haselden was not surprised at all by the suggestion. "Get the prints as soon as you can," he said.

* * *

The suits filed by the United States asked for immediate, emergency relief. Judge Green refused to accept the government's arguments that he should act at once. Instead, he scheduled a hearing for the second Monday after the explosion. The notice of the hearing explained that both sides would be expected to present factual and legal arguments in support of their position. It also contained a xeroxed sheet explaining that federal court had been relocated away from the contamination.

Jim McNeely and Drew Holland arrived at the courthouse at 10:00. Already seated at the government table was a young man. Tony DeSilva, ashen-faced and worn-looking, was seated behind the state's table. Shortly after they took their seats, Governor Haselden entered the rear of the courtroom accompanied by five highway patrolmen. Jim and Drew looked at one another. Green walked to his chair behind the bench unannounced. "Be seated, please," he said.

The young man introduced himself as another attorney from the Justice Department. He handed the judge a number of affidavits documenting the fact that the railcars were federal property and that two of them contained plutonium, which was uniquely and exclusively subject to federal control. He concluded by asking the court to order the cars returned to federal control at once.

Holland stood and addressed the court. "Your Honor, these railcars are vital evidence in the most serious murders ever committed in South Carolina. The state needs to examine them carefully." The young Justice Department lawyer argued that the United States government had as much reason to want to know what happened as the state. Green listened patiently until both men seemed to have finished speaking.

"Is that all you gentlemen have to say before I rule?" he asked.

Blackie stood, smiling at the judge. "Judge, it probably isn't necessary for you to rule, unless you really want to. The federal government is welcomed to take their railcars away whenever they want them." All the lawyers in the courtroom turned to look in surprise at the governor.

"Very well," Green said, "the issue of the railcars has been rendered moot by a settlement, which I will enter into the record. The state agrees to release the cars immediately to federal control. Now, the matter of the ocean dumping." He looked expectantly at the lawyer from Justice.

The young man rose, "If it please the court. Your Honor, these affidavits will confirm that the dumping of radioactive materials in the ocean is contrary to treaty and statutory law of the United States, and is harmful to marine life. The environment will suffer irreparable harm, and, there-fore, so will the people of the United States from the continuation of this illegal activity. This is a simple question, Judge Green. An order must be issued halting the dumping immediately."

"Mr. Holland?"

"Judge, if the radioactive materials are left in place, there will be irreparable harm to the citizens of Florence. People are more important than fish. Dr. DeSilva is prepared to testify that the material must be removed from the center of town as soon as possible to avoid further human contamination."

"Judge, the government will stipulate that Dr. DeSilva is right," the Justice Department lawyer said. "The material must be removed as quickly as possible. But it must be done in accord with proper legal procedures established to protect the environment and the long-term health of all people. Now that the matter of the rail cars is resolved, there is no impedi-ment to full federal cooperation with the state in cleaning up this tragic accident."

Green looked from table to table.

Blackie slowly rose again. "Judge, I may be able to help you out here, too." Both tables turned to face the governor. "It doesn't matter what you rule. The state is going to get that poison out of the middle of Florence the best way it can. Order whatever you want. The dumping will con-tinue until it's gone." Blackie stepped into the aisle and turned to leave the courtroom.

"You're in contempt, Governor." Blackie faced the bench, far more than contempt in his bitter stare.

"Yes, I am."

*   *   *

In a small office at the other end of the city, Julieanne Harris and Tommy Littlejohn watched the videotape made of the inside of the two railcars. Early in the morning, two men dressed in lead-lined suits climbed to the top of both cars. Armed with a power drill, one of the men cut a three-inch hole into the top of the car, taking care to avoid letting the severed piece fall inside. When the hole was cut, the second man extended a light into the center of the car illuminating the interior. A camera was carefully lowered and the entire interior filmed.

The video was clear. Large explosive charges, sufficient to blast the cars and disintegrate the fuel rod casks, were wrapped closely around the casks. Littlejohn didn't recognize the devices attached to the doors of each of the cars, but Julieanne immediately identified the thin red line of the laser trigger, set to detonate the explosives if anything blocked the laser beam, such as the car doors being forced inward.

* * *

"I feel the same as you do, Mike. But there's nothing I can do. Nothing either of us can do. The president won't authorize the release of any funds for the cleanup until Governor Haselden 'gets back into line,' as he says." The energy secretary listened while Mike O'Connelly railed against the president's pettiness. "Nevertheless, Mike, Roger's the only one who can release the money. And without it, nothing goes to South Carolina."

O'Connelly could see the images from the television news. Smoldering wreckage, poison spreading through the center of a small southern city. Anger and impotence washed over him as he listened to the secretary's anguished recitation of yet another mean-spirited and foolish act by Roger Seekings.

"Mike, is there anything anyone can do to defuse this mess? What about the governor? Can he be reasoned with?"

Reason? Was she serious? "Dear, I'm afraid there isn't much of the fuse left."

* * *

She found him sitting alone in the dark. The hall leaked only a little light into the den, enough to silhouette him at the far corner near the glass doors to the porch. She hadn't heard him come in, and she had only wondered where he was when she woke and saw that it was after one o'clock. His head was laid back on the chair and his eyes faced the ceiling.

"I was worried," Alicia said, standing at the other end of the room. "I knew you were going to Florence." She paused, wrapping her arms around herself. "What could have taken so long?"

"We lost ... in Florence ... the judge ordered us to stop dumping the radioactive waste offshore.... The governor told him to go to hell." Still, his eyes had not opened.

"I was worried ... so much has happened...."

"I couldn't get the faces of those boys out of my mind. I just had to drive a while. He shook his head and, rubbing his face, said, "Nothing we did mattered at all. Nothing."

She sat in a chair, still holding her shoulders tight. "We matter." He turned to look at her now. "I matter." She stood and walked back to the hall.

"I'm sorry," he said.

"I'm frightened. I've never seen you like this. Please don't push us away." She walked to him and slid her arms around his chest, holding him close.

Chapter 24

The children were the first to die. Their smaller bodies and still-developing organs succumbed rapidly to the disintegrating effects of the radiation. Death comes in many forms. But no loss is so keenly felt as the unexpected, unexplainable ending of lives not yet full. And through the ages, no crimes have galvanized the hatred of the bereaved like those that take the lives of children.

In the third week after the explosion, the first Scouts died, the hearts of the two boys finally unable to function — so great was the destruction of fiber. In turn, their mothers, having secretly rejected the idea that their boys might truly be lost, became hysterical when the inevitable finally came. One of the fathers, nearly crazed with grief, carried a photograph of his son to the reporters drinking coffee in the hospital lounge. "Show them what they did to my boy!" he cried. "Show them what they did!" The picture was reproduced in every major paper and magazine and shown repeatedly on television broadcasts around the world. The once healthy thirteen-year-old, on the brink of adulthood, was at his death a shriveled, terrifying figure.

One by one, the other boys followed their comrades in death. One day before Billy Harris died, Blackie Haselden visited him. Blackie was seized by the fantasy that he could lift him from the bed and rush him away from the horror. But there was no escape possible. On this, his last visit, Blackie was overcome with panic, with the realization that nothing would save the boy — that the evil thing consuming him would really take away his precious life. Billy was unable to speak. His body was dying and the pain was unbearable. Yet from his blackened face, the boy's eyes fixed on the governor's, and he smiled.

Four days later, Blackie came back to the hospital to see Watson Harris. He felt he was going mad. Watson had not spoken to him in almost a week, so advanced was the destruction of his throat and tongue. Blackie knew it could not be much longer. The specter of his friend's ravaged body was no longer a surprise, but it still shocked him. He closed the door behind him and took a seat next to the bed. Watson was agitated and suddenly jerked his head to look at Blackie.

His mouth opened, revealing the terrible sores, and he began to force the painful words, "Billy ... Billy is ... dead ..."

Blackie was stunned. No one had told the dying man about his son, Blackie was certain. But he knew Billy was dead nonetheless. "Dead ...," he whispered.

Watson's eyes stared at Blackie, pleading for the truth. "Yes, Bud. Two days ago." Watson closed his eyes tight and gripped the sheets hard with his withered hands.

Suddenly, his eyes flew open, bulging. He held out his hand to Blackie who took it in his own. The long, thin fingers closed tight around Blackie's hand. Struggling, Watson forced himself to speak, "Blackie ... don't let this happen ... anymore ... not again ..." All at once, the energy his friend had summoned was gone. The grip on his hand loosened, and the hand fell away. The mouth remained open, the familiar blue eyes staring at him, but Blackie knew the life was gone from them forever.

*   *   *

Tommy Littlejohn picked up his mail. Inside was the FBI's response to his request for an identification of the fingerprints on the doors of the railcars in Florence. He hadn't expected any response at all, much less one so quick. And there was more than the usual information on the owners of the two sets of prints. There were two dossiers, complete with photographs of the two young men — two young soldiers, he saw, in the United States Army. Captain Timothy Giordono, 30, and Lieutenant Erick Gilbert, 26, were officers in Army Intelligence, their biographical summaries said. What was most incredible to the veteran detective, they looked familiar. It took him a few moments. Then he realized why.

From a filing cabinet next to the wall, Littlejohn retrieved a packet of photographs. They were greatly blown up copies of frames from a surveillance camera — the camera from the bank across Broad Street from the law offices of Holland, Rollins, Jerald, & McNeely. The man with the tripod patiently positioning his camera for the perfect shot of St. Michael's Church was unmistakably Giordono. Quickly, Littlejohn sifted through the prints until he found the three frames that showed the face of the second man — the one leaving the law office's back door. He laid the clearest photo next to the photo of Gilbert. "Son of a bitch!" he said. He grabbed his phone and called Kevin McClure. "Get your ass down here.... No, I mean now, God damn it!"

*   *   *

The light penetrated through the opening as he lifted his eyelids. The dull gray walls of the same room were still there. The pain was still there, too. He moved his arm and felt the tug of the IV needle taped to his wrist. The nausea had been gone for a week or more. He couldn't remember. The days all ran together now. The ache in his feet and legs began to throb. *The narcotics must be wearing off,* he thought. *Soon, I'll be screaming again.*

The burning in his legs and perineum was worse than ever. His chest hurt. He punched the button to call the pretty young nurse. Her face appeared shortly at the door, looking tentatively at him, unsmiling. "Mr. Plekanov. How are you?"

She picked up his chart while he answered, "Tatyana, the pain is worse." The words came harder, too. It was as though sand soaked in acid had been poured down his throat. The young nurse looked up, apprising him clinically.

Mikail had been in this room in the hospital since the Aeroflot airliner from Bermuda landed in St. Petersburg. He and Matveev and the others were met by ambulances and paramedics as soon as they were carried from the plane into the terminal. The alarmed pilot had radioed ahead a report hours before they landed about the violently ill passengers. The paramedics noted the peculiar dark color of their skin, not at all like a healthy tan from a tropical vacation. One of the men knew exactly what it was. The Soviet army veteran recognized the telltale mark of the nuclear tan. What he could not understand was how a rich Russian businessman would become irradiated in Bermuda.

Within two hours after the patients' admission to the huge medical complex on the outskirts of the city, the hospital administrator contacted state security and advised officials of the strange cases of acute radiation sickness. And that all of the cases had arrived sick on a flight from Bermuda. As is the way with bureaucracies, particularly Russian ones, it took several days for the two reports — the one of several Russian businessmen afflicted with radiation sickness and the one about an explosion of a trainload of nuclear fuel rods and plutonium — to be correlated by someone. The someone was Major Anatoly Gregarian. For almost two years now, he had coordinated with the American FBI on the joint effort to prevent theft of Russian plutonium and uranium 238 from old Soviet stockpiles by Russian gangsters. Now an attempt to steal it on American soil had resulted in a dramatic tragedy. And five Russians had arrived from Bermuda, an island a short flight from the place where the train had exploded in — what was it called? — South Carolina. The Russians included Mikail Plekanov and his right-hand man, Yigor Matveev. Major Gregarian lit another bitter Turkish cigarette. It would be wise to think carefully over the next move. He pulled out the number he had not called in several months.

"Yes, Mrs. Plekanov, I'm trying to locate Alexis. Is he at home this evening?"

Alexis was in St. Petersburg. At the hospital, or his apartment, perhaps. "Thank you," the major said.

He tried another number. "Hello?"

"Hello, Alexis. I am sorry to hear about your brother." Months later, the cool, sarcastic voice was no less familiar and no less frightening to Alexis.

"Who are you? You call me now! What do you want, you bastard?"

The sarcasm left the major's voice, and it was no longer cool, but hard and demanding. "I want the truth, Alexis. How has Mikail become sick with radiation?"

The following day, Gregarian flew to St. Petersburg, and just before noon entered a small room in state security's office, there to sit face-to-face before Alexis Plekanov for the first time. The younger man wore a fine suit — *Italian, perhaps*, the major thought. But Alexis' face showed the rigors of worry and fear. *He was a mobster, but he was a man*, Gregarian reminded himself. Before Gregarian could begin, Alexis turned to face him, surprising strength in his voice, his stare calm and unwavering.

"Major," Alexis said, seeing the emblems of the man's rank and the blue trim of state security on the uniform jacket of the broad-shouldered man, "we can make a deal, I think."

A deal. "So, Alexis, you wish to bargain with me?"

Alexis ignored him. "I will tell you all you want to know. And my brother will give you a statement. Give one to the Americans, too, if you wish. It will leave no questions unanswered in your curious policeman's mind, Major."

Gregarian pulled a cigarette from a pack with his lips and offered one to Alexis. He lit Alexis' and then his own. "And this is a deal, Banker?"

"My brother will die from the radiation. They say he may live some weeks yet, but no longer. The damage is too great. The same is true of Yigor and the others. You and the government will tell the Americans that Mikail and Yigor alone are responsible — they and their allies — and leave me to run my business and take care of my family — and my brother's. If you do so, there will be no more Plekanovs for you to keep track of, Major. I will be too busy making money." Alexis summoned all the courage he could muster and forced a smile.

"Is that all?"

"One more thing. Mikail's customers. I don't want to have to worry about them."

Major Gregarian contacted his superiors while Alexis listened. After a series of discussions, the matter was put before the Foreign Ministry. After more consultations with the Americans, the answer finally came back to Major Gregarian. He nodded to Alexis.

Two hours later, Alexis slowly opened his brother's hospital room door. "Mikail?" The blackening face turned toward him. The site shocked Gregarian who stood behind Alexis. The color alone was strange, but it was the lack of any hair, eyelashes, or eyebrows, that gave Mikail's face its appalling, alien appearance. "I have brought the men from state security, Mikail."

His weakness was so great that Major Gregarian and his assistant with the video camera and tape recorder were required to make four visits to record all the details of Mikail Plekanov's story. Nothing was left out. It was all that Mikail could offer to the brother he would soon leave behind. In the end, he was no longer soldier nor criminal, only Alexis' big brother.

All of the information, except the means by which Mikail had learned the route and schedule of the train, was shared immediately with the Americans, who explained that they understood the situation, and would not ask for extradition. There was no sense in that, they agreed. The Russians elected to allow the Americans to make all the public statements about the raid in South Carolina. It was decided by the president and the foreign minister that the embarrassment of Russian involvement in the radiation disaster was best handled by maintaining a contrite and low profile. This remained the Russian posture, until the American president and the local leader in the state where the accident had occurred began a very public argument about how the train had come to explode.

The governor claimed the trains had exploded from the inside. The Russians noted that Mikail had indeed told them this before he died, but they thought it only the skewed memory of a pain-wracked mind. Then the governor showed the press a film of the inside of the two railcars that did not explode. There, unmistakably, were large quantities of explosives wrapped around the casks of fuel rods and plutonium — and incredibly, a laser trigger rigged to set off the powerful explosives when the doors of the car were forced open. This man Haselden appeared on television, showed the film and explained what it meant. It was calculated, the president thought, to infuriate Haselden's citizens. He demanded the truth from President Seekings. The American president denied the accuracy of the film, claiming it was a fake. And then the Americans issued the statement that infuriated the Russian president. It said the Russian Mafia was running out of control, able to launch the most vicious operations at home and even in the United States. It was all the doing of the Russians, President Seekings said.

The Russian president consulted his intelligence experts. The governor's video was accurate, they said. Not a fabrication. The Americans had blown up a train filled with the most dangerous radioactive materials on their own soil, but their government wanted to hide this fact and blame the entire incident on Russians. When his rage subsided, he summoned his spokesman and together they drafted a statement for the world press. They said Russia was deeply sorry that Russian criminals, long sought by the police, had participated in causing such horror. But Russia had carefully studied the video of the inside of the train and regretted to say that it was accurate. The Russian president could not imagine how such a thing could have been done, but it was clear that the American government had rigged the train to explode and scatter the radiation among its own citizens. He closed by solemnly offering to the governor of South Carolina all the help his nation could give. Their terrible experience at Chernobyl had taught them much, he said. The Russians decided it was not yet time to use the information they possessed about the American president's special assistant for policy and security — and his soldier friend.

In spite of the friction over the president's announcement, the Russians and Americans continued to cooperate on one important matter. Weeks after the major interviewed Mikail Plekanov, a team of Russian and American assault troops converged on the mountain in the far northern province of Yemen. Within minutes, the old tunnel containing the Arabs' carefully collected material for the construction of nuclear weapons was crushed, collapsing from the powerful explosives delivered by the commandos. At his small house in a village nearby, Marwan Atta awoke to the sound of a nearly silent, rapid entry on the floor below his bedroom. The angry Egyptian snatched the automatic rifle from under his bed, flicked off the safety and lunged into the hall just as the four black-clad soldiers reached the middle of the stairs. No bullets left his rifle. It fell from his hands, blood spurting from the many holes carefully and silently pumped into his chest by the soldiers.

The NATO command could not keep its raid a secret. But by the time Marwan Atta lay dead in the hall outside his bedroom, the world's attention was focused on a much larger drama unfolding in America.

*   *   *

Judge Stephen L. Green's order requiring the state to cease dumping the radioactive debris was flamboyantly ignored. Governor Haselden personally called the supervisors of the cleanup operation. He told them to go on doing exactly what they had been doing.

Four days after Judge Green's injunction was filed in the records of the United States District Court, the USS *John Rogers*, recently directed to take up patrol duty off the coast of South Carolina, detected on radar the ship making its way from the mouth of Charleston Harbor towards the edge of the Continental Shelf, carrying another load of containers to sea. Coming to full speed, the destroyer closed fast on the slow-moving cargo ship. The captain's instructions were strange, but clear. When the black hull of the cargo ship and the containers stacked on deck were visible from the bridge of the *John Rogers*, the captain called the officer in control of the ship's weapons systems. The surprise of the young lieutenant was something the captain expected. He repeated his directions to the weapons officer. "Aye, aye, sir," came the answer.

At the captain's direction, the warship turned to port and made a straight course across the gray water for the cargo ship. "Captain, should we contact the vessel?"

"No."

The paths of the two ships converged, more quickly now as the distance shortened to hundreds of yards. The warship's bow sliced through the water, moving at flank speed to cross the path of the smaller cargo vessel. The captain of the cargo ship slowed his speed but did not alter course. He also had his orders. And he intended to carry them out. When the *John Rogers* was two hundred yards from the cargo ship, the captain gave the order to the lieutenant manning the five-inch gun. The barrel of the gun recoiled and the deep report echoed across the open water between the two ships. The shell screamed over the bow of the cargo vessel, splashing and detonating in the water several hundred yards in the distance. "Now, call her up," the captain on the *John Rogers* said, smiling to the sailor beside him.

"You are directed to turn back to Charleston immediately. Acknowledge."

There was silence. The officers and crew on the destroyer could not hear the captain of the cargo ship finish the string of violent curses that erupted when the shell was fired across his bow. "A shot across my fucking bow! What does the bastard think this is, the fucking War of 1812?" he yelled in a syrupy Charleston accent.

The cargo ship did not vary her course. The destroyer circled to starboard and closed on the slower ship again. Once more in control of his temper, the captain of the cargo ship called over his radio, "*John Rogers*, I may not return this cargo to port. Do you read me?"

"Our orders are clear. You may not deposit the containers in the open sea. Return to port now."

"Negative. If they don't go off the shelf, they go right here. They ain't going back. Got it, asshole?"

There was silence on the bridge of the destroyer. The captain had no authorization to attack the civilian ship and was not about to do so. As he thought about his dilemma, he saw that the cargo ship had fallen behind and was riding in the gentle waves. The destroyer circled around again. In his binoculars, the captain saw the shipboard crane moving on the now stationary ship. One of the containers rose above the rest, swung over the side, dangled briefly ... and then fell into the water. The crane swung back to the stack of containers, the hook lowering to a second metal box. "What's the depth here?" the captain yelled.

"Sir, sixty feet." Another container dropped into the sea.

"Captain! Stop ... stop immediately!" Another container splashed through the surface of the rolling water. The captain had no choice. "We agree to let you take the rest of the containers to the shelf. *John Rogers* will escort you."

"Escort yourself to hell!"

The next morning the *John Rogers* waited at the mouth of Charleston Harbor. There would be no more shipments of radioactive waste dumped in the ocean. The captain of the little cargo ship was an instant celebrity, praised across South Carolina for standing up to the bullying of the warship. His final challenge to the navy warship was broadcast in banner headlines across the front page of every newspaper. Celebration turned to anger as people learned the navy had formed a blockade and would prevent any further removal of the still plentiful radioactive rubble from the site of the train. For the time being, the stories explained, the dangerous waste would be stored in the same kind of lead-capped containers as before in a remote warehouse outside the city. The walls of the warehouse would also be lined with lead, and access to the building would be forbidden for a radius of a half mile.

* * *

There was a raw sore inside Jimmy Dodds, and it was more inflamed with each passing day. His son was one of the Boy Scouts at the train. Every day for two weeks he went to see his boy at the hospital, and each time he saw his child it was worse. When his son died, there was no relief from the pain. None of the consolations people sometimes offered one another — that the suffering of the dead was over at last — eased his agony. He couldn't get the picture of his boy's face out of his mind.

What he saw on television at first seemed like a hallucination, like something dreamt in the midst of a high fever, almost believed, until the fever was finally gone. But what blared from every television and radio station and every newspaper was no dream; it was an ugly tutorial on how his wonderful son was killed. The government killed him — by arrogance or stupidity, it made no difference. The pictures the governor showed of the lethal casks of fuel rods covered with slabs of explosives changed something deep inside Dodds. His rage crystallized and fixed on the man who was the real killer.

On this night, he finally could not stand to be in his house. He had to breathe. His wife's sister came to console and grieve with them. But his grief was more private, more profound — and more violent. He slipped from the house, walking quietly out the back screen door. Without knowing where he was going, he climbed into his truck and drove. The lights of the bar lit up a dark corner of the suburban strip. Everything else was long closed down by the time he drove into the parking lot. A dozen men and three women lounged at the bar or the scattered rough tables that surrounded the pool table. Dodds spotted his brother at one of the tables with two men who worked at the same lumberyard. He joined them and the bartender brought him a glass to share the pitcher of beer. "Bourbon. Straight," he said.

The bartender kept the liquor coming. He knew — they all knew about the boy. And they were all angry. They all remembered the red-haired thirteen-year-old. He was a good kid. The men at the table were already talking about the bastards who stopped the disposal of the contaminated debris from the middle of their town. Like all of Florence, indeed like all of South Carolina, they were frustrated, angry and scared. They told Dodds how sorry they were, how tragic it was about his son. The liquor spread through him with liberating warmth. The tight coils of tension began to unwind. But there was no relaxation. *Not tonight. Not ever again*, he thought. He listened to the bitter complaints about how they had been victimized. How the government had lied and cheated to break the laws designed to prevent this kind of tragedy, to prevent the poisoning of fine boys like his son. He listened until he couldn't bear it any longer.

"Talk! It's all talk! For Christ's sake, don't make me listen to any more fucking talk!" he shouted, his deep, strong voice silencing the room. "We sit around and tell each other what a damn shame it all is. What about the dirty bastards that killed our boys? What about them? They don't hurt any, do they? They sleep in their clean, comfortable beds, so safe and secure! Don't make me listen to any more talk about what a shame it is. They murdered my son, same as if they put a rope around his neck and hung him!" He looked at their eyes, all turned to him. Tears rolled down his unshaven face. "We know what happened. That bastard judge who lives right over there — he made some kind of deal — and he fixed it so they could bring that poison ... bring it here and kill my boy!" He stared wild-eyed at the men around him. For the first time in weeks, he could think clearly. "The son of a bitch deserves to die!" he shouted. He shoved the chair back and it flew, crashing loudly into the empty table behind him. Dodds marched for the door, his heavy steps on the wooden planks the only sound. In the cold night air, he walked to his truck, possessing no idea where he would drive it. He turned at the sounds of the bar emptying and the other men joining him in the parking lot.

His brother called to him, "We ain't gonna let you go by yourself," and climbed into the truck. Dodds really hadn't thought about going to Judge Green's house. But now it seemed that was where he was meant to go all along. His mind was filled with a remarkable clarity, and he felt for the first time since the explosion that he might be able to rest again. He was very drunk. He knew where the judge lived. He had driven by it many times, in fact, since the explosion. It wasn't far. A chain of ten other vehicles followed him along the winding streets to the judge's home. It was two stories, brick, and finer than any of the men assembling in front imagined they might own.

Parked in front of the house was a single car with two U.S. marshals inside. One dozed while the other watched. He shook the other one awake as the trucks and cars began to line up along the street beside them. "Trouble," he said. Dodds jumped from his truck and strode across the lawn to the front door. The marshals quickly stepped outside their car and started to run toward him, when they were halted by two of the other men.

"Hold it right there, assholes," the voice belonged to a man holding a twelve-gauge shotgun that was aimed straight at the marshals. A second man aimed another rifle at the two suddenly very frightened men. "Just get in the back of this truck right here, fellas."

The marshals climbed into the back of one of the trucks, where their hands and feet were bound with wire. Dodds was pounding the doorknocker against the door of the house. Soon, it opened, and Green stood in the door, wrapped in a bathrobe. "What the hell is the meaning of this?" He glanced over Dodds' shoulder and saw the marshals' car empty. His eyes widened with fear.

It was all so clear to the grieving father in that moment. As fear flickered in the smaller man's eyes, he realized the only way to give his son justice, and himself peace, was to punish his son's murderer. With one strong hand, he grabbed the judge's neck and threw him to the concrete walkway. "You're coming with me, you bastard!" He picked Green up and dragged him to his truck. In the bed of the truck was rope he always kept there. Dodds tied Green's hands together, then lifted him and dropped him heavily into the bed of the truck.

Green was terrified into silence. His mind raced. He was grateful he had sent his family to Greenville.

Dodds raced toward the mall. The same string of headlights followed close behind. As the other cars and trucks circled him, he collected the rope lying next to the judge's prone body. He tossed one end, weighted with a hammer, over the arm of the lamppost nearest to him. He grabbed the hammer and fashioned a loop in the rope. It wasn't fancy, but it would work, he was certain. The other men watched, electrified by what they now knew was going to happen. Four of the men, including Dodds' brother, hauled the judge from the truck. Green realized their intentions and panicked, thrashing wildly, screaming, his shrill voice echoing across the empty mall parking lot. One of the men backhanded his face with a beefy hand, knocking his head to one side like a doll's. Green tasted the blood and was silenced by the sharp pain.

Dodds pulled the rope and the noose he had fashioned to Green and placed it around the horrified man's neck. "This is for my son," he said evenly, staring into Green's eyes. He spit into Green's face and tightened the noose roughly. Stepping back from Green and gathering the loose end of the rope, he began to pull it tight. Six other men joined him, grabbing the rope. Easily, they pulled the end of the rope to the next lamppost. Green rose swiftly, his feet kicking wildly, and he struggled futilely against the rope that bound his hands. The men tied the rope to the lamppost. Green jerked his body violently, the sound of his feet against the pole making a dull ringing sound. He moaned and gasped, but could no longer scream because of the choking rope that was crushing his neck. The men watched until the body no longer moved.

Without speaking, they hauled the two terrified U.S. marshals out of the truck and laid them gently on the pavement under the still body of the judge. Then they climbed back into their cars and trucks and drove from the parking lot, leaving the body of Judge Stephen L. Green hanging under the lamplight.

Dodds drove back to the middle of the city toward the exclusion zone. When the convoy of trucks and cars reached the National Guard cordon blocking their way, Dodds walked up to the two soldiers, "We don't want any trouble guys. Just let us go in there to the federal building. We'll take our chances."

The two soldiers had their orders, and they were clear. No one was to go inside the cordon. "I'm sorry, sir. We can't."

"Bullshit. Get out of the way!" The voice belonged to one of the men who had followed Dodds, and he was pointing his shotgun at the chest of the first soldier. A half dozen other guns appeared and the metallic clicks of the rifles being cocked announced the men were serious. The two soldiers laid their M-16s on the pavement.

"O.K. Go on and fuck yourselves up," the first one said to Dodds.

He drove his truck through the rope barrier and the others followed him three blocks to the federal building. He reached into the bed of the pickup and lifted a sledgehammer and two cans of gasoline. Others carried more cans of fuel toward the building. Dodds walked resolutely to the glass wall of the building and with one full swing of the sledgehammer shattered the glass. He walked into the hall and began to throw the gasoline on the walls of the first floor. Two of the men, carrying three more cans of gasoline, rode the elevator to the top floor. There, they smashed into one of the offices and poured the cans across the carpeted floor and curtains. When the cans were empty, one of the men tossed a match and the room burst into brilliant blue flames. The men ran down the stairs to the lobby. As they stepped over the broken glass and through the shattered wall, Dodds tossed a match onto the gasoline.

In seconds the building was illuminated in flame, top and bottom. The flames spread until the entire structure was ablaze. The men watched the hated symbol burn. For hours after they drove back through the cordon to their homes, the federal building lit up the Florence night. There was plenty of time for reporters to capture the dramatic event on film, pictures for the front pages of every morning paper.

It was not until sunrise that the security guard at the mall found the body of Stephen Green dangling from a lamppost in the vacant parking lot.

*   *   *

Thaddeus pulled a paper from the vending machine on the corner. He had been back in South Carolina for a week. The picture of the federal building in flames excited him. It was happening already, and without any encouragement from his militia allies, who were now streaming into the state. For weeks, e-mail messages had flown among the Northwest Territorial Militia and like-minded groups from the Rockies to South Florida. The opportunity they had anticipated for so long was unfolding in South Carolina. The momentum toward rebellion was already building. With the right fuel, it would become the avalanche that would bury the hated federal tyranny forever. Thaddeus hurried back to the sparse room he rented in the old mill district on the south side of Columbia. He flipped on his computer and signaled his contacts in Charleston, Greenville, Myrtle Beach, and Spartanburg. They must not let this moment slip away, he said. Tomorrow, at the latest, they must act.

*   *   *

The body of Judge Green was filmed by a local television cameraman. The security guard did not dare lower the body until police arrived, and the police waited for the fingerprint technician to finish. The cameraman had plenty of time to capture the macabre scene. Across the nation, shock greeted the ugly picture of the dead man, his bathrobe hanging loosely from his shoulders, his neck pulled to a wicked angle by the rope. But in South Carolina, there was little sympathy. After all, wasn't this the guy caught making a deal with the president's man to fix it so the government could ignore the law? Wasn't he the man responsible for the grisly deaths of so many firemen and children?

Thaddeus and his friends decided they needed to act. Dozens of militiamen fanned out in the major cities of the state, planting their flyers and posters. They called for a meeting at 8:00 p.m. near the federal building in each city. As the men made their rounds leaving the flyers in prominent places, they were surprised at the interest they received. Anger was in the air. They could feel it; they were certain. It was their natural element, after all.

In Charleston and Greenville, the police provided only token security at the locations of the rallies advertised in the flyers. In Columbia, there were more police, but the crowd that gathered on Assembly Street was much larger, and arrived so quickly that the dozen police officers retreated when the crowd moved toward the federal courthouse and office building. More police came, but not enough to stem the tide, which by 8:30 rose to nearly fourteen thousand enraged men and women. No bullhorns instructed the crowd what to do. They moved as if driven by a single mind. At the doors to the complex, men in the front of the crowd pulled hammers from their coat pockets and smashed the glass panels. Alarms sounded throughout the building, calling uselessly to the police, who had already retreated before the mob.

Arms shot upward from the throng as rocks, bottles, any missile within reach, was hurled at the windows of the building. Through the broken doors, a dozen or more men moved with more certain purpose. They carried plastic bottles of gasoline, which they rushed to designated sections of the complex and poured on flammable surfaces. Checking their watches to be sure they were coordinating their actions with friends on other floors, they tossed matches onto the gasoline-soaked floors and rushed back to the entrance. In surprisingly little time, the office tower was a soaring mass of flame. The crowd backed away from the inferno but stayed to watch its handiwork. Fire engine sirens shrieked from four directions and converged on the fire.

The crowd warned the firemen to stay back. They would brook no interference in their night's work. Frustrated and helpless — and fascinated nonetheless — the firemen removed their helmets and bright yellow coats and watched the largest concentration of federal offices in the state disappear in flames. As the fire's intensity grew, floors collapsed, throwing flaming debris into the night sky. Finally, the firemen convinced the crowd to allow them to protect nearby buildings and prevent the fire from spreading.

In Charleston and Greenville, the scene was repeated at very nearly the same time. The Charleston mob was larger, some said nearly twenty thousand, that set fire to the federal building, the eerie orange glow illuminating the statue of John C. Calhoun standing high above the square. Only a dramatic appeal by Mayor Patrick Collins convinced the rioters to let firemen save the collection of historic buildings that stood nearby. Collins was the rarest of men in turn of the century America, a politician not only trusted, but loved. He was the long-time mayor of Charleston, and father of most of the innovations that had created a renaissance for the old city. The police reached him at his Gibbes Street home immediately after the mob began to gather. The crowd easily recognized him as he climbed on top of the fire engine, silhouetted against the wall of fire. He clutched the loudspeaker a fireman handed him. His voice was the same one that had calmed most of these same people, giving them hope when so much of their community lay ruined by a great hurricane.

"We can't let anything hurt us any more than we've already been hurt. Look around you!" he yelled at them. "Citadel Square Church, Second Presbyterian, The Old Citadel are all part of the soul of this city. We can't let our heritage burn." Collins paused, then challenged the crowd, "I'm going to work with these men to stop the fire from spreading.... I want you to help me. Now, come on!" He waved to the firemen, who drove the trucks through the crowd that gave way and to the curbs next to the flaming building. The men rushed to hook their hoses to the hydrants and began to bathe the walls of the adjoining church in jets of water. Collins hurried to help the crew preparing the hoses to do the same to the walls of The Old Citadel across the street. In twos and threes and then by the score, men from the crowd helped the crews of the fire trucks that continued to arrive. In the end, only the federal building burned.

A smaller mob attacked the building in North Charleston that housed the Internal Revenue Service and a few other federal agencies. The fire in Greenville quickly destroyed the federal building and courthouse, and spread to three other buildings before the angry crowd of ten thousand finally allowed the frightened firemen to attack the secondary fires spawned by the flaming office tower.

Thaddeus and his friends were very pleased. They congratulated each other profusely in a series of late night e-mail messages.

*   *   *

The flames from the Thurmond Federal Building lit up the sky. Blackie and June Haselden stood at the front window of the governor's mansion and watched the fire rage out of control. A stream of calls told the governor that similar fires were being set by rioting crowds in Charleston and Greenville. The next call was from the commander of the National Guard.

"Governor, it's General Demers." The voice belonged to one of his staff who had rushed to the mansion in response to the news of the chaos in the streets.

"General. I want the guard called up this evening. I won't let the state be taken over by a mob."

"How much of a call up do you want, sir?"

"All of it."

"Sir? All of it?"

"Every man and woman."

"Governor, we have nearly ten thousand soldiers in the National Guard. And a thousand more in the Air National Guard."

"I know that. Call them all to duty, General. And draw all the ammunition you can get from the army."

"Yes, sir." Demers hung up the phone. *Jesus Christ*, he thought.

* * *

A year ago, he might have joked about another funeral. The vice president always goes to funerals, but O'Connelly had to fight hard to come to this one.

The sleek jet, one of the fleet of presidential planes, glided towards the runway of the Florence airport. There was no band to greet him and no dignitaries at the end of a red carpet. He spotted a contingent of National Guard troops at the terminal building as the plane taxied into place. The second plane carrying the limousine had already landed and discharged his car. The secret service agents on his detail escorted him to the car where a man in fatigue uniform waited. He saw he was a colonel in the guard. The colonel saluted smartly. "Mr. Vice President, if you will follow me, sir."

The limousine fell in behind the green Bronco as they made their way to the cemetery where the memorial service would be held. At the gate, among a circle of highway patrolmen and National Guard soldiers, stood Blackie Haselden, waiting. O'Connelly, followed by three of the agents on his detail, walked toward Blackie and extended his hand. "Governor, thank you for letting me come."

They shook hands before Blackie spoke. "Mr. O'Connelly, please ride with us." O'Connelly glanced at the secret service agents standing behind him. "They will wait here." One of the agents moved protectively to O'Connelly's shoulder and started to speak to him.

O'Connelly held up his hand, "It's all right. Governor Haselden and I are old friends."

"Sir ..."

"You boys stay here. I'll be fine." A highway patrolman opened a door to the governor's car and O'Connelly stepped inside. "They get nervous," he said to Blackie.

"There are certain symbols I didn't want at this service. Secret service agents are some of them, and your car is another."

The ride was short to the small stand set up at the end of the cemetery. Seated in front were the families of the firemen and Boy Scouts; all of the firemen and Scouts that were exposed to the radiation were now dead, except for five firemen whose prognosis was still in doubt. Enough time had passed, Blackie decided, and there needed to be a public memorial to the innocent lives lost. He needed to speak to them. The minister from Central Methodist, his church now sealed off by the safety cordon, spoke briefly and solemnly on the trial of faith they all faced from the inexplicable events of the last weeks. From the platform, O'Connelly watched the faces of the stricken — the wives and children of the firemen, the parents, brothers and sisters of the boys. "Simple people" is what was often said of such gatherings. What was simple about their lives? What was uncomplicated about the agony etched on their faces? He fought to make himself understand how they felt, all the people of this place struggling to come to terms with what had happened — and, he remembered bitterly, why it had happened. He realized he could never fathom their grief — or their anger.

Blackie rose and addressed the small crowd. He spoke of his hometown and his ties to so many of the people gathered on the lawn before him. They could never say enough about the quality of those who were so cruelly taken, he said. The world was a finer, brighter place because they had lived here. Then he spoke of his friend and his voice began to waiver. O'Connelly studied the governor's face. For so long he had seen men in Washington feign emotion, even tears. Blackie spoke of Billy Harris, and of his own long-dead infant son. O'Connelly knew his tears were very real.

"Life didn't end on those railroad tracks," he said. "The lives of those we loved so much were precious, but no more so than our own lives and those of the friends and family who are still with us. We will go on, and we must dedicate ourselves to paying tribute to those wonderful men and boys by living it to the fullest, and the best way we can."

Blackie returned to his seat and faced O'Connelly. "Would you like to speak?"

He had notes for remarks in his pocket. They said nothing these people needed to hear. "No, Governor. Thank you."

In the governor's car, Blackie said, "You seem like a decent man, Mr. Vice President. But you must know what the government did that led to this." He looked at O'Connelly and continued, "I appreciate that you had the courage to come here." Blackie picked up a manila folder and handed it to O'Connelly. It was a pair of subpoenas, one each for Captain Timothy Giordono and Lieutenant Erick Gilbert. The attorney general needed to question them about the explosion of the train in Florence. Their fingerprints were found on the doors of two of the cars. "These men are officers in the U.S. Army and they have information about how this happened. I insist they be made available to us immediately. Please deliver these to the president for me."

O'Connelly stared blankly at the subpoenas. "Bill, we have to avoid a worse crisis. It will not be easy. They mean to run the trains through South Carolina again." He closed his eyes in embarrassment. "There is nothing I can do to prevent it. All I can do is tell you to try and keep a cool head." He held up his hand when he saw Blackie's eyes flash. "I'm only trying to tell you to be careful. Remember who you're dealing with."

* * *

The Catholic priest returned to his church after attending the memorial service. As he entered the sanctuary, he noticed a lone figure seated in one of the back pews. It was a slender man with long gray hair pulled into a ponytail. He wore the look a priest learns to recognize, the look of the dying.

"Father, will you hear my confession?"

The priest nodded and led the way to the confessional.

"How long has it been since you last confessed?"

"Twenty years."

He paused a moment, but it wasn't the first long overdue request for forgiveness he had heard.

"Father, my life has been spent in evil work. I wanted to prove I was a great scientist. I wanted to master the secrets of God. It took me so long to understand that His secrets are meant for Him alone. Our meddling has always been wrong. And my hands are unclean with meddling. I knew from the beginning the evil that was hidden in our work. But I was silent. And I worked on, expanding the evil, perfecting it, polishing its claws. All when I should have helped those who tried to sound the alarm." The priest heard the man sobbing through the wall between them.

"God always forgives, my son. But you have to forgive yourself." He paused. "The work was with radiation?"

"All those dead boys, Father. How many more will there be? How many more towns poisoned?"

The priest answered gently, "Those towns and those boys need you to be strong, so you can work to prevent more tragedy. It's a sin as great as an other to wallow in our transgressions. The capable have an obligation to use their strength to do God's work. Forgive yourself."

Anthony DeSilva leaned his head against the polished wooden back of the confessional, tears streaming down his thin cheeks.

* * *

The phones started ringing all over the state within twelve hours of the governor's order. Henry Staggers was helping his brother cut wood on his farm near Greeleyville when his sister-in-law ran from the house to the edge of the field. There was a phone call from the guard, she said. He walked to the house to take the call, knowing what it meant.

Nat Engle was standing in the room they had selected for the nursery when the phone rang. It had been a week since he asked Susan about the radiation. She assured him she had researched it all. There was no need to worry. It was a lie, but it was one she had to tell. The truth was there was no way to know what harm had been done by the radiation in the time her baby was exposed. All the experts said the same thing. She had been tormented by the thought that she should abort the child, and they could try again. The thought of it caused her to shiver in fear. She was seized with a powerful conviction not to lose this child. Her faith and determination would keep it healthy, protect it from whatever conspired against it. She had to.

At the table in the bedroom, Nat listened, saying only that he understood. "Thank you, Sergeant. Call the others. I'll see you in the morning." He walked into the hall, where Susan looked alarmed.

"What is that about?" she asked, already knowing.

"A call up. The governor wants to stop the rioting. We report tomorrow." He saw the confusion on her face. "It isn't so bad. We'll probably just go to Florence or Charleston. How bad can it be? We'll get to see Mark and Beth. Besides, it'll be over soon."

She frowned, worried by the unknown and resentful of this intrusion into the new life they were building together.

"Come on. Let's finish figuring out what we're going to do with this room. Blue or yellow?"

* * *

Two weeks after the train exploded in South Carolina, Terry Wilkins finally left the farm. He moved out while Moore was in the District. It was easier that way. He called Paul Gregg and asked if he could stay with him for a while. It was his only option. He told his wife not to come to Washington. He couldn't face his family. Not now.

Wilkins was obsessed with news about the radiation accident. When Gregg asked him the reason, Wilkins became agitated. "Moore," he said. "He planned the whole thing. I was there, you know, I heard him talk about it. Only I didn't know he had rigged the train to blow up. I didn't know that!" Wilkins' eyes flashed as he talked.

"Terry, why was C. A. telling you these things? He didn't talk about his business to me. Ever."

"He just started telling me. All I did was ask a few questions. It was easy. Then he couldn't tell me enough."

Easy? What the hell did that mean?

Pictures of the rioting in South Carolina filled the screen of the television as the nightly news recounted the call up of National Guard troops across the state to quell the violence.

Gregg watched Wilkins staring at the screen, transfixed, and worried.... What had his friend done?

*   *   *

The emptiness of the house seemed to follow him. He resented this as much as any other part of what Wilkins' leaving had done to him. It never occurred to Moore that he would care. He knew he should try to look for someone else, but the motivation eluded him.

Certainly, there was plenty to occupy him. His orders to rig the trains carrying Russian plutonium were carried out by incompetents. Instead of simple booby traps designed to kill thieves, they created a catastrophe. He did not recall his directives to Hubbard to ensure that the fuel rod and plutonium casks would be utterly destroyed by explosives should there be any intrusion into the railcars.

Two weeks after Wilkins' departure, Moore found himself headed toward a confrontation with Governor Haselden. . Now, it was up to him to fix things again. Moore pulled out the little tin he carried in his coat pocket and snapped it open. He picked two of the little pills from the tin and tossed them into his mouth. They would be landing in Columbia in half an hour. These would help ensure his composure for the meeting with Haselden. The trains were coming again, and this would be the meeting that would end this nonsense once and for all.

Blackie Haselden sat in his office with two men from his staff and his press secretary. "Are the cameras ready?" he asked.

"Yes, Governor. They are in place."

"Fine. Our guest will be here in fifteen minutes. I'll meet with him alone."

"Governor, do you still want to announce a press conference tomorrow?"

"Yes. At 6:15 in the evening. I want the local news to carry it during their regular broadcast. Tell them it will be a short announcement, no more than five minutes, and important."

"Yes, sir." They left him alone to wait for Moore. *Maybe O'Connelly is wrong about the trains,* he told himself. *How could anyone decide to run them through this state again?* he wondered angrily. He asked himself what he would do if Moore told him more trains were coming. Again and again since the explosion he had vowed he would not permit it. But how would he stop it?

The intercom buzzed. Moore was in the reception area. "Bring him in, please."

The door opened, and the man he felt certain was responsible for the tragedy that had taken the lives of Watson and Billy Harris walked into his office, smiling and extending his hand in greeting. Blackie offered him a seat across from his desk. "Governor Haselden, I'm sure the vice president has expressed the deep sorrow all of us in the administration feel for the loss of so many innocent people in Florence. President Seekings has asked me to reiterate his personal condolences for the deaths of your friend and his son."

Blackie ignored Moore's remarks and looked at him impassively.

"But there is a very serious matter that I know you wish to resolve as much as the president. If you will allow me, I believe I can work with you to resolve the matter of the plutonium shipments and allow the government to bring all of its resources to bear in helping South Carolina recover from this terrible tragedy."

"Your government should be here repairing the damage and cleaning up the contamination right now. Your government caused it."

"We deeply regret what happened. But it was the result of a despicable terrorist attack on the train." Moore raised his arms in a helpless gesture. "Who could have imagined anyone would blow up a train like this?"

"You imagined it. You planned it. Why do you come here and pretend otherwise? The video we took of the inside of the surviving freight cars proves that they were rigged with sophisticated triggering mechanisms and enough explosives to shatter the fuel rod and plutonium casks. Look around you, Mr. Moore. We don't have any federal buildings in South Carolina anymore. The people have burned them down because they're mad as hell about what your government did. When will the two army officers be provided to us for questioning?"

"They are unavailable. Your people have been incited by your irresponsible allegations. Unproven and unprovable allegations. That is the situation we must resolve. We must bring this state back to normalcy."

"Bring back the firemen and Boy Scouts in Florence, Mr. Moore."

Moore stared over Blackie's shoulder to the portrait of someone in colonial uniform. This was tiresome. "Governor, here is our message, undiluted. The trains are going to run again. They will be guarded. And there will be no risk of attack or theft. You will be provided with a complete schedule and can take whatever additional security precautions you desire."

"They will not run, Mr. Moore."

Moore's eyes sparkled with fury. "The first train will leave Sunny Point tomorrow night. There is nothing you can do to stop it."

"It will not enter South Carolina."

Moore began to laugh, lightly at first. Then he put his head in his hands and laughed louder. He regained his voice to say, "Look you dull-witted hick, do I need to draw you a picture? The train is coming. O.K.? You can't stop it. The most powerful government in the world wills that this will happen. Not only do you have no power to stop it, you are a minimally important part of this country." He began to laugh again. "Surely even you understand that. You don't matter. Get it! You and this whole miserable, vacuous hole of a state are not on the map. The last time the rest of the country has to think about this worthless little place is when they have to memorize the states and capitals in the fourth grade! Why in the hell do you think we are so insistent that this shit come here to good old South Carolina? Because nobody who does matter wants it in their state, and nobody gives a preacher's damn about you! Now, let me tell you how it's going to be. You are going to get the hell out of our way, or you are going to be crushed. It's just that simple."

"This country is built on the mutual respect of all of its people for one another."

"I don't need a civics lesson from a two-bit redneck politician. You're a bigger fool than I thought." Moore stood and leaned over the governor's desk, thrusting his finger into Blackie's face. "Get the fuck out of the way! Then you can go back to eating grits and screwing your cousins, or whatever the hell it is you like to do." Moore walked to the door and turned to face Blackie again. "Just back off and you won't get hurt, understand?" Then he pulled the door open and walked out.

Blackie picked up the phone. "Did you get it all?"

"Yes, Governor," the still-shocked voice replied.

*　*　*

There was no moon the next night as the train approached the border. Helicopters flew overhead guarding the short line of cars. In the tree line, out of sight, was a company of Bradley fighting vehicles. When the train was within five hundred yards, one of the Bradleys lurched out of the tree line and aimed its machine gun at the tracks in front of the train. Sparks jumped from the metal rails as bullets ricocheted. Splinters from the wood ties flew against the front of the engine. The terrified engineer activated the brake immediately. Inside the Bradley, the crew waited, hoping the Apaches did not fire an anti-tank missile. They understood that the helicopters would have no trouble seeing their vehicle.

The train slowed to a stop just before the line separating North and South Carolina. The commander of the Bradley activated his loud speaker. "Remain inside the train. Repeat. Remain inside the train. We are going to blow the track. Stay clear. Stay clear." Then the Bradley lumbered off the track back into the wood line. Again the commander yelled into the loudspeaker, "Fire in the hole!" At his signal, three charges detonated, ripping the track in three separate places along one hundred yards. The train began to back away from the explosions.

Gratefully, the Bradley crews watched the Apache helicopters circle overhead. They had not yet been given the orders to use deadly force.

•

Chapter 25

"Governor Haselden, the president will be with you in just one minute," the disembodied voice said. Blackie felt his pulse quicken from the reality of the night's events.

He heard the phone click and knew Seekings was on the line. There was no sound for thirty seconds save the president's breathing; Seekings was gathering himself, still too angry to speak. "Yes."

"Roger, I regret what happened tonight. But you left me no choice. I made myself clear to Mr. Moore."

"Do you have any idea what you've done?"

"You will not bring any more nuclear material into this state as long as I have the power to prevent it."

"You don't have that power." Seekings took a deep breath. "Are you a student of history, Governor?"

"Roger—"

"I took an oath to protect this nation ..." Seekings' voice betrayed the barely controlled rage exploding inside him, "... an oath to defend it against all threats, including rebellion."

"Your government has forfeited any claim to loyalty here. You've murdered our citizens and poisoned the heart of one of our cities. And your only response is to arrogantly insist that you be allowed to continue. History teaches that free people can only be shoved so far. We have been pushed exactly to that point."

"You're insane."

* * *

White House aides frantically made calls to the names on the list. Most were not in their offices, but all were in the city or nearby. Each of the young staffers knew the president was furious, and all dreaded having to report that any of the names on their list could not be found for the emergency meeting the president had ordered for 10:00 a.m. They knew what his temper was like. Soon, two dozen frightened aides were scurrying around the capital city, all anxious to ensure that the handful of men the president had summoned would be in the Cabinet Room by 10:00.

Roger Seekings walked purposefully to his seat at the table and laid a small notepad on the polished surface. Around him sat the secretaries of defense and state, the national security advisor, the attorney general, the chairman of the joint chiefs, and C. A. Moore. Before Seekings began to speak, Mike O'Connelly entered the room. Seekings watched dispassionately as his vice president took a chair, carefully concealing his anger at the unwelcome intrusion. O'Connelly returned his gaze with an expressionless mask.

"Gentlemen, last night the National Guard of South Carolina attacked a United States government train carrying nuclear materials, preventing it from crossing into that state," Seekings began, telling them what they already knew. "The state is in rebellion, and its governor has committed treason.

"I have resolved to move to end this insurrection," he said. "First, the Eighty-second Airborne Division at Fort Bragg and the Third Infantry Division at Fort Stewart will be mobilized and prepare to occupy the state as soon as possible." He paused looking around the table. "Second, the National Guard of South Carolina will be brought under direct presidential command. The commander of that organization will be arrested for treason. Third, all federal reservists of all services will be mobilized for 180 days and placed under command of the Third Infantry Division commander.

"I will issue the order federalizing the National Guard tomorrow morning, along with the call up of reservists, both to be effective on Monday, six days from now. I want the occupation force ready to move by then as well. Is that clear, General Cramer?"

"Yes, sir."

"There will be no public discussion of the attack on the train last night. I will make a public announcement that the steps we are taking are required to restore order in the wake of the rioting. I will delay my declaration that a state of rebellion exists until the occupation is completed. Martial law will be instituted for an indefinite period."

The attorney general looked nervously at Seekings and asked, "And Governor Haselden. What action will we take in his case?"

Moore grinned behind Seekings, who turned to face the attorney general. "Wasn't I clear? I want the son of a bitch in jail!"

The president shoved his chair backwards and started to rise from the table.

"It's a mistake." Seekings stopped, still bent over the table and jerked his head toward Mike O'Connelly. "Don't do this."

Stretched beyond its limit, Seekings' control snapped. With reddening face and clenched fists, he turned on O'Connelly. "I didn't ask you what you thought, you washed-up old bastard! It's *my responsibility* to maintain order in this country. Not yours!"

"These people have been pushed far enough. It was your obsession with secrecy that led to this. And the explosives, my God—"

"Shut the fuck up, God damn it! Mike, I want your resignation by this afternoon."

"No."

"What!"

"I won't resign. And I won't be silent."

Seekings turned to the attorney general. "I want to know by tonight exactly what options I have to prevent any official of this government, including the *vice* president, from interfering in my efforts to deal with a national crisis." Casting a final furious glance at O'Connelly, Seekings walked from the room. The others avoided looking at O'Connelly, except General Cramer. The chairman of the joint chiefs calmly looked him in the eye before gathering his folder and striding to the door.

* * *

At 6:15 that evening, in the middle of local news programs, as had been announced, Governor Haselden began his speech.

"Since the terrible tragedy in Florence, we have pursued every effort to accomplish two vital goals. One is to discover the cause of the explosion of the nuclear train. The other is to ensure that no more such trains come into our state. You are entitled to know the facts on both counts. They are profoundly saddening.

"Our law enforcement agencies have identified two sets of fingerprints on the doors of the railcars that did not explode. The prints belong to two U.S. Army officers, both of whom have been subpoenaed for questioning. Photographs of these same men have been matched to pictures of the men who broke into the offices of the lawyers hired by the state to handle our effort to prevent exactly this type of tragedy. The White House has refused to allow these men to be interviewed by us.

"Two days ago, I was visited by a member of the president's staff. He informed me that more trains filled with the same kind of plutonium and nuclear fuel rods would be routed through South Carolina very soon. What you will now see is a tape of my meeting with this man, C. A. Moore, in my office." The image of the governor was replaced by the short videotape showing Moore seated across from Blackie. Soon, Moore's face curled into an ugly snarl and he began to shout, "... a minimally important part of this country ... this whole miserable, vacuous hole of a state are not on the map ... nobody who does matter wants it in their state, and nobody gives a preacher's damn about you...." When the tape ended, the sober face of the governor once again filled the screen.

"I expect that all of you will be as angry and saddened as I am by what you just saw. Let there be no doubt that I am committed to ensuring that we will never again be victimized by the venal and insidious attitude you just saw, by the notion that this state is some kind of inferior partner in the federal union, fit only as a depository for the nation's or the world's nuclear poison. We demand that we be treated as an equal. We must never forget that men from South Carolina signed the documents that gave birth to this nation. I appeal to you for faith that your state government will protect you and, more important, that we will protect one another. We must not resort to mob violence as a substitute for the spirit of community and the determination to preserve our dignity. We need only to be united to be strong and secure. We have no need for the torch or the noose. Good night and God bless you all."

The number of South Carolinians who watched the governor was probably not greater than 15 percent of the population of 3½ million people. Within minutes of the broadcast, however, those who watched were making telephone calls, explaining in animated and angry language what they had seen. Television stations ran the tape over and over, and again as part of their 11:00 news. By morning, it would have been difficult to find anyone who hadn't seen it. The national networks picked up the extraordinary tape and broadcast special news bulletins. Most played the bitter exchange between the governor and Moore in its entirety.

As soon as the camera light indicated he was no longer on the air, he removed the microphone and turned to his chief of staff, "Is General Demers waiting?"

"Yes, Governor."

Demers waited for Blackie in a small conference room. The door was guarded by three armed soldiers, who accompanied the general. Spread before him were detailed maps and two copies of a one-page briefing.

"General, will this work?" Blackie asked Demers when the general had finished his briefing.

Demers could not conceal his nervousness, and his hands fumbled with the papers in front of him as he prepared to answer Blackie's question. "I'm scared too, Harrison," Blackie said. "We never thought we'd be talking about anything like this, did we?" The general smiled and shook his head slowly. "Relax. What can we do to make this work, if we have to?"

"I need to know exactly where they are, and how to neutralize their automatic tracking mechanisms."

*   *   *

Moore didn't see the tape that night. He was at the farm alone. It would not be until the next day that he was told about the broadcast. While Blackie spoke to his citizens, Moore drank. He knew it was a mistake to drink *and* take the pills, but he was certain he could handle the mixture. Control was his greatest strength, and all that was required to walk the delicate balance between alcohol and drugs was control, after all. Fear was for the weak.

He basked in the quiet as the twin elements of release and contentment coursed through his body. As his mind hovered between the music from his CDs and a gentle, gauzy connection with the world, he began to think again about Terry Wilkins. He closed his eyes and could see the square, smiling face of the young soldier. He felt himself begin to stir. His hands could almost feel the taught, smooth skin pulled over the muscular—

Suddenly, terribly, questions exploded in his mind.... Who knew about the schedule and route of the train? How did the Russians know where to strike? How did they know when? He struggled to grasp the next even more terrible question, more frightening for its implications.

Where did Terry inherit the money?

Then he knew, as clearly as if a picture were flashed before him. A picture, the thought. He jumped from the couch and looked fanatically around the den. He ran up the stairs to the bedroom and flicked on the light. His eyes scanned the ceiling from corner to corner of the large room. From the desk by the window he dragged a chair to the furthest corner and stepped up to examine the light panel there. He quickly moved to the next. At the third panel he saw it. The dust on the outside of the panel was disturbed, the print of a hand was clearly visible on the surface. He ripped the panel from the ceiling, and it fell crashing to the wooden floor below, shattering into a hundred opaque fragments. The answer to his question stared back at him. A small camera had been fixed to the inside of the light fixture by two bolts, drilled into the supports. It was pointed to the bed he had shared with Terry. He grabbed the small box and yanked it. At first, it didn't give, and he pulled again, hard, furiously. The sharp edges of the box sliced the skin of his hand and blood ran down his arm and onto the floor, but the bolts gave way, the camera falling to the floor. Deeper was the cut that could not be seen.

* * *

Blackie was leading nearly a third of the way between second and third bases. Bud Harris waved the bat haughtily at the pitcher, his head cocked deep to his chest, daring him to throw a strike. "Knock me home, Bud," Blackie yelled. The pitch was a bold fastball straight to the center of the strike zone. With a grace and artistry only he brought to the diamond, Bud Harris swung the bat strong and level to meet the ball. When he heard the crack of wood on the ball, Blackie was already within reach of the base at third. Out of the corner of his eye he saw Bud round first, his thick legs pumping, carrying him at a remarkable speed over the dusty base line. Blackie could hear the cheers from the bleachers as he turned and headed for home plate. He saw that Bud was already at second, and was not stopping, heading strong for third. He forced more energy into his stride. Ahead of Blackie, the catcher was poised to receive the ball for the tag that would end his race for glory. Blackie dove into a slide. I might as well make it hard for him, he thought. But the throw went to third instead, the outfielder thinking to catch Bud. As Blackie rolled over and away from home plate, he saw Bud charging home. The ball had been overthrown. Bud slid into home, at no risk of being tagged out. His dust-covered body stopped next to Blackie's, and they jumped from the ground together, embracing joyously in their double triumph. Then he remembered. He opened his eyes to the blackness of the bedroom around him. The wonderful, painful dream had come again. He pulled the covers from his sweating body, careful not to wake June curled on the opposite side of the bed.

There was a chill in the night air, but he left his robe on the rack and walked quietly down the hall in his shorts to the television room at the front of the mansion. The cold air surrounded his skin, caressing it, calming him. In the dark, he poured a short glass of bourbon from the decanter on the sideboard and sipped it. Through the windows he saw the lights of Columbia in the distance. The false reality of the dream clung to him. But reality called to him... chided him. It will never be real again. He began to sweat again. His body tensed as he stood in the middle of the blackened room. His hands began to tremble; then his arms began to shake. He clasped his arms around himself to stop the frightened shivering. He needed to hold something.

On the table under the window he spotted the baseball bat that lay there. He picked up the bat. The smooth-grained wood felt good in his hands. Then he saw the images of truth again in his mind's eye. Bud and Billy dying. Dying horribly. Dottie, her eyes vacant, crazed, and alone. Suddenly, his hands were gripped tightly around the bat, and he was holding it straight out in front of him, over the small table. He swung the bat high over him and brought it crashing down onto the table. The crack of wood on wood resounded in the mansion. Blackie raised the bat and brought it down again, his muscles flexed and driving all of his strength into the shattered table. Again and again he brought the bat down onto the table surface, smashing the table into fragments. Lights clicked on, rapidly moving from the first floor up the staircase and down the hall to the television room. An agent assigned to the mansion staff leapt into the room, his revolver drawn, and turned on the light. The governor turned, his face red, his hair wet and matted to his head, the bat resting on the ruined table. June Haselden slid between the agent and the doorframe, wrapped in her robe, and quickly moved to her husband. "It's O.K... It's O.K.," she said. The agent lowered his gun and backed from the room. June took the bat from Blackie's hands. "It's all right."

He sank to his knees on the carpet, crying. She kneeled beside him and circled him in her arms. "They're dead, June. They're never coming back."

She held his head tight to her breast. "I know, Blackie."

"*You don't understand*," he said bitterly. "I *hate* the men who did this. I wanted to kill them. I can't stop hating them. I don't know what I'm going to do."

She stroked his damp hair. "You have to be strong for all of us, Blackie. Strong for me." She held his head and looked into his eyes. "I still need you." He stared into her eyes, finding again the love for her that had been pushed aside since the tragedy, lost to him for too long. "Just do what's right, Blackie. Leave the hate behind. Bud's always right here," she said, placing her hand over his bare chest. "He'll always be part of you. You're a lucky man, Blackie. You have the strength of two men. And we need you both."

*   *   *

The president wasted no time making his intentions clear. In a televised address, he explained that events in South Carolina were now reaching crisis proportions. *Now reaching a crisis*, Jim thought as he watched. The governor and the leadership in the state seemed unable to control the spiraling violence, and he was left with no choice but to assume responsibility for maintaining order.

"... There have been confirmed reports of violence by the National Guard itself directed at officials of the United States government. The nation cannot tolerate ... I will not tolerate any action that undermines our government. Today, I have ordered the FBI and the Justice Department to investigate these incidents and have asked that General Harrison Demers, commander of the South Carolina National Guard, and Governor Bill Haselden meet with my representatives in Atlanta on Thursday to begin a thorough investigation.

"I believe it is necessary for the protection of all the people in South Carolina that I assume direct control of the National Guard forces in that state. On Monday, command of the guard and the Air National Guard will be assumed by my office directly. This step will alleviate the pressure on Governor Haselden in his efforts to manage the relief effort. I remain committed to bringing all necessary assistance to that effort and look forward to working with the governor to relieve the suffering of the people in the affected area.

"On Monday I will be ordering a call to active duty of all federal reservists in all three military services. Their talents are vital if we are to clean up and rebuild the area devastated by the terrible terrorist attack last month. This will be a temporary call up, and I will strive to shorten the time required as much as possible."

Jim was stunned. There were twenty thousand reservists in the state. The call to active duty would strip these people from countless businesses, government offices, and families. And he wondered what it meant for him.

* * *

Throughout the day, President Seekings' twin announcements were denounced by every radio announcer in the state. In offices, on assembly lines, in break rooms, and over backyard fences little else was discussed. Shortly after noon, a radio show in Columbia broadcast a call from a man suggesting that people ought to show the president they were behind the governor and were not going to be pushed around. By mid-afternoon, his suggestion matured into a call, repeated on all the state's radio stations, for rallies at the courthouses of all forty-six counties.

The crowds grew in small town and city alike, until every court-house was an island in a sea of humanity. Some came with flashlights. Some held candles, signs or flags. In many places they sang. In all the squares and in front of antebellum porticos, as many of the faces were black as were white. No accounts were kept of how many people answered the call to rally in defense of the state. But the best guess was that by 9:00 p.m. nearly a million people had turned out.

It was in Charleston during that remarkable night, in the center of the crowd far up Meeting Street from the courthouse, that the flag first appeared. It was familiar to some students of history, but most didn't recognize it. The television camera crew illuminated it with their spot-light. Someone directed the reporter's attention to the blue flag with a single white star in the center and told him what it was. He added the explanation to his report. By morning the picture was on the front page of every paper, and the tape was shown on every television station. They all reported the rallies by leading with the same statement about the flag ... the banner of secession had been raised again in South Carolina.

*   *   *

Somehow the pills didn't seem to be working. Moore wondered if he was growing immune. Perhaps it was just the anticipation of meeting with the president later in the day.

It was a day for reminders. He reached for the safe next to his desk. Inside he retrieved a metal box, unlocked the lid, and pulled out a computer disk. He scanned the list of documents. Selecting one he printed it, folded the pages carefully and slid them into his vest pocket. The president, he felt certain, would need to see this sample from his files this afternoon.

*   *   *

Matt Reicher reached for his list of phone numbers.

"How's life at the pinnacle of power?" he asked his long-time friend in the Pentagon.

The response was loud laugher. "Too hard for all the little people like you to understand."

"I need to tell you something. But you need to understand that the captain has forbidden me to make this recommendation."

"O.K. Go ahead."

"We need to get the intel folks to set up twenty-four hour surveillance by satellite over the entire State of South Carolina. There is no way to tell where this trouble down here is going to end up. If we get overrun, there has to be a way to track any specials that get taken out of here."

Overrun? He didn't understand. He couldn't imagine such a thing, but he knew better than to question Matt Reicher's judgment. "I'll have to go through the admiral, and then their boss at intel will have to approve it. It's a pretty simple thing to shift a bird's orbit. I'll put it to them, Matt. No promises."

"Good man. And ..."

"Yeah."

"What *do* you wear for knee protection?"

"Go to hell, Matt."

The officer hesitated a moment after hanging up; then he reached for his navy directory. This would take some time. And he'd be putting his neck out, way out there. Too bad. If Matt Reicher was worried about security of nuclear weapons, there was a good reason.

* * *

Julieanne Harris drove early to Columbia. Blackie said there was little time, and he needed her expertise. She had received another telephone call from Leo Scardato two days before. She knew it would be the last for quite a while. The president intended to arrest the governor and the commander of the National Guard, he said. Blackie had not been surprised when she told him.

"We don't have long to decide what to do. Either we're going to give in or we're going to have to do something that used to be unthinkable."

"Everything that's happened used to be unthinkable."

"Julie, I mean taking control of our own destiny."

"What do you mean?" Then she saw it ... felt it. "Rebellion?"

"Independence."

She would have thought her senses were deadened to any shock. But the word stunned her. Its sound was alien and ugly ... vaguely resonate of tragedy and death from another time. Yet it was not the faintly remembered past they were discussing. The deaths that summoned the frightening word were still fresh.

"If there were other answers ..." He looked away for a moment. "But there aren't. I'm going to ask the legislature to vote on the question. I've already talked to the leadership and they agree with me. If they vote to give in to the president, I'll step aside, go to Atlanta and let them arrest me."

"You can't make it work unless you seize the nuclear weapons at the Weapons Station in Charleston. Seekings will move heaven and earth to stop you. But not even he will risk nuclear war."

"I know, Julieanne. I need your help to plan how to do that. There will be so little time."

It surprised her how this filled her with new pain. Still, the anger flashed inside her. "We didn't ask for this."

* * *

For ten days Captain Nat Engle and his company had been in Charleston, rotated between the air force base and the federal courthouse. Susan, now halfway through her pregnancy, had joined him four days ago. Mark and Beth Killian insisted they stay with them, and they made as much of the situation as possible. Several times, late at night, Mark and Nat asked themselves where it all might lead.

The call that would tell Nat exactly where the crisis was about to take him came shortly after 10:00 a.m. General Demers called Nat and ordered him to meet a helicopter that was waiting to take him to Columbia.

For General Demers and the small staff working on the governor's special operation, the choice of Engle was an easy one. Not only had he earned an uncommon degree of loyalty from his soldiers that summer at the NTC, but he knew transportation, and he knew the Weapons Station. At National Guard Headquarters, General Demers and three other guard officers waited for Nat. He recognized them all, but not the woman in civilian clothes sitting at the table with them.

"This is Julieanne Harris. She's an expert in weapons security and will help us plan the mission I want to talk to you about."

Demers took a deep breath before continuing. "Captain Engle, on Saturday night a decision will be made as to whether this state will secede from the United States." The shock was visible in Nat's eyes. "Should the decision be to secede, it will be our job to seize the nuclear weapons stored at the Naval Weapons Station in Charleston. Forces will be deployed to take all federal installations, and first priority will naturally be the military bases. For obvious reasons, securing the nuclear devices is key to the success of this operation. I want you to lead the mission at the Weapons Station." The general paused, studying the face of the captain. "Can you carry out this mission without hesitation... without any reservations?"

Adrenaline surged through Nat's body. "Yes, sir. My men and I can accomplish the mission. If the order is given, they will do what has to be done." Nat thought of his men. All of them knew someone who had been touched by the tragedy in Florence. His mind reeled from the incomprehensible thing they might do. A thousand questions cried out for answers. But he remembered his own child. And he was certain there would be no hesitation.

Julieanne explained that it was vital to move quickly. They had to assume satellites would watch everything. She drew him detailed pictures of the transponders that she said they must locate and destroy on each of the weapons. Failure to do that would mean certain catastrophe, she said.

When they were finished reviewing the surprisingly simple plan, Nat asked, "General, who will be in charge of transportation of the weapons once they are secure?"

"No one's been assigned yet."

"General. Can I recommend someone. Nobody knows transportation better than he does."

*   *   *

Mark Killian listened in stunned silence to Nat. "Someone needs to be responsible for transporting the weapons to their hiding places ... if we take the damn things." They stood in the far corner of the backyard of Mark's house. "You're the best man I know at transporting anything. Do you want the job?"

Mark regarded him soberly, "Isn't there any other way, Nat? My God. Secession."

Nat leaned on the planks of the fence, "I don't know. When you boil it all down, I'm just a soldier now. If I think about it, I'll never be able to do my job, will I?"

"But ... this is extreme ... to leave ... to *try* to leave the country. They'll try to stop us, Nat, you know that."

"That's why our mission is so important. If we get our hands on all the nukes, they won't mess with us. Nobody in their right mind would risk nuclear war."

Mark thought a moment, watching the last rays of the sun disappear below the trees. "How can we make it on our own? I mean ... our own country ... Jesus!"

"Maybe, once we have the nukes, they'll cut a deal with us. Then, settle down."

Mark looked at Nat a moment, and then nodded silently. "O.K., country boy."

*   *   *

After the yelling stopped, Moore waited for the president to deliver the message he expected. He was calm. The pills were working after all — or maybe it was the confidence he had in the message he was about to deliver to Roger Seekings.

Seekings regained his composure. "C. A., I just can't keep you in the White House any longer. Not after that tape of you and that redneck bastard Haselden. You know the rules here."

"And what do you propose, Mr. President?"

"I intend to keep you doing the same things for me you've always done, but not here. Not in the House."

"Where?"

"In the Defense Intelligence Agency over at Bolling."

"I see. I think it would be difficult for me to do all the things I have been doing from there. My status would be quite a bit diminished."

"You can't stay here."

"I'm not so easy to dispose of, Mr. President."

Seekings was shocked. Never had Moore spoken to him with anything but deference. "What the hell do you mean by that?"

"I mean, Mr. President, if you'll pardon a trite expression, I know too much. You can't afford to have me anywhere but in this house. Here, take a look at this. Look familiar?" He pulled the pages from his vest pocket and tossed them to Seekings. The president scanned the pages and closed his eyes. "Remember that, sir? The senator didn't want to play ball when it came time for the convention. The records of the illegal campaign contribution — not to say bribe — he received convinced him. Of course, we arranged the contribution for just that purpose. This is just one of the jobs I've done for you, Mr. President."

"What are you saying?"

"I'm saying that unless you're willing to have me killed, you simply *can't afford* to have me anywhere else but right here."

Roger Seekings had nearly forgotten how to be afraid, but he was afraid now. "I see."

"I knew you would once you understood the facts, Mr. President."

Seekings sat silently, staring from the window.

"Besides, Mr. President, I think soon you may need me now more than ever."

*　*　*

On Friday morning Mark Killian, dressed in his uniform, walked into the operations office of the army's Military Traffic Management Command on the South Annex of the Weapons Station. In a manila folder were the orders Nat brought back with him from Columbia. They announced that his company was scheduled to be deployed to Egypt. There was a ship arriving in a week, or so they had been told. The operations sergeant checked the log of expected arrivals. There was nothing there to indicate such a vessel. Well, it wouldn't be the first time that the Marine Sealift Command had thrown them a curve ball, would it? "Fucking navy," the sergeant said.

"Maybe, there is no ship and they just intend for the guard to get some practice in staging their shit," Mark suggested. "Our unit intends to get a little training helping them stage and document the equipment."

"O.K. There's nothing in the lot over by Pier Alpha. When will the convoy be here?"

"Tomorrow. At 0700 hours."

The sergeant printed a form from his computer and handed it to Mark. "Just be sure the convoy commander has this with him to show security at the gate. Probably better to use the Remount gate and go across the bridge."

"I agree. Thanks, Sergeant."

It was a strange time for the guard to be training in ship-loading operations. But that wasn't a sergeant's business. It was Friday, and he intended to be gone as soon after noon as he could get away.

*　*　*

"Thanks for coming up on short notice."

Jim McNeely wasn't nearly finished with the division of his cases among his partners, or with a thousand other loose ends he needed to take care of before Monday morning, when he would report for active duty in response to the president's order. The governor called him the afternoon before and told him it was vital that they meet. He hadn't wanted to see Drew Holland. Just him.

"You know as well as anyone the situation we are in. In three days we will be required to turn over direct control of the state to the federal government. I'm sure you realize it won't just be the National Guard. And I'm certain you know the call up of reservists has nothing to do with cleaning up Florence."

Jim nodded.

"I have also been informed that the president intends to arrest General Demers and I for treason. That was why I declined to go to Atlanta yesterday. There must be a resolution to this, but there are only two choices." He watched Jim's face closely as he continued. "One is to give in. The people are near revolt. And it's clear the president means to impose martial law." He paused and looked, Jim felt, even more deeply into his eyes, "The only other choice is to take control of our own destiny."

"My God," Jim breathed.

"To make this work, we will need to seize all the military installations at once, including the Weapons Station. And that is the key. We must secure the nuclear devices there if we are to protect our independence. I know what I am about to ask will be hard. I want you to accompany the guard unit to the Weapons Station. I want you be my representative." He handed Jim a sheet of paper. "This is a commission in the guard, already executed." Jim glanced at it. *A lieutenant colonel.*

"Jim, it's important that we get this done without any loss of life or mistreatment of people on these bases. I want people I trust at each one. I know how close you are to Commander Reicher. I want you to look after him and his family. That's important. Will you do it?"

"How is this decision being made?"

"Not by me alone. I'm calling the General Assembly into session Saturday night. They will have to decide. If they say secede, we'll be ready. All the forces will be in place. If they say no, we'll just stand down. I'll turn myself over to the federal government." His eyes strayed to the window as he said this.

"All right, Governor." He rubbed his eyes. "There are so many questions...."

"I know there are. Too many to answer now. The answer to the most important one has been forced on us." He reached for Jim's shoulder. "The guard commander will be Captain Nathan Engle, and the transportation of the weapons will be the job of Captain Mark Killian."

* * *

The pines along the Interstate back to Charleston were all familiar. He had watched them grow for twenty-five years. So familiar they seemed. So real.

But the world around them suddenly wasn't familiar at all. It was eerily foreign. He remembered what DeSilva said, standing at Trinity Site, passionately trying to explain the terrible nature of radioactivity. It doesn't stop, he had said, radioactive particles from one damaged, unstable substance contaminate another. And it goes on and on ... ripping apart lives ... and nations. More than atoms were contaminated by the radiation in Florence. One evil had spawned another, and now an even greater cataclysm was upon them, far beyond their control.

*   *   *

It was nearly four o'clock. Carol wondered if the call was from one of her boss' clients with a closing for Monday. "Hello," she said professionally.

"Hey, guess who?" Her heart skipped.

"Dave! Where are you?"

"New York. Almost home. We'll be back in Norfolk next Friday. You still coming?"

"Try to keep me away. I can't believe the time's almost here."

"Have you thought about what I said in Charleston?"

"About what? You said a lot of strange things."

"Very funny. About you and me. Do you think we can make it work?"

"I thought I told you, sailor. Whatever it takes. Whatever it takes."

"I love you."

"I love you, sailor."

*   *   *

Shortly after dawn on Saturday morning, the flatbed trucks arrived at the gate of the Naval Weapons Station, each one carrying a single Bradley fighting vehicle from Captain Engle's company. The security guard glanced at the form handed him by the convoy commander and waved them through. One by one, the trucks led by Henry Staggers snaked their way through the Weapons Station to the bridge across Goose Creek. One-half mile across the bridge, they reached the staging area adjacent to Pier

Alpha and began to unload the Bradleys in neat rows. When they were all staged, Nat Engle drove up in his Humvee. He looked up the paved road that led away from the pier. They were only five miles from the gate that led to the bunkers of nuclear weapons.

Six miles on the other side of the Weapons Station, Mark Killian watched as the largest number of rental trucks he had ever seen began to arrive at the empty lot next to the Department of Transportation maintenance shed. They were from every rental service he had heard of, and from some that he hadn't. By the time they stopped arriving, the lot was full, with nearly one hundred trucks parked in ten straight rows. All the drivers were National Guard soldiers. Tomorrow, they might be very busy, he reminded himself.

Chapter 26

Flags on either side of the podium flapped in the late autumn wind. In front of the stand — which was decorated in red, white, and blue crepe paper — dozens of chairs were filled with reporters, friends and family. Behind the chairs another hundred people stood. Television cameras flanked the rectangle of chairs. Behind the podium hung a banner proclaiming in bold white letters on a blue background: "O'CONNELLY FOR CONGRESS."

The band from the high school played its heart out for the small crowd. At strategic locations, campaign regulars watched the crowd, trying to discern anything that might help them in the election that waited a year away. The crowd stirred as it perceived movement from the courthouse to the platform. A ripple turned into a line of heads making its way to the steps. At the front appeared Marilyn O'Connelly, smiling broadly and waving to the crowd with both hands, just as she had seen her father do so many times. Following were her children and husband. Finally, came the vice president, waving only one hand, desperate not to upstage his daughter. The crowd, which had begun to cheer enthusiastically when Marilyn appeared, erupted when Michael O'Connelly reached the platform. He was their man — would always be their man. Many among them couldn't remember a time when Michael O'Connelly was not a force in politics. He had long ago proved his decency to them, and his good humor.

When they all stood on the platform, the vice president walked to the podium and motioned for the crowd's attention. How sweet this was, the sight of so many faces, trusting him, and waiting to hear him speak.

"That was nice.... Maybe this O'Connelly will run for congress again." They loved it and stood to cheer him again. He turned to his daughter, his eyes saying he was sorry, but not really. How he missed these people. "For a generation... and maybe a little more... you honored me with your trust. I took every vote you offered me to Washington. I never forgot a single one. We had a singular bond, you and I. We meant something to each other." His eyes scanned the crowd. "Those years were the best of my life. Now, the time has come for you to pick another to take your votes ... your trust ... your hopes and concerns to Washington. Today, my daughter begins the hardest challenge she will ever face, earning your trust. She has a year to do that, just as you have a year to select your next congressman. I believe she is the person to carry your votes to congress. But she has to prove that to you. I can't. And I know she is as new to you as I am old. I won't insult you by asking for your votes for my daughter. What I will ask is that you listen to her, look into her eyes. I believe you will see that she has the mettle and the heart to serve you for the next generation. I give you Marilyn O'Connelly." He raised his hand as Marilyn walked to the podium. She kissed him on the cheek. The crowd rose to its feet and cheered wildly. He could say what he wanted, but if Michael O'Connelly wanted them to vote for his daughter, they would gladly do it.

He took his seat and turned to listen to the speech he helped write. Her delivery was flawless. It would play well on TV. But as she spoke, he began to think again about the crisis that was fast spinning out of control. He knew the president's plans, which would be set in motion in only two days, would spawn untold danger.

He saw that the crowd was on its feet and realized Marilyn was finished speaking. She kissed her husband and hugged the kids. He walked towards her and took her hand. Together they faced the cheering people below them, and he raised their hands together, holding them triumphantly over their heads.

* * *

The first platoon of Nat Engle's troops began arriving at the South Annex of the Naval Weapons Station just after four o'clock on Saturday afternoon. Their arrival was staggered to make less noticeable the fact that an entire company of National Guard infantrymen was moving into the army reserve center for the night. By nine o'clock, well after dark, the entire company would be in the center, preparing and waiting for word from Columbia. Only then would the M-16s be unloaded from the trucks parked at the rear of the center.

* * *

Jim McNeely watched the sun touch the horizon of trees in the west. The last rays bathed the streaks of clouds in bright orange, white, and gray, making an artist's canvas of the sky. He asked Alicia to join him on the dock. That was where he waited for her now, unsure what to tell her about the reason he must be gone for the night. It was cruel to leave her alone and unprepared for the news that might come. He couldn't do that, but how to prepare her without revealing the terrible secret that he had to keep for one more day?

Her footsteps caused him to look up the length of the narrow walkway over the marsh. She approached him, illuminated in the sinking sun's light. Behind her rose the house they built, their safe haven. "So. What's this extra duty for the reserves all about? You'll be on duty Monday as it is."

There was still enough light for her to see the anguish in his face. "I'm not in the reserves any longer. I'm in the guard." She stared at him, perplexed, and beginning to be frightened.

"What's going on, Jim?"

"Please, Ally. I can't tell you. There may be trouble tomorrow." Her hand covered her mouth. Everything was happening so fast. There was no time. "I'll be all right. You have to trust me. Don't worry. Promise me you'll stay close to the house tomorrow until I call."

"If you think it's best." Her voice shook. She was scared now and knew she would stay that way until it was over. "Will there be fighting?"

He didn't answer. The truth was written plainly enough in his eyes, eyes she had long ago learned to read. "Oh my God," she moaned, and reached for him. "This has to end," she said. The chill that crept along her arms wasn't from the November air. He took her in his arms and pulled her close to the camouflage uniform jacket he wore, the jacket from which the U.S. Army patch would soon be torn. They kissed long and passionately, the tide turning to ebb now, running under them, fast away to the creek and river beyond.

He walked through the house and kissed his children, both enthralled in a television program. For a moment he paused, staring at the normalcy all around him, the pain of leaving them almost unbearable. In the living room he picked up the small overnight bag by the window and stepped into the cold air of the most frightening night of his life.

*   *   *

The members of the South Carolina General Assembly began arriving after dark. Members of both houses filed into the House chamber, the only one big enough to hold all of the legislators. Over the long, high-paneled rostrum hung the Stars and Stripes of the United States and the blue palmetto flag of the state. Below it rested the giant and ornate eighteenth-century mace, the symbol of the House since colonial times.

Seated in the high-backed chairs behind the rostrum were the aging lieutenant governor, the speaker pro tem of the senate, and the speaker of the house. The legislators milled about in the chamber. The backslapping and loud banter that usually characterized their gatherings was missing tonight. A crisis they had never imagined was bearing down on them like a monster storm, and what they sought above anything else on this night was a direction that would take them out of harm's way.

Theodore Gourdine, the lieutenant governor, lifted the gavel at the rostrum and slammed it heavily three times, the noise carrying solemnly throughout the chamber. The House members took their usual seats, and the senators found seats behind them. Only five House members and one senator were missing.

Gourdine, looking unusually pale, addressed them briefly. The governor had called them back for a special session, he said, to make a fundamental decision about the future of the state. His few sentences seemed to drain the energy from the old man, and he sank back into his chair. The governor walked onto the rostrum behind Gourdine and moved to the microphone. Blackie looked out over the old chamber, his face drawn and his jaw set defiantly.

"There is no time, ladies and gentlemen. There should be long and careful debate over what I am going to propose to you. All of our futures will be determined by what you decide tonight. In less than forty-eight hours, the president will send two divisions of the United States Army into South Carolina with the purpose of occupying this state. Martial law will be imposed for a period that only he will determine. General Demers and myself will be arrested and charged with treason. I can only presume we will be removed to a federal prison in another part of the country." He paused and looked into the faces that watched him. Many were surprised. He knew most had been told exactly what he was going to say. "It goes without saying that this state will remain the storage site for whatever waste the nation finds inconvenient, no matter how horrific the risk to our health or the future of our children.

"You must decide what course we will take. You can elect to give the president what he wants. In that case, the period of martial law and the disruption it would entail would probably be shortened significantly. If that is your choice, the general and I will fly to Atlanta tomorrow and report to the FBI office there.

"The time has come when negotiation is no longer possible. And the choice is harsh, for the only other option for you to consider tonight is the unthinkable. Unthinkable until our lives and well-being became unworthy of protection by the government with which we believed we were an equal partner."

He saw that they were beginning to shift nervously in their chairs. "We must face the fact that our only alternative to subordination to the status of a hazardous and radioactive waste heap is to reclaim direct control over our own affairs." He paused and looked at them. The chamber was still.

"There are many things to consider about independence for our state, but we have only a little time to make this terrible decision. A choice to secede from the Union would be fraught with hardship and the risk of confrontation with the most powerful nation in the world. Tonight, the soldiers of our National Guard are in position to take the weapons to guarantee our independence. If your decision is to claim independence for South Carolina, they will move swiftly to secure every military installation in the state. That will include one of the largest collections of nuclear weapons in the world.

"For myself, I have seen enough to know what I believe should be done. The arrogance and callousness of the people who control the federal government is so great that we must either tear ourselves away to remain a free and secure people, or forfeit the freedom that we have always believed was our birthright. But the decision must be yours, for you are the voice of the people." He looked around the chamber a last time before adding, "Don't delay. There must be an answer by dawn, or events will commit us by default to the course of acquiescence." Blackie left the rostrum and walked to the back of the chamber.

The speaker of the house rose to address the legislators. "We will conduct this session as a committee of the whole General Assembly. It's appropriate that there be a motion to debate, and I'll make it." He had prepared the words days ago, but now they came with difficulty. "I move that this assembly declare that the State of South Carolina is a free and independent nation, free to manage our own affairs among the world's family of sovereign states."

Silence filled the vast room for a full minute. "How will we live?" asked a House delegate from Laurens.

"Like we always have. Hell, in New Hampshire, they print on their license plates, 'Live Free or Die.' We used to feel that way. When did we stop?" The white-haired senator from Hartsville, added, "We can't live the way things are now. How long before there's another accident?"

The questions about how they would live, how they could protect themselves became a flood that spilled across the chamber for two hours, questions without answers. When the torrent subsided, the speaker spread his arms over the rostrum. "We could fill this place up with answerless questions tonight, folks. The one question we know the answer to is what happens when we trust this government to bring nuclear waste into our cities."

A seven-year senator from Hilton Head rose. "What if they fight? Nuclear weapons can't protect us from being crushed — from our soldiers being killed — by a force many times stronger. They only protect us if the other side believes we will use them. But will we? Could we? Against the people who are our countrymen?"

It was just one more question with no answer, at least, not yet.

Again silence fell on the assembly. Ever man and woman felt the current of history running around them, carrying them swirling to an uncertain future.

The speaker looked at his watch. It was nearly two o'clock in the morning. "It's late. We need to call for a vote."

"I move to amend the motion, to call for negotiation of a new arrangement with the United States," a House member said, "One that protects us as equals in the Union." The motion was seconded by a half dozen senators and representatives.

"As amended, the motion is that we declare independence and call for a new contract between this state and the United States. We will call the roll." One by one, the names were called. There were no "nay" votes. All voted "aye," except a dozen, who asked to be skipped.

The speaker looked at the electronic tally of the votes. "We need to be unanimous. No abstentions." The twelve who didn't vote the first time stood. Each called out his vote. Each voted for independence. The last with tears streaming down his cheeks. Stanislas Gamulka came to South Carolina as a child when his parents escaped from Poland after the first anti-Communist uprising in the 1950s, and the flag of the United States was a holy thing to him. His pain at what he had done was profound, but he had no regrets. He knew the evils of a government without compassion or respect for its own people.

Once more, the speaker faced his colleagues. He took a deep breath. Trying to slow the pounding of his heart made him fear it might be his last. "By unanimous vote of the General Assembly, the State of South Carolina is declared to be a free and independent nation, as of 4:00 a.m. today. God be with us."

The legislators stood slowly and began to leave the chamber. A National Guard captain rushed to relay the message to General Demers. Within minutes the task forces gathered at each military installation across the state had received the message.

*   *   *

The phone buzzed next to the sergeant who was keeping the watch. Most of the soldiers were sleeping restlessly along the carpeted halls of the reserve center. After nightfall, there had been a frenzy of activity as the soldiers unloaded their weapons from the trucks, being careful to do so in the dark. They were confused by the secrecy but followed the captain's orders strictly, all under Henry Staggers' watchful eye. Only after the weapons were removed, checked, and loaded, did Nat Engle gather them together in one of the large training rooms. "In a few hours we will know whether we are to carry out the mission I am about to brief you on." Behind him was hung a large map of the Weapons Station. He explained the extraordinary deliberations then underway in Columbia. "If the decision is to secede, it will be our job to take this installation — and the nuclear weapons stored here...." he jabbed his finger at their location on the map. "There's no time to practice or drill this operation. We have surprise. You just need to follow your orders. Second only to accomplishing our mission is this goal: No casualties, ours or theirs." He scanned their faces, trying to look each one in the eye.

In the late afternoon he had returned to the Killians' house to see Susan. For days, the adrenaline had lifted him above the point where he could sense any danger. But as he had walked toward his wife, her image, round with their child, had changed that. Suddenly, the frailty of life and the risk he would soon take had seemed very real. As she had taken him into her arms, she had sensed the change, the softening of confidence. "What's wrong, Nat?" she had asked, her brilliant eyes looking up at him.

"Not a thing. I just missed you. It'll be a long night." She had chuckled softly, her cheek resting against his chest. Her hands had slid between them.

"There'll be tomorrow night. You better be this glad to see me then," she had said.

He had thrown his head back and had laughed loud and deep. "I knew there was a reason I fell in love with you." They had fallen silent a moment, lost in each other's eyes. "I love you," he had said pulling her to him and kissing her desperately. "I love you both."

As he readied his men for their mission, much of the excitement returned to him, though the memory of Susan in his arms was never far away. His soldiers were the best, he told them, and they would do the job. They were going to make history. None accepted his invitation to stay behind. As they went about their work, there was an eerie unspoken sense that it had all been inevitable — ever since the train.

The hand shaking his shoulder meant only one thing, Nat knew as he awoke from the light sleep. "Captain," the excited sergeant said, "the message from Columbia is 'A Single Star,' sir." Secession. So, that was it, then. "Get the unit up, Sergeant. Time to go." The soldiers were up in minutes. They were quiet, and there was little light. The security guards were still patrolling the station. Nat checked his watch. Ninety more minutes. Time to begin the first phase. He saw the armbands were being handed out. The soldiers had already removed the "U.S. Army" patches from above the breast pockets of their uniforms. Now they slid the wide, bright blue bands over their left arms. Painted on the armbands was a bright white crescent, like that on the state flag.

"Lieutenant Rickenbacker, it's time." The younger man saluted and moved to the door. A company of military police had been attached to him for the night's operation. The Humvees carrying the military police filed out of the parking lot behind the reserve center. The lieutenant stepped from his Humvee and walked to the guardhouse at the entrance to the Weapons Station.

"Hi, Lieutenant," the civilian guard said sleepily. "What are you guys up to tonight?"

The lieutenant smiled. "Taking over," he answered. The cold muzzle of the pistol he laid next to the guard's throat said the rest. The older man started to back away, but froze as Rickenbacker shoved the gun deeper into the soft skin. "I'll take this," he lifted the guard's pistol from its holster. "Walk with me over here, and you can have the rest of the night off."

Rickenbacker walked him the few yards to the small guard office. Inside, three of his soldiers were applying the last of the tape to the mouths of two more civilian guards who already had their hands tied. Soon all three were locked in the back room. Rickenbacker's radio came alive again. "Everything's checked out, sir." It was the signal that the main gate of the Weapons Station and the main security office were now controlled by his men.

"Let's gather the rest of the loose straps," Rickenbacker responded.

"Roger that, sir." It was time to call in the security guards who were still roaming the station. In thirty minutes, all of the security guards were tied, gagged, and locked safely away in their own buildings. All of the gates were manned by Lieutenant Rickenbacker's military policemen.

Nat glanced at his watch. On schedule. It was time for the second phase. "First Sergeant, I want you to take the third platoon and secure this area. Second Platoon will cover the pier where that navy ammunition ship is berthed. The rest of the platoons are with me. Don't let that ship on berth at the Transportation Corps dock leave." Berthed at the army's dock one mile away was the *Capricorn*, one of the army's fleet of prepositioned ships kept at sea loaded with a full complement of combat equipment and ammunition, and regularly rotated into port for maintenance. She was nearly loaded again and would be ready to sail on Monday. "We can make use of the cargo on both those ships."

"Yes, sir." Staggers smiled.

Nat settled his helmet on his head and snapped the chinstrap. He stepped into the Humvee that waited for him. The line of vehicles snaked its way to the bridge over Goose Creek and along the wharves to the staging area at the foot of Pier Alpha, where Nat's twenty-one Bradleys waited. The gates were already open and his men were swarming over the armored vehicles, preparing them to move. On the turret of each was a 25-mm cannon and a machine gun. Gun ports on the sides allowed the three-man crew to bathe the entire area around the Bradley in gunfire. In less than ten minutes, the Bradleys were turning toward the gate, moving in a steady line onto the road leading to the main portion of the base.

Soon they were speeding toward their objective at forty-five miles an hour and would travel the five miles in only a few minutes. The first light of dawn was brightening the sky over the Cooper River as the noise of the heavy tracks roaring along the road shook the houses along the river. Matt Reicher leapt from bed and ran to the kitchen phone. No one answered him at the security office. He hurried to pull on clothes and called Captain Kratz.

On the road the Bradleys rushed past the main gate, the two helmeted military policemen there jutting thumbs-up greetings as they passed. From the hatch of the third Bradley, a soldier stood and fixed a blue flag to the top of the turret. The fabric flapped stiffly in the wind, showing a single white star in the center.

As the last Bradley in the line reached the main gate, it pulled to the front of the command building and turned its turret to face the street. Inside the Bradley, Jim McNeely crouched in the unfamiliar surroundings, waiting for Matt. He knew it wouldn't be long. His friend for so long would come, and would be a friend no more, he was certain.

At exactly the scheduled time, the lead Bradley reached the entrance to the weapons storage area that contained the "special weapons." The vehicles behind it raced into their positions inside the gate. The marines had rapidly retreated from the gate to their own armored car several yards behind the gate. Their message to the barracks further down the road was being answered by the arrival of many of their fellow marines in full battle dress, all of them frightened by the armored column they saw arrayed just beyond the fence. It was then that the sound of the rotor blades of the helicopters first thundered over head. The squadron of Apaches made their appearance in perfect time. The marines jerked their heads up at the dark shapes zooming over them in the thin light. Nat flicked the switch of his loudspeaker and announced, "Lay down your arms. We are taking possession of this facility for the State of South Carolina. The forces against you are overwhelming. Lay down your weapons now."

There was no response from the marines.

* * *

At the Transportation Corps dock on the South Annex, the four Bradleys of Third Platoon pulled up to the *Capricorn*. The gangway was unguarded, and no one seemed to be stirring on board. First Sergeant Henry Staggers had never been on a ship in his life. It had never occurred to him that he would ever be asked to commandeer one. He glanced at the four fighting vehicles, their turrets turned to face the side of the ship, and walked up the steep steps to the deck. Behind him were two soldiers, each carrying M-16s. On the deck he found a lone crewman. "Take me to the captain of the ship."

The man at first sneered at the helmeted soldier, assuming him to be another overwrought toy soldier, like those that always seemed to be sticking their noses into the business of the ship. Staggers repeated his demand, this time loudly, and the seaman saw the automatic rifles with clips in place. Then he saw what looked to him like little tanks on the pier. "Sure, man," follow me. He led Staggers and the two armed soldiers into a series of passageways to the cabin of the ship's captain.

"I'm taking charge of this ship, sir, for the State of South Carolina," Staggers barked at the shocked captain, still in shorts and tee shirt, and not yet fully awake. "These soldiers will take you to the control room — or bridge — or whatever you call the place where you drive this damn thing. Make no mistake. If you or anyone try to move this motherfucker, we'll open fire. Understand?"

The stunned captain looked from Staggers to his crewman and nodded slowly.

At Pier Alpha the noise of the Bradleys firing their engines woke many on the USS *Mount McKinley*. The ship's captain had moved back onto her ship anticipating that she would set sail in three days. The ship was nearly loaded with a new cargo of ammunition for delivery to the fleet. The watch woke the captain as soon as the Bradleys of Second Platoon pulled to the edge of the pier. The platoon leader walked to the gangway of the ship and demanded to see the captain. When a junior officer greeted him, the lieutenant informed the surprised young man that the state was seizing the *Mount McKinley*. The ensign hurried to the captain and relayed the strange demand.

Picking up the phone next to her, she ordered, "Get us underway at once.... I don't give a damn.... Get us into the river NOW!" Then she ran to the bridge. The lieutenant, waiting on the gangway saw sailors, most half dressed, appear seemingly from nowhere and begin attacking the lines that bound the ship to the pier. Then he heard the unmistakable sound of the ship's engines. He ran back to his Bradley and grabbed his radio. Frantically, he called the designated point of contact for their air support from the Apache squadron. He was assured they would be there in three minutes. As the last lines were tossed from the ship, it began to float with the incoming tide up the river. Lights quickly illuminated the ship as it floated farther away.

The lieutenant ordered his Bradleys to open fire on the ship, at what he thought must be the bridge. The four vehicles swung their turrets to point at the slowly drifting vessel and began a withering fire at the well-lit row of windows in the forward superstructure of the *Mount McKinley*. On the bridge, people threw themselves to the deck as the hail of bullets shattered the windows and ripped the bulkheads around them. The ship's captain heard the firing and waited to enter the bridge until the Bradleys stopped shooting. No one was hit by the bullets. Only two men were cut by the flying glass. "Get us underway, damn it!" she yelled.

"Aye, Aye, Ma'am," came the answer. The officer steering the great ship wondered if he could take the ship down the tricky river against the tide without running her aground. Everyone on the bridge looked up as the Apaches made their first low pass over the bow of the ship. At the same time, they felt the screws finally begin to dig into the water and push them down the river. Their thoughts were exactly the same at that moment. *Who are the soldiers?* And far more important, *on whose side are the helicopters?* On their second pass over the bow of the ship, the four Apaches raked the empty deck with machine gun fire.

From the pier, the lieutenant called to the ship from his loudspeaker, "Turn back and return to the pier!" Now the frightened sailors and officers on the bridge knew on whose side the helicopters were.

*　*　*

The thirteen Bradleys facing the marines didn't wait long for a response. There was no time. Mark Killian's trucks needed to be loaded and on their way soon. At Nat's signal, the Bradleys lurched forward across the drainage ditch and pushed the chain-link fence to the ground under their tracks. In minutes they surrounded both the marines' armored car and the blockhouse across the road. Nat's own vehicle turned its turret to face the guardhouse behind them. A single round from the 25-mm cannon exploded against the side of the structure, blowing it into splinters and crushed concrete. The turret hummed as it swung back to join the other twelve facing the marines. "Give it up," Nat's voice boomed over the loudspeaker. In less than a minute, the hatch of the armored car opened, and the marines slowly emerged, hands raised in surrender. Immediately, they were followed by those in the blockhouse. Last to walk from the blockhouse was their commander. He threw his pistol to the ground next to Nat's vehicle, but did not raise his hands.

Nat sat in the hatch looking down on him. "You'll hang for this!" the marine commander shouted.

"Stay out of my way, Major, and nobody gets hurt, O.K." Lieutenant Rickenbacker's men collected the marines, this time all with hands held over their heads, and marched them away. They didn't need to see what was about to happen to the weapons they had been guarding.

Nat switched his radio on, "Choirboy, you there?"

"Right here, cowboy. Are the cattle ready?"

"Come get 'em. And hurry." Mark Killian put the radio down on the seat of his Blazer and gave the signal to the trucks. They were less than two miles from the gate to the storage area. He glanced at his watch. On schedule. They should be headed to their various destinations in less than an hour.

* * *

"Captain, should we tie her up at the pier again?" the chief asked his captain.

"Chief, I don't know what navy you've been in all these years, but in my navy we don't surrender to a grunt with a bullhorn."

"Ma'am, the helicopters ..."

"That's enough, Chief. We're going to get to sea. I won't let these people have this ship."

The *Mount McKinley* was making all the speed it dared in the dark, strong currents of the upper Cooper River. The Bradleys were far behind them now, as the ship rounded the bend and neared the Transportation Corps dock. Sharp eruptions of sound rippled from the dock. Fairchild turned to the sound and saw the last of the flashes from the barrels of the four Bradleys of Third Platoon. Each had fired a round from its 25-mm cannon, and she knew they would be loading again. Two of the rounds screamed over the bridge and into the marsh beyond. One exploded into the superstructure behind the bridge, and one into the end of the bow itself. The vessel shook, but did not veer from its course. The captain braced herself for the second, better-aimed round from the four armored vehicles, but it didn't come, and they slipped silently past the Transportation Corps dock and the Westvaco plant. As the ship emerged from underneath the span of the expressway bridge, they heard the helicopters again. In turn, each of the four flew directly towards the bridge of the ship, its machine gun flickering bright orange flashes. The fourth Apache fired several rounds from its 30-mm cannon at the deck. The helicopters circled around to follow the ship and prepare for another strike.

The tall gray vessel, now completely visible in the morning light, gradually slowed in the swirling river. The frantic calls for help to all of the nearest military installations went unanswered. Carefully, the officer guiding her movements steered the *Mount McKinley* alongside an empty pier. The pilots circled their Apaches around the ship, but were now sure the escape to sea had been abandoned. They could not see the captain, lying still on the deck of the bridge, her lifeblood spilling onto the deck, fast and unstoppable from the fatal wounds in her chest.

* * *

Before he started the jeep, Matt Reicher flipped his cellular telephone open and dialed the home number for the navy watch officer in the Pentagon. As the phone began to ring, he backed the jeep quickly into the street and sped towards the command building. He had heard the Bradley's cannon fire from the nuclear storage area, and from Pier Alpha. He had seen the Apaches. *Be home*, he raged to himself. "Answer!" he yelled.

"Hello." The voice was half asleep.

"This is Commander Reicher, XO of the Weapons Station in Charleston. We are under attack.... My guess is the station has already been taken."

"What?" the watch officer asked, shocked into consciousness. "Who?"

"The state! There are Bradley fighting vehicles all over the place. They have to be at the nuclear area. And fucking Apaches!" He rounded the curve in the road and saw the single armored vehicle sitting in front of the command building. "Shit!"

"What is it?"

"Hold on, you need...." Matt was racing along the road preparing to turn toward the driveway of the parking lot. Behind him Captain Kratz was driving just as fast. Suddenly, the barrel of the Bradley's machine gun flashed. The bullets ripped across the grass and onto the pavement in front of the jeep. "God damn!" Matt yelled, and pulled the steering wheel violently to the left. The jeep turned sharply, leaning over on its two right tires. Jumping the curb, Matt and the jeep slid to a stop a few yards from the Bradley. Behind him, Kratz veered sharply to the right, driving his front wheels hard into the curb, exploding both, and sliding the car into the drainage ditch that sloped down on the other side.

"Are you all right?" the watch officer shouted.

"Shit! They shot a damn machine gun in front of me!" The officer could hear Matt's labored breathing. "Look, they are going to take the nukes. That's why they're here. Get the word out! NOW!" He threw the phone down and jumped from the jeep, enraged, walking up to the Bradley, holding his hands up to show he was unarmed. Behind him, Captain Kratz, wearing his loaded pistol around his waist, walked more slowly toward the doors of the command building.

At the Pentagon, the stunned officer clutched the phone. "God damn," he breathed.

*　*　*

At the head of the long line of rental trucks, Mark drove his Blazer to the entrance of the weapons storage area. Standing in the hatch of his Bradley, Nat waited for him at the gate. Jumping into the passenger seat of the Blazer, Nat shouted, "Let's go! The boys should have your cargo ready to pick up by the time we get there."

Within the weapons storage area reserved for nuclear weapons there were a number of missiles tipped with multiple warheads. The two men had no use for these, as they were designed only for submarines. It was the fifty-two other smaller bombs and artillery rounds, all unimaginably deadly, that would be loaded into the trucks and dispatched to predesignated destinations. "How are you going to keep straight which ones you load the weapons in?" Nat asked.

"This," Mark answered, holding up a rectangular device that looked like a large calculator. "I just punch in which bumper numbers get what as they're loaded. It won't be pretty, but it'll work."

At the first bunker, the soldiers were already waiting for the trucks. Mark directed the trucks he designated to carry the weapons back into position. Quickly the soldiers loaded three bombs into the empty space, sliding wooden crates and blankets between them, and to the rear so that they wouldn't slide. Each of the bunkers was breached in turn. Following the careful instructions prepared by Julieanne Harris, they found the transponder signaling device on each weapon and destroyed it. The bombs being loaded into the trucks would not be tracked by the satellites. If Mark's drivers could get their trucks to the hiding places without being detected, the location would be known to only a few.

There were three bunkers. Ten trucks were loaded with the precious cargo from the first two bunkers. They and sixty empty trucks were already speeding away from Charleston when the last group backed to the third and final bunker. This bunker contained a mixture of bombs, Tomahawk cruise missiles, and artillery warheads. The last weapon was slid carefully into the last "delivery" truck. Mark entered the data into his little black box, and the trucks carrying the weapons, along with another larger group of empty decoys, rushed toward the main road. He and four other officers, all National Guard transportation specialists, headed for the four hiding places selected by General Demers and his staff. They would check to make sure that the trucks designated for each site got to their destinations and that the weapons were stored and guarded. Along the roads of the state, if any satellite had been watching, it would have seen a hundred trucks racing to every corner of South Carolina, each one stopping at multiple locations. Only fifteen carried the nuclear arsenal of a newly independent South Carolina. In one, a transponder under the belly of one of the Tomahawks was scratched, but not broken, by the soldier's screwdriver, and it continued to send its silent signals into the air.

*　*　*

"Come out here, God damn it!" Matt yelled at the faceless armored machine in front of him.

Inside the Bradley, Sergeant Morris turned to Jim, the unknown lieutenant colonel with whom Captain Engle had stuck him. "Open it," Jim said to the sergeant, motioning to the hatch. Morris unlocked the hatch and pushed it open. Jim climbed through the open circle and sat on the edge of the turret, gazing down at Matt.

Matt's eyes fixed on him, but there was no change in his furious expression. The only indication of his shock was the halt to his yelling. The rage in his face turned colder, and deeper, as he glared at the man who had been his friend.

The soldiers in the Bradley exchanged confused looks as Jim began to speak to the crazy naval officer, "Matt, it's over. There's nothing to be done."

Wallace Kratz stood behind Matt. No one noticed while he unbuttoned the cover over his pistol.

"Fuck you," Matt said quietly.

Behind Jim came the rumble from the line of tracked vehicles moving back down the road toward them. He climbed down from the turret and jumped the short distance to the ground, to stand in front of Matt. "We're all fucked, Matt." Jim shook his head. From the direction of the housing area across the road, a truck sped to the curb and stopped. Three sailors ran from the truck towards Captain Kratz, each carrying M-16s, all with ammunition clips. Seemingly oblivious to the armored vehicle, they lined up behind Kratz holding their rifles chest high. "This is stupid, Matt. Don't you think we ought to end this before someone else gets hurt?"

Reicher looked at the sailors and at Captain Kratz whose hand was on the handle of his pistol. The line of Bradleys reached the command building and the two lead vehicles pulled onto the grass. Nat Engle pulled himself through the hatch and vaulted to the ground. He walked purposefully to Reicher and Kratz. Saluting, he addressed Kratz, "Captain, the State of South Carolina has taken over this base, sir. You and I should discuss how to best look after your people."

Kratz stared at Nat. "You mean to take my base?"

"It's already been taken, sir. Now, we need to talk about avoiding a worse tragedy."

Jim saw something change in Matt's expression. The rage was replaced with something else. It was alarm. Following Matt's stare, he saw to his horror that Kratz was raising the pistol from its holster. Pointing it at Nat, he barked, "No one is taking this base!"

The sailors behind Kratz raised their rifles and aimed at the soldiers in front of them. Inside the Bradley, the men manning the machine guns pointing from the gun ports cocked their weapons. Backing away from Kratz and Matt several steps, Nat said, "Listen, it's over, Captain. There is no reason now to get anybody hurt."

Suddenly, the loudspeaker on the side of the building erupted with the programmed playing of reveille. The shock of the sudden noise made Captain Kratz jump, and he pulled the trigger of his pistol. The shot rang out loud and sharp across the lawn in front of his headquarters. Reflexively, the men in the Bradley fired at the group of naval officers and sailors. As they fell, the M-16s clutched by the sailors sputtered in the direction of Nat and the soldiers around him. It only took seconds. The sailors rolled on the ground, all wounded painfully, but not critically. Captain Kratz died before he began to fall from the bullet that entered his temple and exploded from the other side of his head.

As Nat cried out and fell beside him, Jim instinctively lurched forward to catch Matt as he crumpled to his knees, clutching his left breast. Red spurted bright and thick through his fingers, and only a low moan escaped from his lips. Jim caught his shoulders, and heard himself screaming far away. "No!" the distant voice cried uselessly. "No, no, no!" Jim lowered his friend to the ground, cradling his head. He looked beside him at Nat sprawled across the grass. Two of the soldiers were rolling him over, his head hanging limply to the side. Blood covered the front of his uniform jacket.

Jim shouted at the Bradley, "Call for the medics!" He felt Matt's head heavy in his hand, the unshaven face suddenly alive, coughing raggedly, groaning. In only minutes, the medics raced up onto the lawn and Jim was replaced by two medical technicians who tore open Matt's shirt, examining the bullet wound over his heart. Two more hovered over Nat. Both men were swiftly lifted into the back of the ambulance and it raced towards Trident Hospital. A second ambulance collected the wounded sailors.

He looked at the shocked soldiers around him and the blood pooled on the ground. There were tears streaming down his cheeks, and blood covered his hands.

Chapter 27

The housing areas on the Weapons Station were blocked by armored vehicles, keeping the thousands of sailors, airmen, and military dependents trapped inside until something could be arranged for their return to the United States. Throughout the weapons storage complex, National Guard soldiers forced open the doors to bunkers. A long line of trucks made its way to each bunker, and the trucks were quickly loaded.

From his Humvee, Jim watched the houses by the river. He had no words to tell Linda Reicher what she must be told. It had been ninety minutes since her husband had been shot. They stopped the vehicle in the driveway of the ranch-style house where he knew she waited, scared and confused.

"Linda, there was an accident. Matt is in Trident Hospital. All I know is he was hit by one bullet and is unconscious." Confusion turned to fear as her eyes studied him.

"I need to go to him."

After a few pained seconds, she began to see the truth. "What happened? And why are you dressed like that?" Understanding a little now, she backed away from the man who began to look alien and dangerous.

"The state has taken over the Weapons Station. There was an accident ... the captain's gun went off ... there was more shooting. The captain is dead. Matt was wounded along with one of our people." His words seemed spoken far away.

"Our people? *You...?*" She leaned towards him. "You were a part of this! You were his friend! Matt loved you ... and *you* came to kill him!" Her angry cries were mixed with sobs. Her face turned violent, and she raised her hands, balled in tight fists, lunging at him, pounding them hard into his chest. As he grabbed her hands and held them together in front of her face, her screaming stopped. He let go of her hands and she drew back. "Damn you! You faithless bastard!" she screeched. She flung her right hand hard against his face, the slap knocking his head to one side, the sting burning like the reality that waited for them outside.

* * *

"All of the installations have been taken, General. The attacks all began at the same time, to the minute, except at the Weapons Station, where the attack began ten minutes earlier. It was all over by sunup. Fort Jackson, the air force bases at Shaw and Charleston, Parris Island and the Marine Corps Air Station in Beaufort. All were approached in similar fashion. Helicopters were used to suppress any resistance, and armored infantry units seized key points on each facility." The colonel spoke in the bloodless tone of a staff officer.

"Casualties?" The chairman of the joint chiefs asked the colonel.

"Low, General."

"Tell me what they are, damn you!"

"The commanding officer of the Weapons Station was killed and his XO is seriously wounded. The captain of the *Mount McKinley* was killed while she tried to run the ship to the open sea. At Shaw Air Force Base, a team of security police ... a sergeant and an airman first class ... tried to block the first Bradley fighting vehicle entering the base. Their car was crushed, and they both suffered broken limbs."

The colonel continued, "The state has gained little from taking these bases, except for ammunition, and the aircraft at Shaw and the Marine Corps Air Station." He pulled a sheet from this folder, "We show the major assets as F16s, F18s and Harriers. Of course, the state is limited in personnel to operate these aircraft."

"And the 'ammunition' from the Weapons Station. Doesn't the state now have enough nuclear punch to incinerate most of the eastern half of the United States?" The general said bitterly. The colonel paled. "They seem to have gained a considerable *asset* there."

"Yes, sir. That is the most serious concern."

"What about the military personnel and dependents?" the general asked.

"There is one more important installation to mention, sir," the colonel said. "The Savannah River Site has also been occupied." The general had forgotten about the bomb plant. "They now control one of the most sophisticated nuclear weapons manufacturing facilities in the world."

* * *

The doctors treating Nat Engle and Matt Reicher were made nervous by the men's injuries and by Josh Cooper's explanation of their cause. Jim arrived at the hospital an hour later and found the doctor. "Commander Reicher received only one bullet to the chest, just above the heart. A fraction of an inch is all that separated him from certain death. He isn't out of the woods yet, but he will recover, although he won't be able to use his left arm for a while. Do you know him?" the doctor asked.

"Yes. For many years."

The doctor looked at the door and back to Jim. "Is it true, colonel, what they say has happened?"

"It's true, Doctor." The doctor noticed the dried blood that covered Jim's BDU jacket and trousers. "Doctor, how is Captain Engle?"

The woman's face was suddenly strained. "I thought you knew. He was shot three times. The damage to his lungs was too great, and by the time he got here, the blood loss was so great.... He's dead, Colonel. I'm sorry. We did everything we could." Jim laid his forehead in his hand. *One mutated piece of matter flings its particles into another and the contamination goes on and on.* "We just lost him."

Jim walked to the room where Matt lay, a confusion of tubes and bottles and monitors surrounding him, ensnaring him. *Thank God you're alive*, Jim thought.

At the end of the hall he saw Cooper, Nat's executive officer, and now commander of the company. That he had been crying was clear from his face. He seemed so young to Jim, his skin smooth and fresh under the close-cropped hair. "Lieutenant, I'm sorry."

"Those bastards. They killed him for nothing! It was all over. They didn't have anything to gain pulling guns on us." There was the tremor of hatred in his voice.

"He was one of the best officers and best men I ever knew. We served together for years," Jim said. The young man looked at him now with recognition. "There's a lot of work to do, and how you do your part will determine if any more people get killed. Hatred in you will ensure that more will die. Make no mistake."

The lieutenant lifted his head and straightened his shoulders. "I should tell Captain Killian. He and Captain Engle were very close."

"I know. Let Captain Killian finish his job. Tell him when he comes back. It's important that he finish." Cooper saw that the coldness of it made Jim's statement no less true. "Mark will tell Nat's wife."

As he walked to the door of the hospital, he wondered how many more young men and women were dead that morning. How many more would be dead before the tears and blood were over?

* * *

The decision to move the surveillance satellites for total coverage of South Carolina was not even halfway through the chain of command. Satellite coverage for the next eighteen hours was minimal. The system just wasn't set up to spy on Americans. Mark Killian's elaborate use of dozens of decoys had never been necessary.

There was absolutely no intelligence at all as to what the South Carolinians had done with the nuclear weapons. The staff of the chief of naval operations pulled up the list of the special weapons in the inventory of the station. They compared them with the list of equipment available to the state's National Guard and Air National Guard, and their conclusions were ominous. The planes could easily deliver the bombs. And their artillery units had guns capable of firing the nuclear shells.

Only the Tomahawk cruise missiles might be useless to them because they required programming and remote guidance capability. But such a weapon would bring a very high price on the world market, and it could buy allies. The list of conventional weapons seized by the state that morning was nearly as impressive. Anyone who cherished the notion that *this* rebellion could be crushed easily was in for a rude shock. The officer responsible for delivering the report to the joint chiefs of staff shook his head. *What a damn mess.*

"Commander, you should see this, sir." It was the marine assigned to his office, Gunnery Sergeant Gregg. "We thought all the transponders on the special weapons had been destroyed. But we just got this report from Defense Intelligence. It looks like one is working."

"Where is the son of a bitch?"

"This is about twenty minutes old. At that point it was at these coordinates." He entered the coordinates and, in seconds, the map appeared, with the location of the coordinates shown as a red dot blinking on Interstate 95 where it crossed Lake Marion.

"Shaw. They're taking it to Shaw Air Force Base, or near by. Sergeant, tell them we need to have updates on that signal every thirty minutes until it stops moving. And when that happens, I want to know exactly what is in, and around, the location. Everything."

"Yes, sir." The marine started to walk away then turned abruptly. "I almost forgot, sir. There is this report about casualties at the Weapons Station." The navy commander read the short message and let it drop to his desk. Matt Reicher, shot in the chest. It didn't say if he survived. He picked up his work again, work designed to find the nuclear weapons. Now, he worked with new determination ... and with anger.

*　*　*

Governor Haselden waited at his desk. The cameras and sound equipment were in place for the address. The short speech had been written days ago. All that was lacking were details from the morning's operations — details of success, and details about casualties. As he waited the final ten minutes, he again read the reports from each task force. All were good news. No one was killed or even seriously wounded. All except the report from Jim McNeely. He knew what McNeely must be feeling. Captain Engle dead and Matt Reicher nearly killed. He prayed this was the end.

At the signal, he looked into the camera. Rumors had flown across the state since the morning seizures of military bases. There were few people not watching when Blackie began to speak.

"Last night, the General Assembly convened in special session to consider what course to pursue to resolve the crisis that began with the explosion of radioactive waste in Florence. Our efforts to convince the federal government to abandon plans to bring more of the same kind of trains into our state have been met with angry refusals and threats. When I refused to permit a second train to enter our state, the president announced plans to assume control over our National Guard and to call into active military service for an indefinite period all twenty thousand reservists in South Carolina.

"All of these measures were intended to frighten and suppress our people. President Seekings also intended to occupy our state with two army divisions and to impose martial law. These actions would have meant the end of our participation in the American Union as an equal partner. It would have meant inferiority and exploitation. It would have meant the end of our dignity as free people.

"It was these issues that the General Assembly considered last night. We know what submission would have meant. To resist, we know that we have no choice but to sever ourselves from the United States. Completely. There is no middle course.

"The General Assembly unanimously accepted my recommendation to declare us an independent nation. As of 4:00 this morning, South Carolina assumed the status of a sovereign state in the world. We remain open to the negotiation of a new contract with the United States, but only one that will return this state to a position of equality in the Union.

"We have secured the means to defend ourselves. This morning the National Guard seized all United States military installations in South Carolina, including the Savannah River Site. The weapons and equipment now in our possession represent our share of the national defense establishment of the United States, and will assure that no power on earth will threaten our territory." He paused and stared into the camera.

"This action was not without cost. There were casualties, both among our soldiers and the federal forces, although they were mercifully light. I ask you all to keep the families of these men and women in your thoughts and prayers.

"The course we take now will not be easy. But there is every reason for hope. I extend my assurance to the business establishment in South Carolina that this government will spare no effort to make this a profitable home. We will prosper, and we will be free. There will be no retreat from the democratic principles that have been our guide for two centuries. We will not abandon this state's commitment to the equality of all of our people.

"I ask you to have faith in yourselves and in your inherent strengths. God bless you all."

The red camera light blinked off. Blackie wondered what they thought, out there beyond the lens.

*   *   *

The extraordinary news transmitted instantly to every corner of the globe transfixed peoples and governments alike. Most had only slender knowledge of the nuclear tragedy in South Carolina. None could have expected that one of the American states would secede from the colossus that dominated them all, in one way or another.

Harold Fraser was watching an old movie with his wife and grandson, enjoying a rare moment free from problems of politics and state. The Canadian prime minister's house was a Tudor mansion not far from the center of Ottawa. He was stretched out on the comfortable carpet, a couch pillow under his head. His grandson, visiting for the week, was enthralled with his first taste of *The Wizard of Oz*. In the way of adults and small children, Fraser felt he too was watching it for the first time.

"Prime Minister." The voice belonged to one of the Royal Canadian Mounted Police posted to the residence. "There is an important message from the defence minister, sir."

Fraser leaned over to peer at the mountie standing in the doorframe. *What the hell? On a Sunday?* "What is it?" He followed the mountie into the hall. When he had eased the door shut, the obviously nervous young man began to explain.

"... It happened last night. It apparently stems from the terrible accident last month with the train of radioactive fuel. Their governor just went on TV and announced that the state was independent."

"But that's crazy. They'll never be allowed to leave the United States."

"The Defence Ministry reports that the militia forces of South Carolina have seized all military bases in the state, including a large cache of nuclear bombs and artillery shells, and nuclear-tipped cruise missiles. The defence minister asks that you call him as soon as is convenient, sir."

"My God." Harold Fraser thought about the likely reaction of the American president. "Tell the minister to meet me in my office in thirty minutes."

* * *

The reaction to the news half a world away was just as acute. As he listened to the briefing from his intelligence chief, the president of the People's Republic of China perceived an opportunity, long awaited. *It was often the way of things*, he thought, *that such opportunities arrived in ways one would never expect.* For many years, China deferred her cherished goal of returning Formosa to the motherland only because of American power. It was far from the last of her lost territories that, sooner or later, would be reclaimed. But it was the wound that festered most painfully. Formosa was where the hated so-called Nationalists maintained their illegitimate regime. He and his predecessors always knew that American power would one day falter. They waited patiently for that day.

He listened carefully to the description of the nuclear weapons the rebels were believed to have seized from an American naval compound, and he smiled. "What is the assessment of how the American president will react to this rebellion?"

The question was expected. "He will not tolerate the rebellious province remaining independent. He will do whatever he must, and use whatever force necessary."

"Will he risk a nuclear attack by the rebels?"

"That is impossible to say. It is more likely that one of the weapons could be used as the result of a miscalculation, or a mistake. The rebels lack the extensive safeguards employed by the governments of the nuclear powers."

The president nodded. He was still smiling. "Yes, I see how that must be so." When their opportunity presented itself, he knew there might not be much time. When the intelligence chief had gone, he turned to his military aide and asked that he plan a conference of the defense minister and the general staff. It was time to review their plans for Formosa.

* * *

C. A. Moore was alerted at the first report of attacks on the military bases. By the time Blackie made his address, Moore was in his office. Now, Seekings would see that he needed him in the White House more than ever.

Ultimately, an invasion would have to be undertaken. Eventually, Roger Seekings would see that as clearly as he saw it now. Moore saw that Blackie and the other leaders of South Carolina would never submit. Even if they were reduced to eating peanuts and pinecones. The conflict was one of blood, now, and could only be ended by force.

Michael O'Connelly stepped into the office unannounced. Moore didn't stand or speak. He had long since dropped any pretext of courtesy to O'Connelly's position.

"Do you read much history, C. A.?" Moore stared at the vice president impassively. "This is a moment of real history, isn't it?" O'Connelly leaned on the back of the chair in front of the desk. His eyes bored into Moore. "I never thought I'd be privy to a moment like this. I wanted to see you, so I can remember the face of the man who instigated the second American Civil War, on the very day it started." Without waiting for a reply, he turned and walked silently from the room.

* * *

His long day was almost over. Mark Killian felt he must have walked a hundred miles. The plans for storage of the bombs and artillery shells required precision, and that meant supervision. If it had been possible, he would have traveled to all four sites. But it was just too many miles. The sites formed an irregular ring, all halfway from the center of the state to one of its borders. And all close to airfields.

In the deep woods of a state park near Sumter, Mark monitored the last delivery truck as it backed up to a maintenance building that had been emptied and cleaned. He noticed that the National Guardsmen assigned to protect this site were already dressed in the uniforms of the game wardens that normally worked there. The bombs were unloaded with great care and carried to their waiting beds.

The other sites were similar to this one. One was an abandoned cotton gin. Another was an empty textile chemical warehouse. The last was a barn on a farm recently leased for long-term research to Clemson University.

The door to the maintenance building was closed and locked, and Mark called Charleston to report he was done. It wasn't Nat Engle's voice that answered, but Cooper, the executive officer.

* * *

By late afternoon it was all over. As he drove toward downtown Charleston, he replayed in his mind, for the first of hundreds of times, the scene of the morning's carnage. Since the train blew up — on that day that seemed an eternity ago — Jim McNeely felt as though he were in a balloon, snapping the ropes that bound it to earth. The last secure lines had finally separated, and the balloon was carrying him skyward — perilously, irretrievably high. He knew it was a trick of his mind, a shield against the horror, like a narcotic fantasy that let him float above the horrendous certainty of the deaths branded forever on his memory — and the death of a friendship that was one of the pillars of his life.

He let the fantasy lift him above it all. Behind him followed a squad of Nat Engle's soldiers. There was one more thing he would accomplish before he went home.

"Break it in," he ordered the soldiers. They slid the crowbars into the crack between the doors and shoved violently. The doors split, opening the main entrance to the federal courthouse. "Take this and find the door to the roof. Put it up there." He handed a folded South Carolina flag to the young soldier. The two men bounded up the stairs of the Victorian courthouse. Jim wandered to the second floor. In the hall outside the clerk's office were stacked jury lists for terms of court that would never be held. At the end of the hall, he found himself standing at the marbleized columns that framed the entrance to the main courtroom.

He opened the tall, polished wooden doors. On the soaring walls hung oil portraits of noted judges who presided there. The quiet of the imposing room washed over him. He stepped to the bench and went behind it to the flag. Lifting it from its pedestal, he began to roll it slowly around the pole until the blue field and the red and white stripes were tightly in place. The sound of someone entering the courtroom from behind the bench made him jump, and he reached for the pistol he wore. Judge Malcolm Richardson walked through the door from the adjoining conference room. He stopped when he spotted Jim.

"Mr. McNeely? Is that you?"

"Yes, Your Honor."

"I don't think I'm 'Your Honor' anymore."

Jim didn't respond.

"I just came to collect some personal items. You're earlier than I expected."

"It was something I needed to do."

Richardson sat behind the bench. "So, Jim, I see you were in the middle of all this."

"Yes."

"I wonder how we got here." Richardson gazed wistfully around the room where so much of his life had been spent. "We are in for a hard time." The judge saw the look in Jim's eyes was distant, frozen. "May I have the flag?"

Jim carried the flag to the bench. Richardson was shocked at the site of the blood that covered Jim's jacket and trousers.

"Are you hurt?" he asked with genuine concern.

"It isn't my blood," Jim answered angrily, his eyes flashing. "Do you really want to know how we got here, Judge?" He clutched the edge of the bench with his hands. The day's terror had been confined for too long, and it was bubbling to the surface. "Remember, Dr. DeSilva told us all." He strode to the witness chair and pounded on the rail. "Right here! He sat right here and told us. When ionizing radiation escapes and comes into contact with normal matter," he said in the even, arcane tone of an expert witness, "the runaway particles slam into the other atoms." He pounded the bench in front of Richardson, yelling now. "And *they contaminate everything they touch!* Normal matter becomes contaminated, too. And it goes on," he pounded, "*and on, and on!*"

Jim, closing his eyes and trying to control his rage, continued. "When we let evil loose, no one can put it back."

"I tried."

"There are too many who aren't like you! That's how we got here. And *here* ... Boy Scouts get incinerated by gamma radiation. *Here* is where we secede!" he yelled at Richardson. "And *here* is where I watch a man's head blown up, where I see one of the finest young men I've ever known torn apart," he fell to the carpeted floor on his knees, his voice cracking, his soul falling back to the inescapable horror, "and where I hold my best friend's head while he bleeds — from the bullet fired by the soldiers *I brought to take his nuclear weapons.*" He wiped the tears across his face, smearing dirt into wild streaks. "It makes quite a circle doesn't it, Judge?"

"I'm sorry, Jim." Korea had been a long time ago, but Malcolm Richardson had seen men in the terrible aftermath of watching friends die. He had been one of those men. The enemy, the weapons and the reasons changed, but not the consequences. And not the wounds of the survivors.

* * *

Mayor Pat Collins and his wife walked along Meeting Street. For hours after the news — he had received a phone call from the governor before the television announcement — Collins tried to assemble the key people on the city's staff he would need to figure out the ramifications. His energy was wasted. Finally, he gave up, resigned like nearly everyone else to waiting for what Monday morning would bring. Pat Collins was not used to being a bystander.

The television reports were repeating themselves, as they always did in times of crisis. At last, Collins couldn't stand the confines of their house. "Let's go for a walk. I've got to get out of here for a while."

As they came within site of the federal courthouse, Pat Collins noticed the flag snapping in the breeze from the roof. It was the blue flag of South Carolina. "Somebody isn't wasting any time," he said, pointing. "Walk down here," he said. They turned down the narrow passage of St. Michael's Alley. Collins stopped in front of a two-story, flat-fronted building that was one of a row with adjoining walls that rose from the edge of the sidewalk. "I wonder what he would have had to say today."

"Who?" his wife asked.

"James Louis Petigrew. This was his law office. In 1860 he thought everybody had lost their minds. He said South Carolina was too small to be a country and too large to be an insane asylum."

"I'm scared, Pat." She took his hand.

"It can't last. It can't. There has to be a way out. After all the posturing is over, both sides will look for a solution. They have to." They walked for two hours through the still quiet, gentle streets of the old city.

* * *

The Blazer raced over the expressway bridge. Below, the black waters of the Cooper flowed, the surface sprinkled with twinkling reflections of the lights around it. His large, strong hands gripped the steering wheel and he shoved the accelerator further to increase his already perilous speed. Inside the truck, sealed from the dark world outside, there was a sound never heard. It was the sound of Mark Killian crying. His life on football fields and container ships provided no guidebook to the country of the bereaved. One hand slammed loudly on the top of the dashboard, threatening to crack the surface. He bellowed violent curses — against the men who killed Nat, against the perverse lunatics who brought them all into this hell, and … against himself for not being there to protect the man whom he never told he loved, but loved all the same.

Country music — played at full volume, as if it would somehow reach the ears of his dead friend — mixed with his cries as he hurtled toward his next job, the final one on this day of new tasks for Mark Killian, newly become a carrier and concealer of nuclear weapons. Now, he would be the ambassador of death, carrying the news of her new status to Nat Engle's widow. He thought of the young, pretty woman he would hurt. He thought of his own children — and the unborn child who would never know the fire, steel and laughter of the man whose love had given him life.

He hurtled, ignoring signs and lights, through streets empty of the frightened people who huddled in their homes, awaiting the uncertain morning. His fear was more immediate, more tangible. She waited for him at his house among the neat suburban rows. Tires screeched as he forced the Blazer to turn, too fast, into his subdivision. Sitting in front of the house where such a short time ago he drank and danced with Nat in celebration, the athlete and loader of great ships struggled to extinguish the conflagration of tears. His shoulders were large, built to give support, and he knew much support would be needed from him that night.

As he stepped into the living room of his house, he found his wife and Susan Engle. He saw they had both been crying. He towered over them, his huge form cloaked in his uniform, splattered with mud and coated with red dust, his boots trailing caked clay onto the carpet. His face concealed nothing from them; the tear-streaked contours of his face, so much older than when he left them, told them everything. Susan bent forward, her already reddened eyes spilling new tears. What she had feared since morning was now manifest, real, and inescapable. Beth slipped an arm around her. Mark sank to his knees in front of them. He would tell them later the details of Nat's death. But now no words could form in the throat that was again choked with sobs. And no words mattered. His arms encircled both women and drew them close.

Chapter 28

Monday morning dawned on a day like no other in their memory. Senators filed into the chamber in unusual numbers. The galleries filled early with press and a large collection of representatives of foreign embassies, all come to see the remarkable story unfold. Fingers pointed from the press gallery as Manning, the junior senator from South Carolina, walked calmly to his desk. His colleagues were more discreet, turning to greet him, their expressions indifferent to the great question they knew would soon be discussed. Shortly, Hampton, South Carolina's senior senator, and one of the oldest ever to serve in that body, strode to his desk on the other side of the aisle from Manning, alert and defiant. The two men nodded to one another as the gavel sounded from the rostrum.

Wielding the gavel was Mike O'Connelly. Though it was his constitutionally appointed role, presiding over the senate was something he, like most vice presidents, rarely did. But this morning he had a reason to take his seat under the marble columns. The senate chaplain walked to the rostrum. O'Connelly rose from his chair, "Reverend, this morning, with your indulgence, I'd like to lead the invocation."

O'Connelly turned to face the nearly full senate chamber. "This morning, it is more important than ever before that we join for a moment of prayer." He bowed his head, and the senators did the same. "Almighty God, this morning our Union is threatened with dissolution. We seek your wisdom, or so much divine insight as we can comprehend, so that we might heal the wounded body of our nation. Help us to still the spiral of anger and create the climate of conciliation. Speak to the hearts of every man and woman in this house and to all the leaders of this country ... and to the leaders of South Carolina. Teach us all the way to understanding — the way back to the Union that has made us the envy of the world."

Seated once again in the high-backed chair, O'Connelly put in motion the plan he had devised the night before. He had told his son, "If I were a betting man, I'd bet against me. But what else can I do?"

Immediately, the senior senator from North Carolina rose. "Mr. President, my colleague and I are proposing a resolution demanding that the administration immediately commence negotiations with the State of South Carolina for the purpose of ending her secession. Those steps are as follows." He picked up a single page and read, "One ... all further shipments of nuclear materials into South Carolina will cease, until a satisfactory arrangement is reached. Two ... the president will issue a declaration that no charges of any kind will be brought against any official of South Carolina for acts during this crisis. Three ... the administration and a joint committee of both houses of congress will draft a comprehensive policy on the transport of all forms of hazardous materials, including nuclear, that provides the states full participation, as a matter of law, in all decisions respecting their disposal."

The junior senator from Georgia was next to speak. "I join with my colleague from North Carolina in sponsoring this resolution. What we must do today is the most important thing any of us will ever do."

O'Connelly recognized the junior senator from New York, whom he knew would be opposed. They might as well get on with the debate.

"Mr. President, this house cannot adopt the resolution. The attempt at rebellion must be ended, unconditionally and immediately. The matter of rebellion by a state was settled long ago, Mr. President."

Six more senators followed him, each opposed to the resolution. After each spoke there were loud murmurs of assent from the other senators. The senator from Idaho turned angrily towards Hampton, who sat only one row behind him, "South Carolina is entitled to no consideration by this house. Yesterday, Idaho paid a heavier price for her treachery. A citizen of my state and a distinguished naval officer was gunned down by the South Carolina National Guard while she captained her ship. Mr. President, Idaho demands accountability from those responsible, not appeasement for their treason." His loud, angry words left the chamber still.

"The chair recognizes the senior senator from South Carolina."

Hampton and Manning both rose and walked to the microphone below the rostrum. Hampton spoke, his old eyes ablaze. "I watched each of you take the oath when you came to the senate. You have shown us that there is truly no hope for resolution aside from an end of our Union. Mr. President, you have our resignations from this house." Hampton and Manning walked silently from the chamber.

One by one, the senators voted. Seventy-eight against the resolution and twenty in favor. Weary and disheartened, O'Connelly left the chamber.

*   *   *

The team of secret service agents cringed as the president threw every breakable glass, vase, and picture frame within his reach against the stone chimney of his lakeside retreat in western Minnesota. The series of telephone calls to Washington that followed was no less violent.

Seated quietly in the corner of the cavernous room, his wife, Melanie, watched and listened. When her husband finished making the calls, he leaned back and, with eyes closed, said, "We have to go back to Washington. Tell them to get the packing started."

Melanie watched a moment longer before answering, "Roger, I need to talk to you in private."

Surprise replaced the anger in his eyes. He nodded to the agents and they discreetly filed out, leaving the president and his wife alone. "What is it?"

"I'll stay here. I don't want to go back," she announced in a carefully measured voice, hands folded in her lap and eyes locked on the shocked face of her husband.

"What are you saying?" She had never once hesitated to accompany him anywhere in their thirty years of marriage.

"I don't want to be there with all this going on, Roger. There will be nothing but tension in that house until this is over, and that won't be soon."

"You have to come back with me."

"No. I don't. Only you do."

"It's important that the nation see us facing this crisis together."

She stood up and walked towards him a few steps. Holding up her hands delicately, she said softly, "Roger, I heard you on the phone. They've taken nuclear weapons.... It isn't safe in Washington. I'll stay here and visit the children. When things get back to normal, I'll come back." Her eyes told him there was no point in arguing with her. "I'm sorry, Dear. I'll go ask them to pack your things." She opened the door to the bedroom hall, and left him.

* * *

Seekings forced the memory from his mind as he walked to the Cabinet Room. No distractions, he told himself. It was vital that they decide on a clear course of action. In a couple of hours he would address the country. Which speech he gave depended on their decision, and he needed consensus among his advisors.

"It's important that they be on the defensive, in every way. If it appears that their government is keeping those people hostage, its support will evaporate. And they will be completely isolated from the world." Moore laid out the approach he had privately explained to Seekings the night before. The idea was that they would not assist in removing the thousands of military servicemen and women and their dependents, other than with minimal actions, sufficient for a photo op, but little else. As soon as the inevitable delay occurred, the president would accuse Haselden of holding them as hostages, just as Iran had held Americans in 1980. The resulting rage would guarantee support for whatever steps he took to crush the rebellion. And it was possible the people in South Carolina would recoil at the prospect of holding, or being blamed for holding, hostages. Seekings approved, but he needed to have consensus. He watched their faces as Moore spoke, especially that of General Cramer, the chairman of the joint chiefs of staff.

"What are your thoughts?" Seekings asked.

"The most important thing to do is get our people out, safely and as quickly as possible," Cramer said immediately.

"Shouldn't we let the state sweat it out? Haselden created this situation. Let him stew in it long enough, and they'll start to cave," Moore said.

The general looked around the table. No one else spoke. He fixed his stare on the president's face. "Is this your plan, Mr. President?"

"I want your input, General."

Cramer watched him in silence a moment before he spoke. When he did, his voice rose slightly, each word fired in Seekings' direction like a well-aimed shot. "Mr. President, I won't have anything to do with this. We owe our soldiers and their families every effort to evacuate them. If your decision is to pursue any other course of action, you may have my resignation."

The president rubbed his chin thoughtfully. "Relax, Norman. I need to look at every option. You'll agree with that, I'm sure. All right. What will it take to get them all out, and how long will it take?"

"Two weeks and every moving van we can get our hands on. We can't expect these people to leave all their possessions behind."

"What about it? Can we afford to let this go that long?"

Cramer replied sharply, "Nothing should be done until the evacuation is complete. Mobs could quickly get out of control and the people on those bases will be easy targets."

"General, I want all the preparations completed for a total blockade of South Carolina. When all of our people are out, impose the blockade."

* * *

The president's face conveyed the seriousness of the moment. His eyes seemed to reach from the television screen into the very heart of every American. The message was strong. "We'll get through this together," the familiar image seemed to say. Seekings crafted his entire presence before the cameras like an artist. It was the single greatest talent he brought to politics, and it had carried him to the apex of power.

"... *One Nation Indivisible.* I know I can count on each of you to rally to those sacred words.

"More is at stake here than political philosophy. There are real people in South Carolina, people whom I have sworn to protect. And they are in real danger. Our first priority will be to rescue the thousands of military personnel and their families who have been trapped there. I have directed General Cramer to move as rapidly as possible to bring them all out safely, along with their possessions." He paused, staring with more intense determination into the cameras, and said, "Let me say this to Governor Haselden and the other rebel leaders. You must treat these people in a civilized manner. I needn't remind you that if any harm comes to them — and disturbing reports have already reached me of abuse. The people of the United States will hold you accountable." It was a lie told with utter sincerity.

"This illegal rebellion was the act of a few, whose motives we can only guess. But what is certain is that millions are now denied their birthrights as citizens, the protection of the Constitution and the Bill of Rights.

Many of you remember, as I do, that not so many years ago, one-half the population of South Carolina, the African-American half, was denied basic human rights by the government of that state just because of the color of their skin. Only through the strong intervention of the federal government were those people allowed decent education, or permitted the most basic right of all Americans, the right to vote. I will not tolerate — and I know you share this determination — a return to the racial oppression of Jim Crow laws and segregation in South Carolina.

"My final words are for the men who have brought about this crisis. I call on the rebel leaders: lay down your weapons. For the sake of your children's future, end this madness now."

* * *

Thaddeus watched transfixed as the president spoke, the image flickering across the dingy little room. He hadn't slept since the first reports of secession the morning before. The conflict he had craved for so long was finally at hand. His computer was alive with messages from every corner of America. The militia faithful were streaming into South Carolina, gathering for the final battle for the soul of the nation. The federal monster now had a viable adversary. And Thaddeus was prepared to provide that adversary with its most powerful ally.

He tipped the bottle of whiskey and drank. Wiping his mouth with the sleeve of his tee shirt, he wound the tape back and watched the president's speech again. There was something he had said. The warning that no harm should come to the military personnel and their families. That bastard Seekings was right this time. If any of the military people were hurt — or killed — Thaddeus smiled as he thought about that, there would be no way to restrain the federal government from invading. He laughed as he wondered if Seekings was issuing an invitation. A few more lives lost would guarantee the war that would topple the unholy Washington tyranny once and for all. He took another long drink from his bottle. In the mirror he saw that he stood taller, and prouder. What he could not see was the dark light shining from his eyes.

* * *

Jim sat with Alicia and watched the president's speech. There was no longer any doubt about what Roger Seekings intended to do. The message of combative determination was clear enough. Since his return home, Jim had grappled with the new reality of conflict and uncertainty. For the children it was simple. There had been shooting, and people had been killed. And their father was in terrible proximity to it all. It terrified them and shattered the filter of security through which they saw the world to know that he could have been killed just as easily. Most immediate for them was the fact that Matt Reicher had been shot. They were desperate to be taken to the hospital to see him.

"They'll never understand that all that's over." He searched her face. "For Matt all that's left is anger. I'm the traitor that assaulted his base. There's no going back."

Alicia took his hands gently. "We'll take the children up to see Matt. It's important to them. They deserve to say goodbye." She started to cry again.

He knew that, at some point, the crying had to end. Life would go on, and his family had to be provided for. Knowing that this most important responsibility would be an ordeal weighed heavily on him. Alicia's instincts were more developed when it came to survival. She saw his burden. "Jim, we're pretty lucky under the circumstances. If things get too bad, we can go to your family's farm. They keep plenty of food put up, and there's room. We can keep up with schoolwork for a while. We won't starve."

He smiled at her, marveling at the simplicity of it. "I thought I'd aspire to more than not starving at his point in my life."

"Will they try to force us to give up?"

"You saw him. Did you hear him talk about racial oppression? He's trying to demonize us. Once all the military people are gone, the pressure will start."

"Do you think there will be more fighting?" She had no instincts for this part of her new world.

He stared from the window. There was no point in lying. "Anything can happen now."

* * *

On the second day, the exodus began. Sleepless nights of work by every Pentagon employee that General Cramer could press into service resulted in a flood of moving vans into South Carolina. First was Shaw

Air Force Base, and then the marine bases in Beaufort. Idle soldiers loaded each family's belongings into the waiting trucks. The activity was a welcome release from the tension that had built steadily among the military communities since they found themselves trapped and made aliens on their own bases overnight.

At the boundaries of the base housing areas, the National Guard watched them. And watched for any sign of looting or mobs.

The exodus wasn't confined to the military. On South Carolina's coast, heavily populated with retirees from across the country, panic took hold. Living on fixed incomes, much of it from the United States government, and obsessed with stability, the cataclysmic change around them was unbearable for many. The national media found no deterrents imposed by the new government of South Carolina, and they rushed into the state. In addition to the obvious backdrops for their coverage — the Capitol building in Columbia and the military bases — many reporters quickly discovered that the plight of the unwilling expatriate retirees was a clever angle. CNN sifted through the reels of footage transmitted by its team, and seized on an interview with an aging veteran outside his beachside condominium. It was played over and over for days. The angry white-haired man became, for much of the rest of the country, the symbol of the "Secession Crisis," as CNN called it.

"This is all I have," the old man spat at the camera, as he pointed to the stucco wall of his condominium. "I fought for this country. I worked and raised a family. And now, a crew of damned criminals and two-bit politicians have made me a foreigner in my own country."

"Where will you go?" the reporter asked in her most solicitous tone.

"Well, we can't stay here, can we? These people probably won't even be able to deliver the mail in a few weeks. How am I going to get the medical care I need? If this isn't the USA anymore, the government sure as hell isn't going run any hospitals." The old man turned to face the beach in front of his condominium. The sea oats waved in the brisk wind blowing from the ocean. He tried to hide his face from the camera as his voice cracked and the tears began to water in his eyes.

The old veteran was joined by many more. Retired stockbrokers, bankers, developers, and entrepreneurs of every description surveyed the tempest around them and decided to move their comfortable lifestyle away from the storm. The few liquid assets they kept inside the state were moved overnight to safety far from South Carolina. The most resourceful found trucks and paid men to load their most valuable possessions for the escape. For weeks they fled, until many of the wealthiest communities from Daufuskie to Little River were deserted.

Unnoticed by the reporters — even by those on the same planes — was the stream of South Carolina natives coming home. Some were drawn by the needs of family caught up in this strangest of exigencies. Some came simply out of loyalty, or to be a part of the most extraordinary event ever to engulf the land they called home. The soldiers came for a more basic reason. As conflict neared, their instincts told them the shooting might involve them. And, like all before them, they found they could not be part of a military machine that waged war on their own people. A trickle became a flood, coming by every conveyance that would carry them. Throughout the ranks of the American military, South Carolina's own abandoned ships, barracks, and offices and headed home.

*   *   *

Four days after the vote for independence, a group of business people convened at a country club on the northeast edge of Columbia. They all belonged to the Business Council, an association of industries and major landowners in South Carolina. Representatives of factories along the I-85 corridor near the mountains — paper companies, chemical manufacturers, and timber companies — had been summoned the day before by the council chairman, a bank executive. Most were not natives of South Carolina. Two were not American citizens. Each worked for a business with hundreds of millions of dollars invested in South Carolina.

Secession — the very word frightened them — threatened to destroy the stability their businesses needed. Unlike retirees, they couldn't simply cut and run away. The plants and machinery, the land itself, could not be moved. They had all spoken with their corporate headquarters and board chairman. There were no good answers in New York or Frankfurt.

"We're all in the same boat;" the banker said, "the question is what do we do about it? All of us answer to boards and stockholders somewhere else, but they're going to look to us for answers."

Stubbing his cigarette in a tray, a German chemical executive smiled and held up his hand. "Perhaps, we aren't taking a broad enough view of the situation. Let's accept that there is nothing we or our superiors, for that matter, can do about the political situation. How will we be affected so long as our products can be exported?" He looked at them and shrugged.

They nodded.

The banker asked the obvious question, "But what if that changes?"

"We will lose huge amounts of money." He smiled again. "Now, think a moment. How will we be affected by this independence, so long as our operations continue undisturbed?"

"We won't be affected. Don't be absurd," the owner of a chain of textile chemical plants responded, irritated by the frivolous chatter.

"You are wrong," the German said, leaning over the table toward him. "There will be no federal regulations. Think about it. There are none now. Right this minute. The only power in South Carolina is the state. The American military is moving its people out as fast as it can."

"Maybe, so it can come back shooting."

"Maybe," the German continued, "but what would be most likely to stop them from doing that — aside from nuclear weapons? Money, ladies and gentlemen. Money is what spins the world on its axis. How much money is represented around this table? How much more is out there in all the other businesses? How many billions?" He waved his hand at the window. "In the meantime, how much more are our enterprises worth without federal regulations. Think about it. No OSHA standards to worry about. No federal clean air, clean water, endangered species regulations. No RCRA. No CERCLA. No IRS. All those letters with no place to go." He laughed at his own joke.

The banker leaned back in his chair, "It would be like an offshore island country. Only we're not offshore."

"And we're a lot bigger than Barbados," the chemical plant owner added. "If this thing got stabilized, we wouldn't be able to find enough room for all the businesses that wanted to come here."

"Exactly," the German said, lighting another cigarette.

"We must educate our boards and chairmen about two things: the absolute necessity of maintaining our operations as before and the incredible benefits of a regulation-free zone on the coast of North America. Then it will be up to them to explain the realities of money to the American president. There is too much to lose to allow him to create chaos here." He leaned back, puffing on the cigarette again.

* * *

Thaddeus was worried at the speed with which the trucks carried the military people and their families away. Shaw and the marine bases were empty in the first week. And there were more trucks. Soon, the Weapons Station and the air base in Charleston would be empty, too. Time was slipping away from him.

* * *

Mark Killian watched the trucks lining up along Red Bank Road, waiting their turn to enter the housing areas at the Weapons Station. He was looking for Cooper. The directions he had were next to useless.

Tempers were running high among the sailors and others waiting to evacuate. Cooper was determined to prevent any screw-ups or friction that might delay their departure. "Fuck 'em," Mark said under his breath as he watched another pair of vans turn into the gate. The wound of Nat's death was still raw. And the infection of hate was flourishing inside that wound. He had thought of little else except his hatred for those responsible, the arrogant sailors who had driven up with their goddamned guns and their dead fool of a captain, now rotting in hell, he hoped.

He spotted Cooper's Humvee. He needed to talk to him about the mess that was building at the interstate. They were going to have to slow it down, or the whole thing was going to grind to a halt.

He caught up with Cooper at the corner of two streets lined with military townhouses. Gathered in the yard were three families surrounding the drivers of two of the vans. Each was yelling at the drivers and at each other. Mark watched, disgusted, as they all demanded to be the next to be loaded. Cooper and his driver waded into the melee shouting for quiet. No one paid him any attention. Finally, Cooper raised the loudspeaker he carried and shouted, "Shut up, God damn it!" The blast of sound at pointblank range caused the arguing men and their wives to cringe and cover their ears. "Now line up in front of your houses. I'll decide who goes next!" Most of the people moved toward their units, but two of the sailors remained and turned to face Cooper and the driver. Mark started walking toward them.

"You stupid asshole! We're next in line! Look at the numbers on the houses! Or can't you read?" The sailor's face was red, the blood vessels pulsing from his forehead. The other sailor took a step toward Cooper. The first lifted the shovel he had been carrying, but he didn't have time to raise it far.

Mark lunged at the sailor who was holding the shovel and snatched it from his hands. With one sweep of his powerful arms he doubled the man over the handle. As the first man crumpled to the ground, gasping for breath, he moved with remarkable speed, landing his huge shoulders into the chest of the second. The man fell hard to the ground, holding the spot where Mark had smashed his chest. Mark lifted him with one large hand by the front of his shirt. The back of his other hand caught the side of the sailor's head, splitting his ear and sending him back down, this time landing on the concrete. Again, Mark lifted him up. The sailor was unconscious, but Mark didn't know it. In fact, he could no longer see him at all, not as a man capable of being conscious, or with feeling. The fury of death consumed him now, blocking out the humanity of the thing he only wanted to punish for killing his friend. Four arms grabbed Mark Killian. They struggled to pull him back. Cooper and the driver finally wrestled him backwards, the three of them falling together on the concrete. Still, he struggled to free himself, roaring like a mad bear.

"Mark ... Mark!" Cooper yelled directly into his ear, "you're going to kill him!" Mark stopped struggling, but his arms and chest stayed tense, and Cooper and the driver held him tightly, fearing he might spring at the man again. Quietly now, Cooper said, "His family's watching Mark. His kids, for God's sake ... Let it go. Let's just get them all out of here ... O.K. ... O.K.?"

* * *

"Does it hurt, Uncle Matt?" Katherine McNeely peered over the hospital bed and pointed to Matt Reicher's heavily bandaged shoulder.

"Not anymore. They give me some good medicine. As long as I don't move it, it's just like new." Matt had always been able to do this, Jim thought. He embraced John and Katherine as the loving uncle he'd always been, while his eyes told Jim there was only enmity between the two men. He made polite conversation, but the coldness and distance were palpable. Jim thought his son sensed it, and that probably made the hug he offered Matt more desperate.

"When do the doctors say you can be released?" Alicia asked.

"In ten days," Matt answered. It was a lie that he was intent on making true. They had told him in no case could he leave in less than three weeks without risking infection and permanent damage to the nerves in his shoulder. Despite Matt's ranting, Linda had already refused evacuation in order to remain with him until he could go. She would stay in the house on the Weapons Station, and when he was free to leave the hospital, they would go.

Alicia promised the children they would see him again and urged them to let their uncle get some rest. Katherine pulled herself up to his pillow and kissed his cheek. John gave him a final hug and shook hands before leaving the room. "Jim, wait a second, please."

When Alicia and the children had filed out and the door closed behind them, Jim looked expectantly at Matt. He was staring at the window. Without turning his head, he said firmly, "Don't come back."

* * *

Thaddeus fingered the grip of the rifle, uncharacteristically nervous. At the tip of the barrel sat the grenade. He reminded himself that all they had to do was get close enough to land the grenade among the soldiers and their families fretting over the packing of their miserable belongings. The pickup truck ahead of him approached the National Guard soldiers on either side of the entrance to Fort Jackson. He watched as they checked his friend's credentials. The papers said they were soldiers who lived off post. His friend would be explaining that they needed to coordinate with the post commander about transportation of their household goods. There were so many soldiers and so much was happening so fast, the guard soldiers paid little attention to them as the four trucks passed through the gates.

Quickly, too quickly he thought, they curled their way towards the family housing area of Fort Jackson. In all of the trucks, his friends checked their grenade launchers and automatic weapons. The tall pine trees followed by the brick duplexes and carports of the homes of the officers slid past the window. At the end of the first street a coterie of men and women was gathered, talking with the drivers of the moving vans. Thaddeus signaled his friends to stop a few dozen yards from the crowd. Only a few guard soldiers stood on the fringe of the group. None paid attention to the trucks.

Quietly, Thaddeus opened his door as his friends stepped to the sidewalk from the other three trucks. All of the men held weapons, a half dozen tipped with the ugly, bulbous ellipses of grenades. The men spread out into a line and kneeled into firing position before the guard soldiers noticed them. Seeing what was happening, the young soldiers reacted, too slowly raising their rifles and stepping between the families and the militiamen who were about to fire. The fusillade of bullets cut down the guard soldiers first and, behind them, the front row of Fort Jackson soldiers and their dependents. Before the echoes of the rifle shots died, Thaddeus and three of his friends fired the barrage of grenades into the shrinking group of men and women. Now, the children, who had been standing next to their parents, could be seen, recoiling from the blast and shrapnel from the grenades, young faces, arms and legs torn by the force of the attack.

Not pausing long enough to hear the shrieks of the wounded and dying, Thaddeus and the others leapt into their trucks and raced towards the gate. One of the wounded guard soldiers was shouting painful warnings to his command post as the trucks sped off. By the time the militiamen reached the gate at Jackson Boulevard, there were no guard soldiers standing on the sides of the road. The ten soldiers were waiting, concealed in firing positions. As the trucks raced toward the gate, their drivers noticed the absence of the soldiers, but not before the hail of bullets shattered the windshields, killing the lead driver. His truck careened over the curb and into the large pine that flanked the guardhouse. The vehicles behind swerved, trying to avoid the fire of the M-16s. Brakes squealed and trucks veered off the pavement, some colliding with each other to avoid the concentrated barrage. Soon, all the trucks were still. The soldiers continued to pour fire into the bodies of the vehicles until the frightened soldiers were certain there was no longer any danger.

One by one, doors of the trucks opened and hands were held high in surrender. The militiamen who were still alive crawled from the trucks and tossed their weapons toward the soldiers. Most were bleeding.

Before long, word had spread of the attack and reporters flocked to the now safe scene of the carnage. The smart ones followed their hunches and met the military trucks carrying the militia prisoners to the state prison an hour later. Their cameras flashed the image of the faces, including that of Thaddeus, arrogant and defiant even in capture, to the networks waiting for more footage for their evening broadcasts. By nightfall, the faces of each were spread before an analyst at FBI Headquarters in Washington. It didn't take her long to recognize the leader of the group as Thaddeus, the same man the Russian, Mikail Plekanov, had identified as his American militia ally, and head of the Northwest Territorial Militia. She picked up the telephone and called Leo Scardato.

* * *

President Seekings followed the evacuation of the military community from South Carolina closely. When the final trucks were being loaded, he summoned General Cramer. It was time to begin the next phase of his plan. He was in no mood to discuss compromise. The weeks since the original humiliation had been an unending series of questions: How had this happened? Would he risk nuclear confrontation? Would he negotiate with the governor? What would be the next step to end the crisis? He was sick of it all.

Cramer entered the Oval Office, as always, erect and arrogant, Seekings thought, staring straight into his eyes, not avoiding them, like most people. The general walked to the desk where Seekings sat, and saluted smartly.

"General Cramer, are you ready?"

"What precisely do you mean, Mr. President?"

Seekings looked around the room for a moment and then responded, "The weapons that have been emitting the signal, are we prepared to destroy them?"

"Yes, sir. But there is only one signal."

"Are you prepared to blockade South Carolina by sea?"

"Yes, sir, if that is the decision of the National Command Authority."

"God damn it, Cramer! Who the hell do you think that authority is? Yes, it's my decision! Can you do it? Just answer the question."

"We can do both, Mr. President."

"Then do it! Destroy the weapons at once, and tell the fleet to seal the coast."

*   *   *

Kevin McClure sat at his desk, as he had done so often for weeks, his mind wandering, unable to focus. The phone rang, a welcome relief. "Mr. McClure?" The voice was strange to McClure.

"Who is this?"

"My name is Scardato. I'm with the FBI. I have some important information for you." McClure sat bolt upright in his chair.

"I'm listening." He grabbed a pen and paper.

"The men who attacked Fort Jackson yesterday.... We have identified most of them from the television pictures. I thought you might be interested."

"I'm listening, Mr. Deputy Director," McClure said, showing that he knew who Scardato was.

"The leader was a man from Indiana who calls himself Thaddeus. He's the leader of a group called the Northwest Territorial Militia."

"O.K."

"The Russian mobsters who attacked the train in South Carolina in October provided detailed statements before they died. Thaddeus was the man who led the assaults on the police stations. He and his men killed the police."

McClure froze.

"You're wondering how to prove this aren't you, Mr. Prosecutor?"

"So. Tell me, Leo."

"I have the Russian's statements."

"Statements of a dead man."

"There is plenty of corroborating evidence in Plekanov's statement. And besides, I believe you have some policemen who survived. Do you think they might recognize our friend?"

"We'll see." McClure scribbled notes as fast as he could write. "Leo, do you suppose you could send me a copy of the Russian's statement? In the interest of international cooperation."

Scardato chuckled. "Sure, Counselor."

In minutes, the fax machine was slowly feeding the pages of Mikail's last statement, given to the state security officer in his St. Petersburg hospital room. McClure pulled each page from the tray as it fell. "Jesus," he said to the empty room. McClure studied the statements and quickly composed a memorandum for the chief criminal attorney in the attorney general's office. Then he called Columbia.

* * *

Blackie Haselden was still reeling from the shock of the attack. Eleven soldiers, wives, and children were dead, and many more horribly injured by the blast and flying metal fragments from grenades. Only hours later came the shattering revelation that the leader of the attack was the same man who had murdered the police in Florence, one of the men who caused this nightmare.

Blackie waited in a tiled anteroom, removed from the inner prison by a wall and a phalanx of armed guards. He told them he wanted to meet with this Thaddeus alone. The guards were not happy, but they took him to a small room, normally used by prisoners and their lawyers. Thaddeus was chained even more securely than the usual maximum-security prisoner, feet and hands closely manacled and bound together. They led him, shuffling, to the little room to meet with Haselden.

Blackie sat as the guards ushered Thaddeus into the room. "That will be fine. Let us speak alone, please," he said. The guards left.

Thaddeus slid the chair on his side of the table far enough back to ease himself down into the seat. He lifted his eyes, "Your Excellency," he said, his lips curling on the ends of his mouth into a parody of a smile.

Blackie was unprepared to sit face to face with the man who had caused so much evil. His stomach threatened to fail him. The walls seemed to close in on him. He resisted the temptation to turn and look at the window to see if the guard was there. Thaddeus' eyes were locked on him, the weird smile never leaving his lips. Blackie scanned the freshly scrubbed face, searching for... what, he wondered. He was suddenly seized by the urge to flee the ugly little room, and the blazing white lights.

"Well, Governor, what exactly did you want to talk about?" Thaddeus asked him, sneering.

Blackie hesitated. He could see that the man was actually enjoying this. "Why? Just tell me why you did it."

Thaddeus tilted his head back as far as it would go and laughed deeply. "Where's my lawyer, Governor? That's pretty incriminating stuff, you're asking me for there." He laughed again.

"So. Do you care? Do you deny what you did?" Blackie asked, the anger building.

Thaddeus stopped laughing and smiled at him. "No." Raising his voice and leaning across the table, he continued, "And why should I? Tell me, Governor Haselden, why should I not be proud of what I've done?"

The blood rushed to Blackie's face. He could feel the anger running uncontrolled through him. "You murdered innocent men, women and children. You're an animal!" Blackie heard himself shout. He wanted to be the man to push the button sending the fatal surge of electricity into the monster that sat before him.

Thaddeus leaned back in his chair. "An animal," he repeated softly. "I'm hurt, Governor. Do you think I'm a worse *beast* than the men who wired those railcars to blow up, and scatter all that radiation all over that little town ... and all over your friend ... and your godson? Am I? You don't think so, do you, *Governor?*" He paused, the luminescent eyes boring into Blackie. "For all you know, I may have just as good a reason to hate the Washington bastards as you do." He threw his head back again and laughed.

"You're a murderer. You're a cheap killer of innocent people, nothing more."

Thaddeus' face twisted into a crazed scowl. His manacled hands grasped the edge of the table. "You think you're so much better, do you?" The eyes that fixed on Blackie were yellow now, wild and alive with hate. "You pitiful prick! I've butchered better than you." He sneered, "And you are the leader of a revolution?" Blackie started to speak, but Thaddeus cut him off, shouting rapidly now. "It's a war! If you don't know that by now, you will soon, won't you? What about all those *nuclear* weapons you have stashed away? What about those, Governor?" He was ranting, his spittle landing on the table. "What do you think you will do with those new toys? What do you think that bastard Seekings will do? I'll tell you! He's going to come down here and cut your nuts off! Unless you stop him by frying the boys he sends to get you."

"You're crazy!" Blackie shouted. The guards heard the clamor in the room and gathered at the door.

Thaddeus calmed himself, the color returning to normal in his agitated face, but never moving his eyes from Blackie. "No. You wish I were." He paused, leaning across the table until their eyes were only inches apart. "You're just like me, Governor. They *killed* your friend and his son, and you hate them as much as I do. When the time comes, you'll *incinerate* them. And you'll *enjoy it,* just like me. You *are* me."

Blackie recoiled, pushing himself away from the deranged face, from the evil laugh that rose unbearably. The guards pushed the doors open as Blackie stood from the table and turned away. The guards pulled Thaddeus out of the room. The door closed behind him, and Blackie heard his shrill cackle echo down the hall as Thaddeus was dragged back to his cell.

*   *   *

When the transponder signal first indicated that the nuclear bomb had ceased moving, the location was soon pinpointed. Those coordinates were plotted into the electronic brain of the Tomahawk cruise missile lying in the launch tube in the forward missile pod of the USS *Deyo.*

The *Deyo* was steaming fourteen miles east of the tip of North Island under a moonless sky. Captain E. J. Horres sipped the fresh cup of coffee he carried with him to the bridge and gave the order to bring the ship into the wind. His own orders from the task force commander were clear enough, but no less extraordinary. His ship had never fired a missile in anger, but tonight he would give the order that would launch one of his Tomahawks and its warhead of 454 kilograms of high explosives into his own country. At least, that's how he thought about it. Secession was just a farce in his mind, a political fluke that would pass if the politicians would just act reasonably and do their jobs. But how long had it been since he assumed they would do that?

He put those thoughts away. He was about to carry out an act of war, one that would kill men, and hopefully destroy all of the nuclear weapons seized by the rebels in South Carolina. It would be quick, but he should have a clear head for what he had to do. It took only six minutes once the ship was in position. Contact was established with the satellite, which would guide the Tomahawk on its way to the interior of South Carolina. Horres gave the order to fire, and in seconds, in a blast of orange-white light, the missile leapt from the tube into the darkness. Out of the tube, the wings deployed and the missile raced upward, illuminating the ship and the ocean below. Quickly, the missile began to respond to the directions transmitted to it by the satellite and dove to the surface of the Atlantic. Now it raced across the waves at seven-tenths the speed of sound.

In less than a minute, the Tomahawk flew over the empty sand-finger of North Island. Wrapped in the dark Carolina night, farms and crossroad hamlets of three counties passed below the missile in twelve minutes. Exactly fifteen minutes after the order to fire, the nose of the missile crashed into the walls of the warehouse deep in a stand of oaks and pines on the state park south of Sumter.

The eruption of sound and flame that followed shook the ground for a mile around the disintegrating building. One of the guards standing watch next to the building was killed instantly by the blast. The three others lived long enough to scream in agony from the terrible destruction to their bodies, rent by flying metal and concrete.

The missile accomplished its mission. All of the nuclear bombs and missiles in the warehouse were destroyed. Their ferocious power would never be unleashed on the United States. The guard lieutenant charged with security for the site arrived minutes after the blast. He had the good sense to isolate the area around the still-burning ruin, for he knew the deadly plutonium fuel from the now useless warheads was probably scattered among the rubble. When he was certain the area was secure, he called Columbia.

Chapter 29

Terry Wilkins sat at his desk and sifted through the telephone memos stacked neatly on his blotter. His wife was calling every day now, leaving messages asking what the hell was going on. How long had it been since he'd talked to her? How much longer would she put up with it? Not much longer, he supposed. Among the messages were several from the bank where all of "his" money was deposited. There was no recorded activity in the account. Had he received all the account information? The checks and personalized register? They could not know that he didn't want the money, that it was soaked in too much blood. And he didn't know how to talk to his wife anymore.

The burden of guilt had been building since the first horrible day in October. Every succeeding page in the still unfolding tragedy bore his imprint, for without him, none of the monstrous things tearing the country apart would have been possible. The weight of self-loathing was now too heavy to bear. He was kidding himself to think anything could change that.

* * *

"... All four guard soldiers are dead. The warehouse with nuclear weapons was completely destroyed." Mayor Collins listened to the governor's summary of the cruise missile attack. Now there had been a direct attack on the state with one of the most sophisticated weapons in the American military's arsenal. Collins was not a student of weaponry, but he remembered the chilling films of missile attacks during the wars in Iraq and Afghanistan. He knew that volleys of such missiles could be launched by the fleet now off the coast.

"Pat, I believe it's important that you try to speak to the vice president." Blackie wanted Collins to find out if there was any hope of negotiating an end to the confrontation. He knew the men were acquainted from many years as leaders in their party.

"But whether you make any progress with him or not, it is vital that he understands this: The cruise missile destroyed *only one* group of the nuclear devices we took. They must understand that the rest are *dispersed* and secured." Blackie continued, his voice becoming more somber, "And tell him I cannot guarantee how many attacks this state is going to absorb without responding with the only deterrent we have."

Collins gasped, "You want me to threaten—?"

"No threats. We are a sovereign nation now. No country will tolerate attacks on its territory or the killing of its citizens. There is no precedent for a military attack on a nuclear power. Remind him of that. If they are banking that I won't use these weapons, tell him it isn't up to me alone."

Collins clutched the telephone receiver in stunned silence. He looked around at the finely detailed ornamentation of his office, a room filled with two decades of labor for his city. He looked, but found no reassurance, nothing to calm the fear quickly turning to panic deep inside him. "Governor, I...." He paused, uncertain what to say. But there was no choice. There had never been. "I'll tell him, Blackie."

* * *

The satellite imagery was pretty good, considering the destruction of the warehouse. It didn't take long for the analysts to make a pretty good guess about what weapons had been stored there, no more than twelve and no fewer than nine. That meant there were between forty and forty-three nuclear weapons still in the hands of the leaders of South Carolina. No one had really believed they would all be in one spot, but it was impossible not to hope.

General Cramer waited to meet with the president. He was the only one waiting. He was learning that Roger Seekings felt no need for advice in matters of retribution.

"So, General, I see we have eliminated less than a quarter of the nuclear devices."

"Yes, Mr. President."

"When can we locate the rest."

"The transponders were all destroyed. There is no way I can guarantee that we will find them. Our people in South Carolina," he said, referring to the nearly two hundred agents who had been sent into the state, "will keep running down every angle they can. But it will be more and more difficult for these people to work. Conflict makes people more clannish. Strangers will stand out. Any agents will be at greater and greater risk. And there is a more serious problem. These weapons are not so large that they can't be moved around. If they have not already done so, the state can put some of them in trucks and just keep them moving."

Seekings stared at him vacantly. Finally, jerking his head to the side, he said, "Just say it, General. The vaunted American military can't find its own nukes, right in its own backyard."

"I wouldn't put it that way. But I suppose that's correct."

"Put it any way you want, General." He shook his head disgustedly. "What about the blockade?"

"The fleet is in place. The sea blockade is in effect. I issued the order this morning to interdict any vessel entering or leaving any port. Small craft may still get through. A total blockade is impossible. But the state will have no ocean-going commerce from this day on."

"What about the next phase?"

"Air interdiction is simply a matter of giving the order, and will be similarly effective, perhaps more so because of radar. Ground isolation is the hardest. The border is long. We can seal off any effective commerce by closing the roads."

"We'll see how the sea blockade works. And there are some other actions I'll be taking today that should start to shut them down. They'll either give up or they'll be starving before long."

"Mr. President, I must ask you, have you considered that we are making war on a power that possesses a major nuclear arsenal? We should not underestimate the destructive—"

"General," Seekings said curtly, "they won't use them. That's bullshit, and we all know it. It's a bluff, and I'm not buying."

"Mr. President, just one of the devices they have is capable of annihilating the entire Third Division at Fort Stewart or the Eighty-second at Bragg. It is possible that one of the weapons could be dismantled, converted into a more portable weapon and transported to any major city in this country, including Washington."

"You watch too many movies. All you guys do. Just do what I tell you, General."

Cramer stared at the president. "Yes, sir."

*   *   *

The Chinese president listened to the briefing from his intelligence chief. So, the American president had fired on the rebels, as he himself had predicted Seekings would do. Now the inevitable chain of events would begin, like carefully stacked dominos falling one into another, leading to the final cataclysm. How fragile the great American monolith was turning out to be after all. The world's historians would write eloquently of these days. It was his intention that those historians be Chinese.

"Make the final preparations for the invasion of Formosa. It won't be long now until our time will come." He thought a minute and added, "Ensure that our satellites monitor the American army bases nearest the border of the rebellious province. If there is any mobilization, I want to know immediately. This information may be useful to us."

*   *   *

The first of the executive orders involved money. The president ordered that no further distributions of United States currency would be made to South Carolina. Even one day's interruption in the supply of currency would cause chaos. But Roger Seekings went further. He ordered that all assets held by South Carolinians in multi-state banks be frozen immediately. These banks would be forbidden to allow any depositor listed on the day of secession as a resident of South Carolina to have access to those accounts. The effect would be to strip most of their wealth from the people of South Carolina. The White House also declared a complete sea blockade of the South Carolina coast.

Another statement declared that an investigation of the murder of the eleven military personnel at Fort Jackson showed the complicity of state National Guard soldiers in the attack. By mid-afternoon, the names of two of the surviving witnesses somehow found their way onto the desks of major news organizations in Washington.

On the evening news that night, and on special reports broadcast later, the witnesses explained how National Guard soldiers greeted the militiamen when they prepared for the attack and actually blocked many from escaping the deadly fire. Both witnesses cried while trying to recount the sight of their friends and comrades falling under the hail of bullets and shrapnel. No other witnesses were available to talk to the media.

The smear was one of C. A. Moore's most masterful. It was so easy to work with military people. No one objected when the two military intelligence operatives, neither of whom was there, told their lies for the cameras. It was nearly a week before General Norman Cramer learned the truth that made him ask himself for the first time in three decades why he wore his nation's uniform.

*   *   *

"Mr. Vice President, there has to be a way to end this. We must start talking. Too many people have died already for no good reason. If this goes on, the tragedy could be repeated many times over," Patrick Collins said soberly, nearly pleading.

O'Connelly listened, knowing that the ways to avoid crisis had been passed by many times since Roger Seekings began to take them down this dark road. "There will be no talks unless all the nuclear weapons are returned to federal control. This president simply will not negotiate, unless that is done." He believed that Seekings would probably refuse to do so in any event.

"That won't happen." Collins took a breath and delivered the message he dreaded. "I must tell you on behalf of Governor Haselden that the cruise missile only destroyed a small number of our weapons. The rest are dispersed and protected. The governor cannot guarantee that he will be able to avoid responding with our deterrent force if there are any further attacks against us."

"Pat, is this a serious threat?" In spite of everything, O'Connelly could not bring himself to believe use of nuclear arms could be contemplated under any circumstances.

"I am told to convey to you that this is not a threat, but the inescapable reality. South Carolina must be regarded by the United States as a sovereign nation. You must realize that it may be impossible to avoid the use of whatever force we possess in defense of our citizens."

"I see," O'Connelly said, still reeling from the unthinkable prospect made more shocking because it was presented by this man, whom he had long known to be credible as well as decent.

"Please understand, Mike, this is all abhorrent to me. But we have to have a way back that is reasonable. And now that people have died in

battle, the way must also be honorable. It gets more difficult the longer
we go on, doesn't it?"

"It always does."

*   *   *

Harold Fraser listened to the colonel summarize the irrefutable intelligence. An American navy destroyer had launched a cruise missile into
the heart of South Carolina and destroyed some, but not all of the nuclear
weapons the state's rebel leaders had seized. Earlier, he had learned of the
blockade and the other economic measures ordered by the president. His
office was already deluged with demands from Canadian interests with
large investments in South Carolina to protest these actions. Hundreds of
millions of dollars were at stake, the angry calls and faxes said.

The Canadian prime minister was concerned about a more terrible
prospect. On opposite ends of the conflict were two irreconcilable forces,
unshakable in their determination ... and in the middle were scores of the
most frightful weapons of destruction ever known.

Canada's policy toward the United States was always one of scrupu-
lous deference, unless they interfered too obscenely in Canada's domestic
affairs. Fraser began to think that his country's policy needed to be
modified in this case. He found it easier to contemplate extraordinary
measures in the face of the appalling specter of nuclear war in North
America. One idea in particular, one that had he proposed only a month
before would have been pure madness, began to take hold. *It was mad,*
Fraser thought, *but no more insane than what was happening only five hundred miles to the south.*

*   *   *

The mere announcement of the sea blockade and cutting off the
flow of Federal Reserve currency effected the isolation of the state's economy
from the rest of North America and the world. Weeks of near normalcy
had left business leaders and workers alike falsely confident that secession
would not disrupt the commerce of the state. President Seekings' pronouncements shattered this illusion and replaced it with chaos.

Frantic messages to corporate headquarters around the world cried
for help. Accounting departments fed the figures to CEOs in every major

industry. Potential losses were staggering. A coalition began to form of those with the largest investments in South Carolina. They would tell the president there had to be a better way. Too many companies and too many people would be hurt, some ruined by isolating the state. Did he realize that he was sealing off fully 2 percent of the industrial capacity of the country? Four percent of the GNP could be traced to the state he was encircling with an economic noose. In board rooms from New York to Zurich, corporate officers used to wielding power sought the best way to make the president see reason. Every day the losses grew.

These things were unknown to Blackie Haselden as he struggled to find a way to keep the state from suffocating. Access to money was their first priority. Through his own executive order, Governor Haselden would declare that all funds of South Carolina residents held in multi-state banks were deemed to be located *in* South Carolina. More difficult was money supply. They would have to face the fact that if no reconciliation was reached soon, South Carolina would simply have to create its own currency.

Blackie's advisors, those inside as well as outside of state government, regarded the blockade of the coast as the first step of a total blockade. "The blockade is a military matter," Blackie replied. The somber faces around the table told him they wondered what he meant to do about it. He supposed they were too frightened of the answer to ask the question. "We will not respond to the blockade at this time. I will release a statement declaring any further blockade to be an act of war. The mayor of Charleston has agreed to see if there are any openings for discussions on a settlement with the federal government. We will wait to see if his efforts bear fruit. In the meantime, General Demers is preparing contingency plans to make the best use of our assets to break the blockade."

The faces around him paled noticeably, but Blackie observed that no one suggested giving up.

* * *

O'Connelly's telephone conversation with Mayor Collins sparked an idea that had been developing in the vice president's mind ever since. He decided to ask his two closest friends in the news media what they thought.

"I had a conversation yesterday with someone in South Carolina," O'Connelly said.

"On the record or off, Mike?" Brent Manzi asked.

"I'm going to let you decide after we finish. Pat Collins called me. He's been the mayor of Charleston for years."

"Yeah, I remember him after the big hurricane. Impressive," Howard Casselman said, remembering how well Collins came across on television.

"Collins was asked by the governor down there to contact me and explore the possibility of settling this mess. I explained the low esteem in which I am currently held by our president, but I think he already knew that. They are desperate for a reasonable resolution."

"But Seekings isn't going to give them one. God, he's calling them racists and murderers. What bullshit," Manzi spat.

"This is still a democracy. You fellas all ran that story, and all the other crap this administration has been putting out. And now the whole country thinks the people down there are all crazed killers or fanatics. They'll give Roger a free hand to do whatever he wants, which is exactly what was supposed to happen."

"So what did the Mayor say?" Casselman asked.

"He says we destroyed only a small fraction of their nuclear weapons, and that if there are any further attacks on South Carolina, they cannot guarantee the governor will be able to avoid using their 'deterrent force.'"

"Jesus H. Christ!" Manzi exploded. "He threatened to use nuclear weapons against the United States!"

"More or less."

"The message sounds pretty damn clear to me," Casselman added.

"Ask yourselves this question: How much killing would you expect any people on earth to take before they used whatever force they had in their power to fight back? Is there any precedent for a nuclear power failing to respond to attacks? The real precedent of the atomic age is simple: Once you have nukes, nobody screws with you anymore. Look at India. What Roger is beginning to do is to screw with people who have nuclear weapons."

"What does Seekings plan to do?" Manzi asked.

"I am the last person in the administration to ask. But look at his pronouncements. He plans to strangle them economically, although I imagine before long there will be quite a howl from Wall Street. It's going to be very expensive for a lot of people."

"He is running a terrible risk," Manzi said.

O'Connelly watched them quietly.

"Mike, you asked us here for a reason, you said. What's on your mind?" Casselman asked.

"How would you guys like to do a great service for your country?"

* * *

"Governor, he's very serious. Brent Manzi, from IPI, and Howard Casselman, the TV anchor, have agreed to come down and interview you. Their organizations will give the interview full coverage. The idea is to allow you to tell our story. I think you should do it," Collins said, not at all sure how Haselden would react.

"What is this supposed to accomplish?"

That was a fair question. "So long as Seekings has people convinced that you're either crazy or a fanatic, he believes he can do whatever he wants. This is your chance to talk directly, to the American public. Take it."

"All right. When?"

"Tomorrow."

"I'll make time. We'll do it in Florence."

* * *

"Mr. President, we appreciate your offering us this time. These are difficult times, sir." Barry Hart had been appointed spokesman for the group of businessmen that had been granted this audience with the president. He was chief executive of one of the largest conglomerates in the country. There were six, including Hart, and each was one of the most powerful men in the American economy, but they spoke for many more.

"Yeah, they are tough, but these problems will pass. I'm optimistic," Seekings said as he greeted his guests. He knew them all. He had solicited and taken huge amounts of campaign money from each one and would again, he was certain. "Now, gentlemen, what can I do for you today?"

Hart spoke again. "Roger," — the familiarity was calculated to remind Seekings of his real relationship with the power they represented

— "the business community is very concerned about what's going on down in South Carolina. There is a lot of money invested there by a lot of people. And this blockade is affecting the market. Did you see the figures from yesterday? Today's will be worse. And tomorrow's, too, unless we can turn things around."

"I hear you. I'm doing everything I can to straighten things out down there. It may take a little longer, but I am sure we will crush this rebellion." He smiled confidently.

Hart cleared his throat before he continued. "Roger, the feeling is that they won't give up. Not short of a fight. All of us," he said, motioning to his colleagues, "have very considerable interests down there. Our local people all say the same thing. South Carolina is united behind this guy Haselden, and they are determined to reclaim what they see as their dignity."

"Their dignity." Seekings smile began to retreat. He wondered why they came to see him. Now, he saw. They were worried over their profits. No matter what crisis afflicted the nation, everything was all right with them so long as they didn't show a loss. "It isn't their dignity that's at stake. It's the Union. People have been killed. I have a responsibility to the people of this country — all the people — and to protect the Constitution."

Hart's face betrayed none of the contempt he felt for this man. *The same petty power addict who groveled for cash to run his campaign now thinks he is Abraham Fucking Lincoln.* "Mr. President, there has to be a way to negotiate this out. It is, after all, a dispute like most others. Each side has things it wants. There must be middle ground here. Perhaps you could appoint a commission to explore alternatives."

"Thank you, but I believe we are on the course that best serves the country."

"Roger," Hart said, his irritation showing now, his face tense and his words terse, "I need to emphasize that we speak for the entire business community. Our concern is very great. A total blockade of South Carolina will cost billions. If there is fighting, the costs will multiply."

"Your message has been received. Tell your friends not to worry." Seekings stood, signaling that their audience was over.

*   *   *

In the car, Hart exploded. "The little shit! It's his ego; that's all this is about! He doesn't give a damn who he ruins, as long as he shows everyone who's boss. And we all helped put him there! God damn it!"

"I keep hearing that Mike O'Connelly has been trying to talk sense into Seekings since all this crap started."

"Yeah, I hear he's got about as much influence around here as the damn yard man."

"Some people are starting to listen to him. Maybe we should go and see Mike."

*   *   *

General Cramer drove himself from his quarters to the Naval Observatory. The vice president's secretary sounded mildly surprised to learn that the chairman of the joint chiefs of staff wanted to visit with her boss that evening. He was surprised, and amused, when Mike O'Connelly answered the door to the official residence himself. Cramer knew about O'Connelly's idiosyncrasies, but had never observed them in person.

"Mr. Vice President, I know this is highly irregular...."

"Highly irregular, Norman? You sound like a second lieutenant talking to your battalion commander. What gives?"

Cramer smiled, in spite of himself. "I'm worried, sir." His normally stoic features betrayed the anxiety that had brought him to Mike O'Connelly's house. "Today, I received confirmation that the Chinese are mounting a full-scale invasion of Taiwan. I think they plan to change its name back to the Province of Formosa. The reports are unequivocal. Everything is in place. The only missing piece of information is what they are waiting for. I believe I know what that is."

"What?"

"They are waiting for word that a nuclear device has been detonated here in the U.S. Then they will move. It's pretty smart, really. At that point, no one will notice, or care."

"What do you think, Norman? Are they just being overly optimistic?"

The general stared at O'Connelly, the chiseled lines of his face mapping the genuine fear that had been growing inside him for weeks. "I think it may be a good bet."

"So, what do we do about this?"

Norman Cramer had never committed a disloyal act in his entire military career. He believed in the necessity of unity to command. There could be only one commander in chief. But he knew in his soldier's mind, and in his heart, that the president was taking the country down a road that led to an unspeakable cataclysm. He didn't know exactly what he expected to accomplish by explaining his fears to the vice president. It certainly was not his way to "share" his burdens with others as therapy. As he told Mike O'Connelly why he believed the president greatly underestimated the danger that the leaders of South Carolina would use nuclear weapons, he allowed himself some hope that this decent, reasonable man would be able somehow to sway the president onto a safer, saner course.

"If there were nukes in Iraq, there would be no embargo. The same is true of Cuba, or Iran, or any number of places in the world. A man with his back against the wall will fight with whatever he has."

"Norman, is the president planning to invade South Carolina?"

Cramer stood and walked to the mantle, gripping the edge. "I have been ordered to prepare plans, yes. But the president is personally directing all of these actions. I do not believe he is receiving counsel from anyone."

"I'm sure he is consulting one man." Cramer nodded. Neither man had to say the name of C. A. Moore.

* * *

After General Cramer left, O'Connelly sat alone in his den, sipping a glass of wine. So often since Governor Haselden's visit in the spring he had resolved to overcome the impotence of his office and force Roger Seekings away from the destructive path that had brought them to a day when he must discuss the chance of nuclear warfare on American soil. All those chances had passed. The last opportunity was nearly at hand. There was a mood for avoiding the coming conflict, and he believed that mood could be tapped. General Cramer and the angry men from Wall Street showed him that. He would wait for the interview with Haselden to be made public in two days. Then he would act.

* * *

"Governor, what do you want to accomplish through independence?" Howard Casselman asked Blackie Haselden, as he and Brent Manzi sat on the bench of the dock on Welch's Creek. Blackie faced them in a chair placed next to the railing. Behind him, the camera captured the gum trees, now colorful, their leaves red in the late fall of the Southeast, with vines spiraling gold into the moss-draped branches. The creek water swirled black past the dock under them. He brought them here after the major portion of the interview was filmed on the edge of the exclusion zone at the center of Florence. If they wanted to capture him as he really was, this was where they could do it. It was the first time he had returned to this special place since Watson and Billy died.

Blackie had already explained in simple, economical terms the evidence proving the government assembled the railcars with the intent to have them explode if breached. He recounted his failed efforts to win an agreement from the president to cease the shipments. In straightforward, compelling language he explained why South Carolina could not permit occupation by the government that could commit such a wrong and fail even to acknowledge the wrong of it.

"I never sought independence. We have come here by default. All countries are founded on the principle that there is a contract between the people and their government. Like other Americans, we believed part of that contract was a promise that our government would hold the safety of our land and our children paramount. We learned at great and painful cost that our government was prepared to discard this most important covenant. We had to secure for ourselves the protection we expected but did not receive from the United States."

Manzi asked him, "What do you see for the immediate future?"

"That depends wholly on the leaders of the United States. We are anxious to reach an honorable, reasonable agreement. If we could do that, we would return happily to the Union. But all of our efforts have been rebuffed. Still, we remain willing to talk. If there is no corresponding willingness on the part of the federal government, we will go on taking care of ourselves. If force is used against us, we will resist."

As broadcast, the interview consumed a full ninety minutes. Casselman imposed on the network to forego commercials. The picture of the leader of an American state in rebellion was spectacular enough to demand the nation's attention. And there were few who missed it. Blackie's sincere, commonsense explication of the events that had led to the crisis was compelling. Casselman's narration told the viewer that the dock on which they concluded the interview was the center of the governor's boyhood

and lifelong friendship with one of the firemen who had been killed by
the radiation from the train. The photo of Watson, Blackie, and Billy
proudly displaying fish on the same dock was resurrected. The network
ended the interview by running the credits over the image of their joyous
faces. The nation was moved. And amazed at a governor whose best friend
had been a fireman. It was hard not to like, and to sympathize with, the
man they saw on their television screens.

*   *   *

At the conclusion of the program, Casselman's network and Manzi's
wire service conducted a joint poll. Overnight, the sense of the country
had reversed. As before, an overwhelming majority, 98 percent, favored
reunification, but the percent believing the rebellion's leaders were responsible for the split had plunged to a mere 7 percent, instead of a majority.
Nearly 80 percent said they were convinced the Seekings Administration
shared equal blame by driving the governor and his state to desperation.
The same majority strongly favored abandoning coercive tactics to end
the rebellion. Nothing about the arguments that led up to the crisis, they
felt, was worth the risks of continued confrontation.

Collins was elated at Blackie's success and the poll results. In a frantic telephone call to Mike O'Connelly, the vice president cautioned him
not to expect too much too soon from this president. But he, too, was
overjoyed. He allowed himself to embrace hope for the first time.

*   *   *

Seekings' response to the interview was swift. In a firestorm of rage,
he ordered that actions originally planned for much later, be taken at
once. On the morning following the broadcast, he called General Cramer
and informed him that the full blockade of South Carolina was to be
implemented at midnight. The only limitation to be placed on the military units was that deadly force not be used unless, as a last resort, it was
required to effect the purpose of the blockade.

*   *   *

The air portion of the blockade was simple to enforce. No planes dared to approach the border of South Carolina. Those needing to reach the major airports at Charlotte or Savannah were tracked closely by the air force and granted individual clearances to land at those places. Air travel simply ceased between the state and the outside world overnight.

The interstates were easy to close. Armored detachments took up positions at both ends of the interstate arteries that crossed the state. The rest of the roads took longer. There were dozens of major roads that connected the state to North Carolina, and a hundred smaller ones. The major ones were closed in a few days, but the army projected that it would be a week before all the paved roads were sealed off, much longer if it was expected to close the border entirely. It did not have the resources to do that. In any event, there was no road that paralleled the borders. Therefore, any patrols would be required to traverse open country, including foothills, ravines and swamps. The task would be enormous. The border with Georgia was no easier, since it consisted of the Savannah River. Crossing at the countless landings that dotted both banks could never be controlled, the army bluntly told the joint chiefs of staff. The directions from the White House were sketchy as to how the land blockade was to be administered. Some crossing was to be permitted for humanitarian purposes, but otherwise, only when it was in the national interest, whatever that meant. The army did the best it could, devising rules of engagement and procedures for monitoring permitted crossings at the scores of established checkpoints. Passes would be issued for specific periods of time.

* * *

"Prime Minister, that's a difficult question. But I'd have to say that I believe the answer is yes. The Americans will invade before long if this blockade doesn't cause the rebels to give it up," the Canadian defense minister said. "Look at it this way. What happens if they don't give up? Soon, the entire economy will collapse in South Carolina. Fuel will run low. Medicines will run out. This means the Americans will have to start making exceptions to the blockade. Next, food will be a problem. Americans will not allow themselves to be put in the position of starving their own citizens, rebels or not. They can't stop the press from covering it — and the American public will recoil at inflicting that kind of misery on anyone, particularly children. Already, public opinion is migrating away from the president. He cannot afford to wait much longer. I believe he will act to end this before Christmas. And that means an invasion."

"What do your people think the South Carolinians will do?"

He stared at the prime minister. "They'll fight."

Fraser turned soberly to the others assembled around the table. "Well, what do you think? Will this plan of mine work?"

The opposition leader in Canada's parliament answered for the group, "Harold, we have to make it work. We can't let their conflict go nuclear … if we can do anything to prevent it."

"All right, then let's get on with it." He picked up his phone. "Call the office of Governor Haselden in South Carolina, right away."

* * *

Jim McNeely got off the elevator and walked to Matt Reicher's room. By now, he knew Linda and the girls would have been there to say their goodbyes and were on their way to the border, back to Pennsylvania. Linda Reicher called him the day after the total blockade was decreed. She and the children couldn't stay any longer, and Matt wasn't ready to travel. It was hard for her, but she asked for help in securing the house. She didn't ask it of him, but Jim promised to get Matt out of the state as soon as he was able to travel.

Jim knocked lightly on the door before opening it. Matt glared at him. "I came to tell you what's going on."

Matt said nothing.

"Your house is sealed. No one is going to get in. The station is guarded. And I've directed the officer in charge to ensure that no one gets near the house. When you're ready to travel, we'll provide a truck and our soldiers will load your things for you. I'll see you to the border."

"I don't want your help."

"Look, make sense."

"I don't want your goddamned help!"

Jim turned to the door. As he slammed it behind him, he shouted, "I guess you don't have any fucking choice!"

* * *

Jim sat in the car, angry and pained by the wreckage of a friendship he had thought would always be his. He turned the ignition, reminded that now he had to think about where the next tank of gas was going to come from. "Stubborn bastard," he said. Could the death of a friend be any more painful than this? His phone beeped.

"Jim?" the governor's voice asked.

"Yes, sir."

"I received a call from the prime minister of Canada this afternoon. He asked me to send a representative to speak with him about a matter he says is of great importance. I spoke to Julieanne."

"She's the best person." In the last weeks, Jim had gained respect for her understanding of international politics.

"It's impossible for her to go." He didn't say that her sister-in-law's depression was too great to risk leaving her alone. "She recommended you. The prime minister is sending a plane to Charleston from Bermuda tomorrow afternoon."

Canada, he thought. *What the hell was this?*

Chapter 30

A freeze and heavy snow had turned Ottawa into a winter postcard. The Rideau Canal below the hotel echoed with voices of skaters. The grounds of Canada's parliament lay under a still fresh white blanket that clung to the gables and corners of the building's roof. The snow accented everything with a natural playfulness. No native of a snowless land can help but be captivated by a real snowfall. As he finished his breakfast in the hotel dining room, Jim was no different. He couldn't help being fascinated by the scene below. In spite of himself, he stopped wondering why he was in Ottawa. He sipped his coffee and wished his family was there, that he could put on ice skates and take them all down to join the crowd on the canal. He thought how good it would be to feel the cold air — to feel free and normal again. How good to teach his children to skate on the thick ice of the frozen canal. He'd tell them it's just like rollerblading....

"Mr. McNeely?" He turned at the sound of the question to find a tall young man in a heavy overcoat.

"I'm Peter Crandal, from the prime minister's office. We thought you might not have planned on our weather, Mr. McNeely." The young man offered a heavy coat on his arm. "There's no need to rush. Whenever you're ready, I can take you up to meet the prime minister."

"You were right. Thanks. Please sit down. How about some coffee?" Jim waved him to the empty chair next to his. Jim, filling his cup, asked, "Tell me, Pete, what is the agenda for this meeting?"

"I really don't know, sir. I'm afraid I'm not privy to those details," he said pleasantly. "I'll be escorting you around. If there is anything you need, let me know and I'll do my best to take care of it. I understand it may be difficult for you to telephone home, although I believe some arrangements have been made through the Ministry of Defence for you to contact your government."

"Thanks. What do you do for the prime minister, Pete?"

"I'm with the RCMP — the mounted police — security for the prime minister, sir. Not exciting, but always interesting. I suppose we're like

the Secret Service in the U.S. Although we do other things, as well —
embassy duty and real police work, for instance."

"A mountie." Crandal smiled. "I apologize for being nosy. I've never
done anything quite like this before." Jim fixed his eyes on the young
man's face, searching for what, he didn't know exactly. An answer as to
why he was here? Well, he wouldn't have to wait long.

They walked to the lobby. The Chateau Laurier was a giant, elegant hotel, built in the last century. It reminded Jim of a castle or a
French chateau. "Shall we walk, then? It isn't far up to parliament," Peter
asked.

"Sure. I don't get to walk in snow often." Jim winced at the curtness
in his voice. He forced himself to control the stress he felt building. "Ottawa is a place I know very little about."

The mountie slipped easily into a guided tour as they crossed the
bridge over the canal, the Ottawa River and Quebec on the other
side. At the path leading up to the parliament buildings, he stopped and
pointed to a large white stone building on the left. The flag flapping in
the brisk wind told Jim what it was before Crandal spoke. "And there is
the Embassy of the United States."

"So," Jim said looking from one building to the other and gesturing
with his hand, "you mean every time the prime minister or a member of
parliament comes out the front door, he has to look at the American
embassy?"

"So it would seem." They both laughed.

*I'll bet there are some folks in there who are wondering what I'm doing
here*, he thought as he stole a last glance at the embassy. It occurred to him
that the Americans might already know what the Canadians wanted, even
if he did not.

Peter ushered him into the front of the huge parliament building. In
the prime minister's office they were greeted by a tall middle-aged man in
uniform, whose insignia was a complete puzzle to Jim. "Mr. McNeely,
I'm to take you up to the prime minister."

The uniform. It's the damn warheads they want, Jim thought angrily.
*How the hell was he going to deal with this? Why hadn't he seen that this was
their reason?*

Neither man spoke as they wound through hallways and finally into
a small conference room with an immaculately polished table.

"Mr. McNeely, may I get you some coffee or tea, sir?" the general asked.

"How about some good Canadian whiskey?" The general looked at him quizzically, as though he thought he might mean it. "I'm just kidding. Really. I'm fine."

The door at the other end of the room swung open and a stocky man in a finely tailored gray suit walked towards him, hand outstretched and smiling. "Mr. McNeely, welcome to Ottawa. I'm Harold Fraser."

He could have been any politician, Jim thought. *They all had the same unmistakable entry.* "Yes, Prime Minister, I recognize you from your pictures."

Laughing and tapping Jim's shoulder, Fraser motioned him to a chair, "My public relations people are doing a better job than I give them credit for, Mr. McNeely. I wouldn't have thought anyone outside the State Department in the U.S. would recognize me."

The group that had followed Fraser into the room surrounded the table. They included three senior military officers, two in different-colored uniforms. There were other gray-suited men and one woman.

"Mr. McNeely, I want to thank you for coming to Ottawa. I know it was not easy. It is important, I believe, that our meeting is in person. I should tell you that this room is as secure a place to speak as we can offer to you in Canada. No doubt the U.S. government would like to know why we have asked to speak with a representative of your government." Jim noted the emphasis he placed on identifying South Carolina as a separate government. "The people I have brought with me are those in whom I have utmost trust."

Motioning around the table, Fraser introduced Jim to the leaders of Canada. They included the foreign minister, the minister of finance, the minister of defence, and the interior minister, as well as senior military leaders. "This gentleman is the leader of the opposition party in parliament. Are you familiar with our parliamentary system, Mr. McNeely?"

"Yes, Prime Minister."

"Good. I want to emphasize that what I propose to you represents the consensus of this government as well as that of the opposition party. You can assure your government that I speak for Canada. Do you understand?"

"Yes."

"Mr. McNeely, I have no desire to meddle in the affairs of South Carolina or the United States. Of course, we have watched with great concern the tragic events of the last months. It appears that South Carolina is determined to sever her ties with the United States. And it appears that your government has secured the military force to protect your independence."

"That is our intention."

"Yes. Of course, the U.S. government seems just as determined to stop you by means that may become ... violent." Fraser paused, looking intently at Jim. His gaze became more penetrating. *Here it comes*, he thought.

"I believe Canada and South Carolina have a mutual interest," Fraser continued. As he said this, one of the military officers opened shutters exposing a display board on which had been posted a map of North America.

"If your state succeeds in leaving the American union, as I am sure you are aware, she will face considerable difficulties economically. Even given the powerful weapons you have acquired, you will also face security challenges in the world community."

"These things have occurred to us, Prime Minister."

"I don't mean to be condescending." Fraser seemed to be genuine in this. "The matter that I want to discuss is an option that will provide South Carolina a way to avoid the serious problems she faces."

He's going to offer to buy warheads from us, Jim told himself angrily.

"Mr. McNeely, Canada is proposing union with South Carolina."

Jim's face froze.

"We want South Carolina to join us as a province of Canada."

Still Jim didn't respond. Union? Is that what he thought he heard?

"Do you understand?"

Jim looked at the map. South Carolina's boundaries were neatly outlined. *They wanted to do what?*

"Mr. McNeely, I would like to present to you our reasoning so that you can present it to your government."

"Mr. Fraser, we are a long way from Canada."

"Let me show you something." Fraser walked to the map. "Alaska is six hundred miles from Washington state. All of those miles are across Canadian territory. South Carolina is only five hundred miles from the southern tip of Ontario."

" Mr. Fraser, what is this about?"

There was anger in Jim's voice.

"Canada has a great interest in stability in North America. If there is an exchange of nuclear weapons here ... well, we don't want that to happen. We will do almost anything to prevent it."

"At the risk of being blunt, Mr. Prime Minister, is it Canada's intention to seek union with my state for the purpose of securing its own nuclear weapons?" As he said this, he turned to look directly at the uniformed officers on the other side of the table.

"No. The warheads must be returned to the U.S. Canada has no desire to have nuclear weapons."

This surprised Jim as much as the proposal for union. His head began to swim.

"Look, there is no reason for this not to work. We are already connected economically, and we are on the same continent, after all. Trade between us is already brisk."

Jim walked to the window. It was snowing again. Figures moved slowly through the white, going about normal lives, while he was in this conference room talking about insanity.

"Mr. Fraser, the United States is the most powerful nation on earth. Do you think it will simply wish us well in our marriage?" He turned and faced the Canadians. "I don't think the president will send us a set of towels or a set of glasses."

"I doubt it."

"Prime Minister, my former country can be one mean son of a bitch. They will turn on you. Don't you understand? Can you imagine the fury in Washington, or in Detroit for that matter? They will not stand by quietly while you absorb one of the states."

"We have given the reaction of the U.S. considerable thought."

Falling into his chair, Jim exclaimed, "My God, I hope so!"

Smiling again, the prime minister placed his hand on Jim's shoulder. "Let me lay it all out for you. It boils down to this. The U.S. will fume for a while, but it won't take action against us. For one thing, until you are securely a part of Canada, you'll still have the nuclear warheads." He paused and smiled. "As part of Canada, you will belong to the British Commonwealth. As you know, that means strong ties between countries like ours and Great Britain. The British have agreed to dispatch a carrier and two destroyers to Charleston along with a small flotilla of our own ships."

"Are you telling me that you have consulted with the British government?"

"Yes, I have. The prime minister agrees with this course of action. And I have consulted with Her Majesty."

"The Queen?"

"Your state is alone, Mr. McNeely. Standing up against, as you put it, the most powerful nation on earth. This is a desperate situation. If your state and the U.S. start fighting — I should say fighting again, since there has already been bloodshed — the result could be catastrophic. There are many reasons why that is a potential disaster for us. It is obviously a potential nightmare for you."

The room fell silent again, more somber this time.

"Let me suggest this. We have arranged for you to meet with the governor general at his residence in a little while. He has agreed to explain how we envision merging South Carolina into our confederation. I hope that you will point out any issues we haven't seen, and discuss ways to solve them. If this is not possible, we shouldn't have to say later we didn't do our best."

"I don't know what to say."

"Right now I'll settle for going to see the governor general."

"I'm not a diplomat. I'm just a lawyer."

"Constable Crandal will take you right over."

Fraser closed the door and looked around the table. "Well?"

* * *

Crandal joined him in the back seat of a black Mercedes. The snow was falling steadily, the flakes blowing in every direction. "Pete, who is the governor general? I hate to be rude, but I don't have much time."

"Right. He is the Queen's representative in Canada." Jim leaned his head back. "He fulfills the same role for us as the Queen in Britain. He is supposed to be above politics. The embodiment of the nation is the Queen and he is her representative. The military and all political leaders swear loyalty to the Queen." Jim squeezed his eyes shut. "Have I been clear?"

"I'm certain you have." They crossed a canal and entered an area of tree-lined streets and landscaped homes. "Pete, you knew what the prime minister was going to propose, didn't you?"

"We're at the residence," Crandal said.

"Good Lord." The car turned into a lane leading to stone columns and high, ornate, wrought-iron gates. On either side were blue boxes with pointed roofs outside of which stood armed guards clad in long coats and black bearskin hats. The high collars of their bright-red uniforms peeked out from the heavy gray coats. "It looks like Buckingham Palace."

"That's the point."

As the car sped through the gate, both guards came to attention and brought the rifles to their chests in salute.

"The license plate tells them it's one of the prime minister's cars," Crandal explained.

Through the gate, the lane was lined with large trees coated in the wet snow. The drive ended in a circle around a frozen fountain fronting the mansion of the governor general. It was a simple, rectangular structure without a portico, adorned only by a fanlight window over the entrance and capped by a pediment with the lion and unicorn of the British coat of arms carved in relief. The twelve flags of Canada's provinces hung from the front. More guards in the same bearskin hats were posted in front. As Jim and Crandal made their way into the mansion, the guards brought their rifles up in salute.

They were met by a uniformed officer in the foyer. "Mr. McNeely, may I take your coat?" Crandal turned to go back outside.

"Wait a second there, Pete. I want you to sit through this with me."

"Mr. McNeely, this is to be a very confidential meeting. Constable Crandal will be at your disposal when the meeting is concluded," the officer explained.

"Nope. I would like to have Crandal here sit in with me. I'm sure he's trustworthy." Crandal and the officer looked at each other, neither sure what to do. "Look, I am the representative of my government in these very unique negotiations. And this is the way we're going to do it, O.K.?"

"Very good, sir." With that decided, the officer led them down a corridor to a large room. Waiting there was a lone man, tall, in his late sixties. Seeing their approach, he smiled broadly and extended his hand.

"Mr. McNeely, welcome to Rideau Hall. I am delighted that you agreed to come." Jim noted an accent in his speech that indicated English was not his first tongue.

"Sir, I have asked Constable Crandal to sit in with me."

"Certainly, we'll get some paper, and the constable can make notes for you." The officer immediately produced a legal pad and pens, which he handed to Crandal, who looked uncomfortable — another departure from the plan. "Mr. McNeely, I'm sure there are many questions you have concerning Mr. Fraser's proposal. It has fallen to me to speak with you about those questions and to sketch out how your state might join the Canadian Confederation."

The governor general retrieved a large leather notebook. For hours, he explained to Jim the details of incorporation of South Carolina into Canada. The plan covered everything. They would send representatives to the Canadian parliament on the same basis as the other provinces. Phased integration into the various national services, national health, defense, etc., would follow — the mail and defense immediately, national health more slowly.

The detail was impressive, the product of a massive effort, like some kind of graduate study in comparative government run amok. But they were quite serious. And none of their ideas seemed unreasonable to him. Except that it all seemed crazy. *But yet no crazier than secession*, he thought, *or pointing nuclear weapons at the United States of America ... or watching your best friend turn into a bitter enemy.* He suddenly felt cold and alone.

The governor general walked to a bookshelf behind the table where they were seated and pulled down three red binders. "Between those and this presentation from the prime minister's office, I believe you have all of our ideas." He handed the binders to Jim. "Is there anything we have not considered, Mr. McNeely?"

"What concerns me is the reaction of the United States, not just the government, but the people. I fear you underestimate the fury this proposal will unleash. Blood has already been shed. Will Canada stay the course if the U.S. turns on her?"

"Unless there is a resolution to this, the U.S. will move to invade your state, and your state may well deliver a nuclear response. That is intolerable for us. We must prevent it. You should not underestimate our determination to avoid nuclear warfare on this continent. Welcoming South Carolina into our confederation will stop this calamity and will do no harm to Canada."

"This is dangerous. I would be a liar if I told you I thought differently."
"This is indeed. There is often danger in doing what must be done.
Let's do what we can together to diffuse it, eh?"

* * *

In the car, Jim said little to Crandal as they drove past the guards and
into rush hour traffic. "Pete, do you skate?"

"Everybody in Ottawa skates. You bet, sir. Why do you ask?"

"I thought you might help me find a place to do a little skating."

"Sure, I'll join you, if you like. We can rent you skates down by the
canal."

"I don't want Mrs. Crandal to hold a grudge against South Carolina."

"I'm afraid there isn't a Mrs. Crandal any longer. She left two years
ago. She was from Quebec. She had strong feelings about independence
and all that. Quebec voted to stay in Canada, but she voted not to stay
married to a mountie. I went to the embassy in Sarajevo and when I came
back, she was gone."

"I'm sorry."

"Don't be. There are a lot worse things than being young and single." He laughed. "I'll let you off at the hotel, and I'll be back with some
sandwiches."

On the ice, Jim felt the tensions melt away. Crandal moved as if he
were born there. Jim supposed he pretty much was. Crandal had played hockey
in school and had been on a team for the mounted police, he had said.
The profound inferiority of his own skating didn't bother Jim. The air was
cold and fresh. The sound of the metal cutting the ice was exhilarating.
There was a large herd of skaters, but the canal accommodated them without crowding. It was different from rink skating, the only kind he had
done in a long while. The laughter of the skaters was muffled by the snow.

"I didn't think it got so cold in South Carolina," Crandal said as he
slid up to Jim, showering his legs with ice. "You do this pretty well. With
a little practice you could join the team, eh."

"Right." Jim frowned at him. "I lived in Maryland for a number of
years when I was a kid, and we did a lot of this in the winter."

"How about something to drink?"

"Sounds good." They made their way to the canal's edge where stands
were set up selling chocolate and coffee.

"Some of these guys have something a little stronger."

They purchased hot rums and claimed a bench by the ice's edge. Jim took a long drink. "O.K., Constable Crandal. What do you think of this business? I don't want any canned crap either. I wanted you to sit there in the big house and listen in so I could talk to someone. So out with it."

"I'm not sure it would be proper." He peered over his Styrofoam cup as he sipped the hot rum.

"Look, I can't call my government. I can't even call my wife. As far as I know, there aren't any other South Carolinians knocking around here in Ottawa. Pete, I've known you a whole day. I trust your judgment. And besides you're all I've got. I have to hear what another rational person thinks. It's important."

"I think the governor general is right. If something isn't done, the U.S. Army is going to invade your state and your people may fire a nuclear weapon. People do terrible things once killing starts. I saw enough in Sarajevo to convince me that nothing is beyond men at war. The death of children and poisoning of a city from stupid mishandling of nuclear material has caused your people to turn against their own government. Men have been killed already. And if a nuclear weapon is detonated, hell will break loose. It will be horrible. That's what I think."

There was a long silence. Neither man spoke. They finished their rums.

Crandal spoke first. Jim saw the seriousness in the young man's expression. "Compared to what will surely happen if something isn't done, it doesn't matter if the union jack flies from the top of your parliament building in Columbia and your kids sing 'God Save the Queen' in school."

"Its called a Capitol building"

"What?"

"The building in Columbia. It's called a Capitol building."

Crandal was silent.

Jim continued, "There really is no question, is there? We have no choice. This is the safe haven we need. Going it alone was never possible."

"Another rum?" Crandal asked. Jim guessed that was his way of saying there wasn't much else for them to say.

"No. I'm whipped. And I have to meet with your Mr. Fraser in the morning. I'd better get some rest. Thanks for the skate, Pete."

"Don't mention it."

"And thanks for speaking your mind."

They turned in the skates and made their way up to the hotel, its towers and spires illuminated brightly against the black sky. Crandal assured Jim he would meet him in the morning and moved off into the night. Jim wondered where he might be headed. Young and single. *Have a good time*, he thought. Glancing at his watch, he saw it was 11:00.

* * *

Jim took the elevator to the fifth floor. As he fished in his jeans pocket for the room key, he jumped at the sound of a voice addressing him from behind. "Mr. McNeely. Good evening."

Jim turned to see three men in dark overcoats. The man speaking was pasty-faced and his coat barely disguised a pronounced middle-age paunch. His gray hair stuck out from under a brown fedora, the only effort at style in his otherwise nondescript appearance. The men flanking him were younger, Jim thought, in their twenties and powerfully built.

The guy with the hat was confident, even cocky. His companions were nervous, their eyes shifting, scanning the hall. They kept their hands shoved deep in the pockets of the bulky overcoats. Suddenly, it occurred to Jim that they might have guns. *Don't be melodramatic*, he told himself. Jim turned toward the man in the middle. "What do you want?"

"We would like to discuss some business with you, Mr. McNeely. May we come in?" He was smiling like he was having the time of his life.

"What kind of business? I have a long day tomorrow."

"We won't be long, but it's of importance to us both I assure you. May I call you Jim?" One of the young men had moved so that he was behind Jim.

" Who are you?"

Felix Hubbard retrieved a small black case from his vest pocket and flung it open. A gold-colored badge flashed in the hall lights. "I'm with the FBI." Jim looked at their faces again. Why were they so familiar? "Now open the door and let's go in and talk, O.K.?" He was getting irritated. Whoever he was, he wasn't used to being told no.

"Look. I don't care who you are. I'm going to bed and I'm going to bed now."

"Not yet."

"All right, you son of a bitch, let's go down to the lobby and talk to hotel security. I think they'll agree with me that you guys are bad for business." Jim wheeled around and found a man behind him blocking his way. Jim grabbed the man's arm and shoved him to the side. The man pulled his hand out of his pocket. He was holding a 9-mm pistol with a stubby attachment of some sort on the end of the barrel. It was a silencer. He raised the pistol and laid it gently against Jim's chest.

"Open the door." The man didn't look nervous anymore. His eyes were steady. Cold.

Jim retrieved the keys from his jeans and began fumbling with the lock. As the door opened, the other young man took the handle of the door and eased it open. The man holding the gun nudged Jim inside. The third man followed.

"Sit down, Mr. McNeely. Your country needs to ask you some questions."

Jim sat on the end of the bed, flanked by the two younger men, one still holding the gun in his direction. "Why did you come to Ottawa?"

"I'm not at liberty to say."

"Actually, you're not at liberty to refuse. I have a federal warrant for your arrest for murder, not to mention treason. I can have you on your way to the States tonight. That's not why we're here, though. Just tell us what you've been talking about with our good friends in Canada."

"It's none of your goddamned business what I've been doing. Now get the hell out of here."

Jim leapt from the bed. The man on his right caught the front of his sweater and shoved him back. He was strong and the force sent Jim onto his back.

"Then we'll just wait a few hours. You will go home with us. You can talk to us in prison." Turning to the man on his right, he said, "Tape his mouth, Erick." Erick produced a roll of heavy blue tape from his pocket and began to peel up the end.

The sound of a key in the door made them jump. The lock clicked and the door flew open. Peter Crandal strode into the room. "Hey guys."

"I think you have the wrong room, sir," the man in the fedora said smoothly.

"No. But I think you have the wrong country. Are you gentlemen carrying guns?"

They stared at him, but did not move.

"Canada has very strong gun control laws, gentlemen. Hand me the pistol, please." Crandal was looking straight at the man on Jim's left, who had returned the gun to his pocket. "Hand it over. I'm Constable Crandal of the RCMP," he declared flipping open his badge cover. "You gentlemen will need to come with me."

Pulling out the gun, the man on Jim's left turned to the older man. "Felix, we have to wrap this up — now. We have to get out of here." His tone was calm, masking the beginning of panic. Turning to Crandal, he said deliberately, "Turn around and put your hands behind your back, Mountie. Erick, tape his wrists and then his mouth."

"You guys aren't going anywhere. My friends are outside. Hand over the gun, Yank."

"He's bluffing. If he wasn't alone, he wouldn't have come in here alone — unarmed." The guy with the gun shoved it into Crandal's ribs. "Felix, you and Erick go get the car and bring it to the back door. Erick, you come up when you get back, we'll take both of them with us."

"No, no, first the tape," Hubbard said. He was rattled.

The telephone rang loudly. Jim saw that the man closest to him momentarily lost concentration and the gun was simply hanging at his side. He lunged and drove his head into the man's stomach, at the same time grabbing the pistol, trying to wrench it out of his grip. They fell onto the bed, the bigger man quickly regaining his breath. Jim saw that the trigger should have been pulled from the force, but it didn't move. *The safety's on*, he realized. The telephone continued to ring as Crandal landed a fist squarely on Erick's jaw, sending him over a chair and onto the floor. Hubbard was a little tougher than he looked, but Crandal deflected his attack and forced his head down, locking it there with his arm; the risk of a snapped neck caused him to be still. Erick raised himself halfway up before Crandal kicked his head hard. He moaned and fell back, blood now flowing from a torn ear. "Get the gun!" Crandal shouted.

The other man was too strong for Jim. He finally tore the gun free and, with his other arm, flung Jim off the bed. Jim fell on the table by the window, shattering the lamp. The American leapt from the bed, clicked the safety off, and pointed the gun at Crandal. "Let him go," he demanded. "Lay down on the floor, face down, and don't move. You, too," he said to Jim. Crandal released Felix and stretched out on the floor, his face in the carpet.

"Now go get the car, and hurry. Forget the damn tape! Just hurry," the man pointing the gun at Jim barked. Felix and Erick quickly left the room.

The American sat in one of the chairs next to the overturned table and pointed the pistol. "Don't make a goddamned move."

"So, are you going to murder us both, or what?" Crandal taunted him.

"Shut up."

The room was silent except for hard breathing from all three. Jim found he was bleeding from cuts on his hands, the sticky ooze covering his fingers.

The young man stiffened at a knock on the door. He walked cautiously around the two men on the carpet in front of him and backed to the door. "Yes?" he said. The only reply was another knock.

"Felix?" he said to the door.

"Yeah."

As peered through the peephole, the door flew open, catching the young man and hurling him to the floor. Six uniformed police charged into the room. Two fell on him, pinning him and grabbing the pistol. The rest fanned out in the room with revolvers drawn. A heavyset man in street clothes came over to where Jim and Crandal lay on the floor. "So Peter, how's it going?"

"What in hell took so long?"

"Ingrate."

Crandal and Jim got up. "Walter, what about the other two guys? Did you get them, as well?" Crandal asked.

"What other two guys? All we knew was you and Mr. McNeely here were in trouble. Your beeper signal got our attention. When no one answered the phone, we got over here."

"This fellow here had two friends with him, Felix and Erick. They left here about twenty minutes ago to get a car. They intended to take Mr. McNeely and I to the U.S."

"I'm sure they didn't come back."

One of the uniformed officers searching the American pulled a folded set of papers, a wallet and a leather folder from his pockets. "Captain Timothy Giordono, United States Army Intelligence. Assigned to the Deputy Chief of Staff for Intelligence. These are directions to the Chateau Laurier and a picture of Mr. McNeely here." He threw the papers onto the bed.

Crandal walked over to Giordono. "So, Captain, what the hell were you doing in this country, armed and trying to kidnap a loyal Canadian subject and a guest of the Canadian government?"

The young man glared in return. "O.K. Do you have a family?" Crandal asked, leaning over and peering into his face. "Listen, dumbass, if you have a family, say so and you can call them. Tell them you're all right. You just won't be home for a while. This is a civilized country."

"A wife. In Bowie, Maryland."

Picking up the phone, Crandal asked, "What's the number?" Crandal dialed the number. A not-quite-awake voice answered. "Hello, Mrs. Giordono? Sorry to bother you so late; your husband asked me to get you on the phone." Crandal handed the phone to the American, who told his wife he was in Canada and would be there for a few days on business. No, he couldn't say what it was, of course. It was business and she understood.

When the officers and Giordono, now in cuffs, were gone, Jim asked, "How did you know to come back?"

"I noticed these guys when we were skating. They followed us up the steps, so I turned back and followed them up to the hotel. I watched from around the corner when they jumped you at the door."

As he talked, Jim reached under the TV and opened the little cabinet stocked with mini-bottles of liquor. He pulled out a fistful and threw them on the bed. Filling two glasses with ice from the bucket, he handed one to Crandal. "If you hadn't been here, I'd be on my way to prison. Hell, they might of put me in front of a firing squad." They poured the little bottles over the ice. "Thanks."

* * *

In the morning the sky was clear, but a fierce, chilling wind caught snow from the drifts and blew it against their faces as they trudged up Parliament Hill. They were quiet as they walked along the icy paths. In the outer office of the prime minister, they were greeted by a young woman, who brought them coffee.

A uniformed man entered from a side door and addressed Crandal. "Constable, the prime minister has been briefed on what happened at the hotel last night. You are free to leave. Get some rest, and make your report as soon as you can."

Jim spoke to the officer, "If Constable Crandal is willing, I would appreciate it if he stayed. Any objections, Pete?"

"No."

Fraser was seated in his office with the ministers of defence and foreign affairs. He had been up since three, when he received the call about three U.S. agents trying to kidnap one of the mounted police and James McNeely at gunpoint. For hours he had gone round and round with two of his most capable ministers, trying to craft the right course. They were no closer now than when they started. One wanted to stick it down the Americans' throats. The other wanted only to run as fast and as far away from this problem as they could. The police and the army had failed to find the other two agents, who presumably were back across the border.

Preparations had been made for his call to the president of the United States. He was going to have to rely on his instincts. There was no precedent for what he was about to do and no consensus among his advisors. The door to the outer office opened, and Jim McNeely and a man in blue jeans and a sweater came into his office.

"Good morning, Mr. McNeely."

"Good morning, sir." Fraser's eyes told Jim how strained he was.

"Are you Crandal?" he asked the young man in the Montreal Canadiens sweater.

"Yes, Prime Minister," Crandal replied standing.

"Well sit down. You did a fine job last night."

"Thank you, sir."

"We have a lot to do. Right now, Jim, I'm about to call the American president. I want you to listen." Jim noticed that one of the men flanking Fraser did not like what the prime minister was about to do.

Fraser punched a button on his desk. "All right. Make the call."

In a few minutes there was a voice from his intercom, "Mr. Prime Minister, President Seekings is on the line."

Fraser picked up the phone, "Roger. How are you this morning?"

Jim marveled at the composure in his voice. What a different story it told from his face. Fraser was about to tell the leader of the most powerful nation in the world that armed agents of his government had violated Canadian sovereignty. But he sounded like he was calling to schedule a real estate closing.

"I'm sure you are. There never seems to be enough time. I have with me a Mr. James McNeely, a guest of our government from South Carolina."

Fraser flipped on the speakerphone. There was no sound from the president. "Can you hear me, Roger?"

"Absolutely, Harold."

"Last night three agents of your government tried to kidnap Mr. McNeely in the Chateau Laurier. You remember. You stayed there last summer for the economic summit. In the process of trying to kidnap our guest, your agents brandished a gun — a 9-mm pistol — threatened one of my security detail, and then tried to kidnap him as well. Are you aware of that?"

There was silence.

"Well, what your intelligence people tell you is your business. We are holding a Captain Timothy Giordono, an officer in your army intelligence service. He's under guard at a Defence Forces Base. He was the one carrying the gun."

"I'm sure there is some explanation. Are you certain you have the facts. You know it's hard for men in our positions to be certain that what we first hear is the truth. It's extraordinary to claim that American military personnel were acting, as you say, on your territory. It's just not possible. I am trying to get the full story now. It seems that an FBI agent was there to serve Mr. McNeely with a warrant and to arrest him for murder and treason. Were you aware of that, Harold?"

"You know, Roger, we have a treaty for extradition. It doesn't provide for shanghaiing a man at gunpoint."

"I am told that our people thought they had gone through the right Canadian channels."

"I don't think that's true. The right procedures would have provided for Mr. McNeely to be detained by our police." Fraser felt the pressure building now. He was becoming angry. He summoned all of his composure. "This morning I ordered all of our defence bases to deny clearance to any American personnel. All of your people serving with our police have likewise been asked to remain home until further notice. I think you owe this country an apology."

"Harold, this is a mistake. James McNeely is wanted for murder and treason, not very pretty crimes. Let me propose that your authorities bring him to the border. I can provide all the documentation of the charges against him. You are probably correct, that our people acted inappropriately. An apology is in order. I certainly would like to extend our regrets to the mounted policeman. I hope he's all right."

"He's fine. Now, about your offer. Canada will not turn over Mr. McNeely. He is our guest, and at the moment there is a dispute as to whether he is subject to U.S. law, given the claim of his state to sovereignty. I'm sure you agree with me on that."

There was silence.

"Until you and I have an agreement that this sort of mistake won't happen again, we will keep your Captain Giordono as our guest."

"This is a matter of purely internal American interest."

"No. Bringing armed agents into our territory to snatch our guest and to threaten our police is a matter of international interest."

"I don't have to tell you that we can't afford to create a rift between our countries. Canada surely stands to lose more if that happens."

"This afternoon the prime minister's jet is leaving Ottawa for Bermuda. Since I don't have your assurance now that there will be no more 'inappropriate' behavior, I will be on the plane with Mr. McNeely. From Bermuda, we will take him home to South Carolina. Until you and I can straighten these things out, all cooperation between Canada and the U.S. on security and military matters will be suspended. I will be phoning this instruction to our representative with NATO."

"Harold, think about what you are doing."

"I've thought of nothing else since three o'clock this morning. Is there anything else we need to talk about?"

"If you change your mind, call me, this is my top priority."

Fraser punched the off button and stared at the phone. "It's reassuring that President Seekings has made this his top priority," Fraser said tautly.

*   *   *

"I want answers right now, God damn it!" President Seekings shouted, slamming his fist on the table. "You sent these men into Canada to find out what Fraser was up to with this, whatever his name is from South Carolina — and we still don't know! We don't know crap, but we've got one man being held a prisoner by the goddamned Canadians! The Canadians, for Christ's sake! The same Canadians who are throwing our people off of their bases. And — do I need to remind you very sharp intelligence men — we still have two men missing? Do you have any idea where they are?"

"Not at this time, Mr. President."

"Then WHEN?" he shouted.

He turned to the national security advisor. "I want Moore up here as soon as you can find him. I want to know where those other two morons are. I want an assessment of what our fine intelligence community thinks the Canuks are doing. Am I clear?"

"Yes, sir."

"I want to know if that son of a bitch is on that plane today or not. And General Cramer, I want a briefing as soon as you can get it of where the Eighty-second Airborne Division and the Third Infantry Division stand. I want to know when they can move with full air cover. Am I clear?"

* * *

The jet rose from the runway and banked right. Jim watched the snowbound city slide away from his view. The landscape was filled with white hills, broken only by the streams curling in frozen, glistening threads. The plane passed above a heavy layer of clouds. All he could see now were the white puffs of the top of the clouds set against a brilliant blue sky. He examined the bandages on his hands.

Fraser left a separate compartment forward and took a seat across from him.

"Eight of our F-18s will go with us to Columbia and then return with me. I want to make my position as clear as I could to President Seekings. After you rest, I would like you to educate me a little. I don't know Governor Haselden, and to be frank, I would like to know more about South Carolina before I meet him. I hadn't planned on this so soon."

As Fraser left him, Jim laid his head against the soft seat back. He needed to sleep. What had the Canadian prime minister said? He hadn't planned on this so soon. What a luxury it seemed to him now — to think life could be planned. He slid away into exhausted sleep, the bitter smile still on his lips.

*   *   *

"General, can you be ready?"

"Yes, Mr. President. We can have two dozen aircraft off the coast when the prime minister's plane approaches."

"Mr. President, there are eight F-18s with the prime minister."

"I don't give a God damn. You have your orders."

Chapter 31

He paced back and forth across the small conference room. "Try again," he barked at the man seated next to the microphone. The man, an army officer detailed to the Defense Intelligence Agency, tried again to get an answer from the phone carried by Lieutenant Erick Gilbert. "What could be the problem?" Moore shouted across the room. "Their instructions were clear, to answer any call from Washington. What the hell's wrong?"

The cellular phone was still tucked inside the pocket of Erick Gilbert's parka, but it could no longer respond to the signals beamed frantically from Washington. Gilbert and Hubbard had watched from their car outside the Chateau Laurier as more than a dozen uniformed Canadian police rushed into the hotel. They didn't need to ask themselves why. They would have to run for the U.S. border before the Canadians caught them, too, as they knew they were at that moment catching Giordono. Gilbert shouted and pounded the side of the car as they drove away from the hotel, and away from the center of the Canadian capital. He was young, Hubbard thought, and not able to accept the reality that their mission had failed, that his friend was captured. "Erick, they'll keep him a few days and let him go. The Canadians aren't going to keep an American officer in custody for long. Relax. We've got to get back across the border."

Hubbard took the wheel as soon as they were a safe distance from the hotel. Gilbert was too excited to drive. From the outskirts of Ottawa he followed only the back roads south towards the bridge over the St. Lawrence at Prescott. The snow that had fallen all day was heavier now. The narrow roads lay under a white coverlet, concealing the sheets of ice underneath. There was no traffic and Hubbard sped through the Ontario countryside quickly. What he feared most was that the Canadians would seal the crossings over the river, and armed with their descriptions, would be certain to arrest them. The tires crunched through the new fallen snow. Suddenly, the headlights seemed to stab into a void, and the road seemed to sink away below them. He realized it was a hill and took his foot from the gas pedal. The hill was steep and the car picked up more speed as it raced into the darkness. Hubbard could see the road ahead curve sharply to the right and slowly pressed the brakes. At the bottom of the hill the tires found the ice, and the car spiraled out of control. After spinning completely around, the car stopped on the shoulder of the country road.

"What the fuck are you trying to do, Felix?" Gilbert shouted.

"Relax, Erick." Hubbard turned the car around slowly. "See where we are. There's a sign." Gilbert pulled the map from the glove compartment. "South Mountain," the sign read.

"Less than thirty miles from the bridge," Gilbert said.

Hubbard drove in silence through the swirling snow over another series of hills and past the small town. Beyond it, the dark rural night swallowed the road. *Thirty minutes,* Hubbard thought, *and they would be home.* The road climbed up a hill and turned to the left. At the top, he suddenly lost sight of the road. Under his headlights, all was white. Quickly, the car was pulled down the much steeper side of the hill. He felt the rough edge of the shoulder under the tires and jerked the wheel to the left. The car slid even more swiftly down the sharp incline. Snow covered the windshield, blurring the scene ahead of him. Hubbard couldn't see the road as they raced out of control. Too late, the headlights illuminated a fence to their right. Hubbard forced the brake to the floor. The tires met the ice and slid fast and free, the car swerving wildly.

As the nose of the car crashed into the heavy wooden planks of the fence, Gilbert yelled, "God damn, Felix!" The splintering of the boards resounded through the car as the hood turned down and fell beyond the ruined fence. Below it, the headlights showed only more white.

A field, Hubbard thought, and braced for the impact. The front of the car crashed into the white surface below, the tires landing hard in the snow. The rear tires landed just as hard, and the car slid further onto the white expanse. Hubbard thought he heard a muffled cracking sound beneath them.

At once, the front of the car leapt downward through the white surface, the headlights disappearing into the dark. The car fell, slowly but steadily, turning on its side as it slid through the dark waters of the pond, swallowed by the hole in the ice. The two men watched the scene in front of them, the realization of what had happened dawning. The bottom of the pond was soft, not yet frozen from the early winter cold. The car sank four feet deep into silt on its right side. The front windshield cracked from the impact, frigid water rushing in. The force of the water anchored the men to their seats, and the freezing water began to sap the life from their bodies. The shock of the cold immobilized Hubbard. He made little effort to escape his fate. Once the water filled the car, Gilbert struggled to push himself through the front windshield and found only cold mud under his clawing hands. His scream never escaped the dark pond.

The cold, dark water ruined the phone in his pocket. Water closed around the car and the bodies of the two Americans. By morning the pond was covered in a thin sheet of ice, snow hiding the surface, and all traces of the hole they had made were gone. In the spring, the farmer who lived on the hill would find them.

* * *

Michael O'Connelly walked calmly to the podium and laid his notes in front of the microphones. The lights from the television cameras were bright. He wore no makeup for this appearance, and he would speak without a Teleprompter. Yet it was the most important speech of his life. As the timer clicked down the seconds, he wondered if the press would have covered his announcement at all if not for Brent Manzi and Howard Casselman. The seconds ticked away and the light went green. It was time.

"This evening, we find ourselves in a crisis unlike any other. It is the role of the vice president to be loyal to the president and to support his policies. I speak to you tonight fully cognizant that this is what you expected when you elected President Seekings and I. But I come to you now to tell you that the policy of this government toward South Carolina is wrong, and I can no longer support it.

"Many of you watched when Governor Haselden explained from his perspective how this crisis came about. He and his people not only came to distrust their government, but to fear it. We must face the truth about what led loyal Americans to rebellion. It was the failure of this government to ensure their safety. Instead of living up to its responsibilities, monstrous risks were taken and an unspeakable disaster was inflicted on innocent men, women and children. All that has followed is the direct result of the failure of this administration.

"Now, our country finds itself in the throes of a conflict unlike any in our history. One of our states, an equal partner in our Union, has not only severed her ties to the nation but has taken up arms against us. Some of those arms include the most hideous instruments of destruction ever devised, nuclear weapons.

"The administration has committed itself to forcing South Carolina to submit to federal authority, thereby disregarding the clear threat posed by those weapons. I can no longer be silent in the face of such a reckless policy. There are vital issues that must be addressed. No one believes more strongly than I in the preservation of the Union. But no question of policy or sovereignty is worth the risk we now face. All that matters is to move us away from the deadly confrontation that looms more threatening each day that we follow the present course.

"I call upon the president to commence negotiations with the people of South Carolina to end this conflict. We must find a way to move away from confrontation.

"The blockade that has been imposed on that state is inflicting terrible consequences on its people, people who are our fellow Americans. It is anathema to me, and I believe to most of you, that the power of the United States should be used to deny food, medicine, and sustenance to Americans. Yet that is what the armed forces of our nation are doing tonight. Every day this situation continues is another day that brings more unwarranted suffering to 3½ million of our countrymen, and that risks the ultimate cataclysm.

"I encourage you to let yourselves be heard. The futures of us all will be determined by what course this government chooses to follow in the coming days."

* * *

"Mr. President, our planes will intercept the Canadians in five minutes."

"What are their orders, Mr. President?" the secretary of defense asked nervously. Seekings ignored the question.

"General, are the planes armed?"

The air force chief of staff stared at the president, perplexed. "Yes, sir. They are fully armed."

Lee A. Brown, the secretary of state, yelled across the table, "Roger, what are you planning to do?" The generals stared at the secretary. Brown's face reddened as Seekings continued to stare at the nautical chart. *My God*, she thought, *he doesn't know what he's going to do.* "Roger, for God's sake!"

"Shut up, Lee!" Seekings turned to the air force colonel holding the headset and asked, "How long now?"

"One minute to station, sir."

"Tell the pilots to do whatever they do to activate their radar and their weapons systems."

The air force general squeezed his eyes, stunned and frightened by the ignorance of the man now leading his pilots toward a mission he had yet to reveal. He looked at the others in the room. Fear etched their faces, except for one man. C. A. Moore stood calmly by the window, arms folded across his chest, watching the president.

"The pilots have the Canadian formation in sight, Mr. President."

"Fly in front of them."

"Sir?"

"Fly in front, God damn it! Tell them to intercept them and fly right in front of the damned Canadians!"

"Mr. President ..." the general exploded, "that's very dangerous. We can't order them to do this!"

"I'm giving the orders, General. Just sit down and be quiet. Colonel tell them!"

The colonel gave the order. He was glad that only he could hear the responses of the pilots.

*　*　*

Jim McNeely saw the formation of jets speeding toward them from the north. The Canadian F-18s pulled away from the prime minister's jet. Across the aisle, he saw that a second group of jets had been spotted racing at them from the south. "Mr. Fraser," the Canadian air force officer said calmly, "two dozen American fighter jets are approaching in formation. Twelve F-18s and twelve F-14s. They appear to be intent on crossing in front of us."

"Get past them and then resume the formation."

"Yes, sir."

The Canadian planes dove below the paths of the Americans, then climbed and resumed their formation. Jim pressed his face against the window straining to see the American jets. He watched as they banked and fell in behind them.

* * *

"They resumed formation, sir."

"Tell them to lock onto the prime minister's jet with their missiles, Colonel."

"Roger! You can't do this!" Brown was screaming at him now. "He's the leader of this country's closest ally! This is madness."

"Not anymore! The bastard's taken sides against me!"

"Are you about to commit murder, Roger?" the defense secretary asked.

"Don't be ridiculous, " Seekings said.

Beads of sweat were beginning to form on the colonel's forehead.

* * *

"Mr. Prime Minister, the Americans have locked onto this plane with their missile radar." Fraser stiffened. The air force officer lifted the microphone and spoke to the pilots of his F-18s flying alongside. "Alpha Flight fall in behind the prime minister's plane. Stay between the Americans and us. Bravo Flight take up positions behind the Americans. Lock onto the planes that have targeted us."

Jim watched as the Canadian F-18s peeled away and raced in the opposite direction. He looked at his right hand, the knuckles tense and pale, and realized he was gripping the armrest. Across the aisle he saw Peter Crandal frozen in the same helpless fear.

* * *

"Tell the man in charge down there to order Fraser to turn back!" Seekings yelled at the air force colonel. Now fighting to stay calm, the colonel gave the order.

"Think what you're doing," the defense secretary said quietly. "Stop this now."

"The Canadians have taken positions behind our planes, Mr. President. They've locked onto us with their own missile radar."

Seekings jerked his head in the direction of the colonel.

"Mr. President, the prime minister will cross over the coast of South Carolina in five minutes."

* * *

"Tell the son of a bitch that the prime minister of Canada does not take orders at the end of a fucking gun! Tell him exactly that, Major!" Fraser shouted. The major nervously repeated the prime minister's exclamation to the American flight leader.

Suddenly, there was a deafening roar, and the jet was buffeted by air wash as twenty-six F-16s sped overhead. Jim strained to see the jets. The twin formations to their rear quickly dispersed in the wake of the new arrivals. Two of the F-16s slid next to the prime minister's jet. Jim saw the blue and white palmetto emblem of South Carolina's Air National Guard on the tail fins. "Prime Minister, the pilot of the jet on our starboard side would like to speak with you, sir."

Fraser took the earphones, "Governor Haselden sends his regards, Mr. Fraser. Welcome to South Carolina. If you all will follow us, we'll be landing in just a few minutes."

* * *

"Mr. President? What are your orders, sir?" The colonel studied Seekings' face expectantly.

Seekings was rigid, his head hung slightly forward and his hands stretched out, the palms pushing down on the table. His answer was nearly a whisper, "Tell them to go the hell home." But for the sound of the colonel conveying the welcome order to break off and return to base, there was utter silence. The two cabinet secretaries walked stiffly from the room followed by the air force general, leaving the president alone with the colonel and Moore.

At four o'clock that afternoon, a single envelope arrived at the White House by special courier from the Pentagon office of the secretary of defense. It contained his resignation. Fifteen minutes later, the resignation of Lee A. Brown was delivered from the State Department. The air force chief of staff handed his resignation personally to Norman Cramer, drove home, and quickly drank four glasses of Scotch before he could steady himself enough to tell his wife what had happened.

* * *

"Roger? Is that you? What time is it?"

"It's one here. Midnight out there." The president sat on the edge of the bed. Sleep would not come even after the drinks he made for himself at the small bar in his bedroom. He had always mistrusted drugs of any kind. Though it would have been a simple matter to order medication to ease him into the rest he needed so badly, he refused to consider it. "Melanie, how are you?"

"Fine, Dear. Is something wrong?"

"No. I just wanted to hear your voice."

His wife had already heard the signals in his voice, and correctly read the reflection of fear in her husband. "What is it, Roger?"

Roger Seekings was frightened as never before in his life. He was acutely sensitive to the feel of the house that surrounded him. Its name alone symbolized what powerful men sacrificed themselves for. It was at once a lifetime's goal and the thief of all that was personal to the one who claimed it as his prize. Its modest lines belied its power. Beyond empire and more profound than the absurd Cold War rubric "Super Power," it was home to a power unique in the history of the world. From this house radiated influence and outright control never before imagined. Few were the stubborn, mostly impotent, corners of the earth beyond the reach of the person who lived here. But the cost was subordination to service of its power. He knew that the only unredeemable failure was one that lessened its reach.

"I'm afraid."

"Of what?"

"I don't have long to end this rebellion. There is no option left ... except the worst of all." He took a swallow from the glass on the table. "If I let them stay out, my political life will be over. And history will remember me as the man who presided over the breakup of the Union."

"Roger, maybe the best thing is to walk away. It's become too personal. Let someone else work this out." It was what she wanted. What she had wanted for a very long time. "Step down, for the sake of the country; tell them that."

"I can't. After all I've invested, to submit — to slink away, a failure — would be too much. My name would be the joke of every school kid for a century."

"Is that what matters now, Roger? Is how history thinks of you really the most important thing?"

Silence greeted her question at first, until finally her husband's voice answered her, strong again, "Yes."

*   *   *

The statements that were issued at noon the following day were brief. The governments of Canada and South Carolina had agreed to explore terms for a union of the two nations, they said. The announcements were released without comment by the prime minister in Ottawa and the governor in Columbia.

The Canadian papers hailed Fraser's courage. In South Carolina there were questions about what such a thing would mean, but the suggestion that there was *any* option for the state gave birth to hope, an almost intoxicating relief from the pervasive fear that had consumed the population since secession. In the U.S., the news incited violent debate. There were few who took the middle ground between anger at the Seekings Administration for provoking the disaster and rage at the Canadians.

*   *   *

At the airport, the Canadian air force major approached Peter Crandal. "Pete, the prime minister wants you to remain here as his liaison. You are to report each day back to Ottawa."

"You want me to report if there's a chance of someone popping a nuke, right?"

The major looked impassively at Crandal. "Yes."

The prime minister's jet rose from the runway, followed by the Canadian F-18s. The formation turned east across the suburbs of the city. As the fields and swamps slid below them, the major turned to Fraser, "Mr. Prime Minister, do you think they will use nuclear weapons if it comes to that?"

Fraser studied the landscape fast disappearing under the clouds. "It isn't 'they,' Major. It's one man. Their governor has the power alone to use them. And I have no idea what he'll do."

* * *

General Cramer walked into the president's office followed by the national security advisor. C. A. Moore was already there.

He had expected a violent tirade in response to the Canadian proposal. The general found himself more alarmed by the unnatural calm in Seekings.

"This afternoon, I will send a private message to Haselden. It will be an ultimatum to end this in five days. No more. If all nuclear weapons seized from our arsenal are not returned by that time, I will recover them by force, and I will restore order in South Carolina."

"Mr. President...."

"I know what you think, General. Here is an order I have signed relieving you of any responsibility over this operation. The same order directs that all command and control for this operation will be from the White House. C. A. will be in charge. The task force and division commanders will take their orders from him."

The NSA interjected. "Mr. President, the risk of a nuclear—"

"There is no risk. What I want from you both is round-the-clock assessment of any place in the world where someone, anyone, appears to be about to take advantage of this distraction. Unless you gentlemen also wish to resign."

Neither man responded.

"Good. At the end of the five days, I will begin a series of attacks to destroy the will of these people. The first attacks will be with warning and without casualties. The later ones, if they are necessary, will be without warning. If that doesn't work, the Eighty-second Division, with elements of the Tenth Division, will proceed from Fort Bragg, and the Third Division will proceed from Savannah — and I will occupy the entire goddamned, godforsaken state. Am I clear, gentlemen?"

*   *   *

Blackie walked to the top of the rostrum in the senate chamber and took his seat. The resignation two days before of the lieutenant governor because of bad health left a gap in leadership that could not be tolerated … not now. The chief justice strode to the center of the rostrum, accompanied by Patrick Collins. Collins placed his hand on the Bible. Collins repeated the oath, "I, Patrick Lloyd Collins, do solemnly swear that I am duly qualified according to the Constitution of South Carolina, to exercise the duties of the office of lieutenant governor.…" Now, it was done, Collins thought. He had accepted Haselden's offer of appointment to a job he never wanted. His professional life had been as a builder, a solver of problems. He couldn't refuse the plea to help solve the most frightening problem of his life. Gone were the old rules and formulas. Collins would devote himself to finding new ones. He turned and faced the senators.

"Ladies and gentlemen, it seems appropriate to dispense with any speech today. Most of you know me already. Our full attention is required by the proposal that is on your desks. He began to read, and the first words made him pause, "The proposal reads, 'Her Majesty's Government in Canada proposes to the State of South Carolina union of the two nations within the Canadian Confederation.…'"

He announced that they must begin debate at once. "I needn't remind you that yesterday the government of the United States issued an ultimatum demanding our submission to federal authority in four days. There is no time to waste."

*   *   *

He was only dimly conscious of Arlington's suburban sprawl of office towers lining both sides of the expressway. They blended unnoticed by him into the gray December sky. The cars rushing impatiently around him seemed part of someone else's world. He told himself it was already a world where he didn't belong. The familiar, terrible guilt embraced him, wrapping him completely in its seductive imitation of comfort. Staff Sergeant Terry Wilkins had made his decision to escape the prison of horror he had constructed for himself.

At the apartment complex, he pulled into a parking space at the far corner of the lot. He paused a moment, looking at the dingy, square, red-brick buildings. Clicking the latch released the door to the glove compartment. He lifted the folded road maps and pulled the gun from underneath. Expertly, he pulled the clip out and made sure it held a full rack of bullets. He slapped the clip back into the handle, shoved the pistol into the pocket of his black uniform jacket, and glanced at his watch. It would be a few minutes before Paul arrived. Paul was the worst part of it, he realized. What a way to repay the compassion of this man who had asked nothing from him.

Wilkins stepped from the car and walked across the parking lot and into the apartment. At the kitchen table that sat behind the couch, he pulled the note from his pocket and carefully unfolded it, smoothing out the creases. It was impossible to convey what he did not fully understand himself. The reasons would die with him. He had told them when to look for the train and where it would come. He had told them because he couldn't face the truth about himself that they threatened to unveil. They had tapes. And he had no courage. He was condemned to see the burned, dying faces of the children every night. When he slept, he heard their voices strained by agony asking him why. He placed a salt shaker on the corner of the single page, looked at the room and walked back into the hallway. At the end of the corridor were the steps to the roof. A few lounge chairs sat around the asphalt surface near the parapet edge. Long-abandoned beer cans were scattered under them.

He sat in the nearest chair and gazed at the gray sky. *It is going to rain all night,* he thought. *Tomorrow will be a bad morning to run.* He pulled the pistol from his pocket. Without hesitation, he cocked the gun, loading a bullet into the chamber. Bending his arm upwards, he laid the barrel next to his temple. The metal was cold against his skin. He removed the gun and laid it in his lap. Then lifting it again, he slid the barrel between his lips and into his mouth.

* * *

Paul Gregg saw Wilkins' car as soon as he turned into the parking lot. He grabbed his bag from the back seat and headed for the front door of the building. His apartment door was open. His call to Wilkins went unanswered. He looked in Wilkins' room. Walking back to the kitchen, he saw the creased paper under the salt shaker. He picked up the note and read the terrifying message so carefully typed. Frantically, he looked around the room. The unlocked door. And no sign that Wilkins had changed out of his uniform.

Gregg ran to the door and flung it open, the knob crashing into the sheetrock wall. He sprinted down the corridor and leapt up the steps three at a time. Grabbing the top step with his hands, he vaulted noisily onto the roof. There he saw Wilkins in one of the lounge chairs. Gregg was looking at his back, but he saw clearly enough the gun in his mouth. He stopped, horrified into stillness by the sight. His breathing was labored, not so much from the run up the stairs, as the effect of what he saw.

"Terry ... it's Paul."

"Go back downstairs, Paul," he slid the gun barrel from his mouth and mumbled without looking.

"No. Put the gun down. Just put it down."

"There's no other way. Go away. I don't want you to see."

"I ain't going anywhere. If you're intent on blowing your brains out, I guess I'll have to watch." Gregg's breathing was even more strained than before.

"Go away," Wilkins said, sobbing now. "Get away from me."

"No." He walked slowly around the chair and stood facing him. He saw the tears running freely down his friend's face. He sank to his knees so that his face was level with the arm that held the pistol, still pointed at Wilkins' mouth. "No."

The young soldier closed his eyes and cried, his arm fixed in its position, the pistol unmoved.

"Give me the gun. You don't want to do this ... think about your boy, Terry."

At that moment, Terry Wilkins resolved not to take the final action, to pull the trigger that would end the nightmares forever. He hesitated a second, long enough to see the face of the son his friend had called on him to remember.

Slowly, the pistol slid from his mouth. Gregg carefully grasped Wilkins' hand and folded his own fingers around the gun. He pushed the safety on and pulled the gun away. "Get up, Terry.... Come on, stand up."

Wilkins looked up at the marine towering over him and stood. "You're going to get through this. Whatever else happens, you're going to get your life back. Trust me." He circled his friend in a powerful embrace. They held each other as the rain that would last all night began to fall.

* * *

"My benefactors have been most impressed with the courage of your people. To face the greatest power on earth is a challenge to make even the bravest falter."

Jim McNeely wondered what this one wanted. *How do they all get here?* he thought. The man seated across from him described himself as a Turkish investor. Only the most recent in the stream of ethereal visitors, this one said he came to bring greetings from one who was interested in doing business with the new republic.

Knowing the answer, Jim asked, "What sort of business is your friend interested in?"

"You have something of great value, my friend. My benefactor is able to pay handsomely. I am sure we can arrange for business that will be of mutual benefit." Jim stared into the dark eyes above the false smile.

"My country will not be selling any nuclear materials. I'm afraid we have nothing to discuss, sir." Jim got up, glad to end this meeting.

"Patience, patience, my friend. You misunderstand me. We will discuss the details of our business another time. That is not my purpose today." Jim resumed his seat. The man reached into this satchel and retrieved a manila envelope. He placed it on the table before them and slid it toward Jim with his finger. "It is an offering of goodwill," he said, waving his hand generously. "Please, have a look. Take them."

Jim opened the envelope and pulled out two stacks of photographs. They were from a satellite. He looked at the smiling man across the table. "Your military people will recognize them, I am sure. These," he said, pointing to the first stack of Chinese photographs, "show the Eighty-second Division mobilizing. These show what I am told is a forward assembly area near a town called — I am not sure of the pronunciation — Laurinburg in North Carolina. These show large elements of the Tenth Division arriving at Fayetteville. The rest show the Third Division in Georgia." He leaned back and smiled broadly at Jim. "It is our gift. A gesture of good will. There will be more as ... matters develop ... to help you see what the Americans are doing."

The man left the small office used by McNeely in the Edgar Brown Building. He was an Iraqi, not a Turk. His government had been happy to assist the Chinese by delivering the photographs, and soon, he would deliver more, as the American army prepared for the inevitable invasion of this American province. He would bring more than photographs next time. His Chinese contact assured him he would be supplied with precise details of the invasion — called an occupation by the Americans. The tens of millions of Chinese dollars invested in American political campaigns was now bearing fruit, the Chinese agent explained. Little information in the American government was beyond their reach.

The means did not matter to the Iraqi. All that mattered was that he could help bring about the long-hoped-for revenge of his country on these most hated of peoples.

* * *

In Fayetteville, the mass movement of equipment and soldiers intensified daily. The units of the Tenth Division arrived and were shuttled quickly to the assembly area on the outskirts of Fort Bragg. Forty miles southwest of Savannah, the scene was the same at Fort Stewart, home of the Third Division. None of the activity was missed by the increasingly nervous people of North Carolina and Georgia and their political leaders.

The governors of both states called the president as soon as they received word of the mobilization. "What was to guarantee that no nuclear weapons would be used?" they asked. Wasn't there some other way to straighten this out? The governor of Georgia became angry at the president's unwillingness to even discuss his concerns. What if he denied the army the ability to stage an invasion from Georgia?

"A traitor? You call me that, you arrogant bastard!" he yelled at the president. The governor had fought his way through Georgia politics all the way from Valdosta, and he was not ready to be condescended to by the president, certainly not over the safety of his own people. "Don't screw with me, Roger."

Seekings asked Moore to establish surveillance on the offices of both governors. It wouldn't be for long. He couldn't afford any more interference.

* * *

The door to the governor's office opened suddenly. A lieutenant walked quickly to General Demers and handed him a single sheet of paper. The young man's face was tense. "Excuse me, Governor," Demers said, and removed his glasses to read the message. He wiped his forehead and turned to Blackie. "Governor, we have received word from the U.S. task force commander that in six hours there will be a series of attacks on some of our installations." He glanced at the sheet again, "The hangers at Charleston Air Force Base, the flight operations building at Beaufort Marine Corps Air Station, the headquarters building at Shaw Air Force Base, and the communications center at McIntyre. Orders have already been issued to evacuate these facilities and surrounding areas."

The faces surrounding him were masks of shock, except for that of the governor. "What can we do to stop the attacks, General?"

Demers answered, clutching the paper, staring at the words he had yet to read. "If they send cruise missiles — nothing. We have no defense against them."

"I see," Blackie said.

"Governor, there is more." The silence around the table became more ominous. "If we do not submit to federal authority by tomorrow at noon, a second series of attacks will be initiated. Those will be without warning. There will be casualties."

"Where are the ships armed with the cruise missiles, General?"

"Offshore, Governor."

"Can our planes reach them? Hit them?" Demers stared at Blackie, the hard lines of his face not concealing the anguish that was roiling inside him.

"They can reach the ships. But the carrier and the rest of the task force would detect them the instant they took off. If any got close enough to fire, it would be suicide. I'm sorry, Governor. They can fire at us with impunity." Collins saw that Demers' hands were tightly balled into fists.

"All right, Harrison. Please give me our options as soon as you can." Blackie looked wearily at the others, "I suppose the president has given us his answer, gentlemen. We'd better get to work. Is there any doubt now about the Canadian proposal?"

* * *

Moore took his seat in the small room in the basement of the White House. It would be only minutes now. Soon, it would all be over. No one in that place would have the balls to stand up to the United States government after they saw what he was about to unleash. A narcotic calm enveloped him.

He handed an envelope to the navy lieutenant behind him. "Get that to the fleet commander. Tell him to ensure that all checkpoints are alerted to the order." His smile made the lieutenant uneasy. "And fax it to this number." As the time for the attacks arrived, the lieutenant sent Moore's message to the admiral aboard the USS *John F. Kennedy*. Then he faxed it to the office being used by Jim McNeely. The great events about to unfold allowed him to settle a much older score. The message was brief:

> *Commander John Matthew Reicher, formerly the executive officer of the Naval Weapons Station, Charleston, is to be apprehended by any American forces that come into contact with him. He is believed to have cooperated with the rebellious forces in South Carolina in their seizure of U.S. nuclear weapons. He is wanted for treason.*

* * *

The admiral glanced one last time at the clock on the bridge of the *Kennedy*. It was clear that no order was going to arrive canceling the strikes. "Commence the operation," he said simply. In seconds, orders were flashed to the destroyers cruising beyond his sight. The captains of the three ships received the order. Each turned into the wind and began the sequence leading to the launch of their Tomahawks. In minutes, three dozen of the missiles, each carrying a 317-kilogram warhead, were speeding across the surface of the Atlantic toward the coast of South Carolina. He noted the timing. *All for effect*, he thought. *Three hours until sunset. Plenty of time to see the effect of the blasts and survey the damage in broad daylight.* Silently, he prayed the people on the other side wouldn't respond.

Twelve minutes after their launch, the missiles directed to the Charleston Air Force Base found their marks. Five hangers dissolved in bright balls of flame, the metal beams and roofing shrieking as they collapsed into useless, smoking mesh. Shortly, after that, Tomahawks pierced the wall of the flight operations building of what had been the Marine Corps Air Station in Beaufort with similar effect. Five minutes later, explosions rocked McIntyre Air Base, outside Columbia, and Shaw, outside Sumter. In less than twenty minutes it was all over. The warning had been heeded and there were no casualties.

Minutes after the cruise missiles destroyed the hangers in Charleston, a pair of Harriers streaked low over the water from the *Kennedy*, ostensibly to observe the damage to the base. Quickly, they circled the burning ruins of the hangers and headed south toward the ocean. Over the peninsula of Charleston's old city, one of the Harriers signaled his partner to proceed and peeled to the left over the Battery, the park of oak trees and Civil War cannon at the city's tip overlooking the harbor. The pilot had special orders. He had studied the map of the city provided with his mission packet the night before and again that morning. It was easy to read the streets, and the hover jet made it simple to "walk" his aircraft to exactly the right spot. *Hell,* he thought, *I could deliver the mail.*

There it was, easy to find. Right at the corner of two narrow streets lined with neat, two-story houses and small, square yards. It reminded him of his grandparents' neighborhood in Columbus. The house looked just like the picture, white, two-story frame, with a columned porch across the first story. Ivy hugged the brick foundation. It was a shame....

The pilot held the Harrier steady, hovering over Gibbes Street and took aim at the corner of the home of Patrick Collins. He pressed the button, and the jet jumped slightly as the 30-mm cannon sent a stream of shells tearing through the thin wooden siding. Shattered boards fell in ragged pieces. The thick, heavy shells ripped into the framing of the old house, finally severing the supports of the front half. As terrified neighbors watched, the building sagged, then rapidly disintegrated, the pieces sliding into a ruined pile of boards, beams, and furniture. The pilot shifted slightly to the right and continued his assault on the Collins home. Quickly, the rear of the structure also collapsed under the ferocious assault of the 30-mm shells. Under the ruins of the house, a broken floor beam crushed the line feeding gas into the kitchen. The next burst of shells from the Harrier ignited the gas in a sudden howling eruption of flame that shattered windows of the neighboring dwellings.

The pilot hadn't expected a gas explosion. The wall of flame to his front nearly caused him to lose control of the jet. Grabbing the throttle, he accelerated and pulled the Harrier rapidly into the sky over the city. Behind him he saw the black smoke of the burning rubble that had been Collins' house.

From blocks away, neighbors gathered and watched as fire trucks raced to the scene. They asked themselves where Liz Collins was. Word spread through the small crowd that she was in Columbia with Pat. The fire hoses extinguished the fire before it engulfed other homes. The stunned observers continued to stare at the smoldering, blackened ruins of thirty years of Liz and Pat Collins' life together.

Their surprise and fear quickly gave way to another, more permanent, emotion. Rage.

*   *   *

The attacks succeeded in one respect. They frightened the people of South Carolina. News of the missile assault reached every corner of the state in minutes. Their message was crystal clear. "We can hit you anywhere... anytime... we want. And with impunity."

Had it not been for news of the other singular attacks by the lone Harrier, the message might have accomplished its goal entirely. But news of the destruction of Patrick Collins' house by a single American jet fighter engendered not more fear, but a wave of violent wrath more intense than any since the crisis had begun. Pictures of the smoking rubble flashed across television screens, and for the first time, there were loud calls from one end of the state to the other, bitter demands that Governor Haselden hit the bastards back.

The radio and television broadcasts were also picked up in North Carolina and Georgia. The news inflamed the panic that had been building in the communities nearest the growing concentrations of troops. Pictures of the destroyed house in Charleston sparked wholesale flight by the frightened residents. Offshore, onboard the American task force ships the sailors and officers also watched and listened. Among them was Petty Officer Dave Walensa on the USS *Deyo*.

*   *   *

Peter Crandal drove Jim McNeely's car down the interstate towards Charleston. The navy's attacks, particularly the destruction of Collins' house, left Jim no choice but to remove his family from Charleston. Alicia had reluctantly agreed when he called her. Crandal offered to help them pack and move to the family's farm outside Andrews. The two men said little on the two-hour drive.

Following Jim's directions, Crandal drove past the office where the sign proclaimed the offices of Holland, Rollins, Jerald, & McNeely. Jim wondered where they all were. His last contact with anyone had been a short telephone call to Drew Holland weeks before. He wondered where they all were… and if they would ever return to the empty old building, to the life that seemed irretrievably remote from the mad world that had taken its place.

"Daddy, Daddy!" Katherine raced from the bottom of the front steps where she had been waiting for his arrival. "Why can't you go with us?" she asked after she released his neck from a crushing hug. "I miss you."

Carrying her toward the house, he said, "I will come and stay with you, but I need to work a while first. O.K.?"

"No," she pouted.

Crandal followed them up the steps to the front door. Standing Katherine carefully on the floor of the hall, Jim took Alicia into his arms. Her hands trembled as she held him, searching for some comfort in a world racing deeper into chaos. Peter stood behind them watching, embarrassed. Letting Jim go at last, Alicia reached for Peter's hand. "I should hug you, Mr. Crandal. We owe you a lot."

When the packing of Jim's van was complete, Alicia set the table for dinner. Jim watched in surprise as she pulled china and crystal from the cabinets. John and Katherine laid silver next to the plates. "I guess this seems odd, doesn't it? But if someone's going to tear down my house, I want to have one more classy meal here first." They ate a leisurely dinner in flickering candlelight. The chaos beyond the walls of the dining room seemed to drift away.

John hadn't said much since his father had arrived. "Dad, are we going to fight back? Why do we have to just keep on taking it?" Jim looked at his son, the anger plain in his young eyes.

"I wish I knew the answer, Son. We just want to be left alone."

"But they won't leave us alone. Next time, what if people get killed?"

There was no answer, he knew. And yet, he had to try. "Those are hard decisions. We have to fight with what we have. If we become part of Canada, we'll be safe. That might be the best way to protect ourselves." The boy pulled part of his lip inside his mouth, a childhood habit that told Jim he was trying hard to understand his father's explanation. The realization that his children needed him — and that he was not there — stung sharply.

Jim looked at Crandal and Alicia. They shared the unspoken understanding that it was much too soon for reassurance.

* * *

DeSilva woke as Jim stepped across the tile floor. "Counselor ... how goes the rebellion?" He had been in the hospital for a week battling the most ferocious attack of the leukemia.

Jim took the hand held up for him, still surprised at the rapid frailty that cancer inflicted on its victims. "I can't lie to you, Doctor." He pointed to the television set. "You see how it's going. There is no reason on their side. It frightens me."

"And your side?"

The eyes that watched him were tired, but knowing. "Reason is perishable."

"A hard lesson."

Tony began to cough, causing Jim to wince. When Tony was quiet, Jim said, "One thing is certain, Doctor. Because of you, the worst of the contamination in Florence is gone. Generations will owe you a debt that can never be repaid." Jim felt the tears come as he spoke.

DeSilva smiled. "Say, do you think they could bring me a little bourbon with my coffee?" Jim laughed.

"All ready taken care of, Doc."

"Matt Reicher is here now. They closed the hospital he was in. Too many doctors have left and there weren't any supplies. Room 907. He's been ready to get out for a week." Jim's face darkened

"I told you I'd ask you for full payment for my services one day. Now's the time," DeSilva added.

"Anything."

"Promise me that if your people decide to fire a nuclear weapon at the other side, you will come and tell me."

Jim stared at the dying man, unable to comprehend his request, but unable to refuse him anything.

"Sure, Doctor."

* * *

The look on the face was no less cold than before. Matt Reicher seemed to have recovered, although Jim knew well enough that if he still suffered any effects from the shooting, he would never show them.

"I have to get out of here. My family needs me." Jim watched him for a moment before handing him the message sent to the task force ordering his arrest for treason. He closed his eyes and his hand crushed the paper into a ball. His chest swelled in anger, "That no-good bastard!"

"Matt, I can smuggle you over into North Carolina. But with this, I can't get your things out." Matt glared at him. "It's dangerous at the border now. It's a no-man's land of smugglers and cutthroats. But with some help on the other side that I believe I can count on, I can get you across. There's a lake up near Mullins. With a boat, you can row across. I'll get you a couple of guns." Matt walked to the window and leaned on the sill. "Is that what you want, Matt?"

"What choice do I have?"

* * *

"Blackie, do you think they'll do it? Kill people, I mean?" The final deadline had passed hours before. Now, in the dark of evening, apprehension began to spread across the state. June Haselden was afraid of many things as the cloudy night sky covered Columbia. She agreed they would not abandon the mansion. Blackie would never have gone in any event. The feel of impending tragedy was palpable, and she was as fearful as anyone over the prospect of the death that another flight of missiles might bring.

But Blackie Haselden's wife was also afraid for the man she loved. Tension accompanied him like a shadow, one that grew longer and darker with each worsening of the crisis. She missed his laugh, but understood these dark times didn't permit it. She missed his touch and the passion of his body, but knew those things had to be stored away until the conflict was over. What she could not accept was the distance between them that grew as he was carried further and further away by the tide of events swirling around them. Only rarely now did his eyes meet hers. His words seemed remote, meant not so much for her as for anyone who happened to listen. He was a man who had never functioned alone, who needed those closest to him for balance. She was worried about what was happening to him as he slipped deeper into isolation.

"Yes. I believe they will do it."

She wrapped her arms around him. "No," she whispered.

"If we have time, we can vote to join the Canadians. It's the only chance we have."

"Love me, Blackie," she cried, unable to control her sorrow any longer. "Hold me."

* * *

"Mr. Prime Minister, there will most certainly be a second attack by the American task force on South Carolina. Constable Crandal's reports confirm that there is a demand for retaliation. We may be close to a nuclear response."

"How soon can our fleet get to Charleston?"

"In two days, Prime Minister. The British will rendezvous from Bermuda."

* * *

This was the worst order. He knew it was coming, but had prayed as earnestly as ever in his life that it would not. The admiral took the message handed to him, flashed from the White House. *From this asshole Moore.* He could not speak the words and could only hand it to the aide next to him. He knew that in minutes, more Tomahawks would streak for the coast — the coast of the United States — and strike targets selected, he was certain, so that people would die. *Damn them,* he railed inside himself. *Damn us all.*

On the *Deyo*, Dave Walensa saw the flash message light up the machine in a sudden static of activity. He was startled by the "flash" identification on the message. It meant the ship's response had to be accomplished in only minutes. Ever since the last launch of missiles, he had feared there would be more. For two nights he worried that the order would come to unleash a strike that would threaten the person who had come to mean everything to him. Carol was there, beyond the coast where they aimed their deadly missiles. The first strike — he learned from the guy who read the OP order — had been with warning, and directed only at empty buildings. Only that knowledge had calmed his panic.

This message was another OP order directing the *Deyo*, along with other ships and planes from the fleet, to launch a second attack, larger and without warning. The time set by the order was less than fifteen minutes away. He scanned the order for the coordinates assigned to the *Deyo*. On his computer, he brought up the mapping program and entered the coordinates. In seconds, the screen filled with a description of the site, a farm of huge storage tanks filled with jet fuel. Filling the bottom of the screen was a map. A cold recognition enveloped him. He knew the streets. He remembered the tanks very well. Carol's condominium was just beyond the fence of the tank farm.

* * *

The planes from the *Kennedy* approached low over the water where the Atlantic met St. Helena Sound. They followed the water and shortly saw ahead of them the lights of the former Beaufort Marine Corps Air Station. It was childishly easy. The base had no early detection. No warning. Prayers filled the cockpits, asking God to please let this be the end, the last sacrifice. Some asked for divine forgiveness.

They found their targets and one by one executed their attack runs. The first missiles struck the fuel storage area with dramatic effect. Plumes of violent orange flame exploded into the night sky until seven of the tanks were raging infernos. The guards nearest the tanks were killed instantly by the blast, others were covered with flaming fuel. Other missiles found their marks in hangers and in jets parked along the runways. More explosions followed. One missile, meant for the headquarters building, missed the corner and instead detonated inside a barracks, bringing mercifully quick deaths to the two dozen guard soldiers sleeping there. The jets left the air station alight with an erratic pattern of fires, and with forty-three dead soldiers.

* * *

Walensa ripped the printed OP order from the machine and ran from the communications center. His heavy footsteps clanked on the deck of the *Deyo* as he ran for the bridge. Bursting onto the bridge, he walked straight to Commander Horres. "Captain, we can't do this!"

Horres took the message and read it impassively. "Why not, Walensa?"

"Captain, there are people who live right here ... look...." He shoved the map he had printed from the computer at his captain. Horres studied the map and the coordinates. He looked up at the excited young sailor. "If we do this, anyone in these buildings will die. Captain, the woman I'm going to marry lives right here!" he shouted. "This is murder! Is that what we are? Murderers?"

A stunned silence settled over the bridge. All eyes turned to Horres, whose calm expression belied the terrible turmoil inside him. He had never disobeyed an order. But the young sailor was right. Their orders *were* murder. And they were orders from a piss-ant civilian asshole. Like every commander in the task force, he knew that the joint chiefs of staff were isolated from this operation. Two cabinet members had resigned. The vice president had declared himself in open opposition to the president. Horres had been stationed in Charleston many years before and could not fathom any justification for killing people there. He had told himself a hundred times since this madness started that it didn't matter, that all he needed to do was follow his orders. But that was a lie. Now here was young Walensa asking him not to kill the woman he loved. *God damn the bastards who brought us to this.*

"Let me see this, Walensa. These coordinates are wrong. Come here." They walked to the chart table and he pulled out the chart of Charleston Harbor. After a moment, Horres pointed to a spot in the center of the shipping channel, just at the head of the harbor where the Cooper and Wando Rivers joined. "This is the correct spot. Replot the coordinates for right there. Then fire the Tomahawks."

Walensa stared at him a moment before he realized what he'd said. "Yes, sir. Right away, sir."

Minutes later, the *Deyo's* forward missile tubes discharged their Tomahawks in blasts of bright orange light. The missiles settled into their paths, skimming the Atlantic's waves, rocketing toward Charleston Harbor. Seven minutes later, they streaked over Fort Sumter, a dozen fingers of light headed for the twin spans over the Wando River.

Driving over the Cooper River span of the bridge, Corporal Chapman, a veteran patrolman on Charleston's police force, was making his late-night round across the bridges. He spotted the streaks of light racing toward the Wando span. Instinctively, he stopped and ran to the rail of the bridge. Before he reached the edge, three explosions — then two more — rocked the bridge, hurling him to the roadway.

Five of the missiles failed to negotiate the openings under the bridge. Five explosions, each throwing 454 kilograms of explosive force against the piers, crushed the concrete structures. Slowly at first, then rapidly, the Wando spans of both bridges began to collapse. The steel girders of the old suspension bridges howled as they twisted and bent under the weight of the dying structure. When Chapman pulled himself up from the roadbed and peered cautiously over the rail, all he saw was a tangle of girders protruding from the dark river where the two soaring spans had stood only minutes before.

* * *

On the *John Rogers,* the captain watched the tracks of the *Deyo's* missiles recorded by his communication center. He saw at once what Ed Horres had done. It resolved his own dilemma. "Lietuenant, get me a chart of the target area, please." After a moment of studying the chart, he said, "These coordinates are wrong. Replot them for this spot here."

"Captain, that's—"

"Yes, Lieutenant, it is. Replot them."

"Yes, sir."

Twenty minutes later a dozen Tomahawk missiles from *John Rogers* skimmed the pine and oak forest around the remote hamlet of Cross. Responding to their new coordinates, they crossed the edge of Lake Marion and, seconds later, plunged themselves harmlessly into the shallow waters of the lake.

Chapter 32

Mark Bryan.

Dean Felbar.

The names spilled from the list, cool and detached from the humanity they represented.

Wade Norton.

Timothy Sommer.

Gene Rankin.

Names of forty-three men who would never answer to them again. The governor studied the list alone in his office and read each one, sounding out the syllables.

Robert Driggers.

Was he one of the Driggers he knew? Farmers from Lake City whom he always visited when he used to campaign for the legislature. How old was this one? A staff sergeant. Forty-three dead soldiers in Beaufort. Sons, fathers, husbands, and brothers gone forever. He had no tears left to shed over the list sent to him by General Demers.

But there was anger enough to take their place. He read the list again, speaking the names aloud, softly — lost names spoken quietly in the governor's office, relics of lives stolen by a monstrous wrong.

With the list were reports of the damage to the base. He scanned the careful paragraphs. Hangers, an office building, and a barracks — God, why did it have to be the barracks? Blackie read the report of the destruction of the Cooper River Bridges and tossed the sheet towards the stack on his desk. *Another perverse message from the president,* he thought bitterly. He ignored the reports of the many missiles that careened aimlessly into the harbor and an entire flight that disappeared into the lake. All he could see were forty-three young faces.

*   *   *

"Sergeant Gregg ... I don't understand how you fit into this."

The navy commander stared at the note Terry Wilkins left on Gregg's table, the cryptic message of farewell. Gregg explained the essential details of Wilkins' dilemma, and how he was blackmailed for details about the nuclear train in South Carolina.

"I was just a friend of Wilkins, and he confided in me. Now, he needs to tell his story, sir. Keeping it all bottled up almost killed him." The big marine studied his boss' confused face. Gregg knew there had only been a slender chance he would avoid revealing his own secret. "This C. A. Moore was keeping guys ... keeping them for sex ... and in return he got them top slots. He put their careers on the fast track. Sergeant Wilkins was one of those guys. And he made a pretty big target for whatever scumbags wanted to get at that train."

"So you're telling me this Wilkins sold out his country. Why should I do anything but turn him in to the FBI?"

Gregg hesitated. "Wilkins isn't the real bad guy, sir." The anger began to rise in Gregg as he spoke. "Moore is this big-shot White House aide, and he's out there buying soldiers to be his playmates. How long was it going to be before somebody took advantage?" He studied the tops of his shoes a moment before going on. "Terry's got a lot to answer for. But he's got the balls to tell the truth. It looks to me like most of what's happening right now started with C. A."

"With C. A.," the officer repeated Gregg's familiar reference to Moore. Now he saw it. *Good God*, he thought. With new, disbelieving eyes, he appraised the marine standing before him. "Gregg, you said Moore was out there buying 'soldiers.' Plural. How do you know Wilkins wasn't the only one?"

This was the moment Gregg had feared for so long. "Because I was there before him. That's how I got my job here." Now his words escaped like water behind a collapsing dam. "He's a crazy motherfucker, Commander. Scary and cruel. He's nothing but danger. I saw what was going on with Wilkins as soon as he got here. So, I warned him. I don't know why. I just couldn't watch somebody get all screwed up out there on the farm and not say something."

"You said this almost cost Wilkins his life."

"I found him on the roof with a pistol in his mouth." The navy officer flinched. "I took it away from him. He blames himself for all those people that died."

"My God." The officer rubbed his chin, lifted his glasses, and ran his hand across his face. "So, Gregg, what was it all about out there on the farm? You guys were just playing along to fast track your careers, or what?"

"You mean, were we gay?"

"I guess that's what I mean, yeah."

"Not Wilkins."

The commander stared at Gregg a moment. Standing from his desk, he tapped the marine's shoulder. "Let's go see the admiral. Shit, this is going to blow the roof off this five-sided box."

* * *

"These are less than twenty-four hours old." Jim McNeely spread the photographs across the small desk. "Everything is in place. I am sure you can see that, as a military man." The Iraqi smiled continuously as he handed Jim more pictures from his satchel. "It is an impressive force the Americans have gathered, is it not?"

Jim arranged the photographs into a mosaic. A force nearly double the size of the Eighty-second Division was deployed in forward positions less than twenty miles from the state border between Laurinburg and Red Springs. He glanced up at the man watching him, the eerie smile frozen below his thick mustache, the eyes piercing and intent.

"I promised you more than pictures. My benefactors wish you to have this information from the most reliable sources, they ask me to assure you."

Jim opened the envelope. It was a warning order to the task force commander for the occupation of South Carolina by the Eighty-second and Third Divisions. He searched for the time and date. In three days at dawn it would begin.

"Mr. McNeely, what you do with the information is not my concern. My benefactor only asks that I assure you it is an expression of their good will." Jim peered into the man's eyes. The intensity was hate, he realized.

When the Iraqi left, Jim called General Demers' office. As he waited for the general to come on the line, Pete Crandal came through the door. The conversation left little for the Canadian to speculate about. The final confrontation his government was risking so much to prevent was very close.

* * *

"What do you mean, they just went off course? They are the most sophisticated guided missiles in the goddamned inventory!" Moore yelled his outrage into the phone. The admiral's explanation that two dozen cruise missiles simply ended up programmed on a different course was nonsense, and he knew it. "How did the wrong coordinates get entered into the guidance program, Admiral? How?"

The admiral knew the answer. Two of his best commanders, or their crews — it wouldn't have been the first time that missile coordinates had been changed by a ship's crew — had decided to nullify Moore's murderous orders. He had seen the damage reports and had heard the intel reports on the forty deaths in Beaufort. Wasn't that enough terror for this son of a bitch? "I've told you all I know." It was all he could manage in reply. He was waiting on his call back from the Chief of Naval Operations. If he was facing a silent mutiny out here, he needed to confer with a sane voice.

"Admiral, I want a full report in twelve hours. I want to know exactly what happened. Every detail." Moore slammed the receiver down. He walked rapidly to the door and left the operations room. Slipping a pill from his pants pocket, he threw it into his mouth and swallowed hard before returning to the room.

The communications technician manning the console near the door watched him discreetly. *I'll bet it ain't no aspirin,* she thought, stifling a smile.

"Lieutenant," Moore called to the young army officer in the opposite corner, "do we know where Felix Hubbard is?"

"No, sir. No word from Hubbard or Gilbert. And no further word from the Canadians."

Moore fumed with frustration. He stepped to one of the secure phones and punched in the numbers to the Defense Intelligence Agency. "This is Moore. When will we be able to locate the rest of the nukes in South Carolina?" He closed his eyes as the same answer he had been given a dozen times came yet again. "What are you buffoons doing? How fucking hard can it be?" He dropped the receiver back into place. How long had it been since he slept? In twelve hours he would have to tell the president they had no choice but to invade. He chuckled, drawing sidelong glances from around the room. Forty-three dead soldiers soon wouldn't seem like all that many.

* * *

Mark Killian removed his cap and ran a hand through his damp hair. The cold of December did little to lessen the humidity of the Carolina forest. It seemed like months instead of just weeks that he had been driving one caravan after another — from dismal spots to even more remote sites. Ever since the Tomahawk missile detonated in the pine woods near Sumter, his job had been to keep the state's cash of "special weapons" moving, elusive and unreachable by more missiles.

What started as four hiding places was now twelve, and they were in constant movement. As he peered out through the thin pine trees, which were wrapped in gray Spanish moss and wet with early morning dew, Mark realized how deeply he missed his wife and children. How long could this go on? The guard headquarters had reported to him that they were certain there were dozens of U.S. agents scouting the state, maybe a hundred, and all searching for "his" weapons. Occasionally, most often in the dead of night, he reminded himself that what he was doing was dangerous. He tried not to think about it. And though he tried very hard not to, sometimes as he chewed on a cigar during a still moment, he thought about Nat Engle, and it was at those times that he felt most alone.

He drew a single sheet of paper from his field pack and began work on his daily report to General Demers. The new locations of all of the weapons were described in code for transmission back to headquarters. As he wrote, the page laid across his knee, his sergeant walked across the pinestraw-laden ground toward him.

"Captain, there's a call from headquarters, sir. They want you in Columbia tomorrow morning."

* * *

The four Canadian frigates fought their way through seas suddenly high and rough in an early winter storm. HMCS *Ville de Quebec* led the formation followed by *Halifax*, *Toronto* and *St. Johns*. Following were the two destroyers HMCS *Iroquois* and *Athabaskan*. By nightfall they would reach the waters west of Bermuda.

The group commander, Captain Defenbaker, hoped the weather would be clear by then. His nerves were strained to their limits at the prospect of taking his little flotilla through the American fleet. He would be grateful for any relief he could get, even from the rain pelting the glass of the bridge. Defenbaker scanned the message from fleet headquarters again. The coordinates of his rendezvous were set, and the time, as well. In a few hours, he would make the final arrangements with the British commander.

Waiting for him west of Bermuda would be the British carrier, HMS *Invincible* and two destroyers, HMS *Cardiff* and *York*. Together, they would aim themselves toward Charleston Harbor. His orders were clear, and unnecessary, he mused. They would not engage the Americans in any way. They were simply to proceed past the blockade of the world's most powerful navy and slip into the harbor of a rebellious American state with whom the Canadian Confederation had proposed union. To establish a "presence," his orders said. Defenbaker sipped on the fresh cup of hot coffee handed him by a sailor and glanced at his watch. *Not a problem*, he laughed to himself.

* * *

O'Connelly listened to General Cramer's dispassionate narrative, wondering at his shock. By now, he should have been immune to any surprise, no matter how deranged or morbid the news. When Cramer came to his house at the Naval Observatory, O'Connelly had just finished a telephone conversation with Brett Manzi describing confirmed reports of a fleet of six Canadian warships headed for a rendezvous with three British vessels, all apparently intending to steam into the harbor at Charleston. Only that morning, Cramer had brought him the dreadful details of the carnage in Beaufort from Moore's attack.

"Mr. Vice President." O'Connelly thought he heard a new seriousness in Cramer's voice. "I have learned the reason for the lack of any other reports of attacks on the South Carolina mainland." He paused, staring at O'Connelly. "Two commanders of ships in the blockade fleet disobeyed their orders to fire on populated areas, Mr. Vice President. They changed the coordinates of their cruise missiles." Cramer walked across the room and looked from the window onto the garden, dormant in the cold of

December. "If not for their ... defiance ... many soldiers and many more civilians would have died last night. As it is, the only damage from their missiles was by accident to two bridges across Charleston Harbor."

"General Cramer, is the—?"

"There is more." O'Connelly leaned back in his chair, bracing himself. "I have learned that *Mr. Moore*, Special White House Assistant" — his words were twisted by the contempt simmering inside him — "has been paying off soldiers to live with him..."— Cramer struggled to make himself say the rest — "...to live with him... for sex. In return, he made sure they were assigned the best jobs in the Pentagon." Cramer turned angrily on O'Connelly, "One of these *men*, an army staff sergeant was blackmailed into finding out from Moore the route and schedule of the nuclear train. He turned this information over to the people who raided the train in October."

"How do we know this, Norman?"

"Another of the men who were kept by him — a marine who is also assigned to the Pentagon — found this sergeant about to blow his brains out. The marine reported the story to his superiors yesterday afternoon. Both of the soldiers are detained at Fort Myers."

"Christ."

"Mr. Vice—"

"General, is there any confirmation from the Russians? When they sent us the information from the men who planned the raid, was there any mention of this?"

"I don't know." This hadn't occurred to Cramer, so overwhelmed had he been with disgust.

"I'll find out. General, keep those two men close by. Keep this locked down tight. Understand. Tight."

"Yes, sir."

Neither man noticed how easily Cramer had begun to take his orders from the vice president.

As Cramer stood next to the mantle and watched, O'Connelly picked up the telephone and dialed Leo Scardato's direct number. "Leo, Mike O'Connelly here. Something's come up. I need you to check on it for me."

When O'Connelly finished speaking with the FBI deputy director, Cramer said, "There is one more thing you should know." O'Connelly looked up at the general. "The Chinese have mobilized a force to invade

Taiwan. There is no question that they mean to do it this time. They expect there will be fighting and they intend to take advantage."

* * *

Major Gregarian was about to leave his sparse Moscow office when the telephone rang. He was already cloaked in his heavy uniform coat to shield him from the frigid temperatures outside. "Major," the voice from the secretary's office said, "we must send the Americans the rest of Plekanov's statement."

Gregarian thought a moment, and remembered which part they withheld. He smiled as he replied, "The portion about the White House apparatchik and his soldier lover?"

"Yes, yes, yes. That is what they want. Somehow, they know about this Moore and his arrangement with the young soldier. They want to know if Plekanov confirmed the story before he died. The president has directed us to give it to them. Do you have the number to the FBI contact in Washington, Major?"

"Yes. I have the number," he was already removing his coat and hat.

Gregarian read over Plekanov's statement again before he fed the pages into the fax machine. He smiled and said quietly, "Mikail, my poor tortured friend. You will have some revenge at last. Maybe you will be the only Russian soldier to bring down an American president. Perhaps now you can rest."

* * *

With the deadly attack by navy planes, a state of near panic seized the coast, particularly communities near military installations. The fear, which had been growing steadily, was rampant. Calls for retaliation were now a shrill avalanche.

General Demers displayed the new set of photographs provided to Jim McNeely by the "Turkish" businessman, pointing out the war preparations they revealed. Last, he flashed onto the overhead screen the copy of the warning order for the occupation of South Carolina. The date and time were no surprise to anyone in the room. In less than three days, nearly forty thousand soldiers would come across their borders, north and south. Before them, swarms of warplanes, like the ones that had killed the soldiers in Beaufort, would rain down terrible destruction. Many thousands would die, and they would not all be soldiers.

Patrick Collins said, "The Canadian ships will arrive before then. We need to move the vote ahead on the Canadian proposal. The president won't attack us if we're already a part of Canada."

"He doesn't care," Blackie replied.

Collins could not bring himself to give up. The alternative was too horrible to contemplate. "We have to try."

"Call them in." Blackie ran his hand tiredly over his face. "Call them in and vote as soon as we can. If the Canadian flotilla makes it in, that will be good." Collins saw that Blackie's mind was focused elsewhere, that he had no hope. He was wrestling with the most terrible of demons. Collins was more terrified than he had ever been in his life.

"General," Blackie said to Demers, "I want to speak with Jim McNeely. Is he here?"

"Yes, sir."

"And I want to be briefed on our contingency plan." Pausing while Demers gave directions to his aides, the governor turned to Collins, "Pat, there isn't much time. Please go and get the General Assembly back in session as soon as you can." Collins stared at Blackie for a moment. There was nothing else he could do.

* * *

In an office near the briefing room, Jim waited with Mark Killian, both summoned by General Demers. Mark explained in oblique terms what his mission had become. Jim guessed the parts Mark left out. He sympathized with him for the time he had been away from his family. Jim suffered the same pangs of separation. "It's going to be a hell of a Christmas," Mark said, staring at the floor.

Jim didn't answer, but reached for his shoulder.

"How can I get in touch with you, Mark?"

Mark handed him a card on which he penned a number to his military cellular phone. Just be careful what you say on here. I'll be here for a couple days, and then I go back out to the circuit." He looked away a moment. "If there were gas, Beth could come up and see me." But there was no gasoline, they both knew. Not for things like that. "I'll be at Fort Jackson. Same old number. Call me."

"Colonel McNeely, could you come in please?" General Demers' aide motioned to him from the door.

*　*　*

The governor waited for him.

"Jim, I want to ask you something," Blackie said. "You have had the most contact with the Canadians." Blackie looked at him steadily. "What will they do if we use a nuclear weapon?"

Jim suddenly felt very cold, as if a blanket of ice had been wrapped around him. It was unthinkable. It was the universally unspoken question. And finally the question was asked of him.

"They will be horrified. Their purpose was always to prevent exactly that."

"Will they still want us to join them to avoid more nuclear attacks, after there's already been one?"

Blackie was asking him about a world without bearings, without seasons or gravity. "Governor, I don't know."

Blackie nodded. "What if they believe it was an accident ... or something that was caused by ... someone out of control?" There was simply no answer.

"All right, Jim. I understand."

Blackie put his hand on Jim's arm. "Governor, may I ask you something? Are we going to submit to the president?"

Blackie's face stiffened. "No. We are not going to submit."

Suddenly, a voice cried out from deep inside Jim McNeely, demanding that he tell Haselden not to use the weapons. "Tell him," the voice insisted, "that they are evil things he must not use." Instead, he left the governor. Walking to the bus that would take him back to his office, he knew with frightening certainty that sometime in the next two days, the governor would hurl a nuclear weapon at the army gathering against them.

*　*　*

Jim raced down the interstate towards Charleston. After the meeting with the governor, he found Pete Crandal. "I have to keep a promise, Peter. Drive with me to Charleston."

The Canadian knew the crisis was reaching its ultimate conclusion. "So, Jim, what's going on?"

Jim drove a few minutes longer in silence before he answered. "They're going to invade in two days."

"And you guys, what will you do?"

"The governor says he won't give in. Your ships won't be in Charleston until after it has started, if the fleet lets them in at all." He looked at Crandal as he drove even faster, "There won't be time to put Mr. Fraser's proposal in place."

"So, what will you do?"

"I don't know," he lied.

At the medical university parking lot, Jim pulled the car to a stop. He laid his head on the steering wheel a moment. "Are you O.K., Jim?" Peter asked.

"No."

Crandal waited in the hall outside Tony DeSilva's room while Jim kept his promise. DeSilva's appearance told him as much as any doctor might have. He slowly turned his head to face Jim as he heard him close the door. In a voice barely a whisper, DeSilva said, "I've been waiting for you." The bright green eyes fixed him with a stare more determined than welcomed. "You have something to tell me."

Now, the fear washed over him. Jim sat heavily in the chair beside the bed. "Yes," he said, looking at DeSilva.

"Your mind is clouded." Jim looked at his eyes. He already knows. He's always known it would come to this, and he's been waiting for me to come and tell him.

"The governor has decided to use a nuclear weapon. I think he will do it tomorrow night." He leaned forward and buried his face in his hands. There were no tears, but he could no longer support the weight of his head, so heavy with thoughts of the coming holocaust.

"And what is to be done?" Jim looked up at DeSilva, stunned by the question. Was DeSilva losing his mind from the pain and the medication?

"I don't understand what you mean."

"Do you believe it is inevitable?"

"Isn't that what it has always been? Isn't that what you taught me? The contamination spreads from one ruined piece of matter to another, contaminating that one, too. And it goes on beyond anyone's power to stop."

"You were a quick study. You learned very well." He began to cough raggedly. "There is one more lesson I have for you, before I go."

Jim saw that he had held the leukemia at bay by force of will, waiting for this moment. "With radiation, we can shield the contamination, surround it with an impenetrable barrier, and prevent it from escaping. But we can never stop the reaction of deteriorating atoms. All we can do is isolate radiation from the healthy world with a strong shield."

"Lead."

DeSilva nodded slowly. "Sometimes lead. Sometimes more is required."

"You're trying to tell me something, but I don't understand."

"You are that shield."

Jim stared at him, incredulous. "You want me to stop this catastrophe?" Jim shook his head violently.

"I will soon be gone. But there are many more whose lives call on you. They want you to do this." He was practically whispering now.

Jim was speechless, convinced DeSilva was hopelessly incoherent. "There is nothing I can do."

"You are wrong. You have always been wrong about yourself ... always waited to be shown by others what you are capable of."

Jim was stung by the penetrating truth of the dying man's words.

DeSilva continued. "Now, there is no one else. You must be the shield that disarms these terrible weapons before many lives are taken before their time."

"Tony, I'm a lawyer. I don't know anything about nuclear weapons."

"Your brother knows." DeSilva rested his head back on the pillow and closed his eyes, smiling. "Matt knows." *Jesus Christ*, Jim suddenly understood.

"My brother? Matt Reicher?" DeSilva nodded. "He hates my guts! He wouldn't...."

DeSilva waved his hand weakly. "He will. He will do it to stop the killing. And because he is your brother."

"Tony...." Jim lifted the frail hand from the edge of the bed.

"Go. It is what you alone can do," he said, fixing Jim with a last look, the eyes bright and suddenly fierce. "Go to Matt. You are the shield," he gasped.

The hand slid from Jim's fingers, the life finally slipping from Anthony DeSilva, his last lesson complete.

"No!" Jim yelled. In seconds, a nurse and an orderly rushed into the room. Jim retreated to the corner as they worked futilely to save the life that DeSilva had already let go.

* * *

Jim knocked on the door and eased it open when there was no answer. On the floor, he saw Matt lying on his back. His legs were stretched out as he raised them a foot from the floor and lowered them again. He was counting the repetitions of the leg lifts. When he reached thirty, he rolled over and began pumping out pushups. His voice betrayed the pain from the still-sore shoulder as he counted to fifty. "Matt...."

Leaping to his feet, he turned quickly to face Jim and Jim's companion, Pete Crandal. "When can I get out of here?"

"Matt, Tony died a few minutes ago."

The angry mask left Matt's face.

"He told me to come and see you."

Matt fixed him with his stare and said, "Well, you've seen me."

"He made me promise to tell him when the state had decided to launch a nuclear attack." Matt's face betrayed his shock. "He told me it was up to me to stop it."

"And why are you unburdening your soul to me?"

"You know how to disarm them. I don't. Tony said you and I needed to neutralize the weapons before they could be used."

Matt began to laugh. "Treason is getting to be habit forming with you. First, you turn on your country. Now, you turn on your state. And you want me to risk certain capture, and probably death, while I try to save a bunch of nuclear weapons that you stole." He jerked his head violently towards Jim, "All to soothe *your* conscience! You're crazy!"

"I probably am," Jim said softly. "Be ready to leave in a couple of hours. I'll go make the arrangements to get you out of here."

"Wait a minute," Crandal said angrily. "Tell your pal here where the weapon is going to be detonated? Go on. Tell him that."

"Who's your friend?" Matt asked.

"He's a Canadian, a liaison from the Mounted Police."

"A mountie!" Matt sneered at Crandal, "O.K., Mountie, tell me what you want me to know."

"Twenty thousand American soldiers and God knows how many civilians in North Carolina. That's where the nuke is headed. You know what that means, eh?" Crandal walked to stand face to face with Matt. He turned to look at Jim, "Your best friend?" Facing Matt again, he said, "Too bad you don't have half the balls of the man who calls you his friend. Too bad you aren't the man he thought you were."

"I'll be back, Matt. Be ready." Jim opened the door to the hall.

"Wait," Matt said. "What did Tony say to you?" The anger was gone from his voice.

Jim eased the door closed again and took a few tentative steps towards Matt. "He said the only way to keep radiation from contaminating everything around it was to shield it ... and he kept talking about you and me being the shield."

"The shield," Matt said. "Tony always knew how to choose his words." He picked up a shirt and pulled it over his head. Slipping on a pair of blue jeans, he said, "There isn't much time. We'd better get started."

*   *   *

"There have to be enough pieces here for a complete set," Matt said as he was rifling through a half dozen open tool kits arrayed on a table before him. Jim watched over his shoulder. Crandal stood inside the open door of the shop of what had been the explosive ordnance disposal unit and watched for anyone approaching the isolated corner of the Naval Weapons Station.

"What are you doing?" Jim asked.

"I need a complete set of special tools." Turning to glance at Jim a second, he added, "A Swiss Army knife won't do. I have to have the right tools or I'll never get into the weapon." He reached from kit to kit grabbing screwdrivers and wrenches and other things Jim didn't recognize. "All right. That's a full kit." He tossed the collection into one of the boxes and slammed it shut. Turning to Jim, he asked, "Now, what weapons do you have?"

Jim hesitated a moment, trying to remember the inventory he prepared with Nat Engle on that night that seemed so long ago. "There are cruise missiles...."

"Forget those. You don't have any way to guide them. What else?"

"There are artillery rounds...."

"Too last minute. Bombs. What bombs are there?"

"O.K.... There were B57s and B61s. And B90s. B86s also. I think that's all."

"All right. Help me find the publications for those over here," Matt led Jim to a shelf of paperback technical manuals. They covered the vast array of explosive weapons of all types, and from most of the world's munitions manufacturing countries. They found the book for each type of air-dropped nuclear device among the weapons seized by the state. Matt tossed them into a leather satchel. Before leaving the shop he grabbed three large packages from the shelf that contained contamination suits.

* * *

Crandal watched Matt search the storage shed. It was an extension of the structure that supported the roof over the carport. "Here they are." He placed three cans of green spray paint into a backpack and handed it to Crandal. Crandal stared at the bottle dangling from Matt's finger — a half-full bottle of Jim Beam.

"O.K. I still don't know what the green paint is for," Crandal said.

"You wouldn't believe me." Matt emerged from the shed carrying two holstered pistols and a box of bullets. Crandal didn't need to ask what these were for.

Jim walked from the house clutching four sets of camouflage uniforms and two pairs of combat boots. "I got a knife to cut the navy patches off. I'll give you guys armbands."

* * *

"We need to know where the B57 and B61 type weapons are. They are the ones the F-15 can deliver. That's the only practical option for your people," Matt explained.

From the exit leading to Fort Jackson, Jim dialed the number for Mark Killian at Fort Jackson. As the number continued to ring, the reality of what they were doing became clear to him. He had to find Mark Killian, and he had to convince him to tell them where the weapons were hidden. "Hello," the familiar voice answered.

Jim felt his heart skip a beat. "Mark, it's Jim McNeely. I thought you were gone." The relief in his voice confused Mark.

"I was in the shower. I haven't seen the inside of one much lately."

"I'm on the way to your place. I need to talk to you. Is that all right?"

"I'll be here at Fort Jackson until tomorrow."

Jim began to consider for the first time what he would do if Mark refused to reveal the locations. For a second, he was struck by the fear that Mark might try to have them arrested. Certainly that would be his duty. If Mark simply refused, Jim realized, he would have to get Crandal and Matt out of South Carolina before morning. In the parking lot, Jim paused a moment trying to decide if only he or all three men should go to Mark's room. "Let's go," he said. There was no time to worry.

Mark Killian opened the door wearing only his uniform trousers. Inside the room, Crandal reflexively noted the power in the arms and chest of the man that towered over them and hoped the big soldier would not turn on them.

"What's up?" Mark asked.

Taking a deep breath, Jim began, "The governor has decided to make a nuclear strike at the troops in North Carolina. The president has issued the order to invade in two days."

"Why are you telling me this?" The eyes of the big man focused intensely on the two strangers. His arms tensed.

"If we do this, Mark, thousands of people will die."

"We didn't start the fighting," Mark snapped.

Jim pressed him. "It won't end with one bomb. You know that." Mark glared at him. "People on the other side won't sit still after twenty thousand men and women go up in a mushroom cloud."

"Why are you here?" Mark demanded.

Jim brushed the question aside. "Every one of those people — and the civilians that get killed because they are too close — all are loved by many more people. The way you loved Nat."

Mark leapt from his chair, his chest swelling and heaving as his breath came in angry gulps of air. "You talk to me about Nat in the same breath you talk about helping the bastards who killed him!" His huge hands clenched themselves into tight fists at the ends of his powerful arms, flexed with rage.

"Nat didn't deserve to die. Neither do the thousands that you know will die if one of these weapons is used." Jim faced Mark. "What would you have done to save Nat? There is nothing you wouldn't have done. You loved him. And I'll tell you something else. If Nat were alive, he'd tell you this has to end now, before a more terrible holocaust is unleashed." The big man turned his back, but Jim followed him, forcing Mark to look into his eyes, "See his face, Mark. Look at that face in your mind, and tell me I'm wrong. Tell me, and I'll take these men to the border so they can go back to their families before things go to hell." Jim reached for his shoulder, as Mark fought back the tears. "You're a good and decent man. None of us wanted this. We've done our duty the best way we knew. But now we have to stop this."

Mark leaned on the table, his hands still balled tightly, his head hanging low. "O.K.," he said softly. Reaching to the floor next to the table, he lifted a green leather bag and laid it on the table. From a clear plastic bag, he pulled a quad sheet map and spread it out. "Here," he pointed to an area circled in red marker. "The bombs that will be used are here. They're all B57s and B61s."

They looked at him in surprise. Mark knew about the attack.

"There isn't much time. The weapons technicians are coming before dawn to arm one and take it to Shaw. Take this chart with you. You won't get in without the password. And it changes every day." He flipped through the pages of a black note pad, "The challenge is 'Blue,' and the answer is 'Arrow.'"

Jim folded the chart and tucked it into his pocket. "Thanks, Mark."

"Keep hiding the weapons, Captain," Matt said. Jim stared at him in amazement. "Whether this works or not, just keep doing your job. If we get it right, the people in North Carolina will never know if the bomb was a dud or a signal from the state. If this bullshit is going to get straightened out, the other side has to believe you guys are serious. If we succeed tonight, it'll be our job to make sure they know that. O.K.?"

Mark reached again into his bag and withdrew a Barretta pistol and two loaded clips. Handing them to Jim, he said, "The border is dangerous as hell."

Jim was all right until they were back in the car. Fishing for his keys, a chill crept along his spine. Turning to Matt, he asked, "What did you mean up there?"

"Disarming one group of these bombs won't end this. And we can't roam around the state looking for them all. If we pull this off, I'll get to the right people in Washington — somehow — and make them understand the next bomb will go off. If the first one's a dud, there will be time while they try to figure out what to do."

Thirty minutes later they were well beyond the edge of Columbia and forty-five minutes away from their destination, a hunting camp deep in the swamps of the Lynches River. Crandal and Matt slipped out of their clothes and put on the uniforms and boots. "Put these on," Jim said, handing them the blue armbands of the state's military forces and collar insignia identifying them as general staff officers. Rain was falling steadily as they sped down the dark miles of tree-lined road.

Chapter 33

There was still time to stop it. All Blackie needed to do was place a call. The terrible responsibility was his. Some men craved the power that tormented him. His people and all of the state's leaders trusted him to be the sole wielder of a frightening prerogative. With no further word from him, tomorrow morning at dawn a single F-15 would take off from the airfield on the outskirts of Sumter. The pilot would fly at tree-top level to the border of North Carolina. Then he would rocket to the designated height above the vast concentration of troops — and he would release the nuclear bomb that would vaporize many, and kill all, of the soldiers preparing to invade his state, before racing back across the border.

The clock in the formal living room struck midnight. *The day of reckoning*, he thought. *Or is it the day of retribution?* He walked around the room, pausing before the encased Revolutionary War saber. He recalled how Billy loved to study that sword, and how he speculated who had wielded the fierce-looking weapon.

"I'll bet it was someone who rode with Marion," he had insisted more than once.

The memories were still so fresh, the pain too raw. Blackie buried his face in his hands. He suddenly knew he had to get out of the house. He summoned his driver. "I need you to take me somewhere."

"Certainly, Governor. I'll be around front in just a minute."

The sleek black car glided through the empty streets outside the mansion's gates. That afternoon, Pat Collins had come to him alone. Collins feared that Blackie had reached the decision he dreaded. "No matter what happens, nothing could be worse, Blackie," he pleaded. "It is the only result that we can't live with." He was a good man, Blackie believed. But he hasn't been wounded as I have, he told himself. And he doesn't bear the responsibility that I do.

The car pulled to the front entrance of the state museum. "Here we are, Governor," the driver said.

"Walk with me."

The surprised guard let them in and hastily turned on the lights to the three floors of the museum. It had been closed for over a month. Blackie walked deliberately to the second floor. His driver sensed his boss needed to be alone, and lagged behind. From the head of the staircase, he watched as Blackie made his way toward an exhibit that had been set up in the spring. It was devoted to the burning of Columbia at the end of the Civil War. The governor stood before a panoramic photograph of the ruined city taken after its capture in 1865. Huge floor-to-ceiling panels flanked three walls of the cavernous exhibit room. The black-and-white image was a chilling scene of empty streets, heaps of brick rubble where houses and commercial buildings once stood. Here and there a wrought iron gate stood as a lonely reminder of the life that had been chased from the desolate streets by the raging fire, a fire set by hate that ran as wild and unstoppable as the flames themselves.

He stared at the scene of utter destruction.

He would bear the burden for what was coming. In the aftermath of the blast that would kill so many, there would be a delay while the other side assessed what had happened, and how to respond. They would understand there were other weapons that might be used. There would be time to complete the arrangement with Canada. Except, he knew the Canadians would not deal with him. He would take the full burden of the decision, which he alone had made; he would take it all with him when he resigned. Collins would finish things with the Canadians. For the first time, he wondered if his wife would leave him. And he wondered if he could ask her to join him in the exile of the pariah he would become. God only knew how much he would need her to be with him, no matter how hard it was certain to be. Still, it was the only way.

The question came to him again, as it had so many times, the question for which there would never be an answer. Was it revenge, after all?

*   *   *

"The turn off should be just ahead, about a hundred meters," Pete Crandal said. He had been following the chart and monitoring the car's mileage meter. The headlights of the car shone on a metal gate that sat about twenty yards off of the narrow pavement across a sandy lane. He glanced at his watch. It was ten minutes after midnight. Taking a deep breath, Jim McNeely stepped from the car and walked toward the gate, waiting to be hailed by the guards he knew were stationed on either side of the road. "Halt," a voice called from the right. "Blue," the unseen young man yelled at Jim.

Jim saw the red light of a night scope glowing through the hedges and brush on the side of the lane. He was in the sights of a loaded rifle. "Arrow," he answered.

"Advance and identify yourself," the voice commanded. A camouflaged soldier slid from the brush on the left and approached him. Jim handed him his identification. The soldier studied it and returned it to him. "Colonel, what can we do for you?"

"I am here with the team to check your special weapons. You were expecting us, right?" Jim could not see the sergeant's face, but could tell he was perplexed.

"You're earlier than we expected, sir."

"We are the first team. A second team is coming later to arm the weapon and take it to the airfield. Didn't you get the word?" Jim knew, as all soldiers knew, that there was always someone who didn't get the word. And he hoped that knowledge and his credentials as a member of the governor's staff would be enough for the soldiers guarding the weapons.

"We'll open the gate for you, sir."

Jim released a sigh of relief as he restarted the car's engine. "Watch your accents." Crandal and Matt looked at each other.

The warehouse at the end of the lane was a concrete cinderblock building used to store grading equipment for maintaining the roads that crisscrossed the hunting preserve. Inside the warehouse they saw the five bombs laid carefully on the concrete floor on wooden pallets, cushioned with wooden bracing. The naked light bulbs filled the windowless enclosure in bright, white light that reflected from the shiny skins of the bombs. The lieutenant followed the men into the windowless warehouse, curious about the experts who understood, as he did not, the deadly things he and his troops had guarded for weeks.

Matt took the contamination suit from under his arm and opened the package. Jim and Crandal did the same, and all three men pulled their one-piece suits from the wrapping. Stepping into the legs of his suit, Matt turned to the lieutenant and asked, "Don't you have a suit?"

The young man looked nervously at the three as they stepped into the heavy white garments. "No. Do I need one?"

Matt snickered, "Not if you don't mind soaking up a few hundred rads if the plutonium cores in one of these babies is leaking. It's up to you, bubba."

Jim winced at Matt's barely disguised New Jersey speech. The lieutenant backed to the door. "I suppose not," he said, "Just let me know when you are done."

"Lieutenant, don't let anyone in while we're working. These cores are probably O.K., but we can't be sure until we're finished. We don't want anybody to get hurt," Jim cautioned the young officer as he closed the door. Outside, the lieutenant posted two guards with instructions to keep it shut until the colonels were through. He thought that one of them looked awfully young, but these were strange days. He was probably some egghead expert on nukes, the lieutenant told himself.

Matt stopped donning the heavy suit as soon as the door closed and rushed to the first bomb. "The tool kit!" he hissed to Crandal. The Canadian opened the kit and laid it next to Matt as he sat in front of the bomb. He retrieved a screwdriver from the kit and loosened the screws to a panel on the front side of the device and lifted it carefully. With a second tool that resembled a small-headed set of pliers, he extracted another panel. "O.K., here we go." He reached into the hole, turning his hand several times, unscrewing something and slowly pulled out a bright red plastic plug about the circumference of a quarter. Holding the plug in the air, he called out to Jim, "Take this and lay it on some newspaper from that satchel. Take the green spray paint and spray the red parts green. Cover all the red and wipe any paint off the shiny parts with that rag. Then set it down on the metal bottom so it'll dry evenly."

Jim took the little plug and did as Matt ordered, careful to get the paint on only the red body of the plug. "Will it dry in time?"

"The can says it will. Here's another one," Matt answered.

"What are we doing?" Jim asked.

"The red plugs tells you a weapon is not armed to explode. A green plug says the weapon is armed. When they check, they will think these are ready to go. But they won't be; they'll still have the safe plugs." It took Matt Reicher thirty minutes to retrieve the plugs from all five bombs. "There just isn't time to disarm the firing mechanism. This is the best we can do."

As he handed over the fifth plug, Jim cursed, "God damn, the paint is gone! In all the cans! What the fuck are we going to do now?"

Matt jumped from the floor and grabbed the can from Jim. It was empty. "All right, plan B. We have four of the motherfuckers on safe. They only want one." Matt stepped to the fifth bomb. Reaching into the tool kit, he retrieved a small hammer. Placing the claw end of the hammer on the skin of the bomb, he pulled it along the surface, digging deep cuts in the shiny metal skin. The sound made Jim and Crandal jump. Grabbing the hammer more securely, Matt hit one of the tail fins of the bomb twice. He repeated the blows to a second fin. Both were bent slightly. Finally, he held a screwdriver to the tip of the bomb, and with the hammer struck the handle tip twice, making deep dents in the surface. Jim and Crandal stared at him, then nervously glanced at the door, expecting the noise to bring the guards back inside. But there was only silence from the door.

After Matt replaced the panels of the fifth bomb, he searched in his bag for a black marker and scrawled "DEADLINED" across the bomb. Turning to Jim, he asked, "Are the plugs dry?"

Jim checked them, the first one was indeed dry. Thankfully, he handed it to Matt. He took the newly painted green plug and tossed the red plug from the fifth bomb to Crandal, "A souvenir, Mountie." Carefully, screwing the plug back into the first bomb, Matt replaced the panels and their screws.

Crandal had watched him carefully remove the panels and reattach the first one, and as Matt took the second plug, Crandal said, "I can attach the panels. You put the plugs in." Working as a team, the two men reassembled the bombs. Jim cleaned up the paint-covered newspaper and stuffed it into the leather satchel. He realized that his hands were covered with the paint. Across the warehouse, Crandal and Matt were dropping the tools back into their box. It was nearly one o'clock.

They pulled the contamination suits back up to their chests, and Jim slowly opened the door.

"They are all in good shape except the one on the end. It's had some pretty rough treatment. Those scratches are probably not a problem, but I don't know about the dents. And it had no safe plug. Don't know what that means," Jim explained as he pulled the contamination suit free of his boots. "We marked it as 'deadlined.' It needs to be examined in a clean, controlled environment."

"Yes, sir."

"All right, Lieutenant, I'll tell Captain Killian we saw you and everything is in order here."

"Thanks, Colonel." They traded salutes.

When the car was out of sight of the warehouse, Jim laid his head back on the headrest. The rain had stopped and left a heavy foglike mist in the air. The tall pines and oaks lining the lane rose over them like a canopy, only a dim gray light ahead was visible at the end of the tunnel of vegetation. Ahead, Jim saw the metal gate again. One of the guards peered in the window and, recognizing Jim, motioned for the gate to be opened. Jim started to drive toward the gate when the same soldier ran back to the side of the car. Noticing the sudden movement out of the corner of his eye, Jim slammed the brakes too hard, throwing Matt and Crandal forward. Calming himself as the sergeant reached the window again, he faced the camouflaged face, "What is it, Sergeant?"

"Sir, the lieutenant wants to talk to you a minute."

Terrified, Jim took the radio the soldier handed him, trying to remember correct radio/telephone procedure, and finally simply answering, "Yes, Lieutenant?" A thousand dark possibilities flashed through his mind.

"Colonel, the second team just checked in. They will be arriving in about twenty minutes. Do you wish to wait and meet with them?" *Don't panic*, Jim told himself. Slow it down. "That's a thought, Lieutenant. Did they ask to see us?"

"No, sir. They seemed surprised to know you were here. I just thought you might want to speak to them about the fifth device."

"Well, it's getting late, Lieutenant. Twenty minutes might turn into an hour and twenty. We've had a long day checking five other sites. Can you remember what we told you?"

"I think so, sir."

"Well, that's all we know to tell them. The other four are good. That's the important thing. We'll go on back to Columbia."

"Very good, sir. Have a safe trip."

"Thanks, Lieutenant." Why did he say anything about other sites? What if this guy checked? *God damn*, he cursed silently, as he drove carefully onto the paved road.

The lieutenant never thought to call any other sites to check on the three-man team of weapons techs. Shortly after they arrived he called for confirmation that they were legitimate, since he had received no advance word about their arrival. "They're legit," Mark Killian told his lieutenant. "It's smart to check, Tom. Good work."

*   *   *

There was no sound in the car for the first thirty minutes after they left, save for Matt and Crandal changing out of their uniforms.

"If you don't mind, I'm going to have a swallow of the bourbon." With that, Crandal tilted the bottle of Jim Beam.

"So, Mountie, any more cracks about my manhood?"

"Have a drink, Yank," he answered and handed Matt the bottle.

Matt turned to Jim. "To Tony," he said as he took a long swallow. Jim took the bottle from him.

"To Tony."

*   *   *

He drove in silence to his uncle's farm. The others were asleep. He could see the single light burning on the front porch from a half-mile down the highway. The pines stood out in the dimly lit sky, the familiar silhouette of home for Jim McNeely.

Matt and Crandal roused themselves, shaking sleep as the car slowly made its way down the sand-and-pine-straw lane. "We'll wait here. No need to wake the whole place up," Matt said. Jim walked up the concrete walk to the old farmhouse. At the side entrance, he eased the door open. Alicia was asleep on the couch and woke as she heard him enter.

"Jim?" She saw it was him and jumped into his arms. She kissed him urgently, her arms wrapped tightly around him, desperate not to let him go again, but knowing it wasn't time for him to stay. "Your uncle has the boat ready. The trailer's hooked up to his truck. Do you have gasoline?" she asked.

"Yeah. All taken care of." He looked at her in the light from the porch and leaned to kiss her again. "Are the children all right?"

"Except they miss you." They walked through the dark house to the room John and Katherine shared. He eased the door open and stepped to the edge of each bed, planting a kiss on the foreheads of both children. As he kissed his daughter, her eyes opened and she flashed her little girl smile at him.

"Hi, Daddy." She closed her eyes and curled herself more tightly in the covers of the narrow bed.

On the porch again, he took Alicia in his arms a final time, "I'll be back by dawn. It'll be O.K. Don't worry."

His uncle pulled the truck to the front of the walk and was talking to Matt and Crandal. Jim saw that they had been passing the bottle of Jim Beam between them. "Aren't you glad you have a designated driver?" he said as he approached them.

"Matt, give Linda our love," Alicia said as she took him in her arms and kissed him. "One day this will all be in the past. We love you."

She walked to Crandal and kissed him, "You, too. And thanks again."

The men slid into the cab of the truck and Jim turned it down the sandy lane. It was a two-hour drive to the lake that sat on the border with North Carolina.

* * *

At the hunting preserve, the weapons team arrived to transport the bomb to Shaw. The major in charge of the team was surprised to learn that an inspection team had just left. His apprehension was lessened by the lieutenant's assurance that Captain Killian confirmed that their visit was expected.

In the warehouse, they looked over the five bombs. "The other team checked them all out. They're all O.K. except the one on the end. The major bent over the bomb and read the word scrawled across the shiny surface. "Deadlined," he read aloud. "Take that one," he said pointing to the one in the middle.

* * *

Jim pushed the button to illuminate his watch. It was 3:30. Matt and Crandal unloaded the jon boat and stashed their few articles of gear in the bottom. Matt examined one of the pistols and made certain it was loaded. On the drive, Jim had explained that the border, particularly places where crossing was still possible, was crawling with smugglers of drugs, gasoline, and even medicine.

He was familiar with the lake and the landing on the opposite side. Many times as a child he had visited cousins nearby to fish and explore the cypress-dotted waters of the lake that sat on the state line.

Jim handed the pistol that Mark had given him to Matt, and said, "You can't go wrong. North Carolina is on the other side. It's not a big lake. Just follow the compass. Just go north. It's less than two miles across. A man named Douglas is expecting you at the store one mile up the road from the landing where I'm going to drop you off. He's a good man. You can trust him." He glanced at his watch again. "Let's get going."

They shoved the little metal boat into the blackness of the lake and jumped inside. Crandal and Jim began digging their paddles into the water. The boat slid quietly away from the landing.

* * *

The bomb, a type B57, was wheeled carefully into the hanger at Shaw Air Force Base. Waiting for it were two weapons experts, formerly with the navy. They carefully removed the panel on the side of the bomb. In a box next to them was one of the green arming plugs seized from one of the federal facilities. The tiny green cylinder would make the bomb ready to detonate.

The plate was lifted free of the bomb and one of the men reached inside the opening. He removed his hand from the opening and shone his light inside. "Shit, look at that!" he exclaimed. "The God damn thing is already armed."

He and his co-worker stared at each other. What the hell was there to do about this? They didn't have long to get the bomb ready.

* * *

As they moved away from the landing, Jim McNeely watched the dim image of the pickup truck disappear in the moonless night. Panic at separation from his family mixed with fear as the boat slipped silently through the black water. The air on the lake was colder, but he couldn't feel its sting on his face.

"We probably ought not use the motor. It's a short distance. Just keep paddling."

"Look, Jim, whatever's going to happen is going to happen in the next few days. Maybe you can hang out over there in North Carolina for a few days. If it's safe to go home, you can slip back across the lake," Crandal said.

The paddles swished through the stillness of the lake as the giant cypress trees slid slowly past on either side of them. Jim and Crandal kept up a steady pace. Normally, there would have been a light on the other side, but it was gone now. Jim hoped his steering directions to Matt were accurate. They scanned the horizon ahead of them searching for the break in the trees signifying the landing. "There it is," Crandal said, pointing to the left.

They steered the little boat in the direction the Canadian was pointing. There it was, a sliver of gray against the inky mass of the lake and the trees. "Matt, when you guys get out, I'm going back," Jim said.

"Jim, Pete's right. Don't do something foolish. This is all going to be over one way or the other soon. Go back tomorrow or the next day," Matt replied.

Before Jim could answer, the sound of a boat motor being cranked broke the stillness of the swamp around them. And a pencil of light swept the surface of the water. "You boys hold up there at the landing!" The voice was rough, mocking. "We want to see maybe we can do a little business. What do you say?"

"They're about a hundred and fifty yards back," Matt said. Crandal already had the motor in place and was cranking it. "Head for the landing!" The boat jumped as the prop began to spin at full speed.

"A race! Come on boys, don't be shy!" a voice out called from the darkness. As the words died in the swamp the first shot rang out. It was a shotgun, Jim thought by the sound. The shot splashed in the water behind them. Two more shots echoed among the trees, ripping into the cypress. The light streaked back and forth searching for them. The bow of the boat ran up the boat ramp, throwing them forward, Matt rolling out into the cold black water. Quickly, he scrambled to his feet. He was followed by the others, each man clutching a pistol now, extra clips stuffed in their pockets. The three men splashed through the shallow water of the landing toward the parking lot. To their horror, they realized that not one, but two boats were sliding onto the landing. "Come on boys, let's see what these sons of bitches don't want us to get!" Jim looked over his shoulder and thought he saw five shapes jogging up from the boat ramp.

Matt ran alongside the tree and brush line next to the right side of the road, and Jim followed suit. Crandal ran along the other side of the dirt road. Two guns fired behind them at once. The shells dug into the ground to Jim's left. Jim thought he saw that Crandal wasn't running to his left any longer. Another shot, a pistol this time, rang out. Behind him, a man screamed and the flashlight fell hard to the ground. "Bastards!" voices yelled angrily. Three guns fired now, the bullets tearing the leaves across the road. More pistol shots sounded, this time from behind their pursuers. Another scream split the night, this one with the ugly sound of finality. The men returned random fire to the woods across the road where Jim knew Crandal had gone. Jim looked ahead and saw that Matt was no longer in front of him.

"In here!" Matt's voice hissed. "Get in the woods!" Jim dived in the direction of the voice, briars ripping his clothes and his skin, blood flowing from his hands. "Stay here," Matt said, and moved behind Jim watching the tree line carefully.

Another well-aimed pistol shot from the other side of the road brought yet another of their pursuers down, this one with a killing wound to the man's head. Now only two voices, more fearful, were talking. One had retrieved the flashlight and was searching the trees and brush, the white light jabbing through the trees to Jim's front. The man didn't hold the flashlight long. Matt aimed his shot to the head he saw illuminated by the light. With the sound of the shot came a dull groan from the man, who dropped the light and crumpled dead to the ground. The remaining man panicked, backing away from his friend, aiming his rifle and firing repeatedly in the direction of the last pistol shot.

This time the cry of pain came from inside the woods. Jim felt the shot tear into his right side, burning like a flame injected by some insane doctor. The pistol nearly fell from his hand with the force of the shot and the pain. He leaned against the tree and balanced the pistol, aimed at the fleeing man, and fired. At the same moment another pistol, or perhaps two others, fired. The man running fell, sliding in the sand. Groaning, he dragged himself from the road and ran, clutching his side. The kick from the pistol was the last thing Jim remembered as he slid from the side of the tree and fell through the briars and brush into the ditch.

Matt jumped into the road, yelling at the retreating man, "You better run, you motherfucker!" He aimed a final shot at the man, now too far away. He heard the engine fire on the man's truck, and the tires screech as he fled the murderous scene at the landing. "Jim, are you all right?" he yelled. When there was no answer, he frantically searched the brush until he found him lying headfirst in the shallow ditch below the hedge of brush. Matt pulled him out onto the road by his arms and turned him over. Jim groaned, but could not speak. Matt searched the dead man, looking for the flashlight. It was broken. "Crandal, let's go! Are you hit?" Matt's voice echoed through the blackness of forest. He waited for an answer that did not come. Matt rushed to the edge of brush on the other side of the road. It was impossible. "Crandal," he yelled desperately. There was only the silence of the swamp. He had no choice. Matt ran back to Jim, lifted him onto his back, and began to jog up the road. He knew his friend was bleeding badly. There was no time to search the dark woods. He would come back after Jim was taken care of.

What did Jim say the distance was to the store? "Shit!" Matt yelled to the uncaring night. His shoulder began to ache, but he jogged on down the road. Around a sharp bend, he spotted a pair of headlights racing down the road. The jeep slid to a stop in front of Matt. The door opened and a man ran towards him. "Matt Reicher?" It was Douglas, their contact.

"We need to get to a doctor right now."

"Damn, what happened?"

They loaded Jim into the car and Douglas raced for the main road to Whiteville.

*　*　*

It was barely four o'clock in the morning when Douglas walked to the door of one of two of Whiteville's family physicians and Douglas' doctor since childhood. The doctor's house flanked the office where he had treated half the population of the small farming town. "What in God's name is wrong?" he said, wrapped in a robe and peering through the screen of his front door.

He didn't wait for an answer. Over Douglas' shoulder, he saw Matt Reicher carrying Jim McNeely and walking towards them up the path. Even in the dark December night, he could see the stain of blood across Jim's chest, blood that was dripping onto the brick walk. "Get him into the examination room."

Matt and Douglas waited in the outer office while the doctor worked to remove the bullet lodged in Jim's right side. "The truck that came tearing down the road. I know who owns it. He and his buddies must have been doing a little smuggling."

"Well, four of his buddies won't be doing any more smuggling."

Douglas nodded soberly. "We need to get you two guys out of here before that asshole decides to get even."

"We left a man out there," Matt said.

"Oh my God. Who?"

"A Canadian cop named Crandal. He took down three of the bastards. I don't know what happened to him." Matt looked at the closed door to the examination room and said, "I had to get Jim out, or maybe lose them both."

"Was he shot, too?"

"I couldn't tell. There was no sign of him."

* * *

The pilot stared at the F-15 Eagle waiting on the tarmac. For fifteen minutes he watched them load the type B57 nuclear bomb under the wing of the plane. The horizon was beginning to glow orange. Soon the sun would ease her arc over the tops of the trees. He glanced at his watch. It was time to go to the plane.

He had not allowed himself much time to think about what he was preparing to do. It had been only ten hours ago that his squadron commander brought him the startling message. Two other pilots had confessed they were not sure if they could bring themselves to drop the terrible weapon. He told himself bitterly that it was only a matter of time before they found him, or someone like him.

He climbed into the cockpit of the sleek jet. The clear, curved shield slowly sealed him into the enclosure of screens and meters. In minutes the tower gave him the signal and he taxied to the end of the runway. He fired the mighty engines that would blast him into the lightening sky. His body was pushed to the back of the molded seat as the jet rocketed from the ground. He banked to the left and dove to the lowest elevation he could fly. The enemy, he knew, had blanketed the state with radar. They would know that he was in the air in less than a minute. But before they could react, it would be too late.

To his right, the sun was illuminating the horizon, a red-orange streak spreading across the earth's edge. Ahead, the darkness was vanishing, though he could still see the white dots of lights in the few houses that scattered the countryside.

As he crossed the border with North Carolina, he executed a rapid climb, reaching in seconds the altitude from which he would drop the bomb. Below him he could see the massive collection of tanks, Bradley fighting vehicles, artillery, helicopters, trucks, and tents of the army ready to invade his home. He swung the jet to the west in a circle that carried him around the marshaling area so that his bombing run would be aimed to the south, back towards South Carolina. The pilot tensed as he saw clearly what he was about to do. He remembered the image of his brother, the young National Guard sergeant burned to death in Beaufort a few days before. He saw the boy's broad grin and red hair. With no thought except contempt for the murderers of so fine a kid brother, the pilot pushed the button that released the pins that held the type B57 bomb to the wing of his plane.

As soon as he knew the bomb was away, there was a shrill beeping indicating enemy radar had found his plane. Immediately, he took evasive action, banking and climbing, then diving. But no missiles followed him. He knew six of his colleagues waited across the border for enemy jets that might follow him. The indicator flashed on his dial telling him the bomb should have impacted, falling in the center of the troop concentration.

Yet there was only silence as he roared across the border. Angrily, he circled to gain a clear view of the horizon. All he saw was the spreading light across the fallow fields and trees. There was no billowing flame rising from the ruined ground and burning people. There was no giant, black mushroom cloud.

* * *

The door to the examination room opened. The doctor said, "He's all right. No broken bones. Although it was close. The bullet grazed a rib pretty bad. The lung's O.K. I didn't have to go too deep to get the damn thing out. He's lost a lot of blood. He really needs a little refill. I don't suppose either of you men are O positive?"

"I am," Matt answered.

"Are you sure?"

"Sure. Can you hook us up?"

"Absolutely."

"Doctor, can he travel? I mean, ride in a car?"

"How far?"

"About four hundred miles."

The doctor stared at Matt. "Is this necessary?" he asked. Then shaking his head, "Never mind. But you promise me that if he starts bleeding … at all … you take him to a hospital right away."

"Agreed." Matt walked into the examination room. Jim was still unconscious from the anesthetic.

"Take off your shirt, please." As Matt removed his shirt, the doctor stared at his left shoulder. "You and your friend like to play rough, don't you. What happened here?" He leaned close and studied the still ugly wound. "How long ago?"

"About a month."

"I shouldn't do this, you know." Matt nodded. "How did you get that, son?"

"They call it civil war, I think."

The doctor smiled. "Lie down over here."

Two hours later, the sun was rising over the tall pines facing the doctor's house. "Take the jeep. Just remember it isn't paid for," Douglas said to Matt. "You're doing the right thing to get out of here." He didn't know that Matt was intent on a mission far more serious than escaping local thugs.

As the jeep drove away, Douglas asked the doctor if he would drive down to the lake. "There's another man down there."

In thirty minutes, they were on the sandy lane leading to the boat landing. The sky was clear; the rain clouds gone. They didn't have to look long. As they passed the store at the bend in the road, they saw the body of a large man.

Peter Crandal lay still next to the long-abandoned pillar of a gas pump, the pistol still clutched in his fist. The pump was decorated with faded red-winged horses, forgotten symbols of the company that built the station. Harper kneeled next to the Canadian, reaching for his wrist. Dried blood stained his blue uniform trousers. A massive bruise covered half of his forehead. "God damn," the doctor said. "Give me a hand."

* * *

The bomb came through the roof of a mess tent twenty minutes before dozens of soldiers reported for breakfast. The soft, sandy soil allowed the nose to bury itself several feet deep. The shell remained intact. And there was no explosion.

When the explosive disposal squad arrived, the sergeant in charge recognized the B57 at once for what it was. "It's a fucking nuke!" he exclaimed. They cleared the area and immediately called for radiation detectors to scan for leaking radiation.

Ten minutes later, the message was flashed to General Cramer's office in Washington. His aide called him at home. The groggy general lifted himself on his elbow. "I'll be right there. Does the president know?"

"No, sir. The message is being transmitted now."

On the USS *John F. Kennedy*, the admiral read the message handed him by the communications technician, who had rushed from the communications center with the astounding news. "Get me the chief of naval operations — the CNO — on the horn, Commander," he said.

Before leaving his home at Fort Myer, General Cramer telephoned the vice president's residence. "Yes, sir. I am certain. One nuclear bomb was dropped by an F-15 of South Carolina's Air National Guard and did not detonate. It was a type B57. Had it detonated, some twenty thousand troops and an undetermined number of civilians would be dead."

"Norman, I will meet you in your office as soon as I can get there."

* * *

"Leo, have you received confirmation from the Russians about Moore?" Mike O'Connelly asked.

"Yes, Mr. Vice President. We received the fax message last night. My people have interviewed the soldier, Sergeant Terry Wilkins, and he confirms all of the details of the Russian's confession. There is no doubt that it is true."

O'Connelly thought a moment. He glanced at the picture of he and his wife, taken years before at a press ball.

"Leo, I want the FBI to search Mr. Moore's office. Search it thoroughly. Do you understand. Open any locked or secured containers."

Scardato understood fully what he was being asked to do. And what it might mean. "Yes, sir."

* * *

Pat Collins gaveled the senate chamber into order. He scanned the men and women heading for their desks across the carpeted floor. They had only one question to consider.

The clerk read the question. "Her Majesty's Government in Canada proposes that the Sovereign State of South Carolina join the Canadian Confederation as a full and equal member of that Confederation."

Collins spoke to the assembled senators. There were none absent, he saw. "The time for debate is past, ladies and gentlemen. The clerk will call the roll." Collins sat in the high-backed chair behind the rostrum and watched the senators, one by one, respond to the call. Not one insisted on making a speech with their vote.

And not one voted no.

When the last vote had been called, Collins forced himself to stand and face the chamber. "The vote is forty-six for the proposal and no votes against. Will the clerk please report the vote in the House." The senate clerk walked from the chamber and crossed the rotunda to the House of Representatives. That proceeding was nearly completed, and she had to wait only a few moments. Except for the three members of the House who had fled the state, the result was the same: a unanimous vote to become part of Canada. The clerk walked back across the rotunda to the senate and carried the results of the House vote to Collins. He read the result to the chamber. Utter stillness settled over the great room.

"Please report the results to the governor," Collins said.

* * *

"Yes, sir. I understand," the admiral said to the CNO. The admiral felt more tired than anything. At least it was nearly over. And no nuclear blast had snuffed out thousands of young lives. He walked to his operations officer. "I want you to send word to the fleet and all elements of the task force to cancel the interdiction order."

The captain studied the admiral's face carefully. "Admiral, this will mean the blockade is ended. The Canadian flotilla will approach the coast in less than two hours, sir."

"Yes, it will. Give the order."

The captain nodded, and passed the directions to the communications center.

"Admiral, the White House is on the line for you, sir."

"Who is it?" the admiral asked, to the surprise of the ensign holding the receiver.

"Mr. Moore, sir."

"Tell Mr. Moore, I will take his call in my quarters. I'm on my way."

He left the bridge and made his way along the carrier's passageways to his cabin. "Yes, sir," he said.

"Admiral, what is your plan to intercept the Canadian flotilla?"

"What exactly do you mean, Mr. Moore? The Canadians are our allies. And as you know they are accompanied by a contingent of British ships."

"Of course I know that! They are not to be allowed to enter our waters. Is that clear?"

"Yes, I understand what you mean."

"Well, what are your plans?"

"Well, Mr. Moore, I think you understand we have more than enough force to convince the flotilla to do as we ask."

"But what action will you take?"

"I think ... can you hear me? ... I believe we are losing the connection ..." The admiral hung up the phone. He called up the communications center. "Take no more voice messages from the White House, do you understand?"

"Yes, sir," the confused voice replied.

* * *

Captain Defenbaker looked at the clock on the bulkhead. They should be close enough now. "Lieutenant, contact the American carrier for me please." His stomach tightened.

"Yes, sir."

In a moment, Defenbaker took the receiver and said, "Admiral, good afternoon, sir."

"Afternoon."

"Sir, we are headed for the port in Charleston. I need to coordinate our passage through your line."

"That will not be a problem. We plot your course as one that will not pose any difficulty. Is there anything else we can do for you, Captain?"

Defenbaker paused. "No, sir. Thank you."

He handed the receiver back to the sailor and stared at the gray sea beyond the window of the bridge. "Make course for Charleston," he said.

Chapter 34

It was nearly two that afternoon when Matt Reicher drove across the Fourteenth Street Bridge into Washington, D.C. During the seven hours, Jim McNeely mostly slept, waking only once and crying out in pain. Matt had pulled to the shoulder long enough to administer the painkiller the doctor gave him. Jim's wound did not bleed at all, thank God.

Twenty-four hours without sleep was beginning to take its toll, but there were two things he had to do before he rested. During his one stop for gasoline, he had called for the address, and now he tried to remember enough about the strange pattern of the capital's streets to find the Canadian Embassy. Driving down the wide thoroughfare of Constitution Avenue, he spotted the red-and-white maple leaf flag flapping in a stiff winter wind. Matt pulled Douglas' jeep to the curb and jogged to the front entrance. "Do you have a service entrance?" he asked the mountie.

The policeman directed him to a side street and watched suspiciously as Matt turned the corner. At the rear entrance, Matt watched carefully until few people were near. Quickly, he opened the back door and lifted Jim McNeely's prone body and carried him to the door where another mountie waited, stunned by the sight of the clearly wounded man being carried up the loading ramp. Matt's appearance didn't give the policeman any greater comfort. His beard was approaching two days' growth, and he was covered with dried mud and dirt.

"Sir, do you have business with the embassy?" the policeman asked.

"Do you know Pete Crandal?" Matt responded.

The mountie was shocked at the question. How did this man know Crandal? "You need to let me bring this man in, or your prime minister is going to be very pissed off. Understand?" The policeman stared at him a moment, absolutely not understanding, but ushered him into the embassy just the same.

* * *

In less than thirty minutes, Matt was pulling the jeep into the parking lot of the Pentagon. He found the spot nearest to an entrance and parked. Matt ran from the jeep to the door, flashed his ID to the guard at the metal detector entrance, and headed for the CNO's suite of offices.

"The bomb was meant to go off. Get it? They meant to do it. And they can do it again. There are another twenty like it scattered around and hidden so we'll never find them."

The shocked navy commander, an aide to the CNO, tried to take in what Matt was telling him. "We need to tell somebody in charge. There might not be much time," Matt insisted. He led Matt down the black-tiled corridor to the office of an assistant to the CNO. Matt stopped him. "I know the chain of command is important around here ... I know it's important to you ... but there just isn't any time. We need to go to the top *right now*."

"O.K. Follow me," he said and led him to the office of the CNO. The secretary regarded Matt with disdain, but delivered the message that Matt had demanded she take to the admiral. When Matt entered the office a few moments later, he was startled to find the chairman of the joint chiefs of staff and the vice president of the United States with the CNO.

When Matt finished his story, the men faced him in silence.

Cramer spoke first, "What type of weapon was it, Commander?"

"A type B57 nuclear bomb, delivered by an F-15 that took off from Shaw in Sumter. How'd I do, General?"

O'Connelly laid his hand on Cramer's shoulder, "Commander, how'd you get access to the bombs?"

"A man I've known for a long time," he corrected himself, "my best friend, James McNeely, was on the governor's staff. He knew the attack was imminent. He came and got me, and he and a Canadian mountie and I went to the place where they were hidden. I made them look like they were already armed. But they weren't. It was all I had time for." Matt ran his hands over his bristled face. Exhaustion was rapidly overtaking him.

"Thank you, Commander Reicher. Your country owes you a great debt," O'Connelly said, extending his hand.

* * *

Before Matt left the Pentagon, he demanded that someone tell him where to find C. A. Moore. At Fort Myer, he was taken to see Paul Gregg. The marine quickly drew him a map of the way to the farm.

* * *

"Mr. Vice President, we can't keep Moore at bay forever. Where is the president?" Cramer asked.

"I don't know. Moore has been running things. He's the only one who reports to Roger on this."

O'Connelly watched the faces around him. They were men accustomed to direction, and now they were looking to him. Men and women had been killed. More would be, unless the right thing was done. He thought about the navy commander and his friend. Was any less expected from him?

* * *

Collins walked into the governor's office. Blackie was seated at his desk staring through the window onto the Capitol grounds.

"The vote is finished, Blackie. Have you called Harold Fraser?"

"No, not yet." Since morning, he had been unable to think about anything but the failure of the bomb to detonate. The hell he had been prepared to inhabit had simply refused to materialize.

"The Canadian flotilla has docked in Charleston. The navy made no effort to stop them. They tell me the city is wild over it. The pier is clogged with people showering the sailors with every kind of food and no small amount of booze." Collins laughed. Blackie realized it was the first time he had heard someone laugh in weeks. He was not a man given to thoughts of Godly intervention in men's affairs ... yet Blackie Haselden could not help feeling the warm breath of divine redemption. His hand had thrown the most terrible of weapons at thousands who should have been doomed ... yet nothing happened. He would always be grateful to a merciful providence, and he would always see the twenty thousand faces that he would have killed. It was a paradox that he would carry forever.

"You call the prime minister, Pat," Blackie said.

* * *

"There is enough evidence here, Mr. Vice President, to convict them both," Leo Scardato said to O'Connelly. General Cramer and the CNO watched from their seats across the table. "In Moore's safe we found this," he said, handing O'Connelly a stack of documents. "They are apparently his record of the things he did for Roger Seekings over the years. His insurance policy. We printed these from the disks we found. Fraud. Bribery. Extortion. Mail fraud. Conspiracy to blackmail. And probably more."

"It's time, gentlemen." O'Connelly rose from the table and walked from his office. The others followed him down the hall to the president's office. Walking into the outer office, O'Connelly asked the receptionist, "Is the president in?"

"Yes, sir—"

Without waiting for her to introduce them, O'Connelly walked into the Oval Office. "Mike? ... What's this?"

"Roger, you know, I assume, that a nuclear bomb was dropped on our troops in North Carolina this morning."

"It didn't detonate. It was a bluff. I told you they wouldn't do it."

"You were wrong, Roger. It didn't go off only because a very brave man risked his life to disarm it."

"That's—"

"Be quiet, Roger. Just shut up! Twenty thousand men and women, our soldiers ... your soldiers, are alive only because of that single act of courage. Before there are other attacks that will succeed, you must resign. The country simply can't afford you anymore."

Seekings exploded. "You stupid old man! Do you think this is some banana republic ... that you can depose me just like that!"

"A banana republic is exactly what you should have been president of, Roger." O'Connelly grabbed the stack of documents from Scardato and tossed them at Seekings. "Recognize these, Roger?" Seekings sank into his chair as he flipped through the damning pages of Moore's files.

"Anyone can manufacture documents like these," Seekings spat. "Come on, Mike. Where are you going to find witnesses. Not much to start a coup over," he sneered, and flung the pages at O'Connelly. "All three of you are going to rot in prison for this." He reached for his phone.

"Not enough, Roger? Let me tell you something you may not know. Your man, C. A. Moore, the man you entrusted with the program to import nuclear materials, and the man you placed in charge of your invasion of South Carolina, was the source for the exact route and schedule of the train that was attacked. Want to know how?" O'Connelly fixed Seekings with a vicious stare, "Moore was keeping soldiers at his house in return for getting them choice assignments in the Pentagon. The Russians blackmailed one of them with a film of he and C. A. together *in bed, Roger*. Here, read the Russian's full statement." He threw Mikail's confession at Seekings. The president picked up the paper with unsteady hands and read the ugly story.

"You can't do this...."

"You will resign now, Roger! I'm not threatening you with some political game. If you don't resign, you are going to be the first American president in history to be deposed. You have taken this nation to the brink of a horrible fate. And I'm not going to let you take it any farther."

Seekings sat still in the chair. "So, what now?" he asked, his voice barely audible.

"Sign this resignation. Then you will get on an air force plane and it will take you to Minnesota. Go home to your wife. Just go home. And thank God that all *you've lost* is your office."

Seekings closed his eyes a moment, and, then, with a single signature, ended his presidency.

* * *

"Governor, it's the vice president." The receptionist stood in the door.

"Yes, Mike. Hello."

"Governor, the president resigned fifteen minutes ago. I will take the oath as soon as the chief justice gets here."

Blackie did not respond.

"We must turn things around. South Carolina should be part of this nation again. Now, we have the chance to do what needs to be done to heal the wounds from so many bad decisions."

"Our legislature has accepted the Canadian proposal to join that country."

"There's no need for that now."

"Mr. ... President ... there must be a clear understanding of this: Never again will we accept *any nuclear waste*. My people have suffered too much."

"You have my word."

Blackie looked at Collins. "Mike, I will be resigning as governor tomorrow. Pat Collins will take over. He's a better man to do the job that will have to be done." Collins' face betrayed his shock. Blackie would never tell Collins of the awful decision he had made, and the desperate need he felt to lay down his burden. Leaving the office of governor would not give him peace, but it was the first step on his journey. "A fresh start will be easier this way."

* * *

Matt pulled the map from his pocket as he warmed the engine of the jeep. He calculated it would take him only forty minutes to reach Moore's farm.

* * *

Moore recovered quickly from the shock. An hour after the army colonel had walked into the operations room and had notified him of Roger Seekings' resignation and of General Cramer's resumption of command of the forces surrounding South Carolina, he had left for the farm. There was no time to waste, not with O'Connelly in power.

He always knew something like this could happen. Seekings was a strong leader as long as things went his way. But there was a fundamental weakness about him. Moore was prepared for exactly this contingency. In the closet that opened onto the bedroom hall, he removed the panel that concealed the safe and spun the dial through the combination. Inside were the papers that would give him a new identity for his flight to Barbados. On that island, whose banks were glad to hide money without questions, he had secreted enough money to be comfortable anywhere he chose. The money was from many sources, few of them legal. Most was from campaign contributions, and part was from the fund that paid for Moore's "dirty" campaign.

He hurriedly stuffed the clothes he would need into two small suitcases. As he zipped the last bag, the beams of two headlights flashed through the front window. A truck of some kind was slowly heading up the lane from the main road. Who the hell was this?

In the dim light of dawn he saw the door to the jeep open. It was just one man in jeans and a short jacket. As the man looked up at the light from the window, Moore saw the face. "Reicher!" he hissed. Bolting to the bedroom, he yanked open a dresser drawer and removed a .38 pistol. He checked to make sure it was loaded. Downstairs, he heard a loud crash as the front door was kicked open.

"Moore where are you?" Matt called from the den. "Planning to go somewhere, aren't you, you worthless bastard? Not today!" Moore walked calmly to the rail overlooking the den and pointed the pistol at Matt.

"Just stand still, Matt," he said. The shot screamed past Matt's ear, smashing the lamp next to the door. Matt dove for the kitchen as another shot rang out, and he pulled the gun from his coat pocket.

Cocking the pistol, he called out, "Give it up. You don't have the guts to fight one on one." The two men stared at the staircase that connected the floors. "I can wait, Moore. I've got all day. You, on the other hand, will be very popular with the FBI. I'll keep you company until they get here. We can talk about old times, eh, buddy."

Moore looked around the hall and bedroom, keeping his gun pointed at the staircase. Behind him was the bedroom window. He pictured the house in his mind. Below the window was the roof of the back porch. It would be an easy jump to the yard. From there, he would need only to get to his car. Slowly, quietly, he backed to the window and raised it. He checked the staircase again. "You're still trying to be a hero, aren't you Matt?" he yelled as he lifted the bag that contained his new identity papers, the ones that would give him freedom and access to his money. "Most men stop when they grow up. But not you! You never figured out how to grow up, did you?" He waited by the window, watching for any movement.

"How does it feel to be responsible for the biggest screw up in a century? Your trial will be the hottest thing since O. J. Simpson." As he spoke, Matt sensed movement above him, then heard a thud outside the kitchen. He leaned to the window and saw Moore land hard on the ground and roll over his side. Moore ran towards the car parked barely twenty yards away.

Matt pulled the door open as Moore reached the car, and aimed his gun at the front tires. Moore dropped behind the car while Matt blew out first one tire and then the other before turning the gun on the windshield, blasting it into shattered fragments. The sharp clicks told him the clip was empty. He yanked the clip out and fumbled with the second one in his coat pocket, finally slamming it into the gun. In the still-dim light, he saw Moore running towards the small barn some sixty yards away. Matt ran after him, careful to keep his pistol ready in case Moore turned his gun on him. Moore disappeared into the barn.

Matt reached the side of the barn and eased himself toward the open door. He picked up a piece of wood and held it in the opening. Two shots were fired from the inside. "Come on, Moore, you're not going anywhere. Just give it up."

"To hell with you!" Moore screamed back. The gun fired from inside again, the bullets piercing the thin door of the barn, one barely missing Matt. The sound of the hammer striking an empty chamber echoed from inside the barn. Matt heard heavy footsteps as Moore ran to the loft. Bending down, Matt ran through the open door.

At the center steps, he aimed his gun upwards and steadily climbed the bare wooden planks. In the loft, he looked around and saw Moore standing by the opening at the end of the barn. He was scrambling to pick up a rope that was tied to a post at the ceiling. As Matt stepped onto the loft floor, Moore lurched backward, the rope slipping from his hands, and fell headfirst through the opening.

Matt ran down the steps to the door of the barn. Moore's body was twisted on the concrete pad by the door. Blood ran from an ugly split in the back of his head. Matt checked his pulse and saw that Moore's head was bent crazily to the side, the neck snapped. The slow pulse weakened rapidly and finally stopped.

*   *   *

General Cramer was not able to convince his new president that he was right about the soldier and the marine. In the general's eyes, neither man was fit to wear the nation's uniform. He was disgusted with what they had done. Mike O'Connelly knew what Cramer felt, but he saw something more in the story of the two men.

"I respect your opinion, Norman. But we can't do that." Cramer had proposed court-martial for Wilkins and the lesser punishment of a dishonorable discharge for Gregg, only because the marine had finally exposed the truth about Moore.

"We can't tolerate something like this, Mr. President."

O'Connelly needed this talented and honorable man to help him return purpose to the nation's military. But he could not countenance the injustice he saw in the general's proposal. "Sergeant Wilkins warrants an honorable discharge, Norman. Nothing more. He has a wife and son to take care of. There have been enough casualties caused by C. A. Moore."

Cramer's face betrayed nothing of his disagreement. O'Connelly hoped it didn't conceal resentment. "And the marine?"

The president shook his head slowly. "No, Norman. Send him back to the corps. Send him to a real job away from the Pentagon." He paused studying the general's impassive face. "I know I can trust you, Norman. No adverse comments secreted somewhere in his records. Send him back to the marines in one piece, and let him find his own way. We owe him that, probably more, but this is the best I can do. He served this country with courage in a way you and I can never understand." O'Connelly could have added that he didn't care what the marine did in private, but it would have made no difference in the way Cramer felt. What mattered was that the new president could trust the general to do as he asked, and that it was the right thing.

"I understand, Mr. President." The general's eyes showed for the briefest of moments the deep respect he felt for Michael O'Connelly. "It will be done as you say, sir."

* * *

Jim McNeely woke to mind-numbing pain. The last medication from the Canadian doctor had worn off. There was no bleeding, and no infection had appeared in the wound. But it would take time for the violence done to his body to heal.

The door to the small bedroom opened, and the doctor greeted his very unusual patient. "How does that hole in your side feel this morning?"

"Not good."

The doctor walked to the television set. "You probably want to see this before we put you back to sleep."

On the screen, Jim saw O'Connelly standing behind a podium in the White House briefing room. The announcer explained that it was his first public comment since assuming the office of president after Roger Seekings' resignation. "Damn," he said.

"... This morning we begin the process of renewal. Since I came to this city, people have spoken dishonestly about renewing their commitment to the core values of America. We have just been through a true nightmare that leaves no doubt that this time there is no alternative except to demand from those who govern this nation a devotion to honesty and duty, standards that were once taken for granted.

"For too many years, it has been said that the American people no longer care about the morals of the men and women who come here, people in congress and the White House sworn to serve the interests of the nation above their own. I don't believe it is true that you ever decided that those oaths didn't mean anything. I think you simply gave up expecting that decent men and women would govern the nation.

"We have seen the cost of failing to select leaders who pass this basic test. We have entrusted men of venal character with our security. They brought us to the brink of catastrophe, and they drove one of our states into violent rebellion.

"This morning the State of South Carolina will consider my invitation to rejoin the union that she helped create. She will come back to us voluntarily as an equal partner, I hope, and into a country that has learned a vital lesson.

"As an important first step, I am committing my administration to this principle: No longer will the handling of nuclear waste be characterized by deceit and arrogance. We have paid too terrible a price.

"Many men and women have died since that train exploded in South Carolina. Even one death would have been too many, and all of them could have been avoided. Foolish pride and addiction to power caused that first terrible tragedy and all of the subsequent catastrophes that spread from the site of that ruined train. Our country was founded by men who knew that no government with contempt for its own people can — or should — survive. Modern history is an anthology of stories about the collapse of empires, kings, dictators, and bureaucracies who ignored this lesson. The pain and tragedy of the last months has shown us that we cannot afford a government led by people who have no regard for the dignity of our own citizens and no respect for the principles of law that protect us all.

"It's an old concept, but no less vital today. We must demand these qualities in our leaders and our public servants. We must end the culture of arrogance that has grown up in this city and the vast government it commands. It is less important to decide whether we have a large government, or one with limited reach, than to ensure that wherever that government is found, it respects the people it serves. There is no alternative if we are to survive as a great and free nation."

Jim watched the new president's earnest speech as the doctor injected more of the pain medication. He knew he would be asleep soon. "Mr. McNeely, there is a call for you," the voice on the intercom said.

He lifted the receiver and heard, "I can forgive you anything, but not for missing the entire hockey season." It was Pete Crandal's voice.

"Where are you, Pete?"

"Someplace called Wilmington, in a hospital with nurses who all sound like Scarlett O'Hara. Your pal and a doctor came and got me yesterday morning."

"Thank God."

"It looks as though things are about to straighten out. Too bad, we won't be able to teach you the words to *O Canada!*"

"I'm glad you're all right."

"Not nearly as glad as I am."

The door opened again as he hung up the telephone. It was Matt Reicher. Jim had not had time to think about what, if anything, was left of his oldest friendship.

"I wanted to see if you were all right," he said.

"I am. You saved my life."

"Ironic, isn't it? Since you almost got me killed."

"Matt...."

"Stow it. We've both been to hell and back. We need to work through all of it ... together. Maybe we'll get a discount on therapy." He started to laugh. "It looks like we'll have time. They're promoting me to captain and sending me back to the station as commander."

"It's the least they can do for a real, live hero."

"True." Matt reached for the door.

"And Matt...." He turned and faced Jim again. "Thanks."

Matt reached for the hand Jim held toward him.

* * *

When she woke — she giggled softly when she glanced at the clock and saw it was nearly ten — her head still swam. It could have been from the champagne. There were several bottles scattered about the hotel room. Or it could have been the same dizzying happiness that had consumed her since she arrived in Virginia the day before. The curtains were pulled open, left from the night, when they lay in bed and admired the lights flickering across Norfolk Harbor. It was a nice room. She'd told Dave it was too much, that they didn't need to waste so much money. And she'd meant not a word of it. It was a marvelous room, with a spectacular view, and the most wonderful way to celebrate that she could imagine.

Still lost in deep sleep, he lay face down in the center of the huge bed. She watched his back rise with each breath, and she admired the fine lines of his shoulders and arms. There was such strength in the sinew and muscle of her young sailor. Carol had never known the feeling of satisfaction that she found in those arms. Late into the night, when they were both well-primed with the champagne he kept pouring, Dave told her about the *Deyo's* Tomahawks and the tanks of fuel so near to her house, about the operations order and the dozen warheads with thousands of kilograms of explosives — and how he couldn't bear to let it happen. She remembered the collapsed bridges in the harbor at Charleston. And she understood with tear-moistened eyes that they lay in those deep waters for her. As she looked at the man she loved, she understood now what deeper strength resided there.

He stretched and turned sleepily to her, the same silly grin from the night spreading across his unshaven face. Without speaking, he reached a large hand and gently pulled her to him. "I thought I'd wake up and it would be a dream."

"If it is, don't wake me up." She curled herself alongside him, their bodies melding themselves into one, and she kissed him passionately.

"Happy new life," he said.

* * *

Before dawn, they led Thaddeus from his cell for the last time. He refused to speak to the minister who came to tell him there was hope for divine reconciliation, reading his Bible alone instead. Clean-shaven and calm, he sat silently as he was fastened to the chair that would send a fatal electric current coursing through his body, snuffing out his mortal life, and sending him to a second one, the men and women observing hoped, of eternal damnation.

The proceedings that brought him to that chair could not correctly be called a trial. Thaddeus put up no defense to the terrible facts set forth by Kevin McClure and the prosecution. Yes, he said, he had organized the killing of the police in Florence. And he had done the same at Fort Jackson, taking many of the lives there with his own hands. He forbade the state-appointed lawyer to mention that he might be insane. When the judge sent a psychiatrist to interview him, he spoke rationally and articulately to the doctor. The chilling session left the doctor convinced that Thaddeus was a frighteningly evil man, but not mad.

His defense was reserved for the closing argument, which he insisted he make himself. His hair was cut conservatively, and he looked more like a businessman than a killer. Gray showed at the temples. The suit provided him by the state was pressed and flattering of the man who seemed transformed before the jury into a dispassionate and seasoned advocate. He offered no apologies for the dozens of dead, for the poisoned city, or the chaos that followed. He denied nothing. For thirty minutes he traced a history of freedom in America they had all heard many times since grammar school. Then he turned on the jury, his face suddenly dark, severe.

"You want me to look different, I know. You want me to look mad, or even bestial. You want me to be an animal, not like you good people at all. But I don't need to dress up my character for you today."

His voice rose until it reverberated around the paneled courtroom, "I did what needed to be done. The few dead police were a small sacrifice," he laughed, "to accomplish the most important mission of my life. You had your chance to escape the corrupt oppressors in Washington — a chance I gave to you — and you have frittered it away. Now, you can rot in the hell of your own making."

It took the jury less than ten minutes to return with a verdict for death. They had forgotten all of Kevin McClure's carefully chosen words. All they could remember was the look on the face of the killer who bragged to them of the rightness of his slaughter.

McClure watched steel-eyed and unflinching as the current of electricity shot through Thaddeus. Blackie Haselden decided at the last minute that he didn't need to witness the death after all.

*   *   *

In Florence the work of Anthony DeSilva was resumed after a careful study to determine how much of the downtown had to be razed and disposed of as radioactive waste. DeSilva's emergency cleanup had minimized the problem. Still, the city/county government complex and most of the stores in the surrounding blocks were demolished, the rubble carefully collected and transported to a storage site in Nevada. The pavement and a shallow layer of soil was similarly collected and shipped away, to be replaced with clean soil in preparation for reconstruction of new buildings. The entire heart of the city was cut out.

More difficult to solve was the problem of the unknown amount of radioactivity that had escaped into the Pee Dee River. Water, soil, and fish were tested to an extent never before known in North America. Access to the contaminated river and its creeks were closed indefinitely. In time the great river would cleanse itself, slowly washing the deadly residue to the ocean. But until the tests confirmed its safety, the river was destined to flow quiet and solitary.

Epilogue

Christmas came to the Haselden farm in Welch's Creek as it always does to those in mourning, both a bitter reminder of lost joy and a confirmation of hope. Stubbornly, June dragged the boxes of decorations from their hiding places in the old house. Blackie returned from a long afternoon walk to find a large spruce tree being erected in the living room. Shock was quickly replaced by the painful reminder that it would be the first Christmas tree he could remember that he did not share with Bud Harris. He knew that in the box of ornaments he saw June opening across the room there was one ornament for each year of Billy's life. A flash of anger at the certainty that there would be no more ornaments made him want to drag the tree that seemed to mock his pain out of the house and destroy it. June looked up from the box of decorations on the floor. She knew the cause of the storm that darkened his eyes. She had known from the beginning that her husband had never come to terms with his loss. There had simply been no time. But there was time, and now there had to be a final reckoning in order for their lives to be more than empty shells.

"Help me put them up, Blackie," she said, getting up from the floor. He stared at her in helpless silence. "Help me," she repeated. "Help us."

They decorated the tree that afternoon, and they decorated the house until late into the night. In the grayness of December afternoons and in the darkness of their bed, they explored all the corners of their new life. Where they found the pain of loss, they faced it and grieved for the love they could now only savor as memories, and where they found happiness, they embraced it hungrily, desperately.

* * *

Just before midnight on Christmas Eve, Julieanne was awakened by the sound of the knocker gently tapping at the door of the house that had been Watson and Dottie Harris' for so long. "Merry Christmas, Julie," Leo Scardato said as she opened the door.

548

"You're out of your mind, Leo, driving down here on Christmas Eve," she said, shaking his hand. But her eyes said so much more.

"A handshake. I bring you this nice present, and all I get is a lousy handshake," he pointed to the car in the drive.

"It's not a present, Leo. It's my car. And we don't say 'lousy' down here."

He closed the door behind him, his face beaming. "What a welcome. I feel like I'm back home in Brooklyn."

Julieanne took his hand again, "Thanks for coming, Leo" — now her eyes were moist — "it's been so awful..."

He took her in his arms before she could finish. Smoothing the hair from her face with one hand and cupping her chin in the other, he bent and kissed her deeply. She didn't move at first but then circled her arms around his shoulders, clutching him to her. "It was more terrible than I thought I could stand, Leo."

"I know. I know, Sweetheart." They kissed again, still standing by the front door. "The car is not your present, Julie," he said reaching into his coat pocket. "This is." He handed her a small box. Inside was another box, covered in felt. She looked at him as if he were a ghost. "Open it," he said, smiling foolishly.

She pulled open the top of the box, the light flashing from the diamond resting on the silk bottom of the box. "Leo, my God!"

"It's a carat-and-a-half!" he whispered. "Do you like it?"

"It's beautiful ... but...."

"Marry me, Julie. Let's quit the bullshit. I never stopped loving you. Let's don't waste any more time. Just marry me."

"Leo, we don't say 'bullshit' down here when we're getting engaged."

"So?"

She put her arms around him again, finding his lips with hers. He felt the tears on her cheeks. "Yes, Leo. Yes. Yes. Yes."

Lying awake in her bed, Dottie Harris listened to the hushed exchanges downstairs. Her eyes began to fill with tears again, but this time, for the first time in so long, with happiness. She exulted to hear the sounds of life in her house again.

* * *

It ended finally for Jim McNeely in the snow, but not in the snow beginning to fall on the capital as the air force jet lifted from Andrews Air Force Base on its way to Charleston. He watched from the window as they rose over the Maryland suburbs, turning white in what would be a heavy covering of snow. He knew the snow would be welcome for Christmas, but all he longed for was home. In the weeks to come, he would force his thoughts to search for the right technology of return to his life before the train... the almost forgotten routine of the law. But now, watching the clouds sink farther away, all that mattered to him was his family.

Alicia, John, and Katherine waited for him at the air base. He could walk again, but with difficulty, and he saw in his wife's eyes that his appearance caused her to cringe. She took him in her arms, a little too tightly, but he didn't let her see the sharp of twinge of pain that shot through his side. The children unleashed a barrage of questions in the car.

Two days before Christmas they drove to Wilmington to pick up Peter Crandal, who had been recovering from the gunshot wound to his thigh. It was a Christmas of uncommon merriment for the McNeelys. The three adults filled the kitchen with happy chaos as they prepared the meal. Generous samples of the Irish whiskey intended for the eggnog spurred Jim's and Pete's enthusiasm.

For an hour, the children spirited their new mountie friend away into the neighborhood to show him off to very impressed friends. When they returned, John announced they had something to show their parents that *Constable* Crandal had taught them. Alicia and Jim leaned on the kitchen island while their two children stood shoulder to shoulder and broke into the first verse of *O Canada!*, leaving Pete collapsed in laughter in the corner.

After the rich and plentiful Christmas Eve dinner, when John and Katherine were in bed, Alicia brought Jim and Pete tall cups of Irish Coffee. "O.K. boys, I want the full story. What happened? You've both got enough liquor in you, it ought to be better than sodium pentothal."

They looked at her in silence, but the grins they shared told her they would soon recount their tale, in every detail. It was mostly Pete who did the talking, and he did not finish until she had handed them both another of the strongly spiked coffees. His speech liberated by the alcohol, Pete vigorously narrated the stirring — and for her, frightening — account. He left out no details, and made no effort to diminish the risks.

His accent thickened along with his tongue. Pete waved his arm grandly and finished, "And that's how it was, Ma'am, that your fine husband here saved us all. For a man not in the RCMP, he's quite a hero, eh." He glanced at his watch, "After midnight. Damn, Santa'll be here soon. Time for this mountie to get a little sleep." He stood unsteadily and turned to Alicia. Bending, he took her hand, and, after a near miss, managed to plant a kiss on her knuckles. In a badly mangled and slurred southern accent he said, "My compliments on a gracious dinner, my dear." Tossing a wave to Jim, he headed for the stairs.

After Pete had climbed the stairs, Alicia turned to Jim, still sipping on the last of the coffee, seeing him as if for the first time. "Is that all true?" she asked.

"He's a mountie. Would Sergeant Preston of the Yukon lie?"

"It is true, then."

"Yes," he said quietly.

There would come a time, many months later, when she tried to express to the man who had been her partner for so long how remarkable a thing it was that he had done. But on this Christmas Eve, she looked at him with only grateful and loving eyes. "Does your side still hurt badly?" she asked.

"Not that bad."

* * *

It was in the heavy snows that fell in the Sacramento Mountains of New Mexico that the long saga ended for Jim McNeely. The flakes flew in the stiff January wind across the burial ground of the Catholic Church nestled in the valley between the spruce-covered slopes of the Mescalero Apache Reservation. The tall adobe spires of the church rose above the sizable crowd that was gathered to listen to the priest lay Doctor Juan Anthony DeSilva's ashes to rest.

Governor Collins asked Jim to lead a small guard of honor to accompany DeSilva's remains home to New Mexico. The dress blue uniform coats offered little comfort from the chill wind, but Jim and the six soldiers standing at rigid attention behind the priest did not shiver. Jim watched the crowd — dozens of high school children whose imaginations DeSilva had fired with the wonders of science, colleagues from the laboratories where men and women still chased the dangerous nuclear phantom, and scores of others touched by the man's life, his humanity, and his style. After the small urn was placed in the grave carved out of the rocky New Mexican ground, Jim watched the waitress from the inn at Cloudcroft reach into her purse and drop a shot glass next to the urn.

Pulled straight from their poles, the three flags held by the South Carolina National Guardsmen flapped stiffly in the wind. The soldiers held the yellow flag of New Mexico — emblazoned with the red sign of the sun — and the blue palmetto flag of South Carolina. In the place of honor was the American flag, its stripes bright beneath the blue field where both states, strangely united by Anthony DeSilva, claimed their place once again with a single star.

*   *   *

Early on a March evening, Mark Killian sat nervously down the hall from the birthing room at McLeod Hospital. Beth Killian was with Susan Engle as she struggled through labor. Mark and Beth had embraced her with unqualified love as she prepared for the birth of the child that should have been hers and Nat's. Mark's mind considered again, as he had countless times since Nat's death, the labyrinth of uncertainties awaiting the young life about to begin.

Susan was young and beautiful. She would not live her life alone, he was certain. That was a good thing, but how would the child fare with a father not his own? He realized, too, that part of his apprehension stemmed from a fear that there might be no place for him. That the last link with the friend he had cherished would be lost.

More frightening, and more real, was what Susan had told them a month before. Tearfully, she explained how she had been exposed to radiation from the injured firemen and Boy Scouts after the train had exploded. The unborn were the most sensitive to the violence of radiation, she said. All the signs were good, but they would not know until the baby arrived, if there were problems. She had not been able to bring herself to tell them what terrible problems they could be. She hadn't told them that some problems might not reveal themselves in her child, that they might not be manifested until her child had grandchildren. Such was the tenacity of radiation's effects.

As the sun set, Mark remembered his friend, as he did every day. The bitterness was gone, but the void left by his loss would never be filled. Mark closed his eyes and heard again Nat's clear voice, loud and buoyant, laughing. The certainty that he had been fortunate to have enjoyed such a friendship seemed at first a slender reed to grasp for consolation. Yet he knew that his life was richer—

"Mark ... come on!" It was Beth shouting from the door of the birthing room. He hurried across the hall and entered to find Susan holding her baby, the baby's black hair wet and matted to the tiny head, the eyes squeezed shut. He walked to the side of the bed. He had been through this twice with his own children, but none of his wonder was diminished.

"It's a boy, Mark," Susan said, smiling, her eyes at once tired and brilliant. "Do you want to hold him?"

Mark bent and lifted the baby, the tiny body swallowed in his huge arms. He gently rocked the child, smiling first at Susan and then at his wife. "Nat and I had already picked out a name," Susan said, "He's Nathan Mark Engle. I'm going to call him Mark."

"Mark ..." he repeated, his smile broadening. "I like it."

"I thought you might."

Nathan Mark Engle was, for all appearances, a perfect baby. There were no fears that night for his health, and Mark Killian stopped worrying about losing touch with so fine a boy, one he would watch live up to both names.

"So, Susan, how are you going to raise him?" It was the old joke they had shared many times with Nat.

"As an American ... I'm going to raise him to be an American ... like his dad."